Patriot Games

Tom Clancy

G. P. PUTNAM'S SONS *New York*

G. P. Putnam's Sons
Publishers Since 1838
200 Madison Avenue
New York, NY 10016

Library of Congress Cataloging in Publication Data

Clancy, Tom, date.
  Patriot games.

  I. Title.
PS3553.L245P38   1987   813'.54   87-6910
ISBN 0-399-13241-4

Printed in the United States of America
1   2   3   4   5   6   7   8   9   10

FOR WANDA

*When bad men combine, the good must associate;
else they will fall one by one, an
unpitied sacrifice in a contemptible struggle.*

—EDMUND BURKE

*Behind all the political rhetoric being hurled at us from
abroad, we are bringing home one unassailable fact—
[terrorism is] a crime by any civilized standard, committed against innocent people, away from the scene
of political conflict, and must be dealt with as a
crime. . . .*

*[I]n our recognition of the nature of terrorism as a
crime lies our best hope of dealing with it. . . .*

*[L]et us use the tools that we have. Let us invoke the
cooperation we have the right to expect around the
world, and with that cooperation let us shrink the dark
and dank areas of sanctuary until these cowardly ma-
rauders are held to answer as criminals in an open and
public trial for the crimes they have committed, and receive the punishment they so richly deserve.*

—WILLIAM H. WEBSTER, Director,
Federal Bureau of Investigation,
October 15, 1985

1

A Sunny Day in Londontown

Ryan was nearly killed twice in half an hour. He left the taxi a few blocks short of his destination. It was a fine, clear day, the sun already low in the blue sky. Ryan had been sitting for hours in a series of straight-back wooden chairs, and he wanted to walk a bit to work the kinks out. Traffic was relatively light on the streets and sidewalks. That surprised him, but he looked forward to the evening rush hour. Clearly these streets had not been laid out with automobiles in mind, and he was sure that the afternoon chaos would be something to behold. Jack's first impression of London was that it would be a fine town to walk in, and he moved at his usual brisk pace, unchanged since his stint in the Marine Corps, marking time unconsciously by tapping the edge of his clipboard against his leg.

Just short of the corner the traffic disappeared, and he moved to cross the street early. He automatically looked left, right, then left again as he had since childhood, and stepped off the curb—

And was nearly crushed by a two-story red bus that screeched past him with a bare two feet to spare.

"Excuse me, sir." Ryan turned to see a police officer—they call them constables over here, he reminded himself—in uniform complete to the Mack Sennett hat. "Please do be careful and cross at the corners. You might also mind the painted signs on the pavement to look right or left. We try not to lose too many tourists to the traffic."

"How do you know I'm a tourist?" He would now, from Ryan's accent.

The cop smiled patiently. "Because you looked the wrong way, sir, and you dress like an American. Please be careful, sir. Good day." The bobby moved off with a friendly nod, leaving Ryan to wonder what there was about his brand-new three-piece suit that marked him as an American.

Chastened, he walked to the corner. Painted lettering on the blacktop warned him to LOOK RIGHT, along with an arrow for the dyslexic. He waited for the light to change, and was careful to stay within the painted lines. Jack remembered that he'd have to pay close attention to the traffic, especially when he rented the car Friday. England was one of the last places in the world where the people drove on the wrong side of the road. He was sure it would take some getting used to.

But they did everything else well enough, he thought comfortably, already drawing universal observations one day into his first trip to Britain. Ryan was a practiced observer, and one can draw many conclusions from a few glances. He was walking in a business and professional district. The other people on the sidewalk were better dressed than their American counterparts would be—aside from the punkers with their spiked orange and purple hair, he thought. The architecture here was a hodgepodge ranging from Octavian Augustus to Mies van der Rohe, but most of the buildings had an old, comfortable look that in Washington or Baltimore would long since have been replaced with an unbroken row of new and soulless glass boxes. Both aspects of the town dovetailed nicely with the good manners he'd encountered so far. It was a working vacation for Ryan, but first impressions told him that it would be a very pleasant one nonetheless.

There were a few jarring notes. Many people seemed to be carrying umbrellas. Ryan had been careful to check the day's weather forecast before setting out on his research trip. A fair day had been accurately predicted—in fact it had been called a hot day, though temperatures were only in the upper sixties. A warm day for this time of year, to be sure, but "hot"? Jack wondered if they called it Indian summer here. Probably not. Why the umbrellas, though? Didn't people trust the local weather service? Was *that* how the cop knew I was an American?

Another thing he ought to have anticipated was the plethora of Rolls-Royces on the streets. He hadn't seen more than a handful in his entire life, and while the streets were not exactly crowded with them, there were quite a few. He himself usually drove around in a five-year-old VW Rabbit. Ryan stopped at a newsstand to purchase a copy of *The Economist,* and had to fumble with the change from his cab fare for several seconds in order to pay the patient dealer, who doubtless also had him pegged for a Yank. He paged through the magazine instead of watching where he was going as he went down the street, and presently found himself halfway down the wrong block. Ryan stopped dead and thought back to the city map he'd inspected before leaving the hotel. One thing Jack could not do was remember street names, but he had a photographic memory for maps. He walked to the end of the block, turned left, proceeded two blocks, then right, and sure enough there was St. James's Park. Ryan checked his watch; he was fifteen minutes early. It was downhill past the monument to a Duke of York, and he crossed the street near a longish classical building of white marble.

Yet another pleasant thing about London was the profusion of green spaces. The park looked big enough, and he could see that the grass was tended with care. The whole autumn must have been unseasonably warm. The trees still bore plenty of leaves. Not many people around, though. Well, he shrugged, it's Wednesday. Middle of the week, the kids were all in school, and it was a normal business day. So much the better, he thought. He'd deliberately come over after the tourist season. Ryan did not like crowds. The Marine Corps had taught him that, too.

"Daddee!" Ryan's head snapped around to see his little daughter running toward him from behind a tree, heedless as usual of her safety. Sally arrived with her customary thump against her tall father. Also as usual, Cathy Ryan trailed behind, never quite able to keep up with their little white tornado. Jack's wife did look like a tourist. Her Canon 35mm camera was draped over one shoulder, along with the camera case that doubled as an oversized purse when they were on vacation.

"How'd it go, Jack?"

Ryan kissed his wife. Maybe the Brits don't do that in public either, he thought. "Great, babe. They treated me like I owned the place. Got all my notes tucked away." He tapped his clipboard. "Didn't you get anything?" Cathy laughed.

"The shops here deliver." She smiled in a way that told him she'd parted with a fairish bit of the money they had allocated for shopping. "And we got something really nice for Sally."

"Oh?" Jack bent over to look his daughter in the eye. "And what might that be?"

"It's a surprise, Daddy." The little girl twisted and giggled like a true four-year-old. She pointed to the park. "Daddy, they got a lake with swans and peccalins!"

"Pelicans," Jack corrected.

"Big white ones!" Sally loved peccalins.

"Uh-huh," Ryan observed. He looked up to his wife. "Get any good pictures?"

Cathy patted her camera. "Oh, sure. London is already Canonized—or would you prefer that we spent the whole day shopping?" Photography was Cathy Ryan's only hobby, and she was good at it.

"Ha!" Ryan looked down the street. The pavement here was reddish, not black, and the road was lined with what looked like beech trees. The Mall, wasn't it? He couldn't remember, and would not ask his wife, who'd been to London many times. The Palace was larger than he'd expected, but it seemed a dour building, three hundred yards away, hidden behind a marble monument of some sort. Traffic was a little thicker here, but moved briskly. "What do we do for dinner?"

"Catch a cab back to the hotel?" She looked at her watch. "Or we can walk."

"They're supposed to have a good dining room. Still early, though. These civilized places make you wait until eight or nine." He saw another Rolls go by in the direction of the Palace. He was looking forward to dinner, though not really to having Sally there. Four-year-olds and four-star restaurants didn't go well together. Brakes squealed off to his left. He wondered if the hotel had a baby-sitting—

BOOM!

Ryan jumped at the sound of an explosion not thirty yards away.

Grenade, something in his mind reported. He sensed the whispering sound of fragments in the air and a moment later heard the chatter of automatic weapons fire. He spun around to see the Rolls turned crooked in the street. The front end seemed lower than it should be, and its path was blocked by a black sedan. There was a man standing at its right front fender, firing an AK-47 rifle into the front end, and another man was racing around to the car's left rear.

"Get down!" Ryan grabbed his daughter's shoulder and forced her to the ground behind a tree, yanking his wife roughly down beside her. A dozen cars were stopped raggedly behind the Rolls, none closer than fifty feet, and these shielded his family from the line of fire. Traffic on the far side was blocked by the sedan. The man with the Kalashnikov was spraying the Rolls for all he was worth.

"Sonuvabitch!" Ryan kept his head up, scarcely able to believe what he saw. "It's the goddamned IRA—they're killing somebody right—" Ryan moved slightly to his left. His peripheral vision took in the faces of people up and down the street, turning and staring, in each face the black circle of a shock-opened mouth. *This is really happening!* he thought, *right in front of me, just like that, just like some Chicago gangster movie. Two bastards are committing murder. Right here. Right now. Just like* that. "Son of a *bitch!"*

Ryan moved farther left, screened by a stopped car. Covered by its front fender, he could see one man standing at the left rear of the Rolls, just standing there, his pistol hand extended as though expecting someone to bolt from the passenger door. The bulk of the Rolls screened Ryan from the AK gunner, who was crouched down to control his weapon. The near gunman had his back to Ryan. He was no more than fifty feet away. He didn't move, concentrating on the passenger door. His back was still turned. Ryan would never remember making any conscious decision.

He moved quickly around the stopped car, head down, keeping low and accelerating rapidly, his eyes locked on his target—the small of the man's back—just as he'd been taught in high school football. It took only a few seconds to cover the distance, with Ryan's mind reaching out, willing the man to stay dumb just a moment longer. At five feet Ryan lowered his shoulder and drove off both legs. His coach would have been proud.

The blind-side tackle caught the gunman perfectly. His back bent like a bow and Ryan heard bones snap as his victim pitched forward and down. A satisfying *klonk* told him that the man's head had bounced off the bumper on the way to the pavement. Ryan got up instantly—winded but full of adrenaline—and crouched beside the body. The man's pistol had dropped from his hand and lay beside the body. Ryan grabbed it. It was an automatic of some sort he had never handled. It looked like a 9mm Makarov or some other East Bloc military issue. The hammer was back and the safety off. He fitted the gun carefully in his right hand—his left hand didn't seem to be working right, but Ryan ignored that. He looked down at the man he'd just tackled and shot him once in the hip. Then he brought the gun up to eye level and moved to the right rear corner of the Rolls. He crouched lower still and peeked around the edge of the bodywork.

The other gunman's AK was lying on the street and he was firing into the car with his own pistol, something else in his other hand. Ryan took a deep breath and stepped from behind the Rolls, leveling his automatic at the man's chest. The other gunman turned his head first, then swiveled off-balance to bring his own gun around. Both men fired at the same instant. Ryan felt a fiery thump in his left shoulder and saw his own round take the man in the chest. The 9mm slug knocked the man backward as though from a hard punch. Ryan brought his own pistol down from recoil and squeezed off another round. The second bullet caught the man under the chin and exploded out the back of his head in a wet, pink cloud. Like a puppet with severed strings, the gunman fell to the pavement without a twitch. Ryan kept his pistol centered on the man's chest until he saw what had happened to his head.

"Oh, God!" The surge of adrenaline left him as quickly as it had come. Time slowed back down to normal, and Ryan found himself suddenly dizzy and breathless. His mouth was open and gasping for air. Whatever force had been holding his body erect seemed to disappear, leaving his frame weak, on the verge of collapse. The black sedan backed up a few yards and accelerated past him, racing down the street, then turning left up a side street. Ryan didn't think to take the number. He was stunned by the flashing sequence of events with which his mind had still not caught up.

The one he'd shot twice was clearly dead, his eyes open and surprised at fate, a foot-wide pool of blood spreading back from his head. Ryan was chilled to see a grenade in his gloved left hand. He bent down to ensure that the cotter pin was still in place on the wooden stick handle, and it was a slow, painful process to straighten up. Next he looked to the Rolls.

The first grenade had torn the front end to shreds. The front wheels were askew, and the tires flat on the blacktop. The driver was dead. Another body was slumped over in the front seat. The thick windshield had been blasted to fragments. The driver's face was—gone, a red spongy mass. There was a red smear on the glass partition separating the driver's seat from the passenger compartment. Jack moved around the car and looked in the back. He saw a man lying prone on the floor, and under him the corner of a woman's dress. He tapped the pistol butt against the glass. The man stirred for a moment, then froze. At least he was alive.

Ryan looked at his pistol. It was empty, the slide locked back on a dry clip. His breath was coming in shudders now. His legs were wobbling under him and his hands were beginning to shake convulsively, which gave his wounded shoulder brief, sharp waves of intense pain. He looked around and saw something to make him forget that—

A soldier was running toward him, with a police officer a few yards behind. One of the Palace guards, Jack thought. The man had lost his bearskin shako but still had an automatic rifle with a half-foot of steel bayonet perched on the muzzle. Ryan quickly wondered if the rifle might be loaded and decided it might be expensive to find out. This was a guardsman, he told himself, a professional soldier from a crack regiment who'd had to prove he had real balls before they sent him to the finishing school that made windup toys for tourists to gawk at. Maybe as good as a Sea Marine. *How did you get here so fast?*

Slowly and carefully, Ryan held the pistol out at arm's length. He thumbed the clip-release button, and the magazine clattered down to the street. Next he twisted the gun so that the soldier could see it was empty. Then he set it down on the pavement and stepped away from it. He tried to raise his hands, but the left one wouldn't move. The guardsman all the time ran smart, head up, eyes tracing left and right but never leaving Ryan entirely. He stopped ten feet away with his rifle at low-guard, its bayonet pointed right at Jack's throat, just like it said in the manual. His chest was heaving, but the soldier's face was a blank mask. The policeman hadn't caught up, his face bloody as he shouted into a small radio.

"At ease, Trooper," Ryan said as firmly as he could. It was not impressive. "We got two bad guys down. I'm one of the good guys."

The guardsman's face didn't change a whit. The boy was a pro, all right. Ryan could hear his thinking—how easy to stick the bayonet right out his target's back. Jack was in no shape to avoid that first thrust.

"DaddeeDaddeeDaddee!" Ryan turned his head and saw his little girl racing past the stalled cars toward him. The four-year-old stopped a few feet away from him, her eyes wide with horror. She ran forward to wrap both arms around her father's leg and screamed up at the guardsman: *"Don't you hurt my daddy!"*

The soldier looked from father to daughter in amazement as Cathy approached more carefully, hands in the open.

"Soldier," she announced in her voice of professional command, "I'm a doctor, and I'm going to treat that wound. So you can put that gun down, right now!"

The police constable grabbed the guardsman's shoulder and said something Jack couldn't make out. The rifle's angle changed fractionally as the soldier relaxed ever so slightly. Ryan saw more cops running to the scene, and a white car with its siren screaming. The situation, whatever it was, was coming under control.

"You lunatic." Cathy surveyed the wound dispassionately. There was a dark stain on the shoulder of Ryan's new suit jacket that turned the gray wool to purple-crimson. His whole body was shaking now. He could barely stand and the weight of Sally hanging on his leg was forcing him to weave. Cathy grabbed his right arm and eased him down to the pavement, sitting him back against the side of the car. She moved his coat away from the wound and probed gently at his shoulder. It didn't feel gentle at all. She reached around to his back pocket for a handkerchief and pressed it against the center of the wound.

"That doesn't feel right," she remarked to no one.

"Daddy, you're all bloody!" Sally stood an arm's length away, her hands fluttering like the wings of a baby bird. Jack wanted to reach out to her, to tell her everything was all right, but the three feet of distance might as well have been a thousand miles—and his shoulder was telling him that things were definitely not all right.

There were now about ten police officers around the car, many of them panting for breath. Three had handguns out, and were scanning the gathering crowd. Two more red-coated soldiers appeared from the west. A police sergeant approached. Before he could say anything Cathy looked up to bark an order.

"Call an ambulance *right now*!"

"On the way, mum," the Sergeant replied with surprising good manners. "Why don't you let us look after that?"

"I'm a doctor," she answered curtly. "You have a knife?"

The Sergeant turned to remove the bayonet from the first guardsman's rifle and stooped down to assist. Cathy held the coat and vest clear for him to cut away, then both cut the shirt free from his shoulder. She tossed the handkerchief clear. It was already blood-sodden. Jack started to protest.

"Shut up, Jack." She looked over to the Sergeant and jerked her chin toward Sally. "Get her away from here."

The Sergeant gestured for a guardsman to come over. The Private scooped Sally up in his arms. He took her a few feet away, cradling her gently to his chest. Jack saw his little girl crying pitifully, but somehow it all seemed to be very far away. He felt his skin go cold and moist—shock?

"Damn," Cathy said gruffly. The Sergeant handed her a thick bandage. She pressed it against the wound and it immediately went red as she tried to tie it in place. Ryan groaned. It felt as though someone had taken an ax to his shoulder.

"Jack, what the hell were you trying to do?" she demanded through clenched teeth as she fumbled with the cloth ties.

Ryan snarled back, the sudden anger helping to block out the pain. "I didn't try—I fucking did it!" The effort required to say that took half his strength away with it.

"Uh-huh," Cathy grunted. "Well, you're bleeding like a pig, Jack."

More men ran in from the other direction. It seemed that a hundred sirens were converging on the scene with men—some in uniform, some not—leaping out to join the party. A uniformed policeman with more ornate shoulder boards began to shout orders at the others. The scene was impressive. A separate, detached part of Ryan's brain catalogued it. There he was, sitting against the Rolls, his shirt soaked red as though blood had been poured from a pitcher. Cathy, her hands covered with her husband's blood, was still trying to arrange the bandage correctly. His daughter was gasping out tears in the arms of a burly young soldier who seemed to be singing to her in a language that

Jack couldn't make out. Sally's eyes were locked on him, full of desperate anguish. The detached part of his mind found all this very amusing until another wave of pain yanked him back to reality.

The policeman who'd evidently taken charge came up to them after first checking the perimeter. "Sergeant, move him aside."

Cathy looked up and snapped angrily: "Open the other side, dammit, I got a bleeder here!"

"The other door's jammed, ma'am. Let me help." Ryan heard a different kind of siren as they bent down. The three of them moved him aside a foot or so, and the senior officer made to open the car door. They hadn't moved him far enough. When the door swung open, its edge caught Ryan's shoulder. The last thing he heard before passing out was his own scream of pain.

Ryan's eyes focused slowly, his consciousness a hazy, variable thing that reported items out of place and out of time. For a moment he was inside a vehicle of some sort. The lateral movements of its passage rippled agony through his chest, and there was an awful atonal sound in the distance, though not all that far away. He thought he saw two faces he vaguely recognized. Cathy was there, too, wasn't she—no, there were some people in green. Everything was soft and vague except the burning pain in his shoulder and chest, but when he blinked his eyes all were gone. He was someplace else again.

The ceiling was white and nearly featureless at first. Ryan knew somehow that he was under the influence of drugs. He recognized the feelings, but could not remember why. It required several minutes of lazy concentration for him to determine that the ceiling was made of white acoustical tiles on a white metal framework. Some of the tiles were waterstained and served to give him a reference. Others were translucent plastic for the soft fluorescent lighting. There was something tied under his nose, and after a moment he began to feel a cool gas tracing into his nostrils—oxygen? His other senses began to report in one at a time. Expanding radially down from his head, they began to explore his body and reported reluctantly to his brain. Some unseen things were taped to his chest. He could feel them pulling at the hairs that Cathy liked to play with when she was drunk. His left shoulder felt . . . didn't really feel at all. His whole body was far too heavy to move even an inch.

A hospital, he decided after several minutes. *Why am I in a hospi-*

tal . . . ? It took an indeterminate period of concentration for Jack to remember why he was here. When it came to him, it was just as well that he could contemplate the taking of a human life from within the protective fog of drugs.

I was shot, too, wasn't I? Ryan turned his head slowly to the right. A bottle of IV fluids was hanging on a metal stand next to the bed, its rubber hose trailing down under the sheet where his arm was tied down. He tried to feel the prick of the catheter that had to be inside the right elbow, but couldn't. His mouth was cottony dry. *Well, I wasn't shot on the right side . . .* Next he tried to turn his head to the left. Something soft but very firm prevented it. Ryan wasn't able to care very much about it. Even his curiosity for his condition was a tenuous thing. For some reason his surroundings seemed much more interesting than his own body. Looking directly up, he saw a TV-like instrument, along with some other electronic stuff, none of which he could make out at the acute angle. *EKG readout? Something like that,* he decided. It all figured. He was in a surgical recovery room, wired up like an astronaut while the staff decided if he'd live or not. The drugs helped him to consider the question with marvelous objectivity.

"Ah, we're awake." A voice other than the distant, muffled tone of the PA system. Ryan dropped his chin to see a nurse of about fifty. She had a Bette Davis face crinkled by years of frowns. He tried to speak to her, but his mouth seemed glued shut. What came out was a cross between a rasp and a croak. The nurse disappeared while he tried to decide what exactly the sound was.

A man appeared a minute or so later. He was also in his fifties, tall and spare, dressed in surgical greens. There was a stethoscope hanging from his neck, and he seemed to be carrying something that Ryan couldn't quite see. He seemed rather tired, but wore a satisfied smile.

"So," he said, "we're awake. How are we feeling?" Ryan managed a full-fledged croak this time. The doctor—?—gestured to the nurse. She came forward to give Ryan a sip of water through a glass straw.

"Thanks." He sloshed the water around his mouth. It was not enough to swallow. His mouth tissues seemed to absorb it all at once. "Where am I?"

"You are in the surgical recovery unit of St. Thomas's Hospital. You are recovering from surgery on your upper left arm and shoulder. I am your surgeon. My team and I have been working on you for, oh, about six hours now, and it would appear that you will probably live,'' he added judiciously. He seemed to regard Ryan as a successful piece of work.

Rather slowly and sluggishly Ryan thought to himself that the English sense of humor, admirable as it might otherwise be, was a little too dry for this sort of situation. He was composing a reply when Cathy came into view. The Bette Davis nurse moved to head her off.

"I'm sorry, Mrs. Ryan, but only medical person—"

"I'm a doctor." She held up her plastic ID card. The man took it.

"Wilmer Eye Institute, Johns Hopkins Hospital." The surgeon extended his hand and gave Cathy a friendly, colleague-to-colleague smile. "How do you do, Doctor? My name is Charles Scott."

"That's right," Ryan confirmed groggily. "She's the surgeon doctor. I'm the historian doctor." No one seemed to notice.

"Sir Charles Scott? Professor Scott?"

"The same." A benign smile. *Everyone likes to be recognized,* Ryan thought as he watched from his back.

"One of my instructors knows you—Professor Knowles."

"Ah, and how is Dennis?"

"Fine, Doctor. He's associate professor of orthopedics now." Cathy shifted gears smoothly, back to medical professional. "Do you have the X-rays?"

"Here." Scott held up a manila envelope and extracted a large film. He held it up in front of a lighting panel. "We took this prior to going in."

"Damn." Cathy's nose wrinkled. She put on the half-glasses she used for close work, the ones Jack hated. He watched her head move slowly from side to side. "I didn't know it was *that* bad."

Professor Scott nodded. "Indeed. We reckon the collarbone was broken before he was shot, then the bullet came crashing through here—just missed the brachial plexus, so we expect no serious nerve damage—and did all this damage." He traced a pencil across the film. Ryan couldn't see any of it from the bed. "Then it did this to the top of the humerus before stopping here, just inside the skin. Bloody powerful thing, the nine millimeter. As you can see, the damage was quite extensive. We had a jolly time finding all these fragments and jigsawing them back into proper place, but—we were able to accomplish this." Scott held a second film up next to the first. Cathy was quiet for several seconds, her head swiveling back and forth.

"That is nice work, Doctor!"

Sir Charles' smile broadened a notch. "From a Johns Hopkins surgeon, yes, I think I'll accept that. Both these pins are permanent, this screw also, I'm afraid, but the rest should heal rather nicely. As you can see, all the large fragments are back where they belong, and we have every reason to expect a full recovery."

"How much impairment?" A detached question. Cathy could be maddeningly unemotional about her work.

"We're not sure yet," Scott said slowly. "Probably a little, but it should not be overly severe. We can't guarantee a complete restoration of function—the damage was far too extensive for that."

"You mind telling me something?" Ryan tried to sound angry, but it hadn't come out right.

"What I mean, Mr. Ryan, is that you'll probably have some permanent loss of use of your arm—precisely how much we cannot determine as yet—and from now on you'll have a permanent barometer. Henceforth, whenever the weather is about to change for the worse, you'll know it before anyone else."

"How long in this cast?" Cathy wanted to know.

"At least a month." The surgeon seemed apologetic. "It is awkward, I know, but the shoulder must be totally immobilized for at least that long. After that we'll have to reevaluate the injury and we can probably revert to a normal cast for another . . . oh, another month or so, I expect. I presume he heals well, no allergies. Looks to be in good health, decent physical shape."

"Jack's in good physical shape, except for a few loose marbles in his head," Cathy nodded, an edge on her weary voice. "He jogs. No allergies except ragweed, and he heals rapidly."

"Yeah," Ryan confirmed. "Her teethmarks go away in under a week, usually." He thought this uproariously funny, but no one laughed.

"Good," Sir Charles said. "So, Doctor, you can see that your husband is in good hands. I will leave the two of you together for five minutes. After that, I wish that he should get some rest, and you look as though you could use some also." The surgeon moved off with Bette Davis in his wake.

Cathy moved closer to him, changing yet again from cool professional to concerned wife. Ryan told himself for perhaps the millionth time how lucky he was to have this girl. Caroline Ryan had a small, round face, short butter-blond hair, and the world's prettiest blue eyes. Behind those eyes was a person with intelligence at least the equal of his own, someone he loved as much as a man could. He would never understand how he'd won her. Ryan was painfully aware that on his best day his own undistinguished features, a heavy beard and a lantern jaw, made him look like a dark-haired Dudley Do-Right of the Mounties. She played pussycat to his crow. Jack tried to reach out for her hand, but was foiled by straps. Cathy took his.

"Love ya, babe," he said softly.

"Oh, Jack." Cathy tried to hug him. She was foiled by the cast that he couldn't even see. "Jack, why the hell did you do that?"

He had already decided how to answer that. "It's over and I'm still alive, okay? How's Sally?"

"I think she's finally asleep. She's downstairs with a policeman." Cathy did look tired. "How do you think she is, Jack? Dear God, she saw you killed almost. You scared us both to death." Her china-blue eyes were rimmed in red, and her hair looked terrible, Jack saw. Well, she never was able to do much of anything with her hair. The surgical caps always ruined it.

"Yeah, I know. Anyway, it doesn't look like I'll be doing much more of that for a while," he grunted. "Matter of fact, it doesn't look like I'll be doing much of anything for a while." That drew a smile. It was good to see her smile.

"Fine. You're supposed to conserve your energy. Maybe this'll teach you a lesson—and don't tell me about all those strange hotel beds going to waste." She squeezed his hand. Her smile turned impish. "We'll probably work something out in a few weeks. How do I look?"

"Like hell." Jack laughed quietly. "I take it the doc was a somebody?"

He saw his wife relax a little. "You might say that. Sir Charles Scott is one of the best orthopeds in the world. He trained Professor Knowles—he did a super job on you. You're lucky to have an arm at all, you know—my God!"

"Easy, babe. I'm going to live, remember?"

"I know, I know."

"It's going to hurt, isn't it?"

Another smile. "Just a bit. Well. I've got to put Sally down. I'll be back tomorrow." She bent down to kiss him. Skin full of drugs, oxygen tube, dry mouth, and all, it felt good. *God,* he thought, *God, how I love this girl.* Cathy squeezed his hand one more time and left.

The Bette Davis nurse came back. It was not a satisfactory trade.

"I'm 'Doctor' Ryan, too, you know," Jack said warily.

"Very good, Doctor. It is time for you to get some rest. I'll be here to look after you all night. Now sleep, Doctor Ryan."

On this happy note Jack closed his eyes. Tomorrow would be a real bitch, he was sure. It would keep.

2

Cops and Royals

Ryan awoke at 6:35 A.M. He knew that because it was announced by a radio disc-jockey whose voice faded to an American Country & Western song of the type which Ryan avoided at home by listening to all-news radio stations. The singer was admonishing mothers not to allow their sons to become cowboys, and Ryan's first muddled thought of the day was, *Surely they don't have that problem over here . . . do they?* His mind drifted along on this tangent for half a minute, wondering if the Brits had C&W bars with sawdust on the floors, mechanical bull rides, and office workers who strutted around with pointy-toed boots and five-pound belt buckles. . . . *Why not?* he concluded. *Yesterday I saw something right out of a Dodge City movie.*

Jack would have been just as happy to slide back into sleep. He tried closing his eyes and willing his body to relax, but it was no use. The flight from Dulles had left early in the morning, barely three hours after he'd awakened. He hadn't slept on the plane—it was something he simply could not do—but flying always exhausted him, and he'd gone to bed soon after arriving at the hotel. Then how long had he been unconscious in the hospital? Too long, he realized. Ryan was all slept out. He would have to begin facing the day.

Someone off to his right was playing a radio just loudly enough to hear. Ryan turned his head and was able to see his shoulder—

Shoulder, he thought, *that's why I'm here. But* where's *here?* It was a different room. The ceiling was smooth plaster, recently painted. It was dark, the only illumination coming from a light on the table next to the bed, perhaps enough to read by. There seemed to be a painting on the wall—at least a rectangle darker than the wall, which wasn't white. Ryan took this in, consciously delaying his examination of his left arm until no excuses remained. He turned his head slowly to the left. He saw his arm first of all. It was sticking up at an angle, wrapped in a plaster and fiberglass cast that went all the way to his hand. His fingers stuck out like an afterthought, about the same shade of gray as the plaster-gauze wrappings. There was a metal ring at the back of the wrist, and in the ring was a hook whose chain led to a metal frame that arced over the bed like a crane.

First things first. Ryan tried to wiggle his fingers. It took several seconds before they acknowledged their subservience to his central nervous system. Ryan let out a long breath and closed his eyes to thank God for that. About where his elbow was, a metal rod angled downward to join the rest of the cast, which, he finally appreciated, began at his neck and went diagonally to his waist. It left his arm sticking out entirely on its own and made Ryan look like half a bridge. The cast was not tight on his chest, but touched almost everywhere, and already he had itches where he couldn't scratch. The surgeon had said something about immobilizing the shoulder, and, Ryan thought glumly, he hadn't been kidding. His shoulder ached in a distant sort of way with the promise of more to come. His mouth tasted like a urinal, and the rest of his body was stiff and sore. He turned his head the other way.

"Somebody over there?" he asked softly.

"Oh, hello." A face appeared at the edge of the bed. Younger than Ryan, mid-twenties or so, and lean. He was dressed casually, his tie loose in his collar, and the edge of a shoulder holster showed under his jacket. "How are you feeling, sir?"

Ryan attempted a smile, wondering how successful it was. "About how I look, probably. Where am I, who are you—first, is there a glass of water in this place?"

The policeman poured ice water from a plastic jug into a plastic cup. Ryan reached out with his right hand before he noticed that it wasn't tied down as it had been the last time he awoke. He could now feel the place where the IV catheter had been. Jack greedily sucked the water from the straw. It was only water, but no beer ever tasted better after a day's yardwork. "Thanks, pal."

"My name is Anthony Wilson. I'm supposed to look after you. You are in the VIP suite of St. Thomas's Hospital. Do you remember why you're here, sir?"

"Yeah, I think so," Ryan nodded. "Can you unhook me from this thing? I have to go." The other reminder of the IV.

"I'll ring the sister—here." Wilson squeezed the button that was pinned to the edge of Ryan's pillow.

Less than fifteen seconds later a nurse came through the door and flipped on the overhead lights. The blaze of light dazzled Jack for a moment before he saw it was a different nurse. Not Bette Davis, this one was young and pretty, with the eager, protective look common to nurses. Ryan had seen it before, and hated it.

"Ah, we're awake," she observed brightly. "How are we feeling?"

"Great," Ryan grumped. "Can you unhook me? I have to go to the john."

"We're not supposed to move just yet, Doctor Ryan. Let me fetch you something." She disappeared out the door before he could object. Wilson watched her leave with an appraising look. Cops and nurses, Ryan thought. His dad had married a nurse; he'd met her after bringing a gunshot victim into the emergency room.

The nurse—her name tag said KITTIWAKE—returned in under a minute bearing a stainless steel urinal as though it were a priceless gift, which under the circumstances, it was, Ryan admitted to himself. She lifted the covers on the bed and suddenly Jack realized that his hospital gown was not really on, but just tied loosely around his neck—worse, the nurse was about to make the necessary adjustments for him to use the urinal. Ryan's right hand shot downward under the covers to take it away from her. He thanked God for the second time this morning that he was able, barely, to reach down far enough.

"Could you, uh, excuse me for a minute?" Ryan willed the girl out of the room, and she went, smiling her disappointment. He waited for the door to close completely before continuing. In deference to Wilson he stifled his sigh of relief. Kittiwake was back through the door after counting to sixty.

"Thank you." Ryan handed her the receptacle and she disappeared out the door. It had barely swung shut when she was back again. This time she stuck a thermometer in his mouth and grabbed his wrist to take his pulse. The thermometer was one of the new electronic sort, and both tasks were completed in fifteen seconds. Ryan asked for the score, but got a smile instead of an answer. The smile remained fixed as she made the entries on his chart. When this task was fulfilled, she made a minor adjustment in the covers, beaming at Ryan. *Little Miss Efficiency,* Ryan told himself. *This girl is going to be a real pain in the ass.*

"Is there anything I might get you, Doctor Ryan?" she asked. Her brown eyes belied the wheat-colored hair. She was cute. She had that dewy look. Ryan was unable to remain angry with pretty women, and hated them for it. Especially young nurses with that dewy look.

"Coffee?" he asked hopefully.

"Breakfast is not for another hour. Can I fetch you a cup of tea?"

"Fine." It wasn't, but it would get rid of her for a little while. Nurse Kittiwake breezed out the door with her ingenuous smile.

"Hospitals!" Ryan snarled when she was gone.

"Oh, I don't know," Wilson observed, the image of Nurse Kittiwake fresh in his mind.

"You ain't the one getting your diapers changed." Ryan grunted and leaned back into the pillow. It was useless to fight it, he knew. He smiled in spite of himself. *Useless to fight it.* He'd been through this twice before, both times with young, pretty nurses. Being grumpy only made them all the more eager to be overpoweringly nice—they had time on their side, time and patience enough to wear anyone down. He sighed out his surrender. It wasn't worth the waste of energy. "So, you're a cop, right? Special Branch?"

"No, sir. I'm with C-13, Anti-Terrorist Branch."

"Can you fill me in on what happened yesterday? I kinda missed a few things."

"How much do you remember, Doctor?" Wilson slid his chair closer. Ryan noted that he remained halfway facing the door, and kept his right hand free.

"I saw—well, I *heard* an explosion, a hand grenade, I think—and when I turned I saw two guys shooting hell out of a Rolls-Royce. IRA, I guess. I took two of them out, and another one got away in a car. The cavalry arrived, and I passed out and woke up here."

"Not IRA. ULA—Ulster Liberation Army, a Maoist offshoot of the Provos. Nasty buggers. The one you killed was John Michael Mc-Crory, a very bad boy from Londonderry—one of the chaps who escaped from the Maze last July. This is the first time he's surfaced since. And the last"—Wilson smiled coldly—"we haven't identified the other chap yet. That is, not as of when I came on duty three hours ago."

"ULA?" Ryan shrugged. He remembered hearing the name, though he couldn't talk about that. "The guy I—killed. He had an AK, but when I came around the car he was using a pistol. How come?"

"The fool jammed it. He had two full magazines taped end to end, like you see all the time in the movies, but like they trained us specifically *not* to do in the paras. We reckon he bashed it, probably when he came out of the car. The second magazine was bent at the top end—wouldn't feed the rounds properly, you see. Damn good luck for you. You *knew* you were going after a chap with a Kalashnikov?" Wilson examined Ryan's face closely.

Jack nodded. "Doesn't sound real smart, does it?"

"You bloody fool." Wilson said this just as Kittiwake came through the door with a tea tray. The nurse flashed the cop an emphatically disapproving look as she set the tray on the bedstand and wheeled it over. Kittiwake arranged things just so, and poured Ryan a cup with delicacy. Wilson had to do his own.

"So who was in the car, anyway?" Ryan asked. He noted strong reactions.

"You didn't know?" Kittiwake was dumbfounded.

"There wasn't much time to find out." Ryan dropped two packets of brown sugar into his cup. His stirring stopped abruptly when Wilson answered his question.

"The Prince and Princess of Wales. And their new baby."

Ryan's head snapped around. "What?"

"You really didn't know?" the nurse asked.

"You're serious," Ryan said quietly. *They wouldn't kid about this, would they?*

"Too bloody right, I'm serious," Wilson went on, his voice very even. Only his choice of words betrayed how deeply the affair disturbed him. "Except for you, they would all three be quite dead, and that makes you a bloody hero, Doctor Ryan." Wilson sipped his tea neat and fished out a cigarette.

Ryan set his cup down. "You mean you let them drive around here without a police or secret service—whatever you call it—without an escort?"

"Supposedly it was an unscheduled trip. Security arrangements for the Royals are not my department in any case. I would speculate, however, that those whose department it is will be rethinking a few things," Wilson commented.

"They weren't hurt?"

"No, but their driver was killed. So was their security escort from DPG—Diplomatic Protection Group—Charlie Winston. I knew Charlie. He had a wife, you know, and four children, all grown."

Ryan observed that the Rolls should have had bulletproof glass.

Wilson grunted. "It *did* have bulletproof glass. Actually plastic, a complex polycarbonate material. Unfortunately, no one seems to have read what it said on the box. The guarantee is only for a year. Turns out that sunlight breaks the material down somehow or other. The windshield was no more use than ordinary safety glass. Our friend McCrory put thirty rounds into it, and it quite simply shattered, killing the driver first. The interior partition, thank God, had not been exposed to sunlight, and remained intact. The last thing Charlie did was push the button to put it up. That probably saved them, too—didn't do Charlie much good, though. He had enough time to draw his automatic, but we don't think he was able to get a shot off."

Ryan thought back. There had been blood in the back of the Rolls— not just blood. The driver's head had been blown apart, and his brains had scattered into the passenger compartment. Jack winced thinking about it. The escort had probably leaned over to push the button before defending himself. . . . *Well,* Jack thought, *that's what they pay them for. What a hell of a way to earn a living.*

"It was fortunate that you intervened when you did. They both had hand grenades, you know."

"Yeah, I saw one." Ryan sipped away the last of his tea. "What the hell was I thinking about?" *You weren't thinking at all, Jack. That's what you were thinking about.*

Kittiwake saw Ryan go pale. "You feel quite all right?" she asked.

"I guess." Ryan grunted in wonderment. "Dumb as I was, I must feel pretty good—I ought to be dead."

"Well, that most emphatically will not happen here." She patted his hand. "Please ring me if you need anything." Another beaming smile and she left.

Ryan was still shaking his head. "The other one got away?"

Wilson nodded. "We found the car near a tube station a few blocks away. It was stolen, of course. No real problem for him to get clean away. Disappear into the underground. Go to Heathrow, perhaps, and catch a plane to the continent—Brussels, say—then a plane to Ulster or the Republic, and a car the rest of the way home. That's one route; there are others, and it's impossible to cover them all. He was drinking beer last night, watching the news coverage on television in his favorite pub, most likely. Did you get a look at him?"

"No, just a shape. I didn't even think to get the tag number—dumb. Right after that the redcoat came running up to me." Ryan winced again. "Christ, I thought he'd put that pigsticker right through me. For a second there I could see it all—I do something right, then get wasted by a good guy."

Wilson laughed. "You don't know how lucky you were. The current guard force is from the Welsh Guards."

"So?"

"His Royal Highness's own regiment, as it were. He's their colonel-in-chief. There you were with a pistol—how would you expect him to react?" Wilson stubbed out his cigarette. "Another piece of good luck, your wife and daughter came running up to you, and the soldier decides to wait a bit, just long enough for things to sort themselves out. Then our chap catches up with him and tells him to stand easy. And a hundred more of my chaps come swooping in.

"I hope you can appreciate this, Doctor. Here we were with three men dead, two others wounded, a Prince and Princess looking as though they'd been shot—your wife examined them on the scene, by the way, and pronounced them fit just before the ambulance arrived— a baby, a hundred witnesses each with his own version of what had just taken place. A bloody Yank—an Irish-American to boot!—whose wife claims he's the chap in the white hat." Wilson laughed again. "Total chaos!

"First order of business, of course, was to get the Royals to safety. The police and guardsmen handled that, probably praying by this time that someone would make trouble. They're still in an evil mood, they tell me, angrier even than from the bandstand bombing incident. Not hard to understand. Anyway, your wife flatly refused to leave your side until you were under doctor's care here. Quite a forceful woman, they tell me."

"Cathy's a surgeon," Ryan explained. "When she plays doc, she's used to having her own way. Surgeons are like that."

"After she was quite satisfied we drove her down to the Yard. Meanwhile we had a merry time identifying you. They called your Legal Attaché at the American Embassy and he ran a check through your FBI, plus a backup check through the Marine Corps." Ryan stole a cigarette from Wilson's pack. The policeman lit it with a butane lighter. Jack gagged on the smoke, but he needed it. Cathy would give him hell for it, he knew, but one thing at a time. "Mind you, we never really thought you were one of them. Have to be a maniac to bring the wife and child along on this sort of job. But one must be careful."

Ryan nodded agreement, briefly dizzy from the smoke. *How'd they know to check through the Corps . . . oh, my Marine Corps Association card. . . .*

"In any event we have things pretty well sorted out. Your government are sending us everything we need—probably here by now, actually." Wilson checked his watch.

"My family's all right?"

Wilson smiled in rather an odd way. "They are being very well looked after, Doctor Ryan. You have my word on that."

"The name's Jack."

"Fine. I'm known to my friends as Tony." They finally got around to shaking hands. "And as I said, you're a bloody hero. Care to see what the press have to say?" He handed Ryan a *Daily Mirror* and a *Times*.

"Dear God!"

The tabloid *Mirror*'s front page was almost entirely a color photograph of himself, sitting unconscious against the Rolls. His chest was a scarlet mass.

ATTEMPT ON HRH—MARINE TO THE RESCUE

A bold attempt to assassinate Their Royal Highnesses the Prince and Princess of Wales within sight of Buckingham Palace was thwarted today by the courage of an American tourist.

John Patrick Ryan, an historian and formerly a lieutenant in the United States Marines, dashed barehanded into a pitched battle on The Mall as over a hundred Londoners watched in shocked disbelief. Ryan, 31, of Annapolis, Maryland, successfully disabled one gunman and, taking his weapon, shot another dead. Ryan himself was seriously wounded in the exchange. He was taken by ambulance to St. Thomas's Hospital, where emergency surgery was successfully performed by Sir Charles Scott.

A third terrorist is reported to have escaped the scene, by running east on The Mall, then turning north on Marlborough Road.

Senior police officials were unanimous in their opinion that, but for Ryan's courageous intervention, Their Highnesses would certainly have been slain.

Ryan turned the page to see another color photograph of himself in happier circumstances. It was his graduation photo from Quantico, and he had to smile at himself, resplendent, then, in blue high-necked blouse, two shiny gold bars, and the Mamaluke sword. It was one of the few decent photographs ever taken of him.

"Where did they get this?"

"Oh, your Marine chaps were most helpful. In fact, one of your Marine ships—helicopter carrier, or something like that—is at Portsmouth right now. I understand that your former colleagues are getting all the free beer they can swill."

Ryan laughed at that. Next he picked up the *Times,* whose headline was marginally less lurid.

The Prince and Princess of Wales escaped certain death this afternoon. Three, possibly four terrorists armed with hand grenades and Kalashnikov assault rifles lay in wait for their Rolls-Royce; only to have their carefully-laid plans foiled by the bold intervention of J. P. Ryan, formerly a second lieutenant in the United States Marine Corps, and now an historian. . . .

Ryan flipped to the editorial page. The lead item, signed by the publisher, screamed for vengeance while praising Ryan, America, and the United States Marine Corps, and thanked Divine Providence with a flourish worthy of a Papal Encyclical.

"Reading about yourself?" Ryan looked up. Sir Charles Scott was standing at the foot of his bed with an aluminum chart.

"First time I ever made the papers." Ryan set them down.

"You've earned it, and it would seem that the sleep did you some good. How do you feel?"

"Now bad, considering. How am I?" Ryan asked.

"Pulse and temperature normal—almost normal. Your color isn't bad at all. With luck we might even avoid a postoperative infection, though I should not wish to give odds on that," the doctor said. "How badly does it hurt?"

"It's there, but I can live with it," Ryan answered cautiously.

"It is only two hours since your last medication. I trust you are not one of those thickheaded fools who do not want pain medications?"

"Yes, I am," Ryan said. He went on slowly. "Doctor, I've been through this twice before. The first time, they gave me too much of the stuff, and coming off was—I'd just as soon not go through that again, if you know what I mean."

Ryan's career in the Marine Corps had ended after a mere three months with a helicopter crash on the shores of Crete during a NATO exercise. The resulting back injury had sent Ryan to Bethesda Naval Medical Center, outside Washington, where the doctors had been a little too generous with their pain medications, and Ryan had taken two weeks to get over them. It was not an experience he wanted to repeat.

Sir Charles nodded thoughtfully. "I think so. Well, it's your arm." The nurse came back in as he made some notations on the chart. "Rotate the bed a bit."

Ryan hadn't noticed that the rack from which his arm hung was actually circular. As the head of the bed came up, his arm dropped to a more comfortable angle. The doctor looked over his glasses at Ryan's fingers.

"Would you wiggle them, please?" Ryan did so. "Good, that's very good. I didn't think there'd be any nerve damage. Doctor Ryan, I am going to prescribe something mild, just enough to keep the edge off it. I will require that you take the medications which I prescribe." Scott's head came around to face Ryan directly. "I've never yet got a patient addicted to narcotics, and I do not propose to start with you.

Don't be pigheaded: pain, discomfort will retard your recovery—unless, that is, you *want* to remain in hospital for several months?''

"Message received, Sir Charles."

"Right." The surgeon smiled. "If you should feel the need for something stronger, I shall be here all day. Just ring nurse Miss Kittiwake here." The girl beamed in anticipation.

"How about something to eat?"

"You think you can keep something down?"

If not, Kittiwake will probably love to help me throw up. "Doc, in the last thirty-six hours I've had a continental breakfast and a light lunch."

"Very well. We'll try some soft foods." He made another notation on the chart and flashed a look to Kittiwake: *Keep an eye on him.* She nodded.

"Your charming wife told me that you are quite obstinate. We'll see about that. Still and all you are doing rather nicely. You can thank your physical condition for that—and my outstanding surgical skill, of course." Scott chuckled to himself. "After breakfast an orderly will help you freshen up for your more, ah, official visitors. Oh, don't expect to see your family soon. They were quite exhausted last night. I gave your wife something to help her sleep; I hope she took it. Your darling little daughter was all done in." Scott gave Ryan a serious look. "I was not misleading you earlier. Discomfort *will* slow your recovery. Do what I tell you and we'll have you out of that bed in a week, and discharged in two—perhaps. But you must do exactly as I say."

"Understood, sir. And thanks. Cathy said you did a good job on the arm."

Scott tried to shrug it off. The smile showed only a little. "One must take proper care of one's guests. I'll be back late this afternoon to see how you are progressing." He left, mumbling instructions to the nurse.

The police arrived in force at 8:30. By this time Ryan had been able to eat his hospital breakfast and wash up. Breakfast had been a huge disappointment, with Wilson collapsing in laughter at Ryan's comment on its appearance—but Kittiwake had been so downcast from this that Ryan had felt constrained to eat all of it, even the stewed prunes that he'd loathed since childhood. Only after finishing had he realized that her demeanor had probably been a sham, a device to get him to eat all the slop. *Nurses,* he reminded himself, *are tricky.* At eight the orderly had arrived to help him clean up. Ryan shaved himself, with the orderly holding the mirror and clucking every time he nicked himself. Four nicks—Ryan customarily used an electric shaver, and hadn't faced a bare blade in years. By 8:30 Ryan felt and looked human again. Kittiwake had brought in a second cup of coffee. It wasn't very good, but it was still coffee.

There were three police officers, very senior ones, Ryan thought, from the way Wilson snapped to his feet and scurried about to arrange chairs for them before excusing himself out the door.

James Owens appeared to be the most senior, and inquired as to Ryan's condition—politely enough that he probably meant it. He reminded Ryan of his own father, a craggy, heavyset man, and, judging from his large, gnarled hands, one who had earned his way to commander's rank after more than a few years of walking the streets and enforcing the law the hard way.

Chief Superintendent William Taylor was about forty, younger than his Anti-Terrorist Branch colleague, and neater. Both senior detectives were well dressed, and both had the red-rimmed eyes that came from an uninterrupted night's work.

David Ashley was the youngest and best-dressed of the three. About Ryan's size and weight, perhaps five years older. He described himself as a representative of the Home Office, and he looked a great deal smoother than either of the others.

"You're quite certain you're up to this?" Taylor asked.

Ryan shrugged. "No sense waiting."

Owens took a cassette tape recorder from his portfolio and set it on the bedstand. He plugged in two microphones, one facing Ryan, the other toward the officers. He punched the record button and announced the date, time, and place.

"Doctor Ryan," Owens asked formally, "do you know that this interview is being recorded?"

"Yes, sir."

"And do you have any objection to this?"

"No, sir. May I ask a question?"

"Certainly," Owens answered.

"Am I being charged with anything? If so, I would like to contact my embassy and have an attor—" Ryan was more than a little uneasy to be the focus of so much high-level police attention, but was cut off by the chuckles of Mr. Ashley. He noted that the other police officers deferred to him for the answer.

"Doctor Ryan, you may just have things the wrong way 'round. For the record, sir, we have no intention whatever of charging you with anything. Were we to do so, I dare say we'd be looking for new employment by day's end."

Ryan nodded, not showing his relief. He'd not yet been sure of this, sure only that the law doesn't have to make sense. Owens began reading his questions from a yellow pad.

"Can you give us your name and address, please?"

"John Patrick Ryan. Our mailing address is Annapolis, Maryland. Our home is at Peregrine Cliff, about ten miles south of Annapolis on the Chesapeake Bay."

"And your occupation?" Owens checked off something on his pad.

"I guess you could say I have a couple of jobs. I'm an instructor in history at the U.S. Naval Academy in Annapolis. I lecture occasionally at the Naval War College in Newport, and from time to time I do a little consulting work on the side."

"That's all?" Ashley inquired with a friendly smile—or was it friendly? Ryan asked himself. Jack wondered just how much they'd managed to find out about him in the past—what? fifteen hours or so— and exactly what Ashley was hinting at. *You're no cop,* Ryan thought. *What exactly are you?* Regardless, he had to stick to his cover story, that he was a part-time consultant to the Mitre Corporation.

"And the purpose of your visit to this country?" Owens went on.

"Combination vacation and research trip. I'm gathering data for a new book, and Cathy needed some time off. Sally is still a pre-schooler, so we decided to head over now and miss the tourist season." Ryan took a cigarette from the pack Wilson had left behind. Ashley lit it from a gold lighter. "In my coat—wherever that is— you'll find letters of introduction to your Admiralty and the Royal Naval College at Dartmouth."

"We have the letters," Owens replied. "Quite illegible, I'm afraid, and I fear your suit is a total loss also. What the blood did not ruin, your wife and our sergeant finished off with a knife. So when did you arrive in Britain?"

"It's still Thursday, right? Well, we got in Tuesday night from Dulles International outside Washington. Arrived about seven-thirty, got to the hotel about nine-thirty or so, had a snack sent up, and went right to sleep. Flying always messes me up—jet lag, whatever. I conked right out." That was not exactly true, but Ryan didn't think they needed to know *everything*.

Owens nodded. They had already learned why Ryan hated flying. "And yesterday?"

"I woke up about seven, I guess, had breakfast and a paper sent up, then just kinda lazed around until about eight-thirty. I arranged to meet Cathy and Sally in the park around four, then caught a cab to the Admiralty building—close, as it turned out, I could have walked it. As I said, I had a letter of introduction to see Admiral Sir Alexander Woodson, the man in charge of your naval archives—he's retired, actually. He took me down to a musty sub-sub-basement. He had the stuff I wanted all ready for me.

"I came over to look at some signal digests. Admiralty signals between London and Admiral Sir James Somerville. He was commander of your Indian Ocean fleet in the early months of 1942, and that's one of the things I'm writing about. So I spend the next three hours reading over faded carbon copies of naval dispatches and taking notes."

"On this?" Ashley held up Ryan's clipboard. Jack snatched it from his hands.

"Thank God!" Ryan exclaimed. "I was sure it got lost." He opened it and set it up on the bedstand, then typed in some instructions. "Ha! It still works!"

"What exactly is that thing?" Ashley wanted to know. All three got out of their chairs to look at it.

"This is my baby." Ryan grinned. On opening the clipboard he revealed a typewriter-style keyboard and a yellow Liquid Crystal Diode display. Outwardly it looked like an expensive clipboard, about an inch thick and bound in leather. "It's a Cambridge Datamaster Model-C Field Computer. A friend of mine makes them. It has an MC-68000 microprocessor, and two megabytes of bubble memory."

"Care to translate that?" Taylor asked.

"Sorry. It's a portable computer. The microprocessor is what does the actual work. Two megabytes means that the memory stores up to two million characters—enough for a whole book—and since it uses bubble memory, you don't lose the information when you switch it off. A guy I went to school with set up a company to make these little darlings. He hit on me for some startup capital. I use an Apple at home, this one's just for carrying around.''

"We knew it was some sort of computer, but our chaps couldn't make it work," Ashley said.

"Security device. The first time you use it, you input your user's code and activate the lockout. Afterward, unless you type in the code, it doesn't work—period.''

"Indeed?" Ashley observed. "How foolproof?''

"You'd have to ask Fred. Maybe you could read the data right off the bubble chips. I don't know how computers work. I just use 'em," Ryan explained. "Anyway, here are my notes.''

"Getting back to your activities of yesterday," Owens said, giving Ashley a cool look. "We now have you to noon."

"Okay. I broke for lunch. A guy on the ground floor directed me to a—a pub, I guess, two blocks away. I don't remember the name of the place. I had a sandwich and a beer while I played with this thing. That took about half an hour. I spent another hour at the Admiralty building before I checked out. Left about quarter of two, I suppose. I thanked Admiral Woodson—very good man. I caught a cab to—don't remember the address, it was on one of my letters. North of—Regent's Park, I think. Admiral Sir Roger DeVere. He served under Somerville. He wasn't there. His housekeeper said he got called out of town suddenly due to a death in the family. So I left a message that I'd been there and flagged another cab back downtown. I decided to get out a few blocks early and walk the rest of the way.''

"Why?" Taylor asked.

"Mainly I was stiff from all the sitting—in the Admiralty building, the flight, the cab. I needed a stretch. I usually jog every day, and I get restless when I miss it.''

"Where did you get out?" Owens asked.

"I don't know the name of the street. If you show me a map I can probably point it out." Owens nodded for him to go on. "Anyway, I nearly got run over by a double-decker bus, and one of your uniformed cops told me not to jaywalk—" Owens looked surprised at that and scribbled some notes. Perhaps they hadn't learned of that encounter. "I picked up a magazine at a street stand and met Cathy about, oh, three-forty or so. They were early, too.''

"And how had she spent her day?" Ashley inquired. Ryan was certain that they had this information already.

"Shopping, mainly. Cathy's been over here a few times, and likes to shop in London. She was last here about three years ago for a surgical convention, but I couldn't make the trip."

"Left you with the little one?" Ashley smiled thinly again. Ryan sensed that Owens was annoyed with him.

"Grandparents. That was before her mom died. I was doing comps for my doctorate at Georgetown, couldn't get out of it. As it was I got my degree in two and a half years, and I sweated blood that last year between the university and seminars at the Center for Strategic and International Studies. This was supposed to be a vacation." Ryan grimaced. "The first real vacation since our honeymoon."

"What were you doing when the attack took place?" Owens got things back on track. All three inquisitors seemed to lean forward in their seats.

"Looking the wrong way. We were talking about what we'd do for dinner when the grenade went off."

"You knew it was a grenade?" Taylor asked.

Ryan nodded. "Yeah. They make a distinctive sound. I hate the damned things, but that's one of the little toys the Marines trained me to use at Quantico. Same thing with the machine-gunner. At Quantico we were exposed to East Bloc weapons. I've handled the AK-47. The sound it makes is different from our stuff, and that's a useful thing to know in combat. How come they didn't both have AKs?"

"As near as we can determine," Owens said, "the man you wounded disabled the car with a rifle-launched antitank grenade. Forensic evidence points to this. His rifle, therefore, was probably one of the new AK-74s, the small-caliber one, fitted to launch grenades. Evidently he didn't have time to remove the grenade-launcher assembly and decided to press on with his pistol. He had a stick grenade also, you know." Jack didn't know about the rifle grenade, but the type of hand grenade he'd seen suddenly leaped out of his memory.

"The antitank kind?" Ryan asked.

"You know about that, do you?" Ashley responded.

"I used to be a Marine, remember? Called the RKG-something, isn't it? Supposed to be able to punch a hole in a light armored vehicle or rip up a truck pretty good." *Where the hell did they get those little rascals— and why didn't they use them . . . ? You're missing something, Jack.*

"Then what?" Owens asked.

"First thing, I got my wife and kid down on the deck. The traffic stopped pretty quick. I kept my head up to see what was happening."

"Why?" Taylor inquired.

"I don't know," Ryan said slowly. "Training, maybe. I wanted to see what the hell was going on—call it stupid curiosity. I saw the one guy hosing down the Rolls and the other one hustling around the back, like he was trying to bag anyone who tried to jump out of the car. I saw that if I moved to my left I could get closer. I was screened by the stopped cars. All of a sudden I was within fifty feet or so. The AK gunner was screened behind the Rolls, and the pistolero had his back to me. I saw that I had a chance, and I guess I took it."

"Why?" It was Owens this time, very quiet.

"Good question. I don't know, I really don't." Ryan was silent for half a minute. "It made me mad. Everyone I've met over here so far has been pretty nice, and all of a sudden I see these two cocksuckers committing murder right the hell in front of me."

"Did you guess who they were?" Taylor asked.

"Doesn't take much imagination, does it? That pissed me off, too. I guess that's it—anger. Maybe that's what motivates people in combat," Ryan mused. "I'll have to think about that. Anyway, like I said, I saw the chance and I took it.

"It was easy—I was very lucky." Owens' eyebrows went up at that understatement. "The guy with the pistol was dumb. He should have checked his back. Instead he just kept looking at his kill zone—*very* dumb. You always 'check-six.' I blindsided him." Ryan grinned. "My coach would have been proud—I really stuck him good. But I guess I ought to have had my pads on, 'cause the doc says I broke something up here when I hit him. He went down pretty hard. I got his gun and shot him—you want to know why I did that, right?"

"Yes," Owens replied.

"I didn't want him to get up."

"He was unconscious—he didn't wake up for two hours, and had a nasty concussion when he did."

If I'd known he had that grenade, I wouldn't have shot him in the ass! "How was I supposed to know that?" Ryan asked reasonably. "I was about to go up against a somebody with a light machine gun, and I didn't need a bad guy behind me. So I neutralized him. I could have put one through the back of his head—at Quantico when they say 'neutralize,' they mean *kill*. My dad was the cop. Most of what I know about police procedures comes from watching TV, and I *know* most of that's wrong. All I knew was that I couldn't afford to have him come at me from behind. I can't say I'm especially proud of it, but at the time it seemed like a good idea.

"I moved around the right-rear corner of the car and looked around. I saw the guy was using a pistol. Your man Wilson explained that to me—that was lucky, too. I wasn't real crazy about taking an AK on with a dinky little handgun. He saw me come around. We both fired about the same time—I just shot straighter, I guess."

Ryan stopped. He hadn't meant it to sound like that. *Is that how it was? If* you *don't know, who does?* Ryan had learned that in a crisis, time compresses and dilates—seemingly at the same time. *It also fools your memory, doesn't it? What else could I have done?* He shook his head.

"I don't know," he said again. "Maybe I should have tried something else. Maybe I should have said, 'Drop it!' or 'Freeze!' like they do on TV—but there just wasn't time. Everything was *right now*— him or me—do you know what I mean? You don't . . . you don't reason all this out when you only have half a second of decision time. I guess you go on training and instinct. The only training I've had was in the Green Machine, the Corps. They don't teach you to arrest people—Christ's sake, I didn't *want* to kill anybody, I just didn't have a hell of a choice in the matter." Ryan paused for a moment.

"Why didn't he—quit, run away, something! He saw I had him. He must have known I had him cold." Ryan slumped back into the pillow. Having to articulate what had happened brought it back all too vividly. *A man is dead because of you, Jack. All the way dead. He had his instincts, too, didn't he? But yours worked better—so why doesn't that make you feel good?*

"Doctor Ryan," Owens said calmly, "we three have personally interviewed six people, all of whom had a clear view of the incident. From what they have told us, you have related the circumstances to us with remarkable clarity. Given the facts of the matter, I—we—do not see that you had any choice at all. It is as certain as such things can possibly be that you did precisely the right thing. And your second shot did not matter, if that is troubling you. Your first went straight through his heart."

Jack nodded. "Yeah, I could see that. The second shot was completely automatic, like my hand did it without being told. The gun came back down and zap! No thought at all . . . funny how your brain works. It's like one part does the doing and another part does the watching and advising. The 'watching' part saw the first round go right through his ten-ring, but the 'doing' part kept going till he went down. I might have tried to squeeze off another round for all I know, but the gun was empty.''

"The Marines taught you to shoot very well indeed," Taylor observed.

Ryan shook his head. "Dad taught me when I was a kid. The Corps doesn't make a big deal about pistols anymore—they're just for show. If the bad guys get that close, it's time to leave. I carried a rifle. Anyway, the guy was only fifteen feet away." Owens made some more notes.

"The car took off a few seconds later. I didn't get much of a look at the driver. It could have been a man or a woman. He or she was white, that's all I can say. The car went whippin' up the street and turned, last I saw of it.''

"It was one of our London taxis—did you notice that?" Taylor asked.

Ryan blinked. "Oh, you're right. I didn't really think about that—that's dumb! Hell, you have a million of the damned things around. No wonder they used one of those.''

"Eight thousand six hundred seventy-nine, to be exact," Owens said. "Five thousand nine hundred nineteen of which are painted black.''

A light went off in Ryan's head. "Tell me, was this an assassination attempt or were they trying to kidnap them?''

"We're not sure about that. You might be interested to know that Sinn Fein, the political wing of the PIRA, released a statement completely disowning the incident.''

"You believe that?" Ryan asked. With pain medications still coursing through his system, he didn't quite notice how skillfully Taylor had parried his question.

"Yes, we are leaning in that direction. Even the Provos aren't this crazy, you know. Something like this has far too high a political price. They learned that much from killing Lord Mountbatten—wasn't even the PIRA who did that, but the INLA, the Irish National Liberation

Army. Regardless, it cost them a lot of money from their American sympathizers,'' Taylor said.

''I see from the papers that your fellow citizens—''

''Subjects,'' Ashley corrected.

''Whatever, your people are pretty worked up about this.''

''Indeed they are, Doctor Ryan. It is rather remarkable how terrorists can always seem to find a way to shock us, no matter what horrors have gone before,'' Owens noted. His voice was wholly professional, but Ryan sensed that the chief of Anti-Terrorist Branch was willing to rip the head right off the surviving terrorist with his bare hands. They looked strong enough to do just that. ''So what happened next?''

''I made sure the guy I shot—the second one—was dead. Then I checked the car. The driver—well, you know about that, and the security officer. One of your people, Mr. Owens?''

''Charlie was a friend of mine. He's been with the Royal Family's security detail for three years now. . . .'' Owens spoke almost as though the man were still alive, and Ryan wondered if they had ever worked together. Police make especially close friendships, he knew.

''Well, you guys know the rest. I hope somebody gives that redcoat a pat on the head. Thank God he took the time to think it all out—at least long enough for your guy to show up and calm him down. Would have been embarrassing for everybody if he'd stuck that bayonet out my back.''

Owens grunted agreement. ''Indeed it would.''

''Was that rifle loaded?'' Ryan asked.

''If it was,'' Ashley replied, ''why didn't he shoot?''

''A crowded street isn't the best place to use a high-powered rifle, even if you're sure of your target,'' Ryan answered. ''It was loaded, wasn't it?''

''We cannot discuss security matters,'' Owens said.

I knew it was loaded, Ryan told himself. ''Where the hell did he come from, anyway? The Palace is a good ways off.''

''Clarence House—the white building adjoining St. James's Palace. The terrorists picked a bad time—or perhaps a bad place—for their attack. There is a guard post at the southwest corner of the building. The guard changes every two hours. When the attack took place, the change was just under way. That meant that four soldiers were there at the time, not just one. The police on duty at the Palace heard the explosion and automatic fire. The Sergeant in charge ran to the gate to see what was going on and yelled for a guardsman to follow.''

"He's the one who sounded the alarm, right? That's how the rest of them arrived so fast?''

"Charlie Winston," Owens said. "The Rolls has an electronic attack alarm—you don't need to tell anyone that. That alerted headquarters. Sergeant Price acted entirely on his own initiative. Unfortunately for him, the guardsman was a hurdler—the lad runs track and field— and vaulted the barriers there. Price tried to do it also, but he fell down and broke his nose. He had a devil of a time catching up, plus sending out his own alarm on his portable radio.''

"Well, I'm glad he caught up when he did. That trooper scared the hell out of me. I hope your Sergeant gets a pat on the head, too.''

"The Queen's Police Medal for starters, and the thanks of Her Majesty," Ashley said. "One thing that has confused us, Doctor Ryan. You left the military with a physical disability, yet you evidenced none of this yesterday.''

"You know that after I left the Corps, I went into the brokerage business. I made something of a name for myself, and Cathy's father came down to talk to me. That's when I met Cathy. I passed on the invitation to move to New York, but Cathy and I hit it right off. One thing led to another, and pretty soon we were engaged. I wore a back brace then, because every so often my back would go bad on me. Well, it happened again right after we got engaged, and Cathy took me into Johns Hopkins to have one of her teachers check me out. One was Stanley Rabinowisz, professor of neurosurgery there. He ran me through three days of tests and said he could fix me good as new.

"It turned out that the docs at Bethesda had goofed my myelogram. No reflection on them, they were sharp young docs, but Stan's about the best there is. Good as his word, too. He opened me up that Friday, and two months later I *was* almost as good as new," Ryan said. "Anyway, that's the story of Ryan's back. I just happened to fall in love with a pretty girl who was studying to be a surgeon.''

"Your wife is certainly a most versatile and competent woman," Owens agreed.

"And you found her pushy," Ryan observed.

"No, Doctor Ryan. People under stress are never at their best. Your wife also examined Their Royal Highnesses on the scene, and that was most useful to us. She refused to leave your side until you were under competent medical care; one can hardly fault her for that. She did find our identification procedures a touch longwinded, I think, and she was quite naturally anxious about you. We might have moved things along more quickly—"

"No need to apologize, sir. My dad was a cop. I know the score. I understand you had trouble identifying us."

"Just over three hours—a timing problem, you see. We had your passport out of your coat, and your driving license, which, we were glad to see, had your photograph. Our initial request to your Legal Attaché was just before five, and that made it noon in America. Lunchtime, you see. He called the FBI's Baltimore field office, who in turn called their Annapolis office. The identification business is fairly straightforward—first they had to find some chaps at your Naval Academy who knew who you were, when you came over, and so forth. Next they found the travel agent who booked your flight and hotel. Another agent went to your motor vehicle registration agency. Many of these people were off eating lunch, and we reckon that cost us roughly an hour. Simultaneously he—the Attaché—sent a query to your Marine Corps. Within three hours we had a fairly complete history on you—including fingerprints. We had your fingerprints from your travel documents and the hotel registration, and they matched your military records, of course."

"Three hours, eh?" *Dinnertime here, and lunchtime at home, and they did it all in three hours. Damn.*

"While all that was going on we had to interview your wife several times to make sure that she related everything she saw—"

"And she gave it to you exactly the same way every time, right?" Ryan asked.

"Correct," Owens said. He smiled. "That is quite remarkable, you know."

Ryan grinned. "Not for Cathy. Some things, medicine especially, she's a real machine. I'm surprised she didn't hand you a roll of film."

"She said that herself," Owens replied. "The photographs in the paper are from a Japanese tourist—that's a cliché, isn't it?—half a block away with a telephoto lens. You might be interested to know that your Marine Corps thinks rather highly of you, by the way." Owens consulted his notes. "Tied for first in your class at Quantico, and your fitness reports were excellent."

"So, you're satisfied I'm a good guy?"

"We were convinced of that from the first moment," Taylor said. "One must be thorough in major felony cases, however, and this one obviously had more than its share of complications."

"There's one thing that bothers me," Jack said. There was more than one, but his brain was working too slowly to classify them all.

"What's that?" Owens asked.

"What the hell were they—the Royals, you call them?—doing out on the street with only one guard—wait a minute." Ryan's head cocked to one side. He went on, speaking rather slowly as his mind struggled to arrange his thoughts. "That ambush was planned—this wasn't any accidental encounter. But the bad guys caught 'em on the fly. . . . They had to hit a particular car in a particular place. Somebody timed this one out. There were some more people involved in this, weren't there?" Ryan heard a lot of silence for a moment. It was all the answer he needed. "Somebody with a radio . . . those characters had to know that they were coming, the route they'd take, and exactly when they got into the kill zone. Even then it wouldn't be all that easy, 'cause you have to worry about traffic. . . ."

"Just an historian, Doctor Ryan?" Ashley asked.

"They teach you how to do ambushes in the Marines. If you want to ambush a specific target . . . first, you have to have intelligence information; second, you choose your ground; third, you put your own security guys out to tell you when the target is coming—that's just the bare-bones requirements. Why here—why St. James's Park, The Mall?" *The terrorist is a political creature. The target and the place are chosen for political effect,* Ryan told himself. "You didn't answer my question before: was this an assassination or an attempted kidnapping?"

"We are not entirely sure," Owens answered.

Ryan looked over his guests. He'd just touched an open nerve. *They disabled the car with an antitank rifle-grenade, and both of them had the hand-thrown kind, too. If they just wanted to kill . . . the grenades would defeat any armor on the car, why use guns at all? No, if this was a straight assassination attempt, they would not have taken so long, would they? You just fibbed to me, Mr. Owens. This was definitely a kidnap attempt and you know it.*

"Why just the one security officer in the car, then? You have to protect your people better than that." *What was it Tony said? An unscheduled trip? The first requirement for a successful ambush is good* intelligence. . . . *You can't pursue this, idiot!* The Commander solved the problem for Jack.

"Well, I believe we covered everything rather nicely. We'll probably be back tomorrow," Owens said.

"How are the terrorists—the one I wounded, I mean."

"He has not been terribly cooperative. Won't speak to us at all, not even to tell us his name—old story dealing with this lot. We've only identified him a few hours ago. No previous criminal record at all—his name appeared as a possible player in two minor cases, but nothing more than that. He is recovering quite nicely, and in three weeks or so," Taylor said coldly, "he will be taken before the Queen's Bench, tried before a jury of twelve good men and true, convicted, and sentenced to spend the remainder of his natural life at a secure prison."

"Only three weeks?" Ryan asked.

"The case is clear-cut," Owens said. "We have three photographs from our Japanese friend that show this lad holding his gun behind the car, and nine good eyewitnesses. There will be no mucking about with this lad."

"And I'll be there to see it," Ryan observed.

"Of course. You will be our most important witness, Doctor. A formality, but a necessary one. And no claim of lunacy like the chap who tried to kill your President. This boy is a university graduate, with honors, and he comes from a good family."

Ryan shook his head. "Ain't that a hell of a thing? But most of the really bad ones are, aren't they?"

"You know about terrorists?" Ashley asked.

"Just things I've read," Ryan answered quickly. *That was a mistake, Jack. Cover it.* "Officer Wilson said the ULA were Maoists."

"Correct," Taylor said.

"That really is crazy. Hell, even the Chinese aren't Maoists anymore, at least the last time I checked they weren't. Oh—what about my family?"

Ashley laughed. "About time you asked, Doctor. We couldn't very well leave them at the hotel, could we? It was arranged for them to be put up at a highly secure location."

"You need not be concerned," Owens agreed. "They are quite safe. My word on it."

"Where, exactly?" Ryan wanted to know.

"A security matter, I'm afraid," Ashley said. The three inquisitors shared an amused look. Owens checked his watch and shot a look to the others.

"Well," Owens said. He switched off the tape recorder. "We do not wish to trouble you further the day after surgery. We will probably be back to check a few additional details. For the moment, sir, you have the thanks of all of us at the Yard for doing our job for us."

"How long will I have Mr. Wilson here?"

"Indefinitely. The ULA are likely to be somewhat annoyed with you," Owens said. "And it would be most embarrassing for us if they were to make an attempt on your life and find you unprotected. We do not regard this as likely, mind, but one must be careful."

"I can live with that," Ryan agreed. *I make a hell of a target here, don't I? A third-grader could kill me with a Popsicle stick.*

"The press want to see you," Taylor said.

"I'm thrilled." *Just what I need*, Ryan thought. "Could you hold them off a bit?"

"Simple enough," Owens agreed. "Your medical condition does not permit it at the moment. But you should get used to the idea. You are now something of a public figure."

"Like hell!" Ryan snorted. "I like being obscure." *Then you should have stayed behind the tree, dumbass! Just what have you got yourself into?*

"You can't refuse to see them indefinitely, you know," Taylor said gently.

Jack let out a long breath. "You're correct, of course. But not today. Tomorrow is soon enough." *Let the hubbub die down some first*, Ryan thought stupidly.

"One cannot always stay in the shadows, Doctor Ryan," Ashley said, standing. The others took their cue from him.

The cops and Ashley—Ryan now had him pegged as some kind of spook, intelligence or counterintelligence—took their leave. Wilson came back in, with Kittiwake trailing behind.

"Did they tire you out?" the nurse asked.

"I think I'll live," Ryan allowed. Kittiwake thrust a thermometer in his mouth to make sure.

*   *   *

Forty minutes after the police had left, Ryan was typing happily away on his computer-toy, reviewing notes and drafting some fresh copy. Cathy Ryan's most frequent (and legitimate) complaint about her husband was that while he was reading—or worse, writing—the world could end around him without his taking notice. This was not entirely true. Jack did notice Wilson jumping to attention out the corner of his eye, but he did not look up until he had finished the paragraph. When he did, he saw that his new visitors were Her Majesty, the Queen of the United Kingdom of Great Britain and Northern Ireland, and her husband, the Duke of Edinburgh. His first coherent thought was a mental curse that no one had warned him. His second, that he must look very funny with his mouth hanging open.

"Good morning, Doctor Ryan," the Queen said agreeably. "How are you feeling?"

"Uh, quite well, thank you, uh, Your Majesty. Won't you, uh, please sit down?" Ryan tried to sit more erect in his bed, but was halted by a flash of pain from his shoulder. It helped to center his thoughts and reminded him that his medication was nearly due.

"We have no wish to impose," she said. Ryan sensed that she didn't wish to leave right away, either. He took a second to frame his response.

"Your Majesty, a visit from a head of state hardly qualifies as an imposition. I would be most grateful for your company." Wilson hustled to get two chairs and excused himself out the door as they sat.

The Queen was dressed in a peach-colored suit whose elegant simplicity must have made a noteworthy dent even in her clothing budget. The Duke was in a dark blue suit which finally made Ryan understand why his wife wanted him to buy some clothes over here.

"Doctor Ryan," she said formally, "on our behalf, and that of our people, we wish to express to you our most profound gratitude for your action of yesterday. We are very much in your debt."

Ryan nodded soberly. He wondered just how awful he looked. "For my own part, ma'am, I am glad that I was able to be of service—but the truth of the matter is that I didn't really do all that much. Anyone could have done the same thing. I just happened to be the closest."

"The police say otherwise," the Duke observed. "And after viewing the scene myself, I am inclined to agree with them. I'm afraid you're a hero whether you like it or not." Jack remembered that this man had once been a professional naval officer—probably a good one. He had the look.

"Why did you do it, Doctor Ryan?" the Queen asked. She examined his face closely.

Jack made a quick guess. "Excuse me, ma'am, but are you asking why I took the chance, or why an Irish-American would take the chance?" Jack was still ordering his own thoughts, examining his own memories. *Why did you do it? Will you ever know?* He saw that he'd guessed right and went on quickly.

"Your Majesty, I cannot speak to your Irish problem. I'm an American citizen, and my country has enough problems of its own without having to delve into someone else's. Where I come from we—that is, Irish-Americans—have made out pretty well. We're in all the professions, business, and politics, but your prototypical Irish-American is still a basic police officer or firefighter. The cavalry that won the West was a third Irish, and there are still plenty of us in uniform—especially the Marine Corps, as a matter of fact. Half of the local FBI office lived in my old neighborhood. They had names like Tully, Sullivan, O'Connor, and Murphy. My dad was a police officer for half his life, and the priests and nuns who educated me were mostly Irish, probably.

"Do you see what I mean, Your Majesty? In America we are the forces of order, the glue that holds society together—so what happens?

"Today, the most famous Irishmen in the world are the maniacs who leave bombs in parked cars, or assassins who kill people to make some sort of political point. I don't like that, and I know my dad wouldn't like it. He spent his whole working life taking animals like that off the street and putting them in cages where they belong. We've worked pretty hard to get where we are—too hard to be happy about being thought of as the relatives of terrorists." Jack smiled. "I guess I understand how Italians feel about the Mafia. Anyway, I can't say that all this stuff paraded through my head yesterday, but I did kind of figure what was going on. I couldn't just sit there like a dummy and let murder be committed before my eyes and not do *something*. So I saw my chance and I took it."

The Queen nodded thoughtfully. She regarded Ryan with a warm, friendly smile for a few moments and turned to look at her husband. The two communicated without words. They'd been married long enough for that, Ryan thought. When she turned back, he could see that a decision had been reached.

"So, then. How shall we reward you?"

"Reward, ma'am?" Ryan shook his head. "Thank you very much, but it's not necessary. I'm glad I was able to help. That's enough."

"No, Doctor Ryan, it is not enough. One of the nicer things about being Queen is that one is permitted to recognize meritorious conduct, then to reward it properly. The Crown cannot appear to be ungrateful." Her eyes sparkled with some private joke. Ryan found himself captivated by the woman's humanity. He'd read that some people found her to be less than intelligent. He already knew they were far off the mark. There was an active brain behind those eyes, and an active wit as well. "Accordingly, it has been decided that you shall be invested as a Knight Commander of the Victorian Order."

"What—er, I beg your pardon, ma'am?" Ryan blinked a few times as his brain tried to catch up with his ears.

"The Victorian Order is a recent development intended to reward those persons who have rendered personal service to the Crown. Certainly you qualify. This is the first case in many years that an heir to the throne has been saved from almost certain death. As an historian yourself, you might be interested to learn that our own scholars are in disagreement as to when was our most recent precedent—in any event, you will henceforth be known as Sir John Ryan."

Again Jack thought that he must look rather funny with his mouth open.

"Your Majesty, American law—"

"We know," she interrupted smoothly. "The Prime Minister will be discussing this with your President later today. We believe that in view of the special nature of this case, and in the interest of Anglo-American relations, the matter will be settled amicably."

"There is ample precedent for this," the Duke went on. "After the Second World War a number of American officers were accorded similar recognition. Your Fleet Admiral Nimitz, for example, became a Knight Commander of the Bath, along with Generals Eisenhower, Bradley, Patton, and a number of others.

"For the purposes of American law, it will probably be considered honorary—but for our purposes it will be quite real."

"Well." Ryan fumbled for something to say. "Your Majesty, insofar as this does not conflict with the laws of my country, I will be deeply honored to accept." The Queen beamed.

"That's settled, then. Now, how are you feeling—really feeling?"

"I've felt worse, ma'am. I have no complaints—I just wish I'd moved a little faster."

The Duke smiled. "Being wounded makes you appear that much more heroic—nothing like a little drama."

Especially if it's someone else's shoulder, my Lord Duke, Ryan thought. A small bell went off in his head. "Excuse me, this knighthood, does it mean that my wife will be called—"

"Lady Ryan? Of course." The Queen flashed her Christmas-tree smile again.

Jack grinned broadly. "You know, when I left Merrill Lynch, Cathy's father was madder than—he was very angry with me, said I'd never amount to anything writing history books. Maybe this will change his mind." He was sure that Cathy would not mind the title— *Lady Ryan.* No, she wouldn't mind that one little bit.

"Not so bad a thing after all?"

"No, sir, and please forgive me if I gave that impression. I'm afraid you caught me a little off balance." Ryan shook his head. *This whole damned affair has me a* lot *off balance.* "Might I ask a question, sir?"

"Certainly."

"The police wouldn't tell me where they're keeping my family." This drew a hearty laugh. The Queen answered.

"It is the opinion of the police that there might exist the possibility of a reprisal against you or your family. Therefore it was decided that they should be moved to a more secure location. Under the circumstances, we decided that they might most easily be moved to the Palace—it was the least thing we could do. When we left, your wife and daughter were fast asleep, and we left strict instructions that they should not be disturbed."

"The Palace?"

"We have ample room for guests, I assure you," the Queen replied.

"Oh, Lord!" Ryan muttered.

"You have an objection?" the Duke asked.

"My little girl, she—"

"Olivia?" the Queen said, rather surprised. "She's a lovely child. When we saw her last night she was sleeping like an angel."

"Sally"—Olivia had been a peace offering to Cathy's family that hadn't worked; it was the name of her grandmother—"is a little angel, asleep, but when she wakes up she's more like a little tornado, and she's very good at breaking things. Especially valuable things.''

''What a dreadful thing to say!'' Her Majesty feigned shock. ''That lovely little girl. The police told us that she broke hearts throughout Scotland Yard last evening. I fear you exaggerate, Sir John.''

''Yes, ma'am.'' There was no arguing with a queen.

3

Flowers
and Families

Wilson had been mistaken in his assessment. The escape had taken longer than anyone at the Yard had thought. Six hundred miles away, a Sabena flight was landing outside of Cork. The passenger in seat 23-D of the Boeing 737 was entirely unremarkable; his sandy hair was cut medium-close, and he was dressed like a middle-level executive in a neat but rumpled suit that gave the entirely accurate impression of a man who'd spent a long day on the job and gotten too little sleep before catching a flight home. An experienced traveler to be sure, with one carry-on flight bag. If asked, he could have given a convincing discourse on the wholesale fish business in the accent of Southwestern Ireland. He could change accents as easily as most men changed shirts; a useful skill, since TV news crews had made the patois of his native Belfast recognizable the world over. He read the *London Times* on the flight, and the topic of discussion in his seat row, as with the rest of the aircraft, was the story which covered the front page.

"A terrible thing, it is," he'd agreed with the man in 23-E, a Belgian dealer in machine tools who could not have known how an event might be terrible in more than one way.

All the months of planning, the painstakingly gathered intelligence, the rehearsals carried out right under the Brit noses, the three escape routes, the radiomen—all for nothing because of this bloody meddler. He examined the photo on the front page.

Who are you, Yank? he wondered. *John Patrick Ryan. Historian—a bloody academic! Ex-Marine—trust a damned bootneck to stick his nose where it doesn't belong!* John Patrick Ryan. *You're a bloody Catholic, aren't you? Well, Johnny nearly put paid on your account. . . . Too bad about Johnny. Good man Johnny was, dependable, loved his guns, and true to the Cause.*

The plane finally came to a stop at the jetway. Forward, the stewardess opened the door, and the passengers rose to get their bags from the overhead stowage. He got his, and joined the slow movement forward. He tried to be philosophical about it. In his years as a "player," he'd seen operations go awry for the most ridiculous of reasons. But this op was so important. So *much* planning. He shook his head as he tucked the paper under his arm. *We'll just have to try again, that's all. We can afford to be patient.* One failure, he told himself, didn't matter in the great scheme of things. The other side had been lucky this time. *We only have to be lucky once.* The men in the H-blocks weren't going anywhere.

What about Sean? A mistake to have taken him along. He'd helped plan the operation from the beginning. Sean knows a great deal about the Organization. He set that worry aside as he stepped off the aircraft. *Sean would never talk. Not Sean, not with his girl in her grave these past five years, from a para's stray bullet.*

He wasn't met, of course. The other men who had been part of the operation were already back, their equipment left behind in rubbish bins, wiped clean of fingerprints. Only he had the risk of exposure, but he was sure that this Ryan fellow hadn't got a good look at his face. He thought back again to be sure. No. The look of surprise on his face, the look of pain he'd seen there. The American couldn't have gotten much of a look—if he had, an identikit composite picture would be in the press already, complete with the moppy wig and fake glasses.

He walked out of the terminal building to the parking lot, his travel bag slung over his shoulder, searching in his pocket for the keys that had set off the airport metal detector in Brussels—what a laugh that was! He smiled for the first time in nearly a day. It was a clear, sunny day, another glorious Irish fall it was. He drove his year-old BMW—a man with a business cover had to have a full disguise, after all—down the road to the safehouse. He was already planning two more operations. Both would require a lot of time, but time was the one thing he had in unlimited quantity.

It was easy enough to tell when it was time for another pain medication. Ryan was unconsciously flexing his left hand at the far end of the cast. It didn't reduce the pain, but did seem to move it about somewhat as the muscles and tendons changed place slightly. It bothered his concentration however much he tried to shut it out. Jack remembered all the TV shows in which the detective or otherwise employed hero took a round in the shoulder but recovered fully in time for the last commercial. The human shoulder—his, at any rate—was a solid collection of bones that bullets—*one* bullet—all too easily broke. As the time for another medication approached it seemed that he could feel every jagged edge of every broken bone grating against its neighbor as he breathed, and even the gentle tapping of his right-hand fingers on the keyboard seemed to ripple across his body to the focus of his pain until he had to stop and watch the wall clock—for the first time he wanted Kittiwake to appear with his next installment of chemical bliss.

Until he remembered his fear. The pain of his back injury had made his first week at Bethesda a living hell. He knew that his present injury paled by comparison, but the body does not remember pain, and the shoulder was *here and now*. He forced himself to remember that pain medications had made his back problem almost tolerable . . . except that the doctors had gotten just a little too generous with his dosages. More than the pain, Ryan dreaded withdrawal from morphine sulphate. That had lasted a week, the wanting that seemed to draw his entire body into some vast empty place, someplace where his innermost self found itself entirely alone and *needing*. . . . Ryan shook his head. The pain rippled through his left arm and shoulder and he forced himself to welcome it. *I'm not going to go through that again. Never again.*

The door opened. It wasn't Kittiwake—the med was still fourteen minutes away. Ryan had noticed a uniform outside the door when it had opened before. Now he was sure. A thirtyish uniformed officer came in with a floral arrangement and he was followed by another who was similarly loaded. A scarlet and gold ribbon decorated the first, a gift from the Marine Corps, followed by another from the American Embassy.

"Quite a few more, sir," one uniformed officer said.

"The room isn't all that big. Can you give me the cards and spread these around some? I'm sure there's people around who'd like them." *And who wants to live in a jungle?* Within ten minutes Ryan had a pile of cards, notes, and telegrams. He found that reading the words of others was better than reading his own when it came to blocking out the ache of his damaged shoulder.

Kittiwake arrived. She gave the flowers only a fleeting glance before administering Ryan's medication, and hustled out with scarcely a word. Ryan learned why five minutes later.

His next visitor was the Prince of Wales. Wilson snapped to his feet again, and Jack wondered if the kid's knees were tiring of this. The med was already working. His shoulder was drifting farther away, but along with this came a slight feeling of lightheadedness as from a couple of stiff drinks. Maybe that was part of the reason for what happened next.

"Howdy." Jack smiled. "How are you feeling, sir?"

"Quite well, thank you." The answering smile contained no enthusiasm. The Prince looked very tired, his thin face stretched an extra inch or so, with a lingering sadness around the eyes. His shoulders drooped within the conservative gray suit.

"Why don't you sit down, sir?" Ryan invited. "You look as though you had a tougher night than I did."

"Yes, thank you, Doctor Ryan." He made another attempt to smile. It failed. "And how are you feeling?"

"Reasonably well, Your Highness. And how is your wife—excuse me, how is the Princess doing?"

The Prince's words did not come easily, and he had trouble looking up to Ryan from his chair. "We both regret that she could not come with me. She's still somewhat disturbed—in shock, I believe. She had a very . . . bad experience."

Brains splattered over her face. I suppose you might call that a bad experience. "I saw. I understand that neither of you was physically injured, thank God. I presume your child also?"

"Yes, all thanks to you, Doctor."

Jack tried another one-armed shrug. The gesture didn't hurt so much this time. "Glad to help, sir—I just wish I hadn't got myself shot in the process." His attempt at levity died on his lips. He'd said the wrong thing in the wrong way. The Prince looked at Jack very curiously for a moment, but then his eyes went flat again.

"We would all have been killed except for you, you know—and on behalf of my family and myself—well, thank you. It's not enough just to say that—" His Highness went on, then halted again and struggled to find a few more words. "But it's the best I can manage. I wasn't able to manage very much yesterday, come to that," he concluded, staring quietly at the foot of the bed.

Aha! Ryan thought. The Prince stood and turned to leave. *What do I do now?*

"Sir, why don't you sit down and let's talk this one over for a minute, okay?"

His Highness turned back. For a moment he looked as though he would say something, but the drawn face changed again and turned away.

"Your Highness, I really think . . ." No effect. *I can't let him go out of here like this. Well, if good manners won't work*—Jack's voice became sharp.

"Hold it!" The Prince turned with a look of great surprise. *"Sit down, goddammit!"* Ryan pointed to the chair. *At least I have his attention now. I wonder if they can take a knighthood back. . . .*

By this time the Prince flushed a bit. The color gave his face life that it had lacked. He wavered for a moment, then sat with reluctance and resignation.

"Now," Ryan said heatedly, "I think I know what's eating at you, sir. You feel bad because you didn't do a John Wayne number yesterday and handle those gunmen all by yourself, right?" The Prince didn't nod or make any other voluntary response, but a hurt expression around his eyes answered the question just as surely.

"Aw, crap!" Ryan snorted. In the corner, Tony Wilson went pale as a ghost. Ryan didn't blame him.

"You oughta have better sense . . . sir," Ryan added hastily. "You've been through the service schools, right? You've qualified as a pilot, parachuted out of airplanes, and even had command of your own ship?" He got a nod. Time to step it up. "Then you've got no excuse, you damned well ought to have better sense than to think like that! You're not really that dumb, are you?"

"What exactly do you mean?" *A trace of anger,* Ryan thought. *Good.*

"Use your head. You've been trained to think this sort of thing out, haven't you? Let's critique the exercise. Examine what the tactical situation was yesterday. You were trapped in a stopped car with two or three bad guys outside holding automatic weapons. The car is armor-plated, but you're stuck. What can you do? The way I see it, you had three choices:

"One. You can just freeze, just sit there and wet your pants. Hell, that's what most normal people would do, caught by surprise like that. That's probably the normal reaction. But you didn't do that.

"Two. You can try to get out of the car and *do something,* right?"

"Yes, I should have."

"Wrong!" Ryan shook his head emphatically. "Sorry, sir, but that's not a real good idea. The guy I tackled was waiting for you to do just that. That guy could have put a nine-millimeter slug in your head before you had both feet on the pavement. You look like you're in pretty good shape. You probably move pretty good—but ain't nobody yet been able to outrun a bullet, sir! That choice might have gotten you killed, and the rest of your family along with you.

"Three. Your last choice, you tough it out and pray the cavalry gets there in time. You know you're close to home. You know there's cops and troops around. So you know that time is on your side if you can survive for a couple of minutes. In the meantime you try to protect your family as best you can. You get them down on the floor of the car and get overtop of them so the only way the terrorists can get them is to go through you first. And *that,* my friend, is what you did." Ryan paused for a moment to let him absorb this.

"You did *exactly* the right thing, dammit!" Ryan leaned forward until his shoulder pulled him back with a gasp. It wasn't all that much of a pain medication. "Jesus, this hurts. Look, sir, you were stuck out in the open—with a lousy set of alternatives. But you used your head and took the best one you had. From where I sit, you could not have done any better than you did. So there is nothing, repeat *nothing,* for you to feel bad about. And if you don't believe me, ask Wilson. He's a cop." The Prince turned his head.

The Anti-Terrorist Branch officer cleared his throat. "Excuse me, Your Royal Highness, but Doctor Ryan is quite correct. We were discussing this, this problem yesterday, and we reached precisely the same conclusion.''

Ryan looked over to the cop. ''How long did you fellows kick the idea around, Tony?''

''Perhaps ten minutes,'' Wilson answered.

''That's six *hundred* seconds, Your Highness. But you had to think and act in—what? Five? Maybe three? Not much time to make a life-and-death decision is it? Mister, I'd say you did damned well. All that training you've picked up along the line worked. And if you were evaluating someone else's performance instead of your own, you'd say the same thing, just like Tony and his friends did.''

''But the press—''

''Oh, screw the press!'' Ryan snapped back, wondering if he'd gone too far. ''What do reporters know about anything? They don't *do* anything, for crying out loud, they just report what other people do. You can fly an airplane, you've jumped out of them—flying scares the hell out of me; I don't even want to think about jumping out of one— and commanded a ship. Plus you ride horses and keep trying to break your neck—and now, finally, you're a father, you got a kid of your own now, right? Isn't that enough to prove to the world that you've got balls? You're not some dumb kid, sir. You're a trained pro. Start acting like one.''

Jack could see his mind going over what he'd just been told. His Highness was sitting a little straighter now. The smile that began to form was an austere one, but at least it had some conviction behind it.

''I am not accustomed to being addressed so forcefully.''

''So cut my head off.'' Ryan grinned. ''You looked like you needed a little straightening out—but I had to get your attention first, didn't I? I'm not going to apologize, sir. Instead, why don't you look in that mirror over there. I bet the guy you see now looks better than the one who shaved this morning.''

''You really believe what you said?''

''Of course. All you have to do is look at the situation from the outside, sir. The problem you had yesterday was tougher than any exercise I had to face at Quantico, but you gutted it out. Listen, I'll tell you a story.

''My first day at Quantico, first day of the officer's course. They line us up, and we meet our Drill Instructor, Gunnery Sergeant Willie King—humongous black guy, we called him Son of Kong. Anyway, he looks us up and down and says, 'Girls, I got some good news, and I got some bad news. The good news is, if you prove that you're good enough to get through this here course, you ain't got nothin' left to prove as long as you live.' And he waits for a couple of seconds. 'The bad news is, you gotta prove it to *me!*'"

"You were top in your class," the Prince said. He'd been briefed, too.

"I was third in that one. I tied for first in the Basic Officer's Course later on. Yeah, I did okay. That course was a gold-plated sonuvabitch. The only easy thing was sleeping—by the time your day was finished, falling asleep was easy enough. But, you know, Son of Kong was almost right.

"If you make it through Quantico, you know you've done something. After that there *was* only one more thing left for me to prove, and the Corps didn't have anything to do with that." Ryan paused for a moment. "Her name is Sally. Anyway, you and your family are alive, sir. Okay, I helped—but so did you. And if any reporter-expert says different, you still have the Tower of London, right? I remember that stuff in the press about your wife last year. Damn, if anybody'd talked that way about Cathy I'd have changed his voice for him."

"Changed his voice?" His Highness asked.

"The *hard* way!" Ryan laughed. "I guess that's a problem with being important—you can't shoot back. Too bad. People in that business could use some manners, and people in your business are entitled to some privacy, just like the rest of us."

"And what of your manners, Sir John?" A real smile now.

"*Mea maxima culpa,* my Lord Prince, you got me there."

"Still, we might not be here except for you."

"I couldn't just sit there and watch some people get murdered. If situations had been reversed, I'll bet you'd have done the same thing I did."

"You really think so?" His Highness was surprised.

"Sir, are you kidding? Anybody dumb enough to jump out of an airplane is dumb enough to try anything."

The Prince stood and walked over to the mirror on the wall. Clearly he liked what he saw there. "Well," he murmured to the mirror. He turned back to voice his last self-doubt.

"And if you had been in my place?"

"I'd probably just've wet my pants," Ryan replied. "But you have an advantage over me, sir. You've thought about this problem for a few years, right? Hell, you practically grew up with it, and you've been through basic training—Royal Marines, too, maybe?''

"Yes, I have."

Ryan nodded. "Okay, so you had your options figured out beforehand, didn't you? They caught you by surprise, sure, but the training shows. You did all right. Honest. Sit back down, and maybe Tony can pour us some coffee."

Wilson did so, though he was clearly uneasy to be close to the heir. The Prince of Wales sipped at his cup while Ryan lit up one of Wilson's cigarettes. His Highness looked on disapprovingly.

"That's not good for you, you know," he pointed out.

Ryan just laughed. "Your Highness, since I arrived in this country, I nearly got run over by one of those two-story buses, I almost got my head blown off by a damned Maoist, then I nearly get myself shish-kabobed by one of your redcoats." Ryan waved the cigarette in the air. "This is the *safest* damned thing I've done since I got here! What a vacation this's turned out to be."

"You do have a point," the Prince admitted. "And quite a sense of humor, Doctor Ryan."

"I guess the valium—or whatever they're giving me—helps. And the name's Jack." He held out his hand. The Prince took it.

"I was able to meet your wife and daughter yesterday—you were unconscious at the time. I gather that your wife is an excellent physician. Your little daughter is quite wonderful."

"Thanks. How do you like being a daddy?"

"The first time you hold your newborn child . . ."

"Yeah," Jack said. "Sir, that's what it's all about." He stopped talking abruptly.

Bingo, Ryan thought. *A four-month-old baby. If they kidnap the Prince and Princess, well, no government can cave in to terrorism. The politicians and police* have to *have a contingency plan already set up for this, don't they? They'd take this town apart one brick at a time, but they wouldn't—couldn't—negotiate anything, and that was just too bad for the grown-ups, but a little baby . . .* damn, *there's a bargaining chip! What kind of people would—*

"Bastards," Ryan whispered to himself. Wilson blanched, but the Prince suspected what Jack was thinking about.

"Excuse me?"

"They weren't trying to kill you. Hell, I bet you weren't even the real objective. . . ." Ryan nodded slowly. He searched his mind for the data he'd seen on the ULA. There hadn't been much—it hadn't been his area of focus in any case—a few tidbits of shadowy intelligence reports, mixed with a lot of pure conjecture. "They didn't want to kill you at all, I bet. And when you covered the wife and kid, you burned their plan . . . maybe, or maybe you just—yeah, maybe you just threw them a curve, and that blew their timing a little bit."

"What do you mean?" the Prince asked.

"Goddamned medications slow your brain down," Ryan said mainly to himself. "Have the police told you what the terrorists were up to?"

His Highness sat upright in the chair. "I can't—"

"You don't have to," Ryan cut him off. "Did they tell you that what you did definitely—*definitely*—saved all of you?"

"No, but—"

"Tony?"

"They told me you were a very clever chap, Jack," Wilson said. "I'm afraid I can't comment further. Your Royal Highness, Doctor Ryan may be correct in his assessment."

"What assessment?" The Prince was puzzled.

Ryan explained. It only took a few minutes.

"How did you arrive at this conclusion, Jack?"

Ryan's mind was still churning through the hypothesis. "Sir, I'm an historian. My business is figuring things out. Before that I was a stockbroker—doing essentially the same thing. It's not all that hard when you think about it. You look for apparent inconsistencies and then you try to figure out why they're not really inconsistent." He concluded, "It's all speculation on my part, but I'm willing to bet that Tony's colleagues are pursuing it." Wilson didn't say anything. He cleared his throat—which was answer enough.

The Prince looked deep into his coffee cup. His face was that of a man who had recovered from fear and shame. Now he contemplated cold anger at what might have been.

"Well, they've had their chance, haven't they?"

"Yes, sir. I imagine if they ever try again, it'll be a lot harder. Right, Tony?"

"I seriously doubt that they will ever try again," Wilson replied. "We should develop some rather good intelligence from this incident.

The ULA have stepped over an invisible line. Politically, success might have enhanced their position, but they didn't succeed, did they? This will harm them, harm their 'popular' support. Some people who know them will now consider talking—not to us, you understand, but some of what they say will get to us in due course. They were outcasts before, they will be outcasts even more now.''

Will they learn from this? Ryan wondered. *If so, what will they have learned? There's a question.* Jack knew that it had only two possible answers, and that those answers were diametrically opposed. He made a mental note. He'd follow up on this when he got home. It wasn't a merely academic exercise now. He had a bullet hole in his shoulder to prove that.

The Prince rose to his feet. ''You must excuse me, Jack. I'm afraid I have rather a full day ahead.''

''Going back out, eh?''

''If I hide, they've won. I understand that fact better now than when I came in here. And I have something else to thank you for.''

''You would have figured it out sooner or later. Better it should be sooner, don't you think?''

''We must see more of each other.''

''I'd like that, sir. Afraid I'm stuck here for a while, though.''

''We are traveling out of the country soon—the day after tomorrow. It's a state visit to New Zealand and the Solomon Islands. You may be gone before we get back.''

''Is your wife up to it, Your Highness?''

''I think so. A change of scenery, the doctor said, is just the ticket. She had a very bad experience yesterday, but''—he smiled—''I think it was harder on me than on her.''

I'll buy that, Ryan thought. *She's young, she'll bounce back, and at least she has something good to remember. Putting your body between your family and the bullets ought to firm up any relationship.* ''Hey, she sure as hell knows you love her, sir.''

''I do, you know,'' the Prince said seriously.

''It's the customary reason to get married, sir,'' Jack replied, ''even for us common folk.''

''You're a most irreverent chap, Jack.''

''Sorry about that.'' Ryan grinned. So did the Prince.

''No, you're not.'' His Highness extended his hand. ''Thank you, Sir John, for many things.''

Ryan watched him leave with a brisk step and a straight back.

"Tony, you know the difference between him and me? I can say that I used to be a Marine, and that's enough. But that poor guy's got to prove it every damned day, to everybody he meets. I guess that's what you have to do when you're in the public eye all the time." Jack shook his head. "There's no way in hell they could pay me enough to take his job."

"He's born to it," Wilson said.

Ryan thought about that. "That's one difference between your country and mine. You think people are born to something. We know that they have to grow into it. It's not the same thing, Tony."

"Well, you're part of it now, Jack."

"I think I should go." David Ashley looked at the telex in his hand. The disturbing thing was that he'd been requested by name. The PIRA knew who he was, and they knew that he was the Security Service executive on the case. *How the hell did they know* that!

"I agree," James Owens said. "If they're this anxious to talk with us, they might be anxious enough to tell us something useful. Of course, there is an element of risk. You could take someone with you."

Ashley thought about that one. There was always the chance that he'd be kidnapped, but . . . The strange thing about the PIRA was that they did have a code of conduct. Within their own definitions, they were honorable. They assassinated their targets without remorse, but they wouldn't deal in drugs. Their bombs would kill children, but they'd never kidnapped one. Ashley shook his head.

"No, people from the Service have met with them before and there's never been a problem. I'll go alone." He turned for the door.

"Daddy!" Sally ran into the room and stopped cold at the side of the bed as she tried to figure a way to climb high enough to kiss her father. She grabbed the side rails and set one foot on the bedframe as if it were the monkey bars at her nursery school and sprang upward. Her diminutive frame bent over the edge of the mattress as she scrambled for a new foothold, and Ryan pulled her up.

"Hi, Daddy." Sally kissed him on the cheek.

"And how are you today?"

"Fine. What's that, Daddy?" She pointed.

"It's called a cast," Cathy Ryan answered. "I thought you had to go to the bathroom."

"Okay." Sally jumped back off the bed.

"I think it's in there," Jack said. "But I'm not sure."

"I thought so," Cathy said after surveying Jack's attachment to the bed. "Okay, come on, Sally."

A man had entered behind his family, Ryan saw. Late twenties, very athletic, and nicely dressed, of course. He was also rather good-looking, Jack reflected.

"Good afternoon, Doctor Ryan," he said. "I'm William Greville."

Jack made a guess. "What regiment?"

"Twenty-second, sir."

"Special Air Service?" Greville nodded, a proud but restrained smile on his lips.

"When you care enough to send the very best," Jack muttered. "Just you?"

"And a driver, Sergeant Michaelson, a policeman from the Diplomatic Protection Group."

"Why you and not another cop?"

"I understand your wife wishes to see a bit of the countryside. My father is something of an authority on various castles, and Her Majesty thought that your wife might wish to have an, ah, escort familiar with the sights. Father has dragged me through nearly every old house in England, you see."

"Escort" is the right word, Ryan thought, remembering what the "Special Air Service" really was. The only association they had with airplanes was jumping out of them—or blowing them up.

Greville went on. "I am also directed by my colonel to extend an invitation to our regimental mess."

Ryan gestured at his suspended arm. "Thanks, but that might have to wait a while."

"We understand. No matter, sir. Whenever you have the chance, we'll be delighted to have you in for dinner. We wanted to extend the invitation before the bootnecks, you see." Greville grinned. "What you did was more our sort of op, after all. Well, I had to extend the invitation. You want to see your family, not me."

"Take good care of them . . . Lieutenant?"

"Captain," Greville corrected. "We will do that, sir." Ryan

watched the young officer leave as Cathy and Sally emerged from the bathroom.

"What do you think of him?" Cathy asked.

"His daddy's a count, Daddy!" Sally announced. "He's nice."

"What?"

"His father's Viscount-something-or-other," his wife explained as she walked over. "You look a lot better."

"So do you, babe." Jack craned his neck up to meet his wife's kiss.

"Jack, you've been smoking." Even before they'd gotten married, Cathy had bullied him into stopping.

Her damned sense of smell, Jack thought. "Be nice, I've had a hard day."

"Wimp!" she observed disgustedly.

Ryan looked up at the ceiling. *To the whole world I'm a hero, but I smoke a couple of cigarettes and to Cathy that makes me a wimp.* He concluded that the world was not exactly overrun with justice.

"Gimme a break, babe."

"Where'd you get them?"

"I have a cop baby-sitting me in here—he had to go someplace a few minutes ago."

Cathy looked around for the offending cigarette pack so that she could squash it. Jack had it stashed under his pillow. Cathy Ryan sat down. Sally climbed into her lap.

"How do you feel?"

"I know it's there, but I can live with it. How'd you make out last night?"

"You know where we are now, right?"

"I heard."

"It's like being Cinderella." Caroline Muller Ryan, MD, grinned.

John Patrick Ryan, PhD, wiggled the fingers of his left hand. "I guess I'm the one who turned into the pumpkin. I guess you're going to make the trips we planned. Good."

"Sure you don't mind?"

"Half the reason for the vacation was to get you away from hospitals, Cathy, remember? No sense taking all the film home unused, is it?"

"It'd be a lot more fun with you."

Jack nodded. He'd looked forward to seeing the castles on the list, too. Like many Americans, Ryan could not have abided the English class system, but that didn't stop him from being fascinated with its trappings. *Or something like that,* he thought. His knighthood, he knew, might change that perspective if he allowed himself to dwell on it.

"Look on the bright side, babe. You've got a guide who can tell you everything you ever wanted to know about Lord Jones's castle on the coast of whatever. You'll have plenty of time for it, too."

"Yeah," she said, "the police said we'd be staying over a while longer than we planned. I'll have to talk to Professor Lewindowski about that." She shrugged. "They'll understand."

"How do you like the new place? Better than the hotel?"

"You're going to have to see—no, you'll have to *experience* it." She laughed. "I think hospitality is the national sport over here. They must teach it in the schools, and have quarterly exams. And guess who we're having dinner with tonight?"

"I don't have to guess."

"Jack, they're so *nice.*"

"I noticed. Looks like you're really getting the VIP treatment."

"What's the Special Air Service—he's some kind of pilot?"

"Something like that," Jack said diffidently. Cathy might feel uncomfortable sitting next to a man who had to be carrying a gun. And was trained to use it with as little compunction as a wolf might use his teeth. "You're not asking how I feel."

"I got hold of your chart on the way in," Cathy explained.

"And?"

"You're doing okay, Jack. I see you can move your fingers. I was worried about that."

"How come?"

"The brachial plexus—it's a nerve junction inside your shoulder. The bullet missed it by about an inch and a half. That's why you can move your fingers. The way you were bleeding, I thought the brachial artery was cut, and that runs right next to the nerves. It would have put your arm out of business for good. But"—she smiled—"you lucked out. Just broken bones. They hurt but they heal."

Doctors are so wonderfully objective, Ryan told himself, even the ones you marry. *Next thing, she'll say the pain is good for me.*

"Nice thing about pain," Cathy went on. "It tells you the nerves are working."

Jack closed his eyes and shook his head. He opened them when he felt Cathy take his hand.

"Jack, I'm so proud of you."

"Nice to be married to a hero?"

"You've always been a hero to me."

"Really?" She'd never said *that* before. What was heroic about being an historian? Cathy didn't know the other stuff he did, but that wasn't especially heroic either.

"Ever since you told Daddy to—well, you know. Besides, I love you, remember?"

"I seem to recall a reminder of that the other day."

Cathy made a face. "Better get your mind off that for a while."

"I know." Ryan made a face of his own. "The patient must conserve his energy—or something. What ever happened to that theory about how a happy attitude speeds recovery?"

"That's what I get for letting you read my journals. Patience, Jack."

Nurse Kittiwake came in, saw the family, and made a quick exit.

"I'll try to be patient," Jack said, and looked longingly at the closing door.

"You turkey," Cathy observed. "I know you better than that."

She did, Jack knew. He couldn't even make that threat work. *Oh, well—that's what you get for loving your wife.*

Cathy stroked his face. "What did you shave with this morning, a rusty nail?"

"Yeah—I need my razor. Maybe my notes, too?"

"I'll bring them over or have somebody do it." She looked up when Wilson came back in.

"Tony, this is Cathy, my wife, and Sally, my daughter. Cathy, this is Tony Wilson. He's the cop who's baby-sitting me."

"Didn't I see you last night?" Cathy never forgot a face—so far as Jack could tell, she never forgot much of anything.

"Possibly, but we didn't speak—rather a busy time for all of us. You are well, Lady Ryan?"

"Excuse me?" Cathy asked. "Lady Ryan?"

"They didn't tell you?" Jack chuckled.

"Tell me what?"

Jack explained. "How do you like being married to a knight?"

"Does that mean you have to have a horse, Daddy?" Sally asked hopefully. "Can I ride it?"

"Is it legal, Jack?"

"They told me that the Prime Minister and the President would discuss it today."

"My God," Lady Ryan said quietly. After a moment, she started smiling.

"Stick with me, kid." Jack laughed.

"What about the horse, Daddy!" Sally insisted.

"I don't know yet. We'll see." He yawned. The only practical use Ryan acknowledged for horses was running at tracks—or maybe tax shelters. *Well, I already have a sword,* he told himself.

"I think Daddy needs a nap," Cathy observed. "And I have to buy something for dinner tonight."

"Oh, God!" Ryan groaned. "A whole new wardrobe."

Cathy grinned. "Whose fault is that, Sir John?"

They met at Flanagan's Steakhouse on O'Connell Street in Dublin. It was a well-regarded establishment whose tourist trade occasionally suffered from being too close to a McDonald's. Ashley was nursing a whiskey when the second man joined him. A third and fourth took a booth across the room and watched. Ashley had come alone. This wasn't the first such meeting, and Dublin was recognized—most of the time—as neutral ground. The two men on the other side of the room were to keep a watch for members of the Garda, the Republic's police force.

"Welcome to Dublin, Mr. Ashley," said the representative of the Provisional Wing of the Irish Republican Army.

"Thank you, Mr. Murphy," the counterintelligence officer answered. "The photograph we have in the file doesn't do you justice."

"Young and foolish, I was. And very vain. I didn't shave very much then," Murphy explained. He picked up the menu that had been waiting for him. "The beef here is excellent, and the vegetables are always fresh. This place is full of bloody tourists in the summer—those who don't want French fries—driving prices up as they always do. Thank God they're all back home in America now, leaving so much money behind in this poor country."

"What information do you have for us?"

"Information?"

"You asked for the meeting, Mr. Murphy," Ashley pointed out.

"The purpose of the meeting is to assure you that we had no part in that bloody fiasco yesterday."

"I could have read that in the papers—I did, in fact."

"It was felt that a more personal communiqué was in order, Mr. Ashley."

"Why should we believe you?" Ashley asked, sipping at his whiskey. Both men kept their voices low and level, though neither man had the slightest doubt as to what they thought of each other.

"Because we are not as crazy as that," Murphy replied. The waiter came, and both men ordered. Ashley chose the wine, a promising Bordeaux. The meal was on his expense account. He was only forty minutes off the flight from London's Gatwick airport. The request for a meeting had been made before dawn in a telephone call to the British Ambassador in Dublin.

"Is that a fact?" Ashley said after the waiter left, staring into the cold blue eyes across the table.

"The Royal Family are strictly off limits. As marvelous a political target as they all are"—Murphy smiled—"we've known for some time that an attack on them would be counterproductive."

"Really?" Ashley pronounced the word as only an Englishman can do it. Murphy flushed angrily at this most elegant of insults.

"Mr. Ashley, we are enemies. I would as soon kill you as have dinner with you. But even enemies can negotiate, can't they, now?"

"Go on."

"We had no part of it. You have my word."

"Your word as a Marxist-Leninist?" Ashley inquired with a smile.

"You are very good at provoking people, Mr. Ashley." Murphy ventured his own smile. "But not today. I am here on a mission of peace and understanding."

Ashley nearly laughed out loud, but caught himself and grinned into his drink.

"Mr. Murphy, I would not shed a single tear if our lads were to catch up with you, but you are a worthy adversary, I'll say that. And a charming bastard."

Ah, the English sense of fair play, Murphy reflected. *That's why we'll win eventually, Mr. Ashley.*

No, you won't. Ashley had seen that look before.

"How can I make you believe me?" Murphy asked reasonably.

"Names and addresses," Ashley answered quietly.

"No. We cannot do that and you know it."

"If you wish to establish some sort of quid pro quo, that's how you must go about it."

Murphy sighed. "Surely you know how we are organized. Do you think we can punch up a bloody computer command and print out our roster? We're not even sure ourselves who they are. Some men, they just drop out. Many come south and simply vanish, more afraid of us than of you, they are—and with reason," Murphy added. "The one you have alive, Sean Miller—we've never even heard the name."

"And Kevin O'Donnell?"

"Yes, he's probably the leader. He dropped off the earth four years ago, as you well know, after—ah, you know the story as well as I."

Kevin Joseph O'Donnell, Ashley reminded himself. *Thirty-four now. Six feet, one hundred sixty pounds, unmarried—this data was old and therefore suspect. The all-time Provo champion at "own-goals." Kevin had been the most ruthless chief of security the Provos had ever had, thrown out after it had been proven that he'd used his power as counterintelligence boss to purge the Organization of political elements he disapproved of. What was the figure—ten, fifteen solid members that he'd had killed or maimed before the Brigade Commander'd found him out? The amazing thing,* Ashley thought, *was that he'd escaped alive at all.* But Murphy was wrong on one thing, Ashley didn't know what had finally tipped the Brigade that O'Donnell was outlaw.

"I fail to see why you feel the urge to protect him and his group." He knew the reason, but why not prod the man when he had the chance?

"And if we turn 'grass,' what becomes of the Organization?" Murphy asked.

"Not my problem, Mr. Murphy, but I do see your point. Still and all, if you want us to believe you—"

"Mr. Ashley, you demonstrate the basis of the entire problem we have, don't you? Had your country ever dealt with Ireland in mutual good faith, surely we would not be here now, would we?"

The intelligence officer reflected on that. It took no more than a couple of seconds, so many times had he examined the historical basis of the Troubles. Some deliberate policy acts, mixed with historical accidents—who could have known that the onset of the crisis that erupted into World War I would prevent a solution to the issue of "Home [or "Rome"] Rule," that the Conservative Party of the time would use this issue as a hammer that would eventually crush the Liberal Party—and who was there to blame now? They were all dead and forgotten, except by hard-core academics who knew that their studies mattered for nothing. It was far too late for that. *Is there a way out of this bloody quagmire?* he wondered. Ashley shook his head. That was not his brief. That was something for politicians. The same sort, he reminded himself, who'd built the Troubles, one small brick at a time.

"I'll tell you this much, Mr. Ashley—" The waiter showed up with dinner. It was amazing how quick the service was here. The waiter uncorked the wine with a flourish, allowing Ashley to smell the cork and sample a splash in his glass. The Englishman was surprised at the quality of the restaurant's cellar.

"This much you will tell me . . ." Ashley said after the waiter left.

"They get very good information. So good, you would not believe it. And their information comes from your side of the Irish Sea, Mr. Ashley. We don't know who, and we don't know how. The lad who found out died, four years ago, you see." Murphy sampled the broccoli. "There, I told you the vegetables were fresh."

"Four years?"

Murphy looked up. "You don't know the story, then? That is a surprise, Mr. Ashley. Yes. His name was Mickey Baird. He worked closely with Kevin. He's the lad who—well, you can guess. He was talking with me over a jar in Derry and said that Kevin had a bloody good new intelligence source. Next day he was dead. The day after, Kevin managed to escape us by an hour. We haven't seen him since. If we find Kevin again, Mr. Ashley, we'll do your work for you, and leave the body for your SAS assassins to collect. Would that be fair enough, now? We cannot exactly tout to the enemy, but he's on our list, too, and if you manage to find the lad, and you don't wish to bring him in yourselves, we'll handle the job for you—assuming, of course, that you don't interfere with the lads who do the work. Can we agree on that?"

"I'll pass that along," Ashley said. "If I could approve it myself, I would. Mr. Murphy, I think we can believe you on this."

"Thank you, Mr. Ashley. That wasn't so painful, was it?" Dinner was excellent.

4
Players

Ryan tried to blink away the blue dots that swirled around his eyes as the television crews set up their own lights. Why the newspaper photographers couldn't wait for the powerful TV lights, he didn't know, and didn't bother asking. Everyone was kind enough to ask how he felt—but nothing short of respiratory arrest would have gotten them out of the room.

It could have been worse, of course. Dr. Scott had told the newspeople rather forcefully that his patient needed rest to recover speedily, and nurse Kittiwake was there to glower at the intruders. So press access to Ryan was being limited to no more than the number of people who would fit into his room. This included the TV crew. It was the best sort of bargain Jack could get. The cameramen and sound technicians took up space that would otherwise be occupied by more inquisitorial reporters.

The morning papers—Ryan had been through the *Times* and the *Daily Telegraph*—had carried reports that Ryan was a former (or current) employee of the Central Intelligence Agency, something that was technically not true, and that Jack had not expected to become public in any case. He found himself remembering what the people at Langley said about leaks, and how pleased they'd been with his off-hand invention of the Canary Trap. *A pity they couldn't use it in my case,* Ryan told himself wryly. *I really need this complication to my life, don't I? For crying out loud, I turned their offer* down. *Sort of.*

"All ready here," the lighting technician said. A moment later he proved this was true by turning on the three klieg lights that brought tears to Jack's squinted eyes.

"They are awfully bright, aren't they?" a reporter sympathized, while the still photographers continued to snap-and-whir away with their strobe-equipped Nikons.

"You might say that," Jack replied. A two-headed mike was clipped to his robe.

"Say something, will you?" the sound man asked.

"And how are you enjoying your first trip to London, Doctor Ryan?"

"Well, I better not hear any complaints about how American tourists are staying away due to panic over the terrorism problem!" Ryan grinned. *You jerk.*

"Indeed," the reporter laughed. "Okay?"

The cameraman and sound man pronounced themselves ready.

Ryan sipped at his tea and made certain that the ashtray was out of sight. One print journalist shared a joke with a colleague. A TV correspondent from NBC was there, along with the London correspondent of the *Washington Post,* but all the others were British. Everything would be pooled with the rest of the media, it had been agreed. There just wasn't room here for a proper press conference. The camera started rolling tape.

They ran through the usual questions. The camera turned to linger on his arm, hanging from its overhead rack. They'd run that shot with the voice-over of Jack's story on when he was shot, he was sure. Nothing like a little drama, as he'd already been told. He wiggled his fingers for the camera.

"Doctor Ryan, there are reports in the American and British press that you are an employee of the Central Intelligence Agency."

"I read that this morning. It was as much a surprise to me as it was to anyone else." Ryan smiled. "Somebody made a mistake. I'm not good-looking enough to be a spy."

"So you deny that report?" asked the *Daily Mirror.*

"Correct. It's just not true. I teach history at the Naval Academy, in Annapolis. That ought to be easy enough to check out. I just gave an exam last week. You can ask my students." Jack waved his left hand at the camera again.

"The report comes from some highly placed sources," observed the *Post.*

"If you read a little history, you'll see that highly placed folks have been known to make mistakes. I think that's what happened here. I teach. I write books. I lecture—okay, I did give a lecture at CIA once, but that was just a repeat of one I delivered at the Naval War College and one other symposium. It wasn't even classified. Maybe that's where the report comes from. Like I said, check it out. My office is in Leahy Hall, at the Naval Academy. I think somebody just goofed." *Somebody goofed, all right.* "I can get you guys a copy of the lecture. It's no big deal."

"How do you like being a public figure, now?" one of the Brit TV people asked.

Thanks for changing the subject. "I think I can live without it. I'm not a movie star, either—again, not good-looking enough."

"You're far too modest, Doctor Ryan," a female reporter observed.

"Please be careful how you say that. My wife will probably see this." There was general laughter. "I suppose I'm good-looking enough for her. That's enough. With all due respect, ladies and gentlemen, I'll be perfectly glad to descend back into obscurity."

"Do you think that likely?"

"That depends on how lucky I am, ma'am. And on whether you folks will let me."

"What do you think we should do with the terrorist, Sean Miller?" the *Times* asked.

"That's for a judge and jury to decide. You don't need me for that."

"Do you think we should have capital punishment?"

"We have it where I live. For your country, that is a question for your elected representatives. We both live in democracies, don't we? The people you elect are supposed to do what the voters ask them to do." *Not that it always works that way, but that's the theory.* . . .

"So you support the idea?" the *Times* persisted.

"In appropriate cases, subject to strict judicial review, yes. Now you're going to ask me about this case, right? It's a moot point.

Anyway, I'm no expert on criminal justice. My dad was a cop but I'm just a historian.''

"And what of your perspective, as an Irish-American, on the Troubles?'' the *Telegraph* wanted to know.

"We have enough problems of our own in America without having to borrow yours.''

"So you say we should solve it, then?''

"What do you think? Isn't that what problems are for?''

"Surely you have a suggestion. Most Americans do.''

"I think I teach history. I'll let other people make it. It's like being a reporter.'' Ryan smiled. "I get to criticize people long after they make their decisions. That doesn't mean I know what to do today.''

"But you knew what to do on Tuesday,'' the *Times* pointed out. Ryan shrugged.

"Yeah, I guess I did,'' Ryan said on the television screen.

"You clever bastard,'' Kevin Joseph O'Donnell muttered into a glass of dark Guinness beer. His base of operations was much farther from the border than any might have suspected. Ireland is a small country, and distances are but relative things—particularly to those with all the resources they need. His former colleagues in the PIRA had extensive safehouses along the border, convenient to a quick trip across from either direction. Not for O'Donnell. There were numerous practical reasons. The Brits had their informers and intelligence people there, always creeping about—and the SAS raiders, who were not averse to a quick snatch—or a quiet kill—of persons who had made the mistake of becoming too well known. The border could be a convenience to either side. A more serious threat was the PIRA itself, which also watched the border closely. His face, altered as it was with some minor surgery and a change in hair color, might still be recognizable to a former colleague. But not here. And the border wasn't all that far a drive in a country barely three hundred miles long.

He turned away from the Sony television and gazed out the leaded-glass windows to the darkness of the sea. He saw the running lights of a car ferry inbound from Le Havre. The view was always a fine one. Even in the limited visibility of an ocean storm, one could savor the fundamental force of nature as the gray waves battered the rocky cliff. Now, the clear, cold air gave him a view to the star-defined horizon, and he spied another merchant ship heading eastward for an unknown port. It pleased O'Donnell that this stately house on the headlands had once belonged to a British lord. It pleased him more that he'd been able to purchase it through a dummy corporation; that there were few questions when cash and a reputable solicitor were involved. So vulnerable this society—all societies were when you had the proper resources . . . and a competent tailor. So shallow they were. So lacking in political awareness. *One must know who one's enemies are,* O'Donnell told himself at least ten times every day. Not a liberal "democratic" society, though. Enemies were people to be dealt with, compromised with, to be civilized, brought into the fold, co-opted.

Fools, self-destructive, ignorant fools who earned their own destruction.

Someday they would all disappear, just as one of those ships slid beneath the horizon. History was a science, an inevitable process. O'Donnell was sure of that.

He turned again to stare into the fire burning under the wide, stone mantel. There had once been stag heads hanging over it, perhaps the lord's favorite fowling piece—from Purdey's, to be sure. And a painting or two. Of horses, O'Donnell was sure—they had to be paintings of horses. The country gentleman who had built this house, he mused, would have been someone who'd been given everything he had. No ideology would have intruded in his empty, useless head. He would have sat in a chair very like this one and sipped his malt whiskey and stared into the fire—his favorite dog at this feet—while he chatted about the day's hunting with a neighbor and planned the hunting for the morrow. *Will it be birds again, or fox, Bertie? Haven't had a good fox hunt in weeks, time we did it again, don't you think?* Or something like that, he was sure. O'Donnell wondered if there was a seasonal aspect to it, or had the lord just done whatever suited his mood. The current owner of the country house never hunted animals. What was the point of killing something that could not harm you or your cause, something that had no ideology? Besides, that was something the Brits did, something the local gentry still did. He didn't hunt the local Irish gentry, they weren't worth his contempt, much less his action. At least, not yet. *You don't hate trees,* he told himself. *You ignore the things until you have to cut them down.* He turned back to the television.

That Ryan fellow was still there, he saw, talking amiably with the press idiots. Bloody hero. *Why did you stick your nose in where it doesn't belong?* Reflex, sounds like, O'Donnell judged. *Bloody meddling fool. Don't even know what's going on, do you? None of you do.*

Americans. The Provo fools still like to talk it up with your kind, telling their lies and pretending that they represent Ireland. What do you Yanks know about anything? *Oh, but we can't afford to offend the Americans,* the Provos still said. Bloody Americans, with all their money and all their arrogance, all their ideas on right and wrong, their childish vision of Irish destiny. Like children dressed up for First Communion. So pure. So naive. So useless with their trickle of money—for all that the Brits complained about NORAID, O'Donnell knew that the PIRA had not netted a million dollars from America in the past three years. All the Americans knew of Ireland came from a few movies, some half-remembered songs for St. Paddy's Day, and the occasional bottle of whiskey. What did they know of life in Ulster, of the imperialist oppression, the way all Ireland was still enslaved to the decaying British Empire, which was, in turn, enslaved to the American one? What did they know about anything? *But we can't offend the Americans.* The leader of the ULA finished off his beer and set it on the end table.

The Cause didn't require much, not really. A clear ideological objective. A few good men. Friends, the right friends, with access to the right resources. That was all. Why clutter things up with bloody Americans? And a public political wing—Sinn Fein electing people to Parliament, what rubbish! They were waiting, *hoping* to be co-opted by the Brit imperialists. Valuable political targets declared off-limits. And people wondered why the Provos were getting nowhere. Their ideology was bankrupt, and there were too many people in the Brigade. When the Brits caught some, a few were bound to turn tout and inform on their comrades. The kind of commitment needed for this sort of job demanded an elite few. O'Donnell had that, all right. *And you need to have the right plan,* he told himself with a wispy smile. O'Donnell had his plan. This Ryan fellow hadn't changed that, he reminded himself.

"Bastard's bloody pleased with himself, isn't he?"

O'Donnell turned to see a fresh bottle of Guinness offered. He took it and refilled his glass. "Sean should have watched his back. Then this bloody hero would be a corpse." *And the mission would have been successful. Damn!*

"We can still do something about that, sir."

O'Donnell shook his head. "We do not waste our energy on the insignificant. The Provos have been doing that for ten years and look where it has gotten them."

"What if he is CIA? What if we've been infiltrated and he was there—"

"Don't be a bloody fool," O'Donnell snapped. "If they'd been tipped, every peeler in London would have been there in plain clothes waiting for us." *And I would have known beforehand,* he didn't say. Only one other member of the Organization knew of his source, and he was in London. "It was luck, good for them, bad for us. Just luck. We were lucky in your case, weren't we, Michael?" Like any Irishman he still believed in luck. Ideology would never change that.

The younger man thought of his eighteen months in the H-Blocks at Long Kesh prison, and was silent. O'Donnell shrugged at the television as the news program changed to another story. Luck. That was all. Some monied Yank with too long a nose who'd gotten very lucky. Any random event, like a punctured tire, a defective radio battery, or a sudden rainstorm, could have made the operation fail, too. And his advantage over the other side was that they had to be lucky all the time. O'Donnell only had to be lucky once. He considered what he had just seen on the television and decided that Ryan wasn't worth the effort.

Mustn't offend the Americans, he thought to himself again, this time with surprise. *Why? Aren't they the enemy, too? Patrick, me boy, now you're thinking like those idiots in the PIRA. Patience is the most important quality in the true revolutionary. One must wait for the proper moment—and then strike decisively.*

He waited for his next intelligence report.

The rare book shop was in the Burlington Arcade, a century-old promenade of shops off the most fashionable part of Piccadilly. It was sandwiched between one of London's custom tailors—this one catered mainly to the tourists who used the arcade to shelter from the elements—and a jeweler. It had the sort of smell that draws bibliophiles as surely as the scent of nectar draws a bee, the musty, dusty odor of dried-out paper and leather binding. The shop's owner-operator was contrastingly young, dressed in a suit whose shoulders were sprinkled with dust. He started every day by running a feather duster over the shelves, and the books were ever exuding new quantities of it. He had grown to like it. The store had an ambience that he dearly loved. The store did a small but lucrative volume of business, depending less on tourists than on a discreet number of regular customers from the upper reaches of London society. The owner, a Mr. Dennis Cooley, traveled a great deal, often flying out on short notice to participate in an auction of some deceased gentleman's library, leaving the shop to the custody of a young lady who would have been quite pretty if she'd worked at it a little harder. Beatrix was off today.

Mr. Cooley had an ancient teak desk in keeping with the rest of the shop's motif, and even a cushionless swivel chair to prove to the customers that nothing in the shop was modern. Even the bookkeeping was done by hand. No electronic calculators here. A battered ledger book dating back to the 1930s listed thousands of sales, and the shop's book catalog was made of simple filing cards in small wooden boxes, one set listing books by title, and another by author. All writing was done with a gold-nibbed fountain pen. A no-smoking sign was the only modern touch. The smell of tobacco might have ruined the shop's unique aroma. The store's stationery bore the "by appointment to" crests of four Royal Family members. The arcade was but a ten-minute uphill walk from Buckingham Palace. The glass door had a hundred-year-old silver bell hanging on the top of the frame. It rang.

"Good morning, Mr. Cooley."

"And to you, sir," Dennis answered one of his regulars as he stood. He had an accent so neutral that his customers had him pegged as a native of three different regions. "I have the first-edition Defoe. The one you called about earlier this week. Just came in yesterday."

"Is this the one from that collection in Cork you spoke about?"

"No, sir. I believe it's originally from the estate of Sir John Claggett, near Swaffham Prior. I found it at Hawstead's in Cambridge."

"A first edition?"

"Most certainly, sir." The book dealer did not react noticeably. The code phrase was both constant and changing. Cooley made frequent trips to Ireland, both north and south, to purchase books from the estates of deceased collectors or from dealers in the country. When the customer mentioned any county in the Irish Republic, he indicated the destination for his information. When he questioned the edition of the book, he also indicated its importance. Cooley pulled the book off the shelf and set it on his desk. The customer opened it with care, running his finger down the title page.

"In an age of paperbacks and half-bound books. . . ."

"Indeed." Cooley nodded. Both men's love for the art of bookbinding was genuine. Any good cover becomes more real than its builders expect. "The leather is in remarkable shape." His visitor grunted agreement.

"I must have it. How much?"

The dealer didn't answer. Instead Cooley removed the card from the box and handed it to his customer. He gave the card only a cursory look.

"Done." The customer sat down in the store's only other chair and opened his briefcase. "I have another job for you. This is an early copy of *The Vicar of Wakefield*. I found it last month at a little shop in Cornwall." He handed the book over. Cooley needed only a single look at its condition.

"Scandalous."

"Can your chap restore it?"

"I don't know. . . ." The leather was cracked, some of the pages had been dog-eared, and the binding was frayed almost to nonexistence.

"I'm afraid the attic in which they found it had a leaky roof," the customer said casually.

"Oh?" *Is the information* that *important?* Cooley looked up. "A tragic waste."

"How else can you explain it?" The man shrugged.

"I'll see what I can do. He's not a miracle worker, you know." *Is it that important?*

"I understand. Still, the best you can arrange." *Yes, it's that important.*

"Of course, sir." Cooley opened his desk drawer and withdrew the cashbox.

This customer always paid cash. Of course. He removed the wallet from his suitcoat and counted out the fifty-pound notes. Cooley checked the amount, then placed the book in a stout cardboard box, which he tied with string. No plastic bags for this shop. Seller and buyer shook hands. The transfer was complete. The customer walked south toward Piccadilly, then turned right, heading west toward Green Park and downhill to the Palace.

Cooley took the envelope that had been hidden in the book and tucked it away in a drawer. He finished making his ledger entry, then called his travel agent to book a flight to Cork, where he would meet a fellow dealer in rare books and have lunch at the Old Bridge restaurant before catching a flight home. Beatrix would have to manage the shop tomorrow. It did not occur to him to open the envelope. That was not his job. The less he knew, the less was vulnerable if he were caught. Cooley had been trained by professionals, and the first rule pounded into his head had been *need-to-know*. He ran the intelligence operation, and he needed to know how to do that. He didn't always need to know what specific information he gathered.

"Hello, Doctor Ryan." It was an American voice, with a South Bay Boston accent that Jack remembered from his college days. It sounded good. The man was in his forties, a wiry, athletic frame, with thinning black hair. He had a flower box tucked under his arm. Whoever he was, the cop outside had opened the door for him.

"Howdy. Who might you be?"

"Dan Murray. I'm the Legal Attaché at the embassy. FBI," he explained. "Sorry I couldn't get down sooner, but things have been a little busy." Murray showed his ID to the cop sitting in with Ryan— Tony Wilson was off duty. The cop excused himself. Murray took his seat.

"Lookin' good, ace."

"You could have left the flowers at the main desk." Ryan gestured around the room. Despite all his efforts to spread the flowers about, he could barely see the walls for all the roses.

"Yeah, I figured that. How's the grub?"

"Hospital food is hospital food."

"Figured that, too." Murray removed the red ribbon and opened the box. "How does a Whopper and fries grab you? You have a choice of vanilla or chocolate shakes."

Jack laughed—and grabbed.

"I've been over here three years," Murray said. "Every so often I have to hit the fast-food joints to remind myself where I come from. You can get tired of lamb. The local beer's pretty good, though. I'd have brought a few of those but—well, you know."

"You just made a friend for life, Mr. Murray, even without the beer."

"Dan."

"Jack." Ryan was tempted to wolf down the burger for fear of having a nurse come through the door and throw an immediate institutional fit. *No,* he decided, *I'll enjoy this one.* He selected the vanilla shake. "The local guys say you broke records identifying me."

"No big deal." Murray poked a straw into the chocolate one. "By the way, I bring you greetings from the Ambassador—he wanted to come over, but they have a big-time party for later tonight. And my friends down the hall send their regards, too."

"Who down the hall?"

"The people you have never worked for." The FBI agent raised his eyebrows.

"Oh." Jack swallowed a few fries. "Who the hell broke that story?"

"Washington. Some reporter was having lunch with somebody's aide—doesn't really matter whose, does it? They all talk too much. Evidently he remembered your name in the back of the final report and couldn't keep his trap shut. Apologies from Langley, they told me to tell you. I saw the TV stuff. You dodged that pretty good."

"I told the truth—barely. All my checks came through Mitre Corporation. Some sort of bookkeeping thing, and Mitre had the consulting contract."

"I understand all your time was at Langley, though."

"Yeah, a little cubbyhole on the third floor with a desk, a computer terminal, and a scratchpad. Ever been there?"

Murray smiled. "Once or twice. I'm in the terrorism business, too. The Bureau has a much nicer decorator. Helps to have a PR department, don't you know?" Murray affected a caricatured London accent. "I saw a copy of the report. Nice work. How much of it did you do?"

"Most. It wasn't all that hard. I just came up with a new angle to look at it from."

"It's been passed along to the Brits—I mean, it came over here two months ago for the Secret Intelligence Service. I understand they liked it."

"So their cops know."

"I'm not sure—well, you can probably assume they do now. Owens is cleared all the way on this stuff."

"And so's Ashley."

"He's a little on the snotty side, but he's damned smart. He's 'Five.'"

"What?" Ryan didn't know that one.

"He's in MI-5, the Security Service. We just call it Five. Has a nice insider feel that way." Murray chuckled.

"I figured him for something like that. The other two started as street cops. It shows."

"It struck a few people as slightly curious—the guy who wrote *Agents and Agencies* gets stuck in the middle of a terrorist op. That's why Ashley showed up." Murray shook his head. "You wouldn't believe all the coincidences you run into in my business. Like you and me."

"I know you come from New England—oh, don't tell me. Boston College?"

"Hey, I always wanted to be an FBI agent. It was either BC or Holy Cross, right?" Murray grinned. That in-house FBI joke went back two generations, and was not without a few grains of truth. Ryan leaned back and sucked the shake up the straw. It tasted wonderful.

"How much do we know about these ULA guys?" Jack asked. "I never saw very much at Langley."

"Not a hell of a lot. The boss-man's a chap named Kevin O'Donnell. He used to be in the PIRA. He started throwing rocks in the streets and supposedly worked his way up to head counterintelligence man. The Provos are pretty good at that. Have to be. The Brits are always working to infiltrate the Organization. The word is that he got a little carried away cleansing the ranks, and barely managed to skip out before they gave him Excedrin Headache number three-five-seven. Just plain disappeared and hasn't been spotted since. A few sketchy reports, like maybe he spent some time in Libya, like maybe he's back in Ulster with a new face, like maybe he has a lot of money—want to guess where from?—to throw around. All we know for sure is that he's one malignant son of a bitch.

"His organization?" Murray set the milk shake down. "It's gotta be small, probably less than thirty. We think he had part of the breakout from Long Kesh last summer. Eleven hard-core Provos got out. The RUC bagged one of 'em two days later and he said that six of the eleven went south, probably to Kevin's outfit. He was a little pissed by that. They were supposed to come back to the PIRA fold, but somebody convinced them to try something different. Some very bad boys—they had a total of fifteen murders among them. The one you killed is the only one to show up since."

"Are they that good?" Ryan asked.

"Hey, the PIRA are the best terrorists in the world, unless you count those bastards in Lebanon, and those are mostly family groups. Hell of a way to describe them, isn't it? But they are the best. Well organized, well trained, and they *believe,* if you know what I mean. They really care about what they're doing. The level of commitment these characters have to the Cause is something you have to see to believe."

"You've been in on it?"

"Some. I've been able to sit in on interrogations—the other side of the two-way mirror, I mean. One of these guys wouldn't talk—wouldn't even give 'em his name!—for a week. Just sat there like a sphinx. Hey, I've chased after bank robbers, kidnappers, mob guys, spies, you name it. These fellows are real pros—and that's the PIRA, maybe five hundred real members, not even as big as a New York Mafia family, and the RUC—that's the Royal Ulster Constabulary, the local cops—is lucky to convict a handful in a year. They have a law of *omertà* up there that would impress the old-time Sicilians. But at least the cops have a handle on who the bastards are. The ULA—we got a couple of names, a few pictures, and that's it. It's almost like the Islamic Jihad bums. You only know them from what they do."

"What do they do?" Ryan asked.

"They seem to specialize in high-risk, high-profile operations. It took over a year to confirm that they exist at all; we thought they were a special-action group of the PIRA. They're an anomaly within the terrorist community. They don't make press releases, they don't take public credit for what they do. They go for the big-time stuff and they cover their tracks like you wouldn't believe. It takes resources to do that. Somebody is bankrolling them in a pretty big way. They've been identified for nine jobs we're sure of, maybe two others. They've only had three operations go bad—quite a track record. They missed killing a judge in Londonderry because the RPG round was a dud—it still took his bodyguard out. They tried to hit a police barracks last February. Somebody saw them setting up and phoned in—but the bastards must have been monitoring the police radio. They skipped before the cavalry arrived. The cops found an eighty-two-millimeter mortar and a box of rounds—high-explosive and white phosphorus, to be exact. And you got in the way of the last one.

"These suckers are getting pretty bold," Murray said. "On the other hand, we got one now."

"We?" Ryan said curiously. "It's not our fight."

"We're talking terrorists, Jack. Everybody wants them. We swap information back and forth with the Yard every day. Anyway, the guy they have in the can right now, they'll keep talking at him. They have a hook on this one. The ULA is an outcast outfit. He is going to be a pariah and he knows it. His colleagues from PIRA and INLA won't circle wagons around him. He'll go to a maximum-security prison, probably to one on the Isle of Wight, populated with some real bad boys. Not all of them are political types, and the ordinary robbers and murderers will probably—well, it's funny how patriotic these guys are. Spies, for example, have about as much fun in the joint as child molesters. This guy went after the Royal Family, the one thing over here that everybody loves. We're talking some serious hard time with this kid. You think the guards are going to bust their ass looking out for his well-being? He's going to learn a whole new sport. It's called *survival*. After he has a taste of it, people will talk to him. Sooner or later that kid's going to have to decide just how committed he is. He just might break down a little. Some have. That's what we play for, anyway. The bad guys have the initiative, we have organization and procedures. If they make a mistake, give us an opportunity, we can act on it."

Ryan nodded. "Yeah, it's all intelligence."

"That's right. Without the right information we're crippled. All we can do is plod along and hope for a break. But give us one solid fact and we'll bring the whole friggin' world down on 'em. It's like taking down a brick wall. The hard part's getting that first brick loose."

"And where do they get their information?"

"They told me you tumbled to that," Murray observed with a smile.

"I don't think it was a chance encounter. Somebody had to tip them. They hit a moving target making an unscheduled trip."

"How the hell did you know that?" the agent demanded.

"Doesn't matter, does it? People talk. Who knew that they were coming in?"

"That is being looked at. The interesting thing is what they were coming in for. Of course, that could just be a coincidence. The Prince gets briefed on political and national security stuff, same as the Queen does. Something happened with the Irish situation, negotiations between London and Dublin. He was coming in for the briefing. All I can tell you."

"Hey, if you checked me out, you know how I'm cleared," Ryan sniffed.

Murray grinned. "Nice try, ace. If you weren't cleared TS, I wouldn't have told you this much. We're not privy to it yet anyway. Like I said, it might just have been a coincidence, but you guessed right on the important part. It was an unscheduled trip and somebody got the word out for the ambush. Only way it could have happened. You will consider that classified information, Doctor Ryan. It doesn't go past that door." Murray was affable. He was also very serious about his job.

Jack nodded agreement. "No problem. It was a kidnap, too, wasn't it?"

The FBI agent grimaced and shook his head. "I've handled about a half-dozen kidnappings and closed every case with a conviction. We only lost one hostage—they killed that kid the first day. Those two were executed. I watched," Murray said coldly. "Kidnapping is a high-risk crime all the way down the line. They have to be at a specific place to get their money—that's usually what gets 'em caught. We can track people like you wouldn't believe, then bring in the cavalry hard and fast. In this case . . . we're talking some impressive bargaining chips, and there would not be a money transfer—the public release of some 'political' prisoners is the obvious objective. The evidence does lean that way, except that these characters have never done one of those. It makes the escape procedures a lot more complex, but these ULA characters have always had their escape routes well planned beforehand. I'd say you're probably right, but it's not as clear-cut as you think. Owens and Taylor aren't completely sure, and our friend isn't talking. Big surprise."

"They've never made a public announcement, you said? Was this supposed to be their break into the big time? Their first public announcement, they might as well do it with something spectacular," Ryan said thoughtfully.

"That's a fair guess." Murray nodded. "It certainly would have put them on the map. Like I said, our intel on these chaps is damned thin; almost all of it's secondhand stuff that comes through the PIRA—which is why we thought they were actually part of it. We haven't exactly figured what they're up to. Every one of their operations has—how do I say this? There seems to be a pattern there, but nobody's ever figured it out. It's almost as though the political fallout isn't aimed at us at all, but that doesn't make any sense—not that it *has* to make sense," the agent grunted. "It's not easy trying to psychoanalyze the terrorist mind."

"Any chance they'll come after me, or—"

Murray shook his head. "Unlikely, and the security's pretty tight. You know who they have taking your wife and kid around?"

"SAS—I asked."

"That youngster's on their Olympic pistol team, and I hear that he has some field experience that never made the papers. The DPG escort is also one of the varsity, and they'll have a chase car everywhere they go. The security on you is pretty impressive, too. You have some big-league interest in your safety. You can relax. And after you get home it's all behind you. None of these groups has *ever* operated in the U.S. We're too important to them. NORAID means more to them psychologically than financially. When they fly to Boston, it's like crawling back into the womb, all the beers people buy for them, it tells them that they're the good guys. No, if they started raising hell out our side of the pond—I don't think they could take being persona non grata in Boston. It's the only real weak point the PIRA and the rest have, and unfortunately it's not one that we can exploit all that well. We've pretty much cut down on the weapons pipeline, but, hell, they get most of their stuff from the other side now. Or they make their own. Like explosives. All you need is a bag of ammonia-based fertilizer and you can make a respectable bomb. You can't arrest a farmer for carrying fertilizer in his truck, can you? It's not as sexy as some good plastique, but it's a hell of a lot easier to get. For guns and heavier stuff— anybody can get AK-47s and RPGs, they're all over the place. No, they depend on us for moral support, and there's quite a few people who'll give it, even in Congress. Remember the fight over the extradition treaty? It's amazing. These bastards kill people.

"Both sides." Murray paused for a moment. "The Protestant crazies are just as bad. The Provisionals waste a prod. Then the Ulster Volunteer Force sends a car through a Catholic neighborhood and pops the first convenient target. A lot of the killing is purely random now. Maybe a third of the kills are people who were walking down the wrong street. The process feeds on itself, and there's not much of a middle ground left anymore. Except the cops—I know, the RUC used to be the bad guys, too, but they've just about ended that crap. The Law has got to be the Law for everyone—but that's too easy to forget sometimes, like in Mississippi back in the sixties, and that's essentially what happened in Northern Ireland. Sir Jack Hermon is trying to turn the RUC into a professional police force. There are plenty of people left over from the bad old days, but the troops are coming around. They must be. The cops are taking casualties from both sides, the last one was killed by prods. They firebombed his house.'' Murray shook his head. "It's amazing. I was just over there two weeks ago. Their morale's great, especially with the new kids. I don't know how they do it—well, I do know. They have their mission, too. The cops and the courts have to reestablish justice, and the people have to see that they're doing it. They're the only hope that place has, them and a few of the church leaders. Maybe common sense'll break out someday, but don't hold your breath. It's going to take a long time. Thank God for Tom Jefferson and Jim Madison, bub. Sometimes I wonder how close we came to that sectarian stuff. It's like a Mafia war that everybody can play in.''

"Well, Judge?'' Admiral James Greer hit the off switch on the remote control as the Cable News Network switched topics. The Director of Central Intelligence tapped his cigar on the cut-glass ashtray.

"We know he's smart, James, and it looks like he knows how to handle himself with reporters, but he's impetuous,'' Judge Arthur Moore said.

"Come on, Arthur. He's young. I want somebody in here with some fresh ideas. You going to tell me now that you didn't like his report? First time at bat, and he turns out something that good!''

Judge Moore smiled behind his cigar. It was drizzling outside the seventh-floor window of the office of the Deputy Director, Intelligence, of the Central Intelligence Agency. The rolling hills of the Potomac Valley prevented his seeing the river, but he could spy the hills a mile or so away on the far side. It was a far prettier view than that of the parking lots.

"Background check?''

"We haven't done a deep one yet, but I'll bet you a bottle of your favorite bourbon that he comes up clean.''

"No bet, James!'' Moore had already seen Jack's service record from the Marine Corps. Besides, he hadn't come to the Agency. They had gone to him and he'd turned them down on the first offer. "You think he can handle it, eh?''

"You really ought to meet the kid, Judge. I had him figured out the first ten minutes he was in here last July."

"You arranged the leak?"

"Me? Leak?" Admiral Greer chuckled. "Nice to know how he can handle himself, though, isn't it? Didn't even blink when he fielded the question. The boy takes his clearance seriously, and"—Greer held up the telex from London—"he's asking good questions. Emil says his man Murray was fairly impressed, too. It's just a damned shame to waste him teaching history."

"Even at your alma mater?"

Greer smiled. "Yes, that does hurt a little. I want him, Arthur. I want to teach him, I want to groom him. He's our kind of people."

"But he doesn't seem to think so."

"He will." Greer was quietly positive.

"Okay, James. How do you want to approach him?"

"No hurry. I want a very thorough background check done first—and who knows? Maybe he'll come to us."

"No chance," Judge Moore scoffed.

"He'll come to us requesting information on this ULA bunch," Greer said.

The Judge thought about that one. One thing about James Greer, Moore knew, was his ability to see into things and people as though they were made of crystal. "That makes sense."

"You bet it does. It'll be a while—the Attaché says he has to stay over for the trial and all—but he'll be in this office two weeks after he gets back, asking for a chance to research this ULA outfit. If he does, I'll pop the offer—if you agree, Arthur. I also want to talk to Emil Jacobs at FBI and compare files on these ULA characters."

"Okay."

They turned to other matters.

5

Perqs and Plots

The day Ryan was released from the hospital was the happiest in his life, at least since Sally had been born at Johns Hopkins, four years before. It was after six in the evening when he finally finished dressing himself—the cast made that a very tricky exercise—and plopped down in the wheelchair. Jack had groused about that, but it was evidently a rule as inviolable in British hospitals as in American ones: patients are not allowed to walk out—somebody might think they were cured. A uniformed policeman pushed him out of the room into the hall. Ryan didn't look back.

Virtually the whole floor staff was lined up in the hall, along with a number of the patients Ryan had met the past week and a half as he'd relearned how to walk up and down the drab corridors—with a ten-degree list from the heavy cast. Jack flushed red at the applause, the more so when people reached out to shake his hand. *I'm not an Apollo astronaut,* he thought. *The Brits are supposed to be more dignified than this.*

Nurse Kittiwake gave a little speech about what a model patient he was. *What a pleasure and an honor* . . . Ryan blushed again when she finished, and gave him some flowers, to take to his lovely wife, she said. Then she kissed him, on behalf of everyone else. Jack kissed back. It was the least he could do, he told himself, and she really was a pretty girl. Kittiwake hugged him, cast and all, and tears started running out of her eyes. Tony Wilson was at her side and gave Jack a surreptitious wink. That was no surprise. Jack shook hands with another ten or so people before the cop got him into the elevator.

"Next time you guys find me wounded in the street," Ryan said, "let me die there."

The policeman laughed. "Bloody ungrateful fellow you are."

"True."

The elevator opened at the lobby and he was grateful to see that it had been cleared except for the Duke of Edinburgh and a gaggle of security people.

"Good evening, My Lord." Ryan tried to stand, but was waved back down.

"Hello, Jack! How are you feeling?" They shook hands, and for a moment he was afraid that the Duke himself would wheel him out the door. That would have been intolerable, but the police officer resumed his pushing as the Duke walked alongside. Jack pointed forward.

"Sir, I will improve at least fifty percent when we make it through that door."

"Hungry?"

"After hospital food? I just might eat one of your polo horses."

The Duke grinned. "We'll try to do a little better than that."

Jack noticed seven security people in the lobby. Outside was a Rolls-Royce . . . and at least four other cars, along with a number of people who did not look like ordinary passersby. It was too dark to see anyone prowling the roofs, but they'd be there, too. *Well*, Ryan thought, *they've learned their lessons on security. Still a damned shame, though, and it means the terrorists have won a victory. If they make society change, even a little, they've won something. Bastards.* The cop brought him right to the Rolls.

"Can I get up now?" The cast was so heavy that it ruined his balance. Ryan stood a little too fast and nearly smashed into the car, but caught himself with an angry shake of the head before anyone had to grab for him. He stood still for a moment, his left arm sticking out like the big claw on a fiddler crab, and tried to figure how to get into the car. It turned out that the best way was to stick the cast in first, then rotate clockwise as he followed it. The Duke had to enter from the other side, and it turned out to be rather a snug fit. Ryan had never been in a Rolls before, and found that it wasn't all that spacious.

"Comfortable?"

"Well—I'll have to be careful not to punch a window out with this damned thing." Ryan leaned back and shook his head with an eyes-closed smile.

"You really are glad to be out of hospital."

"My Lord, on that you can wager one of your castles. This makes three times I've been in the body and fender shop, and that's enough." The Duke motioned for the driver to pull out. The convoy moved slowly into the street, two lead cars and two chase cars surrounding the Rolls-Royce. "Sir, may I ask what's happening this evening?"

"Very little, really. A small party in your honor, with just a few close friends."

Jack wondered what "a few close friends" meant. Twenty? Fifty? A hundred? He was going to dinner at . . . *Scotty, beam me up!* "Sir, you know that you've really been too kind to us."

"Bloody rubbish. Aside from the debt we owe you—not exactly what one would call a small debt, Jack. Aside from that, it's been entirely worthwhile to meet some new people. I even finished your book Sunday night. I thought it was excellent; you must send me a copy of your next one. And the Queen and your wife have got on marvelously. You are a very lucky chap to have a wife like that—and that little imp of a daughter. She's a gem, Jack, a thoroughly wonderful little girl."

Ryan nodded. He often wondered what he had done to be so lucky. "Cathy says that she's seen about every castle in the realm, and thanks a lot for the people you put with her. It made me feel much better about having them run all over the place."

The Duke waved his hand dismissively. It wasn't worth talking about. "How did the research go on your new book?"

"Quite well, sir." The one favorable result of his being in the hospital was that he'd had the time to sift through all of it in detail. His computer had two hundred new pages of notes stored in its bubble chips, and Ryan had a new perspective on judging the actions of others. "I guess I've learned one thing from my little escapade. Sitting in front of a keyboard isn't quite the same as looking into the front end of a gun. Decisions are a little different from that perspective.'' Ryan's tone made a further statement.

The Duke clapped him on the knee. ''I shouldn't think that anyone will fault yours.''

''Maybe. The thing is, my decision was made on pure instinct. If I'd known what I was doing—what if I had done the *wrong* thing on instinct?'' He looked out the window. ''Here I am, supposed to be an expert on naval history, with special emphasis on how decisions are made under stress, and I'm still not satisfied with my own. Damn.'' Jack concluded quietly: ''Sir, you don't forget killing somebody. You just don't.''

''You oughtn't to dwell on it, Jack.''

''Yes, sir.'' Ryan turned back from the window. The Duke was looking at him much the same way his father had, years before. ''A conscience is the price of morality, and morality is the price of civilization. Dad used to say that many criminals don't have a conscience, not much in the way of feelings at all. I guess that's what makes us different from them.''

''Exactly. Your introspection is a fundamentally healthy thing, but you should not overdo it. Put it behind you, Jack. It was my impression of Americans that you prefer to look to the future rather than the past. If you cannot do that professionally, at least try to do it personally.''

''Understood, sir. Thank you.'' *Now if I could just make the dreams stop.* Nearly every night Jack relived the shoot-out on The Mall. Almost three weeks now. Something else they didn't tell you about on TV. The human mind has a way of punishing itself for killing a fellow man. It remembers and relives the incident again and again. Ryan hoped it would stop someday.

The car turned left onto Westminster Bridge. Jack hadn't known exactly where the hospital was, just that it was close to a railway station and close enough to Westminster to hear Big Ben toll the hours. He looked up at the gothic stonework. ''You know, besides the research I wanted to do, I actually wanted to see part of your country, sir. Not much time left for that.''

''Jack, do you really think that we will let you return to America without experiencing British hospitality?'' The Duke was greatly amused. ''We are quite proud of our hospitals, of course, but tourists don't come here to see those. Some small arrangements have been made.''

"Oh."

Ryan had to think a moment to figure where they were, but the maps he'd studied before coming over came back to him. It was called Birdcage Walk—he was only three hundred yards from where he'd been shot . . . there was the lake that Sally liked. He could see Buckingham Palace past the head of the security officer in the left front seat. Knowing that he was going there was one thing, but now the building loomed in front of him and the emotional impact started to take hold.

They entered the Palace grounds at the northeast gate. Jack hadn't seen the Palace before except from a distance. The perimeter security didn't seem all that impressive, but the Palace's hollow-square design hid nearly everything from outside view. There could easily be a company of armed troops inside—and who could tell? More likely civilian police, Ryan knew, backed up by a lot of electronic hardware. But there would be some surprises hidden away, too. After the scares in the past, and this latest incident, he imagined that this place was as secure as the White House—or even better, given greater space in and around the buildings.

It was too dark to make out many details, but the Rolls pulled through an archway into the building's courtyard, then under a canopy, where a sentry snapped to present-arms in the crisp three-count movement the Brits used. As the car stopped, a footman in livery pulled the door open.

Getting out was the reverse of getting in. Ryan turned counterclockwise, stepped out backwards, and pulled his arm out behind. The footman grabbed his arm to help. Jack didn't want the help, but this wasn't a good time to object.

"You'll need a little practice on that," the Duke observed.

"I think you're right, sir." Jack followed him to the door, where another servant did his duty.

"Tell me, Jack—the first time we visited you, you seemed far more intimidated by the presence of the Queen than of me. Why is that?"

"Well, sir, you used to be a naval officer, right?"

"Of course." The Duke turned and looked rather curious.

Ryan grinned. "Sir, I work at Annapolis. The Academy crawls with naval officers, and remember I used to be a Marine. If I let myself get intimidated by every swabbie who crossed my path, the Corps would come and take my sword back.''

"You cheeky bugger!" They both had a laugh.

Ryan had expected to be impressed by the Palace. Even so, it was all he could manage to keep from being overwhelmed. Half the world had once been run from this house, and in addition to what the Royal Family had acquired over the centuries had come gifts from all over the world. Everywhere he looked the wide corridors were decorated with too many masterpieces of painting and sculpture to count. The walls were mainly covered with ivory-colored silk brocaded with gold thread. The carpets, of course, were imperial scarlet over marble or parquet hardwood. The money manager that Jack had once been tried to calculate the value of it all. He overloaded after about ten seconds. The paintings alone were so valuable that any attempt to sell them off would distort the world market in fine art. The gilt frames alone. . . . Ryan shook his head, wishing he had the time to examine every painting. *You could live here five years and not have time to appreciate it all.* He almost fell behind, but managed to control his gawking and kept pace with the older man. Ryan's discomfiture was growing. To the Duke this was home—perhaps one so large as to be something of a nuisance, but nonetheless home, routine. The Rubens masterpieces on the wall were part of the scenery, as familiar to him as the photographs of wife and kids on any man's office desk. To Ryan the impact of where he was, an impact made all the more crushing by the trappings of wealth and power, made him want to shrink away to nothingness. It was one thing to take his chance on the street—the Marines, after all, had prepared and trained him for that—but . . . *this.*

Get off it, Jack, he told himself. *They're a royal family, but they're not* your *royal family.* This didn't work. They were *a* royal family. That was enough to lacerate most of his ego.

"Here we are," the Duke said after turning right through an open door. "This is the Music Room."

It was about the size of the living/dining room in Ryan's house, the only thing he had seen thus far that could be so compared with any part of his $300,000 home on Peregrine Cliff. The ceiling was higher here, domed with gold-leaf trim. There were about thirty people, Ryan judged, and the moment they entered all conversation stopped. Everyone turned to stare at Ryan—Jack was sure they'd seen the Duke before—and his grotesque cast. He had a terrible urge to slink away. He needed a drink.

"If you'll excuse me for a moment, Jack, I must be off. Back in a few minutes."

Thanks a lot, Ryan thought as he nodded politely. *Now what do I do?*

"Good evening, Sir John," said a man in the uniform of a vice admiral of the Royal Navy. Ryan tried not to let his relief show. Of course, he'd been handed off to another custodian. He realized belatedly that lots of people came here for the first time. Some would need a little support while they got used to the idea of being in a palace, and there would be a procedure to take care of them. Jack took a closer look at the man's face as they shook hands. There was something familiar about it. "I'm Basil Charleston."

Aha! "Good evening, sir." His first week at Langley he'd seen the man, and his CIA escort had casually noted that this was "B.C." or just "C," the chief of the British Secret Intelligence Service, once known as MI-6. *What are you doing here?*

"You *must* be thirsty." Another man arrived with a glass of champagne. "Hello. I'm Bill Holmes."

"You gentlemen work together?" Ryan sipped at the bubbling wine.

"Judge Moore told me you were a clever chap," Charleston observed.

"Excuse me? Judge who?"

"Nicely done, Doctor Ryan," Holmes smiled as he finished off his glass. "I understand that you used to play football—the American kind, that is. You were on the junior varsity team, weren't you?"

"Varsity and junior varsity, but only in high school. I wasn't big enough for college ball," Ryan said, trying to mask his uneasiness. "Junior Varsity" was the project name under which he'd been called in to consult with CIA.

"And you wouldn't happen to know anything about the chap who wrote *Agents and Agencies*?" Charleston smiled. Jack went rigid.

"Admiral, I cannot talk about that without—"

"Copy number sixteen is sitting on my desk. The good judge told me to tell you that you were free to talk about the 'smoking word-processor.'"

Ryan let out a breath. The phrase must have come originally from

James Greer. When Jack had made the Canary Trap proposal to the Deputy Director, Intelligence, Admiral James Greer had made a joke about it, using those words. Ryan was free to talk. Probably. His CIA security briefing had not exactly covered this situation.

"Excuse me, sir. Nobody ever told me that I was free to talk about that."

Charleston went from jovial to serious for a moment. "Don't apologize, lad. One is supposed to take matters of classification seriously. That paper you wrote was an excellent bit of detective work. One of our problems, as someone doubtless told you, is that we take in so much information now that the real problem is making sense of it all. Not easy to wade through all the muck and find the gleaming nugget. For the first time in the business, your report was first-rate. What I didn't know about was this thing the Judge called the Canary Trap. He said you could explain it better than he." Charleston waved for another glass. A footman, or some sort of servant, came over with a tray. "You know who I am, of course."

"Yes, Admiral. I saw you last July at the Agency. You were getting out of the executive elevator on the seventh floor when I was coming out of the DDI's office, and somebody told me who you were."

"Good. Now you know that all of this remains in the family. What the devil is this Canary Trap?"

"Well, you know about all the problems CIA has with leaks. When I was finishing off the first draft of the report, I came up with an idea to make each one unique."

"They've been doing that for years," Holmes noted. "All one must do is misplace a comma here and there. Easiest thing in the world. If the newspeople are foolish enough to print a photograph of the document, we can identify the leak."

"Yes, sir, and the reporters who publish the leaks know that, too. They've learned not to show photographs of the documents they get from their sources, haven't they?" Ryan answered. "What I came up with was a new twist on that. *Agents and Agencies* has four sections. Each section has a summary paragraph. Each of those is written in a fairly dramatic fashion."

"Yes, I noticed that," Charleston said. "Didn't read like a CIA document at all. More like one of ours. We use people to write our reports, you see, not computers. Do go on."

"Each summary paragraph has six different versions, and the mixture of those paragraphs is unique to each numbered copy of the paper. There are over a thousand possible permutations, but only ninety-six numbered copies of the actual document. The reason the summary paragraphs are so—well, lurid, I guess—is to entice a reporter to quote them verbatim in the public media. If he quotes something from two or three of those paragraphs, we know which copy he saw and, therefore, who leaked it. They've got an even more refined version of the trap working now. You can do it by computer. You use a thesaurus program to shuffle through synonyms, and you can make every copy of the document totally unique.''

''Did they tell you if it worked?'' Holmes asked.

''No, sir. I had nothing to do with the security side of the Agency.'' *And thank God for that.*

''Oh, it worked.'' Sir Basil paused for a moment. ''That idea is bloody simple—and bloody brilliant! Then there was the substantive aspect of the paper. Did they tell you that your report agreed in nearly every detail with an investigation we ran last year?''

''No, sir, they didn't. So far as I know, all the documents I worked with came from our own people.''

''Then you came up with it entirely on your own? Marvelous.''

''Did I goof up on anything?'' Ryan asked the Admiral.

''You should have paid a bit more attention to that South African chap. That is more our patch, of course, and perhaps you didn't have enough information to fiddle with. We're giving him a very close look at the moment.''

Ryan finished off his glass and thought about that. There had been a good deal of information on Mr. Martens . . . *What did I miss?* He couldn't ask that, not now. Bad form. But he could ask—

''Aren't the South African people—''

''I'm afraid the cooperation they give us isn't quite as good now as it once was, and Erik Martens is quite a valuable chap for them. One can hardly blame them, you know. He does have a way of procuring what their military need, and that rather limits the pressure his government are willing to put on him,'' Holmes pointed out. ''There is also the Israeli connection to be considered. They occasionally stray from the path, but we—SIS and CIA—have too many common interests to rock the boat severely.'' Ryan nodded. The Israeli defense establishment had orders to generate as much income as possible, and this occasionally ran contrary to the wishes of Israel's allies. *I remember Martens' connections, but I must have missed something important . . . what?*

"Please don't take this as criticism," Charleston said. "For a first attempt your report was excellent. The CIA must have you back. It's one of the few Agency reports that didn't threaten to put me to sleep. If nothing else, perhaps you might teach their analysts how to write. Surely they asked if you wanted to stay on?"

"They asked, sir. I didn't think it was a very good idea for me."

"Think again," Sir Basil suggested gently. "This Junior Varsity idea was a good one, like the Team-B program back in the seventies. We do it also—get some outside academics into the shop—to take a new look at all the data that cascades in the front door. Judge Moore, your new DCI, is a genuine breath of fresh air. Splendid chap. Knows the trade quite well, but he's been away from it long enough to have some new ideas. You are one of them, Doctor Ryan. You belong in the business, lad."

"I'm not so sure about that, sir. My degree's history and—"

"So is mine," Bill Holmes said. "One's degree doesn't matter. In the intelligence trade we look for the right sort of mind. You appear to have it. Ah, well, *we* can't recruit you, can we? I would be rather disappointed if Arthur and James don't try again. Do think about it."

I have, Ryan didn't say. He nodded thoughtfully, mulling over his own thoughts. *But I like teaching history.*

"The hero of the hour!" Another man joined the group.

"Good evening, Geoffrey," Charleston said. "Doctor Ryan, this is Geoffrey Watkins of the Foreign Office."

"Like David Ashley of the 'Home Office'?" Ryan shook the man's hand.

"Actually I spend much of my time right here," Watkins said.

"Geoff's the liaison officer between the Foreign Office and the Royal Family. He handles briefings, dabbles in protocol, and generally makes a nuisance of himself," Holmes explained with a smile. "How long now, Geoff?"

Watkins frowned as he thought that over. "Just over four years, I think. Seems like only last week. Nothing like the glamour one might expect. Mainly I carry the dispatch box and try to hide in corners." Ryan smiled. He could identify with that.

"Nonsense," Charleston objected. "One of the best minds in the Office, else they wouldn't have kept you here."

Watkins made an embarrassed gesture. "It does keep me rather busy."

"It must," Holmes observed. "I haven't seen you at the tennis club in months."

"Doctor Ryan, the Palace staff have asked me to express their appreciation for what you have done." He droned on for a few more seconds. Watkins was an inch under Ryan's height and pushing forty. His neatly trimmed black hair was going gray at the sides, and his skin was pale in the way of people who rarely saw the sun. He looked like a diplomat. His smile was so perfect that he must have practiced it in front of a mirror. It was the sort of smile that could have meant anything. Or more likely, nothing. There was interest behind those blue eyes, though. As had happened many times in the past few weeks, this man was trying to decide what Dr. John Patrick Ryan was made of. The subject of the investigation was getting very tired of this, but there wasn't much Jack could do about it.

"Geoff is something of an expert on the Northern Ireland situation," Holmes said.

"No one's an 'expert,'" Watkins said with a shake of his head. "I was there at the beginning, back in 1969. I was in uniform then, a subaltern with—well, that hardly matters now, does it? How do you think we should handle the problem, Doctor Ryan?"

"People have been asking me that question for three weeks, Mr. Watkins. How the hell should I know?"

"Still looking for ideas, Geoff?" Holmes asked.

"The right idea is out there somewhere," Watkins said, keeping his eyes on Ryan.

"I don't have it," Jack said. "And even if someone did, how would you know? I teach history, remember, I don't make it."

"Just a history teacher, and these two chaps descend on you?"

"We wanted to see if he really works for CIA, as the papers say," Charleston responded.

Jack took the signal from that. Watkins wasn't cleared for everything, and was not to know about his past association with the Agency—not that he couldn't draw his own conclusions, Ryan reminded himself. Regardless, rules were rules. *That's why I turned Greer's offer down,* Jack remembered. *All those idiot rules. You can't talk to anybody about this or that, not even to your wife. Security. Security. Security . . . Crap! Sure, some things have to stay secret, but if nobody gets to see them, how is anyone supposed to make use of them—and what good is a secret you can't use?*

"You know, it'll be nice to get back to Annapolis. At least the mids believe I'm a teacher!"

"Quite," Watkins noted. *And the head of SIS is asking you for an opinion on Trafalgar. What exactly are you, Ryan?* After leaving military service in 1972 and joining the Foreign Office, Watkins had often played the foreign service officer's embassy game: *Who's the spook?* He was getting mixed signals from Ryan, and this made the game all the more interesting. Watkins loved games. All sorts.

"How do you keep yourself busy now, Geoff?" Holmes asked.

"You mean, aside from the twelve-hour days? I do manage to read the occasional book. I just started going through *Moll Flanders* again."

"Really?" Holmes asked. "I just started *Robinson Crusoe* a few days ago. One sure way of getting one's mind off the world is to return to the classics."

"Do you read the classics, Doctor Ryan?" Watkins asked.

"Used to. Jesuit education, remember? They don't let you avoid the old stuff." *Is* Moll Flanders *a classic?* Jack wondered. *It's not in Latin or Greek, and it's not Shakespeare. . . .*

"'Old stuff.' What a terrible attitude!" Watkins laughed.

"Did you ever try to read Virgil in the original?" Ryan asked. *"Arma virumque cano, trojae qui primus ab oris . . . ?"*

"Geoff and I attended Winchester together," Holmes explained. *"Contiquere omnes, intenteque ora tenebant. . . ."* Both public school graduates had a good chuckle.

"Hey, I got good marks in Latin, I just don't remember any of it," Ryan said defensively.

"Another colonial philistine," Watkins observed.

Ryan decided that he didn't like Mr. Watkins. The foreign-service officer was deliberately hitting him to get reactions, and Ryan had long since tired of this game. Ryan was happy with what he was, and didn't need a bunch of amateur pshrinks, as he called them, to define his personality for him.

"Sorry. Where I live we have slightly different priorities."

"Of course," Watkins replied. The smile hadn't changed a whit. This surprised Jack, though he wasn't sure why.

"You live not far from the Naval Academy, don't you? Wasn't there some sort of incident there recently?" Sir Basil asked. "I read about it in some report somewhere. I never did get straight on the details."

"It wasn't really terrorism—just your basic crime. A couple of midshipmen saw what looked like a drug deal being made in Annapolis, and called the police. The people who got arrested were members of a local motorcycle gang. A week later, some of the gang members decided to take the mids out. They got past the Jimmy Legs—the civilian security guards—about three in the morning and sneaked into Bancroft Hall. They must have assumed that it was just another college dorm—not hardly. The kids standing midwatch spotted them, got the alarm out, and then everything came apart. The intruders got themselves lost—Bancroft has a couple of miles of corridors—and cornered. It's a federal case since it happened on government property, and the FBI takes a very dim view of people who try to tamper with witnesses. They'll be gone for a while. The good news is that the Marine guard force at the Academy has been beefed up, and it's a lot easier to get in and out now."

"Easier?" Watkins asked. "But—"

Jack smiled. "With Marines on the perimeter, they leave a lot more gates open—a Marine guard beats a locked gate any day."

"Indeed. I—" Something caught Charleston's eye. Ryan was facing the wrong way to see what it was, but the reactions were plain enough. Charleston and Holmes began to disengage, with Watkins making his way off first. Jack turned in time to see the Queen appear at the door, coming past a servant.

The Duke was at her side, with Cathy trailing a diplomatically defined distance behind and to the side. The Queen came first to him.

"You are looking much better."

Jack tried to bow—he thought he was supposed to—without endangering the Queen's life with his cast. The main trick was standing still, he'd learned. The weight of the thing tended to induce a progressive lean to the left. Moving around helped him stay upright.

"Thank you, Your Majesty. I feel much better. Good evening, sir."

One thing about shaking hands with the Duke, you knew there was a man at the other end. "Hello again, Jack. Do try to be at ease. This is completely informal. No receiving line, no protocol. Relax."

"Well, the champagne helps."

"Excellent," the Queen observed. "I think we'll let you and Caroline get reacquainted for the moment." She and the Duke moved off.

"Easy on the booze, Jack." Cathy positively glowed in a white cocktail dress so lovely that Ryan forgot to wonder what it had cost. Her hair was nicely arranged and she had makeup on, two things that her profession regularly denied her. Most of all, she was Cathy Ryan. He gave his wife a quick kiss, audience and all.

"All these people—"

"Screw 'em," Jack said quietly. "How's my favorite girl?"

Her eyes sparkled with the news, but her voice was deadpan-professional:

"Pregnant."

"You sure—*when?*"

"I'm sure, darling, because, A, I'm a doctor, and B, I'm two weeks late. As to when, Jack, remember when we got here, as soon as we put Sally down to bed. . . . It's those strange hotel beds, Jack." She took his hand. "They do it every time."

There wasn't anything for Jack to say. He wrapped his good arm around her shoulders and squeezed as discreetly as his emotions would allow. If she was two weeks late—well, he knew Cathy to be as regular as her Swiss watch. *I'm going to be a daddy—again!*

"We'll try for a boy this time," she said.

"You know that's not important, babe."

"I see you've told him." The Queen returned as quietly as a cat. The Duke, Jack saw, was talking to Admiral Charleston. About what? he wondered. "Congratulations, Sir John."

"Thank you, Your Majesty, and thank you for a lot of things. We'll never be able to repay you for all your kindness."

The Christmas-tree smile again. "It is we who are repaying you. From what Caroline tells me, you will now have at least one positive reminder of your visit to our country."

"Indeed, ma'am, but more than one." Jack was learning how the game was played.

"Caroline, is he always so gallant?"

"As a matter of fact, ma'am, no. We must have caught him at a weak moment,'' Cathy said. ''Or maybe being over here is a civilizing influence.''

''That is good to know, after all the horrid things he said about your little Olivia. Do you know that she refused to go to bed without kissing me goodnight? Such a lovely, charming little angel. And *he* called her a menace!''

Jack sighed. It wasn't hard for him to get the picture. After three weeks in this environment, Sally was probably doing the cutest curtsies in the history of Western Civilization. By this time the Palace staff was probably fighting for the right to look after her. Sally was a true daddy's girl. The ability to manipulate the people around her came easily. She'd practiced on her father for years.

''Perhaps I exaggerated, ma'am.''

''Libelously.'' The Queen's eyes flared with amusement. ''She has not broken a single thing. Not one. And I'll have you know that she's turning into the best equestrienne we have seen in years.''

''Excuse me?''

''Riding lessons,'' Cathy explained.

''You mean on a horse?''

''What else would she ride?'' the Queen asked.

''Sally, on a horse?'' Ryan looked at his wife. He didn't like that idea very much.

''And doing splendidly.'' The Queen sprang to Cathy's defense. ''It's quite safe, Sir John. Riding is a fine skill for a child to learn. It teaches discipline, coordination, and responsibility.''

Not to mention a fabulous way to break her pretty little neck, Ryan thought. Again he remembered that one does not argue with a queen, especially under her own roof.

''You could even try to ride yourself,'' the Queen said. ''Your wife rides.''

''We have enough land now, Jack,'' Cathy said. ''You'd love it.''

''I'd fall off,'' Ryan said bleakly.

''Then you climb back on again until you get it right,'' said a woman with over fifty years of riding behind her.

It's the same with a bike, except you don't fall as far off a bike, and Sally's too little *for a bike,* Ryan told himself. He got nervous watching Sally move her Hotwheel trike around the driveway. *For God's sake, she's so little the horse wouldn't even know if she was there or not.* Cathy read his mind.

"Children do have to grow up. You can't protect her from everything," his wife pointed out.

"Yes, dear, I know." *The hell I can't. That's my job.*

A few minutes later everyone headed out the room for dinner. Ryan found himself in the Blue Drawing Room, a breathtaking pillared hall, and then passed through mirrored double doors into the State Dining Room.

The contrast was incredible. From a room of muted blue they entered one ablaze with scarlet, fabric-covered walls. Overhead the vaulted ceiling was ivory and gold, and over the snow-white fireplace was a massive portrait—of whom? Ryan wondered. It had to be a king, of course, probably 18th or 19th century, judging by his white . . . pantyhose, or whatever they'd called them then, complete with garter. Over the door they'd entered was the royal cipher of Queen Victoria, VR, and he wondered how much history had passed through—or been made right in this single room.

"You will sit at my right hand, Jack," the Queen said.

Ryan took a quick look at the table. It was wide enough that he didn't have to worry about clobbering Her Majesty with his left arm. That wouldn't do.

The worst thing about the dinner was that Ryan would be forever unable to remember—and too proud to ask Cathy—what it was. Eating one-handed was something he'd had a lot of practice at, but never had he had such an audience, and Ryan was sure that everyone was watching him. After all, he was a Yank and would have been something of a curiosity even without his arm. He constantly reminded himself to be careful, to go easy on the wine, to watch his language. He shot the occasional glance at Cathy, sitting at the other end of the table next to the Duke and clearly enjoying herself. It made her husband slightly angry that she was more at ease than he was. *If there was ever a pig in the manger,* Ryan thought while chewing on something he immediately forgot, *it's me.* He wondered if he would be here now, had he been a rookie cop or a private in the Royal Marines who just happened to be at the right place. Probably not, he thought. *And why is that?* Ryan didn't know. He did know that something about the institution of nobility went against his American outlook. At the same time, being knighted—even honorarily—was something he liked. It was a contradiction that troubled him in a way he didn't understand. All this attention was too seductive, he told himself. *It'll be good to get away from it. Or will it?* He sipped at a glass of wine. *I know I don't belong here, but do I* want *to belong here? There's a good question.* The wine didn't give him an answer. He'd have to find it somewhere else.

He looked down the table to his wife, who did seem to fit in very nicely. She'd been raised in a similar atmosphere, a monied family, a big house in Westchester County, lots of parties where people told one another how important they all were. It was a life he'd rejected, and that she had walked away from. They were both happy with what they had, each with a career, but did her ease with this mean that she missed . . . Ryan frowned.

"Feeling all right, Jack?" the Queen asked.

"Yes, ma'am, please excuse me. I'm afraid it will take me a while to adjust to all of this."

"Jack," she said quietly, "the reason everyone likes you—and we all do, you know—is because of who and what you are. Try to keep that in mind."

It struck Ryan that this was probably the kindest thing he'd ever been told. Perhaps nobility was supposed to be a state of mind rather than an institution. His father-in-law could learn from that, Ryan thought. His father-in-law could learn from a lot of things.

Three hours later Jack followed his wife into their room. There was a sitting room off to the right. In front of him the bed had already been turned down. He pulled the tie loose from his collar and undid the button, then let out a long, audible breath.

"You weren't kidding about turning into pumpkins."

"I know," his wife said.

Only a single dim light was lit, and his wife switched it off. The only illumination in the room was from distant streetlights that filtered through the heavy curtains. Her white dress stood out in the darkness, but her face showed only the curve of her lips and the sparkle of her eyes as she turned away from the light. Her husband's mind filled in the remaining details. Jack wrapped his good arm around his wife and cursed the monstrosity of plaster that encased his left side as he pulled her in close. She rested her head on his healthy shoulder, and his cheek came down to the softness of her fine blond hair. Neither said anything for a minute or two. It was enough to be alone, together in the quiet darkness.

"Love ya, babe."

"How are you feeling, Jack?" The question was more than a simple inquiry.

"Not bad. Pretty well rested. The shoulder doesn't hurt very much anymore. Aspirin takes care of the aches." This was an exaggeration, but Jack was used to the discomfort.

"Oh, I see how they did it." Cathy was exploring the left side of his jacket. The tailors had put snap closures on the underside so that it would not so much conceal the cast as make it look dressed. His wife removed the snaps quickly and pulled the coat off. The shirt went next.

"I am able to do this myself, you know."

"Shut up, Jack. I don't want to have to wait all night for you to undress." He next heard the sound of a long zipper.

"Can I help?"

There was laughter in the darkness. "I might want to wear this dress again. And be careful where you put that arm."

"I haven't crunched anyone yet."

"Good. Let's try to keep a perfect record." A whisper of silk. She took his hand. "Let's get you sitting down."

After he sat on the edge of the bed, the rest came easy. Cathy sat beside him. He felt her, cool and smooth at his side, a hint of perfume in the air. He reached around her shoulder, down to the soft skin of her abdomen.

It's happening right now, growing away while we sit here. "You're going to have my baby," Jack said softly. *There really is a God, and there really are miracles.*

Her hand came across his face. "That's right. I can't have anything to drink after tonight—but I wanted to enjoy tonight."

"You know, I really do love you."

"I know," she said. "Lie back."

6

Trials
and Troubles

Preliminary testimony lasted for about two hours while Ryan sat on a
marble bench outside Old Bailey's number two courtroom. He tried to
work on his computer, but he couldn't seem to keep his mind on it, and
found himself staring around the hundred-sixty-year-old building.

Security was incredibly tight. Outside, numerous uniformed police
constables stood about in plain sight, small zippered pistol cases dangling from their hands. Others, uniformed and not, stood on the buildings across Newgate Street like falcons on the watch for rabbits.
Except rabbits don't carry machine guns and RPG-7 bazookas, Ryan
thought. Every person who entered the building was subjected to a
metal detector sensitive enough to *ping* on the foil inside a cigarette
pack, and nearly everyone was given a pat-down search. This included
Ryan, who was surprised enough at the intimacy of the search to tell
the officer that he went a bit far for a first date. The grand hall was
closed off to anyone not connected with the case, and less prominent
trials had been switched among the building's nineteen courtrooms to
accommodate *Crown v Miller*.

Ryan had never been in a courthouse before. He was amused by the fact that he'd never even had a speeding ticket, his life had been so dull until now. The marble floor—nearly everything in sight was marble—gave the hall the aspect of a cathedral, and the walls were decorated with aphorisms such as Cicero's THE WELFARE OF THE PEOPLE IS THE HIGHEST LAW, a phrase he found curiously—or at least potentially—expedient in what was certainly designed as a temple to the idea of law. He wondered if the members of the ULA felt the same way, and justified their activities in accordance with their view of the welfare of the people. *Who doesn't?* Jack asked himself. *What tyrant ever failed to justify his crimes?* Around him were a half-dozen other witnesses. Jack didn't talk with them. His instructions were quite specific: even the appearance of conversation might give cause to the defense attorneys to speculate that witnesses had coached one another. The prosecution team had bent every effort to make their case a textbook example of correct legal procedure.

The case was being handled on a contradictory basis. The ambush had taken place barely four weeks ago, and the trial was already under way—an unusually speedy process even by British standards. Security was airtight. Admittance to the public gallery (visitors entered from another part of the building) was being strictly controlled. But at the same time, the trial was being handled strictly as a criminal matter. The name "Ulster Liberation Army" had not been mentioned. The prosecutor had not once used the word terrorist. The police ignored—publicly—the political aspects of the case. Two men were dead, and this was a trial for first-degree murder—period. Even the press was playing along, on the theory that there was no more contemptuous way to treat the defendant than to call him a simple criminal, and not sanctify him as a creature of politics. Jack wondered about additional political or intelligence-related motives in this treatment, but no one was talking along those lines, and the defense attorney certainly couldn't defend his client better by calling him a member of a terrorist group. In the media, and in the courtroom, this was a case of murder.

The truth was different, of course, and everyone knew it. But Ryan knew enough about the law to remember that lawyers rarely concern themselves with truth. The rules were far more important. There would therefore be no official speculation on the goal of the criminals, and no involvement of the Royal Family, aside from depositions that they could not identify the living conspirator and hence had no worthwhile evidence to offer.

It didn't matter. From the press coverage of the evidence it seemed clear enough that the trial was as airtight as was possible without a videotape of the entire event. Similarly, Cathy was not to testify. In addition to forensic experts who had testified the day before, the Crown had eight eyewitnesses. Ryan was number two. The trial was expected to last a maximum of four days. As Owens had told him in the hospital, there would be no mucking about with this lad.

"Doctor Ryan? Would you please follow me, sir?" The VIP treatment continued here also. A bailiff in short sleeves and tie came over and led him into the courtroom through a side door. A police officer took his computer after opening the door. "Showtime," Ryan whispered to himself.

Old Bailey #2 was an extravagance of 19th-century woodworking. The large room was paneled with so much solid oak that the construction of a similar room in America would draw a protest from the Sierra Club for all the trees it required. The actual floorspace was surprisingly small, scarcely as much as the dining room in his house, a similarity made all the more striking by a table set in the center. The judge's bench was a wooden fortress adjacent to the witness box. The Honorable Mr. Justice Wheeler sat in one of the five high-backed chairs behind it. He was resplendent in a scarlet robe and sash, and a horsehair wig, called a "peruke," Ryan had been told, that fell to his narrow shoulders and clearly looked like something from another age. The jury box was to Ryan's left. Eight women and four men sat in two even rows, each face full of anticipation. Above them was the public gallery, perched like a choir loft and angled so that Ryan could barely see the people there. The barristers were to Ryan's right, across the small floorspace, wearing black robes, 18th-century cravats, and their own, smaller wigs. The net effect of all this was a vaguely religious atmosphere that made Ryan slightly uneasy as he was sworn.

William Richards, QC, the prosecutor, was a man of Ryan's age, similar in height and build. He began with the usual questions: your name, place of residence, profession, when did you arrive, for what purpose? Richards predictably had a flair for the dramatic, and by the time the questions carried them to the shooting, Ryan could sense the excitement and anticipation of the audience without even looking at their faces.

"Doctor Ryan, could you describe in your own words what happened next?"

Jack did exactly this for ten minutes, without interruption, all the while half-facing the jury. He tried to avoid looking into their faces. It seemed an odd place to get stage fright, but this was precisely what Ryan felt. He focused his eyes on the oak panels just over their heads as he ran through the events. It was almost like living it again, and Ryan could feel his heart beating faster as he concluded.

"And, Doctor Ryan, can you identify for us the man whom you first attacked?" Richards finally asked.

"Yes, sir." Ryan pointed. "The defendant, right there, sir."

It was Ryan's first really good look at him. His name was Sean Miller—not a particularly Irish name to Ryan's way of thinking. He was twenty-six, short, slender, dressed neatly in a suit and tie. He was smiling up at someone in the visitors' gallery, a family member perhaps, when Ryan pointed. Then his gaze shifted, and Ryan examined the man for the first time. What sort of person, Jack had wondered for weeks, could plan and execute such a crime? What was missing in him, or what terrible thing lived in him that most civilized people had the good fortune to lack? The thin, acne-scarred face was entirely normal. Miller could have been an executive trainee at Merrill Lynch or any other business concern. Jack's father had spent his life dealing with criminals, but their existence was a puzzlement to Ryan. *Why are you different? What makes you what you are?* Ryan wanted to ask, knowing that even if there were an answer the question would remain. Then he looked at Miller's eyes. He looked for . . . something, a spark of life, humanity—something that would say that this was indeed another human being. It could only have been two seconds, but for Ryan the moment seemed to linger into minutes as he looked into those pale gray eyes and saw . . .

Nothing. Nothing at all. And Jack began to understand a little.

"The record will show," the Lord Justice intoned to the court reporter, "that the witness identified the defendant, Sean Miller."

"Thank you, My Lord," Richards concluded.

Ryan took the opportunity to blow his nose. He'd acquired a head cold over the preceding weekend.

"Are you quite comfortable, Doctor Ryan?" the judge inquired. Jack realized that he'd been leaning on the wooden rail.

"Excuse me, your hon—My Lord. This cast is a little tiring."

Every time Sally came past her father, she had taken to singing, "I'm a little teapot . . ."

"Bailiff, a stool for the witness," the judge ordered.

The defense team was seated adjacent to the prosecution, perhaps fifteen feet farther away in the same row of seats, green leather cushions on the oak benches. In a moment the bailiff arrived with a simple wooden stool, and Ryan settled down on it. What he really needed was a hook for his left arm, but he was gradually becoming used to the weight. It was the constant itching that drove him crazy, though there was nothing anybody could do about that.

The defense attorney—barrister—rose with elegant deliberation. His name was Charles Atkinson, more commonly known as Red Charlie, a lawyer with a penchant for radical causes and radical crimes. He was supposed to be an embarrassment to the Labour Party, which he had served until recently in Parliament. Red Charlie was about thirty pounds overweight, his wig askew atop a florid, strangely thin face for the ample frame. Defending terrorists must have paid well enough, Ryan thought. *There's a question Owens must be looking into,* Ryan told himself. *Where is your money coming from, Mr. Atkinson?*

"May it please Your Lordship," he said formally to the bench. He walked slowly towards Ryan, a sheaf of notes in his hand.

"Doctor Ryan—or should I say Sir John?"

Jack waved his hand. "Whatever is convenient to you, sir," he answered indifferently. They had warned him about Atkinson. *A very clever bastard,* they'd said. Ryan had known quite a few clever bastards in the brokerage business.

"You were, I believe, a *lef*tenant in the United States Marine Corps?"

"Yes, sir, that is correct."

Atkinson looked down at his notes, then over at the jury. "Blood-thirsty mob, the U.S. Marines," he muttered.

"Excuse me, sir? Bloodthirsty?" Ryan asked. "No, sir. Most of the Marines I know are beer drinkers."

Atkinson spun back at Ryan as a ripple of laughter came down from the gallery. He gave Jack a thin, dangerous smile. They'd warned Jack most of all to beware his word games and tactical skill in the courtroom. *To hell with it,* Ryan told himself. He smiled back at the barrister. *Go for it, asshole. . . .*

"Forgive me, Sir John. A figure of speech. I meant to say that the U.S. Marines have a reputation for aggressiveness. Surely this is true?"

"Marines are light infantry troops who specialize in amphibious assault. We were pretty well trained, but when you get down to it we weren't all that different from any other kind of soldier. It's just a matter of specialization in a particularly tough field," Ryan answered, hoping to throw him a little off balance. Marines were supposed to be arrogant, but that was mostly movie stuff. If you're really good, they'd taught him at Quantico, you don't have to be arrogant. Just letting people know you're a Marine was usually enough.

"Assault troops?"

"Yes, sir. That's basically correct."

"So, you commanded assault troops, then?"

"Yes, sir."

"Try not to be too modest, Sir John. What sort of man is selected to lead such troops. Aggressive? Decisive? Bold? Certainly he would have more of these qualities than the average foot soldier?"

"As a matter of fact, sir, in my edition of *The Marine Officer's Guide,* the foremost of the qualities that the Corps looks for in an officer is *integrity*." Ryan smiled again. Atkinson hadn't done his homework on that score. "I commanded a platoon, sure, but as my captain explained to me when I came aboard, my principal job was to carry out the orders he gave me, and to lean on my gunny—my platoon sergeant—for his practical experience. The job I was in was supposed to be as much a learning experience as a command slot. I mean, in business it's called an entry-level position. You don't start shaking the world your first day on the job in any business."

Atkinson frowned a bit. This was not going as he'd expected.

"Ah, then, Sir John, a *lef*tenant of American Marines is really a leader of Boy Scouts. Surely you don't mean that?" he asked, a sarcastic edge on his voice.

"No, sir. Excuse me, I did not mean to give that impression, but we're not a bunch of hyperaggressive barbarians either. My job was to carry out orders, to be as aggressive as the situation called for, and to exercise some amount of judgment, like any officer. But I was only there three months, and I was still learning how to be an officer when I was injured. Marines follow orders. Officers give orders, of course, but a second lieutenant is the lowest form of officer. You take more than you give. I guess you've never been in the service,'' Ryan tagged on the barb at the end.

"So, what sort of training *did* they give you?'' Atkinson demanded, either angry or feigning it.

Richards looked up to Ryan, a warning broadcast from his eyes. He'd emphasized several times that Jack shouldn't cross swords with Red Charlie.

"Really, basic leadership skills. They taught us how to lead men in the field,'' Ryan replied. "How to react to a given tactical situation. How to employ the platoon's weapons, and to a lesser extent, the weapons in a rifle company. How to call in outside support from artillery and air assets—''

"To react?''

"Yes, sir, that is part of it.'' Ryan kept his answers as long as he thought he could get away with, careful to keep his voice even, friendly, and informative. "I've never been in anything like a combat situation—unless you count this thing we're talking about, of course—but our instructors were very clear about telling us that you don't have time to think very much when bullets are flying. You have to know what to do, and you have to do it fast—or you get your own people killed.''

"Excellent, Sir John. You were trained to react quickly and decisively to tactical stimuli, correct?''

"Yes, sir.'' Ryan thought he saw the ambush coming.

"So, in the unfortunate incident before this court, when the initial explosion took place, you have testified that you were looking in the wrong direction?''

"I was looking away from the explosion, yes, sir.''

"How soon afterwards did you turn to see what was happening?''

"Well, sir, as I said earlier, the first thing I did was to get my wife and daughter down under cover. Then I looked up. How long did that take?'' Ryan cocked his head. "At least one second, sir, maybe as many as three. Sorry, but as I said earlier, it's hard to recall that sort of thing—you don't have a stopwatch on yourself, I mean.''

"So, when you *finally* did look up, you had not seen what had immediately transpired?''

"Correct, sir.'' *Okay, Charlie, ask the next question.*

"You did not, therefore, see my client fire his pistol, nor throw a hand grenade?"

Cute, Ryan thought, surprised that he'd try this ploy. *Well, he has to try something, doesn't he?* "No, sir. When I first saw him, he was running around the corner of the car, from the direction of the other man, the one who was killed—the one with the rifle. A moment later he was at the right-rear corner of the Rolls, facing away from me, with the pistol in his right hand, pointed forward and down, as if—"

"Assumption on your part," Atkinson interrupted. "As if what? It could have been any one of several things. But what things? How could you tell what he was doing there? You did not see him get out of the car, which later drove off. For all you know he might have been another pedestrian racing to the rescue, just as you did, mightn't he?"

Jack was supposed to be surprised by this.

"Assumption, sir? No, I'd call it a judgment. For him to have been racing to the rescue as you suggest, he would have had to come from across the street. I doubt that anyone could have reacted anywhere near fast enough to do that at all, not to mention the fact that there was a guy there with a machine gun to make you think twice about it. Also, the direction I saw him running from was directly away from the guy with the AK-47. If he was running to the rescue, why away from him? If he had a gun, why not shoot him? At the time I never considered this possibility, and it seems pretty unlikely now, sir."

"Again, a *conclusion,* Sir John," Atkinson said as though to a backward child.

"Sir, you asked me a question, and I tried to answer it, with the reasons to back up my answer."

"And you expect us to believe that all this flashed through your mind in a brief span of seconds?" Atkinson turned back to the jury.

"Yes, sir, it did," Ryan said with conviction. "That's all I can say—it did."

"I don't suppose you've been told that my client has never been arrested, or accused of any crime?"

"I guess that makes him a first offender."

"It's for the jury to decide that," the lawyer snapped back. "You did not see him fire a single shot, did you?"

"No, sir, but his automatic had an eight-shot clip, and there were only three rounds in it. When I fired my third shot, it was empty."

"So what? For all you know someone else could have fired that gun. You did not see him fire, did you?"

"No, sir."

"So it might have been dropped by someone in the car. My client might have picked it up and, I repeat, been doing the same thing you were doing—this could all be true, but you have no way of knowing this, do you?"

"I cannot testify about things I didn't see, sir. However, I *did* see the street, the traffic, and the other pedestrians. If your client did what you say, where did he come from?"

"Precisely—you don't know, do you?" Atkinson said sharply.

"When I saw your client, sir, he was coming from the direction of the stopped car." Jack gestured to the model on the evidence table. "For him to have come off the sidewalk, then gotten the gun, and then appeared where I saw him—there's just no way unless he's an Olympic-class sprinter."

"Well, we'll never know, will we—you fixed that. You reacted precipitously, didn't you? You reacted as you were trained to by the U.S. Marines, never stopping to assess the situation. You raced into the fray quite recklessly, attacked my client and knocked him unconscious, then tried to kill him."

"No, sir, I did not try to kill your client. I've already—"

"Then why did you shoot an unconscious, helpless man?"

"My Lord," prosecutor Richards said, standing up, "we have already asked that question."

"The witness may answer on further reflection," Justice Wheeler intoned. No one would say that this trial was unfair.

"Sir, I did not know he was unconscious, and I didn't know how long it would be before he got up. So, I shot to disable him. I just didn't want him to get back up for a while."

"I'm sure that's what they said at My Lai."

"That wasn't the Marines, Mr. Atkinson," Ryan shot back.

The lawyer smiled up at Jack. "I suppose your chaps were better trained at keeping quiet. Indeed, perhaps you yourself have been trained in such things. . . ."

"No, sir, I have not." *He's making you angry, Jack.* He took his handkerchief out and blew his nose again. The two deep breaths helped. "Excuse me, I'm afraid the local weather has given me a bit of a head cold. What you just said—if the Marines trained people in that sort of stuff, the newspapers would have plastered it on their front pages years ago. No, moral issues aside for the moment, the Corps has a much better sense of public relations than that, Mr. Atkinson.''

"In*deed*." The barrister shrugged. "And what about the Central Intelligence Agency?''

"Excuse me?''

"What of the press reports that you've worked for the CIA?''

"Sir, the only times I've been paid by the U.S. government," Jack said, choosing his words very carefully, "the money came from the Navy Department, first as a Marine, then later—now, that is, as an instructor at the United States Naval Academy. I have never been employed by any other government agency, period.''

"So you are not an agent of the CIA? I remind you that you are under oath.''

"No, sir. I am not now, and I never have been any kind of agent— unless you count being a stockbroker. I don't work for the CIA.''

"And these news reports?''

"I'm afraid that you'll have to ask the reporters. I don't know where that stuff comes from. I teach history. My office is in Leahy Hall on the Naval Academy grounds. That's kind of a long way from Langley.''

"Langley? You know where CIA is, then?''

"Yes, sir. It's on record that I have delivered a lecture there. It was the same lecture I delivered the month before at the Naval War College at Newport, Rhode Island. My paper dealt with the nature of tactical decision-making. I have never worked for the Central Intelligence Agency, but I did, once, give a lecture there. Maybe that's where all these reports started.''

"I think you're lying, Sir John," Atkinson observed.

Not quite, Charlie. "I can't help what you think, sir. I can only answer your questions truthfully.''

"And you never wrote an official report for the government entitled *Agents and Agencies*?''

Ryan did not allow himself to react. *Where did you get that bit of data, Charlie?* He answered the question with great care.

"Sir, last year—that is, last summer, at the end of the last school year—I was asked to be a contract consultant to a private company that does government work. The company is the Mitre Corporation, and I was hired on a temporary basis as part of one of their consulting contracts with the U.S. government. The work involved was classified, but it obviously had nothing at all to do with this case."

"Obviously? Why don't you let the jury decide that?"

"Mr. Atkinson," Justice Wheeler said tiredly, "are you suggesting that this work in which the witness was involved has a direct connection with the case before the court?"

"I think we might wish to establish that, My Lord. It is my belief that the witness is misleading the court."

"Very well." The judge turned. "Doctor Ryan, did this work in which you were engaged have anything whatever to do with a case of murder in the city of London, or with any of the persons involved in this case?"

"No, sir."

"You are quite certain?"

"Yes, sir."

"Are you now or have you ever been an employee of any intelligence or security agency of the American government?"

"Except for the Marine Corps, no, sir."

"I remind you of your oath to tell the truth—the whole, complete truth. Have you misled the court in any way, Doctor Ryan?"

"No, sir, absolutely not."

"Thank you, Doctor Ryan. I believe that question is now settled." Mr. Justice Wheeler turned back to his right. "Next question, Mr. Atkinson."

The barrister had to be angry at that, Ryan thought, but he didn't let it show. He wondered if someone had briefed the judge.

"You say that you shot my client *merely* in the hope that he would not get up?"

Richards stood. "My Lord, the witness has already—"

"If His Lordship will permit me to ask the next question, the issue will be more clear," Atkinson interrupted smoothly.

"Proceed."

"Doctor Ryan, you said that you shot my client in the hope that he would not get up. Do the U.S. Marine Corps teach one to shoot to disable, or to kill?"

"To kill, sir."

"And you are telling us, therefore, that you went against your training?"

"Yes, sir. It is pretty clear that I was not on a battlefield. I was on a city street. It never occurred to me to kill your client." *I wish it* had, *then I probably wouldn't be here,* Ryan thought, wondering if he really meant it.

"So you reacted in accordance with your training when you leaped into the fray on The Mall, but then you *disregarded* your training a moment later? Do you think it reasonable that all of us here will believe *that*?"

Atkinson had finally succeeded in confusing Ryan. Jack had not the slightest idea where this was leading.

"I haven't thought of it that way, sir, but, yes, you are correct," Jack admitted. "That is pretty much what happened."

"And next you crept to the corner of the automobile, saw the second person whom you had seen earlier, and instead of trying to disable him, you shot him dead without warning. In this case, it is clear that you reverted again to your Marine training, and shot to kill. Don't you find this inconsistent?"

Jack shook his head. "Not at all, sir. In each case I used the force necessary to—well, the force I had to use, as I saw things."

"I think you are wrong, Sir John. I think that you reacted like a hotheaded officer of the United States Marines throughout. You raced into a situation of which you had no clear understanding, attacked an innocent man, and tried then to kill him while he lay helpless and unconscious on the street. Next you coldly gunned down someone else without the first thought of trying to disarm him. You did not know then, and you do not know now what was really happening, do you?"

"No, sir, I do not believe that was the case at all. What was I supposed to have done with the second man?"

Atkinson saw an opening and used it. "You just told the court that you only wished to disable my client—when in fact you tried to kill him. How do you expect us to believe that when your next action had not the first thing to do with such a *peaceful* solution?"

"Sir, when I saw McCrory, the second gunman, for the first time, he had an AK-47 assault rifle in his hands. Going up against a light machine gun with a pistol—"

"But by this time you saw that he didn't have the Kalashnikov, didn't you?"

"Yes, sir, that's true. If he'd still had it—I don't know, maybe I wouldn't have stepped around the car, maybe I would have shot from cover, from behind the car, that is."

"Ah, I see!" Atkinson exclaimed. "Instead, here was your chance to confront and kill the man in true cowboy fashion." His hands went up in the air. "Dodge City on The Mall!"

"I wish you'd tell me what you think I should have done," Jack said with some exasperation.

"For someone able to shoot straight through the heart on his first shot, why not shoot the gun from his hand, Sir John?"

"Oh, I see." Atkinson had just made a mistake. Ryan shook his head and smiled. "I wish you'd make up your mind."

"What?" The barrister was caught by surprise.

"Mr. Atkinson, a minute ago you said that I tried to kill your client. I was at arm's-length range, but I *didn't* kill him. So I'm a pretty lousy shot. But you expect me to be able to hit a man in the hand at fifteen or twenty feet. It doesn't work that way, sir. I'm either a good shot or a bad shot, sir, but not both. Besides, that's just TV stuff, shooting a gun out of somebody's hand. On TV the good guy can do that, but TV isn't real. With a pistol, you aim for the center of your target. That's what I did. I stepped out from behind the car to get a clear shot, and I aimed. If McCrory had not turned his gun towards me—I can't say for sure, but probably I would not have shot. But he did turn and fire, as you can see from my shoulder—and I did return fire. It is true that I might have done things differently. Unfortunately I did not. I had—I didn't have much time to take action. I did the best I could. I'm sorry the man was killed, but that was his choice, too. He saw I had the drop on him, but he turned and fired—and he fired first, sir."

"But you never said a word, did you?"

"No, I don't think I did," Jack admitted.

"Don't you wish you'd done things differently?"

"Mr. Atkinson, if it makes you feel any better, I have gone over that again and again for the past four weeks. If I'd had more time to think, perhaps I would have done something different. But I'll never know, because I didn't have more time." Jack paused. "I suppose the best thing for all concerned would be if all this had never happened. But I didn't make it happen, sir. He did.'' Jack allowed himself to look at Miller again.

Miller was sitting in a straight-back wooden chair, his arms crossed in front of him, and head cocked slightly to the left. A smile started to take shape at one corner of his mouth. It didn't go very far, and wasn't supposed to. It was a smile for Ryan alone . . . or maybe not me alone, Jack realized. Sean Miller's gray eyes didn't blink—he must have practiced that—as they bored in on him from thirty feet away. Ryan returned the stare, careful to keep his face without expression, and while the court reporter finished up his transcription of Jack's testimony, and the visitors in the overhead gallery shared whispered observations, Ryan and Miller were all alone, testing each other's wills. *What's behind those eyes?* Jack wondered again. No weakling, to be sure. This was a game—Miller's game that he'd practiced before, Ryan thought with certainty. There was strength in there, like something one might encounter in a predatory animal. But there was nothing to mute the strength. There was none of the softness of morality or conscience, only strength and will. With four police constables around him, Sean Miller was as surely restrained as a wolf in a cage, and he looked at Ryan as a wolf might from behind the bars, without recognition of his humanity. He was a predator, looking at a . . . thing—and wondering how he might reach it. The suit and the tie were camouflage, as had been his earlier smile at his friends in the gallery. He wasn't thinking about them now. He wasn't thinking about what the court would decide. He wasn't thinking about prison, Jack knew. He was thinking only about something named Ryan, something he could see just out of his reach. In the witness box, Jack's right hand flexed in his lap as though to grasp the pistol which lay in sight on the evidence table a few feet away.

This wasn't an animal in a cage, after all. Miller had intelligence and education. He could think and plan, as a human could, but he would not be restrained by any human impulses when he decided to move. Jack's academic investigation of terrorists for the CIA had dealt with them as abstractions, robots that moved about and did things, and had to be neutralized one way or another. He'd never expected to meet one. More important, Jack had never expected to have one look at him in this way. Didn't he know that Jack was just doing his civic duty?

You could care less about that. I'm something that got in your way. I hurt you, killed your friend, and defeated your mission. You want to get even, don't you? A wounded animal will always seek out its tormentor, Jack told himself. *And this wounded animal has a brain. This one has a memory.* Out of sight to anyone else, he wiped a sweaty hand on his pants. *This one is* thinking.

Ryan was frightened in a way that he'd never known before. It lasted several seconds before he reminded himself that Miller *was* surrounded by four cops, that the jury would find him guilty, that he would be sentenced to prison for the remainder of his natural life, and that prison life would change the person or thing that lived behind those pale gray eyes.

And I used to be a Marine, Jack told himself. *I'm not afraid of you. I can handle you, punk. I took you out once, didn't I?* He smiled back at Sean Miller, just a slight curve at the corner of his own mouth. *Not a wolf—a weasel. Nasty, but not that much to worry about,* he told himself. Jack turned away as though from an exhibit in the zoo. He wondered if Miller had seen through his quiet bravado.

"No further questions," Atkinson said.

"The witness may step down," Mr. Justice Wheeler said.

Jack stood up from the stool and turned to find the way out. As he did so, his eyes swept across Miller one last time, long enough to see that the look and the smile hadn't changed.

Jack walked back out to the grand hall as another witness passed in the other direction. He found Dan Murray waiting for him.

"Not bad," the FBI agent observed, "but you want to be careful locking horns with a lawyer. He almost tripped you up."

"You think it'll matter?"

Murray shook his head. "Nah. The trial's a formality, the case is airtight."

"What'll he get?"

"Life. Normally over here 'life' doesn't mean any more than it does stateside—six or eight years. For this kid, 'life' means *life*. Oh, there you are, Jimmy."

Commander Owens came down the corridor and joined them. "How did our lad perform?"

"Not an Oscar winner, but the jury liked him," Murray said.

"How can you tell that?"

"That's right, you've never been through this, have you? They sat perfectly still, hardly even breathed while you were telling your story. They believed everything you said, especially the part about how you've thought and worried about it. You come across as an honest guy.''

"I am," Ryan said. "So?"

"Not everybody is," Owens pointed out. "And juries are actually quite good at noticing it. That is, some of the time."

Murray nodded. "We both have some good—well, not so good— stories about what a jury can do, but when you get down to it, the system works pretty well. Commander Owens, why don't we buy this gentleman a beer?"

"A fine idea, Agent Murray." Owens took Ryan's arm and led him to the staircase.

"That kid's a scary little bastard, isn't he?" Ryan said. He wanted a professional opinion.

"You noticed, eh?" Murray observed. "Welcome to the wonderful world of the international terrorist. Yeah, he's a tough little son of a bitch, all right. Most of 'em are, at first."

"A year from now he'll have been changed a bit. He's a hard one, mind, but the hard ones are often rather brittle," Owens said. "They sometimes crack. Time is very much on our side, Jack. And even if he doesn't, that's one less to worry about."

"A very confident witness," the TV news commentator said. "Doctor Ryan fended off a determined attack by the defense counsel, Charles Atkinson, and identified defendant Sean Miller quite positively in the second day of The Mall Murder trial in Old Bailey Number Two." The picture showed Ryan walking down the hill from the courthouse with two men in attendance. The American was gesturing about something, then laughed as he passed the TV news camera.

"Our old friend Owens. Who's the other one?" O'Donnell asked.

"Daniel E. Murray, FBI representative at Grosvenor Square," replied his intelligence officer.

"Oh. Never saw his face. So that's what he looks like. Going out for a jar, I'll wager. The hero and his coat-holders. Pity we couldn't have had a man with an RPG right there. . . ." They'd scouted James Owens once, trying to figure a way to assassinate him, but the man always had a chase car and never used the same route twice. His house was always watched. They could have killed him, but the getaway would have been too risky, and O'Donnell was not given to sending his men on suicide missions. "Ryan goes home either tomorrow or next day."

"Oh?" The intelligence officer hadn't learned that. *Where does Kevin get all his special information . . . ?*

"Too bad, isn't it? Wouldn't it be grand to send him home in a coffin, Michael?"

"I thought you said he was not a worthwhile target," Mike McKenney said.

"Ah, but he's a proud one, isn't he? Crosses swords with our friend Charlie and prances out of the Bailey for a pint of beer. Bloody American, so sure of everything." *Wouldn't it be nice to . . .* Kevin O'Donnell shook his head. "We have other things to plan. Sir John can wait, and so can we."

"I practically had to hold a gun on somebody to get to do this," Murray said over his shoulder. The FBI agent was driving his personal car, with a Diplomatic Protection Group escort on the left front seat, and a chase car of C-13 detectives trying to keep up.

Keep your eyes on the damned road, Ryan wished as hard as he could. His exposure to London traffic to this point had been minimal, and only now did he appreciate that the city's speed limit was considered a matter of contempt by the drivers. Being on the wrong side of the road didn't help either.

"Tom Hughes—he's the Chief Warder—told me what he had planned, and I figured you might want an escort who talks right."

And drives right, Ryan thought as they passed a truck—lorry—on the wrong side. *Or was it the right side? How do you tell?* He could tell that they'd missed the truck's taillights by about eighteen inches. English roads were not impressive for their width.

"Damned shame you didn't get to see very much."

"Well, Cathy did, and I caught a lot of TV."

"What did you watch?"

Jack laughed. "I caught a lot of the replays of the cricket championships."

"Did you ever figure out the rules?" Murray asked, turning his head again.

"It has rules?" Ryan asked incredulously. "Why spoil it with rules?"

"They say it does, but damn if I ever figured them out. But we're getting even now."

"How's that?"

"Football is becoming pretty popular over here. Our kind, I mean. I gave Jimmy Owens a big runaround last year on the difference between offside and illegal procedure."

"You mean encroachment and false start, don't you?" the DPG man inquired.

"See? They're catching on."

"You mean I could have gotten football on TV, and nobody told me!"

"Too bad, Jack," Cathy observed.

"Well, here we are." Murray stood on the brakes as he turned downhill toward the river. Jack noticed that he seemed to be heading the wrong way down a one-way street, but at least he was going more slowly now. Finally the car stopped. It was dark. The sunset came early this time of year.

"Here's your surprise." Murray jumped out and got the door, allowing Ryan to repeat his imitation of a fiddler crab exiting from a car. "Hi, there, Tom!"

Two men approached, both in Tudor uniforms of blue and red. The one in the lead, a man in his late fifties, came directly to Ryan.

"Sir John, Lady Ryan, welcome to Her Majesty's Tower of London. I am Thomas Hughes, this is Joseph Evans. I see that Dan managed to get you here on time." Everyone shook hands.

"Yeah, we didn't even have to break mach-1. May I ask what the surprise is?"

"But then it wouldn't be a surprise," Hughes pointed out. "I had hoped to conduct you around the grounds myself, but there's something I must attend to. Joe will see to your needs, and I will rejoin you shortly." The Chief Warder walked off with Dan Murray in his wake.

"Have you been to the Tower before?" Evans asked. Jack shook his head.

"I have, when I was nine," Cathy said. "I don't remember very much."

Evans motioned for them to come along with him. "Well, we'll try to implant the knowledge more permanently this time."

"You guys are all soldiers, right?"

"Actually, Sir John, we are all ex-sergeant majors—well, two of us were warrant officers. I was sergeant major in 1 Para when I retired. I had to wait four years to get accepted here. There is quite a bit of interest in this job, as you might imagine. The competition is very keen."

"So, you were what we call a command sergeant-major, sir?"

"Yes, I think that's right."

Ryan gave a quick look to the decorations on Evans' coat—it looked more like a dress, but he had no plans to say that. Those ribbons didn't mean that Evans had come out of the dentist's office with no cavities. It didn't take much imagination to figure what sort of men got appointed to this job. Evans didn't walk; he marched with the sort of pride that took thirty years of soldiering to acquire.

"Is your arm troubling you, sir?"

"My name's Jack, and my arm's okay."

"I had a cast just like that one back in sixty-eight, I think it was. Training accident," Evans said with a rueful shake of his head. "Landed on a stone fence. Hurt like the very devil for weeks."

"But you kept jumping." *And did your push-ups one-handed, didn't you?*

"Of course." Evans stopped. "Right, now this imposing edifice is the Middle Tower. There used to be an outer structure right there where the souvenir shop is. They called it the Lion Tower, because that's where the royal menagerie was kept until 1834."

The speech was delivered as perfectly as Evans had done, several times per day, for the past four years. *My first castle,* Jack thought, looking at the stone walls.

"Was the moat for-real?"

"Oh, yes, and a very unpleasant one at that. The problem, you see, was that it was designed so that the river would wash in and out every day, thereby keeping it fresh and clean. Unfortunately the engineer didn't do his sums quite right, and once the water came in, it stayed in. Even worse, everything that got thrown away by the people living here was naturally enough thrown into the moat—and stayed there, and rotted. I suppose it served a tactical purpose, though. The smell of the moat alone must have been sufficient to keep all but the most adventurous chaps away. It was finally drained in 1843, and now it serves a really useful purpose—the children can play football there. On the far side are swings and jungle gyms. Do you have children?''

"One and a ninth," Cathy answered.

"Really?" Evans smiled in the darkness. "Bloody marvelous! I suppose that's one Yank who will be forever—at least a little—British! Moira and I have two, both of them born overseas. Now this is the Byward Tower.''

"These things all had drawbridges, right?" Jack asked.

"Yes, the Lion and Middle towers were essentially islands with twenty or so feet of smelly water around them. You'll also notice that the path into the grounds has a right-angle turn. The purpose of that, of course, was to make life difficult for the chaps with the battering ram.''

Jack looked at the width of the moat and the height of the walls as they passed into the Tower grounds proper. "So nobody ever took this place?''

Evans shook his head. "There has never been a serious attempt, and I wouldn't much fancy trying today.''

"Yeah," Ryan agreed. "You sweat having somebody come in and bomb the place?''

"That's happened, I am sorry to say, in the White Tower, over ten years ago—terrorists. Security is somewhat tighter now," Evans said.

In addition to the Yeoman Warders there were uniformed guards like those Ryan had encountered on The Mall, wearing the same red tunics and bearskin hats, and carrying the same kind of modern rifle. It was rather an odd contrast to Evans' period uniform, but no one seemed to notice.

"You know, of course, that this facility served many purposes over the years. It was the royal prison, and as late as World War Two, Rudolf Hess was kept here. Now, do you know who was the first Queen of England to be executed here?''

"Anne Boleyn," Cathy answered.

"Very good. They teach our history in America?" Evans asked.

"*Masterpiece Theater*," Cathy explained. "I saw the TV show.''

"Well, then you know that all the private executions were carried out with an ax—except hers. King Henry had a special executioner imported from France; he used a sword instead of an ax.''

''He didn't want it to hurt?'' Cathy asked with a twisted smile. ''Nice of him.''

''Yes, he was a considerate chap, wasn't he? And this is Traitor's Gate. You might be interested to know that it was originally called the Water Gate.''

Ryan laughed. ''Lucky for you guys too, eh?''

''Indeed. Prisoners were taken through this gate by boat to Westminster for trial.''

''Then back here for their haircuts?''

''Only the really important ones. Those executions—they were private instead of public—were done on the Tower Green. The public executions were carried out elsewhere.'' Evans led them through the gate in the Bloody Tower, after explaining its history. Ryan wondered if anyone had ever put all this place's history into one book, and if so, how many volumes it required.

The Tower Green was far too pleasant to be the site of executions. Even the signs to keep people off the grass said *Please*. Two sides were lined with Tudor-style (of course) houses, but the northern edge was the site where the scaffolding was erected for the high-society executions. Evans went through the procedure, which included having the executionee pay the headsman—in advance—in the hope that he'd do a proper job.

''The last woman to be executed here,'' Evans went on, ''was Jane, Viscountess Rochford, 13 February, 1542.''

''What did she do?'' Cathy asked.

''What she didn't do, actually. She neglected to tell King Henry the Eighth that his fifth wife, Catherine Howard, was, uh, amorously engaged with someone other than her husband,'' Evans said delicately.

''That was a real historic moment,'' Jack chuckled. ''That's the last time a woman was ever executed for keeping her mouth *shut*.''

Cathy smiled at her husband. ''Jack, how about I break your other arm?''

''And what would Sally say?''

''She'd understand,'' his wife assured him.

''Sergeant major, isn't it amazing how women stick together?''

''I did not survive thirty-one years as a professional soldier by being so foolish as to get involved in domestic disputes,'' Evans said sensibly.

I lose, Ryan told himself. The remainder of the tour lasted about twenty minutes. The Yeoman led them downhill past the White Tower, then left toward an area roped off from the public. A moment later Ryan and his wife found themselves in another of the reasons that men applied for the job.

The Yeoman Warders had their own little pub hidden away in the 14th-century stonework. Plaques from every regiment in the British Army—and probably gifts from many others—lined the walls. Evans handed them off to yet another man. Dan Murray reappeared, a glass in his hand.

"Jack, Cathy, this is Bob Hallston."

"You must be thirsty," the man said.

"You could talk me into a beer," Jack admitted. "Cathy?"

"Something soft."

"You're sure?" Hallston asked.

"I'm not a temperance worker, I just don't drink when I'm pregnant," Cathy explained.

"Congratulations!" Hallston took two steps to the bar and returned with a glass of lager for Jack, and what looked like ginger ale for his wife. "To your health, and your baby's."

Cathy beamed. There was something about pregnant women, Jack thought. His wife wasn't just pretty anymore. She glowed. He wondered if it was only for him.

"I understand you're a doctor?"

"I'm an ophthalmic surgeon."

"And you teach history, sir?"

"That's right. I take it you work here, too."

"Correct. There are thirty-nine of us. We are the ceremonial guardians of the Sovereign. We have invited you here to thank you for doing our job, and to join us in a small ceremony that we do every night."

"Since 1240," Murray said.

"The year 1240?" Cathy asked.

"Yeah, it's not something they cooked up for the tourists. This is the real thing," Murray said. "Right, Bob?"

"Quite real. When we lock up for the night, this museum collection becomes the safest place in England."

"I'll buy that," Jack tossed off half his beer. "And if they get past those kids out there, the bad guys have you fellows to worry about."

"Yes." Hallston smiled. "One or two of us might remember our basic skills. I was in the original SAS, playing hare and hounds with Rommel in the Western Desert. Dreadful place, the desert. Left me with a permanent thirst."

They never lose it, Ryan thought. They never lose the look, not the real professionals. They get older, add a few pounds, mellow out a little, but beneath all that you can still see the discipline and the essential toughness that makes them different. And the pride, the understated confidence that comes from having done it all, and not having to talk about it very much, except among themselves. It never goes away.

"Do you have any Marines in here?"

"Two," Hallston said. "We try to keep them from holding hands."

"Right! Be nice, I used to be a Marine."

"No one's perfect," Hallston sympathized.

"So, what's this Key Ceremony?"

"Well, back in the year 1240, the chap whose job it was to lock up for the night was set upon by some ruffians. Thereafter, he refused to do his duty without a military escort. Every night since, without interruption, the Chief Warder locks the three principal gates, then places the keys in the Queen's House on the Tower Green. There's a small ceremony that goes along with this. We thought that you and your wife might like to see it." Hallston sipped his beer. "You were in court today, I understand. How did it go?"

"I'm glad it's behind me. Dan says I did all right." Ryan shrugged. "When Mr. Evans showed us the block topside—I wonder if it still works," Ryan said thoughtfully, remembering the look on that young face. *Is Miller sitting in his cell right now, thinking about me?* Ryan drank the last of his beer. *I'll bet he is.*

"Excuse me?"

"That Miller kid. It's a shame you can't take him up there for a short haircut."

Hallston smiled coldly. "I doubt anyone here would disagree with you. We might even find a volunteer to swing the ax."

"You'd have to hold a lottery, Bob." Murray handed Ryan another glass. "You still worrying about him, Jack?"

"I've never seen anybody like that before."

"He's in jail, Jack," Cathy pointed out.

"Yeah, I know." *So why are you still thinking about him?* Jack asked himself. *The hell with it. The hell with him.* "This is great beer, Sar-major."

"That's the real reason they apply for the job," Murray chuckled.

"One of the reasons." Hallston finished his glass. "Almost time."

Jack finished off his second glass with a gulp. Evans reappeared, now wearing street clothes, and led them back out to the chilled night air. It was a clear night, with a three-quarters moon casting muted shadows on the stone battlements. A handful of electric lights added a few isolated splashes of light. Jack was surprised how peaceful it was for being in the center of a city, like his own home over the Chesapeake. Without thinking, he took his wife's hand as Evans led them west toward the Bloody Tower. A small crowd was already there, standing by Traitor's Gate, and a Warder was giving them instructions to be as quiet as possible, and not, of course, to take any photographs. A sentry was posted there, plus four other men under arms, their breath illuminated by the blue-white floodlights. It was the only sign of life. Otherwise they might have been made of stone.

"Right about now," Murray whispered.

Jack heard a door close somewhere ahead. It was too dark to see very much, and the few lights that were turned on only served to impair his night vision. He heard the sound of jingling keys first of all, like small bells rattling to the measured tread of a walking man. Next he saw a point of light. It grew into a square lantern with a candle inside, carried by Tom Hughes, the Chief Warder. The sound of his footsteps was as regular as a metronome as he approached, his back ramrod-straight from a lifetime of practice. A moment later the four soldiers formed up on him, the warder between them, and they marched off, back into the tunnel-like darkness to the fading music of the rattling keys and cleated shoes clicking on the pavement, leaving the sentry at the Bloody Tower.

Jack didn't hear the gates close, but a few minutes later the sound of the keys returned, and he glimpsed the returning guards in the irregular splashes of light. For some reason the scene was overpoweringly romantic. Ryan reached around his wife's waist and pulled her close. She looked up.

Love you, he said with his lips as the keys approached again. Her eyes answered.

To their right, the sentry snapped to on-guard: "Halt! Who goes there?" His words reverberated down the corridor of ancient stone.

The advancing men stopped at once, and Tom Hughes answered the challenge: "The keys!"

"Whose keys?" the sentry demanded.

"Queen's Anne's keys!"

"Pass, Queen Anne's keys!" The sentry brought his rifle to present-arms.

The sentries, with Hughes in their midst, resumed their march and turned left, up the slope to the Tower Green. Ryan and his wife followed close behind. At the steps that capped the upward slope waited a squad of riflemen. Hughes and his escort stopped. The squad on the steps came to present-arms, and the Chief Warder removed his uniform bonnet.

"God preserve Queen Anne!"

"Amen!" the guard force replied.

Behind them, a bugler stood. He blew Last Post, the British version of Taps. The notes echoed against the stones in a way that denoted the end of day, and when necessary, the end of life. Like the circular waves that follow a stone's fall into the water, the last mournful note lingered until it faded to nothingness in the still air. Ryan bent down to kiss his wife. It was a magical moment that they would not soon forget.

The Chief Warder proceeded up the steps to secure the keys for the night, and the crowd withdrew.

"Every night since 1240, eh?" Jack asked.

"The ceremony was interrupted during the Blitz. A German bomb fell into the Tower grounds while things were under way. The warder was bowled over by the blast, and the candle in his lantern was extinguished. He had to relight it before he could continue," Evans said. That the man had been wounded was irrelevant. Some things are more important than that. "Shall we return to the pub?"

"We don't have anything like this at home," Cathy said quietly.

"Well, America isn't old enough, is she?"

"It would be nice if we had something like this, maybe at Bunker Hill or Fort McHenry," Jack said quietly.

Murray nodded agreement. "Something to remind us why we're here."

"Tradition is important," Evans said. "For a soldier, tradition is often the reason one carries on when there are so many reasons not to. It's more than just yourself, more than just your mates—but it's not just something for soldiers, is it? It is true—or should be true—of any professional community."

"It is," Cathy said. "Any good medical school beats that into your head. Hopkins sure did."

"So does the Corps," Jack agreed. "But we don't express it as well as you just did."

"We've had more practice." Evans opened the door to the pub. "And better beer to aid in our contemplation."

"Now, if you guys could only learn how to fix beef properly. . . ." Jack said to Murray.

"That's telling 'em, ace," the FBI agent chuckled.

"Another beer for a brother Marine." A glass was handed to Ryan by another of the warders. "Surely you've had enough of this para prima donna by now."

"Bert's one of the Marines I told you about," Evans explained.

"I never say bad things about somebody who buys the drinks," Ryan told Bert.

"That is an awfully sensible attitude. Are you sure you were only a lieutenant?"

"Only for three months." Jack explained about the helicopter crash.

"That *was* bad luck. Bloody training accidents," Evans said. "More dangerous than combat."

"So you guys work as tour guides here?"

"That's part of it," the other warder said. "It's a good way to keep one's hand in, and also to educate the odd lieutenant. Just last week I spoke to one of the Welsh Guards chaps—he was having trouble getting things right, and I gave him a suggestion."

"The one thing you really miss," Evans agreed. "Teaching those young officers to be proper soldiers. Who says the best diplomats work at Whitehall?"

"I never got the feeling that I was completely useless as a second lieutenant," Jack observed with a smile.

"All depends on one's point of view," the other yeoman said.

"Still and all, you might have worked out all right, judging by what you did on The Mall."

"I don't know, Bert. A lieutenant with a hero complex is not the sort of chap you want to be around. They keep doing the damnedest things. But I suppose the ones who survive, and learn, do work out as you say. Tell me, Lieutenant Ryan, what have you learned?"

"Not to get shot. The next time I'll just shoot from cover."

"Excellent." Bob Hallston rejoined them. "And don't leave one alive behind you," he added. The SAS wasn't noted for leaving people alive by accident.

Cathy didn't like this sort of talk. "Gentlemen, you can't just kill people like that."

"The Lieutenant took rather a large chance, ma'am, not the sort of chance that one will walk away from very often. If there is ever a next time—and there won't be, of course. But if there is, you can act like a policeman or a soldier, but not both. You're very lucky to be alive, young man. You have that arm to remind you just how lucky you are. It is good to be brave, Lieutenant. It is better to be smart, and much less painful for those around you," Evans said. He looked down at his beer. "Dear God, how *many* times have I said that!"

"How many times have we all said it?" Bert said quietly. "And the pity is, so many of them didn't listen. Enough of that. This lovely lady doesn't want to hear the ramblings of tired old men. Bob tells me that you are expecting another child. In two months, I shall be a grandfather for the first time."

"Yes, he can hardly wait to show us the pictures." Evans laughed. "A boy or a girl this time?"

"Just so all the pieces are attached, and they all work." There was general agreement on the point. Ryan finished off his third beer of the evening. It was pretty strong stuff, and he was getting a buzz from it. "Gentlemen, if any of you come to America, and happen to visit the Washington area, I trust you will let us know."

"And the next time you are in London, the bar is open," Tom Hughes said. The Chief Warder was back in civilian clothes, but carrying his uniform bonnet, a hat whose design went back three or four centuries. "And perhaps you'll find room in your home for this. Sir John, with the thanks of us all."

"I'll take good care of this." Ryan took the hat, but couldn't bring himself to put it on. He hadn't earned that right.

"Now, I regret to say that if you don't leave now, you'll be stuck here all night. At midnight all the doors are shut, and that is that."

Jack and Cathy shook hands all around, then followed Hughes and Murray out the door.

The walk between the inner and outer walls was still quiet, the air still cold, and Jack found himself wondering if ghosts walked the Tower Grounds at night. It was almost—

"What's that?" He pointed to the outer wall. A spectral shape *was* walking up there.

"A sentry," Hughes said. "After the Ceremony of the Keys, the guards don their pattern-disruptive clothing." They passed the sentry at the Bloody Tower, now dressed in camouflage fatigues, with web gear and ammo pouches.

"Those rifles are loaded now, aren't they?" Jack asked.

"Not very much use otherwise, are they? This is a very safe place," Hughes replied.

Nice to know that some places are, Ryan thought. *Now why did I think that?*

7

Speedbird Home

The Speedway Lounge at Heathrow Airport's Terminal 4 was relaxing enough, or would have been had Jack not been nervous about flying. Beyond the floor-to-ceiling windows he could see the Concorde he'd be taking home in a few minutes. The designers had given their creation the aspect of a living creature, like some huge, merciless bird of prey, a thing of fearful beauty. It sat there at the end of the jetway atop its unusually high landing gear, staring at Ryan impassively over its daggerlike nose.

"I wish the Bureau would let me commute back and forth on that baby," Murray observed.

"It's pretty!" Sally Ryan agreed.

It's just another goddamned airplane, Jack told himself. *You can't see what holds it up.* Jack didn't remember whether it was Bernoulli's Principle or the Venturi Effect, but he knew that it was something *inferred,* not actually seen, that enabled aircraft to fly. He remembered that something had interrupted the Principle or Effect over Crete and nearly killed him, and that nineteen months later that same something had reached up and killed his parents five thousand feet short of the runway at Chicago's O'Hare International Airport. Intellectually he knew that his Marine helicopter had died of a mechanical failure, and that commercial airliners were simpler and easier to maintain than CH-46s. He also knew that bad weather had been the main contributing factor in his parents' case—and the weather here was clear—but to Ryan there was something outrageous about flying, something unnatural.

Fine, Jack. Why not go back to living in caves and hunting bear with a pointed stick? What's natural about teaching history, or watching TV, or driving a car? Idiot.

But I hate to fly, Ryan reminded himself.

"There has never been an accident in the Concorde," Murray pointed out. "And Jimmy Owens's troops gave the bird a complete checkout." The possibility of a bomb on that pretty white bird was a real one. The explosives experts from C-13 had spent over an hour that morning making sure that nobody had done that, and now police dressed as British Airways ground crewmen stood around the airliner. Jack wasn't worried about a bomb. Dogs could find bombs.

"I know," Jack replied with a wan smile. "Just a basic lack of guts on my part."

"It's only lack of guts if you don't go, ace," Murray pointed out. He was surprised that Ryan was so nervous, though he concealed it well, the FBI agent thought. Murray enjoyed flying. An Air Force recruiter had almost convinced him to become a pilot, back in his college days.

No, it's lack of brains if I do, Jack told himself. *You really are a wimp,* another part of his brain informed him. *Some Marine you turned out to be!*

"When do we blast off, Daddy?" Sally asked.

"One o'clock," Cathy told her daughter. "Don't bother Daddy."

Blast off, Jack thought with a smile. *Dammit, there is* nothing *to be afraid of and you know it!* Ryan shook his head and sipped at his drink from the complimentary bar. He counted four security people in the lounge, all trying to look inconspicuous. Owens was taking no chances on Ryan's last day in England. The rest was up to British Airways. He wasn't even being billed for the extra cost. Ryan wondered if that was good luck or bad.

A disembodied female voice announced the flight. Jack finished off the drink and rose to his feet.

"Thanks for everything, Dan."

"Can we go now, Daddy?" Sally asked brightly. Cathy took her daughter's hand.

"Wait a minute!" Murray stooped down to Sally. "Don't I get a hug and a kiss?"

"Okay." Sally obliged with enthusiasm. "G'bye, Mr. M'ray."

"Take good care of our hero," the FBI man told Cathy.

"He'll be all right," she assured him.

"Enjoy the football, ace!" Murray nearly crushed Jack's hand. "That's the one thing I really miss."

"I can send you tapes."

"It's not the same. Back to teaching history, eh?"

"That's what I do," Ryan said.

"We'll see," Murray observed cryptically. "How the hell do you walk with that thing on?"

"Badly," Ryan chuckled. "I think the doc installed some lead weights, or maybe he left some tools in there by mistake. Well, here we are." They reached the entrance to the jetway.

"Break a leg." Murray smiled and moved off.

"Welcome aboard, Sir John," a flight attendant said. "We have you in 1-D. Have you flown Concorde before?"

"No." It was all Jack could muster. Ahead of him, Cathy turned and grinned. The tunnel-like jetway looked like the entrance to the grave.

"Well, you are in for the thrill of your life!" the stewardess assured him.

Thanks a lot! Ryan nearly choked at the outrage, and remembered that he couldn't strangle her with one hand. Then he laughed. There wasn't anything else to do.

He had to duck to avoid crunching his head at the door. It was tiny inside; the cabin was only eight or nine feet across. He looked forward quickly and saw the flight crew in impossibly tight quarters—getting into the pilot's left seat must have been like putting on a boot, it seemed so cramped. Another attendant was hanging up coats. He had to wait until she saw him, and walked sideways, his plaster-encased arm leading the way into the passenger cabin.

"Right here," his personal guide said.

Jack got into the right-side window seat in the front row. Cathy and Sally were already in their seats on the other side. Jack's cast stuck well over seat 1-C. No one could have sat there. It was just as well that British Airways wasn't charging the difference between this and their L-1011 tickets; there would have been an extra seat charge. He immediately tried to snap on his seat belt and found that it wasn't easy with only one hand. The stewardess was ready for this, and handled it for him.

"You are quite comfortable?"

"Yes," Jack lied. *I am quite terrified.*

"Excellent. Here is your Concorde information kit." She pointed toward a gray vinyl folder. "Would you like a magazine?"

"No, thank you, I have a book in my pocket."

"Fine. I'll be back after we take off, but if you need anything, please ring."

Jack pulled the seat belt tighter as he looked forward and left at the airplane's door. It was still open. He could still escape. But he knew he wouldn't do that. He leaned back. The seat was gray, too, a little on the narrow side but comfortable. His placement in the front row gave him all the legroom he needed. The airplane's inside wall—or whatever they called it—was off-white, and he had a window to look out of. Not a very large one, about the size of two paperback books, but better than no window at all. He looked around. The flight was about three-quarters full. These were seasoned travelers, and wealthy ones. Business types mostly, Jack figured, many were reading their copies of the *Financial Times.* And none of them were afraid of flying. You could tell from their impassive faces. It never occurred to Jack that his face was set exactly the same.

"Ladies and gentlemen, this is Captain Nigel Higgins welcoming you aboard British Airways Flight 189, Concorde Service to Washington, D.C., and Miami, Florida. We'll begin taxiing in approximately five minutes. Weather at our first stop, Washington's Dulles International Airport, is excellent, clear, with a temperature of fifty-six degrees. We will be in the air a total of three hours and twenty-five minutes. Please observe that the no-smoking sign is lighted, and we ask that while you are seated you keep your seat belts fastened. Thank you," the clipped voice concluded.

The door had been closed during the speech, Ryan noted sourly. A clever distraction, as their only escape route was eliminated. He leaned back and closed his eyes, resigning himself to fate. One nice thing about being up front was that no one could see him except Cathy—

Sally had the window seat—and his wife understood, or at least pretended to. Soon the cabin crew was demonstrating how to put on and inflate life jackets stowed under the seats. Jack watched without interest. Concorde's perfect safety record meant that no one had the first idea on how to ditch one safely, and his position near the nose, so far from the delta-shaped wing, ensured that if they hit the water he'd be in the part of the fuselage that broke off and sank like a cement block. Not that this would matter. The impact itself would surely be fatal.

Asshole, if this bird was dangerous, they would have lost one by now.

The whine of the jet turbines came next, triggering the acid glands in Jack's stomach. He closed his eyes again. *You can't run away.* He commanded himself to control his breathing and relax. That was strangely easy. Jack had never been a white-knuckled flier. He was more likely to be limp.

Some unseen tractor-cart started pushing the aircraft backward. Ryan looked out of the window and watched the scenery move slowly forward. Heathrow was quite a complex. Aircraft from a dozen airlines were visible, mainly sitting at the terminal buildings like ships at a dock. *Wish we could take a ship home,* he thought, forgetting that he'd been one seasick Marine on *Guam,* years ago. The Concorde stopped for a few seconds, then began moving under its own power. Ryan didn't know why the landing gear was so high, but this factor imparted an odd sort of movement as they taxied. The captain came on the intercom again and said something about taking off on afterburners, but Ryan didn't catch it, instead watching a Pan Am 747 lift off. The Concorde was certainly prettier, Ryan thought. It reminded him of the models of fighter planes he'd assembled as a kid. *We're going first class.*

The plane made a sweeping turn at the end of the runway and stopped, bobbing a little on the nose gear. *Here we go.*

"Departure positions," the intercom announced. Somewhere aft the cabin crew strapped into their jump seats. In 1-D, Jack fitted himself into his seat much like a man awaiting electrocution. His eyes were open now, watching out the window.

The engine sounds increased markedly, and Speedbird started to roll. A few seconds later the engine noise appeared to pick up even more, and Ryan was pressed back into the fabric and vinyl chair. *Damn,* he told himself. The acceleration was impressive, about double anything he'd experienced before. He had no way of measuring it, but an invisible hand was pressing him backward while another pushed at his cast and tried to turn him sideways. The stew had been right. It was a thrill. The grass was racing by his window, then the nose came up sharply. A final bump announced that the main gear was off the ground. Jack listened for its retraction into the airframe, but the sheer power of the takeoff blocked it out. Already they were at least a thousand feet off the ground and rocketing upward at what seemed an impossible angle. He looked over to his wife. Wow, Cathy mouthed at him. Sally had her nose against the plastic inside window.

The angle of climb eased off slightly. Already the cabin attendants were at work, with a drink cart. Jack got himself a glass of champagne. He wasn't in a celebrating mood, but bubbly wines always affected him fast. Once Cathy had offered to prescribe some Valium for his flying jitters. Ryan had an ingrained reluctance to take drugs. But booze was different, he told himself. He looked out the window. They were still going up. The ride was fairly smooth, no bumps worse than going over the tar strip on a concrete highway.

Jack felt every one, mindful of the fact that he was several thousand feet over—he checked—still the ground.

He fished the paperback out of his pocket and started reading. This was his one sure escape from flying. Jack slouched to his right, his head firmly wedged into the place where the seat and white plastic wall met. He was able to rest his left arm on the aisle seat, and that took the weight off the place on his waist where the cast dug in hard. His right elbow was planted on the armrest, and Ryan made himself a rigid part of the airframe as he concentrated on his book. He'd selected well for the flight, one of Alistair Horne's books on the Franco-German conflicts. He soon found another reason to hate his cast. It was difficult to read and turn pages one-handed. He had to set the book down first to do it.

A brief surge of power announced that first one, then the other pair of afterburners had been activated on the Concorde's Olympus engines. He felt the new acceleration, and the aircraft began to climb again as she passed through mach-1, and the airliner gave meaning to her call sign prefix: "Speedbird." Jack looked out the window—they were over water now. He checked his watch: less than three hours to touchdown at Dulles. *You can put up with anything for three hours, can't you?*

Like you have a choice. A light caught his eye. *How did I miss that before?* On the bulkhead a few feet from his head was a digital speed readout. It now read 1024, the last number changing upward rapidly.

Damn! I'm going a thousand miles per hour. What would Robby say about this? I wonder how Robby's doing. . . . He found himself mesmerized by the number. Soon it was over 1300. The rate of change dropped off nearly to zero, and the display stopped at 1351. *One thousand three hundred fifty-one miles per hour.* He did the computation in his head: nearly two thousand feet per second, almost as fast as a bullet, about twenty miles per minute. *Damn.* He looked out the window again. *But why is it still noisy? If we're going supersonic, how come the sound isn't all behind us? I'll ask Robby. He'll know.*

The puffy, white, fair-weather clouds were miles below and sliding by at a perceptible rate nevertheless. The sun glinted off the waves, and they stood out like shiny blue furrows. One of the things that annoyed Jack about himself was the dichotomy between his terror of flying and his fascination with what the world looked like from up here. He pulled himself back to the book and read of a period when a steam locomotive was the leading edge of human technology, traveling at a thirtieth of what he was doing now. *This may be terrifying, but at least it gets you from place to place.*

Dinner arrived a few minutes later. Ryan found that the champagne had given him an appetite. Jack was rarely hungry on an airplane, but much to his surprise he was now. The menu carried on the annoying, and baffling, English habit of advertising their food in French, as if language had any effect on taste. Jack soon found that the taste needed no amplification. Salmon gave way to a surprisingly good steak— something the Brits have trouble with—a decent salad, strawberries and cream for dessert, and a small plate of cheese. A good port replaced the champagne, and Ryan found that forty minutes had slipped by. Less than two hours to home.

"Ladies and gentlemen, this is the captain speaking. We are now cruising at fifty-three thousand feet, with a ground speed of thirteen hundred fifty-five miles per hour. As we burn off fuel, the aircraft will float up to a peak altitude of roughly fifty-nine thousand feet. The outside air temperature is sixty degrees below zero Celsius, and the aircraft skin temperature is about one hundred degrees Celsius, this caused by friction as we pass through the air. One side effect of this is that the aircraft expands, becoming roughly eleven inches longer in midflight—"

Metal fatigue! Ryan thought bleakly. *Did you have to tell me that?* He touched the window. It felt warm, and he realized that one could boil water on the outside aluminum skin. He wondered what effect that had on the airframe. *Back to the 19th century,* he commanded himself again. Across the aisle his daughter was asleep, and Cathy was immersed in a magazine.

The next time Jack checked his watch there was less than an hour to go. The captain said something about Halifax, Nova Scotia, to his right. Jack looked but saw only a vague dark line on the northern horizon. *North America—we're getting there.* That was good news. As always, his tension and the airliner seat conspired to make his back stiff, and the cast didn't help at all. He felt a need to stand up and walk a few steps, but that was something he tried not to do on airplanes. The steward refilled his port glass, and Jack noticed that the angle of the sun through the window had not changed since London. They were staying even, the aircraft keeping up with the earth's rotation as it sped west. They would arrive at Dulles at about noon, the pilot informed them. Jack looked at his watch again: forty minutes. He stretched his legs and went back to the book.

The next disturbance was when the cabin crew handed out customs and immigration forms. As he tucked his book away, Jack watched his wife go to work listing all the clothes she'd bought. Sally was still asleep, curled up with an almost angelic peace on her face. They made landfall a minute later somewhere over the coast of New Jersey, heading west into Pennsylvania before turning south again. The aircraft was lower now. He'd missed the transonic deceleration, but the cumulus clouds were much closer than they'd been over the ocean. *Okay, Captain Higgins, let's get this bird back on the ground in one solid piece.* He found a silver luggage tag that he was evidently supposed to keep. In fact, he decided to keep the whole package, complete with a certificate that identified him as a Concorde passenger—*or veteran,* he thought wryly. *I survived the British Airways Concorde.*

Dumbass, if you'd flown the 747 back home, you'd still be over the ocean.

They were low enough to see roads now. The majority of aircraft accidents came at landing, but Ryan didn't see it that way. They were nearly home. His fear was nearly at an end. That was good news as he looked out the window at the Potomac. Finally the Concorde took a large nose-high angle again, coming in awfully fast, Jack thought, as she dropped gently toward the ground. A second later he saw the airport perimeter fence. The heavy bumps on the airliner's main gear followed at once. They were down. They were safe. Anything that happened now was a vehicle accident, not an aircraft one, he told himself. Ryan felt safe in cars, mainly because he was in control. He remembered that Cathy would have to drive today, however.

The seat belt sign came off a moment after the aircraft stopped, and the forward door was opened. Home. Ryan stood and stretched. It was good to be stationary. Cathy had their daughter in her lap, running a brush through her hair as Sally rubbed the sleep from her eyes.

"Okay, Jack?"

"Are we home *already*?" Sally asked.

Her father assured her that they were. He walked forward. The stewardess who'd led him aboard asked if he'd enjoyed the ride, and Jack replied, truthfully, that he had. *Now that it's over.* He found a seat in the mobile lounge, and his family joined him.

"Next time we go across, that's how we do it," Ryan announced quietly.

"Why? Did you like it?" Cathy was surprised.

"You better believe I like it. You only have to be up there half as long." Jack laughed, mainly at himself. As with every flight he took, being back on the ground alive carried its own thrill. He had survived what was patently an unnatural act, and the exhilaration of being alive, and home, gave him a quiet glow of his own. The stride of passengers off an airplane is always jauntier than the stride on. The lounge pulled away. The Concorde looked very pretty indeed as they drew away from it and turned toward the terminal.

"How much money did you spend on clothes?" Jack asked as the lounge stopped at the arrival gate. His wife just handed him the form. "That much?"

"Well, why not?" Cathy grinned. "I can pay for it out of *my* money, can't I?"

"Sure, babe."

"And that's three suits for you, too, Jack," his wife informed him.

"What? How did you—"

"When the tailor set you up for the tux, I had him do three suits.

Your arms are the same length, Jack. They'll fit, as soon as we get that damned cast off you, that is.''

Another nice thing about the Concorde: the airliner carried so few people, compared to a wide-body, that getting the luggage back was a snap. Cathy got a wheeled cart—which Sally insisted on pushing—while Jack retrieved their bags. The last obstacle was customs, where they paid over three hundred dollars' worth of penance for Cathy's purchases. Less than thirty minutes after leaving the aircraft, Jack proceeded to his left out the door, helping Sally with the luggage cart.

"Jack!" It was a big man, taller than Jack's six-one, and broader across the shoulders. He walked badly due to a prosthetic leg that extended above where he had once had a left knee, a gift from a drunken driver. His artificial left foot was a squared-off aluminum band instead of something that looked human. Oliver Wendell Tyler found it easier to walk on. But his hand was completely normal, if rather large. He grabbed Ryan's and squeezed. "Welcome home, buddy!"

"How's it goin', Skip?" Jack disengaged his hand from the grip of a former offensive tackle and mentally counted his fingers. Skip Tyler was a close friend who never fully appreciated his strength.

"Good. Hi, Cathy." His wife got a kiss. "And how's Sally?"

"Fine." She held up her arms, and got herself picked up as desired. Only briefly, though; Sally wriggled free to get back to the luggage cart.

"What are you doing here?" Jack asked. *Oh, Cathy must have called. . . .*

"Don't worry about the car," Dr. Tyler said. "Jean and I retrieved it for you, and dropped it off home. We decided we'd pick you up in ours—more room. She's getting it now."

"Taking a day off, eh?"

"Something like that. Hell, Jack, Billings has been covering your classes for a couple of weeks. Why can't I take an afternoon off?" A skycap approached them, but Tyler waved him off.

"How's Jean?" Cathy asked.

"Six more weeks."

"It'll be a little longer for us," Cathy announced.

"Really?" Tyler's face lit up. "Outstanding!"

It was cool, with a bright autumn sun, as they left the terminal. Jean Tyler was already pulling up with the Tyler family's full-size Chevy wagon. Dark-haired, tall, and willowy, Jean was pregnant with their third and fourth children. The sonogram had confirmed the twins right before the Ryans had left for England. Her otherwise slender frame would have seemed grotesque with the bulge of the babies except for the glow on her face. Cathy went right to her as she got out of the car and said something. Jack knew what it was immediately—their wives immediately hugged: Me, too. Skip wrenched the tailgate open and tossed the luggage inside like so many sheets of paper.

"I gotta admire your timing, Jack. You made it back almost in time for Christmas break," Skip observed as everyone got in the car.

"I didn't exactly plan it that way," Jack objected.

"How's the shoulder?"

"Better'n it was, guy."

"I believe it," Tyler laughed as he pulled away from the terminal. "I was surprised they got you on the Concorde. How'd you like it?"

"It's over a lot faster."

"Yeah, that's what they say."

"How are things going at school?"

"Ah, nothing ever changes. You heard about The Game?" Tyler's head came around.

"No, as a matter of fact." *How did I ever forget about that?*

"Absolutely great. Five points down with three minutes left, we recover a fumble on our twelve. Thompson finally gets it untracked and starts hitting sideline patterns—boom, boom, boom, eight-ten yards a pop. Then he pulls a draw play that gets us to the thirty. Army changes its defense, right? So we go to a spread. I'm up in the press box, and I see their strong-side safety is favoring the outside—figures we gotta stop the clock—and we call a post for the tight end. Like a charm! Thompson couldn't have *handed* him the ball any better! Twenty-one to nineteen. What a way to end the season."

Tyler was an Annapolis graduate who'd made second-string All-American at offensive tackle before entering the submarine service. Three years before, when he'd been on the threshold of his own command a drunk driver had left him without half his leg. Amazingly, Skip hadn't looked back. After taking his doctorate in engineering from MIT, he'd joined the faculty at Annapolis, where he was also able to scout and do a little coaching in the football program. Jack wondered how much happier Jean was now. A lovely girl who had once worked as a legal secretary, she must have resented Skip's enforced absences on submarine duty. Now she had him home—surely he wasn't straying far; it seemed that Jean was always pregnant—and they were rarely separated. Even when they walked in the shopping malls, Skip and Jean held hands. If anyone found it humorous, he kept his peace about it.

"What are you doing about a Christmas tree, Jack?"

"I haven't thought about it," Ryan admitted.

"I found a place where we can cut 'em fresh. I'm going over tomorrow. Wanna come?"

"Sure. We have some shopping to do, too," he added quietly.

"Boy, you've really been out of it. Cathy called last week. Jean and I finished up the, uh, the important part. Didn't she tell you?"

"No." Ryan turned to see his wife smile at him. *Gotcha!* "Thanks, Skip."

"Ah." Tyler waved his hand as they pulled onto the D.C. beltway. "We're going up to Jean's family's place—last chance for her to travel before the twins arrive. And Professor Billings says you have a little work waiting for you."

A little, Ryan thought. *More like two months' worth.*

"When are you going to be able to start back to work?"

"It'll have to wait until he gets the cast off," Cathy answered for Jack. "I'll be taking Jack to Baltimore tomorrow to see about that. We'll get Professor Hawley to check him out."

"No sense hurrying with that kind of injury," Skip acknowledged. He had ample personal experience with that sort of thing. "Robby says hi. He couldn't make it. He's down at Pax River today on a flight simulator, learning to be an airedale again. Rob and Sissy are doing fine, they were just over the house night before last. You picked a good weather day, too. Rained most of last week."

Home, Jack told himself as he listened. Back to the mundane, day-to-day crap that grates on you so much—until somebody takes it away from you. It was so nice to be back to a situation where rain was a major annoyance, and one's day was marked by waking up, working, eating, and going back to bed. Catching things on television, and football games. The comics in the daily paper. Helping his wife with the wash. Curling up with a book and a glass of wine after Sally was put to bed. Jack promised himself that he'd never find this a dull existence again. He'd just spent over a month on the fast track, and was grateful that he'd left it three thousand miles behind him.

*　　*　　*

"Good evening, Mr. Cooley." Kevin O'Donnell looked up from his menu.

"Hello, Mr. Jameson. How nice to see you," the book dealer replied with well-acted surprise.

"Won't you join me?"

"Why, yes. Thank you."

"What brings you into town?"

"Business. I'm staying overnight with friends at Cobh." This was true; it also told O'Donnell—known locally as Michael Jameson—that he had the latest message with him.

"Care to look at the menu?" O'Donnell handed it over. Cooley inspected it briefly, closed it, and handed it back. No one could have seen the transfer. "Jameson" let the small envelope inside the folder drop to his lap. The conversation which ensued over the next hour drifted through various pleasantries. There were four Gardai in the next booth, and in any case Mr. Cooley did not concern himself with operational matters. His job was that of contact agent and cutout. A weak man, O'Donnell thought, though he'd never told this to anyone. Cooley didn't have the right qualities for real operations; he was better suited to the role of intelligence. Not that he'd ever asked, and surely the smaller man had passed through training well enough. His ideology was sound, but O'Donnell had always sensed within him a weakness of character that accompanied his cleverness. No matter. Cooley was a man with no record in any police station. He'd never even thrown a rock, much less a cocktail, at a Saracen. He'd preferred to watch and let his hate fester without an emotional release. Quiet, bookish, and unobtrusive, Dennis was perfect for his job. If Cooley was unable to shed blood, O'Donnell knew, he was also unlikely to shed tears. *You bland little fellow, you can organize a superb intelligence-gathering operation, and so long as you don't have to do any of the wet-work yourself, you can—you have helped cause the death of . . . ten or twelve, wasn't it?* Did the man have any emotions at all? Probably not, the leader judged. Perfect. He had his own little Himmler, O'Donnell told himself—or maybe Dzerzhinsky would be a more apt role model. Yes, "Iron Feliks" Dzerzhinsky: that malignant, effective little man. It was only the round, puffy face that reminded him of the Nazi Himmler—and a man couldn't choose his looks, could he? Cooley had a future in the Organization. When the time came, they'd need a real Dzerzhinsky.

They finished their talking over after-dinner coffee. Cooley picked up the check. He insisted: business was excellent. O'Donnell pocketed the envelope and left the restaurant. He resisted the urge to read the report. Kevin was a man to whom patience came hard, and as a consequence he forced himself to it. Impatience had ruined more operations that the British Army ever had, he knew. Another lesson from his early days with the Provos. He drove his BMW through the old streets at the legal limit, leaving the town behind as he entered the narrow country roads to his home on the headlands. He did not take a direct route, and kept an eye on his mirror. O'Donnell knew that his security was excellent. He also knew that continued vigilance was the reason it remained so. His expensive car was registered to his corporation's head office in Dundalk. It was a real business, with nine bluewater trawlers that dragged purse-seine nets through the cold northern waters that surrounded the British Isles. The business had an excellent general manager, a man who had never been involved in the Troubles and whose skills allowed O'Donnell to live the life of a country gentleman far to the south. The tradition of absentee ownership was an old one in Ireland—like O'Donnell's home, a legacy from the English.

It took just under an hour to reach the private driveway marked by a pair of stone pillars, and another five minutes to reach the house over the sea. Like any common man, O'Donnell parked his car in the open; the carriage house that was attached to the manor had been converted to offices by a local contractor. He went at once to his study. McKenney was waiting for him there, reading a recent edition of Yeats' poetry. Another bookish lad, though he did not share Cooley's aversion to the sight of blood. His quiet, disciplined demeanor concealed an explosive capacity for action. A man very like O'Donnell himself, Michael was. Like the O'Donnell of ten or twelve years before, his youth needed tempering; hence his assignment as chief of intelligence so that he could learn the value of deliberation, of gathering all the information he could get before he committed himself to action. The Provos never really did that. They used tactical intelligence, but not the strategic kind—a fine explanation, O'Donnell thought, for the mindlessness of their overall strategy. Another of the reasons he had left the Provisionals—but he would return to the fold. Or more properly, the fold would return to him. Then he would have his army. Kevin already had his plan, though not even his closest associates knew it—at least not all of it.

O'Donnell sat in the leather chair behind the desk and took the envelope from his coat pocket. McKenney discreetly went to the corner bar and got his superior a glass of whiskey. With ice, a taste Kevin had acquired in hotter climes several years before. He set the glass on the desk, and O'Donnell took it, sipping off a tiny bit without a word.

There were six pages to the document, and O'Donnell read through the single-spaced pages as slowly and deliberately as McKenney had just been doing with the words of Yeats. The younger man marveled at the man's patience. For all his reputation as a fighter capable of ruthless action, the chief of the ULA often seemed a creature made of stone, the way he would assemble and process data. Like a computer, but a malignant one. He took fully twenty minutes to go through the six pages.

"Well, our friend Ryan is back in America, where he belongs. Flew the Concorde home, and his wife arranged for a friend to meet them at the airport. Next Monday I expect he'll be back teaching those fine young men and women at their Naval Academy." O'Donnell smiled at the humor of his words. "His Highness and his lovely bride will be back home two days late. It seems that their aircraft developed electrical problems, and a new instrument had to be flown in all the way from England—or so the public story will go. In reality, it would seem that they like New Zealand so much that they wanted some additional time to enjoy their privacy. Security on their arrival will be impressive.

"In fact, looking this over, it would seem that their security for the next few months at least will be impenetrable."

McKenney snorted. "No security's impenetrable. We've proven that ourselves."

"Michael, we do not wish to kill them. Any fool can do that," he said patiently. "Our objective demands that we take them alive."

"But—"

Would they never learn? "No buts, Michael. If I wanted to kill them, they would already be dead, and this Ryan bastard along with them. It is easy to kill, but that will not achieve what we wish."

"Yes, sir." McKenney nodded his submission. "And Sean?"

"They will be processing him in Brixton Prison for another two weeks or so—our friends in C-13 don't want him far from their reach for the moment.''

"Does that mean that Sean—"

"Most unlikely," O'Donnell cut him off. "Still and all, I think the Organization is stronger with him than without him, don't you?''

"But how will we know?''

"There is a great deal of high-level interest in our comrade," O'Donnell half-explained.

McKenney nodded thoughtfully. He concealed his annoyance that the Commander would not share his intelligence source with his own intelligence chief. McKenney knew how valuable the information was, but where it came from was the deepest of all the ULA's secrets. The younger man shrugged it off. He had his own information sources, and his skill at using their information was growing on a daily basis. Having always to wait so long to act on it chafed on him, but he admitted to himself—grudgingly at first, but with increasing conviction—that full preparation had allowed several tricky operations to go perfectly. Another operation that had not gone so well had landed him in the H-Blocks of Long Kesh prison. The lesson he'd learned from this miscued op was that the revolution needed more competent hands. He'd come to hate the PIRA leadership's ineffectiveness even more than he did the British Army. The revolutionary often had more to fear from friends than enemies.

"Anything new with our colleagues?'' O'Donnell asked.

"Yes, as a matter of fact," McKenney answered brightly. *Our colleagues* were the Provisional Wing of the Irish Republican Army. "One of the cells of the Belfast Brigade is going to go after a pub, day after tomorrow. Some UVF chaps have been using it of late—not very smart of them, is it?''

"I think we can let that one pass," O'Donnell judged. It would be a bomb, of course, and it would kill a number of people, some of whom might be members of the Ulster Volunteer Force, whom he regarded as the reactionary forces of the ruling bourgeoisie—no more than thugs, since they lacked any ideology at all. So much the better that some UVF would be killed, but really any prod would suffice, since then other UVF gunmen would slink into a Catholic neighborhood and kill one or two people on the street. And the detectives of the RUC's Criminal Investigation Division would investigate, as always, and no one would admit to have seen much of anything, as usual, and the Catholic neighborhoods would retain their state of revolutionary instability. Hate was such a useful asset. Even more than fear, hate was what sustained the Cause. "Anything else?"

"The bombmaker, Dwyer, has dropped out of sight again," McKenney went on.

"The last time that happened . . . yes, England, wasn't it? Another campaign?"

"Our man doesn't know. He's working on it, but I have told him to be careful."

"Very good." O'Donnell would think about this one. Dwyer was one of the best PIRA bombers, a genius with delayed fuses, someone Scotland Yard's C-13 branch wanted as badly as they wanted anyone. Dwyer's capture would be a serious blow to the PIRA leadership. . . . "We want our chap to be very careful indeed, but it would be useful to know where Dwyer is."

McKenney got the message loud and clear. It was too bad about Dwyer, but that colleague had picked the wrong side. "And the Belfast brigadier?"

"No." The chief shook his head.

"But he'll slip away again. We needed a month to—"

"No, Michael. Timing—remember the importance of timing. The operation is an integrated whole, not a mere collection of events." The commander of the PIRA's Belfast Brigade—*Brigade, less than two hundred men,* O'Donnell thought wryly—was the most wanted man in Ulster. Wanted by more than one side, though for the moment the Commander perforce had to let the Brits have him. *Too bad. I will dearly love to make you pay personally for casting me out, Johnny Doyle, for putting a price on my head. But on this I, too, must be patient. After all, I want more than your head.* "You might also keep in mind that our chaps have their own skins to protect. The reason timing is so important is that what we have planned can only work once. That is why we must be patient. We must wait for exactly the right moment."

What right moment? *What plan?* McKenney wanted to know. Only weeks before, O'Donnell had announced that "the moment" was at hand, only to call things off with a last-second telephone call from London. Sean Miller knew, as did one or two others, but McKenney didn't even know who those privileged fellows were. If there was anything the Commander believed in, it was security. The intelligence officer acknowledged its importance, but his youth chafed at the frustration of knowing the importance of what was happening without knowing *what it was*.

"Difficult, isn't it, Mike?"

"Yes, sir, it is," McKenney admitted with a smile.

"Just keep in mind where impatience has gotten us," the leader said.

8

Information

"I guess that about covers it, Jimmy. Thanks from the Bureau for tracking that guy down."

"I really don't think he's the sort of tourist we need, Dan," Owens replied. A Floridian who'd embezzled three million dollars from an Orlando bank had made the mistake of stopping off in Britain on his way to another European country, one with slightly different banking laws. "I think the next time we'll let him do some shopping on Bond Street before we arrest him, though. You can call that a fee—a fee for apprehending him."

"Ha!" The FBI representative closed the last folder. It was six o'clock local time. Dan Murray leaned back in his chair. Behind him, the brick Georgian buildings across the street paled in the dusk. Men were discreetly patrolling the roofs there, as with all the buildings on Grosvenor Square. The American Embassy was not so much heavily guarded as minorly fortified, so many terrorist threat warnings had come and gone over the past six years. Uniformed police officers stood in front of the building, where North Audley Street was closed off to traffic. The sidewalk was decorated with concrete "flowerpots" that a tank could surmount only with difficulty, and the rest of the building had a sloped concrete glacis to fend off car bombs. Inside, behind bullet-resistant glass, a Marine corporal stood guard beside a wall safe containing a .357 Magnum Smith & Wesson revolver. *A hell of a thing,* Murray thought. *A hell of a thing. The wonderful world of the international terrorist.* Murray hated working in a building that seemed part of the Maginot Line, hated wondering if there might be some Iranian, or Palestinian, or Libyan, or whatever madman of a terrorist, with an RPG-7 rocket launcher in a building across the street from his office. It wasn't fear for his life. Murray had put his life at risk more than once. He hated the injustice, the insult to his profession, that there were people who would kill their fellow men as a part of some form of political expression. *But they're not madmen at all, are they? The behavioral specialists say that they're not. They're romantics— believers, people willing to commit themselves to an ideal, and to commit any crime to further it.* Romantics!

"Jimmy, remember the good old days when we hunted bank bandits who were just in the business for a fast buck?"

"I've never done any of those. I was mainly concerned with ordinary thievery until they sent me to handling murders. But terrorism does make one nostalgic for the day of the common thug. I can even remember when *they* were fairly civilized." Owens refilled his glass with port. A growing problem for the Metropolitan Police was that the criminal use of firearms was no longer so rare as it had once been, this new tool made more popular by the evening news reports on terrorism within the U.K. And while the streets and parks of London were far safer than their American counterparts, they were not as safe as they'd only recently been. The times were changing in London, too, and Owens didn't like it at all.

The phone rang. Murray's secretary had just left for the night, and the agent lifted it.

"Murray. Hi, Bob. Yeah, he's right here. Bob Highland for you, Jimmy." He handed the phone over.

"Commander Owens here." The officer sipped at his port, then set the glass down abruptly and waved for a pen and pad. "Where exactly? And you've already—good, excellent. I'm coming straightaway."

"What gives?" Murray asked quickly.

"We've just had a tip on a certain Dwyer. Bomb factory in a flat on Tooley Street."

"Isn't that right across from the river from the Tower?"

"Too bloody right. I'm off." Owens rose and grabbed for his coat.

"You mind if I tag along?"

"Dan, you must remember—"

"To keep out of the way." Murray was already on his feet. One hand unconsciously checked his left hip, where his service revolver would be, had the agent not been in a foreign country. Owens had never carried a gun. Murray wondered how you could be a cop and not be armed with something. Together they left Murray's office and trotted up the corridor, turning left for the elevators. Two minutes later they were in the Embassy's basement parking garage. The two officers from Owens' chase car were already in their vehicle, and the Commander's driver followed them out.

Owens was on the radio the instant the car hit the street, with Murray in the back seat.

"You have people rolling?" Murray asked.

"Yes. Bob will have a team there in a few minutes. Dwyer, by God! The description fits perfectly." As much as he tried to hide it, Owens was as excited as a kid on Christmas morning.

"Who tipped you?"

"Anonymous. A male voice, claimed to have seen wiring, and something that was wrapped up in small blocks, when he looked in the window."

"I love it! Peeping Tom cues the cops—probably afraid his wife'll find out what he's been up to. Well, you take what you get." Murray grinned. He'd had cases break on slimmer stuff than this.

The evening traffic was curb-to-curb, and the police siren could not change that. It took fully twenty frustrating minutes to travel the five miles to Tooley Street, with Owens listening to the radio, his fist beating softly on the front door's armrest while his men arrived at the suspect house. Finally the car darted across the Tower Bridge and turned right. The driver parked it on the sidewalk alongside two other police cars.

It was a three-story building of drab, dirty brick, in a working class neighborhood. Next door was a small pub with its daily menu scrawled on a blackboard. Several patrons were standing at the door, pints in their fists as they watched the police, and more stood across the street. Owens ran to the door. A plainclothes detective was waiting for him.

"All secure, sir. We have the suspect in custody. Top floor, in the rear."

The Commander trotted up the stairs with Murray on his heels. Another detective met him on the top-floor landing. Owens proceeded the last thirty feet with a cruel, satisfied smile on his face.

"It's all over, sir," Highland said. "Here's the suspect."

Maureen Dwyer was stark naked, spread-eagled on the floor. Around her was a puddle of water, and a trail of wet footprints coming from the adjacent bathroom.

"She was taking a bath," Highland explained. "And she'd left her pistol on the kitchen table. No trouble at all."

"Do you have a female detective on the way?"

"Yes, sir. I'm surprised she's not here already."

"Traffic is bloody awful," Owens noted.

"Any evidence of a companion?"

"No, sir. None at all." Highland answered. "Only this."

The bottom drawer of the only bureau in the shabby apartment was lying on the floor. It contained several blocks of what looked like plastic explosive, some blasting caps, and what were probably electronic timers. Already a detective was doing a written inventory while another was busily photographing the entire room with a Nikon camera and strobe. A third was breaking open an evidence kit. Everything in the room would be tagged, dropped in a clear plastic bag, and stored for use in yet another terrorist trial in the Old Bailey. There were smiles of satisfaction everywhere—except for Maureen Dwyer's face, which was pressed to the floor. Two detectives stood over the girl, their service revolvers holstered as they watched the naked, wet figure without a trace of sympathy.

Murray stood in the doorway to keep out of everyone's way while his eyes took in the way Owens' detectives handled the scene. There wasn't much to criticize. The suspect was neutralized, the area secured, and now evidence was being collected; everything was going by the book. He noted that the suspect was kept stationary. A woman officer would perform a cavity search to ensure that she wasn't "holding" something that might be dangerous. This was a little hard on Miss Dwyer's modesty, but Murray didn't think a judge would object. Maureen Dwyer was a known bomber, with at least three years' work behind her. Nine months before, she'd been seen leaving the site of a nasty one in Belfast that minutes later had killed four people and maimed another three. No, there wouldn't be all that much sympathy for Miss Dwyer. After another several minutes, a detective took the sheet off the bed and draped it over her, covering her from her knees to her shoulders. Through it all, the suspect didn't move. She was breathing rapidly, but made no sound.

"This is interesting," one man said. He pulled a suitcase from under the bed. After checking it for booby traps, he opened it and extracted a theatrical makeup case complete with four wigs.

"Goodness, I could use one of those myself." The female detective squeezed past Murray and approached Owens. "I came as fast as I could, Commander."

"Carry on." Owens smiled. He was too happy to let something this minor annoy him.

"Spread 'em, dearie. You know the drill." The detective put on a rubber glove for her search. Murray didn't watch. This was one thing he'd always been squeamish about. A few seconds later, the glove came off with a snapping sound. A detective handed Dwyer some clothes to put on. Murray watched the suspect dress herself as unselfconsciously as if she'd been alone—no, he thought, alone she'd show more emotion. As soon as her clothes were on, a police officer snapped steel handcuffs on her wrists. The same man informed Dwyer of her rights, not very differently from the way American cops did it. She did not acknowledge the words. Maureen Dwyer looked about at the police, no expression at all on her face, not even anger, and was taken out without having said a single word.

That's a cold piece of work, Murray told himself. Even with her hair wet, with no makeup, she was pretty enough, he thought. Nice complexion. It wouldn't hurt her to knock off eight or ten pounds, but in nice clothes that wouldn't matter very much. *You could pass her on the street, or sit next to her in a bar and offer to buy her a drink, and you'd never suspect that she was carrying two pounds of high explosives in her purse. Thank God we don't have anything like that at home. . . .* He wondered how well the Bureau would do against such a threat. Even with all their resources, the scientific and forensic experts who back up the special agents in the field, this was no easy crime to deal with. For any police force, the name of the game was wait for the bad guys to make a mistake. You had to play for the breaks, just like a football team waited for a turnover. The problem was, the crooks kept getting better, kept learning from their mistakes. It was like any sort of competition. Both sides became increasingly sophisticated. But the criminals always had the initiative. The cops were always playing catchup ball.

"Well, Dan, any critique? Do we measure up to FBI standards?" Owens inquired with the slightest amount of smugness.

"Don't give me that crap, Jimmy!" Murray grinned. Things were settled down now. The detectives were fully engaged in cataloging the physical evidence in the confidence that they already had a solid criminal case. "I'd say you have this one pretty cold. You know how lucky you are not to have our illegal-search-and-seizure rules?" *Not to mention some of our judges.*

"Finished," the photographer said.

"Excellent," replied Sergeant Bob Highland, who was running the crime scene.

"How'd you get here so fast, Bob?" Murray wanted to know. "You take the tube, or what?"

"Why didn't I think of that?" Highland laughed. "Perhaps we caught the traffic right. We were here within eleven minutes. You weren't that far behind us. We booted the door and had Dwyer in custody in under five seconds. Isn't it amazing how easy it can be—if you have the bloody information you need!"

"Can I come in now?"

"Certainly." Owens waved him into the apartment.

Murray went right to the bureau drawer with the explosives. The FBI man was an expert on explosive devices. He and Owens crouched over the collection.

"Looks like Czech," Murray muttered.

"It is," another detective said. "From Skoda works, you can tell from the wrapping. These are American, though. California Pyronetics, model thirty-one electronic detonator." He tossed one—in a plastic bag—to Murray.

"Damn! They're turning up all over the place—a shipment of these little babies got hijacked a year and a half ago. They were heading for an oil field in Venezuela, and got taken outside Caracas," Murray explained. He gave the small black device a closer look. "The oil field guys love 'em. Safe, reliable, and damned near foolproof. This is as good as the stuff the Army uses. State of the art."

"Where else have they turned up?" Owens asked.

"We're sure about three or four. The problem is, they're so small that it's not always possible to identify what's left. A bank in Puerto Rico, a police station in Peru—those were political. The other one—maybe two—were drug related. Until now they've all been on the other side of the Atlantic. As far as I know, this is the first time they've showed up here. These detonators have lot numbers. You'll want to check them against the stolen shipment. I can get a telex off tonight, have you an answer inside an hour."

"Thank you, Dan."

Murray counted five one-kilo blocks of explosive. The Czech plastique had a good reputation for quality. It was as potent as the stuff Du Pont made for American military use. One block, properly placed, could take a building down. With the Pyronetics timers, Miss Dwyer could have placed five separate bombs, set them for delayed detonation—as much as a month—and been a thousand miles away when they went off.

"You saved some lives tonight, gentlemen. Good one." Murray looked up. The apartment had a single window facing to the rear. The window had a pull-down blind that was all the way down, and some cheap, dirty curtains. Murray wondered what this flat cost to rent. Not much, he was sure. The heat was turned way up, and the room was getting stuffy. "Anybody mind if I let some air in here?"

"Excellent idea, Dan," Owens answered.

"Let me do it, sir." A detective with gloves on put up the blind and then the window. Everything in the room would be dusted for fingerprints also, but opening the window wouldn't harm anything. A breeze cooled things off in an instant.

"That's better." The FBI representative took a deep breath, scarcely noticing the smell of diesel exhaust from the London cabs. . . .

Something was wrong.

It hit Murray as a surprise. Something *was* wrong. *What?* He looked out the window. To the left was a—probably a warehouse, a blank four-story wall. Past it on the right, he could see the outline of the Tower of London, standing over the River Thames. That was all. He turned his head to see Owens, also staring out the window. The Commander of C-13 turned his head and looked at Murray, a question on his face also.

"Yes," Owens said.

"What was it that guy on the phone said?" Murray muttered.

Owens' head bobbed. "Exactly. Sergeant Highland?"

"Yes, Commander?"

"The voice on the phone. What exactly did it say, and what exactly did it sound like?" Owens kept looking out the window.

"The voice had . . . a Midlands accent, I should think. A man's voice. He said that he was looking in the window, and saw explosives and some wires. We have it all on tape, of course."

Murray reached through the open window and ran a finger along the outside surface of the glass. It came back dirty. "It sure wasn't a window-washer who called in." He leaned out the window. There was no fire escape.

"Someone atop the warehouse, perhaps—no," Owens said at once. "The angle isn't right, unless she had the material spread out on the floor. That is rather odd."

"Break-in? Maybe someone got in here, saw the stuff, and decided to call in like a good citizen?" Murray asked. "That doesn't sound very likely."

Owens shrugged. "No telling, is there? A boyfriend she dumped—I think for the moment we can be content with counting our blessings, Dan. There are five bombs that will never hurt anyone. Let's get out of everyone's way and send that telex off to Washington. Sergeant Highland, gentlemen, this was well done! Congratulations to you all for some splendid police work. Carry on."

Owens and Murray left the building quietly. Outside they found a small crowd being restrained by about ten uniformed constables. A TV news crew was on the scene with its bright lights. These were enough to keep them from seeing across the street. This block had three small pubs. In the doorway of one stood a soft-looking man with a pint of bitter in his hand. He showed no emotion, not even curiosity, as he looked across the street. His memory recorded the faces he saw. His name was Dennis Cooley.

Murray and Owens drove to New Scotland Yard headquarters, where the FBI agent made his telex to Washington. They didn't discuss the one anomaly that the case had unexpectedly developed, and Murray left Owens to his work. C-13 had broken yet another bomb case—and done so in the best way, without a single casualty. It meant that Owens and his people would have a sleepless night of paperwork, and preparing reports for the Home Office bureaucracy, and press releases for Fleet Street, but that was something they would gladly accept.

Ryan's first day back at work was easier than he had expected. His prolonged absence had forced the History Department to reassign his classes, and in any case it was almost time for Christmas break, and nearly all of the mids were looking forward to being home for the holidays. Class routine was slightly relaxed, and even the plebes enjoyed a respite from the upperclassmen's harassment in the wake of the win over Army. For Ryan, the result was a fairish collection of letters and documents piled on his In tray, and a quiet day with which to deal with them. He'd arrived in his office at 7:30; by quarter to five he'd dealt with most of his paperwork, and Ryan felt that he'd delivered an honest day's work. He was finishing a series of test questions for the semester's final exam when he smelled cheap cigar smoke and heard a familiar voice.

"Did you enjoy your vacation, boy?" Lieutenant Commander Robert Jefferson Jackson was leaning against the door frame.

"It had a few interesting moments, Robby. The sun over—or under—the yardarm yet?"

"Damn straight!" Jackson set his white cap on top of Ryan's filing cabinet and collapsed unceremoniously into the leather chair opposite his friend's desk.

Ryan closed the file folder on his draft exam and shoved it into a desk drawer. One of the personal touches in his office was a small refrigerator. He opened it and took out a two-liter bottle of 7-Up, along with an empty bottle of Canada Dry ginger ale, then removed a bottle of Irish whiskey from his desk. Robby got two cups from the table by the door and handed them to Jack. Ryan mixed two drinks to the approximate color of ginger ale. It was against Academy policy to have liquor in one's office—a stance Ryan found curious, given the naval orientation of the institution—but drinking "ginger ale" was a winked-upon subterfuge. Besides, everyone recognized that the Officer and Faculty Club was only a minute's walk away. Jack handed one drink over and replaced everything but the empty ginger ale bottle.

"Welcome home, pal!" Robby held his drink up.

"Nice to be back." The two men clicked their cups together.

"Glad you made it, Jack. You kind of worried us. How's the arm?" Jackson gestured with his cup.

"Better than it was. You oughta see the cast I started out with. They took it off at Hopkins last Friday. I learned one thing today, though, driving a stick shift through Annapolis with one arm is a bitch."

"I'll bet," Robby chuckled. "Damn if you ain't crazy, boy."

Ryan nodded agreement. He'd met Jackson the previous March at a faculty tea. Robby wore the gold wings of a naval aviator. He'd been assigned to the nearby Patuxent River Naval Air Test Center, Maryland, as an instructor in the test pilot school until a faulty relay had unexpectedly blasted him clear of the Buckeye jet trainer he'd been flying one fine, clear morning. Unprepared for the event, he'd broken his leg badly. The injury had been serious enough to take him off flight status for six months, and the Navy had assigned him to temporary duty as an instructor in Annapolis, where he was currently in the engineering department. It was an assignment which Jackson regarded as one step above pulling oars in a galley.

Jackson was shorter than Ryan, and much darker. He was the fourth son of a Baptist preacher in southern Alabama. When they'd first met, the officer was still in a cast, and Jackson had asked Ryan if he might want to try his hand at kendo. It was something that Ryan had never tried, the Japanese fencing sport in which bamboo staves are used in place of samurai swords. Ryan had used pugil sticks in the Marines and figured it wouldn't be too different. He'd accepted the invitation, thinking that his longer reach would be a decisive advantage, particularly on top of Jackson's reduced mobility. It hadn't occurred to him that Jackson would first have asked a brother officer for a kendo match. In fact, Ryan later learned, he had. He'd also learned by then that Robby had the blinding quickness and killer instinct of a rattlesnake. By the time the bruises had faded, they were fast friends.

For his part, Ryan had introduced the pilot to the smoky flavor of good Irish whiskey, and they'd evolved the tradition of an afternoon drink or two in the privacy of Jack's office.

"Any news on campus?" Ryan asked.

"Still teachin' the boys and girls," Jackson said comfortably.

"And you've started to like it?"

"Not exactly. The leg's finally back in battery, though. I've been spending my weekends down at Pax River to prove I still know how to fly. You know, you made one hell of a flap hereabouts."

"When I was shot?"

"Yeah, I was in with the Superintendent when the call came in. The 'soop' put it on speaker, and we got this FBI-guy askin' if we got a nut-case teacher in London playing cops and robbers. I said, sure, I know the jerk, but they wanted somebody in the History Department to back me up—mainly they wanted the name of your travel agent, I suppose. Anyway, everybody was out to lunch, and I had to track Professor Billings down in the O-Club, and the superintendent did some runnin' around, too. You almost ruined the boss's last golf day with the Governor.''

"Damned near ruined my day, too.''

"Was it like they said in the papers?''

"Probably. The Brit papers got it pretty straight.''

Jackson nodded as he tapped the cigar on Ryan's ashtray. "You're lucky you didn't come home parcel post, boy,'' he said.

"Don't you start, Robby. One more guy tells me I'm a hero, and I'll flatten him—''

"Hero? Hell, no! If all you honkies were that dumb, my ancestors would have imported yours.'' The pilot shook his head emphatically. "Didn't anybody ever tell you, that hand-to-hand stuff is *dangerous*?''

"If you'd been there, I bet you'd have done the same—''

"No chance! God Almighty, is there anything dumber than a Marine? This hand-to-hand stuff, Jeez, you get blood on your clothes, mess up the shine on your shoes. No way, boy! When I do my killin', it'll be with cannon shells and missiles—you know, the civilized way.'' Jackson grinned. "The safe way.''

"Not like flying an airplane that decides to blast you loose without warning you first,'' Ryan scoffed.

"I dinged my leg some, sure, but when I got my Tomcat strapped to my back, I'm hummin' along at six hundred-plus knots. Anybody who wants to put a bullet in me, fella, he can do it, but he's gonna have to work at it.''

Ryan shook his head. He was hearing a safety lecture from someone who just happened to be in the most dangerous business there was—a carrier aviator *and* a test pilot.

"How's Cathy and Sally?'' Robby asked, more seriously. "We meant to come over Sunday, but we had to drive up to Philadelphia on short notice.''

"It was kinda tough on them, but they came through all right.''

"You got a family to worry about, Jack,'' Jackson pointed out.

"Leave that rescue stuff to the professionals." The funny thing about Robby, Jack knew, was his caution. For all the down-home bantering about his life as a fighter pilot, Jackson never took a risk he didn't have to. He'd known pilots who had. Many were dead. There was not a single man wearing those gold wings who had not lost a friend, and Jack wondered how deeply that had affected Jackson over the years. Of one thing he was sure, though Robby was in a dangerous business, like all successful gamblers he thought things over before he moved his chips. Wherever his body went, his mind had already gone.

"It's all over, Rob. It's all behind me, and there won't be a next time."

"We'll put a big roger on that. Who else am I gonna drink with? So how'd you like it over there?"

"I didn't see very much, but Cathy had a great time, all things considered. I think she saw every castle in the country—plus the new friends we made."

"That must have been right interesting," Robby chuckled. The flyer stubbed out his cigar. They were cheap, crooked, evil-smelling little things, and Jack figured that Jackson puffed on them only as part of the Image of the Fighter Pilot. "Not hard to understand why they took a liking to you."

"They took a liking to Sally, too. They got her started riding horses," Jack added sourly.

"Oh, yeah? So what are they like?"

"You'd like 'em," Ryan assured him.

Jackson smiled. "Yeah, I imagine I would. The Prince used to drive Phantoms, so he must be a right guy, and his dad's supposed to know his way around a cockpit, too. I hear you took the Concorde back. How'd you like it?"

"I meant to ask you about that. How come it was so noisy? I mean, if you're doing mach-2-plus, why isn't all the noise behind you?"

Jackson shook his head sadly. "What's the airplane made out of?"

"Aluminum, I suppose."

"You suppose the speed of sound is faster in metal than it is in air, maybe?" Jackson asked.

"Oh. The sound travels through the body of the airplane."

"Sure, engine noise, noise from the fuel pumps, various other things."

"Okay." Ryan filed that away.

"You didn't like it, did you?" Robby was amused at his friend's attitude toward flying.

"Why does everybody pick on me for that?" Ryan asked the ceiling.

"Because it's so funny, Jack. You're the last person in the world who's afraid to fly."

"Hey, Rob, I do it, okay? I get aboard, and strap in, and do it."

"I know. I'm sorry." Jackson eased off. "It's just that it's so easy to needle you on this—I mean, what are friends for? You done good, Jack. We're proud of you. But for Christ's sake, be careful, okay? This hero shit gets people killed."

"I hear you."

"Is it true about Cathy?" Robby asked.

"Yep. The doc confirmed it the same day they took the cast off."

"Way to go, pop! I'd say that calls for another—a light one." Robby held his cup out, and Jack poured. "Looks like the bottle's about had it, too."

"It's my turn to buy the next one, isn't it?"

"It's been so long, I don't remember," Robby admitted. "But I'll take your word for it."

"So they have you back in airplanes?"

"Next Monday they'll let me back in a Tomcat," Jackson replied. "And come summer, it's back to the work they pay me for."

"You got orders?"

"Yeah, you're looking at the prospective XO of VF-41." Robby held his cup up in the air.

The executive officer of Fighter Squadron 41, Ryan translated. "That's all right, Rob!"

"Yeah, it's not bad, considering I've been a black shoe for the past seven months."

"Right out on carriers?"

"No, we'll be on the beach for a while, down at Oceana, Virginia. The squadron's deployed now on *Nimitz*. When the boat comes back for refit, the fighters stay on the beach for refresher training. Then we'll probably redeploy on *Kennedy*. They're reshuffling the squadron assignments. Jack, it'll be good to strap that fighter back on! I've been here too long."

"We're gonna miss you and Sissy."

"Hey, we don't leave till summer—they're making me finish out the school year—and Virginia Beach isn't all that far away. Come on down and visit, for crying out loud. You don't have to fly, Jack. You can drive," Jackson pointed out.

"Well, you'll probably be around for the new kid."

"Good." Jackson finished off his drink.

"Are you and Sissy going anywhere for Christmas?"

"Not that I know of. I can't, really; most of the holidays I'm gonna be flying down at Pax."

"Okay, come on over to our place for dinner—three-ish."

"Cathy's family isn't—"

"No," Ryan said as he tucked everything back where it belonged. Robby shook his head.

"Some folks just don't catch on," the pilot observed.

"Well, you know how it is. I don't worship at the temple of the Almighty Dollar anymore."

"But you managed to do a job on the collection basket."

Jack grinned. "Yeah, you might say that."

"That reminds me. There's a little outfit outside Boston that's gonna hit it big."

"Oh?" Jack's ears perked up.

"It's called Holoware, Ltd., I think. They came up with new software for the computers on fighter planes—really good stuff, cuts a third off the processing time, generates intercept solutions like magic. It's set up on the simulator down at Pax, and the Navy's going to buy it real soon."

"Who knows?"

Jackson laughed as he got his things. "The company doesn't know yet. Captain Stevens down at Pax just got the word from the guys out at Topgun. Bill May out there—I used to fly with Bill—ran the stuff for the first time a month ago, and he liked it so much that he almost got the Pentagon boys to cut through all the bullshit and just buy the stuff. It got hung up, but DCNO-Air is on it now, and they say Admiral Rendall is really hot for it. Thirty more days, and that little company is going to get a Christmas present. A little late," Robby said, "but it'll fill one big stocking. Just for the hell of it, I checked the paper this morning, and sure enough, they're listed on the American Exchange. You might want to check it out."

"What about you?"

The pilot shook his head. "I don't play the market, but you still fool around there, right?"

"A little. Is this classified or anything?" Jack asked.

"Not that I know of. The classified part is how the software is written, and they got a real good classification system on that—nobody understands it. Maybe Skip Tyler could figure it out, but I never will. You have to be a nuc to think in ones and zeros. Pilots don't think digital. We're analog." Jackson chuckled. "Gotta run. Sissy's got a recital tonight."

" 'Night, Rob."

"Low and slow, Jack." Robby closed the door behind him. Jack leaned back in his chair for a moment. He smiled to himself, then rose and packed some papers into his briefcase.

"Yeah," he said to himself. "Just to show him that I still know how."

Ryan got his coat on and left the building, walking downhill past the Preble Memorial. His car was parked on Decatur Road. Jack drove a five-year-old VW Rabbit. It was a very practical car for the narrow streets of Annapolis, and he refused to have a Porsche like his wife used for commuting back and forth to Baltimore. It was dumb, he'd told Cathy about a thousand times, for two people to have three cars. A Rabbit for him, a 911 for her, and a station wagon for the family. Dumb. Cathy's suggestion that he should sell the Rabbit and drive the wagon was, of course, unacceptable. The little gas engine fired up at once. It sounded too noisy. He'd have to check the muffler. Jack pulled out, turning right, as always, onto Maryland Avenue through Gate Three in the grimly undecorous perimeter wall that surrounded the Academy. A Marine guard saluted him on the way out. Ryan was surprised by that—they'd never done it before.

Driving wasn't easy. When he shifted, Ryan twisted his left hand inside the sling to grab the wheel while his right hand worked the gearshift. The rush-hour traffic didn't help. Several thousand state workers were disgorging themselves from various government buildings, and the crowded streets gave Ryan plenty of opportunity to stop and restart from first gear. His Rabbit had five, plus reverse, and by the time he got to the Central Avenue light he was asking himself why he hadn't gotten the Rabbit with an automatic. Fuel efficiency was the answer—*is this worth an extra two miles per gallon*? Ryan laughed at himself as he headed east toward the Chesapeake Bay, then right onto Falcon's Nest Road.

There was rarely any traffic back here. Falcon's Nest Road came to a dead end not too far down from Ryan's place, and on the other side of the road were several farms, also dormant at the beginning of winter. The stubby remains of cornstalks lay in rows on the brown, hard fields. He turned left into his driveway. Ryan had thirty acres on Peregrine Cliff. His nearest neighbor, an engineer named Art Palmer, was half a mile away through heavily wooded slopes and across a murky stream. The cliffs on the western shore of the Chesapeake Bay were nearly fifty feet high where Jack lived—those farther south got a little higher, but not much—and made of crumbly sandstone. They were a paleontologist's delight. Every so often a team from a local college or museum would scour at the base and find fossilized shark teeth that had once belonged to a creature as large as a midget submarine, along with the bones of even more unlikely creatures that had lived here a hundred million years earlier.

The bad news was that the cliffs were prone to erosion. His house was built a hundred feet back from the edge, and his daughter was under strict orders—twice enforced with a spanking—not to go anywhere near the edge. In an attempt to protect the cliff face, the state environmental-protection people had persuaded Ryan and his neighbors to plant kudzu, a prolific weed from the American South. The weed had thoroughly stabilized the cliff face, but it was now attacking the trees near the cliff, and Jack periodically had to go after them with a weed-eater to save the trees from being smothered. But that wasn't a problem this time of year.

Ryan's lot was half open and half wooded. The part near the road had once been farmed, though not easily, as the ground was not flat enough to drive a tractor across it safely. As he approached his house, the trees began, some gnarled old oaks, and other deciduous trees whose leaves were gone now, leaving skeletal branches to reach out into the thin, cold air. As he approached the carport, he saw that Cathy was already home, her Porsche and the family wagon parked in the carport. He had to leave his Rabbit in the open.

"Daddy!" Sally yanked open the door and ran out without her jacket to meet her father.

"It's too cold out here," Jack told his daughter.

"No, isn't," Sally replied. She grabbed his briefcase and carried it with two hands, puffing as she climbed up the three steps into the house.

Ryan got out of his coat and hung it in the entry closet. As with everything else, it was hard to do with one hand. He was cheating a little now. As with steering the car, he was starting to use his left hand, careful to avoid putting any strain on his shoulder. The pain was completely gone now, but Ryan was sure that he could bring it back quickly enough if he did something dumb. Besides which, Cathy would yell at him. He found his wife in the kitchen. She was looking at the pantry and frowning.

"Hi, honey."

"Hi, Jack. You're late."

"So are you." Ryan kissed his wife. Cathy smelled his breath. Her nose crinkled.

"How's Robby?"

"Fine—and I just had two very light ones."

"Uh-huh." She turned back to the pantry. "What do you want for dinner?"

"Surprise me," Jack suggested.

"You're a big help! I ought to let you fix it."

"It's not my turn, remember?"

"I knew I should have stopped at the Giant," Cathy groused.

"How was work?"

"Only one procedure. I assisted Bernie on a cornea transplant, then I had to take the residents around for rounds. Dull day. Tomorrow'll be better. Bernie says hi, by the way. How does franks and beans grab you?"

Jack laughed. Ever since they came back, their diet had consisted mainly of basic American staples, and it was a little late for something fancy.

"Okay. I'm going to change and punch up something on the computer for a few minutes."

"Careful with the arm, Jack."

Five times a day she warns me. Jack sighed. *Never marry a doctor.* The Ryan home was a deckhouse design. The living/dining room had a cathedral ceiling that peaked sixteen feet over the carpeted floor with an enormous wood beam. A wall of triple-paned windows faced the bay, with a large deck beyond the sliding glass doors. Opposite the glass was a massive brick fireplace that reached through the roof. The master bedroom was half a level above the living room, with a window that enabled one to look down into it. Ryan trotted up the steps. The house design accommodated large closets. Ryan selected casual clothes, and went through the annoying ritual of changing himself one-handed. He was still experimenting, trying to find an efficient way to do it.

Finished, he went back down, and curved around the stairs to the next level down, his library. It was a large one. Jack read a lot, and also purchased books he didn't have time to read, banking against the time when he would. He had a large desk up against the windows on the bay side of the house. Here was his personal computer, an Apple, and all of its peripheral equipment. Ryan flipped it on and started typing in instructions. Next he put his modem on line and placed a call into CompuServe. The time of day guaranteed easy access, and he selected MicroQuote II from the entry menu.

A moment later he was looking at Holoware, Ltd.'s stock performance over the past three years. The stock was agreeably unimpressive, fluctuating from two dollars to as much as six, but that was two years back—it was a company which had once held great promise, but somewhere along the way investors had lost confidence. Jack made a note, then exited the program and got into another, Disclosure II, to look at the company's SEC filings and last annual report. *Okay,* Ryan told himself. The company was making money, but not very much. One problem with hi-tech issues was that so many investors wanted big returns very quickly, or they'd move on to something else, forgetting that things didn't necessarily happen that way. This company had found a small though somewhat precarious niche, and was ready to try something bold. Ryan made a mental estimate of what the Navy contract would be worth and compared it with the company's total revenues. . . .

"Okay!" he told himself before exiting the system completely and shutting his computer down. Next he called his broker. Ryan worked through a discount brokerage firm that had people on duty around the clock. Jack always dealt with the same man.

"Hi, Mort, it's Jack. How's the family?"

"Hello again, Doctor Ryan. Everything's fine with us. What can we do for you tonight?"

"An outfit called Holoware, one of the hi-tech bunch on Highway 128 outside Boston. It's on the AMEX."

"Okay." Ryan heard tapping on a keyboard. Everyone used comput-

ers. "Here it is. Going at four and seven-eighths, not a very active issue
. . . until lately. There has been some modest activity over the past
month."

"What kind?" Ryan asked. This was another sign to look for.

"Oh, I see. The company is buying itself back a little. No big deal,
but they're buying their own stock out."

Bingo! Ryan smiled to himself. *Thank you, Robby. You gave me a tip
on a real live one.* Jack asked himself if this constituted trading on inside
information. His initial tip might be called that, but his decision to buy
was based on confirmation made legally, on the basis of his experience
as a stock trader. *Okay, it's legal.* He could do whatever he wanted.

"How much do you think you can get for me?"

"It's not a very impressive stock."

"How often am I wrong, Mort?"

"How much do you want?"

"At least twenty-K, and if there's more, I want all of it you can find."
There was no way he'd get hold of more than fifty thousand shares, but
Ryan made a snap decision to grab all he could. If he lost, it was only
money, and it had been over a year since he'd last had a hunch like this
one. If they got the Navy contract, that stock would increase in value
tenfold. The company must have had a tip, too. Buying back their own
stock on the slim resources they had would, if Ryan was guessing right,
dramatically increase the firm's capital, enabling a rapid expansion of
operations. Holoware was betting on the future, and betting big.

There was five seconds of silence on the phone.

"What do you know, Jack?" the broker asked finally.

"I'm playing a hunch."

"Okay . . . twenty-K plus . . . I'll call you at ten tomorrow. You
think I should . . . ?"

"It's a toss of the dice, but I think it's a good toss."

"Thanks. Anything else?"

"No. I have to go eat dinner. Good night, Mort."

"See ya." Both men hung up. At the far end of the phone, the broker
decided that he'd go in for a thousand shares, too. Ryan was occasionally wrong, but when he was right, he tended to be very right.

"Christmas Day," O'Donnell said quietly. "Perfect."

"Is that the day they're moving Sean?" McKenney asked.

"He leaves London by van at four in the morning. That's bloody good news. I was afraid they'd use a helicopter. No word on the route they'll use. . . ." He read on. "But they're going to take him across on the Lymington ferry at eight-thirty Christmas morning. Excellent timing, when you think about it. Too early for heavy traffic. Everyone'll be opening his presents and getting dressed for church. The van might even have the ferry to itself—who'd expect a prisoner transfer on Christmas Day?"

"So, we are going to break Sean out, then?"

"Michael, our men do us little good when they're inside, don't they? You and I are flying over tomorrow morning. I think we'll drive down to Lymington and look at the ferry."

9

A Day for Celebration

"God, it'll be nice to have two arms again," Ryan observed.

"Two more weeks, maybe three," Cathy reminded him. "And keep your hand still inside the damned sling!"

"Yes, dear."

It was about two in the morning, and things were going badly—and well. Part of the Ryan family tradition—a tradition barely three years old, but a tradition nevertheless—was that after Sally was in bed and asleep, her parents would creep down to the basement storage area—a room with a padlocked door—and bring the toys upstairs for assembly. The previous two years, this ceremony had been accompanied by a couple of bottles of champagne. Assembling toys was a wholly different sort of exercise when the assemblers were half blasted. It was their method of relaxing into the Christmas spirit.

So far things had gone well. Jack had taken his daughter to the seven o'clock children's mass at St. Mary's, and gotten her to bed a little after nine. His daughter had slid her head around the fireplace wall only twice before a loud command from her father had banished her to her bedroom for good, her arm clasping an overly talkative AG Bear to her chest. By midnight it was decided that she was asleep enough for her parents to make a little noise. This had begun the toy trek, as Cathy called it. Both parents removed their shoes to minimize noise on the hardwood steps and went downstairs. Of course, Jack forgot the key to the padlock, and had to climb back upstairs to the master bedroom to search for it. Five minutes later the door was opened and the two of them made four trips each, setting up a lavish pile of multicolored boxes near the tree, next to Jack's tool kit.

"You know what the two most obscene words in the English language are, Cathy?" Ryan asked nearly two hours later.

"'Assembly required,'" his wife answered with a giggle. "Honey, last year I said that."

"A small Phillips." Jack held his hand out. Cathy smacked the screwdriver into his hand like a surgical instrument. Both of them were sitting on the rug, fifteen feet from the eight-foot tree. Around them was a crescent of toys, some in boxes, some already assembled by the now-exasperated father of a little girl.

"You ought to let me do that."

"This is man's work," her husband said. He sat the screwdriver down and sipped at a glass of champagne.

"You chauvinist pig! If I let you do this by yourself, you wouldn't be finished by Easter."

She was right, Jack told himself. Doing it half-drunk wasn't all that hard. Doing it one-handed was hard but not insurmountable. Doing it one-handed *and* half-drunk was. . . . The damned screws didn't want to stay in the plastic, and the instructions for putting a V-8 engine together had to be easier than this!

"Why is it that a doll needs a house?" Jack asked plaintively. "I mean, the friggin' doll's already *in* a house, isn't she?"

"It must be hard, being a chauvinist pig. You dodos just don't understand anything," Cathy noted sympathetically. "I guess men never get over baseball bats—all those simple, one-piece toys."

Jack's head turned slowly. "Well, the least you could do is have another glass of wine."

"One's the weekly limit, Jack. I did have a big glass," she reminded him.

"And made me drink the rest."

"You bought the bottle, Jack." She picked it up. "Big one, too."

Ryan turned back to the Barbie Doll house. He thought he remembered when the Barbie Doll had been invented, a simple, rather curvy doll, but still just a damned doll, something that girls played with. It hadn't occurred to him then that he might someday have a little girl of his own. *The things we do for our kids,* he told himself. Then he laughed quietly at himself. *Of course we do, and we enjoy it. Tomorrow this will be a funny memory, like the Christmas morning last year when I nearly put this very screwdriver through the palm of my hand.* If he didn't enlist his wife's assistance, Ryan told himself, Santa would be planning next year's flight before he finished. Jack took a deep breath and swallowed his pride.

"Help."

Cathy checked her watch. "That took about forty minutes longer than I expected."

"I must be slowing down."

"Poor baby, having to drink all that champagne all by himself." She kissed him on the forehead. "Screwdriver."

He handed it to her. Cathy took a quick look at the plans. "No wonder, you dummy. You're using a short screw when you're supposed to use a long one."

"I keep forgetting that I'm married to a high-priced mechanic."

"That's real Christmas spirit, Jack." She grinned as she turned the screw into place.

"A very pretty, smart, and extremely lovable high-priced mechanic." He ran a finger down the back of her neck.

"That's a *little* better."

"Who's better with tools than I am, one-handed."

Her head turned to reveal the sort of smile a wife saves only for the husband she loves. "Give me another screw, Jack, and I'll forgive you."

"Don't you think you should finish the doll house first?"

"Screw, dammit!" He handed her one. "You have a one-track gutter, but I forgive you anyway."

"Thanks. If it didn't work, though, I had something else planned."

"Oh, did Santa come for me, too?"

"I'm not sure. I'll check in a few minutes."

"You didn't do bad, considering," his wife said, finishing off the orange plastic roof. "That's it, isn't it?"

"Last one," Jack confirmed. "Thanks for the assist, babe."

"Did I ever tell you what—no, I didn't. It was one of the ladies-in-waiting. I never did find out what they were waiting for. Anyway, this one countess . . . she was right out of *Gone With the Wind*," Cathy said with a chuckle. It was his wife's favorite epithet for useless women. "She asked me if I did needlepoint."

Not the sort of thing you ask my wife. Jack grinned at the windows. "And you said . . ."

"Only on eyeballs." A sweet, nasty smile.

"Oooh. I hope that wasn't over lunch."

"Jack! You know me better than that. She was nice enough, and she played a pretty good piano."

"Good as yours?"

"No." His wife smiled at him. Jack reached out to squeeze the tip of her nose.

"Caroline Ryan, MD, liberated woman, instructor in ophthalmic surgery, world-famous player of classical piano, wife and mother, takes no crap off anybody."

"Except her husband."

"When's the last time I ever won an exchange with you?" Jack asked.

"Jack, we're not in competition. We're in love." She leaned toward him.

"I won't argue with you on that," he said quietly before kissing his wife's offered lips. "How many people do you suppose are still in love after all the time we've been married?"

"Just the lucky ones, you old fart. 'All the time we've been married'!"

Jack kissed her again and rose. He walked carefully around the sea of toys toward the tree and returned with a small box wrapped in green Christmas paper. He sat down beside his wife, his shoulder against hers as he dropped the box in her lap.

"Merry Christmas, Cathy."

She opened the box as greedily as a child, but neatly, using her nails to slit the paper. She found a white cardboard box, and inside it, a felt-covered one. This she opened slowly.

It was a necklace of fine gold, more than a quarter-inch wide, designed to fit closely around the neck. You could tell the price by the workmanship and the weight. Cathy Ryan took a deep breath. Her husband held his. Figuring out women's fashions was not his strongest point. He'd gotten advice from Sissy Jackson, and a very patient clerk at the jewelry store. *Do you like it?*

"I better not swim with this on."

"But you won't have to take it off when you scrub," Jack said. "Here." He took it from the box and put it around her neck. He managed to clasp it one-handed on the first try.

"You practiced." One hand traced over the necklace while her eyes looked deeply into his. "You practiced, just so you could put it on me yourself, didn't you?"

"For a week at the office." Jack nodded. "Wrapping it was a bitch, too."

"It's wonderful. Oh, Jack!" Both her arms darted around his neck, and he kissed the base of hers.

"Thanks, babe. Thanks for being my wife. Thanks for having my kids. Thanks for letting me love you."

Cathy blinked away a tear or two. They gave her blue eyes a gleam that made him happier than any man on earth. *Let me count the ways . . .*

"Just something I saw," he explained casually, lying. It was something he'd seen after looking for nine hours, through seven stores in three shopping malls. "And it just said to me, 'I was made for her.'"

"Jack, I didn't get you anything like—"

"Shut up. Every morning I wake up, and I see you next to me, I get the best present there is."

"You are a sentimental jerk right out of some book—but I don't mind."

"You do like it?" he asked carefully.

"You dummy—I love it!" They kissed again. Jack had lost his parents years before. His sister lived in Seattle, and most of the rest of his relations were in Chicago. Everything he loved was in this house: a wife, a child—and a third of another. He'd made his wife smile on Christmas, and now this year went into the ledger book as a success.

About the time Ryan started assembling the doll house, four identical blue vans left the Brixton Prison at five-minute intervals. For each, the first thirty minutes involved driving through the side streets of suburban London. In each, a pair of police officers sat looking out the small windows in the rear doors, watching to see if there might be a car trailing the truck on its random path through the city.

They'd picked a good day for it. It was a fairly typical morning for the English winter. The vans drove through patches of fog and cold rain. There was a moderate storm blowing in from the Channel, and best of all, it was dark. The island's northern latitude guaranteed that the sun would not be up for some hours yet, and the dark blue vans were invisible in the early morning.

Security was so strict that Sergeant Bob Highland of C-13 didn't even know that he was in the third van to leave the jail. He did know that he was sitting only a few feet from Sean Miller, and that their destination was the small port of Lymington. They had a choice of three ports to take them to the Isle of Wight, and three different modes of transport: ordinary ferry, hovercraft, and hydrofoil. They might also have chosen a Royal Navy helicopter out of Gosport, but Highland needed only a quick look at the starless sky to rule that one out. *Not a good idea*, he thought to himself. Besides, security is airtight. Not more than thirty people knew that Miller was being moved this morning. Miller himself hadn't known until three hours before, and he still didn't know what prison he was heading to. He'd only learn when he got to the island.

Embarrassments to the British prison system had accumulated over the years. The old, forbidding structures that inhabited such desolate places as Dartmoor in Cornwall had turned out to be amazingly easy to escape from, and as a result two new maximum-security facilities, Albany and Parkhurst, had been built on the Isle of Wight. There were many advantages to this. An island by definition was easier to secure, and this one had only four regular entry points. More importantly, this island was a clannish place even by English standards, and any stranger on the loose would at least be noticed, and might even be commented upon. The new prisons were somewhat more comfortable than those constructed in the previous century. It was an accident, but one to which Highland did not object. Along with the better living conditions for the prisoners came facilities designed to make escape very difficult—nothing made them impossible, but these new prisons had television cameras to cover every inch of wall, electronic alarms in the most unlikely of places, and guards armed with automatic weapons.

Highland stretched and yawned. With luck he'd get home by early afternoon and still salvage something of Christmas Day with his family.

"I don't see anything at all to concern us," the other constable said, his nose against the small glass rectangle in the door. "Only a handful of vehicles on the street, and none are following us."

"I shouldn't complain," Highland observed. He turned around to look at Miller.

The prisoner sat all the way forward on the left-hand bench. His hands were manacled, a chain running from the cuffs to a similar pair on his ankles. With luck and a little assistance, a man so restrained might be able to keep pace with a crawling infant, but he'd have little chance of outracing a two-year-old. Miller just sat there, his head back against the wall of the van, his eyes closed as the vehicles bounced and jolted over the road. He looked to be asleep, but Highland knew better. Miller had withdrawn into himself again, lost in some kind of contemplation.

What are you thinking about, Mr. Miller? the policeman wanted to ask. It wasn't that he'd failed to ask questions. Almost every day since the incident on The Mall, Highland and several other detectives had sat across a rugged wood table from this young man and tried to start some kind of conversation. He was a strong one, Highland admitted to himself. He had spoken but one unnecessary word, and that only nine days before. A jailer with more indignation than professionalism had used the excuse of a plumbing problem in Miller's cell to move him temporarily to another. In the other were two ODCs, as they were called: Ordinary Decent Criminals, as opposed to the political kind that C-13 dealt with. One was awaiting sentencing for a series of vicious street robberies, the other for the gun-murder of a shop owner in Kensington. Both knew who Miller was, and hated him enough to look at the small young man as a way to atone for the crimes which they little regretted in any case. When Highland had shown up for yet another fruitless interrogation session, he'd found Miller facedown on the floor of the cell, his pants gone, and the robber sodomizing him so brutally that the policeman had actually felt sympathy for the terrorist.

The Ordinary Decent Criminals had withdrawn at Highland's command, and when the cell door was opened, Highland had himself picked Miller up and helped him to the dispensary. And there Miller had actually spoken to him as though to another human being. A single word from the puffy, split lips: "Thanks."

Cop rescues terrorist, Highland thought to himself, *some headline that would be.* The jailer had pleaded innocence, of course. There *was* a problem with the plumbing in Miller's cell—somehow the work order had got mislaid, you see—and the jailer had been called to quell a disturbance elsewhere. Hadn't heard a sound from that end of the cell block. Not a sound. Miller's face had been beaten to a bloody pulp, and certainly he'd have no toilet problems for a few more days. His sympathy for Miller had been short-lived. Highland was still angry with the jailer. It was his professionalism that was offended. What the jailer had done was, quite simply, wrong, and potentially the first step on a path that could lead back to the rack and hot pincers. The law was not so much designed to protect society from the criminals, but more profoundly to protect society from itself. This was a truth that not even all policemen understood fully, but it was the single lesson that Highland had learned from five years in the Anti-Terrorist Branch. It was a hard lesson to believe when you'd seen the work of the terrorists.

Miller's face still bore some of the marks, but he was a young man and he was healing quickly. Only for a brief few minutes had he been a victim, a human victim. Now he was an animal again. Highland was hard-pressed to think of him as a fellow man—but that was what his professionalism was for. *Even for the likes of you.* The policeman looked back out the rear window.

It was a boring drive, as it had to be with no radio, no conversation, only vigilance for something that almost certainly wasn't out there. Highland wished that he'd put coffee in his thermos instead of tea. They watched the truck pass out of Woking, then Aldershot and Farnham. They were in the estate country of Southern England now. All around them were stately homes belonging to the horse crowd, and the less stately homes of those whom they employed. It was a pity it was dark, Highland thought, this could be a very pleasant drive. As it was, the fog hung in the numerous valleys, and rain pelted the flat metal top of the van, and the van's driver had to be especially careful as he negotiated the narrow, twisting roads that characterize the English countryside. The only good news was the near-total absence of traffic. Here and there Highland saw a solitary light over some distant door, but there was little more than that.

An hour later, the van used the M-27 motorway to bypass Southampton, then turned south on a secondary—"Class A"—road for Lymington. Every few miles they passed through a small village. There were the beginnings of life here and there. A few bakeries had cars parked outside while their owners got fresh, hot bread for the

day's dinner. Early church services were under way already, but the
real traveling wouldn't start until the sun was up, and that was still
over two hours off. The weather was worsening. They were only a few
miles from the coast now, and the wind was gusting at thirty miles per
hour. It blew away the fog, but also drove sheets of cold rain and
rocked the van on its wheels.

"Miserable bloody day to take a boat ride," the other cop in the
back commented.

"Only supposed to be thirty minutes," Highland said, his own
stomach already queasy at the thought. Born in a nation of seamen,
Bob Highland detested traveling on the water.

"On a day like this? An hour, more like." The man started humming "A Life on the Rolling Wave" while Highland started regretting
the large breakfast he'd fixed before leaving home.

Nothing for it, he told himself. *After we deliver young Mr. Miller,
it's home for Christmas and two days off. I've bloody earned it.* Thirty
minutes later they arrived in Lymington.

Highland had been there once before, but he remembered more than
he could see. The wind off the water was now a good forty miles per
hour, a full gale out of the southwest. He remembered from the map
that most of the boat ride to the Isle of Wight was in sheltered waters—
a relative term, but something to depend on nonetheless. The ferry
Cenlac waited at the dock for them. Only half an hour before, the
boat's captain had been told that a special passenger was en route. That
explained the four armed officers who stood or sat in various places
around the ferry. A low-profile operation, to be sure, and it didn't
interfere with the ferry's other passengers, many of them carrying
bundles whose identity didn't need to be guessed at.

The Lymington to Yarmouth ferry cast off her lines at 8:30
exactly. Highland and the other officer remained in the van while the
driver and another armed constable who'd ridden in front stood outside. *Another hour,* he told himself, *then a few more minutes to deliver Miller to the prison, and then a leisurely drive back to London.
I might even stretch out and get a few winks.* Christmas Dinner was
scheduled for four in the afternoon—his contemplation of that event
stopped abruptly.

The *Cenlac* entered the Solent, the channel between the English
mainland and the Isle of Wight. If these waters were sheltered, Highland didn't want to think what the open ocean was like. The *Cenlac*

wasn't all that large, and the ferry lacked the weatherly lines of a blue-water craft. The channel gale was broad on her starboard beam, as were the seas, and the boat was already taking fifteen-degree rolls.

"Bloody hell," the Sergeant observed to himself. He looked at Miller. The terrorist's demeanor hadn't changed a whit. He sat there like a statue, head still against the van's wall, eyes still closed, hands in his lap. Highland decided to try the same thing. There was nothing to be gained by staring out the back window. There wasn't any traffic to worry about now. He sat back and propped his feet on the left-side bench. Somewhere he'd once read that closing one's eyes was an effective defense against motion sickness. He had nothing to fear from Miller. Highland was not carrying a gun, of course, and the keys to the prisoner's manacles were in the driver's pocket. So he did close his eyes, and let his inner ear come to terms with the rolling motion of the ferry without the confusion that would come from staring at the un-moving interior of the truck. It helped a little. His stomach soon started to inform him of its dissatisfaction with the current scheme of things, but it didn't get too bad. Highland hoped that the rougher seas farther out wouldn't change this. They wouldn't.

The sound of automatic weapons fire jerked his head up a moment later. The screams came next, from women and children, followed by the rough shouts of men. Somewhere an automobile horn started blar-ing and didn't stop. More guns started. Highland recognized the short bark of some detective's service automatic—answered at once by the staccato of a submachine gun. It couldn't have lasted more than a minute. The *Cenlac*'s own horn started blowing short, loud notes, then stopped after a few seconds while the auto's horn kept going. The screams diminished. No longer shrill cries of alarm, they were now the deeper cries of comprehended terror. A few more bursts of machine-gun fire crashed out, then stopped. Highland feared the silence more than the noise. He looked out the window and saw nothing but a car and the dark sea beyond. There would be more, and he knew what it would be. Uselessly his hand went inside his jacket for the pistol that wasn't there.

How did they know—how did the bastards know we'd be here!

Now came more shouts, the sound of orders that would not be disobeyed by anyone who wanted to live through this Christmas Day. Highland's hands balled into fists. He turned to look again at Miller. The terrorist was staring at him now. The Sergeant would have preferred a cruel smile to the empty expression he saw on that young, pitiless face.

The metal door shook to the impact of an open hand.

"Open the bloody door or we'll blow it off!"

"What do we do?" the other cop asked.

"We open the door."

"But—"

"But *what*? Wait for them to hold a gun at some baby's head? They've won." Highland twisted the handles. Both doors were yanked open.

There were three men there, ski masks pulled down over their faces. They held automatic weapons.

"Let's see your guns," the tall one said. Highland noted the Irish accent, not that he was very surprised by it.

"We are both unarmed," the Sergeant answered. He held both hands up.

"Out. One at a time, and flat on the deck." The voice didn't bother to make any threats.

Highland stepped out of the truck and got to his knees, then was kicked down on his face. He felt the other cop come down beside him.

"Hello, Sean," another voice said. "You didn't think we'd forget you, did you now?"

Still Miller didn't say anything, Highland thought in wonderment. He listened to the flat jingle of his chains as he hobbled out of the van. He saw the shoes of a man step to the doors, probably to help him down.

The driver must be dead, Highland thought. The gunmen had his keys. He heard the manacles come off, then a pair of hands lifted Miller to his feet. Miller was rubbing his wrists, finally showing a little emotion. He smiled at the deck before looking up at the Sergeant.

There wasn't much point in looking at the terrorist. Around them he saw at least three men dead. One of the black-clad gunman pulled a shattered head off a car's wheel, and the horn finally stopped. Twenty feet away a man was grasping at a bloody stomach and moaning, a woman—probably his wife—trying to minister to him. Others lay about on the deck in small knots, each watched by an armed terrorist as their hands sweated on the backs of their necks. There was no unnecessary noise from the gunmen, Highland noted. They were trained men. All the noise came from the civilians. Children were crying, and their parents were faring better than the childless adults. Parents had to be brave to protect their kids, while the single had only their own lives to fear for. Several of these were whimpering.

"You are Robert Highland," the tall one said quietly. "Sergeant Highland of the famous C-13?"

"That's right," the policeman answered. He knew that he was going to die. It seemed a terrible thing to die on Christmas Day. But if he was going to die, there was nothing left to lose. He wouldn't plead, he wouldn't beg. "And who might you be?"

"Sean's friends, of course. Did you really think that we'd abandon him to your kind?" The voice sounded educated despite the simple diction. "Do you have anything to say?"

Highland wanted to say something, but he knew that nothing would really matter. He wouldn't even entertain them with a curse—and it came to him that he understood Miller a little better now. The realization shocked him out of his fear. Now he knew why Miller hadn't spoken. *What damned fool things go through your head at a time like this,* he thought. It was almost funny, but more than that it was disgusting.

"Get on with it and be on your way."

He could only see the tall one's eyes, and was robbed of the satisfaction he might have had from seeing the man's reactions. Highland became angry at that. Now that death was certain, he found himself enraged by the irrelevant. The tall one took an automatic pistol from his belt and handed it to Miller.

"This one's yours, Sean."

Sean took the gun in his left hand and looked one last time at Highland.

I might as well be a rabbit for all that little fucker cares.

"I should have left you in that cell," Highland said, his own voice now devoid of emotion.

Miller considered that for a moment, waiting for a fitting reply to spring from his brain as he held the gun at his hip. A quote from Josef Stalin came to mind. He raised his gun. "Gratitude, Mr. Highland . . . is a disease of dogs." He fired two rounds from a distance of fifteen feet.

"Come on," O'Donnell said from behind his mask. Another black-clad man appeared on the vehicle deck. He trotted to the leader.

"Both engines are disabled."

O'Donnell checked his watch. Things had gone almost perfectly. A good plan, it was—except for the bloody weather. Visibility was under a mile, and—

"There it is, coming up aft," one man called.

"Patience, lads."

"Just who the hell are you?" the cop at their feet asked.

O'Donnell fired a short burst for an answer, correcting this oversight. Another chorus of screams erupted, then trailed quickly away into the shriek of the winds. The leader took a whistle from inside his sweater and blew it. The assault group formed up on the leader. There were seven of them, plus Sean. Their training showed, O'Donnell noted with satisfaction. Every man of them stood facing outward around him, gun at the ready in case one of these terrified civilians might be so foolish as to try something. The ferry's captain stood on the ladder sixty feet away, clearly worrying about his next hazard, handling his craft in a storm without engine power. O'Donnell had considered killing all aboard and sinking the boat, but rejected the idea as counterproductive. Better to leave survivors behind to tell the tale, otherwise the Brits might not know of his victory.

"Ready!" the man at the stern announced.

One by one the gunmen moved aft. There was an eight-foot sea rolling, and it would get worse farther out beyond the shelter of Sconce Point. It was a hazard that O'Donnell could accept more readily than the *Cenlac*'s captain.

"Go!" he ordered.

The first of his men jumped into the ten-meter Zodiac. The man at the controls of the small boat took alee from the ferry and used the power of his twin outboards to hold her in close. The men had all practiced that in three-foot seas, and despite the more violent waves, things went easily. As each man jumped aboard, he rolled to starboard to clear a path for the next. It took just over a minute. O'Donnell and Miller went last, and as they hit the rubber deck, the boat moved alee, and the throttles cracked open to full power. The Zodiac raced up the side of the ferry, out of her wind shadow, and then southwest toward the English Channel. O'Donnell looked back at the ferry. There were perhaps six people watching them pull away. He waved to them.

"Welcome back to us, Sean," he shouted to his comrade.

"I didn't tell them a bloody thing," Miller replied.

"I know that." O'Donnell handed the younger man a flask of whiskey. Miller lifted it and swallowed two ounces. He'd forgotten how good it could taste, and the cold sheets of rain made it all the better.

The Zodiac skimmed over the wavetops, almost like a hovercraft, driven by a pair of hundred-horsepower engines. The helmsman stood at his post 'midships, his knees bent to absord the mild buffeting as he piloted the craft through the wind and rain toward the rendezvous. O'Donnell's fleet of trawlers gave him a wide choice of seamen, and this wasn't the first time he'd used them in an operation. One of the gunmen crawled around to pass out life jackets. In the most unlikely event that someone saw them, they would look like a team from the Royal Marines' Special Boat Service, running an exercise on Christmas morning. O'Donnell's operations always covered the angles, were always planned down to the last detail. Miller was the only man he'd ever had captured; and now his perfect record was reestablished. The gunmen were securing their weapons in plastic bags to minimize corrosion damage. A few were talking to each other, but it was impossible to hear them over the howl of wind and outboard motors.

Miller had hit the boat pretty hard. He was rubbing his backside. "Bloody faggots!" he snarled. It was good to be able to talk again.

"What's that?" O'Donnell asked over the noise. Miller explained for a minute. He was sure it had all been Highland's idea, something to soften him up, make him grateful to the cop. That was why both his shots had gone into Highland's guts. There was no sense in letting him die fast. But Miller didn't tell his boss that. That sort of thing was not professional. Kevin might not approve.

"Where's that Ryan bastard?" Sean asked.

"Home in America." O'Donnell checked his watch and subtracted six hours. "Fast asleep in his bed, I wager."

"He set us back a year, Kevin," Miller pointed out. "A whole bloody year!"

"I thought you'd say that. Later, Sean."

The younger man nodded and took another swig of whiskey. "Where are we going?"

"Someplace warmer than this!"

The *Cenlac* drifted before the wind. As soon as the last terrorist had left, the captain had sent his crew below to check for bombs. They'd found none, but the Captain knew that could just mean they were hidden, and a ship was the perfect place to hide anything. His engineer and another sailor were trying to repair one of his diesels while his three deckhands rigged a sea anchor that now streamed over the stern to steady the ferry on the rolling seas. The wind drove the boat closer to land. That did give them more moderate seas, but to touch the coast in this weather was death for all aboard. He thought he might launch one of his lifeboats, but even that entailed dangers that he prayed he might yet avoid.

He stood alone in the pilothouse and looked at his radios—smashed. With them he could call for help, a tug, a merchantman, anything that could put a line on his bow and pull him to safe harbor. But all three of his radio transmitters were wrecked beyond repair by a whole clip of machine gun bullets.

Why did the bastards leave us alive? he asked himself in quiet, helpless rage. His engineer appeared at the door.

"Can't fix it. We just don't have the tools we need. The bastards knew exactly what to break."

"They knew exactly what to do, all right," the Captain agreed.

"We're late for Yarmouth. Perhaps—"

"They'll write it off to the weather. We'll be on the rocks before they get their thumbs out." The Captain turned and opened a drawer. He withdrew a flare pistol and a plastic box of star shells. "Two-minute intervals. I'm going to see to the passengers. If nothing happens in . . . forty minutes, we launch the boats."

"But we'll kill the wounded getting them in—"

"We'll lose bloody everyone if we don't!" The Captain went below.

One of the passengers was a veterinarian, it turned out. Five people were wounded, and the doctor was trying to treat them, assisted by a member of the crew. It was wet and noisy on the vehicle deck. The ferry was rolling twenty degrees, and a window had been smashed by the seas. One of his deck crew was struggling to put canvas over the hole. The Captain saw that he would probably succeed, then went to the wounded.

"How are they?"

The veterinarian looked up, the anguish plain on his face. One of his patients was going to die, and the other four . . .

"We may have to move them to the lifeboats soon."

"It'll kill them. I—"

"Radio," one of them said through his teeth.

"Lie still," the doctor said.

"Radio," he persisted. The man's hands were clasping bandages to his abdomen, and it was all he could do not to scream out his agony.

"The bastards wrecked them," the Captain said. "I'm sorry—we don't have one."

"The truck—a radio in the fucking truck!"

"What?"

"Police," Highland gasped. "Police van—prisoner transport . . . *radio. . . ."*

"Holy Jesus!" He looked at the van—the radio might not work from inside the ferry. The Captain ran back to the pilothouse and gave an order to his engineer.

It was an easy enough task. The engineer used his tools to remove the VHF radio from the truck. He was able to hook it up to one of the ferry's antennas, and the Captain was using it within five minutes.

"Who is this?" the police dispatcher asked.

"This is the *Cenlac,* you bloody fool. Our marine radios are out. We are disabled and adrift, three miles south of Lisle Court, and we need assistance at once!"

"Oh. Very well. Stand by." The desk sergeant in Lymington was no stranger to the sea. He lifted his telephone and ran his finger down a list of emergency numbers till he found the right one. Two minutes later he was back to the ferry.

"We have a tugboat heading towards you right now. Please confirm your position three miles south of Lisle Court."

"That is correct, but we are drifting northeast. Our radar is still operating. We can guide the tug in. For Christ's good sake, tell him to hurry. We have wounded aboard."

The Sergeant bolted upright in his chair. "Say again—repeat your last."

The Captain explained in as few words as possible now that help was en route to his ship. Ashore, the Sergeant called his superior, then the local superintendent. Another call went to London. Fifteen minutes later, a Royal Navy flight crew was warming up a Sea King rescue helicopter at Gosport. They flew first to the naval hospital at Portsmouth to pick up a doctor and a medical orderly, then reversed course into the teeth of the gale. It took twenty dreadful minutes to find her, the pilot fighting his aircraft through the buffeting winds while the copilot used the look-down radar to pick the ferry's profile out from the sea return on the scope. That was the easy part.

He had to give his aircraft more than forty knots of forward speed just to hold her steady over the boat—and the wind never stayed the same for more than a few seconds, veering a few degrees in direction, changing ten knots in speed as he struggled with the controls to maintain something like a hover over her. Aft, the crew chief wrapped the rescue sling around the doctor first, holding him at the open door. Over the intercom, the pilot told the chief to lower away. At least they had a fairly large target. Two crewmen waited on the top deck of the ferry to receive the doctor. They'd never done it before, but the helicopter crew had, dropping him rapidly to ten feet over the rocking deck, then more easily the last few feet. One crewman tackled the doctor and detached the collar. The medical orderly came next, cursing fate and nature all the way down. He too arrived safely, and the helicopter shot upward to get away from the dangerous surface.

"Surgeon Lieutenant Dilk, Doctor."

"Welcome. I'm afraid my practice is usually limited to horses and dogs," the vet replied at once. "One sucking chest, the other three are belly wounds. One died—I did my best, but—" there wasn't much else to say. "Fucking murderers!"

The sound of a diesel horn announced the arrival of the tugboat. Lieutenant Dilk didn't bother looking while the Captain and crew caught the messenger line and hauled in a towing wire. Together, the doctors administered morphine and worked to stabilize the wounded.

The helicopter was already gone southwest, a grimmer purpose to their second mission for the day. Another helicopter, this one with armed Marines aboard, was lifting off from Gosport while the first searched the surface with radar and eyes for a black ten-meter zodiac-type rubber boat. Orders had come from the Home Office with record speed, and for once they were orders that men in uniform were trained and equipped to handle: *Locate and destroy.*

"The radar's hopeless," the copilot reported over the intercom.

The pilot nodded agreement. On a calm day they'd have a good chance to pick the rubber boat out, but the return from the confused seas and the flying spray made radar detection impossible.

"They can't have gone too far, and visibility isn't all that bad from up here. We'll do a quartering search and eyeball the bastards."

"Where do we start?"

"Off the Needles, then inward to Christchurch Bay, then we'll work west if we have to. We'll catch the bastards before they make landfall and have the bootnecks meet them on the beach. You heard the orders."

"Indeed." The copilot activated his tactical navigation display to set up the search pattern. Ninety minutes later it was plain that they'd searched in the wrong place. Surprised—baffled—the helicopters returned to Gosport empty-handed. The pilot went into the ready shack and found two very senior police officers.

"Well?"

"We searched from the Needles to Poole Bay—we didn't miss a thing." The pilot traced his flight path on the chart. "That type of boat can make perhaps twenty knots in these sea conditions—at most, and then only with an expert crew. We should not have missed them." The pilot sipped at a mug of tea. He stared at the chart and shook his head in disbelief. "No *way* we could have missed them! Not with two machines up."

"What if they went seaward, what if they went south?"

"But where? Even if they carried enough fuel to cross the Channel, which I doubt, only a madman would try it. There will be twenty-foot seas out there, and the gale is still freshening. Suicide," the pilot concluded.

"Well, we know that they're not madmen, they're too damned smart for that. No way they could have gotten past you, made landfall before you caught up with them?"

"Not a chance. None." The flyer was emphatic.

"Then where the hell are they?"

"I'm sorry, sir, but I haven't a clue. Perhaps they sank."

"Do you believe that?" the cop demanded.

"No, sir."

Commander James Owens turned away. He looked out the windows. The pilot was right; the storm was worsening. The phone rang.

"For you, sir." A petty officer held it up.

"Owens. Yes?" His face changed from sadness to rage and back. "Thank you. Please keep us posted. That was the hospital. Another of the wounded died. Sergeant Highland's in surgery now. One of the bullets hit his spine. That's a total of nine dead, I believe. Gentlemen, is there anything you can suggest to us? I'd be quite willing to hire a gypsy fortune teller at the moment."

"Perhaps they made south from the Needles, then curved east and made landfall on the Isle of Wight."

Owens shook his head. "We have people there. Nothing."

"Then they might have rendezvoused with a ship. There is the usual amount of traffic in the Channel."

"Any way to check that?"

The pilot shook his head. "No. There's a ship-traffic-control radar at Dover Strait, but not here. We can't board every ship, can we?"

"Very well. Gentlemen, thank you for your efforts, particularly getting your surgeon out as quickly as you did. I was told that this action saved several lives." Commander Owens walked out of the building. Those left behind marveled at his self-control. Outside, the senior detective looked up into the leaden sky and swore a mental curse at fortune, but he was too consumed by anger to show what he felt. Owens was a man accustomed to concealing what he thought and felt. Emotions, he often lectured his men, had no place in police work. Of course that was false, and like many cops Owens only succeeded in turning his rage inward. That accounted for the packet of antacid pills always in his coat pocket, and the quiet spells at home that his wife had learned to live with. He reached in his shirt pocket for a cigarette that wasn't there, then snorted to himself—*how did you ever break that habit, Jimmy?* He stood alone in the parking lot for a moment, as though the cold rain would dampen his anger. But it only gave him a chill, and he couldn't afford that. He'd have to answer for this, answer to the Commissioner of the Metropolitan Police, answer to the Home Office. Someone—*not me, thank God*—would also have to answer to the Crown.

That thought hammered home. He had failed *them*. He'd failed them twice. He had failed to detect and prevent the original attack on The Mall, and only the incredible luck of that Yank's intervention had saved the day. Then, when everything had subsequently gone right, this failure. Nothing like this had ever happened before. Owens was responsible. It had all happened on his watch. He had personally set up the transport scheme. The method was of his choosing. He had established the security procedures. Picked the day. Picked the routes. Picked the men, all dead now, except for Bob Highland.

How did they know? Owens demanded of himself. *They knew when, they knew where. How did they know? Well,* he told himself, *that's one place to start looking.* The number of people who had this information was known to Owens. Somehow it had been leaked. He remembered the report Ashley had brought back from Dublin. "So good, you would not believe it," that PIRA bastard had said of O'Donnell's intelligence source. Murphy was wrong, the detective thought. Everyone will believe it now.

"Back to London," he told the driver.

"Great day, Jack," Robby observed on the couch.

"Not bad at all," Ryan agreed. *Of course the house looks like a Toys 'R Us that got nuked. . . .*

In front of them, Sally was playing with her new toys. She particularly liked the doll house, Jack was gratified to see. His daughter was winding down, having gotten her parents up at seven that morning. Jack and Cathy were winding down also after only five hours of sleep. That was a little tough on a pregnant wife, Jack had thought an hour earlier, and he and Robby had cleared away the dishes, now being processed by the dishwasher in the kitchen. Now their wives were on the other couch talking while the menfolk sipped at some brandy.

"Not flying tomorrow?"

Jackson shook his head. "The bird went tits-up, take another day or so to fix. Besides, what's Christmas without a good brandy? I'll be back in the simulator tomorrow, and regs don't prevent me from drinking before I do that. I don't strap in until three tomorrow, I ought to be fairly sober by then." Robby'd had one glass of wine with dinner, and had limited himself to only one Hennessy.

"God, I need a stretch." Jack stood up and beckoned his friend to the stairs.

"How late were you up last night, sport?"

"I think we hit the sack a little after two."

Robby checked to see that Sally was out of earshot. "Being Santa is a bitch, isn't it? If you can put all those toys together, maybe I ought to turn you loose on my broke airplane."

"Wait till I have both arms back." Jack pulled his arm out of the sling and moved it around as they went down to the library level.

"What's Cathy say about that?"

"What docs always say—hell, if you get well too soon, they lose money!" He moved his wrist around. "This thing knots up like you wouldn't believe."

"How's it feel?"

"Pretty good. I think I might get full use back. At least I haven't had it quit on me yet." Jack checked his watch. "Want to catch the news?"

"Sure."

Ryan flipped on the small TV on his deck. Cable had finally made it down his road, and he was already hooked on CNN. It was so nice to get the national and world news whenever you wanted. Jack dropped into his swivel chair while Robby selected another in the corner. It was a few minutes short of the hourly headlines. Jack left the sound down.

"How's the book coming?"

"Getting there. I have all the information in line, finally. Four more chapters to write, and two I have to change around some, and it's done."

"What did you change?"

"Turned out that I got bum data. You were right about that deck-spotting problem on the Japanese carriers."

"I didn't think that sounded right," Robby replied. "They were pretty good, but they weren't that good—I mean, we took 'em at Midway, didn't we?"

"What about today?"

"The Russians? Hey, Jack, anybody wants to fool with me and my Tomcat better have his will fixed up. They don't pay me to lose, son." Jackson grinned like a sleepy lion.

"Nice to see such confidence."

"There's better pilots than me," Robby admitted. "Three, as a matter of fact. Ask me again in a year, when I'm back in the groove."

"Oh, yeah!" Jack laughed. The laugh died when he saw the picture on the TV screen. "That's him—I wonder why—" He turned the sound up.

". . . killed, including five police officers. An intensive land, sea, and air search is under way for the terrorists who snatched their convicted comrade while en route to a British prison on the Isle of Wight. Sean Miller was convicted only three weeks before in the daring attack on the Prince and Princess of Wales within sight of Buckingham Palace. Two police officers and one of the terrorists were killed before the attack was broken up by American tourist Jack Ryan of Annapolis, Maryland."

The picture changed to show the weather on the Channel and a

Royal Navy helicopter, evidently searching for something. It changed again to a file tape of Miller being taken out of the Old Bailey. Just before he was put in the police van, Miller turned to face the camera, and now weeks later his eyes stared again into those of John Patrick Ryan.

"Oh, my God . . ." Jack muttered.

10

Plans and Threats

"You shouldn't blame yourself, Jimmy," Murray said. "And Bob's going to make it. That's something."

"Certainly," Owens replied sardonically. "There's even a fifty-percent chance that he'll learn to walk again. What of the others, Dan? Five good men gone, and four civilians along with them."

"And maybe the terrorists, too," Murray pointed out.

"You don't believe that any more than I do!"

It had come as a piece of blind luck. A Royal Navy mine-hunter ship conducting an ongoing sonar survey of the English Channel had found a new object on the bottom and immediately sent a camera sled down to classify it. The videotape showed the remains of a ten-meter zodiac-type inflatable boat, with two hundred-horse outboard motors. It had clearly sunk as the result of an explosion near the gas tanks, but there was no evidence of the men who'd been aboard, or their weapons. The vessel's skipper had immediately grasped the importance of the discovery and informed his superiors. A salvage crew was preparing now to go out and raise the wreck.

"It's a possibility. One of them might have screwed up, the boat blew, the bad guys get dumped in the drink . . ."

"And the bodies?"

"Fish food." Murray smirked. "Makes a nice image, doesn't it?"

"You are so fond of punting, Dan. Just what percentage of your salary would you wager on that hypothesis?" Owens wasn't in the mood for humor. Murray could see that the head of C-13 still looked on this as a very personal defeat.

"Not very much," the FBI representative conceded. "So you think a ship picked them up."

"It's the only thing that makes the least bit of sense. Nine merchant vessels were close enough to have been involved. We have the list."

So did Murray. It had already been forwarded to Washington, where the FBI and CIA would both work on it. "But why not recover the boat, too?"

"Obvious, isn't it? What if one of our helicopters saw them doing it? Or it might have been too difficult for the weather conditions. Or they might just not have wished to trouble themselves. They do have ample financial resources, don't they?"

"When will the Navy raise the wreck?"

"If the weather holds, day after tomorrow," Owens said. That was the one thing to be happy about. Then they'd have physical evidence. Everything made in the world carried trademarks and serial numbers. Somewhere there would be records of sale. That was how many successful investigations had started—a single sales slip in a single shop had often led to the conviction of the most dangerous criminals. From the videotape, the outboards on the boat looked like American Mercury motors. The Bureau had already been alerted to run that lead down as soon as the engine numbers were in. Murray had already learned that Mercury motors were a favorite all over the world. It would make matters harder, but it was still something; and something was always better than nothing. The resources of the Metropolitan Police and the Bureau were designed for precisely such a task.

"Any breaks on the leak?" Murray asked. This touched the rawest nerve of all.

"He'd better pray we don't find him," Owens said quietly. There was as yet no danger that this would happen. There had been a total of thirty-one people who'd known the time and route for the prisoner transfer, and five of them were dead—even the driver of the van hadn't known beforehand. That left twenty-six, ranging from a few members of C-13, two more high officials in the Metropolitan Police, ten in the Home Office, a few more in MI-5, the Security Service, and various others. Every one of them had a top-drawer security clearance. *Not that a clearance matters a damn,* Owens told himself again. *By definition a leak had to come from some bastard with a top-drawer clearance.*

But this was different. This was treason—it was *worse* than treason—a concept that Owens hadn't even thought possible until the last week. Whoever had leaked this had also to have been involved in the attack on the Royal Family. To betray national security secrets to a foreign power was sufficiently heinous to make the Commander think in unprofessional terms. But deliberately to endanger the Royal Family itself was so incomprehensible a crime that Owens had scarcely been able to believe it possible. This wasn't someone of dubious mental state. This was a person with intelligence and considerable skill at dissimulation, someone who had betrayed a trust both personal and national. There had been a time in his country when such people died by torture. It was not a fact that Owens was proud of, but now he understood why it had happened, how easily one might countenance such punishment. The Royal Family served so many functions for the United Kingdom, was so greatly loved by the people. And someone, probably someone very close to them, was quite willing to betray them to a small band of terrorists. Owens wanted that person. Wanted to see him dead, wanted to watch him die. There could be no other punishment for this kind of crime.

His professionalism returned after the few seconds of grim revelry. *We won't find the bastard by wishing him dead. Finding him means police work—careful, painstaking, thorough investigation.* Owens knew how to do that. Neither he nor the elite team of men on the investigation would rest until they succeeded. But none of them doubted that they would ultimately succeed.

"That's two breaks you have, Jimmy," Murray said after reading his friend's mind. It wasn't hard to do. Both men had handled hard cases, and police differ little over the world.

"Indeed," Owens said, almost smiling. "They ought not to have tipped their hand. They should have bent every effort to protect their source. We can compare the lists of who knew that His Highness was coming in that afternoon, and who knew that young Mr. Miller was going to Lymington.''

''And the telephone operators who put the calls through,'' Murray reminded him. ''And the secretaries and co-workers who might have overheard, and the girlfriends, or boyfriends, who might have heard during some horizontal conversation.''

''Thank you ever so much for that, Dan. One needs encouragement at a time like this.'' The Englishman walked over to Murray's cabinet and found a bottle of whiskey—a Christmas present, still unopened on New Year's Eve.

''You're right that they should have protected their intel source. I know you'll get him, Jimmy. I will put some money down on that.''

Owens poured the drinks. It was gratifying to see that the American had finally learned to drink his whiskey decently. In the past year Owens had broken Murray of the need to put ice in everything. It was shameful to contaminate single-malt Scotch whiskey. He frowned at another recurring thought. ''What does that tell us about Sean Miller?''

Murray stretched his arms out. ''More important than you thought, maybe? Maybe they were afraid you'd break information out of him. Maybe they just wanted to keep their perfect record. Maybe something else?''

Owens nodded. In addition to the close working relationship Scotland Yard had with the FBI, Owens valued the opinions of his colleague. Though both were experienced cops, Murray could always be trusted to have a slightly different slant on things. Two years before Owens had been surprised to learn how valuable this might be. Though he never had thought about it, Murray had used his colleague's brain the same way on several occasions.

''So what might that make Miller?'' Owens wondered aloud.

''Who can say? Chief of operations?'' Murray waved his glass.

''Awfully young for that.''

''Jimmy, the guy who dropped the atomic bomb on Hiroshima was a full colonel in the Air Force, and twenty-nine years old. Hell, how old is this O'Donnell character?''

''That's what Bob Highland thinks.'' Owens stared into his glass for a moment, frowning again.

''Bob's a smart kid, too. God, I hope you can put him back on the street.''

"If not, we can still use him in the office," Commander Owens said positively. "He does have a fine brain for the business of investigations—too good to be lost now. Well, I must be off. New Year's Eve, Dan. What do we drink to?"

"That's obvious. A successful investigation. You're going to get that source, Jimmy, and he's going to give you the information you need." Murray held his glass up. "To a closed case."

"Yes." Both men emptied their glasses.

"Jimmy, do yourself a favor and give it a night off. Clear the old head out and start fresh in the morning."

Owens smiled. "I'll try." He picked up his overcoat and walked toward the door. "One last thing. It hit me on the drive over. These chaps, the ULA, have broken all the rules, haven't they?"

"That's true enough," Murray replied as he locked up his files.

"There's only one rule they haven't broken."

Murray turned. "Oh? What's that?"

"They've never done anything in America."

"None of them do that." Murray dismissed the idea.

"None have had much of a reason before."

"So?"

"Dan, the ULA might have a reason now—and they've never been reticent about breaking the rules. It's just a feeling, no more than that." Owens shrugged. "Well. Good night, and a happy new year to you, Special Agent Murray."

They shook hands ceremonially. "And to you, Commander Owens. Give my love to Emily."

Dan saw him to the door, locked it, and returned to his office to make sure all his secure files were locked up properly. It was pitch dark outside at—he checked his watch—quarter to six.

"Jimmy, why did you say that?" Murray asked the darkness. He sat back down in his swivel chair.

No Irish terrorist group had ever operated in the United States. Sure, they raised money there, in the Irish neighborhoods and saloons of Boston and New York, made the odd speech about their vision for the future of a free, united Ireland—never bothering to say that as committed Marxist-Leninists, their vision of Ireland was of another Cuba. They had always been shrewd enough to know that Irish-Americans might not feel comfortable with that little detail. And there was the gun-running. That was largely something in the past. The PIRA and

INLA currently got most of their weapons on the open world market. There were also reports that some of their people had gotten training in Soviet military camps—you couldn't tell a man's nationality from a satellite photograph, nor could you recognize a specific face. These reports had never been confirmed sufficiently to be released to the press. The same was true of the camps in Libya, and Syria, and Lebanon. Some people, fair-skinned people, were being trained there—but who? The intelligence got a little confused on this point. It was different with the European terrorists. The Arabs who got caught often sang like canaries, but the captured members of the PIRA and INLA, and the Red Army Faction, and *Action-Directe* of France, and all the other shadowy groups gave up their information far more grudgingly. A cultural thing, or maybe they could simply be more certain that their captors would not—could not—use interrogation measures still common in the Middle East. They'd all been raised under democratic rules, and knew precisely the weaknesses of the societies they sought to topple. Murray thought of them as strengths, but recognized the inconveniences that they imposed on law-enforcement professionals. . . .

The bottom line was still that PIRA and INLA had never committed a violent crime in America. Never. Not once.

But Jimmy's right. The ULA has never hesitated to break a rule. The Royal Family was off-limits to everyone else, but not the ULA. The PIRA and INLA never hesitated to advertise its operations—every terrorist group advertises its operations. But not the ULA. He shook his head. There wasn't any evidence to suggest that they'd break this rule. It was simply the one thing that they hadn't done . . . yet. Not the sort of thing to start an investigation with.

"But what are they up to?" he said aloud. Nobody knew that. Even their name was an anomaly. Why did they call themselves the *Ulster* Liberation Army? The nationalist movement always focused on its Irishness, it was an Irish nationalist movement, but the ULA's very name was a regional expression. "Ulster" was invariably the prefix of the reactionary *Protestant* groups. Terrorists didn't have to make all that much sense in what they did, but they did have to make *some* sense. Everything about the ULA was an anomaly. They did the things no one else would do, called themselves something no else would.

They did the things no one else would. That's what was chewing on Jimmy, Murray knew. Why did they operate that way? There had to be a reason. For all the madness of their actions, terrorists were rational by their own standards. However twisted their reasoning appeared to an outsider, it did have its own internal logic. The PIRA and INLA had such logic. They had even announced their rationales, and their actions could be seen to fit with what they said: To make Northern Ireland ungovernable. If they succeeded, the British would finally have enough of it and leave. Their objective, therefore, was to sustain a low-level conflict indefinitely and wait for the other side to walk away. It did make conceptual sense.

But the ULA has never said what it's up to. Why not? Why should their objective be a secret? Hell, why should the existence of a terrorist group be a secret—if they're running operations, how can it be a secret; then why have they never even announced their existence, except within the PIRA/INLA community itself? This can't be completely unreasoned action, he reminded himself. *They can't be acting completely without reason and still be as effective as they've been.*

"Damn!" The answer was there. Murray could feel it floating at the edge of his consciousness, but his mind couldn't quite reach that far. The agent left his office. Two Marines were already patrolling the corridors, checking that the doors were locked. Dan waved to them on the way to the elevator, his mind still trying to assemble the pieces into a unified picture. He wished that Owens hadn't left so soon. He wanted to talk this one over with Jimmy. Maybe the two of them could make sense of it all. No, he told himself, not "maybe." They'd find it. It was there, waiting to be found.

I bet Miller knew, Murray thought.

"What a dreadful place," Sean Miller said. The sunset was magnificient, almost like one at sea. The sky was clear of the usual urban pollution, and the distant dunes gave a crisp, if crenelated, line for the sun to slide behind. The odd thing was the temperature range, of course. The noon temperature had reached ninety-two—and the locals thought of this as a cool day!—but now as the sun sank, a cool wind came up, and soon the temperature would drop to freezing. The sand couldn't hold the heat, and with the clear, dry air, it would just radiate away, back to the stars.

Miller was tired. It had been that sort of day: refresher training. He hadn't touched a weapon in nearly two months. His reactions were off, his marksmanship abysmal, his physical condition little better. He'd actually gained a few pounds on prison food, something that had come as quite a surprise. In a week he'd have that run off. The desert was good for that. Like most men born in the higher latitudes, Miller had trouble tolerating this sort of climate. His physical activity made him thirsty, but he found it difficult to eat when it was so hot. So he drank water and allowed his body to turn in on itself. He'd lose the weight and harden his body more quickly here than anywhere else. But that didn't make him like the place.

Four more of their men were here also, but the remainder of the rescue force had immediately flown home via Rome and Brussels, putting a new string of entry stamps on their "travel" passports.

"It's not Ireland," O'Donnell agreed. His nose crinkled at the smell of dust, and his own sweat. Not like home. No smell of the mist over the peat, or coke fires on the hearths, or the alcoholic ambience of the local pub.

That was an annoying development: no liquor. The locals had got another attack of Allah and decided that even the fellow members of the international revolutionary community could not break God's law. *What a bloody nuisance.*

It wasn't much of a camp. Six buildings, one of them a garage. An unused helicopter pad, a road half-covered with sand from the last storm. One deep well for water. A firing range. Nothing else. In the past as many as fifty people had cycled through here at a time. Not now. This was the ULA's own camp, well separated from camps used by other groups. Every one of them had learned the importance of security. On a blackboard in hut #1 was a schedule provided by other fair-skinned friends that gave the pass-over times for American reconnaissance satellites; everyone knew when to be out of sight, and the camp's vehicles were under cover.

Two headlights appeared on the horizon, heading south toward the camp. O'Donnell noted their appearance, but said nothing about it. The horizon was far away. He put his arms into the sleeves of his jacket to ward off the gathering chill as he watched the lights slide left and right, their conical beams tracing over the dunes. The driver was taking his time, Kevin saw. The lights weren't bouncing about. The climate made it hard for a man to push himself hard. Things would get done tomorrow, God willing. *Insh'Allah,* a Latin colleague had once told him, meant the same thing as mañana—but without the urgency.

The vehicle was a Toyota Land Cruiser, the four-wheel-drive that had replaced the Land-Rover in most places. The driver took it right into the garage before getting out. O'Donnell checked his watch. The next satellite pass was in thirty minutes. Close enough. He rose and walked into hut #3. Miller followed, waving to the man who'd just come into the camp. A uniformed soldier from the camp's permanent force closed the garage door, and otherwise ignored them.

"Glad to see you got out, Sean," the visitor said. He carried a small satchel.

"Thank you, Shamus."

O'Donnell held open the door. He was not one to stand on ceremony.

"Thank you, Kevin."

"You're just in time for dinner," the chief of the ULA said.

"Well, one can't always be lucky," Shamus Padraig Connolly said. He looked around the inside of the hut. "No wogs about?"

"Not in here," O'Donnell assured him.

"Good." Connolly opened his satchel and brought out two bottles. "I thought you might like a drop of the pure."

"How did you get it past the bastards?" Miller asked.

"I heard about the new rule. I told them I was bringing in a gun, of course." Everyone laughed as Miller fetched three glasses and ice. You always used ice in this place.

"When are you supposed to arrive at the camp?" O'Donnell referred to the one forty miles away used by the PIRA.

"I'm having some car trouble, and staying the night with our uniformed friends. The bad news is that they've confiscated my whiskey."

"Bloody heathens!" Miller laughed. The three men toasted one another.

"How was it inside, Sean?" Connolly asked. The first round of drinks was already gone.

"Could have been worse. A week before Kevin came for me, I had a bad time with some thugs—the peelers put them up to it, of course, and they had a merry time. Bloody faggots. Aside from that, ah, it is so entertaining to sit there and watch them talk and talk and talk like a bunch of old women."

"You didn't think that Sean would talk, did you?" O'Donnell asked reprovingly. The smile covered his feelings—of course they had all worried about that; they had worried most of all what might happen when the PIRA and INLA lads in Parkhurst Prison got hold of him.

"Good lad!" Connolly refilled the glasses.

"So, what's the news from Belfast?" the chief asked.

"Johnny Doyle is not very pleased with having lost Maureen. The men are becoming restless—not much, mind, but there is talk. Your op in London, Sean, in case you've not been told, had glasses filled and raised throughout the Six Counties." That most citizens in Northern Ireland, Protestant and Catholic, had been disgusted by the operation mattered not to Connolly. His small community of revolutionaries was the entire world.

"One does not get drunk for a failure," Miller observed sourly. *That bastard Ryan!*

"But it was a splendid attempt. It is clear enough that you were unlucky, no more than that, and we are all slaves to fortune."

O'Donnell frowned. His guest was too poetic for Kevin's way of thinking, despite the fact, as Connolly was fond of pointing out, that Mao himself had written poetry.

"Will they try to spring Maureen?"

Connolly laughed at that one. "After what you did with Sean here? Not bloody likely. How ever did you pull that off, Kevin?"

"There are ways," O'Donnell let it go at that. His intelligence source was under strict orders not to do a thing for two months. Dennis's bookstore was closed so far as he was concerned. The decision to use him to get information for the rescue operation hadn't come easy. That was the problem with good intelligence, his teachers had hammered into his head years before. The really valuable stuff was always a risk to the source itself. It was a paradox. The most useful material was often too dangerous to use, but at the same time intelligence information that could not be used had no value at all.

"Well, you've gotten everyone's attention. The reason I'm here is to brief our lads on your operation."

"Really!" Kevin laughed. "And what does Mr. Doyle think of us?"

The visitor crooked a comically accusing finger. "You are a counterrevolutionary influence whose objective is to wreck the movement. The op on The Mall has had serious repercussions on the other side of the Atlantic. We'll—excuse me, *they'll* be sending some of their chaps to Boston in another month or so to set things right, to tell the Yanks that they had nothing to do with it," Connolly said.

"Money—we don't need their bloody money!" Miller objected. "And they can put their 'moral support' up—"

"Mustn't offend the Americans," Connolly pointed out.

O'Donnell raised his glass for a toast: "The devil with the bloody Americans."

As he drank off the last of his second whiskey, Miller's eyes snapped open sharply enough to make a *click.*

"Kevin, we won't be doing much in the U.K. for a while. . . ."

"Nor in the Six Counties," O'Donnell said thoughtfully. "This is a time to lie low, I think. We'll concentrate on our training for the moment and await our next opportunity."

"Shamus, how effective might Doyle's men be in Boston?"

Connolly shrugged his shoulders. "Get enough liquor into them and they'll believe anything they're told, and toss their dollars into the hat as always."

Miller smiled for a moment. He refilled his own glass this time as the other two talked on. His own mind began assembling a plan.

Murray had had a number of assignments in the Bureau over his many years of service, ranging from junior agent involved in chasing down bank robbers to instructor in investigation procedures at the FBI Academy at Quantico, Virginia. One thing he'd always told the youngsters in the classroom was the importance of intuition. Law enforcement was still as much art as science. The Bureau had immense scientific resources to process evidence, had written procedures for everything, but when you got down to it, there was never a substitute for the mind of an experienced agent. It was mostly experience, Murray knew, the way you fitted evidence together, the way you got a feel for the mind of your target and tried to predict his next move. But more than experience, there was intuition. The two qualities worked together until you couldn't separate them in your own mind.

That's the hard part, Murray told himself on the drive home from the embassy. *Because intuition can run a little wild if there's not enough evidence to hold on to.*

"You will learn to trust your instincts," Murray told the traffic, quoting from his memorized class notes. "Instinct is never a substitute for evidence and procedure, but it can be a very useful tool in adapting one to another—oh, Dan, you would have made a hell of a Jesuit.'' He chuckled to himself, oblivious of the stare he was getting from the car on his right.

If it's so damned funny, why does it bother you?

Murray's instinct was ringing a quiet but persistent bell. Why had Jimmy said that? Obviously it was bothering him, too—but what the hell was it?

The problem was, it wasn't just one thing. He saw that now. It was several things, and they were interrelated like some kind of three-dimensional crossword puzzle. He didn't know the number of blanks, and he didn't have any of the clues to the words, but he did know roughly the way they fitted together. That was something. Given time, it might even be enough, but—

"Damn!" His hands gripped tight on the steering wheel as good humor again gave way to renewed frustration. He could talk it over with Owens tomorrow or the next day, but the bell told him that it was more urgent than that.

Why is it so damned urgent? There is no *evidence of anything to get excited about.*

Murray reminded himself that the first case that he'd broken more or less on his own, ten months after hitting the street as a special agent, had begun with a feeling like this one. In retrospect the evidence had seemed obvious enough once he'd put the right twist on it, but that twist hadn't occurred to anyone else. And with Murray himself it had begun as nothing more than the same sort of intellectual headache he was suffering through in his car. Now he was really mad at himself.

Fact: The ULA broke all the rules. Fact: No Irish terrorist organization had ever run an operation in the U.S. There were no more Facts. If they ran an op in America . . . well, they were undoubtedly mad at Ryan, but they hadn't made a move against him over here, and that would have been a hell of a lot easier than staging one in the U.S. What if Miller really was their chief of operations—no, Murray told himself, terrorists don't usually take things personally. It's unprofessional, and the bastards *are* professional. They'd have to have a better reason than that.

Just because you don't know what the reason is doesn't mean they don't have one, Danny. Murray found himself wondering if his intuition hadn't transformed itself into paranoia with increasing age. *What if there's more than one reason to do it?*

"There's a thought," he said to himself. One could be an excuse for the other—but what's the *it* that they want to do? *Motive*, all the police procedure manuals said, was the main thing to look for. Murray didn't have a clue on their motive. "I could go crazy doing this."

Murray turned left off Kensington Road, into the upscale neighborhood of flats where he had his official residence. Parking was the usual problem. Even when he'd been assigned to the counterespionage section of the New York City Field Office, parking hadn't been this bad. He found a space perhaps two feet longer than his car and spent nearly five minutes fitting the vehicle into it.

Murray hung his coat on the peg beside the door and walked right into the living room. His wife found him dialing the phone, a ferocious scowl on his face. She wondered what was wrong.

It took a few seconds for the overseas call to go into the proper office.

"Bill, this is Dan Murray . . . we're fine," his wife heard him say. "I want you to do something. You know that guy Jack Ryan? Yeah, that's the one. Tell him—hell, how do I say this? Tell him that maybe he should watch his back. . . . I know that, Bill. . . . I can't say, something's bothering me, and I can't—something like that, yeah. . . . I know they've never done it before, Bill, but it's still bothering me. . . . No, nothing specific that I can point to, but Jimmy Owens brought it up, and now he's got me worrying about it. Oh, you got the report already? Good, then you know what I mean."

Murray leaned back and stared at the ceiling for a moment. "Call it feeling, or instinct—call it anything you want, it's bothering me. I want somebody to act on it. . . . Good man. How's the family? Oh, yeah? Great! Well, I guess it'll be a happy new year for you. Okay. Take care. 'Bye." He set the phone down. "Well, that feels a little better," he said quietly to himself.

"The party starts at nine," his wife said. She was used to his bringing work home. He was used to having her remind him of his social obligations.

"I guess I better get dressed, then." Murray rose and kissed his wife. He did feel better now. He'd done *something*—probably no more than having people in the Bureau wonder what was happening to him over here, but he could live with that. "Bill's oldest is engaged.

He's going to marry her off to a young agent in the D.C. Field Office."

"Anyone we know?"

"New kid."

"We have to leave soon."

"Okay, okay." He walked to the master bedroom and started to change for the big embassy party.

11

Warnings

"As you see, ladies and gentlemen, the decision Nelson made in this case had the long-term effect of finally putting an end to the stultifying influence of the Royal Navy's formal tactics." Ryan closed his note folder. "There is nothing like a decisive victory to teach people a lesson. Questions?"

It was Jack's first day back at teaching class. The room had forty students, all third classmen (that title included the six female mids in the class), or sophomores in civilian terms, taking Ryan's introductory course in naval history. There were no questions. He was surprised. Jack knew he was a pretty good teacher, but not that good. After a moment, one of the students stood up. It was George Winton, a football player from Pittsburgh.

"Doctor Ryan," he said stiffly, "I've been asked to make a presentation on behalf of the class."

"Uh-oh." Jack took half a step backward and scanned the body of students theatrically for the advancing threat.

Mid/3 Winton walked forward and produced a small box from behind his back. There was a typed sheet on the top. The young man stood at attention.

"Attention to orders: For service above and beyond the duty of a tourist—even a brainless Marine—the class awards Doctor John Ryan the Order of the Purple Target, in the hope that he will duck the next time, lest he become a part of history rather than a teacher of it."

Winton opened the box and produced a purple ribbon three inches across on which was inscribed in gold: SHOOT ME. Below it was a brass bull's-eye of equal size. The mid pinned it to Ryan's shoulder so that the target portion almost covered where he'd been shot. The class stood and applauded as Ryan shook hands with the class spokesman.

Jack fingered the "decoration" and looked up at his class. "Did my wife put you up to this?" They started converging on him.

"Way to go, Doc!" said an aspiring submarine driver.

"Semper fi!" echoed a would-be Marine.

Ryan held up his hands. He was still getting used to the idea of having his left arm back. The shoulder ached now that he was really using it, but the surgeon at Hopkins had told him that the stiffness would gradually fade away, and the net impairment to his left shoulder would be less than five percent.

"Thank you, people, but you still have to take the exam next week!"

There was general laughter as the kids filed out of the room to their next class. This was Ryan's last for the day. He gathered up his books and notes and trailed out of the room for the walk uphill to his office in Leahy Hall.

There was snow on the ground this frigid January day. Jack had to watch for patches of ice on the brick sidewalk. Around him the campus of the Naval Academy was a beautiful place. The immense quadrangle bordered by the chapel to the south, Bancroft Hall to the east, and classroom buildings on the other sides, was a glistening white blanket with pathways shoveled from one place to another. The kids—Ryan thought of them as kids—marched about as they always did, a little too earnest and serious for Jack's liking. They saved their smiles for places where no outsiders might notice. Each of them had his (or her) shoes spit-shined, and they moved about with straight backs, books tucked under the left arm so as not to interfere with saluting. There was a lot of that here. At the top of the hill, at Gate #3, a Marine lance corporal stood with the "Jimmy Legs" civilian guard. A normal day at the office, Jack told himself. It was a good place to work. The mids were easily the equal of the students of any school in the country, always ready with questions, and, once you earned their trust, capable of some astonishing horseplay. This was something a visitor to the Academy might never suspect, so serious was the kids' public demeanor.

Jack got into the steam-heated warmth of Leahy Hall and bounded up the steps to his office, laughing to himself at the absurd award that dangled from his shoulder. He found Robby sitting opposite his desk.

"What in the hell is that?" the pilot inquired. Jack explained as he set his books down. Robby started laughing.

"It's nice to see the kids can unwind a little, even in exam season. So what's new with you?" Jack asked his friend.

"Well, I'm a Tomcat driver again," Robby announced. "Four hours over the weekend. Oh, man! Jack, I'm telling you, I had that baby talking to me. Took her offshore, had her up to mach one-point-four, did a midair refueling, then I came back for some simulated carrier landings, and—it was good, Jack," the pilot concluded. "Two more months and I'll be back where I belong."

"That long, Rob?"

"Flying this bird is not supposed to be easy or they wouldn't need people of my caliber to do it," Jackson explained seriously.

"It must be hard to be so humble."

Before Robby could respond, there came a knock on the opened door and a man stuck his head in. "Doctor Ryan?"

"That's right. Join us."

"I'm Bill Shaw, FBI." The visitor came all the way in and held up his ID card. About Robby's height, he was a slender man in his mid-forties with eyes so deep set that they almost gave him the look of a raccoon, the kind of eyes that got that way from sixteen-hour days. A sharp dresser, he looked like a very serious man. "Dan Murray asked me to come over to see you."

Ryan rose to take his hand. "This is Lieutenant Commander Jackson."

"Howdy." Robby shook his hand, too.

"I hope I'm not interrupting anything."

"Not at all—we're both finished teaching for the day. Grab a chair. What can I do for you?"

Shaw looked at Jackson but didn't say anything.

"Well, if you guys have to talk, I can mosey on over to the O-Club—"

"Relax, Rob. Mr. Shaw, you're among friends. Can I offer you anything?"

"No, thank you." The FBI agent pulled the straight-back chair from next to the door. "I work in the counterterrorism unit at FBI headquarters. Dan asked me to—well, you know that the ULA rescued their man Miller from police custody."

Now Ryan was completely serious. "Yeah—I caught that on TV. Any idea where they took him to?"

Shaw shook his head. "They just disappeared."

"Quite an operation," Robby noted. "They escaped to seaward, right? Some ship pick them up maybe?" This drew a sharp look. "You notice my uniform, Mr. Shaw? I earn my living out there on the water."

"We're not sure, but that is a possibility."

"Whose ships were out there?" Jackson persisted. This wasn't a law-enforcement problem to Robby. It was a naval matter.

"That's being looked at."

Jackson and Ryan traded a look. Robby fished out one of his cigars and lit it.

"I got a call last week from Dan. He's a little—I wish to emphasize this, only a little—concerned that the ULA might . . . well, they don't have much of a reason to like you, Doctor Ryan."

"Dan said that none of these groups has ever operated over here," Ryan said cautiously.

"That's entirely correct." Shaw nodded. "It's never happened. I imagine Dan explained why this is true. The Provisional IRA continues to get money from over here, I am sorry to say, not much, but some. They still get some weapons. There is even reason to believe that they have some surface-to-air missiles—"

"What the hell!" Jackson's head snapped around.

"There have been several thefts of Redeye missiles—the man-portable one the Army's phasing out now. They were stolen from a couple of National Guard armories. This isn't new. The RUC has captured M-60 machine guns that got over to Ulster the same way. These weapons were either stolen or bought from some supply sergeants who forgot who they were working for. We've convicted several of them in the past year, and the Army's setting up a new system things. Only one missile has turned up. They—the PIRA—tried to shoot down a British Army helicopter a few months back. It never made the papers over here, mainly because they missed, and the Brits were able to hush it up.

"Anyway," Shaw went on, "if they were to conduct actual terrorist operations over here, the money and the weapons would probably dry up quite a bit. The PIRA knows that, and it stands to reason that the ULA does, too."

"Okay," Jack said. "They've never operated over here. But Murray asked you to come here and warn me. How come?"

"There isn't any reason. If this had come from anyone except Dan, I wouldn't even be here, but Dan's a very experienced agent, and he's a little bit concerned that maybe you should be made aware of his—it's not even enough to be a suspicion, Doctor Ryan. Call it insurance, like checking the tires on your car before a long drive."

"Then what the hell are you telling me?" Ryan said testily.

"The ULA has dropped out of sight—that's not saying much, of course. I guess it's the way they dropped out of sight. They pulled a pretty bold operation, and"—he snapped his fingers—"disappeared back under their rock."

"Intel," Jack muttered.

"What's that?" Shaw asked.

"It happened again. The thing in London that I got in the way of, it resulted from very good intelligence information. This did, too, didn't it? They were moving Miller secretly, but the bad guys penetrated Brit security, didn't they?"

"I honestly don't know the specifics, but I'd say you probably had that one figured out pretty well," Shaw conceded.

Jack picked up a pencil in his left hand and started twirling it. "Do we know anything about what we're up against here?"

"They're professionals. That's bad news for the Brits and the RUC, of course, but it's good news for you."

"How's that?" Robby asked.

"Their disagreement with Doctor Ryan here is more or less a 'personal' matter. To take action against him would be unprofessional."

"In other words," the pilot said, "when you tell Jack that there's nothing for him to really worry about, you're betting on the 'professional' conduct of terrorists."

Errata

The following corrections pertain to a portion of the first printing of *Patriot Games:*

P. 218: At the beginning of the first line, add the words: ''to keep track of''.

P. 228: Delete the top line, which repeats the last line of p. 227. At the bottom of the page, add, as a new paragraph: *''Information—it's all a battle for information. You have to know''*.

P. 231: Delete the top line, which repeats the last line of p. 230.

P. 232: At the bottom of the page, add, as a new paragraph: '' 'I can't say.' ''

These errors are being corrected in subsequent printings.

"That's one way to put it, Commander. Another way is to say that we have long experience dealing with this type of person."

"Uh-huh." Robby stabbed out his cigar. "In mathematics that's called inductive reasoning. It's a conclusion inferred, rather than deduced from specific evidence. In engineering we call it a WAG."

"Wag?" Shaw shook his head.

"A Wild-Ass Guess." Jackson turned to stare into the FBI man's eyes. "Like most operational intelligence reports—you can't tell the good ones from the bad ones until it's too damned late. Excuse me, Mr. Shaw, I'm afraid that we operators aren't always impressed with the stuff we get from the intelligence community."

"I knew it was a mistake to come here," Shaw observed. "Look, Dan told me over the phone that he doesn't have a single piece of evidence to suggest that there is any chance something unusual will happen. I've spent the last couple of days going over what we have on this outfit, and there just isn't any real evidence. He's responding to instinct. When you're a cop, you learn to do that."

Robby nodded at that one. Pilots trust their instinct, too. Now, his were telling him something.

"So," Jack leaned back. "What should I do?"

"The best defense against terrorists—what the security schools teach business executives, for example—is to avoid patterns. Take a slightly different route to work every day. Alter your time of departure somewhat. When you drive in, keep an eye on the mirror. If you see the same vehicle three or more days in a row, take the tag number and call me. I'll be glad to have it run through the computer—no big deal. It's probably nothing to be worried about, just be a little bit more alert. With luck, in a few days or weeks we'll be able to call you and tell you to forget the whole thing. What I am almost certainly doing is alarming you unnecessarily, but you know the rule about how it's better to be safe than sorry, right?"

"And if you get any information the other way?" Jack asked.

"I'll be on the phone to you five minutes later. The Bureau doesn't like the idea of having terrorists operate here. We work damned hard to keep it from happening, and we've been very effective so far."

"How much of that is luck?" Robby asked.

"Not as much as you think," Shaw replied. "Well, Doctor Ryan, I'm really sorry to have worried you about what is probably nothing at

220 • TOM CLANCY

all. Here's my card. If there is anything we can do for you, don't hesitate to call me.''

"Thank you, Mr. Shaw." Jack took the card and watched the man leave. He was silent for a few seconds. Then he flipped open his phone list and dialed 011-44-1-499-9000. It took a few seconds for the overseas call to get through.

"American Embassy," the switchboard operator answered after the first ring.

"Legal Attaché, please."

"Thank you. Wait, please." Jack waited. The operator was back in fifteen seconds. "No answer. Mr. Murray has gone home for the day—no, excuse me, he's out of town for the remainder of the week. Can I take a message?"

Jack frowned for a moment. "No, thank you. I'll call back next week."

Robby watched his friend hang up. Jack drummed his fingers on the phone and again remembered what Sean Miller's face had looked like. *He's three thousand miles away, Jack,* Ryan told himself. "Maybe," he breathed aloud.

"Huh?"

"I never told you about the one I . . . captured, I guess."

"The one they sprung? The one we saw on TV?"

"Rob, you ever seen—how do I say it? You ever see somebody that you're just automatically afraid of?"

"I think I know what you mean," Robby said to avoid the question. Jackson didn't know how to answer that. As a pilot, he'd known fear often enough, but always there was training and experience to deal with it. There was no *man* in the world he'd ever been afraid of.

"At the trial, I looked at him, and I just knew that—"

"He's a terrorist, and he kills people. That would bother me, too." Jackson stood up and looked out the window. "Jesus, and they call 'em professionals! *I'm* a professional. I have a code of conduct, I train, I practice, I adhere to standards and rules."

"They're real good at what they do," Jack said quietly. "That's what makes them dangerous. And this ULA outfit is unpredictable. That's what Dan Murray told me." Jackson turned away from the window.

"Let's go see somebody."

"Who?"

"Just come along, boy." Jackson's voice had the ring of command when he wanted it to. He set his white officer's cap on his head just so.

They took the stairs down and walked east, past the chapel and Bancroft Hall's massive, prisonlike bulk. Ryan liked the Academy campus except for that. He supposed it was necessary for all the mids to experience the corporate identity of military life, but Jack would not have cared to live that way as a college student. The odd mid snapped a salute at Robby, who returned each with panache as he proceeded in total silence with Jack trying to keep up. Ryan could almost hear the thoughts whirring through the aviator's head. It took five minutes to reach the new LeJeune Annex across from the Halsey field house.

The large glass and marble edifice contrasted with Bancroft's stolid gray stone. The United States Naval Academy was a government complex, and hence exempt from the normal standards of architectural good taste. They entered the ground floor past a gaggle of midshipmen in jogging suits, and Robby led him down a staircase into the basement. Jack had never been here before. They ended up in a dimly lit corridor whose block walls led to a dead end. Ryan imagined he heard the crack of small-bore pistol fire, and it was confirmed when Jackson opened a heavy steel door to the Academy's new pistol range. They saw a lone figure standing in the center lane, a .22 automatic steady in his extended right hand.

Sergeant Major Noah Breckenridge was the image of the Marine noncommissioned officer. Six-three, the only fat on his two-hundred-pound frame was in the hot dogs he'd had for lunch in the adjacent Dalgren Hall. He was wearing a short-sleeved khaki shirt. Ryan had seen but never met him, though Breckenridge's reputation was well known. In twenty-eight years as a Marine, he had been everywhere a Marine can go, done everything a Marine can do. His "salad bar" of decorations covered five even rows, topmost among them the Navy Cross, which he'd won while a sniper in Vietnam, part of 1st Force Recon. Beneath the ribbons were his marksmanship medals—"shooting iron"—the least of which was a "Master" rating. Breckenridge was known for his weapons proficiency. Every year he went to the national championships at Camp Perry, Ohio, and in two of the past five years he had won the President's Cup for his mastery of the .45 Colt automatic. His shoes were so shiny that one could determine only with difficulty that the underlying leather was actually black. His brass shone like stainless steel, and his hair was cut so close that if any gray were in there, the casual observer could never have seen it. He had begun his career as an ordinary rifleman, been an Embassy Marine and a Sea Marine. He had taught marksmanship at the sniper school, been a drill instructor at Parris Island and an officer instructor at Quantico.

When the Marine detail at the Academy had been augmented, Breckenridge had been the divisional Sergeant Major at Camp Le-Jeune, and it was said that when he left Annapolis, he would complete his thirty-year tour of duty as Sergeant Major of the Corps, with an office adjoining that of the Commandant. His presence at Annapolis was no accident. As he walked about the campus, Breckenridge was himself an eloquent and unspoken challenge to whichever midshipman might still be undecided on his career goals: *Don't even think about being a Marine officer unless you are fit to command a man like this.* It was the sort of challenge that few mids could walk away from. The Marine force that backed up the civilian guards was technically under the command of a captain. In fact, as was so often the case with the Corps, the Captain had the good sense to let Breckenridge run things. The traditions of the Corps were not passed on by officers, but rather by the professional NCOs who were the conservators of it all.

As Ryan and Jackson watched, the Sergeant Major took a fresh pistol from a cardboard box and slipped a clip into it. He fired two rounds, then checked his target through a spotting scope. Frowning, he pulled a tiny screwdriver from his shirt pocket and made an adjustment to the sights. Two more rounds, check, another adjustment. Two more shots. The pistol was now perfectly sighted, and went back into the manufacturer's box.

"How's it going, Gunny?" Robby asked.

"Good afternoon, Commander," Breckenridge said agreeably. His southern Mississippi accent spilled across the naked concrete floor. "And how are you today, sir?"

"No complaints. I got somebody I want you to meet. This here's Jack Ryan."

They shook hands. Unlike Skip Tyler, Breckenridge was a man who understood and disciplined his strength.

"Howdy. You're the guy was in the papers." Breckenridge examined Ryan like a fresh boot.

"That's right."

"Pleased to meet you, sir. I know the guy who ran you through Quantico."

Ryan laughed. "And how is Son of Kong?"

"Willie's retired now. He runs a sporting goods store down in Roanoke. He remembers you. Says you were pretty sharp for a college boy, and I imagine you remember mosta what he taught you." Breckenridge gazed down at Jack with a look of benign satisfaction, as though Ryan's action in London was renewed proof that everything the Marine Corps said and did, everything to which he had dedicated his life, really meant something. He would not have believed otherwise in any case, but incidents like this further enhanced his belief in the image of the Corps. "If the papers got things straight, you did right well, Lieutenant."

"Not all that well, Sergeant Major—"

"Gunny," Breckenridge corrected. "Everybody calls me Gunny."

"After it was all over," Ryan went on, "I shook like a baby's rattle."

Breckenridge was amused by this. "Hell, sir, we all do that. What counts is gettin' the job done. What comes after don't matter a damn. So, what can I do for you gentlemen? You want a few rounds of small-bore practice?"

Jackson explained what the FBI agent had said. The Sergeant Major's face darkened, the jaw set. After a moment he shook his head.

"You're sweatin' this, eh? Can't say that I blame you, Lieutenant. 'Terrorists!'" he snorted. "A 'terrorist' is a punk with a machine gun. That's all, just a well-armed punk. It doesn't take much to shoot somebody in the back or hose down an airport waiting room. So. Lieutenant, you'll be thinkin' about carrying some protection, right? And maybe something at home."

"I don't know . . . but I guess you're the man to see." Ryan hadn't thought about it yet, but it was clear that Robby had.

"How'd you do at Quantico?"

"I qualified with the .45 automatic and the M-16. Nothing spectacular, but I qualified."

"Do you do any shootin' now, sir?" Breckenridge asked with a frown. Just qualifying wasn't a very hopeful sign to a serious marksman.

"I usually get my quota of ducks and geese. I missed out this season, though," Jack admitted.

"Uplands game?"

"I had two good afternoons after dove in September. I'm a pretty fair wing-shot, Gunny. I use a Remington 1100 automatic, 12-gauge."

Breckenridge nodded. "Good for a start. That's your at-home gun. Nothing beats a shotgun at close range—short of a flamethrower, that is." The Sergeant Major smiled. "You have a deer/slug barrel? No? Well, you're gonna get one of those. It's twenty inches or so, with a cylinder bore and rifle-type sights. You pull the magazine plug, and you got five-round capacity. Now most people'll tell you to use double-ought buck, but I like number four better. More pellets, and you're not giving any range away. You can still hit out to eighty, ninety yards, and that's all you'll ever need. The important thing is, anything you hit with buckshot's goin' down—period." He paused. "As a matter of fact, I might be able to get you some flechette rounds."

"What's that?" Ryan asked.

"It's an experimental thing they foolin' with down at Quantico for military police use, and maybe at the embassies. Instead of lead pellets, you shoot sixty or so darts, about three-caliber diameter, like little arrows. You gotta see what those little buggers do to believe it. Nasty. So that'll take care of home. Now, you gonna want to carry a handgun with you?"

Ryan thought about that. It would mean getting a permit. He thought he could apply to the state police for one . . . or maybe to a certain federal agency. Already his mind was mulling over *that* question.

"Maybe," he said finally.

"Okay. Let's do a little experiment." Breckenridge walked into his office. He returned a minute later with a cardboard box.

"Lieutenant, this here's a High-Standard target pistol, a .22 built on a .45 frame." The Sergeant Major handed it over. Ryan took it, ejected the magazine, and pulled the slide back to make sure the pistol was unloaded. Breckenridge watched and nodded approvingly. Jack had been taught range safety by his father twenty years before. After that he fitted the weapon in his hand, then sighted down the range to get used to the feel. Every gun is a little different. This was a target pistol, with nice balance and pretty good sights.

"Feels okay," Ryan said. "Little lighter than a Colt, though."

"This'll make it heavier." Breckenridge handed over a loaded clip. "That's five rounds. Insert the clip in the weapon, but do not chamber a round until I tell you, sir." The Sergeant Major was accustomed to giving orders to officers, and knew how to do so politely. "Step to lane four. Relax. It's a nice day in the park, okay?"

"Yeah. That's how this whole mess started," Ryan observed wryly.

The Gunny walked over to the switch panel and extinguished most of the lights in the room.

"Okay, Lieutenant, let's keep the weapon pointed downrange and at the floor, if you please, sir. Chamber your first round, and relax."

Jack pulled the slide back with his left hand, then let it snap forward. He didn't turn around. He told himself to relax and play the game. He heard a cigarette lighter snap shut. Maybe Robby was lighting up one of his cigars.

"I saw a picture of your little girl in the papers, Lieutenant. She's a pretty little thing."

"Thank you, Gunny. I've seen one of yours on campus, too. Cute, but not very little. I heard she's engaged to a mid."

"Yes, sir. That's my little baby," Breckenridge said, like a father rather than a Marine. "The last of my three. She'll be married—"

Ryan nearly jumped out of his skin as a string of firecrackers began exploding at his feet. He started to turn when Breckenridge screamed at him:

"There, there, there's your target!"

A light snapped on to illuminate a silhouette target fifty feet away. One small part of Ryan's mind knew this was a test—but most of him didn't care. The .22 came up and seemed to aim itself at the paper target. He loosed all five rounds in under three seconds. The noise was still echoing when his trembling hands set the automatic down on the table.

"Jesus Christ, Sar-major!" Ryan nearly screamed.

The rest of the lights came back on. The room stank of gunpowder, and paper fragments from the firecrackers littered the floor. Robby, Jack saw, was standing safely at the entrance to the Gunny's office, while Breckenridge was right behind him, ready to grab Ryan's gun hand if he did anything foolish.

"One of the other things I do is moonlight as an instructor for the Annapolis City Police. You know, it's a real pain in the ass trying to figure a way to simulate the stress of combat conditions. This here's what I came up with. Okay, let's get a look at the target."

Breckenridge punched a button, and a hidden electric motor turned the pulley for lane four.

"Damn!" Ryan growled, looking at the target.

"Not so bad," Breckenridge judged. "We got four rounds on the paper. Two snowbirds. Two in the black, both in the chest. Your target is on the ground, Lieutenant, and he's hurt pretty bad."

"Two rounds out of five—must be the last two. I settled down on them and took some more time."

"I noticed that." Breckenridge nodded. "Your first round was high and to the left, missed the card. Your next two came in here and here. The last two were on the money fairly well. That's not too bad, Lieutenant."

"I did a hell of a lot better in London." Ryan was not convinced. The two holes outside the black target silhouette mocked at him, and one round hadn't even found the target at all. . . .

"In London, if the TV got it right, you had a second or two to figure out what you were gonna do," the Gunny said.

"That's pretty much the way it was," Ryan admitted.

"You see, Lieutenant, that's the real important part. That one or two seconds makes all the difference, because you have a little time to think things over. The reason so many cops get killed is because they don't have that little bit of time to think it out—but the crooks have done that already. That one second lets you figure what's happening, select your target, and decide what you're gonna do about it. Now, what I just made you do was go through all three steps, all at once. Your first round went wild. The second and third were better, and your last two were good enough to put the target on the ground. That's not bad, son. That's about as well as a trained cop does—but you gotta do better than that."

"What do you mean?"

"A cop's job is to keep the peace. Your job is just staying alive, and that's a little easier. That's the good news. The bad news is, those bad guys ain't gonna give you two seconds to think unless you make them, or you're real lucky." Breckenridge waved for the men to follow him into his office. The Sergeant Major plopped down in his cheap swivel chair. Like Jackson, he was a cigar smoker. He lit up something better than what Robby smoked, but it still stank up the room.

"Two things you gotta do. One, I want to see you here every day for a box of .22; that's every day for a month, Lieutenant. You have to learn to shoot better. Shootin' is just like golf. You want to be good at it, you gotta do it every day. You have to work at it, and you need somebody to teach you right.'' The Gunny smiled. ''That's no problem; I'll teach you right. The second thing, you have to buy time for yourself if the bad guys come lookin' for you.''

''The FBI told him to drive like the embassy guys do,'' Jackson offered.

''Yeah, that's good for starters. Same as in Nam—you don't settle into patterns. What if they try to hit you at home?''

''Pretty isolated, Gunny,'' Robby said.

''You got an alarm?'' Breckenridge asked Ryan.

''No, but I can fix that pretty easy,'' Ryan said.

''It's a good idea. I don't know the layout of your place, but if you can buy yourself a few seconds, and you got that shotgun, Lieutenant, you can make 'em wish they never came calling—at least you can hold them off till the police come. Like I said, the name of the game's just staying alive. Now, what about your family?''

''My wife's a doc, and she's pregnant. My little girl—well, you saw her on TV, I guess.''

''Does your wife know how to shoot?''

''I don't think she's ever touched a gun in her life.''

''I teach a class in firearms safety for women—part of the work I do with the local police.''

Ryan wondered how Cathy would react to all this. He put that one off. ''What sort of handgun you think I oughta get?''

''If you come by tomorrow, I'll try you out on a couple of 'em. Mainly you want something you're comfortable with. Don't go out and get a .44 Magnum, okay? I like automatics, myself. The springs eat up a lot of the recoil, so they're easier to get comfortable with. You want to buy something that's fun to shoot, not something that beats up on your hand and wrist. Me, I like the .45 Colt, but I been shooting that little baby for twenty-some years.'' Breckenridge grabbed Ryan's right hand and flexed it around roughly. ''I think I'll start you off on a 9-millimeter Browning. Your hand looks big enough to hold it right— the Browning's got a thirteen-shot clip, you need a fair-sized hand to control it proper. Got a nice safety, too. If you have a kid in the house, Lieutenant, you'd better think about safety, okay?''

''No problem,'' Ryan said. ''I can keep it where she can't reach it—

"No problem," Ryan said. "I can keep it where she can't reach it—we got a big closet, and I can keep them there, seven feet off the floor. Can I practice with a big-bore handgun in here?"

The Sergeant Major laughed. "That backstop we got used to be the armor plate on a heavy cruiser. Mainly we use .22's in here, but my guards practice with .45's all the time. Sounds to me like you know shotgunnin' pretty good. Once you have that skill with pistol too, you'll be able to do it with any gun you pick up. Trust me, sir, this is what I do for a living."

"When do you want me here?"

"Say about four, every afternoon?"

Ryan nodded. "Okay."

"About your wife—look, just bring her over some Saturday maybe. I'll sit her down and talk to her about guns. Lots of women, they're just afraid of the noise—and there's all that crap on TV. If nothing else, we'll get her used to shotgunning. You say she's a doc, so she's gotta be pretty smart. Hell, maybe she'll like it. You'd be surprised how many of the gals I teach really get into it."

Ryan shook his head. Cathy had never once touched his shotgun, and whenever he cleaned it, kept Sally out of the room. Jack hadn't thought much about it, and hadn't minded having Sally out of the way. Little kids and firearms were not a happy mixture. At home he usually had the Remington disassembled and the ammunition locked away in the basement. How would Cathy react to having a loaded gun in the house?

What if you start carrying a gun around? How will she react to that? What if the bad guys are interested in going after them, too . . . ?

"I know what you're thinkin', Lieutenant," Breckenridge said. "Hey, the Commander said the FBI didn't think any of this crap was gonna happen, right?"

"Yeah."

"So what you're doin' is buyin' insurance, okay?"

"He said that, too," Ryan replied.

"Look—we get intel reports here, sir. Yeah, that's right. Ever since those bike bums broke in, we get stuff from the cops and the FBI, and from some other places—even the Coast Guard. Some of their guys come here for firearms training, 'cause of the drug stuff they got 'em doing now. I'll keep an ear out, too," Breckenridge assured him.

what's happening if you're going to do anything about it. Jack turned back to look at Jackson while he made a decision that he'd been trying to avoid ever since he got back from England. He still had the number in his office.

"And if they tell you those bike bums are coming back?" Ryan asked with a smile.

"They'll wish they didn't," the Sergeant Major said seriously. "This is a U.S. Navy reservation, guarded by the United States Marine Corps."

And that's the name of that tune, Ryan thought. "Well, thanks, Gunny. I'll get out of your way."

Breckenridge saw them to the door. "Sixteen hundred tomorrow, Lieutenant. How about you, Commander Jackson?"

"I'll stick to missiles and cannons, Gunny. Safer that way. G'night."

"Good night, sir."

Robby walked Jack back to his office. They had to pass on the daily drinks. Jackson had to do some shopping on the way home. After his friend left, Jack stared at his telephone for several minutes. Somehow he'd managed to avoid doing this for several weeks despite his wish to track down information on the ULA. But it wasn't just curiosity anymore. Ryan flipped open his telephone book and turned to the "G" page. He was able to call the D.C. area direct, though his finger hesitated before it jabbed down on each button.

"This is Mrs. Cummings," a voice answered after the first ring. Jack took a deep breath.

"Hello, Nancy, this is Doctor Ryan. Is the boss in?"

"Let me check. Can you hold for a second?"

"Yes."

They didn't have one of the new musical hold buttons there, Ryan noted. There was just the muted chirp of electronic noise for him to listen to. *Am I doing the right thing?* he wondered. He admitted to himself that he didn't know.

"Jack?" a familiar voice said.

"Hello, Admiral."

"How's the family?"

"Fine, thank you, sir."

"They came through all the excitement all right?"

"Yes, sir."

"And I understand that your wife's expecting another baby. Congratulations."

And how did you know that, Admiral? Ryan did not ask. He didn't have to. The DDI was supposed to know everything, and there were at least a million ways he might have found out.

"Thank you, sir."

"So, what can I do for you?"

"Admiral, I . . ." Jack hesitated. "I want to look into this ULA bunch."

"Yeah, I thought you might. I have here on my desk a report from the FBI's terrorism unit about them, and we've been coordinating lately with the SIS. I'd like to see you back here, Jack. Maybe even on a more permanent basis. Have you thought our offer over any more since we last spoke?" Greer inquired innocently.

"Yes, sir, I have, but . . . well, I am committed to the end of the school year." Jack temporized. He didn't want to have to face that particular question. If forced, he'd just say no, and that would kill his chance to get into Langley.

"I understand. Take your time. When do you want to come over?"

Why are you making it so easy? "Could I come over tomorrow morning? My first class isn't until two in the afternoon."

"No problem. Be at the main gate at eight in the morning. They'll be waiting for you. See ya."

"Goodbye, sir." Jack hung up.

Well, that was easy. Too easy, Jack thought. *What's he up to?* Ryan dismissed the thought. He wanted to look at what CIA had. They might have stuff the FBI didn't; at the least he'd get a look at more data than he had now, and Jack wanted to do that.

Nevertheless the drive home was a troubled one. Jack watched his rearview mirror after remembering that he'd left the Academy the same way he always did. The hell of it was, he *did* see familiar cars. That was a problem with making your commute about the same time every day. There were at least twenty cars that he had learned to recognize. There was someone's secretary driving her Camaro Z-28. She had to be a secretary. She was dressed too well to be anything else. Then there was the young lawyer in his BMW—the car made him a lawyer, Ryan thought, wondering how he had ever assigned tags to his fellow commuters. *What if a new one shows up?* he wondered. *Will you be able to tell which one is a terrorist?* Fat chance, he knew.

you be able to tell which one is a terrorist? Fat chance, he knew. Miller, for all the danger that lay on his face, would look ordinary enough with a jacket and tie, just another state employee fighting his way up Route 2 into Annapolis. . . .

"Paranoid, all this is paranoid," Ryan murmured to himself. Pretty soon he'd check the rear seat in his car before he got in, to see if someone might be lurking back there like on TV, with a pistol or garrote! He wondered if the whole thing might be a stupid, paranoid waste of time. What if Dan Murray just had a bug up his ass or was simply being cautious? The Bureau probably taught its men to be cautious on these things, he was sure. Do I scare Cathy over this? What if that's all there is to it?

What if it's not?

That's why I'm going to go to Langley tomorrow, Ryan answered himself.

They sent Sally to bed at 8:30, dressed in her bunny-rabbit sleeper, the flannel pajamas with feet that keep kids warm through the night. She was getting a little old for that, Jack thought, but his wife insisted on them, since their daughter had a habit of kicking the blankets on the floor in the middle of the night.

"How was work today?" his wife asked.

"The mids gave me a medal," he said, and explained on for a few minutes. Finally he pulled the Order of the Purple Target out of his briefcase. Cathy found it amusing. The smiling stopped when he related the visit from Mr. Shaw of the FBI. Jack ran through the information, careful to include everything the agent had said.

"So, he doesn't really think it'll be a problem?" she asked hopefully.

"We can't ignore it."

Cathy turned away for a moment. She didn't know what to make of this new information. *Of course,* her husband thought. *Neither do I.*

"So what are you going to do?" she asked finally.

"For one thing I'm going to call an alarm company and have the house wired. Next, I've already put my shotgun back together, and it's loaded—"

"No, Jack, not in this house, not with Sally around," Cathy said at once.

"It's on the top shelf in my closet. It's loaded, but it doesn't have a round chambered. She can't possibly get to it, not even with a stool to stand on. It stays loaded, Cathy. I'm also going to start practicing some with it, and maybe get a pistol, too. And"—he hesitated—"I want you to start shooting, too."

"No! I'm a doctor, Jack. I don't use guns."

"They don't bite," Jack said patiently. "I just want you to meet a guy I know who teaches women to shoot. Just meet the guy."

"No." Cathy was adamant. Jack took a deep breath. It would take an hour to persuade her, that was the usual time required for her common sense to overcome her prejudices. The problem was, he didn't want to spend an hour on the subject right now.

"So you're going to call the alarm company tomorrow morning?" she asked.

"I have to go somewhere."

"Where? You don't have any classes until after lunch."

Ryan took a deep breath. "I'm going over to Langley."

"What's at Langley?"

"The CIA," Jack answered simply.

"What?"

"Remember last summer? I got that consulting money from Mitre Corporation?"

"Yeah."

"All the work was at CIA headquarters."

"But—you said over in England that you never—"

"That's where the checks came from. That's who I was working for. But CIA was where I was working *at*."

"You lied?" Cathy was astounded. "You lied in a courtroom?"

"No. I said that I was never employed by CIA, and I wasn't."

"But you never told me."

"You didn't need to know," Jack replied. *I knew this wasn't a good idea. . . .*

"I'm your wife, dammit! What were you doing there?"

"I was part of a team of academics. Every few years they bring in outsiders to look at some of their data, just as sort of a check on the regular people who work there. I'm not a spy or anything. I did all the work sitting at a little desk in a little room on the third floor. I wrote a report, and that was that." There was no sense in explaining the rest to her.

"What was the report about?"

"Jack!" She was really mad now.

"Look, babe, I signed an agreement that I would never discuss the work with anybody who wasn't cleared—I gave my word, Cathy." That calmed her down a bit. She knew that her husband was a real stickler for keeping his word. It was actually one of the things she loved about him. It annoyed her that he used this as a defense, but she knew that it was a wall she couldn't breach. She tried another tack.

"So why are you going back?"

"I want to see some information they have. You ought to be able to figure out what that information is."

"About these ULA people, then."

"Well, let's just say that I'm not worried about the Chinese right now."

"You really are worried about them, aren't you?" She was starting to worry, finally.

"Yeah, I guess I am."

"But why? You said the FBI said they weren't—"

"I don't know—hell, yes, I *do* know. It's that Miller bastard, the one at the trial. He wants to kill me." Ryan looked down at the floor. It was the first time he'd said it aloud.

"How do you know that?"

"Because I saw his face, Cathy. I saw it, and I'm scared—not just for me."

"But Sally and I—"

"Do you really think he cares about that?" Ryan snapped angrily. "These bastards kill people they don't even know. They almost do it for fun. They want to change the world into something they like, and they don't give a damn who's in the way. *They just don't care.*"

"So why go to the CIA? Can they protect you—us—I mean. . . ."

"I want a better feel for what these guys are all about."

"But the FBI knows that, don't they?"

"I want to see the information for myself. I did pretty good when I worked there," Jack explained. "They even asked me to, well, to take a permanent position there. I turned them down."

"You never told me any of this," Cathy grumped.

"You know now." Jack went on for a few minutes, explaining what Shaw had told him. Cathy would have to be careful driving to and from work. She finally started smiling again. She drove a six-cylinder bomb of a Porsche 911. Why she never got a speeding ticket was always a source of wonderment to her husband. Probably her looks didn't hurt, and maybe she flashed her Hopkins ID card, with a story that she was heading to emergency surgery. However she did it, she was in a car with a top speed of over a hundred twenty miles per hour and the maneuverability of a jackrabbit. She'd been driving Porsches since her sixteenth birthday, and Jack admitted to himself that she knew how to make the little green sports car streak down a country road—enough to make him hold on pretty tight. This, Ryan told himself, was probably a better defense than carrying a gun.

"So, you think you can remember to do that?"

"Do I really have to?"

"I'm sorry I got us into this. I never—I never knew that anything like this would happen. Maybe I just should have stayed put."

Cathy ran her hand across his neck. "You can't change it now. Maybe they're wrong. Like you said, probably they're just acting paranoid."

"Yeah."

12

Homecoming

Ryan left home well before seven. First he drove to U.S. Route 50 and headed west toward D.C. The road was crowded, as usual, with the early morning commuters heading to the federal agencies that had transformed the District of Columbia from a picturesque plot of real estate into a pseudo-city of transients. He got off onto I-495, the beltway that surrounds the town, heading north through even thicker traffic whose more congested spots were reported on by a radio station's helicopter. It was nice to know why the traffic was moving at fifteen miles per hour on a road designed for seventy.

He wondered if Cathy was doing what she was supposed to do. The problem was that there weren't that many roads for her to use to get to Baltimore. The nursery school that Sally attended was on Ritchie Highway, and that precluded use of the only direct alternate route. On the other hand, Ritchie Highway was always a crowded and fast-moving road, and intercepting her wouldn't be easy there. In Baltimore itself, she had a wide choice of routes into Hopkins, and she promised to switch them around. Ryan looked out at the traffic in front of him and swore a silent curse. Despite what he'd told Cathy, he didn't worry overly much about his family. He was the one who'd gotten in the way of the terrorists, and if their motivation was really personal, then he was the only target. Maybe. Finally he crossed the Potomac River and got on the George Washington Parkway. Fifteen minutes later he took the CIA exit.

He stopped his Rabbit at the guard post. A uniformed security officer came out and asked his name, though he'd already checked Ryan's license plate against a computer-generated list on his clipboard. Ryan handed his driver's license to the guard, who scrupulously checked the photograph against Jack's face before giving him a pass.

"Sir, the visitors' parking lot is to the left, then the second right—"

"Thanks, I've been here before."

"Very well, sir." The guard waved him on.

The trees were bare. CIA headquarters was built behind the first rank of hills overlooking the Potomac Valley, in what had once been a lush forest. Most of the trees remained, to keep people from seeing the building. Jack took the first left and drove uphill on a curving road. The visitor parking lot was also attended by a guard—this one was a woman—who waved him to an open slot and made another check of Ryan before directing him toward the canopied main entrance. To his right was "the Bubble," an igloo-shaped theater that was connected to the building by a tunnel. He'd once delivered a talk there, a paper on naval strategy. Before him, the CIA building was a seven-story structure of white stone, or maybe prestressed concrete. He'd never checked that closely. As soon as he got inside, the ambience of spook-central hit him like a club. He saw eight security officers, all in civilian clothes now, their jackets unbuttoned to suggest the presence of side-arms. What they really carried was radios, but Jack was sure that men with guns were only a few feet away. The walls had cameras that fed into some central monitoring room—Ryan didn't know where that was; in fact, the only parts of the building he actually knew were the path to his erstwhile cubbyhole of an office, from there to the men's room, and the route to the cafeteria. He'd been to the top floor several times, but each time he'd been escorted since his security pass didn't clear him for that level.

"Doctor Ryan." A man approached. He looked vaguely familiar, but Jack couldn't put a name on the face. "I'm Marty Cantor—I work upstairs."

The name came back as they shook hands. Cantor was Admiral

Greer's executive assistant, a preppy type from Yale. He gave Jack a security pass.

"I don't have to go through the visitor room?" Jack waved to his left.

"All taken care of. You can follow me."

Cantor led him to the first security checkpoint. He took the pass from the chain around his neck and slid it into a slot. A small gate with orange and yellow stripes, like those used for parking garages, snapped up, then down again as Ryan stuck his card in the slot. A computer in a basement room checked the electronic code on the pass and decided that it could safely admit Ryan to the building. The gate went back up. Already Jack was uncomfortable here. *Just like before,* he thought, *like being in a prison—no, security in a prison is nothing compared to this.* There was something about this place that made Jack instantly paranoid.

Jack slung the pass around his neck. He gave it a quick look. It had a color photograph, taken the previous year, and a number, but no name. None of the CIA passes had names on them. Cantor led off at a brisk walk to the right, then left toward the elevators. Ryan noticed the kiosk where you could buy a Coke and a Snickers bar. It was staffed by blind workers, yet another of the oddly sinister things about the CIA. Blind people were less likely to be security risks, he supposed, though he wondered how they drove in to work every day. The building was surprisingly shabby, the floor tile never quite shiny, the walls a drab shade of yellow-beige; even the murals were second-rate. It surprised a lot of people that the Agency spent little on the outward trappings of importance. The previous summer Jack had learned that the people here took a perverse pride in the place's seediness.

Everywhere people walked about with anonymous haste. They walked so fast in the building that most corners had hubcap-shaped mirrors to warn you of possible collision with a fellow spook . . . or to alert you that someone might be lurking and listening around the corner.

Why did you come here?

Jack shook the thought off as he entered the elevator. Cantor pushed the button for the seventh floor. The door opened a minute later to expose yet another drab corridor. Ryan vaguely remembered the way now. Cantor turned left, then right, as Ryan watched people walking about with a speed that would impress a recruiter for the Olympic

Team's heel-and-toe crew. He had to smile at it until he realized that none of them were smiling. A serious place, the Central Intelligence Agency.

The executive row of CIA had its own private corridor—this one had a rug—that paralleled the main one and led to offices facing the east. As always, there were people just standing about and watching. They inspected Ryan and his pass, but showed no reaction, which was good enough news for Jack. Cantor took his charge to the proper door and opened it.

Admiral James Greer was in civilian clothes, as usual, leaning back in a high-backed swivel chair, reading an inevitable folder and sipping at inevitable coffee. Ryan had never seen him otherwise. He was in his middle sixties, a tall, patrician-looking man whose voice could be as courtly or harsh as he wished. His accent was that of Maine, and for all his sophistication, Ryan knew him to be a farmer's son who'd earned his way into the Naval Academy, then spent forty years in uniform, first as a submarine officer, then as a full-time intelligence specialist. Greer was one of the brightest people Ryan had ever met. And one of the trickiest. Jack was convinced that this gray-haired old gentleman could read minds. Surely that was part of the job description for the Deputy Director, Intelligence, of the Central Intelligence Agency. All the data gathered by spies and satellites, and God only knew what else, came across his desk. If Greer didn't know it, it wasn't worth knowing. He looked up after a moment.

"Hello, Doctor Ryan." The Admiral rose and came over. "I see you're right on time."

"Yes, sir. I remembered what a pain the commute was last summer." Without being asked, Marty Cantor got everyone coffee as they sat on chairs around a low table. One nice thing about Greer was that he always had good coffee, Jack remembered.

"How's the arm, son?" the Admiral asked.

"Almost normal, sir. I can tell you when it's going to rain, though. They say that may go away eventually, but it's like arthritis."

"And how's your family?"

The man doesn't miss a trick, Jack thought. But Jack had one of his own. "A little tense at the moment, sir. I broke the news to Cathy last night. She's not real happy about it, but then neither am I." *Let's get down to business, Admiral.*

"So what exactly can we do for you?" Greer's demeanor changed from pleasant old gentleman to professional intelligence officer.

"Sir, I know this is asking a lot, but I'd like to see what the Agency has on these ULA characters."

"Not a hell of a lot." Cantor snorted. "These boys cover their tracks like real pros. They're being bankrolled in a pretty big way—that's inferred, of course, but it has to be true."

"Where does your data come from?"

Cantor looked over to Greer and got a nod. "Doctor, before we go any further, we have to talk about classification."

Resignedly: "Yeah. What do I have to sign?"

"We'll take care of that before you leave. We'll show you just about everything we've got. What you have to know now is that this stuff is classified SI-codeword."

"Well, that's no surprise." Ryan sighed. Special-Intelligence-Codeword was a level of classification higher than top secret. People had to be individually cleared for the data, which was identified by a special codeword. Even the codeword itself was secret. Ryan had only twice before seen data of this sensitivity. *But now they're going to lay it all out in front of me,* he thought as he looked at Cantor. *Greer must really want me back to open a door like this.* "So, like I said, where does it come from?"

"Some from the Brits—actually from the PIRA via the Brits. Some new stuff from the Italians—"

"Italians?" Ryan was surprised for a moment, then realized what the implications of that were. "Oh. Okay, yeah, they have a lot of people down in sand-dune country, don't they?"

"One of them ID'd your friend Sean Miller last week. He was getting off a certain ship that was, miraculously enough, in the English Channel on Christmas Day," Greer said.

"But we don't know where he is?"

"He and an unknown number of associates headed south." Cantor smiled. "Of course the whole country is south of the Med, so that's not much of a help."

"The FBI has everything we have, and so do the Brits," Greer said. "It's not much to go on, but we do have a team sifting through it."

"Thanks for letting me take a look, Admiral."

"We're not doing this out of charity, Doctor Ryan," the Admiral pointed out. "I'm hoping that you might find something useful. And this thing has a price for you, too. If you want in, you will be an Agency employee by the end of the day. We can even arrange for you to have a federal pistol permit."

"How did you know—"

"It's my job to know, sonny." The old man grinned at him. Ryan didn't think this situation was the least bit funny, but he granted the Admiral his points.

"When can I start?"

"How does your schedule look?"

"I can work on that," Jack said cautiously. "I can be here Tuesday morning, and maybe work one full day per week, plus two half-days. In the mornings. Most of my classes are in the afternoon. Semester break is coming up, and then I can give you a full week."

"Very well. You can work out the details with Marty. Go take care of the paperwork. Nice to see you again, Jack."

Jack shook his hand once more. "Thank you, sir."

Greer watched the door close before he went back to the desk. He waited a few seconds for Ryan and Cantor to clear the corridor, then walked out to the corner office that belonged to the Director of Central Intelligence.

"Well?" Judge Arthur Moore asked.

"We got him," Greer reported.

"How's the clearance procedure going?"

"Clean. He was a little too sharp doing his stock deals a few years back, but, hell, he was supposed to be sharp."

"Nothing illegal?" Judge Moore asked. The Agency didn't need someone who might be investigated by the SEC. Greer shook his head.

"Nah, just very smart."

"Fine. But he doesn't see anything but this terrorist stuff until the clearance procedures are complete."

"Okay, Arthur!"

"And I don't have Deputy Directors to do our recruiting," the DCI pointed out.

"You're taking this awfully hard. Does a bottle of bourbon put that much of a dent in your bank account?"

The Judge laughed. The day after Miller had been sprung from British custody, Greer had made the gentlemanly wager. Moore didn't like losing at anything—he'd been a trial lawyer before becoming a

jurist—but it was nice to know that his DDI had a head for prog-
nostication.

"I'm having Cantor get him a gun permit, too," Greer added.

"You sure that's a good idea?"

"I think so."

"So it's decided, then?" Miller asked quietly.

O'Donnell looked over at the younger man, knowing why the plan
had been formulated. It was a good plan, he admitted to himself, an
effective plan. It had elements of brilliance in its daring. But Sean had
allowed personal feelings to influence his judgment. That wasn't so
good.

He turned toward the window. The French countryside was dark,
thirty thousand feet below the airliner. All those peaceful people,
sleeping in their homes, safe and secure. They were on a red-eye
flight, and the plane was nearly empty. The stewardess dozed a few
rows aft, and there was no one about to hear what they were saying.
The whine of the jet engines would keep any electronic listening device from working, and they'd been very careful to cover their tracks.
First the flight to Bucharest, then to Prague, then to Paris, and now the
flight home to Ireland, with only French entry stamps on their passports. O'Donnell was a careful man, to the point of carrying notes on
his fictitious business meetings in France. They'd get through customs
easily enough, O'Donnell was sure. It was late, and the clerks at
passport control were scheduled to go home right after this flight
arrived.

Sean had a completely new passport, with the proper stamps, of
course. His eyes were now brown, courtesy of some contact lenses, his
hair changed in color and style, a neatly trimmed beard changing the
shape of his face. Sean hated the beard for its itching, O'Donnell
smiled at the darkness. Well, he'd have to get used to that.

Sean didn't say anything else. He sat back and pretended to read
through the magazine he'd found in the seat pocket. The pretended
patience was gratifying to his chief. The young man had gone through
his refresher training (O'Donnell thought in military terms for this sort
of thing) with a passion, trimming off the excess weight, reacquainting
himself with his weapons, conferring with the intelligence officers
from other fair-skinned nations, and living through their critique of the
failed operation in London. These "friends" had not acknowledged

the luck factor, and pointed out that another car of men had been needed to ensure success. Through all of it, Sean had kept his peace and listened politely. And now he waited patiently for the decision on his proposed operation. Perhaps the young man had learned something in that English jail.

"Yes."

Ryan signed the form, acknowledging receipt of the cartful of information. He was back in the same cubbyhole office he'd had the previous summer, a windowless, closet-sized room on the third floor of CIA's main building. His desk was about the smallest size made—in federal prison workshops—for office use, and the swivel chair was a cheap one. CIA chic.

The messenger stacked the documents on the corner of Ryan's desk and wheeled the cart back out of the room. Jack went to work. He took the top off a Styrofoam cup of coffee bought at the kiosk around the corner, dumped in the whole container of creamer and two envelopes of sugar, and stirred it with a pencil as he often did. It was a habit his wife loathed.

The pile was about nine inches high. The files were in oversized envelopes, each of which had an alpha-numeric code stamped on in block figures. The file folders he removed from the top envelope were trimmed with red tape so as to look important—the visual cues were designed to be noticed, to stand out visually. Such files had to be locked up in secure cabinets every night, never left on a desk where someone might take an unauthorized look at them. The papers inside each were held in place with Acco fasteners, and all had numbers. The cover of the first file had its codeword neatly typed on a paper label: FIDELITY. Ryan knew that the code names were assigned at random by a computer, and he wondered how many such files and names there were, if the dictionary of the English language that resided in the computer's memory had been seriously depleted by the elimination of words for the thousands of secret files that sat in cabinets throughout the building. He hesitated for a moment before opening it, as though doing so would irrevocably commit him to employment at CIA; as though the first step on that path had not already been taken. . . .

Enough of that, he told himself, and opened the file. It was the first official CIA report on the ULA, barely a year old.

"Ulster Liberation Army," the title of the report read. "Genesis of an Anomaly."

"Anomaly." That was the word Murray had used, Ryan remembered. The first paragraph of the report stated with disarming honesty that the information contained in the following thirty single-spaced pages was more speculation than fact, based principally on data gotten from convicted PIRA members—specifically on denials they'd made. *That wasn't* our *operation,* some of them had said after being caught for another. Ryan frowned. Not exactly the most reliable of evidence. The two men who'd done the report, however, had done a superb job of cross-referencing. The most unlikely story, heard from four separate sources, changed to something else. It was particularly true since the PIRA was, technically speaking, a professional outfit. Jack knew from his own research the previous year that the Provisional Wing of the Irish Republican Army was superbly organized, along the classic cellular lines. It was just like any intelligence agency. With the exception of a handful of top people, the specifics of any particular operation were compartmentalized: known only to those who really needed to know. "Need-to-know" was the catch phrase in any intelligence agency.

Therefore, if the details of an operation are *widely known,* the report argued, *it can only be because it was not a PIRA op. Otherwise they would not have known or talked about the details, even among themselves.* This was twisted logic, Jack thought, but fairly convincing nonetheless. The theory held insofar as the PIRA's main rival, the less well organized Irish National Liberation Army, the gang that had killed Lord Louis Mountbatten, had often had its operations identified in the same way. The rivalry between PIRA and INLA had turned vicious often enough, though the latter, with its lack of internal unity and generally amateurish organization, was not nearly as effective.

It was barely a year since the ULA had emerged from the shadows to take some kind of shape. For the first year they'd operated, it was thought by the British that they were a PIRA Special Action Group, a Provo hit squad, a theory broken when a captured PIRA member had indignantly denied complicity in what had turned out to be a ULA assassination. The authors of the report then examined suspected ULA operations, pointing to operational patterns. These, Ryan saw, were quite real. For one thing, they involved more people, on average, than PIRA ops.

That's interesting. . . . Ryan walked out of the room, heading down the corridor to the kiosk, where he bought a pack of cigarettes. In under a minute he was back to his office, fumbling with the cipher lock on the door.

More people per operation. Ryan lit one of the low-tar smokes. That was a violation of ordinary security procedures. The more people involved in an operation, the greater the risk of its being blown. What did this mean? Ryan examined three separate operations, looking for his own patterns.

It was clear after ten minutes of examination. The ULA was more of a military organization than PIRA. Instead of the small, independent groups typical of urban terrorists, the ULA organized itself more on classic military lines. The PIRA often depended on a single "cowboy" assassin, less often on the special action groups. There were many cases Ryan knew of, where the one "designated hitter"—a term popular in CIA the previous year—had his own special gun, and lay in wait like a deer hunter, often for days, to kill a specific target. But the ULA was different. For one thing they didn't generally go for individual targets. They relied, it seemed, on a reconnaissance team and an assault team that worked in close cooperation—the operative word here was "seemed," Ryan read, since this, again, was something inferred from scanty evidence. When they did something, they usually got away cleanly. Planning and resources.

Classic military lines. That implied a great deal of confidence by the ULA in its people—and in its security. Jack started making notes. The actual facts in the report were thin—he counted six—but the analysis was interesting. The ULA showed a very high degree of professionalism in its planning and execution of operations, more so than the PIRA, which was itself proficient enough. Instead of a small number of really sharp operatives, it appeared that weapons expertise was uniform throughout the small organization. The uniformity of expertise was interesting.

Military training? Ryan wrote down. *How good? Where done? What source?* He looked at the next report. It was dated some months after "Genesis" and showed a greater degree of institutional interest. CIA had begun to take a closer look at the ULA, starting seven months previously. *Right after I left here,* Jack noted. *Coincidence.*

This one concentrated on Kevin O'Donnell, the suspected leader of the ULA. The first thing Ryan saw was a photograph taken from a British intelligence-gathering team. The man was fairly tall, but otherwise ordinary. The photo was dated years before, and the next thing Jack read was that the man had reportedly had plastic surgery to change his face. Jack studied the photo anyway. He'd been at a funeral for a PIRA member killed by the Ulster Defense Regiment. The face was solemn enough, with a hardness around the eyes. He wondered how much he could draw from a single photo of a man at a funeral for a comrade, and set the picture aside to read the biography of the man.

A working-class background. His father had been a truck driver. His mother had died when he was nine. Catholic schools, of course. A copy of his college transcript showed him to be bright enough. O'Donnell had graduated from university with honors, and his degree was in political science. He'd taken every course on Marxism that the institution had offered, and been involved on the fringes of civil-rights groups in the late sixties and early seventies. This had earned him attention from the RUC and British intelligence agencies. Then, after graduating, he'd dropped out of sight for a year, reappearing in 1972 after the Bloody Sunday fiasco when British Army paratroopers had gotten out of control and fired into a crowd of demonstrators, killing fourteen people, none of whom had been proven to have a gun.

"There's a coincidence," Ryan whispered to himself. The paratroopers still claimed that they'd been fired upon from someone in the crowd and merely returned fire to defend themselves. An official government report done by the British backed this up—of course, what else could they say? Ryan shrugged. It might even have been true. The biggest mistake the English had ever made was to send troops into Northern Ireland. What they'd needed was good cops to reestablish law and order, not an army of occupation. But with the RUC out of control then, and supplemented by the B-Special thugs, there hadn't been a real alternative. So soldiers had been sent in, to a situation for which they were unsuited by training . . . and vulnerable to provocation.

Ryan's antennae twitched at that.

Political-science major, heavy course-load in Marxism. O'Donnell had dropped out of sight, then reappeared about a year later immediately after the Bloody Sunday disaster, and soon thereafter was identified by an informer as the PIRA's chief of internal security. He didn't get that job on the basis of college classwork. He'd had to work to earn that. Terrorism, like any other profession, has its apprenticeship. Somehow this Kevin Joseph O'Donnell had earned his spurs. *How did you do that? Were you one of the guys who stage-managed the provocations? If so, where did you learn how, and does that missing year have anything to do with it? Were you trained in urban insurgency tactics . . . in the Crimea maybe . . . ?*

Too much of a coincidence, Jack told himself. The idea of Soviet training for the hard-core members of the PIRA and INLA had been bandied about so much that it had lost credibility. Besides, it didn't have to be something that dramatic. They might just have figured out the proper tactics for themselves, or read them in books. There were plenty of books on the subject of how to be an urban guerrilla. Jack had read several of them.

He flipped forward in time to O'Donnell's second disappearance. Here the information from British sources was fairly complete for once. O'Donnell had been remarkably effective as chief of internal security. Nearly half the people he'd killed really had been informers of one sort or another, not a bad percentage in this sort of business. He found a couple of new pages at the end of the report, and read the information that David Ashley had gathered a few months before in Dublin. . . . *He got a little carried away.* . . . O'Donnell had used his position to eliminate Provos whose politics didn't quite agree with his. It had been discovered, and he'd vanished for a second time. Again the data was speculative, but it tracked with what Murray had told him in London. O'Donnell *had* gone somewhere.

Surely he'd convinced someone to provide his nascent organization with financing, training, and support. *His nascent organization,* Ryan thought. *Where had it come from?* There was a lapse of two years before O'Donnell's disappearance from Ulster and the first positively identified operation of the ULA. Two complete years. The Brit intel data suggested plastic surgery. Where? Who paid for it? *He didn't do that in some jerkwater third-world country,* Ryan told himself. He wondered if Cathy could ask her colleagues at Hopkins about the availability of good face-cutters. *Two years to change his face, get financial backing, recruit his troops, establish a base of operations, and begin to make his impact.* . . . *Not bad,* Ryan thought with grudging admiration. All that in two years.

Another year before the name of the outfit surfaces. . . .

Ryan turned when he heard someone working the lock on his office door. It was Marty Cantor.

"I thought you stopped smoking." He pointed at the cigarette.

Ryan crushed it out. "So does my wife. Have you seen all this stuff?"

"Yeah." Cantor nodded. "The boss had me run through it over the weekend. What do you think?"

"I think this O'Donnell character is one formidable son of a bitch. He's got his outfit organized and trained like a real army. It's small enough that he knows every one of them. His ideological background tells me he's a careful recruiter. He has an unusually high degree of trust in his troops. He's a political animal, but he knows how to think and plan like a soldier. Who trained him?"

"Nobody knows," Cantor replied. "I think you can overestimate that factor, though."

"I know that," Ryan agreed. "What I'm looking for is . . . flavor, I guess. I'm trying to get a feel for how he thinks. It would also be nice to know who's bankrolling him." Ryan paused, and something else leaped into his mind. "What are the chances that he has people inside the PIRA?"

"What do you mean?"

"He runs for his life when he finds out that the PIRA leadership is out for his ass. Two years later, he's back in business with his own organization. Where did the troops come from?"

"Some pals from inside the PIRA, obviously," Cantor said.

"Sure." Jack nodded. "People he knew to be reliable. But we also know that he's a counterintelligence type, right?"

"What do you mean?" Cantor hadn't been down this road yet.

"Who's the main threat to O'Donnell?"

"Everybody wants him—"

"Who wants to kill him?" Jack refocused the question. "The Brits don't have capital punishment—but the PIRA does."

"So?"

"So if you were O'Donnell, and you recruited people from inside the PIRA, and you knew that the PIRA was interested in having your head on a wall plaque, you think you'd leave people inside to cue you in?"

"Makes sense," Cantor said thoughtfully.

"Next, who is the ULA's political target?"

"We don't know that."

"Don't give that crap, Marty!" Ryan snapped. "Most of the information in these documents comes from inside the Provos, doesn't it? How the hell do these people know what the ULA is up to? How does the data get to them?"

"You're pushing, Jack," Cantor warned. "I've seen the data, too. It's mainly negative. The Provos who had the information sweated out of them mainly said that certain operations weren't theirs. The conclusion that ULA did 'em is inferential—circumstantial. I don't think that this stuff is as clear as you do."

"No, the two guys who did this report make a good case for putting the ULA fingerprint on these ops. What the ULA has is its own *style*, Marty! We can identify that, can't we?"

"You've constructed a circular argument," Cantor pointed out. "O'Donnell comes from the Provos, therefore he must have recruited from there, therefore he must have people in there, et cetera. Your basic arguments are logical, but try to remember that they're based on a very shaky foundation. What if the ULA really is a special-action group of the Provisionals? Isn't it in their interest to have something like that?" Cantor was a splendid devil's advocate, one of the reasons he was Greer's executive assistant.

"Okay, there is some truth to that," Ryan admitted. "Still, everything I say makes sense, assuming that the ULA is real."

"Granted that it's logical. But not proven."

"So it's the first logical thing we have for these characters. What else does that tell us?"

Cantor grinned. "Let me know when you figure it out."

"Can I talk to anybody about this?"

"Like who—I just want to ask before I say no."

"The Legal Attaché in London—Dan Murray," Ryan said. "He's supposed to be cleared all the way on this material, isn't he?"

"Yeah, he is, and he works with our people, too. Okay, you can talk with him. That keeps it in the family."

"Thanks."

Five minutes later Cantor was sitting across from Admiral Greer's desk.

"He really knows how to ask the right questions."

"So what did he tumble to?" the Admiral asked.

"The same questions that Emil Jacobs and his team have been asking: What's O'Donnell up to? Does he have the PIRA infiltrated? If so, why?"

"And Jack says . . . ?"

"Same as Jacobs and the FBI evaluation: O'Donnell is a counterintelligence type by training. The Provos want his hide on the barn door, and the best way to keep his hide where it belongs is to have people inside to warn him if they get too close."

The Admiral nodded agreement, then looked away for a moment. That was only part of an answer, his instincts told him. There had to be more. "Anything else?"

"The training stuff. He hasn't sifted through all the data yet. I think we should give him some time. But you were right, sir. He's pretty sharp."

Murray lifted his phone and pushed the right button without paying much attention. "Yeah?"

"Dan? This is Jack Ryan," the voice on the phone said.

"How's it going, teacher?"

"Not bad. Something I want to talk over with you."

"Shoot."

"I think the ULA has the PIRA infiltrated."

"What?" Murray snapped upright in his chair. "Hey, ace, I can't—" He looked at the telephone. The line he was talking on was— "What the hell are you doing on a secure line?"

"Let's say that I'm back in government service," Ryan replied coyly.

"Nobody told me."

"So what do you think?"

"I think it's a possibility. Jimmy came up with the idea about three months back. The Bureau agrees that it makes sense. There is no objective evidence to support the theory, but everybody thinks it's a logical—I mean, it would be a smart thing for our friend Kevin to do, if he can. Remember that the PIRA has very good internal security, Jack."

"You told me that most of what we know about the ULA comes from PIRA sources. How do they get the info?" Ryan asked rapidly.

"What? You lost me."

"How does the PIRA find out what the ULA is doing?"

"Oh, okay. That we don't know." It was something that bothered Murray, and James Owens, but cops deal all the time with anonymous information sources.

"Why would they be doing that?"

"Telling the Provos what they're up to? We have no idea. If you have a suggestion, I'm open to it."

"How about recruiting new members for his team?" Ryan asked.

"Why don't you think that one over for a few seconds," Murray replied immediately. Ryan had just rediscovered the flat earth theory.

There was a moment of silence. "Oh—then he'd risk being infiltrated by the Provisionals."

"Very good, ace. If O'Donnell's got them infiltrated as a security measure to protect himself, why invite members of the group that wants his ass into his own fold? If you want to kill yourself, there're simpler ways, Jack." Murray had to laugh. He could hear Ryan deflate over the phone.

"Okay, I guess I had that coming. Thanks."

"Sorry to rain on your parade, but we buried that idea a couple of months ago."

"But he must have recruited his people from the Provisionals to begin with," Ryan objected belatedly. He cursed himself for being so slow, but remembered that Murray had been an expert on this subject for years.

"Yeah, I'll buy that, but he kept the numbers very low," Murray said. "The bigger the organization gets, the greater the risk that the Provos will infiltrate—and destroy—him. Hey, they really want his ass on a platter, Jack." Murray stopped short of revealing the deal David Ashley had cut with the PIRA. CIA didn't know about that yet.

"How's the family?" he asked, changing the subject.

"Fine."

"Bill Shaw says he talked to you last week. . . ." Murray said.

"Yeah. That's why I'm here now. You've got me looking over my shoulder, Dan. Anything else that you've cued in on?"

It was Murray's turn to deflate. "The more I think about it, the more it looks like I got worried over nothing. No evidence at all, Jack. It was just instinct, you know, like from an old woman. Sorry. I think I just overreacted to something Jimmy said. Hope I didn't worry you too much."

"Don't sweat it," Jack replied. "Well, I have to clear out of here. See ya."

"Yeah. 'Bye, Jack.'" Murray replaced the phone in the holder and went back to his paperwork.

Ryan did much the same. He had to leave by noon in order to make his first class of the day. The messenger came back with his cart and took the files away, along with Jack's notes, which, of course, were also classified. He left the building a few minutes later, his mind still sifting through the data he'd read.

What Jack didn't know was that in the new annex to the CIA headquarters building was the headquarters of the National Reconnaissance Office. This was a joint CIA–Air Force agency that managed the data from satellites and, to a lesser degree, high-altitude reconnaissance aircraft.

The new generation of satellites used television-type scanning cameras instead of photographic film. One consequence of this was that they could be used almost continuously instead of husbanding their film for coverage of the Soviet Union and its satellites. This allowed the NRO to assemble a much better data base on world trends and events, and had generated scores of new projects for hundreds of new analysts—explaining the newly built annex behind the original CIA building.

One junior analyst's brief was coverage on camps suspected to be used for the training of terrorists. The project had not yet shown enough results to be treated more importantly, though the data and photographs were passed on to the Task Force on Combating Terrorism. TFCT used the satellite photos, as was the norm in government circles. The staffers oohed and ahhed over the clarity of the shots, were briefed on the new charge-coupled devices that enabled the cameras to get high-resolution pictures despite atmospheric disturbances, noted that, despite all the hoopla, you really couldn't read the numbers on a license plate—and promptly forgot about them as anything more than pictures of camps where terrorists might be training. Photoreconnaissance interpretation had always been a narrow field for experts only. The analysis work was simply too technical.

And as was so often the case, here was the rub. The junior analyst was better described as a technician. He collected and collated data, but didn't really analyze it. That was someone else's job, for when the project was finished. In this particular case the data being processed noted infrared energy. The camps he examined on a daily basis—there were over two hundred—were mainly in deserts. That was remarkably good luck. While everyone knew that deserts suffer from blistering daylight heat, it was less appreciated that they can get quite cold at night—falling below freezing in many cases. So the technician was trying to determine the occupancy of the camps from the number of buildings that were heated during the cool nights. These showed up quite well on the infrared: bright blobs of white on a cold, black background.

A computer stored the digital signals from the satellite. The technician called up the camps by code number, noted the number of heated buildings in each, and transferred the data to a second data file. Camp 11-5-18, located at 28° 32' 47" North Latitude, 19° 07' 52" East Longitude, had six buildings, one of which was a garage. This one had at least two vehicles in it; though the building was unheated, the thermal signatures of two internal-combustion engines radiated clearly through the corrugated steel roofs. Of the other five buildings, only one had its heater on, the technician noted. The previous week—he checked—three had been warm. The warm one now, the data sheet said, was occupied by a small guard and maintenance group, thought to be five men. It evidently had its own kitchen, since one part of the building was always a little warmer than the rest. Another building was a full-sized dining hall. That and the dormitories were now empty. The technician made the appropriate notations, and the computer assigned them to a simple line graph that peaked when occupancy was high and fell when it was low. The technician didn't have the time to check the patterns on the graph, but he assumed, wrongly, that someone else did.

"You remember, Lieutenant," Breckenridge said. "Deep breath, let it half out, and squeeze gently."

The 9mm Browning automatic had excellent sights. Ryan centered them on the circular target and did what the Gunny said. He did it right. The flash and sound of the shot came almost as a surprise to him. The automatic ejected the spent round and was ready to fire again as Jack brought the pistol down from recoil. He repeated the procedure four more times. The pistol locked open on the empty clip and Ryan set it down. Next he took off the muff-type ear protectors. His ears were sweaty.

"Two nines, three tens, two of them in the X-ring." Breckenridge stood away from the spotting scope. "Not as good as the last time."

"My arm's tired," Ryan explained. The pistol weighed almost forty ounces. It didn't seem like much weight until you had to hold it stone-steady at arm's length for an hour.

"You can get some wrist weights—you know, like joggers use. It'll build up your forearm and wrist muscles." Breckenridge slipped five rounds into the clip of Ryan's pistol and stepped to the line to aim at a fresh target.

The Sergeant Major fired all five in under three seconds. Ryan looked in the spotting scope. There were five holes within the target's X-ring, clustered like the petals on a flower.

"Damn, I forgot how much fun a nice Browning could be." He ejected the clip and reloaded. "The sights are right on, too."

"I noticed," Jack replied lamely.

"Don't feel too bad, Lieutenant," Breckenridge said. "I've been doin' this since you were in diapers." Five more rounds and the center was effectively removed from the target, fifty feet away.

"Why are we doing round targets anyway?" Jack asked.

"I want you to get used to the idea of placing your shots exactly where you want them to go," the Gunny explained. "We'll sweat the fancy stuff later. For now we'll work on basic skills. You look a little looser today, Lieutenant."

"Yeah, well, I talked to the FBI guy who originated the warning. Now he says he might have overreacted—maybe I did, too."

Breckenridge shrugged. "You never been in combat, Lieutenant. I have. One thing you learn: the first twitch you have is usually right. Keep that in mind."

Jack nodded, not believing it. He'd accomplished much today. His look at the ULA data told him a lot about the organization, but there was not the first inkling that they had ever operated at all in America. The Provisional IRA had plenty of American connections, but no one believed that the ULA did. Even if they planned to do something here, Ryan judged, they'd need the connections. It was possible that O'Donnell might call on some of his previous PIRA friends, but that seemed most unlikely. He was a dangerous man, but only on his own turf. And

America wasn't his turf. That's what the data said. Jack knew that this was too broad a conclusion to base on one day's work, of course. He'd keep looking—it seemed that his investigation would last two or three weeks, the way he was going. If nothing else, he wanted to look into the relationship between O'Donnell and the Provos. He did have a feeling that something odd was going on, just as Murray evidently did, and he wanted to examine the data fully, in the hope of coming up with a plausible theory. He owed CIA something for its courtesy.

The storm was magnificent. Miller and O'Donnell stood by the leaded-glass windows and watched as the Atlantic gale beat the sea to foaming waves that slammed against the base of the cliff on which the house stood. The crash of the breaking waves provided the bass notes, while the wind howled and whistled through the trees and raindrops beat their tattoo against the house itself.

"Not a day to be sailing, Sean," O'Donnell said as he sipped at a whiskey.

"When do our colleagues go to America?"

"Three weeks. Not much time. Do you still want to do it?" The chief of the ULA thought the timing marginal for what Sean planned.

"This is not an opportunity to be missed, Kevin," Miller answered evenly.

"Do you have another motive?" O'Donnell asked. Better to get it in the open, he decided.

"Consider the ramifications. The Provisionals go over to proclaim their innocence and—"

"Yes, I know. It is a fine opportunity. Very well. When do you want to leave?"

"Wednesday morning. We must move quickly. Even with our contacts, it won't be easy."

13

Visitors

The two men hunched over the blow-up of the map, flanked by several eight-by-ten photographs.

"This is going to be the hard one," Alex said. "This one I can't help you with."

"What's the problem?" Sean could see it, but by asking the question he could also gauge the skill of his new associate. He'd never worked with a black before, and though he'd met Alex and members of his group the year before, both were unknown quantities, at least in an operational sense.

"He always comes out by Gate Three, here. This street, as you see, is a dead end. He has to go straight west or turn north coming out. He has done both. This street here is wide enough to do the job from a car, but this one—too narrow, and it leads the wrong way. That means the only sure spot is right here, at the corner. Traffic lights here and here." Alex pointed. "Both these streets are narrow and always have cars parked on both sides. This building is apartments. These are houses— expensive ones. There isn't much pedestrian traffic here, oddly enough. One man can probably get by. Two or more, uh-uh." He shook his head. "And it's a white area. A black man would be conspicuous. Your guy has to wing this one alone, pal, and he's gotta be on foot. Probably inside this door is the best place, but he'll have to be on his toes or the target will get away."

"How does he get out?" Sean asked.

"I can park a car around this corner, or this one. Timing for that is not a concern. We can wait all day for the right slot. We have a choice of escape routes. That's no problem either. At rush hour the streets are crowded. That actually works for us. The cops will have trouble responding, and we can use a car that looks ordinary, like a state-owned one. They can't stop all of them. Getaway is easy. The problem is your man. He has to be right here."

"Why not catch him in his car at a different place?"

Alex shook his head. "Too hard. The roads are too crowded to be sure, and it'd be too easy to lose him. You've seen the traffic, Sean, and he never goes exactly the same way twice. If you want my opinion, you should split the operation, do it one part at a time."

"No." Miller was adamant. "We'll do it the way I want."

"Okay, man, but I'm telling you, this man is exposed."

Miller thought that one over for a moment. Finally he smiled. "I have just the right man for it.

"The other part?"

Alex switched maps. "Easy. The target can take any route at all, but they all come to this place here at exactly four forty-five. We've checked six days in the past two weeks, never been off by more than five minutes. We'll do the job right along here, close to the bridge. Anybody could handle this one. We can even rehearse it for you."

"When?"

"This afternoon good enough?" Alex smiled.

"Indeed. Escape route?"

"We'll show you. We might as well make it a real rehearsal."

"Excellent." Miller was well pleased. Getting here had been complicated enough. Not difficult, just complicated, involving six separate flights. It hadn't been without humor, though. Sean Miller was traveling on a British passport at the moment, and the immigration clerk at Miami had taken his Belfast accent for Scottish. It hadn't occurred to him that to an American ear there isn't much difference between a brogue and a burr. *If that's the skill level in American law-enforcement officials,* Miller told himself, *this op should go easily enough.*

They'd do the run-through today. If it looked good he'd summon the team, and they'd go in . . . four days, he judged. The weapons were already in place.

"Conclusions?" Cantor asked.

Ryan picked up a sixty-page sheaf of paper. "Here's my analysis, for what it's worth—not much," Jack admitted. "I didn't turn up anything new. The reports you already have are pretty good, given the lack of real evidence to go on. The ULA is a really kinky bunch. On one hand their operations don't seem to have a real purpose that we can discern—but this kind of skill. . . . They're too professional to be operating without an objective, dammit!"

"True enough," Cantor said. They were in his office, across the hall from the DDI's. Admiral Greer was out of town. "You come up with anything at all?"

"I've mapped their operations geographically and against time. No pattern there that I can see. The only visible pattern is in the type of operation, and the execution, but that doesn't mean anything. They like high-profile targets, but—hell, what terrorist doesn't? That's the whole point of being a terrorist, going after the really big game, right? They mostly use East Bloc weapons, but most of the groups do. We infer that they're well financed. That's logical, given the nature of their activity, but again there isn't any substantive evidence to confirm it.

"O'Donnell has a real talent for dropping out of sight, both personally and professionally. There are three whole years we can't account for, one before he turned up around the time of Bloody Sunday and two years after the Provos tried to punch his ticket. They're both complete blanks. I talked to my wife about the plastic surgery angle—"

"What?" Cantor didn't react favorably to that.

"She doesn't know why I wanted the information. Give me a break, Marty. I'm married to a surgeon, remember? One of her classmates is a reconstructive surgeon, and I had Cathy ask her where you can get a new face. Not many places that can really do it—I was surprised. I have a list of where they are in here. Two are behind the Curtain. It turns out that some of the real pioneering work was done in Moscow before World War Two. Hopkins people have been to the institute— it's named for the guy, but I can't recall the name—and they found a few odd things about the place."

"Like what?" Cantor asked.

"Like two floors that you can't get onto. Annette DiSalvi—Cathy's classmate—was there two years ago. The top two floors of the place can be reached only by special elevators, and the stairways have barred gates. Odd sort of thing for a hospital. I thought that was a funny bit of information. Maybe it'll be useful to somebody else."

Cantor nodded. He knew something about this particular clinic, but the closed floors were something new. It was amazing, he thought, how new bits of data could turn up so innocently. He also wondered why a surgical team from Johns Hopkins had been allowed into the place. He made a mental note to check that out.

"Cathy says this 'getting a new face' thing isn't what it's cracked up to be. Most of the work is designed to correct damage from trauma—car accidents and things like that. The job isn't so much to change as to repair. There is a lot of cosmetic work—I mean aside from nose jobs and face-lifts—but that you can accomplish almost as well with a new hair style and a beard. They can change chins and cheekbones pretty well, but if the work is too extensive it leaves scars. This place in Moscow is good, Annette says, almost as good as Hopkins or even UCLA. A lot of the best reconstructive surgeons are in California," Jack explained. "Anyway, we're not talking a face-lift or a nose job here. Extensive facial surgery involves multiple procedures and takes several months. If O'Donnell was gone for two years, a lot of the time was spent in the body shop."

"Oh." Cantor got the point. "He really is a fast worker, then?"

Jack grinned. "That's what I was really after. He was out of sight for two years. At least six months of that time must have been spent in some hospital or other. So in the other eighteen months, he recruited his people, set up a base of operations, started collecting operational intelligence, and ran his first op."

"Not bad," Cantor said thoughtfully.

"Yeah. So he had to have recruited people from in the Provos. They must have brought some stuff with them, too. I'll bet that his initial operations were things the PIRA had already looked at and set aside for one reason or another. That's why the Brits thought they were actually part of the PIRA to begin with, Marty."

"You said you didn't find anything important," Cantor said. "This sounds like pretty sharp analysis to me."

"Maybe. All I did was reorder stuff you already had. Nothing new is in here, and I still haven't answered my own question. I don't have much of an idea what they're really up to." Ryan's hand flipped through the pages of manuscript. His voice showed his frustration. Jack was not accustomed to failure. "We still don't know where these bastards are coming from. They're up to something, but damned if I know what it is."

"American connections?"

"None—none at all that we know of. That makes me feel a lot better. There's no hint of a contact with American organizations, and lots of reasons for them not to have any. O'Donnell is too slick to play with his old PIRA contacts."

"But his recruiting—" Cantor objected. Jack cut him off.

"Over here, I mean. As chief of internal security, he could know who was who in Belfast and Londonderry. But the American connections to the Provisionals all run through Sinn Fein, the Provos' political wing. He'd have to be crazy to trust them. Remember, he did his best to restructure the political leanings in the outfit and failed."

"Okay. I see what you mean. Possible connections with other groups?"

Ryan shook his head. "No evidence. I wouldn't bet against contact with some of the European groups, maybe some of the Islamic ones even, but not over here. O'Donnell's a smart cookie. To come over here means too many complications—hey, they don't like me, I can dig that. The good news is that the FBI's right. We're dealing with professionals. I am not a politically significant target. Coming after me has no political value, and these are political animals," Jack observed confidently. "Thank God."

"Did you know that the PIRA—well, Sinn Fein—has a delegation coming over day after tomorrow?"

"What for?"

"The thing in London hurt them in Boston and New York. They've denied involvement about a hundred times, and they have a bunch coming over for a couple of weeks to tell the local Irish communities in person."

"Aw, crap!" Ryan snarled. "Why not keep the bastards out of the friggin' country?"

"Not that easy. The people coming over aren't on the Watch List. They've been here before. They're clean, technically. We live in a free democracy, Jack. Remember what Oliver Wendell Holmes said: the

Constitution was written for people of fundamentally differing views—or something like that. The short name is Freedom of Speech.''

Ryan had to smile. The outside view of the Central Intelligence Agency people was often one of bumbling fascists, threats to American freedom, corrupt but incompetent schemers, a cross between the Mafia and the Marx brothers. In fact, Ryan had found them to be politically moderate—more so than he was. If the truth ever got out, of course, the press would think it was a sinister ruse. Even he found it very odd.

"I hope somebody will keep an eye on them," Jack observed.

"The FBI will have people in every bar, swilling their John Jameson and singing 'The Men Behind the Wire.' And keeping an eye on everything. The Bureau's pretty good at that. They've just about ended the gun-running. The word's gotten out on that—must be a half-dozen people who got sent up the river for sending guns and explosives over.''

"Fine. So now the bad guys use Kalashnikovs, or Armalites made in Singapore.''

"That," Cantor said, "is not our responsibility.''

"Well, this here's all that I was able to come up with, Marty. Unless there's other data around, that's all I can give you.'' Jack tossed the report in Cantor's lap.

"I'll read this over and get back to you. Back to teaching history?''

"Yep.'' Ryan stood and got his coat from the back of the chair. He paused. "What if something about these guys turns up in a different place?''

"This is the only compartment you can see, Jack—''

"I know that. What I'm asking is, the way this place is set up, how do you connect things from different compartments?''

"That's why we have supervisory oversight teams, and computers,'' Cantor answered. *Not that the system always works. . . .*

"If anything new turns up—''

"It's flagged," Cantor said. "Both here and at the FBI. If we get any sort of twitch on these fellows, you'll be warned the day we get it.''

"Fair enough.'' Ryan made sure his pass was hanging in plain view before going out into the corridor. "Thanks—and please thank the

Admiral for me. You guys didn't have to do this. I wouldn't feel this good if somebody else had told me what I saw for myself. I owe you.''

"You'll be hearing from us," Cantor promised him.

Ryan nodded and went out the door. He'd be hearing from them, all right. They'd make the offer again, and he'd turn it down again—with the greatest reluctance, of course. He'd gone out of his way to be humble and polite with Cantor. In truth, he thought his sixty-page report did a pretty good job of organizing what data they did have on the ULA. That squared matters. He didn't really think he owed any-body.

Caroline Muller Ryan, MD, FACS, lived a very controlled and structured life. She liked it that way. In surgery she always worked with the same team of doctors, nurses, and technicians. They knew how she liked to work, how she liked her instruments arranged. Most surgeons had their peculiarities, and the ophthalmic specialists were unusually fastidious. Her team tolerated it because she was one of the best technical surgeons of her age group and also one of the easiest to like. She rarely had problems with her temper, and got along well with her nurses—something that female doctors often had trouble with. Her current problem was her pregnancy, which forced her to limit her exposure to certain operating-room chemicals. Her swelling abdomen was beginning to alter her stance at the table—actually eye surgeons usually sit, but the principle was the same. Cathy Ryan had to reach a little farther now, and joked about it constantly.

These traits carried over to her personal life also. She drove her Porsche with mechanistic precision, always shifting the gears at ex-actly the right RPM setting, taking corners on a line as regular as a Formula One driver's. Doing things the same way every time wasn't a rut for Cathy Ryan; it was perfection. She played the piano that way also. Sissy Jackson, who played and taught professionally, had once remarked that her playing was too perfect, lacking in soul. Cathy took that as a compliment. Surgeons don't autograph their work; they do it the right way, every time.

Which was why she was annoyed with life at the moment. It was a minor annoyance having to take a slightly different route to work every day—in fact it was something of a challenge, since she gave herself the goal of not allowing it to affect her schedule. Driving to and from work never took more than fifty-seven minutes, nor less than forty-nine (unless she came in on a weekend, when different traffic rules applied). She always picked up Sally at exactly quarter to five. Taking new routes, mainly inside Baltimore, threatened to change this segment of her life, but there weren't many driving problems that a Porsche 911 couldn't solve.

Her route this day was down state Route 3, then across a secondary road. That brought her out onto Ritchie Highway, six miles above the Giant Steps Nursery School. She caught the light just right and took the turn in second gear, working quickly up to third, then fourth. The feline growl of the six-cylinder engine reached through the sound insulation as a gentle purr. Cathy Ryan loved her Porsche. She'd never driven anything else until after she was married—a station wagon was useful for shopping and family drives, unfortunately—and wondered what she'd do when her second child arrived. That, she sighed, would be a problem. It depended on where the sitter was, she decided. Or maybe she could finally convince Jack to get a nanny. Her husband was a little too working-class in that respect. He'd resisted the idea of hiring a part-time maid to help with the housework—that was all the more crazy since Cathy knew her husband tended to be something of a slob, slow to hang up his clothing. Getting the maid had changed that a little. Now, nights before the maid was due in, Jack scurried around picking things up so that she wouldn't think the Ryans were a family of slovens. Jack could be so funny. *Yes,* she thought, *we'll get a nanny. After all, Jack's a knight now.* Cathy smiled at the traffic. Pushing him in the right direction wouldn't be all that hard. Jack was very easy to manipulate. She changed lanes and darted past a dump truck in third gear. The Porsche made it so easy to accelerate around things.

She turned right into the Giant Steps parking lot two minutes later. The sports car bumped over the uneven driveway and she brought it to a stop in the usual spot. Cathy locked the car on getting out, of course. Her Porsche was six years old, but meticulously maintained. It had been her present to herself on getting through her intern year at Hopkins. There wasn't a single scratch on the British Racing Green finish, and only a Hopkins parking sticker marred the gleaming chrome bumper.

"Mommy!" Sally met her at the door.

Cathy bent to pick her up. It was getting harder to bend over, and harder still to stand up with Sally around her neck. She hoped that their daughter would not feel threatened by the arrival of the baby. Some kids were, she knew, but she had already explained to the little girl what was going on, and Sally seemed to like the idea of a new brother or sister.

"So what did my big girl do today?" Dr. Ryan asked. Sally liked being called a Big Girl, and this was Cathy's subterfuge for ensuring that sibling rivalry would be minimized by the arrival of a "little" boy or girl.

Sally wriggled free to drop back to the floor, and held up a finger painting done on what looked like wide-carriage computer paper. It was a credible abstract work of purple and orange. Together, mother and daughter went to the back and got her coat and lunch box. Cathy made sure that Sally's coat was zipped and the hood up—it was only a few degrees above freezing outside, and they didn't want Sally to get another cold. It took a total of five minutes from the time Cathy stopped the car until she was back out the door, walking toward it again.

She didn't really notice the routineness of her daily schedule. Cathy unlocked the door, got Sally into her seat, and made sure the seat belt was fastened snugly before closing and locking the door and going around to the left side of the car.

She looked up briefly. Across Ritchie Highway was a small shopping center, a 7-Eleven Store, a cleaners, a video store, and a hardware dealer. There was a blue van parked at the 7-Eleven again. She'd noticed it twice the previous week. Cathy shrugged it off. 7-Eleven was a convenience store, and lots of people made it a regular stop on the way home.

"Hello, Lady Ryan," Miller said inside the van. The two windows in the rear doors—they reminded Miller of the police transport van; he smiled to himself at that—were made of coated glass so that an outsider couldn't see in. Alex was in the store getting a six-pack of Cokes, as he'd done on a fairly regular basis the previous two weeks.

Miller checked his watch: She'd arrived at 4:46 and was leaving at 4:52. Next to him, a man with a camera was shooting away. Miller raised binoculars. The green Porsche would be easy to spot, plus it had a customized license plate, CR-SRGN. Alex had explained how license plates in Maryland could be bought to individual specifications, and Sean wondered who'd be using that code next year. Surely there was another surgeon with the initials CR.

Alex got back in and started the engine. The van left the parking lot just as the target's Porsche did. Alex did his own driving. He went north on Ritchie Highway, hung a quick U-turn, and raced south to keep the Porsche in sight. Miller joined him in the right-side seat.

"She takes this road south to Route 50, across the Severn River bridge, then gets off 50 onto Route 2. We want to hit her before she does that. We'll proceed, take the same exit, and switch cars where I showed you. Too bad," Alex said. "I was beginning to like this here van."

"You can buy another with what we're paying you."

A grin split the black face. "Yeah, I 'spect so. Have a better interior on the next one, too." He turned right, taking the exit onto Route 50. It was a divided, multilane highway. Traffic was moderate to heavy. Alex explained that this was normal.

"No problem getting the job done," he assured Miller.

"Excellent," Miller agreed. "Good work, Alex." *Even if you do have a big mouth.*

Cathy always drove more sedately with Sally aboard. The little girl craned her neck to see over the dashboard, her left hand fiddling with the seat belt buckle as it usually did. Her mother was relaxing now. It generally took her about this length of time to settle down from a hard day—there were few easy ones—at the Wilmer Eye Institute. It wasn't stress so much. She'd had two procedures today and would have two more the next day. She loved her work. There were a lot of people now who could see only because of her professional skill, and the satisfaction of that was not something easily communicated, even to Jack. The price of it was that her days were rarely easy ones. The minute precision demanded by ophthalmic surgery denied her coffee—she couldn't risk the slight tremor in her hands that might come from caffeine—and imposed a degree of concentration on her that few professions demanded. There were more difficult medical skills, but not many. This was the main reason she drove her 911. It was as though in pushing through the air, or taking a tight corner at twenty-five in second gear, the car drained the excess energy from the driver and spread it into the environment. She almost always got home in a good mood. Tonight would be better still since it was Jack's turn to fix dinner. If the car had been built with a brain, it would have noticed the reduced pressure on accelerator and brakes as they took the Route 2 exit. It was being pampered now, like a faithful horse that had jumped all the fences properly.

"Okay?" Alex asked, keeping west on Route 50 toward Washington.

The other man in the back handed Miller the clipboard with the new time notation. There was a total of seven entries, all but the last complete with photographs. Sean looked at the numbers. The target was on a beautifully regular schedule.

"Fine," he said after a moment.

"I can't give you a precise spot for the hit—traffic can make things go a little funny. I'd say we should try on the east side of the bridge."

"Agreed."

Cathy Ryan walked into her house fifteen minutes later. She unzipped Sally's coat and watched her little—"big"—girl struggle out of the sleeves, a skill she was just beginning to acquire. Cathy took it and hung it up before getting out of her coat. Mother and daughter then proceeded to the kitchen, where they heard the unmistakable noise of a husband trying to fix dinner and a television tuned to the *MacNeil-Lehrer Report*.

"Daddy, look what I did!" Sally said first.

"Oh, great!" Jack took the picture and examined it with great care. "I think we'll hang this one up." All of them got hung up. The art gallery in question was the front of the family refrigerator. A magnetized holder gave the finger painting a semipermanent place over the ice and cold-water dispenser. Sally never noticed that there was a new hanging spot every day. Nor did she know that every such painting was saved, tucked away in a box in the foyer closet.

"Hi, babe." Jack kissed his wife next. "How were things today?"

"Two cornea replacements. Bernie assisted on the second one—it was a bear. Tomorrow, I'm scheduled for a vitrectomy. Bernie says hi, by the way."

"How's his kid?" Jack asked.

"Just an appendectomy, she'll be climbing the monkey bars next week," Cathy replied, surveying the kitchen. She often wondered if having Jack fix dinner was worth the wreckage he made of her room. It appeared that he was fixing pot roast, but she wasn't sure. It wasn't that Jack was a bad cook—with some things he was pretty good—he was just so damned sloppy about it. Never kept his utensils neat. Cathy always had her knives, forks, and everything else arranged like a surgical instrument tray. Jack would just set them anywhere and spent half of his time looking for where they were.

Sally left the room and found a TV that didn't have a news show on.

"Good news," Jack said.

"Oh?"

"I finished up at CIA today."

"So what are you smiling about?"

"There just isn't anything I see to make me suspect that we have anything to worry about." Jack explained for several minutes, keeping within the bounds of classification—mostly. "They've never operated over here. They don't have any contacts over here that we know of. The real thing is that we're not good targets for them."

"Why?"

"We're not political. The people they go after are soldiers, police, judges, mayors, stuff like that—"

"Not to mention the odd prince," Cathy observed.

"Yeah, well, we're not one of those either, are we?"

"So what are you telling me?"

"They're a scary bunch. That Miller kid—well, we've talked about that. I'll feel a little better when they have him back in the can. But these guys are pros. They're not going to mount an op three thousand miles from home for revenge."

Cathy took his hand. "You're sure?"

"Sure as I can be. The intelligence biz isn't like mathematics, but you get a feel for the other guy, the way his head works. A terrorist kills to make a political point. We ain't political fodder."

Cathy gave her husband a gentle smile. "So I can relax now?"

"I think so. Still, keep an eye on the mirror."

"And you're not going to carry that gun anymore," she said hopefully.

"Babe, I like shooting. I forgot what fun a pistol can be. I'm going to keep shooting at the Academy, but, no, I won't be wearing it anymore."

"And the shotgun?"

"It hasn't hurt anybody."

"I don't *like* it, Jack. At least unload it, okay?" She walked off to the bedroom to change.

"Okay." It wasn't that important. He'd keep the box of shells right next to the gun, on the top shelf of the closet. Sally couldn't reach it. Even Cathy had to stretch. It would be safe there. Jack reconsidered all his actions over the past three and a half weeks and decided that they had been worthwhile, really. The alarm system on the house wasn't such a bad idea, and he liked his new 9mm Browning. He was getting pretty good scores. If he kept at it for a year, maybe he could give Breckenridge a run for his money.

He checked the oven. Another ten minutes. Next he turned up the TV. The current segment on the *MacNeil-Lehrer News Hour* was—*I'll be damned.*

"Joining us from our affiliate WGBH in Boston is Padraig—did I pronounce that right?—O'Neil, a spokesman for Sinn Fein and an elected member of the British Parliament. Mr. O'Neil, why are you visiting America at this time?"

"I and many of my colleagues have visited America many times, to inform the American people of the oppression inflicted upon the Irish people by the British government, the systematic denial of economic opportunity and basic civil rights, the total abrogation of the judicial process, and the continuing brutality of the British army of occupation against the people of Ireland," O'Neil said in a smooth and reasonable voice. He had done all this before.

"Mr. O'Neil," said someone from the British Embassy in Washington, "is the political front-man for the Provisional Wing of the so-called Irish Republican Army. This is a terrorist organization that is illegal both in Northern Ireland and in the Irish Republic. His mission in the United States is, as always, to raise money so that his organization can buy arms and explosives. This source of income for the IRA was damaged by the cowardly attack against the Royal Family in London last year, and his reason for being here is to persuade Irish-Americans that the IRA had no part in that."

"Mr. O'Neil," MacNeil said, "how do you respond to that?"

The Irishman smiled at the camera as benignly as Bob Keeshan's Captain Kangaroo. "Mr. Bennett, as usual, skirts over the legitimate political issues here. Are Northern Ireland's Catholics denied economic and political opportunity—yes, they are. Have the legal processes in Northern Ireland been subverted for political reasons by the

British government—yes, they have. Are we any closer to a political settlement of this dispute that goes back, in its modern phase, to 1969—no, I regret to say we are not. If I am a terrorist, why have I been allowed into your country? I am, in fact, a member of the British Parliament, elected by the people of my parliamentary district.''

"But you don't take your seat in Parliament," MacNeil objected.

"And join the government that is killing my constituents?"

"Jesus," Ryan said, "what a mess." He turned the TV off.

"Such a reasonable man," Miller said. Alex's house was outside the D.C. beltway. "Tell your friends how reasonable you are, Paddy. And when you get to the pubs tonight, be sure to tell your friends that you have never hurt anyone who was not a genuine oppressor of the Irish people." Sean watched the whole segment, then placed an overseas call to a pay phone outside a Dublin pub.

The next morning—only five hours later in Ireland—four men boarded a plane for Paris. Neatly dressed, they looked like young executives traveling with their soft luggage to business appointments overseas. At Charles de Gaulle International Airport they made connections to a flight to Caracas. From there they flew Eastern Air Lines to Atlanta, and another Eastern flight to National Airport, just down the Potomac from the memorial to Thomas Jefferson. The four were jet-lagged out and sick of airliner seats when they arrived. They took an airport limousine to a local hotel to sleep off their travel shock. The young businessmen checked out the next morning and were met by a car.

14

Second Chances

There ought to be a law against Mondays, Ryan thought. He stared at what had to be the worst way to start any day: a broken shoelace that dangled from his left fist. Where were the spares? he asked himself. He couldn't ask Cathy; she and Sally had left the house ten minutes before on the way to Giant Steps and Hopkins. Damn. He started rummaging through his dresser drawers. Nothing. The kitchen. He walked downstairs and across the house to the kitchen drawer that held everything that wasn't someplace else. Hidden beneath the notepads and magnets and scissors he found a spare pair—no, one white lace for a sneaker. He was getting warmer. Several minutes of digging later, he found something close enough. He took one and left the other. After all, shoelaces broke one at a time.

Next Jack had to select a tie for the day. That was never easy, though at least he didn't have his wife around to tell him he'd picked the wrong one. He was wearing a gray suit, and picked a dark blue tie with red stripes. Ryan was still wearing white, button-down shirts made mostly of cotton. Old habits die hard. The suit jacket slid on neatly. It was one of the suits Cathy had bought in England. It was painful to admit that her taste in clothing was far better than his. That London tailor wasn't too bad, either. He smiled at himself in the mirror—*you handsome devil!*—before heading downstairs. His briefcase was waiting on the foyer table, full of the draft quizzes he'd be giving today. Ryan took his overcoat from the closet, checked to see his keys were in the right pocket, got the briefcase, and went out the door.

"Oops!" He unlocked the door and set the burglar alarm before going back outside.

Sergeant Major Breckenridge walked down the double line of Marines, and his long-practiced eyes didn't miss a thing. One private had lint on his blue, high-necked blouse. Another's shoes needed a little more work, and two needed haircuts; you could barely see their scalps under the quarter-inch hair. All in all, there wasn't much to be displeased with. Every one would have passed a normal inspection, but this wasn't a normal post, and normal rules didn't apply. Breckenridge was not a screamer. He'd gotten past that. His remonstrations were more fatherly now. They carried the force of a command from God nevertheless. He finished the inspection and dismissed the guard detail. Several marched off to their gate posts. Others rode in pickups to the more remote posts to relieve the current watch standers at eight o'clock exactly. Each Marine wore his dress blues and a white pistol belt. Their pistols were kept at the posts. They were unloaded, in keeping with the peaceful nature of their duty, but full clips of .45 ACP cartridges were always nearby, in keeping with the nature of the Marines.

Did I really look forward to this? It took all of Ryan's energy just to think that question of himself. But he didn't have any further excuses. In London his injuries had prevented him from doing it. The same had been true of the first few weeks at home. Then he'd spent the early mornings traveling to CIA. That had been his last excuse. None were left.

Rickover Hall, he told himself. *I'll stop when I get to Rickover Hall.* He had to stop soon. Breathing the cold air off the river was like inhaling knives. His nose and mouth were like sandpaper and his heart threatened to burst from his chest. Jack hadn't jogged in months, and he was paying the price for his sloth.

Rickover Hall seemed a thousand miles away, though he knew it was only a few hundred more yards. As recently as the previous October, he'd been able to make three circuits of the grounds and come away with nothing more than a good sweat. Now he was only at the halfway mark of his first lap, and death seemed amazingly attractive. His legs were already rubbery with fatigue. His stride was off; Ryan was weaving slightly, a sure sign of a runner who was beyond his limit.

Another hundred yards. About fifteen seconds more, he told himself. All the time he'd spent on his back, all the time sitting down, all the cigarettes he'd sneaked at CIA were punishing him now. The runs he'd had to do at Quantico had been nothing like this. *You were a lot younger then,* Ryan's mind pointed out gleefully.

He turned his head left and saw that he was lined up on the building's east wall. Ryan leaned back and slowed to a walk, hands supported on his hips as his chest heaved to catch up on the oxygen it needed.

"You okay, Doc?" A mid stopped—his legs still pumping in double-time—to look Jack over. Ryan tried to hate him for his youth and energy, but couldn't summon enough energy.

"Yeah, just out of training," Jack gasped out over three breaths.

"You gotta work back into it slowly, sir," the twenty-year-old pointed out, and sped off, leaving his history teacher scornfully in his dust. Jack started laughing at himself, but it gave him a coughing fit. The next one to pass him was a girl. Her grin really made things worse.

Don't sit down. Whatever you do, don't sit down.

He turned and moved away from the seawall. Just walking on his wobbly legs was an effort. He took the towel from around his neck to wipe the sweat from his face before he got too much of a chill. Jack held the towel taut between his hands and stretched his arms high. He'd caught his breath by now. A renewed supply of oxygen returned to his limbs, and most of the pain left. The rubberiness would go next, he knew. In another ten minutes he'd feel pretty good. Tomorrow he'd make it a little farther—to the Nimitz Library, he promised himself. By May he wouldn't have the mids—at least not the girls—racing past him. Well, not all of the girls, anyway. He was spotting a minimum of ten years to the midshipmen, something that would only get worse. Jack had already passed thirty. Next stop: forty.

*   *   *

Cathy Ryan was in her greens, scrubbing at the special basin outside the surgical suite. The elastic waistband of the pants was high, above the curve of her abdomen, and that made the pants overly short, like the clamdiggers that had been fashionable in her teenage years. A green cap was over her hair, and she wondered yet again why she bothered to brush it out every morning. By the time the procedure was finished, her hair would look like the snaky locks of the Medusa.

"Game time," she said quietly to herself. She hit the door-opening switch with her elbow, keeping her hands high, just like it was done in the movies. Bernice, the circulating nurse, had her gloves ready, and Cathy reached her hands into the rubber until the tops of the gloves came far up on her forearms. Because of this, she was rarely able to wear her engagement ring, though her simple wedding band posed no problem. "Thanks."

"How's the baby?" Bernice asked. She had three of her own.

"At the moment he's learning to jog." Cathy smiled behind her mask. "Or maybe he's lifting weights."

"Nice necklace."

"Christmas present from Jack."

Dr. Terri Mitchell, the anesthesiologist, hooked the patient up to her various monitors and went to work as the surgeons looked on. Cathy gave the instruments a quick look, knowing that Lisa-Marie always got things right. She was one of the best scrub nurses in the hospital and was picky on the doctors she'd work with.

"All ready, Doctor?" Cathy asked the resident. "Okay, people, let's see if we can save this lady's eyesight." She looked at the clock. "Starting at eight forty-one."

Miller assembled the submachine gun slowly. He had plenty of time. The weapon had been carefully cleaned and oiled after being test fired the night before at a quarry twenty miles north of Washington. This one would be his personal weapon. Already he liked it. The balance was perfect, the folding stock, when extended, had a good, solid feel to it. The sights were easy to use, and the gun was fairly steady on full-automatic fire. All in all, a nice combination of traits for such a small, deadly weapon. He palmed back the bolt and squeezed the trigger to get a better feel for where it broke. He figured it at about twelve pounds—perfect, not too light and not too heavy. Miller left the bolt closed on an empty chamber and loaded the magazine of thirty 9mm rounds. Then he folded the stock and tried the hanging hook inside his topcoat. A standard modification to the Uzi, it allowed a person to carry it concealed. That probably wouldn't be necessary, but Miller was a man who planned for all the contingencies. He'd learned that lesson the hard way.

"Ned?"

"Yes, Sean?" Eamon Clark, known as Ned, hadn't stopped going over the maps and photographs of his place since arriving in America. One of the most experienced assassins in Ireland, he was one of the men the ULA had broken from Long Kesh Prison the previous year. A handsome young man, Clark had spent the previous day touring the Naval Academy grounds, carrying his own camera as he'd photographed the statue of Tecumseh . . . and carefully examined Gate Three. Ryan would drive straight uphill, giving him roughly fifteen seconds to get ready. It would demand vigilance, but Ned had the necessary patience. Besides, they knew the target's schedule. His last class ended at three that afternoon and he hit the gate at a predictable time. Alex was even now parking the getaway car on King George Street. Clark had misgivings, but kept them to himself. Sean Miller had masterminded the prison break that had made him a free man. This was his first real operation with the ULA. Clark decided that he owed them loyalty. Besides, his look at the Academy's security had not impressed him. Ned Clark knew that he was not the brightest man in the room, but they needed a man able to work on his own, and he did know how to do that. He'd proven this seven times.

Outside the house were three cars, the van and two station wagons. The van would be used for the second part of the operation, while the station wagons would take everyone to the airport when the operation was finished.

Miller sat down in an overstuffed chair and ran over the entire operation in his mind. As always, he closed his eyes and visualized every event, then he inserted variables. What if the traffic were unusually heavy or unusually light? What if . . .

One of Alex's men came through the front door. He tossed Miller a Polaroid.

"Right on time?" Sean Miller asked.

"You got it, man."

The photograph showed Cathy Ryan leading her daughter by the hand into—what was the name of the place? Oh, yes, Giant Steps. Miller smiled at that. Today would be a giant step indeed. Miller leaned back again, eyes closed, to make sure.

"But there wasn't a threat," a mid objected.

"That's correct. Which is to say we know that *now*. But how did it look to Spruance? He knew what the Japanese fleet had in surface ships. What if they *had* come east, what if the recall order had never been issued?" Jack pointed to the diagram he'd drawn on the blackboard. "There would have been contact at about oh-three-hundred hours. Who do you think would have won that one, mister?"

"But he blew his chance for a good air strike the next day," the midshipman persisted.

"With what? Let's look at the losses in the air groups. With all the torpedo craft lost, just what losses do you think he could have inflicted?" Jack asked.

"But—"

"You remember the Kenny Rogers song: You have to know when to walk away, and know when to run. Buck fever is a bad thing in a hunter. In an admiral commanding a fleet it can be disastrous. Spruance looked at his information, looked at his capabilities, and decided to call it a day. A secondary consideration was—what?"

"To cover Midway?" another mid asked.

"Right. What if they had carried on with the invasion? That was gamed out at Newport once and the invasion was successful. Please note that this is a manifestation of logic overpowering reality, but it was a possibility that Spruance could not afford to dismiss. His primary mission was to inflict damage on a superior Japanese fleet. His secondary mission was to prevent the occupation of Midway. The balance he struck here is a masterpiece of operational expertise. . . ." Ryan paused for a moment. What was it that he'd just said? *Logic overcoming reality*. Hadn't he just come to the logical conclusion that the ULA wouldn't—no, no, a different situation entirely. He shook off the thought and kept going on the lessons from the Battle of Midway. He had the class going now, and ideas were crackling across the room like lightning.

* * *

"Perfect," Cathy said as she pulled her mask down around her neck. She stood up from the stool and stretched her arms over her head. "Nice one, folks."

The patient was wheeled out to the recovery room while Lisa-Marie made a final check of her instruments. Cathy Ryan pulled off her mask and rubbed her nose. Then her hands went down to her belly. The little guy really was kicking up a storm.

"Football player?" Bernice asked.

"Feels like a whole backfield. Sally wasn't this active. I think this one's a boy," Cathy judged, knowing that there was no such correlation. It was good enough that the baby was very active. That was always a positive sign. She smiled, mostly to herself, at the miracle and the magic of motherhood. Right there inside her was a brand-new human being waiting to be born, and by the feel of it, rather impatient. "Well. I have a family to talk to."

She walked out of the operating room, not bothering to change out of her greens. It always looked more dramatic to keep them on. The waiting room was a mere fifty feet away. The Jeffers family—the father and one of their daughters—was waiting on the inevitable couch, staring at the inevitable magazines but not reading them. The moment she came through the swinging door, both leaped to their feet. She gave them her best smile, always the quickest way to convey the message.

"Okay?" the husband asked, his anxiety a physical thing.

"Everything went perfectly," Cathy said. "No problems at all. She'll be fine."

"When will she be able—"

"A week. We have to be patient on this. You'll be able to see her in about an hour and a half. Now, why don't you get yourselves something to eat. There's no sense having a healthy patient if the family is worn out, I—"

"Doctor Ryan," the public address speaker said. "Doctor Caroline Ryan."

"Wait a minute." Cathy walked to the nurses' station and lifted the phone. "This is Doctor Ryan."

"Cathy, this is Gene in the ER. I've got a major eye trauma. Ten-year-old black male, he took his bike through a store window," the voice said urgently. "His left eye is badly lacerated."

"Send him up to six." Cathy hung up and went back to the Jeffers family. "I have to run, there's an emergency case coming up. Your wife will be fine. I'll be seeing you tomorrow." Cathy walked as quickly as she could to the OR.

"Heads up, we have an emergency coming in from ER. Major eye trauma to a ten-year-old." Lisa-Marie was already moving. Cathy walked to the wall phone and punched the number for surgeons' lounge. "This is Ryan in Wilmer six. Where's Bernie?"

"I'll get him." A moment later: "Doctor Katz."

"Bernie, I have a major eye trauma coming into six. Gene Wood in ER says it's a baddie."

"On the way." Cathy Ryan turned.

"Terri?"

"All ready," the anesthesiologist assured her.

"Give me another two minutes," Lisa-Marie said.

Cathy went into the scrub room to rewash her hands. Bernie Katz arrived before she started. He was a thoroughly disreputable-looking man, only an inch taller than Cathy Ryan, with longish hair and a Bismarck mustache. He was also one of the best surgeons at Hopkins.

"You'd better lead on this one," she said. "I haven't done a major trauma in quite a while."

"No problem. How's the baby coming?"

"Great." A new sound arrived, the high-pitched shrieks of a child in agony. The doctors moved into the OR. They watched dispassionately as two orderlies were strapping the child down. *Why weren't you in school?* Cathy asked him silently. The left side of the boy's face was a mess. The reconstructive teams would have to work on that later. Eyes came first. The child had already tried to be brave, but the pain was too great for that. Terri did the first medication, with both orderlies holding the child's arm in place. Cathy and Bernie hovered over the kid's face a moment later.

"Bad," Dr. Katz observed. He looked to the circulating nurse. "I have a procedure scheduled for one o'clock. Have to bump it. This one's going to take some time."

"All ready on this side," the scrub nurse said.

"Two more minutes," the anesthesiologist advised. You had to be careful medicating kids.

"Gloves," Cathy said. Bernie came over with them a moment later. "What happened?"

"He was riding his bike down the sidewalk on Monument Street," the orderly said. "He hit something and went through an appliance-store window."

"Why wasn't he in school?" she asked, looking back at the kid's left eye. She saw hours of work and an uncertain outcome.

"President's Day, Doc," the orderly replied.

"Oh. That's right." She looked at Bernie Katz. His grimace was visible around the mask.

"I don't know, Cathy." He was examining the eye through the magnifying-glass headset. "Must have been a cheap window—lots of slivers. I count five penetrations. Jeez, look at how that one's extended into the cornea. Let's go."

The Chevy pulled into one of Hopkins' high-rise parking garages. From the top level the driver had a perfect view of the door leading from the hospital to the doctors' parking area. The garage was guarded, of course, but there was plenty of traffic in and out, and it was not unusual for someone to wait in a car while another visited a family member inside. He settled back and lit a cigarette, listening to music on the car radio.

Ryan put roast beef on his hard roll and selected iced tea. The Officer and Faculty Club had an unusual arrangement for charging: he set his tray on a scale and the cashier billed him by weight. Jack paid up his two dollars and ten cents. The price for lunch was hardly exorbitant, but it did seem an odd way to set the price. He joined Robby Jackson in a corner booth.

"Mondays!" he observed to his friend.

"Are you kidding? I can relax today. I was up flying Saturday and Sunday."

"I thought you liked that."

"I do," Robby assured him. "But both days I got off before seven. I actually got to sleep until six this morning. I needed the extra two hours. How's the family?"

"Fine. Cathy had a big procedure today—had to be up there early. The one bad thing about being married to a surgeon, they always start early. Sometimes it's a little hard on Sally."

"Yeah, early to bed, early to rise—might as well be dead," Robby agreed. "How's the baby coming?"

"Super." Jack smiled. "He's an active little bugger. I never figured how women can take that—having the kid kick, turn and like that, I mean."

"Mind if I join you?" Skip Tyler slipped into the booth.

"How are the twins?" Jack asked at once.

The reply was a low moan, and a look at the circles under Tyler's eyes provided the answer. "The trick is getting both of them asleep. You just get one quieted down, then the other one goes off like a damned fire alarm. I don't know how Jean does it. Of course"—Tyler grinned—"she can walk the floor with them. When I do it it's step-*thump*, step-*thump*."

All three men laughed. Skip Tyler had never been the least sensitive about losing his leg.

"How's Jean holding up?" Robby asked.

"No problem—she sleeps when they do and I get to do all the housework."

"Serves you right, turkey," Jack observed. "Why don't you give it a rest?"

"Can I help it if I'm hot-blooded?" Skip demanded.

"No, but your timing sucks," Robby replied.

"My timing," Tyler said with raised eyebrows, "is perfect."

"I guess that's one way to look at it," Jack agreed.

"I heard you were out jogging this morning." Tyler changed subjects.

"So did I." Robby laughed.

"I'm still alive, guys."

"One of my mids said tomorrow they're going to follow you around with an ambulance just in case." Skip chuckled. "I suppose it's nice for you to remember that most of the kids know CPR."

"Why are Mondays always like this?" Jack asked.

Alex and Sean Miller made a final run along Route 50. They were careful to keep just under the speed limit. The State Police radar cars were out in force today for some reason or other. Alex assured his colleague that this would end around 4:30. Rush hour had too many cars on the road for efficient law enforcement. Two other men were in the back of the van, each with his weapon.

"Right about here, I think," Miller said.

"Yeah, it's the best place," Alex agreed.

"Escape route." Sean clicked on a stopwatch.

"Okay." Alex changed lanes and kept heading west. "Remember, it's gonna be slower tonight."

Miller nodded, getting the usual pre-op butterflies in his stomach. He ran through his plan, thinking over each contingency as he sat in the right-front seat of the van, watching the way traffic piled up at certain exits off the highway. The road was far better than the roads he was accustomed to in Ireland, but people drove on the wrong side here, he thought, though with pretty good traffic manners compared to Europe. Especially France and Italy . . . he shook off the thought and concentrated on the situation at hand.

Once the attack was completed, they would reach the getaway vehicles in under ten minutes. The way it was timed, Ned Clark would be waiting for them. Miller completed his mental run-through, satisfied that his plan, though a hasty one, was effective.

"You're early," Breckenridge said.

"Yeah, well, I have a couple of mids coming in this afternoon to go over their term papers. Any problem?" Jack took the Browning from his briefcase.

The Sergeant Major grabbed a box of 9mm rounds. "Nope. Mondays are supposed to be screwed up."

Ryan walked to lane three and pulled the gun from the holster. First he ejected the empty clip and pulled the slide back. Next he checked the barrel for obstructions. He knew the weapon was fine mechanically, of course, but Breckenridge had range-safety rules that were inviolable. Even the Superintendent of the Academy had to follow them.

"Okay, Gunny."

"I think today we'll try rapid fire." The Sergeant Major clipped the appropriate target on the rack, and the motorized pulley took it fifty feet downrange. Ryan loaded five rounds into the clip.

"Get your ears on, Lieutenant." Breckenridge tossed the muff-type protectors. Ryan put them on. He slid the clip into the pistol and thumbed down the slide release. The weapon was now "in battery," ready to fire. Ryan pointed it downrange and waited. A moment later the light over the target snapped on. Jack brought the gun up and set the black circle right on the top of his front sight blade before he squeezed. Rapid-fire rules gave him one second per shot. This was more time than it sounded like. He got the first round off a little late, but most people did. The gun ejected the spent case and Ryan pulled it down for the next shot, concentrating on the target and his sights. By the time he counted to five, the gun was locked open. Jack pulled off the ear protectors.

"You're getting there, Lieutenant," Breckenridge said at the spotting scope. "All in the black: a nine, four tens, one of 'em in the X-ring. Again."

Ryan reloaded with a smile. He'd allowed himself to forget how much fun a pistol could be. This was a pure physical skill, a man's skill that carried the same sort of satisfaction as a just-right golf shot. He had to control a machine that delivered a .357-inch bullet to a precise destination. Doing this required coordination of eye and hand. It wasn't quite the same as using a shotgun or a rifle. Pistol was much harder than either of those, and hitting the target carried a subintellectual pleasure that was not easily described to someone who hadn't done it. His next five rounds were all tens. He tried the two-hand Weaver stance, and placed four out of five in the X-ring, a circle half the diameter of the ten-ring, used for tie-breaking in competition shoots.

"Not bad for a civilian," Breckenridge said. "Coffee?"

"Thanks, Gunny." Ryan took the cup.

"I want you to concentrate a little more on your second round. You keep letting that one go off to the right some. You're rushing it a little." The difference, Ryan knew, was barely two inches at fifty feet. Breckenridge was a stone perfectionist. It struck him that the Sergeant Major and Cathy had very similar personalities: either you were doing it exactly right or you were doing it completely wrong. "Doc, it's a shame you got hurt. You would have made a good officer, with the right sergeant to bring you along—they all need that of course."

"You know something, Gunny? I met a couple of guys in London that you'd just love." Jack slipped the magazine back into his automatic.

"Ryan is rather a clever lad, isn't he?" Owens handed the document back to Murray.

"Nothing really new in here," Dan admitted, "but at least it's well organized. Here's the other thing you wanted."

"Oh, our friends in Boston. How is Paddy O'Neil doing?" Owens was more than just annoyed at this. Padraig O'Neil was an insult to the

British parliamentary system, an elected mouthpiece for the Provisional IRA. In ten years of trying, however, neither Owens' Anti-Terror Branch nor the Royal Ulster Constabulary had ever linked him to an illegal act.

"Drinking a lot of beer, talking to a lot of folks, and raising a little money, just like always." Murray sipped at his port. "We have agents following him around. He knows they're there, of course. If he spits on the sidewalk, we'll put him on the next bird home. He knows that, too. He hasn't broken a single law. Even his driver—the guy's a teetotaler. I hate to say it, Jimmy, but the bum's clean, and he's making points."

"Oh, yes, he's a charming one, Paddy is." Owens flipped a page and looked up. "Let me see that thing your Ryan fellow did again."

"The guys at Five glommed your copy. I expect they'll give it to you tomorrow."

Owens grunted as he flipped to the summary at the back of the document. "Here it is. . . . Good God above!"

"What?" Murray snapped forward in his chair.

"The link, the bloody link. It's right here!"

"What are you talking about, Jimmy? I've read the thing twice myself."

" 'The fact that ULA personnel seem to have been drawn almost entirely from "extreme" elements within the PIRA itself,' " he read aloud, " 'must have a significance beyond that established by existing evidence. It seems likely that since the ULA membership has been so recruited, some ULA "defectors-in-place" remain within the PIRA, serving as information sources to their actual parent organization. It follows that such information may be of an operational nature in addition to its obvious counterintelligence value.' *Operational*," Owens said quietly. "We've always assumed that O'Donnell was simply trying to protect himself . . . but he could be playing another game entirely."

"I still haven't caught up with you, Jimmy." Murray set his glass down and frowned for a moment. "Oh. Maureen Dwyer. You never did figure out that tip, did you?"

Owens was thinking about another case, but Murray's remark exploded like a flashbulb in front of his eyes. The detective just stared at his American colleague for a moment while his brain raced down a host of ideas.

"But why?" Murray asked. "What do they gain?"

"They can do great embarrassment to the leadership, inhibit operations."

"But what material good does that do for the ULA? O'Donnell's too professional to screw his old friends just for the hell of it. The INLA might, but they're just a bunch of damned-fool cowboys. The ULA is too sophisticated for that sort of crap."

"Yes. We've just surmounted one wall to find another before us. Still, that's one more wall behind us. It gives us something to question young Miss Dwyer about, doesn't it?"

"Well, it's an idea to run down. The ULA has the PIRA penetrated, and sometimes they feed information to you to make the Provos look bad." Murray shook his head. *Did I just say that one terrorist outfit was trying to make another one look bad?* "Do you have enough evidence to back that idea up?"

"I can name you three cases in the last year where anonymous tips gave us Provos who were at the top of our list. In none of the three did we ever learn who the source was."

"But if the Provos suspect it—oh, scratch that idea. They want O'Donnell anyway, and that's straight revenge for all the people he did away with within the organization. Okay, embarrassing the PIRA leadership may be an objective in itself—*if* O'Donnell was trying to recruit some new members. But you've already discarded that idea."

Owens swore under his breath. Criminal investigation, he often said, was like doing a jigsaw puzzle when you didn't have all the pieces and never really knew their shapes. But telling that to his subordinates wasn't the same thing as experiencing it himself. If only they hadn't lost Sean Miller. Maybe they might have gotten something from him by now. His instinct told him that one small, crucial fact would make a complete picture of all the rubbish he was sorting through. Without that fact, his reason told Owens, everything he thought he knew was nothing more than speculation. But one thought kept repeating itself in his mind:

"Dan, if you wanted to embarrass the Provisionals' leadership politically, how and where would you do it?"

"Hello, this is Doctor Ryan."

"This is Bernice Wilson at Johns Hopkins. Your wife asked me to tell you that she's in an emergency procedure and she'll be about a half hour late tonight.''

"Okay, thank you.'' Jack replaced the phone. *Mondays,* he told himself. He went back to discussing the term paper projects with his two mids. His deck clock said four in the afternoon. Well, there was no hurry, was there?

The watch changed at Gate Three. The civilian guard was named Bob Riggs. He was a retired Navy chief master at arms, past fifty, with a beer belly that made it hard for him to see his shoes. The cold affected him badly, and he spent as much time as possible in the guardhouse. He didn't see a man in his late twenties approach the opposite corner and disappear into a doorway. Neither did Sergeant Tom Cummings of the Marine guard force, who was checking some paperwork just after relieving the previous watch-stander. The Academy was good duty for the young Marine NCO. There were a score of good saloons within easy walking distance, and plenty of unattached womenfolk to be sampled, but the duty at Annapolis was pretty boring when you got down to it, and Cummings was young enough to crave some action. It had been a typical Monday. The previous guard had issued three parking citations. He was already yawning.

Fifty feet away, an elderly lady approached the entrance to the apartment building. She was surprised to see a handsome young man there and dropped her shopping bag while fumbling for her key.

"Can I help you with that, now?'' he asked politely. His accent made him sound different, but rather kind, the lady thought. He held the bag while she unlocked the door.

"I'm afraid I'm a little early—waiting to meet my young lady, you see,'' he explained with a charming smile. "I'm sorry if I startled you, ma'am—just trying to keep out of this bitter wind.''

"Would you like to wait inside the door?'' she offered.

"That's very kind indeed, ma'am, but no. I might miss her and it's a bit of a surprise, you see. Good day to you.'' His hand relaxed around the knife in his coat pocket.

Sergeant Cummings finished going over the papers and walked outside. He noticed the man in the doorway for the first time. Looked like he was waiting for someone, the Sergeant judged, and trying to keep out of the cold north wind. That seemed sensible enough. The Sergeant checked his watch. Four-fifteen.

"I think that does it," Bernie Katz said.

"We did it," Cathy Ryan agreed. There were smiles all around the OR. It had taken over five hours, but the youngster's eye was back together. He might need another operation, and certainly he'd wear glasses for the rest of his life, but that was better than having only one eye.

"For somebody who hasn't done one of these in four months, not bad, Cath. This kid will have both his eyes. You want to tell the family? I have to go to the john."

The boy's mother was waiting exactly where the Jeffers family had been, the same look of anxiety on her face. Beside her was someone with a camera.

"We saved the eye," Cathy said at once. After she sat down beside the woman, the photographer—he said he was from the *Baltimore Sun*—fired away with his Nikon for several minutes. The surgeon explained the procedure to the mother for several minutes, trying to calm her down. It wasn't easy, but Cathy'd had lots of practice.

Finally someone from Social Services arrived, and Cathy was able to head for the locker room. She pulled off her greens, tossing them in the hamper. Bernie Katz was sitting on the bench, rubbing his neck.

"I could use some of that myself," Cathy observed. She stood there in her Gucci underwear and stretched. Katz turned to admire the view.

"Getting pretty big, Cath. How's the back?"

"Stiff. Just like it was with Sally. Avert your gaze, Doctor, you're a married man."

"Can I help it if pregnant women look sexy?"

"I'm glad I look it, 'cause I sure as hell don't feel like it at the moment." She dropped to the bench in front of her locker. "I didn't think we could do that one, Bernie."

"We were lucky," Katz admitted. "Fortunately the dear Lord looks after fools, drunks, and little children. Some of the time, anyway."

Cathy pulled open the locker. In the mirror she had inside, she saw that her hair did indeed look like the Medusa's. She made a face at herself. "I need another vacation."

"But you just had one," Katz observed.

"Right," Dr. Ryan snorted. She slid her legs into her pants and reached for her blouse.

"And when that fetus decides to become a baby, you'll have another."

The jacket came next. "Bernie, if you were in OB, your patients would kill you for that sort of crap."

"What a loss to medicine that would be," Katz thought aloud.

Cathy laughed. "Nice job, Bern. Kiss Annie for me."

"Sure, and you take it a little easy, eh, or I'll tell Madge North to come after you."

"I see her Friday, Bernie. She says I'm doing fine." Cathy breezed out the door. She waved to her nurses, complimenting them yet again for a superb job in the OR. The elevator was next. Already she had her car keys in her hand.

The green Porsche was waiting for her. Cathy unlocked the door and tossed her bag in the back before settling in the driver's seat. The six-cylinder engine started in an instant. The tachymeter needle swung upward to the idle setting. She let the engine warm up for a minute while she buckled her seat belt and slipped off the parking brake. The throaty rumble of the engine echoed down the concrete walls of the parking garage. When the temperature needle started to move, she shifted into reverse. A moment later she dropped the gear lever into first and moved toward Broadway. She checked the clock on the dashboard and winced—worse, she had to make a stop at the store on the way home. Well, she did have her 911 to play catch-up with.

"The target is moving," a voice said into a radio three levels up. The message was relayed by telephone to Alex's safehouse, then by radio again.

"About bloody time," Miller growled a few minutes later. "Why the hell is she late?" The last hour had been infuriating for him. First thirty minutes of waiting for her to be on time, then another thirty minutes while she wasn't. He told himself to relax. She had to be at the day-care center to pick up the kid.

"She's a doc. It happens, man," Alex said. "Let's roll."

The pickup car led off first, followed by the van. The Ford would be at the 7-Eleven across from Giant Steps in exactly thirty minutes.

*   *   *

"He must be waiting for somebody pretty," Riggs said when he got back into the guard shack.

"Still there?" Cummings was surprised. Three weeks before, Breckenridge had briefed the guard force about the possible threat to Dr. Ryan. Cummings knew that the history teacher always went out this gate—he was late today, though. The Sergeant could see that the light in his office was still on. Though the duty here was dull, Cummings was serious about it. Three months in Beirut had taught him everything he would ever need to know about that. He walked outside and took a place on the other side of the road.

Cummings watched the cars leaving. Mostly they were driven by civilians, but those driven by naval officers got a regulation Marine salute. The wind only got colder. He wore a sweater under his blouse. This kept his torso warm, but the white kid gloves that went with the dress-blue uniform were the next thing to useless. He made a great show of clapping his hands together as he turned around periodically. He never stared at the apartment building, never acted as though he knew anybody were there. It was getting dark now, and it wasn't all that easy to see him anyway. But somebody was there.

"That was fast," the man in the pickup car said. He checked his watch. She'd just knocked five minutes off her fastest time. *Damn,* he thought, *must be nice to have one of those little Porsches.* He checked the tag: CR-SRGN. Yep, that was the one. He grabbed the radio.

"Hi, Mom, I'm home," he said.

"It's about time," a male voice answered. The van was half a mile away, sitting on Joyce Lane, west of Ritchie Highway.

He saw the lady come out of the day-care center less than two minutes later. She was in a hurry.

"Rolling."

"Okay," came the answer.

"Come on, Sally, we're late. Buckle up." Cathy Ryan hated to be late. She restarted the engine. She hadn't been this late in over a month, but she could still make it home before Jack if she hustled.

The rush hour was under way in earnest, but the Porsche was small, fast, and agile. In a minute from sitting in the parking lot she was doing sixty-five, weaving through traffic like a race driver at Daytona.

*   *   *

For all their preparation, Alex almost missed her. An eighteen-wheeler was laboring up the hill in the right lane when the distinctive shape of the Porsche appeared next to it. Alex floored the van and darted out onto the road, causing the semi to jam his brakes and horn at the same time. Alex didn't look back. Miller got out of the right-front seat and went back to the window on the sliding door.

"Whooee, this lady's in a hurry tonight!"

"Can you catch her?" Miller asked.

Alex just smiled. "Watch."

"Damn, look at that Porsche!" Trooper First Class Sam Waverly was driving J-30, a State Police car coming off an afternoon of pursuit-radar work on U.S. Route 50. He and Larry Fontana of J-19 were heading back to the Annapolis police barracks off Rowe Boulevard after a long day's work when they saw the green sports car take the entrance ramp off Ritchie Highway. Both troopers were driving about sixty-five miles per hour, a privilege that accrued only to police officers. Their cars were unmarked. This made them and their radar guns impossible to spot until it was too late. They usually worked in pairs, and took turns, with one working his radar gun and the other a quarter mile down the road to wave the speeders over for their tickets.

"Another one!" Fontana said over the radio. A van swerved into the highway's left lane, forcing somebody in a Pontiac to jam on his brakes. "Let's get 'em." They were both young officers and while, contrary to legend, the State Police didn't assign ticket quotas to its officers, everyone knew that one sure way to promotion was to write a lot of them. It also made the roads safer, and that was their mission as state troopers. Neither officer really enjoyed giving out traffic citations, but they enjoyed responding to major accidents far less.

"Okay, I got the Porsche."

"You get all the fun," Fontana noted. He'd gotten a quick look at the driver.

It was a lot harder than one might imagine. First they had to clock the speeding vehicles to establish how far over the limit they were going—the greater the speed, the greater the fine, of course—then they had to close and switch on their lights to pull them over. Both subject vehicles were two hundred yards ahead of the police cruisers now.

*   *   *

Cathy checked her clock again. She'd managed to cut nearly ten minutes off her trip time. Next she checked her rearview mirror for a police car. She didn't want to get a ticket. There was nothing that looked like a cop car, only ordinary cars and trucks. She had to slow as the traffic became congested approaching the Severn River bridge. She debated getting over into the left lane, but decided against it. Sometimes it was hard to get back into the right lane in time to take the Route 2 exit. Beside her, Sally was craning her neck to see over the dash, as usual, and playing with the seat-belt buckle. Cathy didn't say anything this time, but concentrated on the traffic as she eased off the pedal.

Miller slipped the door latch and moved the door an inch backward. Another man took hold of the door as he knelt and thumbed the safety forward on his weapon.

He couldn't get her for speeding now, Trooper Waverly noted sourly. She'd slowed before he could establish her speed. He was a hundred yards back. Fontana could, however, ticket the van for improper lane-changing, and one out of two wasn't bad. Waverly checked his mirror. J-19 was catching up, about to pull even with his J-30. There was something odd about the blue van, he saw . . . like the side door wasn't quite right.

"Now!" Alex called.

Cathy Ryan noted that a van was pulling up on her left side. She took a casual look in time to see the van's door slide back. There was a man kneeling, holding something. There came a chilling moment of realization. She stomped her foot on the brake a fraction of a second before she saw the white flash.

"What!" Waverly saw a foot-long tongue of flame spit out from the side of the van. The windshield of the Porsche went cloudy and the car swerved sideways, straightened out, then slammed into the bridge's concrete work at over fifty miles per hour. Instantly cars in both lanes slammed on their brakes. The van kept going.

"Larry, shots fired—shots fired from the van. The Porsche was hit!" Waverly flipped on his lights and stood on his brakes. The police car skidded right and nearly slid sideways into the wrecked Porsche. "Get the van, get the van!"

"I'm on him," Fontana replied. He suddenly realized that the gout of flame he'd seen could only mean some kind of machine gun. "Holy shit," he said to himself.

Waverly returned his attention to the Porsche. Steam poured from the rear engine compartment. "J-30, Annapolis, officer reports shots fired—looked like automatic weapons fire—and a PI accident westbound Route 50 on Severn River bridge. Appears to be serious PI. J-19 in pursuit of vehicle 2. Stand by."

"Standing by," the dispatcher acknowledged. *What the hell . . .*

Waverly grabbed his fire extinguisher and ran the fifteen feet to the wreck. Glass and metal were scattered as far as he could see. The engine, thank God, wasn't on fire. He checked the passenger compartment next.

"Oh, Jesus!" He ran back to his car. "J-30, Annapolis. Call fireboard, officer requests helicopter response. Serious PI, two victims, a white female adult and a white female child, repeat we have a serious PI accident westbound Route 50 east side of Severn River bridge. Officer requests helicopter response."

"J-19, Annapolis," Fontana called in next. "I am in pursuit of a dark van, with handicap tag number Henry Six-Seven-Seven-Two. I am westbound on Route 50 just west of the Severn River bridge. Shots fired from this vehicle. Officer requests assistance," he said coolly. He decided against turning his lights on for the moment. *Holy shit . . .*

"You get her?" Alex called back.

Miller was breathing heavily. He wasn't sure—he wasn't sure about his shots. The Porsche had slowed suddenly just as he squeezed the trigger, but he saw the car hit the bridge and spring up into the air like a toy. No way they could walk away from that sort of accident, he was sure of that.

"Yes."

"Okay, let's boogie." Alex didn't let his emotions interfere with his work. This job meant weapons and money for his movement. It was too bad about the woman and the kid, but it wasn't his fault that they made the wrong kind of enemies.

*   *   *

The Annapolis dispatcher was already on his UHF radio to the State Police helicopter. Trooper-1, a Bell JetRanger-II was just lifting off from a refueling stop at Baltimore-Washington International Airport.

"Roger that," the helicopter pilot replied, turning south and twisting the throttle control to full power. The paramedic in the left seat leaned forward to change the transponder "squawk" setting from 1200 to 5101. This would inform air traffic controllers that the helicopter was on an emergency medivac mission.

"Trooper-1, J-30, we are en route to your position, ETA four minutes."

Waverly didn't acknowledge. He and two civilians were prying the driver's side window off the car with a tire iron. The driver and passenger were both unconscious, and there was blood all over the interior of the car. She was probably pretty, Waverly thought, looking at the driver, but her head was covered with glistening blood. The child lay like a broken doll, half on the seat, half on the floor. His stomach was a tight cold ball just below his pounding heart. *Another dead kid,* he thought. *Please, God, not another one.*

"Trooper-2, Annapolis," came the next call to the dispatcher.

"Annapolis, Trooper-2, where are you?"

"We are over Mayo Beach, northbound. I copied your medivac call. I have the Governor and Attorney General aboard. Can we help, over."

The dispatcher made a quick decision. Trooper-1 would be at the accident scene in three more minutes. J-19 needed backup in a hurry. This was real luck. Already he had six state vehicles converging on the area, plus three more from the Anne Arundel County Police station at Edgewater. "Trooper-2, contact J-19."

"Trooper-2, J-19, please advise your location," the radio squawked in Fontana's car.

"Westbound Route 50, just passing Rowe Boulevard. I am in pursuit of a dark van with a handicap tag. J-30 and I observed automatic weapons fire from this vehicle, repeat automatic weapons fire. I need some help, people."

*   *   *

It was easy to spot. The Sergeant flying Trooper-2 saw the other helicopter circling over the accident to the east, and Route 50 was nearly bare of cars from west of the accident to Rowe Boulevard. The police car and the van were on the back edge of the moving traffic.

"What gives?" the Governor asked from the back. The paramedic in the left-front seat filled them in as the pilot continued his visual search for . . . there! *Okay, sucker . . .*

"J-19, this is Trooper-2, I got you and the subject car visual." The pilot dropped altitude to five hundred feet. "Trooper-2, Annapolis, I got 'em. Black, or maybe blue van westbound on 50, with an unmarked car in pursuit."

Alex was wondering who the car was. It was unmarked, but a cheap-body car, with dull, monocolor paintwork. *Uh-oh.*

"That's a cop behind us!" he shouted. One of Miller's men looked out the window. Unmarked cars were nothing new where they came from.

"Get rid of him!" Alex snarled.

Fontana held at fifty yards from the van. This was far enough, he thought, to keep himself out of danger. The trooper was listening to continuous chatter on his radio as additional cars announced that they were inbound on the call. The distraction of the radio made him a second late on seeing the van's door fly open. Fontana blanched and hit the brakes.

Miller handled this one too. The moment the door was open, he leveled his machine gun and loosed ten rounds at the police car. He saw it dip when the driver tried to panic-stop, swerve sideways in the road, and flip over. He was too excited even to smile, though inwardly he was awash with glee. The door came back shut as Alex changed lanes.

Fontana felt the bullet hit his chest before he realized that the car's windshield was shattering around him. His right arm jerked down, turning the car too rapidly to the right. The locked-up rear wheels gave the car a broadside skid, a tire blew out, and the car flipped over.

Fontana watched in fascination the world rotate around him as the car's top crumpled. Like most policemen he never bothered with his seat belt, and he fell on his neck. The collapsing car top broke it. It didn't matter. A car that had been following his crashed into the police cruiser, finishing the work begun by Miller's submachine gun.

"Shit!" the pilot of Trooper-2 cursed. "Trooper-2, Annapolis, J-19 is wrecked with serious PI on 50 west of the Route 2 exit. Where the hell are the other cars!"

"Trooper-2, advise condition of J-19."

"He's dead, man—I'm on that fucking van! Where's the goddamned backup!"

"Trooper-2, be advised we have eleven cars converging. We have a roadblock setting up now on 50 at South Haven Road. There are three cars westbound on 50 about half a mile back of you and two more eastbound approaching the exit to General's Highway."

"Roger that, I am on the van," the pilot responded.

"Come on, Alex!" Miller shouted.

"Almost there, man," the black man said, changing to the right lane exit. About a mile ahead he saw the blue and red flashing lights of two police cars coming east toward him, but there was no eastbound exit here. *Tough luck, pigs.* He didn't feel very happy about doing the Porsche, but a dead cop was always something to feel good about. "Here we go!"

"Annapolis, Trooper-2," the pilot called, "the subject van is turning north off of Route 50." It took a moment to register. "Oh, no!" He gave a quick order. The eastbound police cars slowed, then darted across the grass median strip into the westbound lanes. These were clear, blocked by a second major accident, but the median was uneven. One car bogged down in the grass and mud while the other bounded up onto the pavement and ran the wrong way on the highway toward the exit.

Alex hit the traffic light exactly right, crossing West Street and heading north. His peripheral vision caught a county police car stuck in the rush-hour traffic on West Street two hundred yards to his right, despite his lights and siren. *Too late, pig.* He proceeded two hundred yards and turned left.

The Sergeant flying Trooper-2 started cursing, oblivious to the Governor and Attorney General in the back. As he watched, the van pulled into the hundred-acre parking lot that surrounded Annapolis Mall. The vehicle proceeded toward the inner ring of parking spaces as three cars turned off West Street in pursuit.

"Son of a *bitch*!" He pushed down on his collective control and dove at the parking lot.

Alex pulled into a handicap parking slot and stopped the van. His passengers were ready, and opened the doors as soon as the vehicle stopped. They walked slowly and normally to the entrance to the mall. The driver looked up in surprise when he heard the whine and flutter of the helicopter. It hovered at about a hundred feet. Alex made sure his hat was in place and waved as he went through the door.

The helicopter pilot looked at the paramedic in the left seat, whose hand was clenched in rage at his shoulder-holstered .357 revolver while the pilot needed both of his on the controls.

"They're gone," the paramedic said quietly over the intercom.

"What do you mean they're gone!" the Attorney General demanded.

Below them, a county and a State Police car screeched to a halt outside the entrance. But inside those doors were about three thousand shoppers, and the police didn't know what the suspects looked like. The officers stood there, guns drawn, not knowing what to do next.

Alex and his men were inside a public rest room. Two members of Alex's organization were waiting there with shopping bags. Each man from the van got a new coat. They broke up into pairs and walked out into the shopping concourse, heading for an exit at the west end of the mall. They took their time. There was no reason to hurry.

"He waved at us," the Governor said. "Do something!"

"What?" the pilot asked. "What do you want us to do? Who do we stop? They're gone, they might as well be in California now."

The Governor was slow to catch on, though faster than the Attorney General, who was still blubbering. What had begun as a routine political meeting in Salisbury, on Maryland's eastern shore, had turned into an exciting pursuit, but one with a most unsatisfactory ending. He'd watched one of his state troopers killed right before his eyes, and neither he nor his people could do a single thing about it. The Governor swore, finally. The voters would have been shocked at his language.

Trooper-1 was sitting on the Severn River bridge, its rotor turning rapidly to stay above the concrete barriers. The paramedic, Trooper Waverly, and a motorist who turned out to be a volunteer fireman, were loading the two accident victims into Stokes litters for transport on the helicopter. The other motorist who had assisted was standing alone by the police car, over a puddle of his own vomit. A fire engine was pulling up to the scene, and two more state troopers were preparing to get traffic moving, once the helicopter took off. The highway was already backed up at least four miles. As they prepared to start directing traffic, they heard on their radios what had happened to J-19 and its driver. The police officers exchanged looks, but no words. They would come later.

As first officer on the scene, Waverly took the driver's purse and started looking for identification. He had lots of forms to fill out, and people to notify. Inside the purse, he saw, was some kind of finger painting. He looked up as the little girl's litter was loaded into the top rack of the helicopter's passenger bay. The paramedic went in behind it, and less than thirty seconds later, Waverly's face stung with the impact of gravel, thrown up by the helicopter's rotor. He watched it lift into the air, and whispered a prayer for the little girl who'd done a painting of something that looked like a blue cow. *Back to work,* he told himself. The purse had a red address book. He checked the driver's license to get a name, then looked in the book under the same letter. Someone with the first name of Jack, but no last name written in, had a number designated "work." It was probably her husband's. Somebody had to call him.

"Baltimore Approach, this is Trooper-1 on a medivac inbound to Baltimore."

"Trooper-1, roger, you are cleared for direct approach, come left to course three-four-seven and maintain current altitude,'' the air controller at Baltimore-Washington International responded. The 5101 squawk number was clear on his scope, and medical emergencies had unconditional priority.

"Hopkins Emergency, this is Trooper-1, inbound with a white female child accident victim.''

"Trooper-1, Hopkins. Divert to University. We're full up here.''

"Roger. University, Trooper-1, do you copy, over.''

"Trooper-1, this is University, we copy, and we're ready for you.''

"Roger, ETA five minutes. Out.''

"Gunny, this is Cummings at Gate Three,'' the Sergeant called on the telephone.

"What is it, Sergeant?'' Breckenridge asked.

"There's this guy, he's been standing on the corner across the street for about forty-five minutes. It just feels funny, you know? He's off the grounds, but it doesn't feel right.''

"Call the cops?'' the Sergeant Major asked.

"What for?'' Cummings asked reasonably. "He ain't even spit far as I can tell.''

"Okay, I'll walk on up.'' Breckenridge stood. He was bored anyway. The Sergeant Major donned his cap and walked out of the building, heading north across the campus. It took five minutes, during which he saluted six officers and greeted a larger number of mids. He didn't like the cold. It had never been like this during his childhood on a Mississippi dirt farm. But spring was coming. He was careful not to look too obviously out of the gate as he crossed the street.

He found Cummings in the guardhouse, standing inside the door. A good young sergeant, Cummings was. He had the new look of the Corps. Breckenridge was built along the classic John Wayne lines, with broad shoulders and imposing bulk. Cummings was a black kid, a runner who had the frame of a Frank Shorter. The boy could run all day, something that the Gunny had never been able to do. But more than all of that, Cummings was a lifer. He understood what the Marine Corps was all about. Breckenridge had taken the young man under his wing, imparting a few important lessons along the way. The Sergeant Major knew that he would soon be part of the Corps' past. Cummings was its future, and he told himself that the future looked pretty good.

"Hey, Gunny,'' the Sergeant greeted him.

"The guy in the doorway?"

"He's been there since a little after four. He don't live here." Cummings paused for a moment. He was, after all, only a "buck" sergeant with no rockers under his stripes, talking to a man whom generals addressed with respect. "It just feels funny."

"Well, let's give him a few minutes," Breckenridge thought aloud.

"God, I hate grading quizzes."

"So go easy on the boys and girls," Robby chuckled.

"Like you do?" Ryan asked.

"I teach a difficult, technical subject. I have to give quizzes."

"Engineers! Shame you can't read and write as well as you multiply."

"You must have taken a tough-pill this afternoon, Jack."

"Yeah, well—" The phone rang. Jack picked it up. "Doctor Ryan. Yes—who?" His face changed, his voice became guarded.

"Yes, that's right." Robby saw his friend go stiff in the chair. "Are you sure? Where are they now? Okay—ah, okay, thank you . . . I, uh, thank you." Jack stared at the phone for a second or two before hanging it up.

"What's the matter, Jack?" Robby asked.

It took him a moment to answer. "That was the police. There's been an accident."

"Where are they?" Robby said immediately.

"They flew them—they flew them to Baltimore." Jack stood shakily. "I have to get there." He looked down at his friend. "God, Robby . . ."

Jackson was on his feet in an instant. "Come on, I'll take you up there."

"No, I'll—"

"Stuff it, Jack. I'm driving." Robby got his coat and tossed Jack's over the desk. "Move it, boy!"

"They took them by helicopter . . ."

"Where? Where to, Jack?"

"University," he said.

"Get it together, Jack." Robby grabbed his arm. "Settle down some." The flyer led his friend down the stairs and out of the building. His red Corvette was parked a hundred yards away.

*   *   *

"Still there," the civilian guard reported when he came back in.

"Okay," Breckenridge said, standing. He looked at the pistol holster hanging in the corner, but decided against that. "This is what we're going to do."

Ned Clark hadn't liked the mission from the first moment. Sean was too eager on this one. But he hadn't said so. Sean had masterminded the prison break that had made him a free man. If nothing else, Ned Clark was loyal to the Cause. He was exposed here and didn't like that either. His briefing had told him that the guards at the Academy gate were lax, and he could see that they were unarmed. They had no authority at all off the grounds of the school.

But it was taking too long. His target was thirty minutes late. He didn't smoke, didn't do anything to make himself conspicuous, and he knew that he'd be hard to spot. The doorway of the tired old apartment building had no light—one of Alex's people had taken care of that with a pellet gun the previous night.

Ought to call this one off, Clark told himself. But he didn't want to do that. He didn't want to fail Sean. He saw a pair of men leave the Academy. Bootnecks, bloody Marines in their Sunday clothes. They looked so pretty without their guns, so vulnerable.

"So the Captain, he says," the big one was saying loudly, "get that goddamned gook off my chopper!" And the other one started laughing.

"I love it!"

"How about a couple of beers?" the big one said next. They crossed the street, heading his way.

"Okay by me, Gunny. You buyin'?"

"My turn, isn't it? I have to get some money first." The big one reached in his pocket for some keys and turned toward Clark. "Excuse me, sir, can I help you?" His hand came out of his pocket without any keys.

Clark reacted quickly, but not quickly enough. The right hand inside his overcoat started moving up, but Breckenridge's own right grabbed it like a vise.

"I asked if I could help you, sir," the Sergeant Major said pleasantly. "What do you have in that hand?" Clark tried to move, but the big man pushed him against the brick wall.

"Careful, Tom," Breckenridge warned.

Cummings' hand searched downward and found the metallic shape of a pistol. "Gun," he said sharply.

"It better not go off," the Gunny announced, his left arm across Clark's throat. "Let the man have it, sonny, real careful, like."

Clark was amazed at his stupidity, letting them get so close to him. His head tried to turn to look up the street, but the man waiting for him in the car was around the corner. Before he could think of anything to do, the black man had disarmed him and was searching his pockets. Cummings removed the knife next.

"Talk to me," Breckenridge said. Clark didn't say anything, and the forearm slid roughly across his throat. "*Please* talk to me, *sir*."

"Get your bloody hands off of me! Who do you think you are?"

"Where you from, boy?" Breckenridge didn't need an answer to that one. The Sergeant wrenched Clark's arm out of the pocket and twisted it behind his back. "Okay, sonny, we're going to walk through that gate over yonder, and you're gonna sit down and be a good boy while we call the police. If you make any trouble, I'm going to tear this arm off and shove it right up your ass. Let's go, boy."

The driver who'd been waiting for Clark was standing at the far corner. He took one look at what had happened and walked to his car. Two minutes later he was blocks away.

Cummings handcuffed the man to a chair while Breckenridge established that he carried no identification—aside from an automatic pistol, which was ID enough. First he called his captain, then the Annapolis City police. It started there, but, though the Gunny didn't know, it wouldn't stop there.

15

Shock and Trauma

If Jack had ever doubted that Robby Jackson really was a fighter pilot, this would have cured him. Jackson's personal toy was a two-year-old Chevrolet Corvette, painted candy-apple red, and he drove it with a sense of personal invincibility. The flyer raced out the Academy's west gate, turned left, and found his way to Rowe Boulevard. The traffic problems on Route 50 west were immediately apparent, and he changed lanes to head east. In a minute he was streaking across the Severn River bridge. Jack was too engrossed in his thoughts to see much of anything, but Robby saw what looked like the remains of a Porsche on the other side of the roadway. Jackson's blood went cold as he turned away. He cast the thoughts aside and concentrated on his driving, pushing the Corvette past eighty. There were too many cops on the other side of the road for him to worry about a ticket. He took the Ritchie Highway exit a minute later and curved around north toward Baltimore. Rush-hour traffic was heavy, though most of it was heading in the other direction. This gave him gaps to exploit, and the pilot used every one. He worked up and down through the gears, rarely touching the brakes.

To his right, Jack simply stared straight ahead, not seeing much of anything. He managed to wince when Robby paused behind two tractor-trailers running side by side—then shot up right between them with scant inches of clearance on either side. The outraged screams of the two diesel horns faded irrelevantly behind the racing 'Vette, and Jack returned to the emptiness of his thoughts.

Breckenridge allowed his captain, Mike Peters, to handle the situation. He was a pretty good officer, the Sergeant Major thought, who had the common sense to let his NCOs run things. He'd managed to get to the guard shack about two minutes ahead of the Annapolis City police, long enough for Breckenridge and Cummings to fill him in.

"So what gives, gentlemen?" the responding officer asked. Captain Peters nodded for Breckenridge to speak.

"Sir, Sergeant Cummings here observed this individual to be standing over at the corner across the street. He did not look like a local resident, so we kept an eye on him. Finally Cummings and I walked over and asked if we might be of assistance to him. He tried to pull this on us"—the Gunny lifted the pistol carefully, so as not to disturb the fingerprints—"and he had this knife in his pocket. Carrying a concealed weapon is a violation of local law, so Cummings and I made a citizen's arrest and called you. This character does not have any identification on him, and he declined to speak with us."

"What kind of gun is that?" the cop asked.

"It's a FN nine-millimeter," Breckenridge answered. "It's the same as the Browning Hi-Power, but a different trademark, with a thirteen-round magazine. The weapon was loaded, with a live round in the chamber. The hammer was down. The knife is a cheap piece of shit. Punk knife."

The cop had to smile. He knew Breckenridge from the department firearms training unit.

"Can I have your name, please," the cop said to Eamon Clark. The "suspect" just stared at him. "Sir, you have a number of constitutional rights which I am about to read to you, but the law does not allow you to withhold your identity. You have to tell me your name."

The cop stared at Clark for another minute. At last he shrugged and pulled a card from his clipboard. "Sir, you have the right to remain silent. . . ." He read the litany off the card. "Do you understand these rights?"

Still Clark didn't say anything. The police officer was getting irritated. He looked at the other three men in the room. "Gentlemen, will you testify that I read this individual his rights?"

"Yes, sir, we certainly will," Captain Peters said.

"If I may make a suggestion, officer," Breckenridge said. "You might want to check this boy out with the FBI."

"How come?"

"He talks funny," the Sergeant Major explained. "He don't come from here."

"Great—two crazy ones in one day."

"What do ya mean?" Breckenridge asked.

"Little while ago a car got machine-gunned on 50, sounds like some kind of drug hit. A trooper got killed by the same bunch a few minutes later. The bad guys got away." The cop leaned down to look Clark in the face. "You better start talkin', sir. The cops in this town are in a mean mood tonight. What I'm tellin' you, man, is that we don't want to put up with some unnecessary shit. You understand me?"

Clark didn't understand. In Ireland carrying a concealed weapon was a serious crime. In America it was rather less so since so many citizens owned guns. Had he said he was waiting for someone and carried a gun because he was afraid of street criminals, he might have gotten out on the street before identification procedures were complete. Instead, his intransigence was only making the policeman angry and ensuring that the identification procedures would be carried out in full before he was arraigned.

Captain Peters and Sergeant Major Breckenridge exchanged a meaningful look.

"Officer," the Captain said, "I would most strongly recommend that you check this character's ID with the FBI. We've, uh, we had a sort of an informal warning about terrorist activity a few weeks back. This is still your jurisdiction since he was arrested in the city, but . . ."

"I hear you, Cap'n," the cop said. He thought for a few seconds and concluded that there was something more here than met the eye. "If you gentlemen will come to the station with me, we'll find out who Mr. Doe here really is."

                    *   *   *

Ryan charged through the entrance of the Shock-Trauma Center and
identified himself to the reception desk, whose occupant directed him
to a waiting room where, she said firmly, he would be notified as soon
as there was anything to report. The sudden change from action to
inaction disoriented Jack enormously. He stood at the entrance to the
waiting room for some minutes, his mind a total blank as it struggled
with the situation. By the time Robby arrived from parking his car, he
found his friend sitting on the cracked vinyl of an old sofa, mindlessly
reading through a brochure whose stiff paper had become as soft as
chamois from the numberless hands of parents, wives, husbands, and
friends of the patients who had passed through this building.

The brochure explained in bureaucratic prose how the Maryland
Institute for Emergency Medical Services was the first and best organization of its kind, devoted exclusively to the most sophisticated emergency care for trauma victims. Ryan knew all this. Johns Hopkins
managed the more recent pediatric unit and provided many of the staff
surgeons for eye injuries. Cathy had spent some time doing that during
her residency, an intense two months that she'd been happy to leave
behind. Jack wondered if she were now being treated by a former
colleague. *Would he recognize her? Would it matter?*

The Shock-Trauma Center—so known to everyone but the billing
department—had begun as the dream of a brilliant, aggressive, and
supremely arrogant heart surgeon who had bludgeoned his way
through a labyrinth of bureaucratic empires to build this 21st-century
emergency room.

It had blossomed into a dazzling, legendary success. Shock-Trauma
was the leading edge of emergency medical technology. It had already
pioneered many techniques for critical care, and in doing so had over-
thrown many historical precepts of conventional medicine—which had
not endeared its founder to his medical brethren. That would have been
true in any field, and Shock-Trauma's founder had not helped the
process with his brutally outspoken opinions. His greatest—but un-
acknowledged—crime, of course, was being right in nearly all details.
And while this prophet was without honor in the mainstream of his
profession, its younger members were easier to convert. Shock-
Trauma attracted the best young surgical talent in the world, and only
the finest of them were chosen.

But will they be good enough? Ryan asked himself.

He lost all track of time, waiting, afraid to look at his watch, afraid to speculate on the significance of time's flight. Alone, completely alone in his circumscribed world, he reflected that God had given him a wife he loved and a child he treasured more than his own life; that his first duty as husband and father was to protect them from an often hostile world; that he had failed; that, because of this, their lives were now in strangers' hands. All his knowledge, all his skills were useless now. It was worse than impotence, and some evil agency in his mind kept repeating over and over the thoughts that made him cringe as he retreated farther and farther into catatonic numbness. For hours he stared at the floor, then the wall, unable even to pray as his mind sought the solace of emptiness.

Jackson sat beside his friend, silent, in his own private world. A naval aviator, he had seen close friends vanish from a trivial mistake or a mechanical glitch—or seemingly nothing at all. He'd felt death's cold hand brush his own shoulder less than a year before. But this wasn't a danger to a mature man who had freely chosen a dangerous profession. This was a young wife and an innocent child whose lives were at risk. He couldn't joke about how "old Dutch" would luck this one out. He knew nothing at all he could say, no encouragement he could offer other than just sitting there, and though he gave no sign of it, Robby was sure that Jack knew his friend was close at hand.

After two hours Jackson quietly left the waiting room to call his wife and check discreetly at the desk. The receptionist fumbled for the names, then identified them as: a Female, Blond, Age Thirty or so, Head; and a Female, Blond, Age Four or so, Flailed Chest. The pilot was tempted to throttle the receptionist for her coldness, but his discipline was sufficient to allow him to turn away without a word. Jackson rejoined Ryan a moment later, and together they stared at the wall through the passage of time. It started to rain outside, a cold rain that perfectly matched what they both felt.

Special Agent Shaw was walking through the door of his Chevy Chase home when the phone rang. His teen-age daughter answered it and just held it out to him. This sort of thing was not the least unusual.

"Shaw here."

"Mr. Shaw, this is Nick Capitano from the Annapolis office. The city police here have in custody a man with a pistol, a knife, but no ID.

He refuses to talk at all, but earlier he did speak to a couple of Marines, and he had an accent.''

"That's nice, he has an accent. What kind?'' Shaw asked testily.

"Maybe Irish,'' Capitano replied. "He was apprehended just outside Gate Three of the U.S. Naval Academy. There's a Marine here who says that some teacher named Ryan works there, and he got some sort of warning from the Anti-Terrorism Office.''

What the hell. "Have you ID'd the suspect yet?''

"No, sir. The local police just fingerprinted him, and they faxed a copy of the prints and photo to the Bureau. The suspect refuses to say anything. He just isn't talking at all, sir.''

"Okay,'' Shaw thought for a moment. *So much for dinner.* "I'll be back in my office in thirty minutes. Have them send a copy of the mug shot and the prints there. You stay put, and have somebody find Doctor Ryan and stay with him.''

"Right.''

Shaw hung up and dialed his office at the Bureau. "Dave, Bill. Call London, and tell Dan Murray I want him in his office in half an hour. We may have something happening over here.''

"'Bye, Daddy,'' his daughter said. Shaw hadn't even had time to take off his coat.

He was at his desk twenty-seven minutes later. First he called Nick Capitano in Annapolis.

"Anything new?''

"No, sir. The security detail at Annapolis can't find this Ryan guy. His car is parked on the Academy grounds, and they've got people looking for him. I've asked the Anne Arundel County Police to send a car to his home in case he got a ride—car broke down, or something like that. Things are a little wild here at the moment. Something crazy happened about the same time this John Doe gunman got picked up. A car got hosed down with a machine gun just outside the city.''

"What the hell was that?''

"The State Police are handling it. We haven't been called in,'' Capitano explained.

"Get a man over there!'' Shaw said at once. A secretary came into the office and handed him a folder. Inside was a facsimile copy of the suspect's mug shot. It showed full face and profile.

"Hold it!'' He caught the secretary before the door was closed. "I want this faxed to London right now.''

"Yes, sir."

Shaw next dialed the tie line to the embassy in London.

"I just got to sleep," the voice answered after the first ring.

"Hi, Dan. I just missed dinner. It's a tough world. I have a photo being faxed to you now." Shaw filled Murray in on what had happened.

"Oh, my God." Murray gulped down some coffee. "Where's Ryan?"

"We don't know. Probably just wandering around somewhere. His car's still parked in Annapolis—at the Academy, I mean. The security guys are looking for him. He's gotta be all right, Dan. If I read this right, the suspect in Annapolis was probably waiting for him."

The photograph of Eamon Clark was already in the embassy. The Bureau's communications unit worked on the same satellite net used by the intelligence services. The embassy communications officers were actually employees of the National Security Agency, which never slept. The facsimile had arrived with a FLASH-priority header, and a messenger ran it up to the Legal Attaché's office. But the door was locked. Murray had to set the phone down to open it.

"I'm back," Murray said. He opened the folder. The photo had suffered somewhat from twice being broken into electronic bits and broadcast, but for all of that it was recognizable. "This one's familiar. I can't put a name on him, but he's a bad guy."

"How fast can you ID him?"

"I can call Jimmy Owens real quick. You in your office?"

"Yeah," Shaw answered.

"I'll be back." Murray changed buttons on his phones. He didn't have Owens' home number memorized and had to look it up.

"Yes?"

"Hi, Jimmy, it's Dan." Murray's voice was actually chipper now. *Have I got something for you.*

Owens didn't know that yet. "Do you know what time it is?"

"Our guys have somebody in custody that you may be interested in."

"Who?" Owens asked.

"I got a picture but no name. He was arrested in Annapolis, outside the Naval Academy—"

"Ryan?"

"Maybe." Murray was worried about that.

"Meet me at the Yard," Owens said.

"On the way." Murray headed downstairs for his car.

It was easier for Owens. His house was always watched by a pair of armed detectives in a police car. All he had to do was step outside and wave, and the Land-Rover came to his door. He beat Murray by five minutes. By the time the FBI agent arrived, Owens had already consumed a cup of tea. He poured two more.

"This guy look familiar?" The FBI agent tossed the photo over. Owens' eyes went wide.

"Ned Clark," he breathed. "In America, you say?"

"I thought he looked familiar. He got picked up in Annapolis."

"This is one of the lads who broke out of Long Kesh, a very bad boy with several murders to his name. Thank you, Mr. Murray."

"Thank the Marines." Murray grabbed a cup of tea. He really needed the caffeine. "Can I make a call?" Within a minute he was back to FBI headquarters. The desk phone was on speaker so that Owens could listen in.

"Bill, the suspect is one Ned Clark, a convicted murderer who escaped from prison last year. He used to be a big-time assassin with the Provos."

"I got some bad news, Dan," Shaw replied. "It appears that there was an attack on this Ryan fellow's family. The State Police are investigating what looks like a machine-gun attack on a car belonging to Doctor Caroline Ryan, MD. The suspects were in a van and made a clean escape after killing a state trooper."

"Where is Jack Ryan?" Murray asked.

"We don't know yet. He was seen leaving the Naval Academy grounds in the car of a friend. The troopers are looking for the car now."

"What about his family?" It was Owens this time.

"They were flown to the Shock-Trauma Center in Baltimore. The local police have been notified to keep an eye on the place, but it's usually guarded anyway. As soon as we find Ryan we'll put some people with him. Okay, on this Clark kid, I'll have him in federal custody by tomorrow morning. I expect that Mr. Owens wants him back?"

"Yes." Owens leaned back in his chair. He had his own call to make now. As often happened in police work, there was bad news to accompany the good.

"Mr. Ryan?" It was a doctor. Probably a doctor. He wore a pink paper gown and strange-looking pink booties over what were probably sneakers. The gown was bloodstained. He couldn't be much over thirty, Ryan judged. The face was tired and dark. DR. BARRY SHAPIRO, the name tag announced, DEPUTY TRAUMA-SURGEON-IN-CHIEF. Ryan tried to stand but found that his legs would not work. The doctor waved for him to remain seated. He came over slowly and fell into the chair next to the sofa.

What news do you bring me? Ryan thought. His mind both screamed for information and dreaded learning what had happened to his family.

"I'm Barry Shapiro. I've been working on your daughter." He spoke quickly, with a curious accent that Ryan noted but discarded as irrelevant. "Okay, your wife is fine. She had a broken and lacerated upper left arm and a nasty cut on her head. When the helicopter paramedic saw the head wound—heads bleed a lot—he brought her here as a precaution. We ran a complete head protocol on her, and she's fine. A mild concussion, but nothing to worry about. She'll be fine."

"She's pregnant. Do—"

"We noticed." Shapiro smiled. "No problem with that. The pregnancy has not been compromised in any way."

"She's a surgeon. Will there be any permanent damage?"

"Oh? I didn't know that. We don't bother very much with patient identification," Shapiro explained. "No, there should be no problem. The damage to her arm is extensive but routine. It should heal completely."

Ryan nodded, afraid to ask the next question. The doctor paused before going on. *Does the bad news come next. . . .*

"Your daughter is a very sick little girl."

Jack nearly choked with his next breath. The iron fist that had clutched his stomach relaxed a millimeter. *At least she's alive. Sally's alive!*

"Apparently she wasn't wearing her seat belt. When the car hit she was thrown forward, very hard." Jack nodded. Sally liked to play with her seat belt buckle—*we thought it was cute,* Ryan reminded himself bitterly. "Okay, tib and fib are broken in both legs, along with the left femur. All of the left-side ribs are broken, and six on the right side—a classic flailed chest. She can't breathe for herself, but she's on respirator; that is under control. She arrived with extensive internal injuries and hemorrhaging, severe damage to the liver and spleen, and the large bowel. Her heart stopped right after she got here, probably—almost certainly—from loss of blood volume. We got it restarted at once and immediately started replacing the blood loss." Shapiro went on quickly. "That problem is also behind us.

"Doctor Kinter and I have been working on her for the best part of five hours. We had to remove the spleen—that's okay, you can live without a spleen." Shapiro didn't say that the spleen was an important part of the body's defense against infections. "The liver had a moderately extensive stellate fracture and damage to the main artery that feeds blood into the organ. We had to remove about a quarter of the liver—again no problem with that—and I *think* we fixed the arterial damage, and I *think* the repair will hold. The liver is important. It has a great deal to do with blood formation and the body's biochemical balance. You can't live without it. If liver function is maintained . . . she'll probably make it. The damage to the bowel was easy to repair. We removed about thirty centimeters. The legs are immobilized. We'll repair them later. The ribs—well, that's painful but not life-threatening. And the skull is relatively minor. I guess her chest took the main impact. She has a concussion, but there's no sign of intercranial bleeding." Shapiro rubbed his hands over his heavily-bearded face.

"The whole thing revolves around her liver function. If the liver continues to work, she will probably recover fully. We're keeping a very close watch on her blood chemistry, and we'll know something in, oh, maybe eight or nine hours."

"Not till then?" Ryan's face twisted into an agonized mass. The fist tightened its grip yet again. *She still might die . . . ?*

"Mr. Ryan," Shapiro said slowly, "I know what you are going through. If it hadn't been for the helicopter bringing your little girl in, well, right now I'd be telling you that she had died. Another five minutes getting here—maybe not that long—and she would not have made it this far. That's how close it was. But she *is* alive now, and I promise you that we're doing our very best to keep her that way. And our best is the best there is. My team of doctors and nurses is the best of its kind in the world—period. Nobody comes close. If there's a way, we'll find it." *And if there's not,* he didn't say, *we won't.*

"Can I see them?"

"No." Shapiro shook his head. "Right now both of them are in the CCRU—the Critical Care Recovery Unit. We keep that as clean as an OR. The smallest infection can be lethal for a trauma patient. I'm sorry, but it would be too dangerous to them. My people are watching them constantly. A nurse—an experienced trauma nurse—is with each of them every second, with a team of doctors and nurses thirty feet away."

"Okay." He almost gasped the word. Ryan leaned his head back against the wall and closed his eyes. *Eight more hours? But you have no choice. You have to wait. You have to do what they say.* "Okay."

Shapiro left and Jackson followed after him, catching him by the elevator.

"Doc, can't Jack see his little girl? She—"

"Not a chance." Shapiro half fell against the wall and let out a long breath. "Look, right now the little girl—what's her name anyway?"

"Sally."

"Okay, right now she's in a bed, stark naked, with IV tubes running into both arms and one leg. Her head's partially shaved. She's wired up to a half-dozen monitors, and we have an Engstrom respirator breathing for her. Her legs are wrapped—all you can see of her is one big bruise from her hips to the top of her head." Shapiro looked down at the pilot. He was too tired to show any emotion. "Look, she might die. I don't think so, but there's no way we can be sure. With liver injuries, you can't tell until the blood-chemistry readings come in, you just can't. If she does die, would you want your friend to see her like that? Would you want him to remember her like that, for the rest of his life?"

"I guess not," Jackson said quietly, surprised at how much he wanted this little girl to live. His wife could not have children, and somehow Sally had become like their own. "What are her chances?"

"I'm not a bookie, I don't quote odds. Numbers don't mean a thing in a case like this. Sorry, but either she makes it or she doesn't. Look, that wasn't a song and dance I gave—Jack, you said? She could not be in a better place." Shapiro's eyes focused on Jackson's chest. He jabbed a finger at the wings of gold. "You a pilot?"

"Yeah. Fighters."

"Phantoms?"

"No, the F-14. Tomcat."

"I fly." Shapiro smiled. "I used to be a flight surgeon in the Air Force. Last year I got a sailplane. Nice and peaceful up there. When I can get away from this madhouse, I go up every time I can. No phones. No hassles. Just me and the clouds." The doctor was not talking to Jackson so much as himself. Robby set his hand on the surgeon's arm.

"Doc, tell you what—you save that little girl, and I'll get you a checkride in any bird you want. Ever been up in a T-38?"

"What's that?" Shapiro was too tired to remember that he'd seen them before.

"A spiffy little supersonic trainer. Two seats, dual controls, and she handles like a wet dream. I can disguise you as one of ours and get you up, no sweat. Ever been past mach-1?"

"No. Can you do some aerobatics?" Shapiro smiled like a tired little boy.

"Sure, Doc." Jackson grinned, knowing that he could do maneuvers to make a quail lose its lunch.

"I'll take you up on that. We work the same way with every patient, but I'll take you up on that anyway. Keep an eye on your friend. He looks a little rocky. That's normal. This sort of thing can be harder on the family than it is on the victims. If he doesn't come around some, tell the receptionist. We have a staff psychiatrist who specializes in working with—the *other* victims, he calls 'em." Yet another new idea at Shock-Trauma was a specialist in helping people cope with the injuries to family and friends.

"Cathy's arm. She's an eye surgeon, lots of fine work, you know? You sure there's no problem with that?"

Shapiro shook his head. "No big deal. It was a clean break to the humerus. Must have been a jacketed slug. The bullet went in clean, went out clean. Pretty lucky, really."

Robby's hand clamped shut on the doctor's arm as the elevator arrived. *"Bullet?"*

"Didn't I say that? God, I must be tireder than I thought. Yeah, it was a gunshot wound, but very clean. Hell, I wish they were all that clean. A nine-millimeter, maybe a thirty-eight, 'bout that size. I have to get back to work." The doctor went into the elevator.

"Shit," Jackson said to the wall. He turned when he heard a man with an English accent—two of them, it turned out—whom the receptionist directed to the waiting room. Robby followed them in.

The taller one approached Ryan and said, "Sir John?"

Ryan looked up. *Sir John?* Robby thought. The Brit drew himself to attention and went on briskly.

"My name is Geoffrey Bennett. I am Chargé d'Affairs at the British Embassy." He produced an envelope from his pocket and handed it to Ryan. "I am directed by Her Majesty to deliver this personally into your hand and to await your reply."

Jack blinked his eyes a few times, then tore open the envelope and extracted a yellow message form. The cable was brief, kind, and to the point. *What time is it over there?* Ryan wondered. *Two in the morning? Three? Something like that.* That meant that she'd been awakened with the news, probably, and cared enough to send a personal message. And was waiting for a reply.

How about that.

Ryan closed his eyes and told himself that it was time to return to the world of the living. Too drained for the tears he needed to shed, he swallowed a few times and rubbed his hands across his face before standing.

"Please tell Her Majesty that I am most grateful for her concern. My wife is expected to recover fully, but my daughter is in critical condition and we will have no definitive word on her for another eight or nine hours. Please tell Her Majesty that . . . that I am deeply touched by her concern, and that all of us value her friendship very highly indeed."

"Thank you, Sir John." Bennett made some notes. "I will cable your reply immediately. If you have no objection, I will leave a member of the embassy staff here with you." Jack nodded, puzzled, as Bennett made his exit.

Robby took all this in with a raised eyebrow and a dozen unasked questions. *Who was this guy?* He introduced himself as Edward Wayson, and took a seat in the corner facing the doorway. He looked over at Jackson. Their eyes met briefly and each man evaluated the other. Wayson had cool, detached eyes, and a wispy smile at the corners of his mouth. Robby gave him a closer look. There was a slight bulge under his left arm. Wayson affected to read a paperback novel, which he held in his left hand, but his eyes kept flickering to the door every

few seconds, and his right hand stayed free in his lap. He caught
Jackson's glance and nodded. So, Robby concluded, a spook, or at
least a security officer. *So that's what this is all about.* The realization
came as a blast of cold air. The pilot's hands flexed as he considered
the type of person who would deliberately attempt to murder a woman
and her child.

Five minutes later three State Police officers made their belated
arrival. They talked to Ryan for ten minutes. Jackson watched with
interest and saw his friend's face go pale with anger as he stammered
answers to numerous questions. Wayson didn't look but heard it all.

"You were right, Jimmy," Murray said. He was standing at the
window, watching the early morning traffic negotiate the corner of
Broadway and Victoria.

"Paddy O'Neil in Boston likes to say what wonderful chaps Sinn
Fein are," Owens said speculatively. "And our friend O' Donnell
decides to embarrass them. We could not have known, Dan. A possibility of a suspicion is not evidence and you know it. There was no
basis in fact for giving them a more serious warning than what you did.
And you *did* warn them, Dan."

"She's a pretty little girl. Gave me a hug and a kiss before they flew
home." Murray looked at his watch again and subtracted five hours.
"Jimmy, there are times . . . Fifteen years ago we arrested this—this
person who went after kids, little boys. I interrogated him. Sang like a
canary, he couldn't be happier with himself. He copped to six cases,
gave me all the details with a big shit-eatin' grin. It was right after the
Supreme Court struck down all the death-penalty laws, so he knew that
he'd live to a ripe old age. Do you know how close I came to—" He
stopped for a moment before going on. "Sometimes we're too damned
civilized."

"The alternative, Dan, is to become like them."

"I know that's true, Jimmy, but I just don't like it right now."

When Barry Shapiro next checked his watch it was five in the
morning. *No wonder I feel so tired,* he thought. *Twenty hours on duty.
I'm too old for this.* He was senior staff. He was supposed to know
better.

The first sign was staying on duty too long, taking on too much
personal responsibility, taking too keen an interest in patients who in

the final analysis were nothing more or less than bruised and broken pieces of meat. Some of them died. No matter how great his skill, how refined his technique, how determined the efforts of his team, some would always die. And when you got this tired, you couldn't sleep. Their injuries—and worse, their faces—were too fresh in your memory, too haunting to go away. Doctors need sleep more than most men. Persistent loss of sleep was the last and most dangerous warning. That was when you had to leave—or risk a breakdown, as had happened all too often to the Shock-Trauma staffers.

It was their grimmest institutional joke: how their patients arrived with broken bodies and mostly went home whole—but the staff doctors and nurses who came in with the greatest energy and highest personal ideals would so often leave broken in spirit. It was the ultimate irony of his profession that success would engender the expectation of still greater success; that failure in this most demanding of medical disciplines could leave almost as much damage on the practitioner as the patient. Shapiro was cynic enough to see the humor of it.

The surgeon reread the print-out that the blood-analyzer unit had spat out a minute before, and handed it back to the nurse-practitioner. She attached it to the child's chart, then sat back down, stroking her dirty hair outside the oxygen mask.

"Her father is downstairs. Get relief here and go down and tell him. I'm going upstairs for a smoke." Shapiro left the CCRU and got his overcoat, fishing in his pockets for his cigarettes.

He wandered down the hall to the fire stairs, then climbed slowly up the six flights to the roof. *God,* he thought. *Dear God, I'm tired.* The roof was flat, covered with tar and gravel, spotted here and there with the UHF antennas for the center's SYSCOM communications net, and a few air-conditioning condensers. Shapiro lit a cigarette in the lee of the stairway tower, cursing himself for his inability to break the noxious habit. He rationalized that, unlike most of his colleagues, he never saw the degenerative effects of smoking. Most of his patients were too young for chronic diseases. Their injuries resulted from the miracles of a technical society: automobiles, motorcycles, firearms, and industrial machinery.

Shapiro walked to the edge of the roof, rested his foot on the parapet as though on a bar rail, and blew smoke into the early-morning air. It wafted away to appear and disappear as a gentle morning breeze carried it past the rooftop lights. The doctor stretched his tired arms and

314 · TOM CLANCY

neck. The night's rain had washed the sky clean of its normal pollu-

neck. The night's rain had washed the sky clean of its normal pollution, and he could see stars overhead in the pre-dawn darkness.

Shapiro's curious accent resulted from his background. His early childhood had been spent in the Williamsburg section of New York, the son of a rabbi who had taken his family to South Carolina. Barry had had good private schooling there, but emerged from it with a mixture of Southern drawl and New York quip. It was further damaged by a prairie twang acquired during his medical training at Baylor University in Texas. His father was a distinguished man of letters in his own right, a frequent lecturer at the University of South Carolina at Columbia. An expert in 19th-century American literature, Rabbi Shapiro's specialty was the work of Edgar Allan Poe. Barry Shapiro loathed Poe. A scribbler of death and perversity, the surgeon called him whenever the subject came up, and he'd been surprised to learn that Poe had died in Baltimore long before, after falling asleep, drunk, in a gutter; and that Poe's home was only a few blocks from the University Hospital complex, a demi-shrine for the local literati.

It seemed to the surgeon that everything about Poe was dark and twisted, always expecting the inevitability of death—violent, untimely death, Shapiro's own very personal enemy. He had come to think of Poe as the embodiment of that enemy, sometimes beaten, sometimes not. It was not something he talked about to the staff psychiatrist, who also kept a close eye on the hospital staff—but now, alone, he looked north to the Poe house.

"You son of a bitch," he whispered. To himself. To Poe. To no one. *"You son of a bitch!* Not this time—you don't get this one! This one goes home."* He flicked the cigarette away and watched the point of orange light fall all the way to the shining, empty street. He turned back to the stairs. It was time to get some sleep.

16

Objectives and Patriots

Like most professional officers, Lieutenant Commander Robby Jackson had little use for the press. The irony of it was that Jack had tried many times to tell him that his outlook was wrong, that the press was as important to the preservation of American democracy as the Navy was. Now, as he watched, reporters were hounding his friend with questions that alternated between totally inane and intrusively personal. Why did everyone need to know how Jack felt about his daughter's condition? What would *any* normal person feel about having his child hovering near death—did they need such feelings explained? How was Jack supposed to know who'd done the shooting—if the police didn't know, how could he?

"And what's *your* name?" one finally asked Robby. He gave the woman his name and rank, but not his serial number.

"What are you doing here?" she persisted.

"We're friends. I drove him up here." *You dumbass.*

"And what do you think of all this?"

"What do you think I think? If that was your friend's little girl up there, what the hell would you think?" the pilot snapped back at her.

"Do you know who did it?"

"I fly airplanes for a living, I'm not a cop. Ask them."

"They're not talking."

Robby smiled thinly. "Well, score one for the good guys. Lady, why don't you leave that man alone? If you were going through what he is, do you think you would want a half-dozen strangers asking you these kind of questions? That's a human being over there, y'know? And he's my friend and I don't like what you people are doing to him."

"Look, Commander, we know that his wife and daughter were attacked by terrorists—"

"Says who?" Jackson demanded.

"Who else would it be? Do you think we're stupid?" Robby didn't answer that. "This is news—it's the first attack by a foreign terrorist group on American soil, if we're reading this right. That is important. The people have a right to know what happened and why," the reporter said reasonably.

She's right, Robby admitted reluctantly to himself. He didn't like it, but she was right. *Damn.*

"Would it make you feel any better to know that I do have a kid about that age? Mine's a boy," she said. The reporter actually seemed sympathetic.

Jackson searched for something to dislike about her. "Answer me this: if you have a chance to interview the people who did this, would you do it?"

"That's my job. We need to know where they're coming from."

"Where they're comin' from, lady, is they kill people for the fun of it. It's all part of their game." Robby remembered intelligence reports he'd seen while in the Eastern Med. "Back a couple of years ago— you never heard this from me, okay?"

"Off the record," she said solemnly.

"I was on a carrier off Beirut, okay? We had intelligence reports— and pictures—of people from Europe who flew in to do some killing. They were mainly kids, musta been from good families—I mean, from the way they dressed. No shit, this is for-real, I saw the friggin' pictures. They joined up with some of the crazies, got guns, and just started blasting away, at random, for the pure hell of it. They shot from those high-rise hotels and office buildings into the streets. With a rifle you can hit from a thousand yards away. Something moves—boom, they blast it with automatic weapons fire. Then they got to go home. They were killing people, for fun! Maybe some of them grew up to be real terrorists, I don't know. It was pretty sickening stuff, not the sort of thing you forget. That's the kind of people we're talking about here, okay?

"I don't give a good goddamn about their point of view, lady! When I was a little kid in Alabama, we had problems with people like that, those assholes in the Klan. I don't give a damn about their point of view, either. The only good thing about the Klan was they were idiots. The terrorists we got running around now are a lot more efficient. Maybe that makes them more legitimate in your eyes, but not mine."

"That thing in Beirut never made the papers," the reporter said.

"I know for a fact that one reporter saw it. Maybe he figured that nobody would believe it. I don't know that I would have without the photos. But I saw 'em. You got my word on that, lady."

"What kind of pictures?"

"That I can't say—but they were good enough to see their shiny young faces." The photos had been made by U.S. and Israeli reconnaissance aircraft.

"So what do you do about it?"

"If you could arrange to have all these bastards in one place, I think we and the Marines could figure something out," Robby replied, voicing a wish common to professional soldiers throughout the world. "We might even invite you newsies to the wake. Who the hell is that?" Two new people came into the room.

Jack was too tired to be fully coherent. The news that Sally was out of immediate danger had been like a giant weight leaving his shoulders, and he was waiting for the chance to see his wife, who would soon be moved to a regular hospital floor. A few feet away, Wayson, the British security officer, watched with unconcealed contempt, refusing even to give his name to the reporters who asked. The State Police officers were unable to keep the press away, though hospital personnel flatly refused to let the TV equipment in the front door, and were able to make that stick. The question that kept repeating was, Who did it? Jack said he didn't know, though he thought he did. It was probably the people he'd decided not to worry about.

It could have been worse, he told himself. At least it was now probable that Sally would be alive at the end of the week. His daughter was not dead because of his misjudgment. That was some consolation.

"Mr. Ryan?" one of the new visitors asked.

"Yeah?" Jack was too exhausted to look up. He was awake only because of adrenaline now. His nerves were too ragged to allow him sleep, much as he needed it.

"I'm Special Agent Ed Donoho, Boston Field Office of the FBI. I have somebody who wants to say something to you."

Nobody ever said that Paddy O'Neil was stupid, Donoho thought. As soon as the report had made the Eleven O'Clock News, the man from Sinn Fein had asked his FBI "escort" if he might fly down to Baltimore. Donoho was in no position to deny him the right, and had been co-opted into bringing the man himself on the first available plane into BWI.

"Mr. Ryan," O'Neil said with a voice that dripped sympathy, "I understand that the condition of your child has been upgraded. I hope that my prayers had something to do with it, and . . ."

It took Ryan over ten seconds to recognize the face that he'd seen a few days before on TV. His mouth slowly dropped open as his eyes widened. For some reason he didn't hear what the man was saying. The words came through his ears, but, as though they were in some unknown tongue, his brain did not assemble them into speech. All he saw was the man's throat, five feet away. *Just about five feet,* was what his brain told him.

"Uh-oh," Robby said on the other side of the room. He stood as his friend went beet-red. Two seconds later, Ryan's face was as pale as the collar on his white cotton shirt. Jack's feet shifted, sliding straight beneath his body as he leaned forward on the couch.

Robby pushed past the FBI agent as Ryan launched himself from the couch, hands stretching out for O'Neil's neck. Jackson's shoulder caught his friend's chest, and the pilot wrapped Jack up in a bear hug, trying to push him backward as three photographers recorded the scene. Jack didn't make a sound, but Robby knew exactly what he wanted to do. Jackson had leverage going for him, and pushed Ryan back, hurling him onto the couch. He turned quickly.

"Get that asshole outa here before *I* kill him!" Jackson was four inches shorter than the Irishman, but his rage was scarcely less than Ryan's. "Get that terrorist bastard out of here!"

"Officer!" Special Agent Donoho pointed to a state trooper, who grabbed O'Neil and dragged him from the room in an instant. For some reason the reporters followed as O'Neil loudly protested his innocence.

"Are you out of your fucking mind!" Jackson snarled at the FBI agent.

"Cool down, Commander. I'm on your side, okay? Cool it down some."

Jackson sat down beside Ryan, who was breathing like a horse at the end of a race while he stared at the floor. Donoho sat down on the other side.

"Mr. Ryan, I couldn't keep him from coming down. I'm sorry, but we can't do that. He wanted to tell you—shit, all the way down on the plane, he told me that his outfit had nothing to do with this; that it would be a disaster for them. He wanted to extend his sympathy, I guess." The agent hated himself for saying that, even though it was true enough. He hated himself even more because he'd almost started to like Paddy O'Neil over the past week. The front man for Sinn Fein was a person of considerable charm, a man with a gift for presenting his point of view in a reasonable way. Ed Donoho asked himself why he'd been assigned to this job. *Why couldn't they have picked an Italian?* He knew the answer to that, of course, but just because there was a reason didn't mean that he had to like it. "I'll make sure he doesn't bother you anymore."

"You do that," Robby said.

Donoho went back into the hall, and unsurprisingly found O'Neil giving his spiel to the reporters. *Mr. Ryan is distraught,* he was saying, *as any family man would be in similar circumstances.* His first exposure to the man the previous week had given him a feeling of distaste. Then he'd started to admire his skill and charm. Now Donoho's reaction to the man's words was one of loathing. An idea blinked on in his head. He wondered if the Bureau would approve and decided it was worth the risk. First the agent grabbed a state trooper by the arm and made sure that the man wouldn't get close to Ryan again. Next he got hold of a photographer and talked to him briefly. Together they found a doctor.

"No, absolutely not," the surgeon replied to the initial request.

"Hey, Doc," the photojournalist said. "My wife's pregnant with our first. If it'll help this guy, I'm for it. This one doesn't make the papers. You got my word, Doc."

"I think it'll help," the FBI agent said. "I really do."

Ten minutes later Donoho and the photographer stripped off their scrub clothing. The FBI agent took the film cassette and tucked it in his pocket. Before he took O'Neil back to the airport, he made a call to headquarters in Washington, and two agents drove out to Ryan's home on Peregrine Cliff. They didn't have any problem with the alarm system.

Jack had been awake for more than twenty-four hours now. If he'd been able to think about it, he would have marveled at the fact that he was awake and functional, though the latter observation would have been a matter of dispute to anyone who saw him walking. He was alone now. Robby was off attending to something that he couldn't remember.

He would have been alone in any case. Twenty minutes earlier, Cathy had been moved into the main University Hospital complex, and Jack had to go see her. He walked like a man facing execution down a drab corridor of glazed institutional brick. He turned a corner and saw what room it had to be. A pair of state troopers was standing there. They watched him approach, and Jack watched their eyes for a sign that they knew all of this was his fault, that his wife and daughter had nearly died because he'd decided that there was nothing to worry about. Not once in his life had Jack experienced failure, and its bitter taste made him think that the whole world would hold him in the same contempt he felt for himself.

You're so fucking smart.

It seemed to his senses that he did not so much approach the door— it approached him, looming ever larger in his sight. Behind the door was the woman he loved. The woman who had nearly died because of his confidence in himself. What would she say to him? Did he dare to find out? Jack stood at the door for a moment. The troopers tried not to stare at him. Perhaps they felt sympathy, Jack thought, knowing that he didn't deserve it. The doorknob was cold, accusing metal in his hand as he entered the room.

Cathy was lying in her single-bed room. Her arm was in a cast. An enormous purple bruise covered the right side of her face and there was a bandage over half her forehead. Her eyes were open but almost lifeless, staring at a television that wasn't on. Jack moved toward her as though asleep. A nurse had set a chair alongside the bed. He sat in it, and took his wife's hand while he tried to think of something he could say to the wife he had failed. Her face turned toward his. Her eyes were blackened and full of tears.

"I'm sorry, Jack," she whispered.

"What?"

"I knew she was fooling with the seat belt, but I didn't do anything because I was in a hurry—and then that truck came, and I didn't have time to—if I had made sure she was strapped in, Sally would be fine . . . but I was in a hurry," she finished, and looked away. "Jack, I'm so sorry."

My God, she thinks it's her fault . . . what do I say now?

"She's going to be okay, babe," Ryan managed to say, stunned at what he'd just heard. He held Cathy's hand to his face and kissed it. "And so are you. That's the only thing that matters now."

"But—" She stared at the far wall.

"No 'buts.'"

Her face turned back. Cathy tried to smile but tears were rolling from her eyes. "I talked to Doctor Ellingstone at Hopkins—he came over and saw Sally. He says—he says she'll be okay. He says that Shapiro saved her life."

"I know."

"I haven't even seen her—I remember seeing the bridge and then I woke up two hours ago, and—*oh, Jack!*" Her hand closed on his like a claw. He leaned forward to kiss her, but before their lips touched, both started weeping.

"It's okay, Cathy," Jack said, and he started to believe that it really was, or at least that it would be so again. His world had not ended, not quite.

But someone else's will, Ryan told himself. The thought was a quiet, distant one, voiced in a part of his mind that was already looking at the future while the present occupied his sight. Seeing his wife weeping tears caused by someone else started a cold rage in him which only that someone's death could ever warm.

The time for grief was already ending, carried away by his own tears. Though it had not yet happened, Ryan's intellect was already beginning to think of the time when his emotions would be at rest—most of them. One would remain. He would control it, but it would also control him. He would not feel like a whole man again until he was purged of it.

One can only weep for so long; it is as though each tear carries a finite amount of emotion away with it. Cathy stopped first. She used her hand to wipe her husband's face. She managed a real smile now. Jack hadn't shaved. It was like rubbing sandpaper.

"What time is it?"

"Ten-thirty." Jack didn't have to check his watch.

"You need sleep, Jack," she said. "You have to stay healthy, too."

"Yeah." Jack rubbed his eyes.

"Hi, Cathy," Robby said as he came through the door. "I've come to take him away from you."

"Good."

"We're checked into the Holiday Inn over on Lombard Street."

"We? Robby, you don't—"

"Stuff it, Jack," Robby said. "How are you, Cathy?"

"I have a headache you wouldn't believe."

"Good to see you smile," Robby said softly. "Sissy'll be up after lunch. Is there anything she can get for you?"

"Not right now. Thanks, Rob."

"Hang in there, Doc." Robby took Jack's arm and hauled him to his feet. "I'll have him back to you later today."

Twenty minutes later Robby led Jack into their motel room. He pulled a pill container from his pocket. "The doc said you should take one of these."

"I don't take pills."

"You're taking one of these, sport. It's a nice yellow one. That's not a request, Jack, it's an order. You need sleep. Here." Robby tossed them over and stared until Jack swallowed one. Ryan was asleep in ten minutes. Jackson made certain that the door was secured before settling down on the other bed. The pilot dreamed of seeing the people who had done all this. They were in an airplane. Four times he fired a missile into their bird and watched their bodies spill out of the hole it made so that he could blast them with his cannon before they fell into the sea.

The Patriots Club was a bar across the street from Broadway Station in one of South Boston's Irish enclaves. Its name harkened not back to the revolutionaries of the 1770s, but rather to the owner's image of himself. John Donoho had served in the First Marine Division on the bitter retreat from the Chosin Reservoir. Wounded twice, he'd never left his squad on the long, cold march to the port of Hungnam. He still walked with a slight limp from the four toes that frostbite had taken from his right foot. He was prouder of this than of his several decorations, framed under a Marine Corps standard behind the bar. Anyone who entered the bar in a Marine uniform always got his first drink free, along with a story or two about the Old Corps, which Corporal John Donoho, USMC (ret.), had served at the ripe age of eighteen.

He was also a professional Irishman. Every year he took an Aer Lingus flight from Boston's Logan International Airport to the old sod, to brush up on his roots and his accent, and sample the better varieties of whiskey that somehow were never exported to America in quantity. Donoho also tried to keep current on the happenings in the North, "the Six Counties," as he called them, to maintain his spiritual connection with the rebels who labored courageously to free their people from the British yoke. Many a dollar had been raised in his bar, to aid those in the North, many a glass raised to their health and to the Cause.

"Hello, Johnny!" Paddy O'Neil called from the door.

"And good evening to you, Paddy!" Donoho was already drawing a beer when he saw his nephew follow O'Neil through the door. Eddie was his dead brother's only son, a good boy, educated at Notre Dame, where he'd played second string on the football team before joining up with the FBI. It wasn't quite as good as being a Marine, but Uncle John knew that it paid a lot better. He'd heard that Eddie was following O'Neil around, but was vaguely sad to see that it was true. Perhaps it was to protect Paddy from a Brit assassin, the owner rationalized.

John and Paddy had a beer together before the latter joined a small group waiting for him in the back room. His nephew stayed alone at the end of the bar, where he drank a cup of coffee and kept an eye on things. After ten minutes O'Neil went back to give his talk. Donoho went to say hello to his nephew.

"Hi, Uncle John," Eddie greeted him.

"Have you set the date yet, now?" John asked, affecting an Irish accent, as he usually did when O'Neil was around.

"Maybe next September," the younger man allowed.

"And what would your father say, you living with the girl for almost a year? And the good fathers at Notre Dame?"

"Probably the same thing they'd say to you for raising money for terrorists," the young agent replied. Eddie was sick and tired of being told how to live his life.

"I don't want to hear any of that in my place." He'd heard that line before, too.

"That's what O'Neil does, Uncle John."

"They're freedom fighters. I know they bend some of our laws from time to time, but the English laws they break are no concern of mine— or yours," John Donoho said firmly.

"You watch TV?" The agent didn't need an answer to that. A wide-screen TV in the opposite corner was used for baseball and football games. The bar's name had also made it an occasional watering hole for the New England Patriots football players. Uncle John's interest in TV was limited to the Patriots, Red Sox, Celtics, and Bruins. His interest in politics was virtually nil. He voted for Teddy Kennedy every six years and considered himself a staunch proponent of national defense. "I want to show you a couple of pictures."

He set the first one on the bar. "This is a little girl named Sally Ryan. She lives in Annapolis."

His uncle picked it up and smiled. "I remember when my Kathleen looked like that."

"Her father is a teacher at the Naval Academy, used to be a Marine lieutenant. He went to Boston College. His father was a cop."

"Sounds like a good Irishman. Friend of yours?"

"Not exactly," Eddie said. "Paddy and I met him earlier today. This is what his daughter looked like then." The second photo was laid on the bar.

"Jesus, Mary, and Joseph." It wasn't easy to discern that there was a child under all the medical equipment. Her feet stuck out from heavy wrappings. An inch-wide plastic pipe was in her mouth, and what parts of her body were visible formed a horribly discolored mass that the photographer had recorded with remarkable skill.

"She's the lucky one, Uncle John. The girl's mother was there, too." Two more photos went onto the bar.

"What happened, car accident—what are you showing me?" John Donoho asked. He really didn't know what this was all about.

"She's a surgeon—she's pregnant, too, the pictures don't show that. Her car was machine-gunned yesterday, right outside of Annapolis, Maryland. They killed a State Police officer a few minutes later." Another picture went down.

"What? Who did it?" the older man asked.

"Here's the father, Jack Ryan." It was the same picture that the London papers had used, Jack's graduation shot from Quantico. Eddie knew that his uncle always looked at Marine dress blues with pride.

"I've seen him before somewhere . . ."

"Yeah. He stopped a terrorist attack over in London a few months back. It looks like he offended the terrorists enough that they came after him and his family. The Bureau is working on that."

"Who did it?"

The last photo went down on the bar. It showed Ryan's hands less than a foot from Paddy O'Neil, and a black man holding him back.

"Who's the jig?" John asked. His nephew almost lost his temper.

"Goddammit, Uncle John! That *man* is a Navy fighter pilot."

"Oh." John was briefly embarrassed. He had little use for blacks, though one who wore a Marine uniform into his bar got his first drink free, too. It was different with the ones in uniform, he told himself. Anyone who served the flag as he had done was okay in his book, John Donoho always said. *Some of my best friends in the Corps. . . .* He remembered how Navy strike aircraft had supported his outfit all the way back to the sea, holding the Chinese back with rockets and napalm. Well, maybe this one was different, too. He stared at the rest of the picture for a few seconds. "So, you say Paddy had something to do with this?"

"I've been telling you for years who the bastard fronts for. If you don't believe me, maybe you want to ask Mr. Ryan here. It's bad enough that O'Neil spits on our whole country every time he comes over here. His friends damned near killed this whole family yesterday. We got one of 'em. Two Marine guards at the Naval Academy grabbed him, waiting to shoot Ryan. His name's Eamon Clark, and we know that he used to work for the Provisional Wing of the IRA—we *know* it, Uncle John, he's a convicted murderer. They caught him with a loaded pistol in his pocket. You still think they're good guys? Dammit, they're going after Americans now! If you don't believe me, believe this!" Eddie Donoho rearranged the photos on the wooden surface. "This little girl, and her mother, and a kid not even born yet almost died yesterday. This state trooper did. He left a wife and a kid behind. That friend of yours in the back room raises the money to buy the guns, he's connected with the people who did this."

"But why?"

"Like I said, this girl's dad got in the way of a murder over in London. I guess the people he stopped wanted to get even with him— not just him, though, they went for his whole family," the agent explained slowly.

"The little girl didn't—"

"Goddammit," Eddie swore again. "That's why they're called terrorists!" It was getting through. He could see that he was finally getting the message across.

"You're sure that Paddy is part of this?" his uncle asked.

"He's never lifted a gun that we know of. He's their mouthpiece, he comes over here and raises money so that they can do things like this at home. Oh, he never gets his hands bloody. He's too smart for that. But this is what the money goes for. We are absolutely sure of that. And now they're playing their games over here." Agent Donoho knew that the money-raising was secondary to the psychological reasons for coming over, but now wasn't the time to clutter the issue with details. He watched his uncle stare at the photos of the little girl. His face showed the confusion that always accompanies a completely new thought.

"You're sure? Really sure?"

"Uncle John, we have over thirty agents on the case now, plus the local police. You bet we're sure. We'll get 'em, too. The Director's put the word out on this case. We want 'em. Whatever it takes, we'll get these bastards," Edward Michael Donoho, Jr., said with cold determination.

John Donoho looked at his nephew, and for the first time he saw a man. Eddie's FBI post was a source of family pride, but John finally knew why this was so. He wasn't a kid anymore. He was a man with a job about which he was deadly serious. More than the photographs, it was this that decided things. John had to believe what he'd been told.

The owner of the Patriots Club stood up straight and walked down the bar to the folding gate. He lifted it and made for the back room, with his nephew trailing behind.

"But our boys are fighting back," O'Neil was telling the fifteen men in the room. "Every day they fight back to—joining us, Johnny?"

"Out," Donoho said quietly.

"What—I don't understand, John," O'Neil said, genuinely puzzled.

"You must think I'm pretty stupid. I guess maybe I was. Leave."
The voice was more forceful now, and the feigned accent was gone.
"Get out of my club and don't ever come back."

"But, Johnny—what are you talking about?"

Donoho grabbed the man by his collar and lifted him off his chair.
O'Neil's voice continued to protest as he was propelled all the way out
the front door. Eddie Donoho waved to his uncle as he followed his
charge out onto the street.

"What was that all about?" one of the men from the back room
asked. Another of them, a reporter for the *Boston Globe,* started making notes as the bar owner stumbled through what he had finally
learned.

To this point no police agency had implicated any terrorist group by
name, and in fact neither had Special Agent Donoho done so. His
instructions from Washington on that score had been carefully given
and carefully followed. But in the translation through Uncle John and a
reporter, the facts got slightly garbled—as surprised no one—and
within hours the story was on the AP wire that the attack on Jack Ryan
and his family had been made by the Provisional Wing of the Irish
Republican Army.

Sean Miller's mission in America had been fully accomplished by
an agency of the United States government.

Miller and his party were already back home. As many people in
this line of work had done before, Sean reflected on the value of rapid
international air travel. In this case it had been off to Mexico from
Washington's Dulles International, from there to the Netherlands An-
tilles, to Schiphol International Airport on a KLM flight, and then to
Ireland. All one needed was correct travel documents and a little
money. The travel documents in question were already destroyed, and
the money untraceable cash. He sat across from Kevin O'Donnell's
desk, drinking water to compensate for the dehydration normal to
flying.

"What about Eamon?" One rule of ULA operations was that no
overseas telephone calls ever came to his house.

"Alex's man says he was picked up." Miller shrugged. "It was a
risk I felt worth taking. I selected Ned for it because he knows very
little about us." He knew that O'Donnell had to agree with that. Clark
was one of the new men brought into the Organization, and more of an

accident than a recruit. He'd come south because one of his friends from the H-blocks had come. O'Donnell had thought him of possible use, since they had no experienced work-alone assassins. But Clark was stupid. His motivations came from emotion rather than ideology. He was, in fact, a typical PIRA thug, little different from those in the UVF for that matter, useful in the same sense that a trained dog was useful, Kevin told himself. He knew but a few names and faces within the Organization. Most damning of all, he had failed. Clark's one redeeming characteristic was his doglike loyalty. He hadn't broken in Long Kesh prison and he probably wouldn't break now. He lacked the imagination.

"Very well," Kevin O'Donnell said after a moment's reflection. Clark would be remembered as a martyr, gaining greater respect in failure than he had managed to earn in success. "The rest?"

"Perfect. I saw the wife and child die, and Alex's people got us away cleanly." Miller smiled and poured some whiskey to follow his liter of ice water.

"They're not dead, Sean," O'Donnell said.

"What?" Miller had been on an airplane less than three hours after the shooting, and hadn't seen or heard a snippet of news since. He listened to his boss's explanation in incredulous silence.

"But it doesn't matter," O'Donnell concluded. He explained that, too. The AP story that had originated in the *Boston Globe* had been picked up by the *Irish Times* of Dublin. "It was a good plan after all, Sean. Despite everything that went wrong, the mission is accomplished."

Sean didn't allow himself to react. Two operations in a row had gone wrong for him. Before the fiasco in London, he'd never failed at all. He'd written that off to random chance, pure luck, nothing more. He didn't even think of that in this case. Two in a row, that wasn't luck. He knew that Kevin would not tolerate a third failure. The young operations officer took a deep breath and told himself to be objective. He'd allowed himself to think of Ryan as a personal target, not a political one. That had been his first mistake. Though Kevin hadn't said it, losing Ned had been a serious mistake. Miller reviewed his plan, rethinking every aspect of the operation. Just going after the wife and child would have been simple thuggery, and he'd never approved of that; it was not professional. Just going after Ryan himself, however, would not have carried the same political impact, which was the whole point of the operation. The rest of the family was—had been necessary. So his objectives had been sound enough, but . . .

"I should have taken more time on this one," he said finally. "I tried to be too dramatic. Perhaps we should have waited."

"Yes," his boss agreed, pleased that Sean saw his errors.

"Any help we can give you," Owens said, "is yours. You know that, Dan."

"Yeah, well, this has attracted some high-level interest." Murray held a cable from Director Emil Jacobs himself. "Well, it was only a matter of time. It had to happen sooner or later." *And if we don't bag these sons of bitches,* he thought, *it'll happen again. The ULA just proved that terrorists could operate in the U.S.* The emotional shock of the event had come as a surprise to Murray. As a professional in the field, he knew that it was mere luck that it hadn't happened already. The inept domestic terrorist groups had set off some bombs and murdered a few people, but the Bureau had experienced considerable success running them to ground. None of them had ever gotten much in the way of foreign support. But that had changed, too. The helicopter pilot had identified one of the escaping terrorists as black, and there weren't many of them in Ireland.

It was a new ball game, and for all his experience in the FBI, Murray was worried about how well the Bureau would be able to handle it. Director Jacobs was right on one thing: this was a top-priority mission. Bill Shaw would run the case personally, and Murray knew him to be one of the best intellects in the business. The thirty agents initially assigned to the case would treble in the next few days, then treble again. The only way to keep this from happening again was to demonstrate that America was too dangerous a place for terrorists. In his heart, Murray knew that this was impossible. No place was too dangerous, certainly no democracy.

But the Bureau did have formidable resources, and it wouldn't be the only agency involved.

17

Recriminations and Decisions

Ryan awoke to find Robby waving a cup of coffee under his nose. Jack had managed to sleep without dreams this time, and the oblivion of undisturbed slumber had worked wonders on him.

"Sissy was over the hospital earlier. She says Cathy looks all right, considering. It's all set up so you can get in to see Sally. She'll be asleep, but you can see her."

"Where is she?"

"Sissy? She's out runnin' some errands."

"I need a shave."

"Me, too. She's getting what we need. First I'm gonna get some food in ya'," Robby said.

"I owe you, man," Jack said as he stood.

"Give it a rest, Jack. That's what the Lord put us here for, like my pappy says. Now, eat!" Robby commanded.

Jack realized that he'd not eaten anything for a long time, and once his stomach reminded itself of this, it cried out for nourishment. Within five minutes he'd disposed of two eggs, bacon, hash-browns, four slices of toast, and two cups of coffee.

"Shame they don't have grits here," Robby observed. A knock came to the door. The pilot answered it. Sissy breezed in with a shopping bag in one hand and Jack's briefcase in the other.

"You better freshen up, Jack," she said. "Cathy looks better than you do."

"Nothing unusual about that," Jack replied—cheerfully, he realized with surprise. Sissy had baited him into it.

"Robby?"

"Yeah?"

"What the hell are grits?"

"You don't want to know," Cecilia Jackson answered.

"I'll take your word for it." Jack walked into the bathroom and started the shower. By the time he got out, Robby had shaved, leaving the razor and cream on the sink. Jack scraped his beard away and patched the bloody spots with toilet paper. A new toothbrush was sitting there too, and Ryan emerged from the room looking and feeling like a human being.

"Thanks, guys," he said.

"I'll take you home tonight," Robby said. "I have to teach class tomorrow. You don't. I fixed it with the department."

"Okay."

Sissy left for home. Jack and Robby walked over to the hospital. Visiting hours were under way and they were able to walk right up to Cathy's room.

"Well, if it isn't our hero!" Joe Muller was Cathy's father. He was a short, swarthy man—Cathy's hair and complexion came from her mother, now dead. A senior VP with Merrill Lynch, he was a product of the Ivy League, and had started in the brokerage business much as Ryan had, though his brief stint in the military had been two years of drafted service in the Army that he'd long since put behind him. He'd once had big plans for Jack and had never forgiven him for leaving the business. Muller was a passionate man who was also well aware of his importance in the financial community. He and Jack hadn't exchanged a civil word in over three years. It didn't look to Jack as though that was going to change.

"Daddy," Cathy said, "we don't need that."

"Hi, Joe." Ryan held out his hand. It hung there for five seconds, all by itself. Robby excused himself out the door, and Jack went to kiss his wife. "Lookin' better, babe."

"What do you have to say for yourself?" Muller demanded.

"The guy who wanted to kill me was arrested yesterday. The FBI has him," Jack said carefully. He amazed himself by saying it so calmly. Somehow it seemed a trivial matter compared with his wife and daughter.

"This is all your fault, you know." Muller had been rehearsing this for hours.

"I know," Jack conceded the point. He wondered how much more he could back up.

"Daddy—" Cathy started to say.

"You keep out of this," Muller said to his daughter, a little too sharply for Jack.

"You can say anything you want to me, but don't snap at her," he warned.

"Oh, you want to protect her, eh? So where the hell were you yesterday!"

"I was in my office, just like you were."

"You had to stick your nose in where it didn't belong, didn't you? You had to play hero—and you damned near got your family killed," Muller went on through his lines.

"Look, Mr. Muller." Jack had told himself all these things before. He could accept the punishment from himself. But not from his father-in-law. "Unless you know of a company on the exchange that makes a time machine, we can't very well change that, can we? All we can do now is help the authorities find the people who did this."

"Why didn't you think about all this before, dammit!"

"Daddy, that's enough!" Cathy rejoined the conversation.

"Shut up—this is between us!"

"If you yell at her again, mister, you'll regret it." Jack needed a release. He hadn't protected his family the previous day, but he could now.

"Calm down, Jack." His wife didn't know that she was making things worse, but Jack took the cue after a moment. Muller didn't.

"You're a real big guy now, aren't you?"

Keep going, Joe, and you might find out. Jack looked over to his wife and took a deep breath. "Look, if you came down here to yell at me, that's fine, we can do that by ourselves, okay?—but that's your daughter over there, and maybe she needs you, too." He turned to Cathy. "I'll be outside if you need me."

Ryan left the room. There were still two very serious state troopers at the door, and another at the nurses' station down the hall. Jack reminded himself that a trooper had been killed, and that Cathy was the only thing they had that was close to being a witness. She was safe, finally. Robby waved to his friend from down the hall.

"Settle down, boy," the pilot suggested.

"He has a real talent for pissing me off," Jack said after another deep breath.

"I know he's an asshole, but he almost lost his kid. Try to remember that. Taking it out on him doesn't help things."

"It might," Jack said with a smile, thinking about it. "What are you, a philosopher?"

"I'm a PK, Jack. Preacher's Kid. You can't imagine the stuff I used to hear from the parlor when people came over to talk with the old man. He isn't so much mad at you as scared by what almost happened," Robby said.

"So am I, pal." Ryan looked down the hall.

"But you've had more time to deal with it."

"Yeah." Jack was quiet for a moment. "I still don't like the son of a bitch."

"He gave you Cathy, man. That's something."

"Are you sure you're in the right line of work? How come you're not a chaplain?"

"I am the voice of reason in a chaotic world. You don't accomplish as much when you're pissed off. That's why we train people to be professionals. If you want to get the job done, emotions don't help. You've already gotten even with the man, right?"

"Yeah. If he'd had his way, I'd be living up in Westchester County, taking the train in every day, and—crap!" Jack shook his head. "He still makes me mad."

Muller came out of the room just then. He looked around for a moment, spotted Jack, and walked down. "Stay close," Ryan told his friend.

"You almost killed my little girl." Joe's mood hadn't improved.

Jack didn't reply. He'd told himself that about a hundred times, and was just starting to consider the possibility that he was a victim, too.

"You ain't thinking right, Mr. Muller," Robby said.

"Who the hell are you!"

"A friend," Robby replied. He and Joe were about the same height, but the pilot was twenty years younger. The look he gave the broker communicated this rather clearly. The voice of reason didn't like being yelled at. Joe Muller had a talent for irritating people. On Wall Street he could get away with it, and he assumed that meant that he could do it anywhere he liked. He was a man who had not learned the limitations of his power.

"We can't change what has happened," Jack offered. "We can work to see that it doesn't happen again."

"If you'd done what I wanted, this never would have happened!"

"If I'd done what *you* wanted, I'd be working with you every day, moving money from Column A to Column B and pretending it was important, like all the other Wall Street wimps—and hating it, and turning into another miserable bastard in the financial world. I proved that I could do that as well as you, but I made my pile, and so now I do something I like. At least we're trying to make the world a better place instead of trying to take it over with leveraged buyouts. It's not my fault that you don't understand that. Cathy and I are doing what we like to do."

"Something you *like*," Muller snapped, rejecting the concept that making money wasn't something to be enjoyed in and of itself. "Make the world a better place, eh?"

"Yeah, because I'm going to help catch the bastards who did this."

"And how is a punk history teacher going to do that!"

Ryan gave his father-in-law his best smile. "That's something I can't tell you, Joe."

The stockbroker swore and stalked away. *So much for reconciliation,* Jack told himself. He wished it had gone otherwise. His estrangement with Joe Muller was occasionally hard on Cathy.

"Back to the Agency, Jack?" Robby asked.

"Yeah."

Ryan spent twenty minutes with his wife, long enough to learn what she'd told the police and to make sure that she really was feeling better. She was dozing off when he left. Next he went across the street to the Shock-Trauma Center.

Getting into scrubs reminded him of the only other time he'd done so, the night Sally was born. A nurse took him into the Critical Care Recover Unit, and he saw his little girl for the first time in thirty-six hours, a day and a half that had stretched into an eternity. It was a thoroughly ghastly experience. Had he not been told positively that her survival chances were good, he might have broken down on the spot. The bruised little shape was unconscious from the combination of drugs and injuries. He watched and listened as the respirator breathed for her. She was being fed from bottles and tubes that ran into her veins. A doctor explained that her condition looked far worse than it was. Sally's liver was functioning well, under the circumstances. In two or three more days the broken legs would be set.

"Is she going to be crippled?" Jack asked quietly.

"No, there isn't any reason to worry about that. Kids' bones—what we say is, if the broken pieces are in the same room, they'll heal. It looks far worse than it is. The trick with cases like this is getting them through the first hour—in her case, the first twelve or so. Once we get kids through the initial crisis, once we get the system working again, they heal fast. You'll have her home in a month. In two months, she'll be running around like it never happened. As crazy as that sounds, it's true. Nothing heals like a kid. She's a very sick little girl right now, but she's going to get well. Hey, I was here when she arrived."

"What's your name?"

"Rich Kinter. Barry Shapiro and I did most of the surgery. It was close—God, it was so close! But we won. Okay? We won. You will be taking her home."

"Thanks—that doesn't cover it, Doc." Jack stumbled over a few more words, not knowing what to say to the people who had saved his daughter's life.

Kinter shook his head. "Bring her back sometime and we're even. We have a party for ex-patients every few months. Mr. Ryan, there is nothing you can do that comes close to what we all feel when we see our little patients come back—walk back. That's why we're here, man, to make sure they come back for cake and juice. Just let us bounce her on our knees after she's better."

"Deal." Ryan wondered how many people were alive because of the people in this room. He was certain that this surgeon could be a rich man in private practice. Jack understood him, understood why he was here, and knew that his father-in-law wouldn't. He sat for a few minutes at Sally's side, listening to the machine breathe for her through the plastic tube. The nurse-practitioner overseeing the case smiled at him around her mask. He kissed Sally's bruised forehead before leaving. Jack felt better now, better about almost everything. But one item remained. The people who had done this to his little girl.

*　　*　　*

"It had wheelchair tags," the clerk in the 7-Eleven was saying, "but the dude who drove it didn't look crippled or anything."

"You remember what he looked like?" Special Agent Nick Capitano and a major from the Maryland State Police were interviewing the witness.

"Yeah, he was 'bout as black as me. Tall dude. He wore sunglasses, the mirror kind. Had a beard, too. There was always at least one other dude in the truck, but I never got a look at him—black man, that's all I can say."

"What did he wear?"

"Jeans and a brown leather jacket, I think. You know, like a construction worker."

"Shoes or boots?" the major asked.

"Never did see that," the clerk said after a moment.

"How about jewelry, T-shirt with a pattern, anything special or different about him?"

"No, nothin' I remember."

"What did he do here?"

"He always bought a six-pack of Coke Classic. Once or twice he got some Twinkies, but he always got hisself the Cokes."

"What did he sound like? Anything special?"

The clerk shook her head. "Nah, just a dude, y'know?"

"Do you think you could recognize him again?" Capitano asked.

"Maybe—we get a lot of folks through here, lotta regulars, lotta strangers, y'know?"

"Would you mind looking through some pictures?" the agent went on.

"Gotta clear it with the boss. I mean, I need the job, but you say this chump tried to kill a little girl—yeah, sure, I'll help ya."

"We'll clear it with the boss," the Major assured her. "You won't lose pay over it."

"Gloves," she said, looking up. "Forgot to say that. He wore work gloves. Leather ones, I think." *Gloves*, both men wrote in their notebooks.

"Thank you, ma'am. We'll call you tonight. A car will pick you up tomorrow morning so you can look at some pictures for us," the FBI agent said.

"Pick me up?" The clerk was surprised.

"You bet." Manpower was not a factor on this case. The agent who picked her up would pick her brain again on the drive into D.C. The two investigators left. The Major drove his unmarked State Police car.

Capitano checked his notes. This wasn't bad for a first interview. He, the Major, and fifteen others had spent the day interviewing people in stores and shops up and down five miles of Ritchie Highway. Four people thought they remembered the van, but this was the first person who had seen one of its occupants closely enough for a description. It wasn't much, but it was a start. They already had the shooter ID'd. Cathy Ryan had recognized Sean Miller's face—thought she did, the agent corrected himself. If it had been Miller, he had a beard now, on the brown side of black and neatly trimmed. An artist would try to re-create that.

Twenty more agents and detectives had spent their day at the three local airports, showing photos to every ticket agent and gate clerk. They'd come up blank, but they hadn't had a description of Miller then. Tomorrow they would try again. A computer check was being made of international flights that connected to flights to Ireland, and domestic flights that connected to international ones. Capitano was happy that he didn't have to run all of those down. It would take weeks, and the chance of getting an ID from an airport worker diminished measurably every hour.

The van had been identified for more than a day, off the FBI's computer. It had been stolen a month before in New York City, repainted—professionally, by the look of it—and given new tags. Several sets of them, since the handicap tags found on it yesterday had been stolen less than two days before from a nursing home's van in Hagerstown, Maryland, a hundred miles away. Everything about the crime said it was a professional job from start to finish. Switching cars at the shopping center had been a brilliant finale to a perfectly planned and executed operation. Capitano and the major were able to restrain their admiration, but they had to make an objective assessment of the people they were after. These weren't common thugs. They were professionals in every perverted sense of the word.

"You suppose they got the van themselves?" Capitano asked the Major.

The State Police investigator grunted. "There's some outfit in Pennsylvania that steals them from all over the Northeast, paints them, reworks the interior, and sells 'em. You guys are looking for them, remember?''

''I've heard a few things about the investigation, but that's not my territory. It's being looked at. Personally, I think they did it themselves. Why risk a connection with somebody else?''

''Yeah,'' the Major agreed reluctantly. The van had already been checked out by state and federal forensic experts. Not a single fingerprint had been found. The vehicle had been thoroughly cleaned, down to the knobs on the window handles. The technicians found nothing that could lead them to the criminals. Now the dirt and fabric fibers vacuumed from the van's carpet were being analyzed in Washington, but this was the sort of clue that worked reliably only on TV. If the people had been smart enough to clean out the van, they were almost certainly smart enough to burn the clothing they'd worn. Everything was being checked out anyway, because even the smartest people did make mistakes.

''You heard anything on the ballistics yet?'' the Major asked, turning the car onto Rowe Boulevard.

''Oughta be waiting for us.'' They'd found almost twenty nine-millimeter cartridge cases to go along with the two usable bullets recovered from the Porsche, and the one that had gone through Trooper Fontana's chest and lodged in the back seat of his wrecked car. These had gone directly to the FBI laboratory in Washington for analysis. The evidence would tell them that the weapon was a submachine gun, which they already knew, but might give them a type, which they didn't yet know. The cartridge cases were Belgian-made, from the Fabrique Nationale at Liège. They might be able to identify the lot number, but FN made so many millions such rounds per year, which were shipped and reshipped all over the world, that the lead was a slim one. Very often such shipments simply disappeared, mainly from sloppy—or creative—bookkeeping.

''How many black groups are known to have contact with these ULA characters?''

''None,'' Capitano replied. ''That's something we are going to have to establish.''

''Great.''

Ryan arrived home to find an unmarked car and a liveried State Police cruiser in his driveway. Jack's own FBI interview wasn't a long one. It hadn't taken long to confirm the fact that he quite simply knew nothing about the attempt on his family or himself.

"Any idea where they are?" he asked finally.

"We're checking airports," the agent answered. "If these guys are as smart as they look, they're long gone."

"They're smart, all right," Ryan noted sourly. "What about the one you caught?"

"He's doing one hell of a good imitation of a clam. He has a lawyer now, of course, and the lawyer is telling him to keep his mouth shut. You can depend on lawyers for that."

"Where'd the lawyer come from?"

"Public defender's office. It's a rule, remember. You hold a suspect for any length of time, he has to have a lawyer. I don't think it matters. He probably isn't talking to the lawyer either. We have him on a state weapons violation and federal immigration laws. He goes back to the U.K. as soon as the paperwork gets done. Maybe two weeks or so, depending on if the attorney contests things." The agent closed his notebook. "You never know, maybe he'll start talking, but don't count on it. The word we get from the Brits is that he's not real bright anyway. He's the Irish version of a street hood, very good with weapons but a little slow upstairs."

"So if he's dumb, how come—"

"How come he's good at what he does? How smart do you have to be to kill somebody? Clark's a sociopathic personality. He has very little in the way of feelings. Some people are like that. They don't relate to the people around them as being real people. They see them as objects, and since they're only objects, whatever happens to them is not important. Once I met a hit man who killed four people—just the ones we know about—and didn't bat an eye, far as I could tell; but he cried like a baby when we told him his cat died. People like that don't even understand why they get sent to prison; they really don't understand," he concluded. "Those are the scary ones."

"No," Ryan said. "The scary ones are the ones with brains, the ones who believe in it."

"I haven't met one of those yet," he admitted.

"I have." Jack walked him to the door and watched him pull away. The house was an empty, quiet place without Sally running around, without the TV on, without Cathy talking about her friends at Hopkins. For several minutes Jack wandered around aimlessly, as though expecting to find someone. He didn't want to sit down, because that would somehow be an admission that he was all alone. He walked into the kitchen and started to fix a drink, but before he was finished, he dumped it all down the sink. He didn't want to get drunk. It was better to keep his mind unimpaired. Finally he lifted the phone and dialed.

"Yes," a voice answered.

"Admiral, Jack Ryan."

"I understand that your girl's going to be all right," James Greer said. "I'm glad to hear that, son."

"Thank you, sir. Is the Agency involved in this?"

"This is an unsecure line, Jack," the Admiral replied.

"I want in," Ryan said.

"Be here tomorrow morning."

Ryan hung up and went looking for his briefcase. He opened it and took out the Browning automatic pistol. After setting it on the kitchen table, he got out his shotgun and cleaning kit. He spent the next hour cleaning and oiling first the pistol, then the shotgun. When he was satisfied, he loaded both.

He left for Langley at five the next morning. Ryan had managed to get four more hours of sleep before rising and going through the usual morning ritual of coffee and breakfast. His early departure allowed him to miss the worst of the traffic, though the George Washington Parkway was never really free of the government workers heading to and from the agencies that were always more or less awake. After getting into the CIA building, he reflected that he had never called here and found Admiral Greer absent. *Well,* he told himself, *that's one thing in this world that I can depend on.* A security officer escorted him to the seventh floor.

"Good morning, sir," Jack said on entering the room.

"You look better than I expected," the DDI observed.

"It's an illusion mostly, but I can't solve my problem by hiding in a corner, can I? Can we talk about what's going on?"

"Your Irish friends have gotten a lot of attention. The President himself wants action on this. We've never had international terrorists play games in our country—at least, not things that ever made the press," Greer said cryptically. "It is now a high-priority case. It's getting a lot of resources."

"I want to be one of them," Ryan said simply.

"If you think that you can be part of an operation—"

"I know better than that, Admiral."

Greer smiled at the younger man. "That's good to see, son. I thought you were smart. So what do you want to do for us?"

"We both know that the bad guys are part of the network. The data you let me look at was pretty limited. Obviously you're going to be trying to collate data on all the groups, searching for leads on the ULA. Maybe I can help."

"What about your teaching?"

"I can be here when I'm not teaching. There isn't much to hold me at home at the moment, sir."

"It isn't good practice to use people who are personally involved in the investigation," Greer pointed out.

"This isn't the FBI, sir. I'm not going out into the field. You just told me that. I know you want me back here on a permanent basis, Admiral. If you really want me, let me start off doing something that's important to both of us." Jack paused, searching for another point. "If I'm good enough, let's find out now."

"Some people aren't going to like it."

"There's things happening to me that I don't like very much, sir, and I have to live with it. If I can't fight back somehow, I might as well stay at home. You're the only chance I have to do something to protect my family, sir."

Greer turned to refill his coffee cup from the drip machine behind his desk. He'd liked Jack almost from the first moment he'd met him. This was a young man accustomed to having his way, though he was not arrogant about it. That was a point in his favor: Ryan knew what he wanted, but wasn't overly pushy. He wasn't a person driven by ambition, another point in his favor. Finally, he had a lot of raw talent to be shaped and trained and directed. Greer was always looking for talent. The Admiral turned back.

"Okay, you're on the team. Marty's coordinating the information. You'll work directly with him. I hope you don't talk in your sleep, son, because you're going to see stuff that you're not even allowed to dream about."

"Sir, there's only one thing that I'm going to dream about."

It had been a very busy month for Dennis Cooley. The death of an earl in East Anglia had forced his heirs to sell off a massive collection of books to pay the death duties, and Cooley had used up nearly all of his available capital to secure no less than twenty-one items for his shop. But it was worth it: among them was a rare first-folio of Marlowe's plays. Better still, the dead earl had been assiduous in protecting his treasures. The books had been deep-frozen several times to kill off the insects that desecrated these priceless relics of the past. The Marlowe was in remarkably good shape, despite the waterstained cover that had put off a number of less perceptive buyers. Cooley was stooped over his desk, reading the first act of *The Jew of Malta,* when the bell rang.

"Is that the one I heard about?" his visitor asked at once.

"Indeed." Cooley smiled to cover his surprise. He hadn't seen this particular visitor for some time, and was somewhat disturbed that he'd come back so soon. "Printed in 1633, forty years after Marlowe's death. Some parts of the text are suspect, of course, but this is one of the few surviving copies of the first printed edition."

"It's quite authentic?"

"Of course," Cooley replied, slightly put off at the question. "In addition to my own humble expertise, it has authentication papers from Sir Edmund Grey of the British Museum."

"One cannot argue with that," the customer agreed.

"I'm afraid I have not yet decided upon a price for it." *Why are you here?*

"Price is not an object. I understand that you may wish to enjoy it for yourself, but I must have it." This told Cooley why he was here. He leaned to look over Cooley's shoulder at the book. "Magnificent," he said, placing a small envelope in the book dealer's pocket.

"Perhaps we can work something out," Cooley allowed. "In a few weeks, perhaps." He looked out the window. A man was window-shopping at the jewelry store on the opposite side of the arcade. After a moment he straightened up and walked away.

"Sooner than that, please," the man insisted.

Cooley sighed. "Come see me next week and we may be able to discuss it. I do have other customers, you know."

"But none more important, I hope."

Cooley blinked twice. "Very well."

Geoffrey Watkins continued to browse the store for another few minutes. He selected a Keats that had also come from the dead earl's estate and paid six hundred pounds for it before leaving. On leaving the arcade he failed to notice a young lady at the newsstand outside and could not have known that another was waiting at the arcade's other end. The one who followed him was dressed in a manner guaranteed to garner attention, including orange hair that would have fluoresced if the sun had been out. She followed him west for two blocks and kept going in that direction when he crossed the street. Another police officer was on the walk down Green Park.

That night the daily surveillance reports came to Scotland Yard where, as always, they were put on computer. The operation being run was a joint venture between the Metropolitan Police and the Security Service, once known as MI-5. Unlike the American FBI, the people at "Five" did not have the authority to arrest suspects, and had to work through the police to bring a case to a conclusion. The marriage was not entirely a happy one. It meant that James Owens had to work closely with David Ashley. Owens entirely concurred with his FBI colleague's assessment of the younger man: "a snotty bastard."

"Patterns, patterns, patterns," Ashley said, sipping his tea while he looked at the print-out. They had identified a total of thirty-nine people who knew, or might have known, information common to the ambush on The Mall and Miller's transport to the Isle of Wight. One of them had leaked the information. Every one of them was being watched. Thus far they had discovered a closet homosexual, two men and one woman who were having affairs not of state, and a man who got considerable enjoyment watching pornographic movies in the Soho theaters. Financial records gotten from Inland Revenue showed nothing particularly interesting, nor did living habits. There was the usual spread of hobbies, taste in theatrical plays, and television shows. Several of the people had wide collections of friends. A few had none at all. The investigators were grateful for these sad, lonely people—many of the other people's friends had to be checked out, too, and this took time and manpower. Owens viewed the entire operation as something necessary but rather distasteful. It was the police equivalent of peering through windows. The tapes of telephone conversations—especially those between lovers—made him squirm on occasion. Owens was a man who appreciated the individual's need for privacy. No one's life could survive this sort of scrutiny. He told himself that one person's life wouldn't, and that was the point of the exercise.

344 • TOM CLANCY

"I see Mr. Watkins visited a rare book shop this afternoon," Owens noted, reading over his own print-out.

"Yes. He collects them. So do I," Ashley said. "I've been in that shop once or twice myself. There was an estate sale recently. Perhaps Cooley bought a few things that Geoffrey wants for himself." The security officer made a mental note to look at the shop for himself. "He was in there for ten minutes, spoke with Dennis—"

"You know him?" Owens looked up.

"One of the best men in the trade," Ashley said. He smiled at his own choice of words: *the Trade.* "I bought a Brontë there for my wife, Christmas two years ago, I think. He's a fat little poof, but he's quite knowledgeable. So Geoffrey spoke with him for about ten minutes, made a purchase, and left. I wonder what he bought." Ashley rubbed his eyes. He'd been on a strict regimen of fourteen-hour days for longer than he cared to remember.

"The first new person Watkins has seen in several weeks," Owens noted. He thought about it for a moment. There were better leads than this to follow up on, and his manpower was limited.

"So can we deal on this immigration question?" the public defender asked.

"Not a chance," Bill Shaw said from the other side of the table. *You think we're going to give him political asylum?*

"You're not offering us a thing," the lawyer observed. "I bet I can beat the weapons charge, and there's no way you can make the conspiracy stick."

"That's fine, counselor. If it will make you any happier we'll cut him loose and give him a plane ticket, and even an escort, home."

"To a maximum-security prison." The public defender closed his file folder on the case of Eamon Clark. "You're not giving me anything to deal with."

"If he cops to the gun charge and conspiracy, and if he helps us, he gets to spend a few years in a much nicer prison. But if you think we're going to let a convicted murderer just walk, mister, you are kidding yourself. What do you think you have to deal with?"

"You might be surprised," the attorney said cryptically.

"Oh, yeah? I'm willing to bet that he hasn't said anything to you either," the agent challenged the young attorney, and watched closely for his reaction. Bill Shaw, too, had passed the bar exam, though he devoted his legal expertise to the safety of society rather than the freedom of criminals.

"Conversations between attorney and client are privileged." The lawyer had been practicing for exactly two and a half years. His understanding of his job was limited largely to keeping the police away from his charges. At first he'd been gratified that Clark hadn't said much of anything to the police and FBI, but he was surprised that Clark wouldn't even talk to him. After all, maybe he could cut a deal, despite what this FBI fellow said. But he had nothing to deal with, as Shaw had just told him. He waited a few moments for a reaction from the agent and got nothing but a blank stare. The public defender admitted defeat to himself. Well, there hadn't been much of a chance on this.

"That's what I thought." Shaw stood. "Tell your client that unless he opens up by the day after tomorrow, he's flying home to finish out a life sentence. Make sure you tell him that. If he wants to talk after he gets back, we'll send people to him. They say the beer's pretty good over there, and I wouldn't mind flying over myself to find out." The only thing the Bureau could use over Clark was fear. The mission he'd been part of had hurt the Provos, and young, dumb Ned might not like the reception he got. He'd be safer in a U.S. penitentiary than he would be in a British one, but Shaw doubted that he understood this, or that he'd crack in any case. Maybe after he got back, something might be arranged.

The case was not going well; not that he'd expected otherwise. This sort of thing either cracked open immediately, or took months—or years. The people they were after were too clever to have left an immediate opening to be exploited. What remained to him and his men was the day-by-day grind. But that was the textbook definition of investigative police work. Shaw knew this well enough: he had written one of the standard texts.

18

Lights

Ashley entered the bookshop at four in the afternoon. A true biblio-phile, he paused on opening the door to appreciate the aroma.

"Is Mr. Cooley in today?" he asked the clerk.

"No, sir," Beatrix replied. "He's abroad on business. May I help you?"

"Yes. I understand that you've made some new acquisitions."

"Ah, yes. Have you heard about the Marlowe first folio?" Beatrix looked remarkably like a mouse. Her hair was exactly the proper drab shade of brown and ill-kept. Her face was puffy, whether from too much food or too much drink, Ashley couldn't say. Her eyes were hidden behind thick glasses. She dressed in a way that fitted the store exactly—everything she had on was old and out of date. Ashley re-membered buying his wife the Brontë here, and wondered if those two sad, lonely sisters had looked like this girl. It was too bad, really. With a little effort she might actually have been attractive.

"A Marlowe?" the man from "Five" asked. "First folio, you said?"

"Yes, sir, from the collection of the late Earl of Crundale. As you know, Marlowe's plays were not actually printed until forty years after his death.'' She went on, displaying something that her appearance didn't begin to hint at. Ashley listened with respect. The mouse knew her business as well as an Oxford don.

"How do you find such things?" Ashley asked when she'd finished her discourse.

She smiled. "Mr. Dennis can smell them. He is always traveling, working with other dealers and lawyers and such. He's in Ireland today, for example. It's amazing how many books he manages to obtain over there. Those horrid people have the most marvelous collections." Beatrix did not approve of the Irish.

"Indeed," David Ashley noted. He didn't react to this bit of news at all. At least not physically, but a switch in the back of his head flipped on. "Well, that is one of the contributions our friends across the water have made. A few rather good writers, and whiskey.''

"And bombers," Beatrix noted. "I shouldn't want to travel there so much myself.''

"Oh, I take my holiday there quite often. The fishing is marvelous.''

"That's what Lord Louis Mountbatten thought," the clerk observed.

"How often does Dennis go over?''

"At least once a month.''

"Well, on this Marlowe you have—may I see it?" Ashley asked with an enthusiasm that was only partially feigned.

"By all means." The girl took the volume from a shelf and opened it with great care. "As you see, though the cover is in poor condition, the pages are in a remarkable state of preservation.''

Ashley hovered over the book, his eyes running down the opened page. "Indeed they are. How much for this one?''

"Mr. Dennis hasn't set a price yet. I believe another customer is already very interested in it, however.''

"Do you know who that is?''

"No, sir, I do not, and I would not be able to reveal his name in any case. We respect our customers' confidentiality," Beatrix said primly.

"Quite so. That is entirely proper," Ashley agreed. "So when will Mr. Cooley be back? I want to talk to him about this myself.''

"He'll be back tomorrow afternoon.''

"Will you be here also?" Ashley asked with a charming smile.

"No, I'll be at my other job."

"Too bad. Well, thank you very much for showing me this." Ashley made for the door.

"My pleasure, sir."

The security officer walked out of the arcade and turned right. He waited for the afternoon traffic to clear before crossing the street. He decided to walk back to Scotland Yard instead of taking a cab, and went downhill along St. James's Street, turning left to go around the Palace to the east, then down Marlborough Road to The Mall.

It happened right there, he thought. *The getaway car turned here to make its escape. The ambush was a mere hundred yards west of where I'm standing now.* He stood and looked for a few seconds, remembering.

The personality of a security officer is much the same all over the world. They do not believe in coincidences, though they do believe in accidents. They lack any semblance of a sense of humor where their work is concerned. This comes from the knowledge that only the most trusted of people have the ability to be traitors; before betraying their countries, they must first betray the people who trust them. Beneath all his charm, Ashley was a man who hated traitors beyond all things, who suspected everyone and trusted no one.

Ten minutes later Ashley got past the security checkpoint at Scotland Yard and took the elevator to James Owens' office.

"That Cooley chap," he said.

"Cooley?" Owens was puzzled for a moment. "Oh, the book dealer Watkins visited yesterday. Is that where you were?"

"A fine little shop. Its owner is in Ireland today," Ashley said deadpan.

Commander Owens nodded thoughtfully at that. What had been unimportant changed with a word. Ashley outlined what he had learned over several minutes. It wasn't even a real lead yet, but it was something to be looked at. Neither man said anything about how significant it might be—there had been many such things to run down, all of which to date had ended at blank walls. Many of the walls had also been checked out in every possible detail. The investigation wasn't at a standstill. People were still out on the street, accumulating information—none of which was the least useful to the case. This was something new to be looked at, nothing more than that; but for the moment that was enough.

*   *   *

It was eleven in the morning at Langley. Ryan was not admitted to the meetings between CIA and FBI people coordinating information on the case. Marty Cantor had explained to him that the FBI might be uneasy to have him there. Jack didn't mind. He'd get the information summaries after lunch, and that was enough for the moment. Cantor would come away both with the information FBI had developed, plus the thoughts and ideas of the chief investigators. Ryan didn't want that. He preferred to look at the raw data. His unprejudiced outsider's perspective had worked before and it might work again, he thought— hoped.

The wonderful world of the international terrorist, Murray had said to him outside the Old Bailey. It wasn't very wonderful, Jack thought, but it was a fairly complete world, including all of what the Greeks and Romans thought the civilized world was. He was going over satellite reconnaissance data at the moment. The bound report he was looking at contained no less than sixteen maps. In addition to the cities and roads shown on them were little red triangles designating suspected terrorist training camps in four countries. These were being photographed on almost a daily basis by the photoreconnaissance satellites (Jack was not allowed to know their number) orbiting the globe. He concentrated on the ones in Libya. They did have that report from an Italian agent that Sean Miller had been seen leaving a freighter in Bengazi harbor. The freighter had been of Cypriot registry, owned by a network of corporations sufficiently complex that it didn't really matter, since the ship was under charter to yet another such network. An American destroyer had photographed the ship in what certainly seemed a chance encounter in the Straits of Sicily. The ship was old but surprisingly well maintained, with modern radar and radio gear. She was regularly employed on runs from Eastern European ports to Libya and Syria, and was known to carry arms and military equipment from the East Bloc to client states on the Mediterranean. This data had already been set aside for further use.

Ryan found that the CIA and National Reconnaissance Office were looking at a number of camps in the North African desert. A simple graph accompanied the dated photos of each, and Ryan was looking for a camp whose apparent activity had changed the day that Miller's ship had docked at Bengazi. He was disappointed to find that four had done so. One was known to be used by the Provisional Wing of the

IRA—this datum had come from the interrogation of a convicted bomber. The other three were unknowns. The people there—aside from the maintenance staff provided by the Libyan armed forces— could be identified from the photos as Europeans from their fair skin, but that was all. Jack was disappointed to see that you couldn't recognize a face from these shots, just color of skin, and if the sun was right, color of hair. You could also determine the make of a car or truck, but not its identifying tag numbers. Strangely, the clarity of the photos was better at night. The cooler night air was less roiled and did not interfere with imaging as much as in the shimmering heat of the day.

The pictures in the heavy binder that occupied his attention were of camps 11-5-04, 11-5-18, and 11-5-20. Jack didn't know how the number designators had been arrived at and didn't really care. The camps were all pretty much the same; only the spacing of the huts distinguished one from another.

Jack spent the best part of an hour looking over the photos, and concluded that this miracle of modern technology told him all sorts of technical things, none of which were pertinent to his purpose. Whoever ran those camps knew enough to keep people out of sight when a reconsat was overhead—except for one which was not known to have photographic capability. Even then, the number of people visible was almost never the same, and the actual occupancy of the camps was therefore a matter for uncertain estimation. It was singularly frustrating.

Ryan leaned back and lit another low-tar cigarette bought from the kiosk on the next floor down. It went well with the coffee that was serving to keep him awake. He was up against another blank wall. It made him think of the computer games he occasionally played at home when he was tired of writing—Zork and Ultima. The business of intelligence analysis was so often like those computer ''head games.'' You had to figure things out, but you never quite knew what it was that you were figuring out. The patterns you had to deduce could be very different from anything one normally dealt with, and the difference could be significant or mere happenstance.

Two of the suspected ULA camps were within forty miles of the known IRA outpost. *Less than an hour's drive,* Jack thought. *If they only knew.* He would have settled for having the Provos clean out the ULA, as they evidently wanted to do. There were indications that the Brits were thinking along similar lines. Jack wondered what Mr.

Owens thought of that one and concluded that he probably didn't know. It was a surprising thought that he now had information that some experienced players did not. He went back to the pictures.

One, taken a week after Miller had been seen in Bengazi, showed a car—it looked like a Toyota Land Cruiser—about a mile from 11-5-18, heading away. Ryan wondered where it was going. He wrote down the date and time on the bottom of the photo and checked the cross-reference table in the front. Ten minutes later he found the same car, the next day, at Camp 11-5-09, a PIRA camp forty miles from 11-5-18.

Jack told himself not to get overly excited: 11-5-18 could belong to the Red Army Faction of West Germany, Italy's resurgent Red Brigade, or any number of other organizations with which the PIRA cross-pollinated. He still made some notes. It was a "datum," a bit of information that was worth checking out.

Next he checked the occupancy graph for the camp. This showed the number of camp buildings occupied at night, and went back for over two years. He compared it with a list of known ULA operations, and discovered . . . nothing, at first. The instances where the number of occupied buildings blipped up did not correlate with the organization's known activities . . . but there was some sort of pattern, he saw.

What kind of pattern? Jack asked himself. Every three months or so the occupancy went up by one. Regardless of the number of the people at the camp, the number of huts being used went up by one, for a period of three days. Ryan swore when he saw that the pattern didn't quite hold. Twice in two years the number didn't change. *And what does* that *mean?*

"You are in a maze of twisty passages, all alike," Jack murmured to himself. It was a line from one of his computer games. Pattern-recognition was not one of his strong points. Jack left the room to get a can of Coke, but more to clear his head. He was back in five minutes.

He pulled the occupancy graphs from the three "unknown" camps to compare the respective levels of activity. What he really needed to do was to make Xerox copies of the graphs, but CIA had strict rules on the use of copying machines. Doing it would take time that he didn't want to lose at the moment. The other two camps showed no recognizable pattern at all, while Camp -18 did seem to lean in that direction. He spent an hour doing this. By the end of it he had all three graphs memorized. He had to get away from it. Ryan tucked the graphs back where they belonged and returned to examining the photographs themselves.

Camp 11-5-20, he saw, showed a girl in one photo. At least there was someone there wearing a two-piece bathing suit. Jack stared at the image for a few seconds, then turned away in disgust. He was playing voyeur, trying to discern the figure of someone who was probably a terrorist. There were no such attractions at camps -04 and -18, and he wondered at the significance of this until he remembered that only one satellite was giving daylight photos with people in them. Ryan made a note to himself to check at the Academy's library for a book on orbital mechanics. He decided that he needed to know how often a single satellite passed over a given spot in a day.

"You're not getting anywhere," he told himself aloud.

"Neither is anybody else," Marty Cantor said. Ryan spun around.

"How did you get in here?" Jack demanded.

"I'll say one thing for you, Jack, when you concentrate you really concentrate. I've been standing here for five minutes." Cantor grinned. "I like your intensity, but if you want an opinion, you're pushing a little hard, fella."

"I'll survive."

"You say so," Cantor said dubiously. "How do you like our photo album?"

"The people who do this full-time must go nuts."

"Some do," Cantor agreed.

"I might have something worth checking out," Jack said, explaining his suspicions on Camp -18.

"Not bad. By the way, number -20 may be *Action-Directe,* the French group that's picked up lately. DGSE—the French foreign intelligence service—thinks they have a line on it."

"Oh. That may explain one of the photos." Ryan flipped to the proper page.

"Thank God Ivan doesn't know what that bird does," Cantor nodded. "Hmm. We may be able to ID from this."

"How?" Jack asked. "You can't make out her face."

"You can tell her hair length, roughly. You can also tell the size of her tits." Cantor grinned ear to ear.

"What?"

"The guys in photointerpretation are—well, they're very technical. For cleavage to show up in these photos, a girl has to have C-cup breasts—at least that's what they told me once. I'm not kidding, Jack. Somebody actually worked the math out, because you can identify people from a combination of factors like hair color, length, and bust size. *Action-Directe* has lots of female operatives. Our French colleagues might find this interesting." *If they're willing to deal,* he didn't say.

"What about -18?"

"I don't know. We've never really tried to identify that one. The thing about the car may count against it, though."

"Remember that our ULA friends have the Provos infiltrated," Jack said.

"You're still on that, eh? Okay, it's something to be considered," Cantor conceded. "What about this pattern thing you talked about?"

"I haven't got anything to point to yet," Jack admitted.

"Let's see the graph."

Jack unfolded it from the back of the binder. "Every three months, mostly, the occupancy rate picks up."

Cantor frowned at the graph for a moment. Then he flipped through the photographs. On only one of the dates did they have a daylight photo that showed anything. Each of the camps had what looked like a shooting range. In the photo Cantor selected, there were three men standing near it.

"You might have something, Jack."

"What?" Ryan had looked at the photo and made nothing of it.

"What's the distinguishing feature of the ULA?"

"Their professionalism," Ryan answered.

"Your last paper on them said they were more militarily organized than some of the others, remember? Every one of them, as far as we can tell, is skilled with weapons."

"So?"

"Think!" Cantor snapped. Ryan gave him a blank look. "Periodic weapons-refresher training, maybe?"

"Oh. I hadn't thought of that. How come nobody ever—"

"Do you know how many satellite photos come through here? I can't say exactly, but you may safely assume that it's a fairly large number, thousands per month. Figure it takes a minimum of five minutes to examine each one. Mostly we're interested in the Russians—missile silos, factories, troop movements, tank parks, you name it. That's where most of the analytical talent goes, and they can't keep up with what comes in. The guys we have on this stuff here are technicians, not analysts.'' Cantor paused. ''Camp -18 looks interesting enough that we might try to figure a way to check it out, see who really lives there. Not bad.''

''He's violated security,'' Kevin O'Donnell said by way of greeting. He was quiet enough that no one in the noisy pub would have heard him.

''Perhaps this is worth it,'' Cooley replied. ''Instructions?''

''When are you going back?''

''Tomorrow morning, the early flight.''

O'Donnell nodded, finishing off his drink. He left the pub and walked directly to his car. Twenty minutes later he was home. Ten minutes after that, his operations and intelligence chiefs were in his study.

''Sean, how did you like working with Alex's organization?''

''They're like us, small but professional. Alex is a very thorough technician, but an arrogant one. He hasn't had a great deal of formal training. He's clever, very clever. And he's hungry, as they say over there. He wants to make his mark.''

''Well, he may just have his chance next summer.'' O'Donnell paused, holding up the letter Cooley had delivered. ''It would seem that His Royal Highness will be visiting America next summer. The Treasure Houses exhibit was such a success that they are going to stage another one. Nearly ninety percent of the works of Leonardo Da Vinci belong to the Royal Family, and they'll be sending them over to raise money for some favored charities. The show opens in Washington on August the first, and the Prince of Wales will be going over to start things off. This will not be announced until July, but here is his itinerary, including the proposed security arrangements. It is as yet undecided whether or not his lovely bride will accompany His Highness, but we will proceed on the assumption that she will.''

''The child?'' Miller asked.

''I rather suspect not, but we will allow for that possibility also.'' He handed the letter to Joseph McKenney. The intelligence officer for the ULA skimmed over the data.

''The security at the official functions will be airtight. The Americans have had a number of incidents, and they've learned from each of them,'' McKenney said. Like all intelligence officers, he saw his potential opponents as overwhelmingly powerful. "But if they go forward with this one . . .''

"Yes," O'Donnell said. "I want you two to work together on this. We have plenty of time and we'll use all of it.'' He took the letter back and reread it before giving it to Miller. After they left, he wrote his instructions for their agent in London.

At the airport the next morning Cooley saw his contact and walked into the coffee shop. He was early for his flight, seasoned traveler that he was, and had a cup while he waited for it to be announced. Finished, he walked outside. His contact was just walking in. The two men brushed by each other, and the message was passed, just as was taught in every spy school in the world.

"He does travel about a good deal," Ashley observed. It had taken Owens' detectives less than an hour to find Cooley's travel agent and to get a record of his trips for the past three years. Another pair was assembling a biographical file on the man. It was strictly routine work. Owens and his men knew better than to get excited about a new lead. Enthusiasm all too easily got in the way of objectivity. His car— parked at Gatwick Airport—had considerable mileage on the clock for its age, and that was explained by his motoring about buying books. This was the extent of the data assembled in eighteen hours. They would patiently wait for more.

"How often does he travel to Ireland?"

"Quite frequently, but he does business in English-language books, and we are the only two countries in Europe that speak English, aren't we?" Ashley, too, was able to control himself.

"America?" Owens asked.

"Once a year, looks like. I rather suspect it's to an annual trade show. I can check that myself.''

"They speak English, too.''

Ashley grinned. "Shakespeare didn't live or print books there. There aren't many examples of American publishing old enough to excite a person like Cooley. What he might do is buy up books of ours that have found their way across the water, but more likely he's looking for buyers. No, Ireland fits beautifully with his cover—excuse me, if it is that. My own dealer, Samuel Pickett and Sons, travel there often also . . . but not as much, I should think,'' he added.

"Perhaps his biography will tell us something," Owens noted.

"One can hope." Ashley was looking for a light at the end of this tunnel, but saw only more tunnel.

"It's okay, Jack," Cathy said.

He nodded. Ryan knew that his wife was right. The nurse-practitioner had positively beamed at the news she gave them on their arrival. Sally was bouncing back like any healthy child should. The healing process had already begun.

Yet there was a difference between the knowledge of the mind and the knowledge of the heart. Sally had been awake this time. She was unable to speak, of course, with the respirator hose in her mouth, but the murmurs that tried to come out could only have meant: *It hurts.* The injuries inflicted on the body of his child did not appear any less horrific, despite his knowledge that they would heal. If anything they seemed worse now that she was occasionally conscious. The pain would eventually go away—but his little girl was in pain now. Cathy might be able to tell herself that only the living could feel pain, that it was a positive sign for all the discomfort it gave. Jack could not. They stayed until she dozed off again. He took his wife outside.

"How are you?" he asked her.

"Better. You can take me home tomorrow night."

Jack shook his head. He hadn't thought about that. Stupid, Ryan told himself. Somehow he'd assumed that Cathy would stay here, close to Sally.

"The house is pretty empty without you, babe," he said after a moment.

"It'll be empty without her," his wife answered, and the tears started again. She buried her face in her husband's shoulder. "She's so little . . ."

"Yeah." Jack thought of Sally's face, the two little blue eyes surrounded by a sea of bruises, the hurt there, the pain there. "She's going to get better, honey, and I don't want to hear any more of that 'it's my fault' crap."

"But it is!"

"No, it isn't. Do you know how lucky I am to have you both alive? I saw the FBI's data today. If you hadn't stomped on the brakes when you did, you'd both be dead." The supposition was that this had thrown off Miller's aim by a few inches. At least two rounds had missed Cathy's head by a whisker, the forensic experts said. Jack could close his eyes and recite that information word for word. "You saved her life and yours by being smart."

It took Cathy a moment to react. "How did you find that out?"

"CIA. They're cooperating with the police. I asked to be part of the team and they let me join up."

"But—"

"A lot of people are working on this, babe. I'm one of them," Jack said quietly. "The only thing that matters now is finding them."

"Do you think . . ."

"Yeah, I do." *Sooner or later.*

Bill Shaw had no such hopes at the moment. The best potential lead they had was the identity of the black man who'd driven the van. This was being kept out of the media. As far as the TV and newspapers were concerned, all the suspects were white. The FBI hadn't so much lied to the press as allowed them to draw a false conclusion from the partial data that had been released—as happened frequently enough. It might keep the suspect from being spooked. The only person who'd seen him at close range was the 7-Eleven clerk. She had spent several hours going over pictures of blacks thought to be members of revolutionary groups and come up with three possibles. Two of these were in prison, one for bank robbery, the other for interstate transport of explosives. The third had dropped out of sight seven years before. He was only a picture to the Bureau. The name they had for him was known to be an alias, and there were no fingerprints. He'd cut himself loose from his former associates—a smart move, since most of them had been arrested and convicted for various criminal acts—and simply disappeared. The best bet, Shaw told himself, was that he was now part of society, living a normal life somewhere with his past activities no more than a memory.

The agent looked over the file once again. "Constantine Duppens," his alias had been. Well-spoken on the few occasions when he'd spoken at all, the informant had said of him. Educated, probably. Attached to the group the Bureau had been watching, but never really part of it, the file went on. He'd never participated in a single illegal act, and had drifted away when the leaders of the little band had started talking about supporting themselves with bank robberies and drug trafficking. Maybe a dilettante, Shaw thought, a student with a radical streak who'd gotten a look at one of the groups and recognized them for what they were—what Shaw thought they were: ineffective dolts, street hoods with a smattering of Marxist garbage or pseudo-Hitlerism.

A few fringe groups occasionally managed to set off a bomb somewhere, but these cases were so rare, so minor, that the American people scarcely knew that they'd happened at all. When a group robbed a bank or armored car to support itself, the public remembered that one need not be politically motivated to rob a bank; greed was enough. From a high of fifty-one terrorist incidents in 1982, the number had been slashed to seven in 1985. The Bureau had managed to run down many of these amateurish groups, preventing more than twenty incidents the previous year, with good intelligence followed by quick action. Fundamentally, the small cells of crazies had been done in by their own amateurism.

America didn't have any ideologically motivated terrorist groups, at least not in the European sense. There were the Armenian groups whose main objective was murdering Turkish diplomats, and the white-supremacist people in the Northwest, but in both cases the only ideology was hatred—of Turks, blacks, Jews, or whatever. These were vicious but not really dangerous to society, since they lacked a shared vision of their political objective. To be really effective, the members of such a group had to believe in something more than the negativity of hate. The most dangerous terrorists were the idealists, of course, but America was a hard place to see the benefits of Marxism or Nazism. When even welfare families had color televisions, how much attraction could there be to collectivism? When the country lacked a system of class distinctions, what group could one hate with conviction? And so most of the small groups found that they were guerrilla fish swimming not in a sea of peasants, but rather a sea of apathy. Not a single group had been able to overcome that fact before being penetrated and destroyed by the Bureau—then to learn that their destruction was granted but a few column inches on page eleven, their defiant manifesto not printed at all. They were judged by faceless editors not to be newsworthy. In so many ways this was the perfect conclusion to a terrorist trial.

In that sense the FBI was a victim of its own success. So well had the job been done that the possibility of terrorist activity in America was not a matter of general public concern. Even the Ryan Case, as it was now being called, was regarded as nothing more than a nasty crime, not a harbinger of something new in America. To Shaw it was both. As a matter of institutional policy, the FBI regarded terrorism as a crime without any sort of political dimension that might lend a perverted respectability to the perpetrators. The importance of this distinction was not merely semantic. Since by their nature, terrorists struck at the foundations of civilized society, to grant them the thinnest shred of respectability was the equivalent of a suicide note for the targeted society. The Bureau recognized, however, that these were not mere criminals chasing after money. Their objective was far more dangerous than that. For this reason, crimes that otherwise would have been in the domain of local police departments were immediately taken under charge by the federal government.

Shaw returned to the photo of "Constantine Duppens" one more time. It was expecting too much for a convenience-store clerk to remember one face from the hundred she saw every day, or at least to remember it well enough to pick out a photo that might be years old. She'd certainly tried to help, and had agreed to tell no one of what she'd done. They had a description of the suspect's clothing—almost certainly burned—and the van, which they had. It was being dismantled piece by piece not far from Shaw's office. The forensic experts had identified the type of gun used. For the moment, that was all they had. All Inspector Bill Shaw could do was wait for his agents in the field to come up with something new. A paid informant might overhear something, or a new witness might turn up, or maybe the forensics team would discover something unexpected in the van. Shaw told himself to be patient. Despite twenty-two years in the FBI, patience was something he still had to force on himself.

"Aw, I was starting to like the beard," a co-worker said.

"Damned thing itched too much." Alexander Constantine Dobbens was back at his job. "I was spending half my time just scratching my face."

"Yeah, same thing when I was on subs," his roommate agreed. "Different when you're young."

"Speak for yourself, grandpop!" Dobbens laughed. "You old married turkey. Just because you're chained doesn't mean I have to be."

"You oughta settle down, Alex."

"The world is full of interesting things to do, and I haven't done them all yet." *Not hardly.* He was a field engineer for Baltimore Gas and Electric Company and usually worked nights. The job forced him to spend much of his time on the road, checking equipment and supervising line crews. Alex was a popular fellow who didn't mind getting his hands dirty, who actually enjoyed the physical work that many engineers were too proud to do. A man of the people, he called himself. His pro-union stance was a source of irritation to management, but he was a good engineer, and being black didn't hurt either. A man who was a good engineer, popular with his people, *and* black was fireproof. He'd done a good deal of minority recruiting, moreover, having brought a dozen good workers into the company. A few of them had shaky backgrounds, but Alex had brought them around.

It was often quiet working nights, and as was usually the case, Alex got the first edition of the *Baltimore Sun*. The case was already off the front page, now back in the local news section. The FBI and State Police, he read, were continuing to investigate the case. He was still amazed that the woman and kid had survived—testimony, his training told him, to the efficacy of seat belts, not to mention the work of the Porsche engineers. *Well,* he decided, *that's okay.* Killing a little kid and a pregnant woman wasn't exactly something to brag about. They had wasted the state trooper, and that was enough for him. Losing that Clark boy to the cops continued to rankle Dobbens, though. *I told the dumb fuck that the man was too exposed there, but no, he wanted to waste the whole family at once.* Alex knew why that was so, but saw it as a case of zeal overcoming realism. *Damned political-science majors, they think you can make something happen if you wish hard enough.* Engineers knew different.

Dobbens took comfort from the fact that all the known suspects were white. Waving to the helicopter had been his mistake. Bravado had no place in revolutionary activity. It was his own lesson to be learned, but this one hadn't hurt anyone. The gloves and hat had denied the pigs a description. The really funny thing was that despite all the screwups, the operation had been a success. That IRA punk, O-something, had been booted out of Boston with his honky tail between his legs. At least the operation had been politically sound. And that, he told himself, was the real measure of success.

From his point of view, success meant earning his spurs. He and his people had provided expert assistance to an established revolutionary group. He could now look to his African friends for funding. They really weren't African to his way of thinking, but they liked to call themselves that. There were ways to hurt America, to get attention in a way that no revolutionary group ever had. What, for example, if he could turn out the lights in fifteen states at once? Alex Dobbens knew how. The revolutionary had to know a way of hitting people where they lived, and what better way, he thought, than to make unreliable something that they took for granted? If he could demonstrate that the corrupt government could not even keep their lights on reliably, what doubts might he put in people's heads next? America was a society of things, he thought. What if those things stopped working? What then would people think? He didn't know the answer to that, but he knew that something would change, and change was what he was after.

19

Tests and Passing Grades

"He is an odd duck," Owens observed. The dossier was the result of three weeks of work. It could have gone faster, of course, but when you don't want the news of an inquiry to reach its subject, you had to be more circumspect.

Dennis Cooley was a Belfast native, born to a middle-class Catholic family, although neither of his deceased parents had been churchgoers, something decidedly odd in a region where religion defines both life and death. Dennis had attended church—a necessity for one who'd been educated at the parish school—until university, then stopped at once and never gone back. No criminal record at all. None. Not even a place in a suspected associates file. As a university student he'd hung around the fringes of a few activist groups, but never joined, evidently preferring his studies in literature. He'd graduated with the highest honors. A few courses in Marxism, a few more in economics, always with a teacher whose leanings were decidedly left of center, Owens saw. The police commander snorted to himself. There were enough of those at the London School of Economics, weren't there?

For two years all they had were tax records. He'd worked in his father's bookshop, and so far as the police were concerned, simply did not exist. That was a problem with police work—you noticed only the criminals. A few very discreet inquiries made in Belfast hadn't turned up anything. All sorts of people had visited the shop, even soldiers of the British Army, who'd arrived there about the time Cooley had graduated university. The shop's window had been smashed once or twice by marauding bands of Protestants—the reason the Army had been called in in the first place—but nothing more serious than that. Young Dennis hadn't frequented the local pubs enough that anyone had noticed, hadn't belonged to any church organization, nor any political club, nor any sports association. "He was always reading something," someone had told one of the detectives. *There's a bloody revelation,* Owens told himself. *A bookshop owner who reads . . .*

Then his parents had died in an auto accident.

Owens was struck by the fact that they'd died in a completely ordinary way. A lorry's brakes had failed and smashed into their Mini one Saturday afternoon. It was hard to remember that some people in Ulster actually died "normally," and were just as dead as those blown up or shot by the terrorists who prowled the night. Dennis Cooley had taken the insurance settlement and continued to operate the store as before after the quiet, ill-attended funeral ceremony at the local church. Some years later he'd sold out and moved to London, first setting up a shop in Knightsbridge and soon thereafter taking over a shop in the arcade where he continued to do business.

Tax records showed that he made a comfortable living. A check of his flat showed that he lived within his means. He was well-regarded by his fellow dealers. His one employee, Beatrix, evidently liked working with him part-time. Cooley had no friends, still didn't frequent local pubs—rarely drank at all, it seemed—lived alone, had no known sexual preferences, and traveled a good deal on business.

"He's a bloody cipher, a zero," Owens said.

"Yes," Ashley replied. "At least it explains where Geoff met him—he was a lieutenant with one of the first regiments to go over, and probably wandered into the shop once or twice. You know what a talker Geoff Watkins is. They probably started talking books—can't have been much else. I doubt that Cooley has any interest beyond that."

"Yes, I believe he's what the Yanks call a nerd. Or at least it's an image he's cultivating. What about his parents?"

Ashley smiled. "They are remembered as the local Communists. Nothing serious, but decidedly bolshie until the Hungarian uprising of 1956. That seems to have disenchanted them. They remained outspokenly left-wing, but their political activities effectively ended then. Actually they're remembered as rather pleasant people, but a little odd. Evidently they encouraged the local children to read—made good business sense, if nothing else. Paid their bills on time. Other than that, nothing."

"This girl Beatrix?"

"Somehow she got an education from our state schools. Didn't attend university, but self-taught in literature and the history of publishing. Lives with her elderly father—he's a retired RAF sergeant. She has no social life. She probably spends her evenings watching the telly and sipping Dubonnet. She rather intensely dislikes the Irish, but doesn't mind working with 'Mr. Dennis' because he's an expert in his field. Nothing there at all."

"So, we have a dealer in rare books with a Marxist family, but no known ties with any terrorist group," Owens summarized. "He was in university about the same time as our friend O'Donnell, wasn't he?"

"Yes, but nobody remembers if they ever met. In fact, they lived only a few streets apart, but again no one remembers if Kevin ever frequented the bookshop." Ashley shrugged. "That goes back before O'Donnell attracted any serious attention, remember. If there were a lead of some sort then, it was never documented. They shared this economics instructor. That might have been a useful lead, but the chap died two years ago—natural causes. Their fellow students have scattered to the four winds, and we've yet to find one who knew both of them."

Owens walked to the corner of his office to pour a cup of tea. *A chap with a Marxist background who attended the same school at the same time as O'Donnell.* Despite the total lack of a connection with a terrorist group, it was enough to follow up. If they could find something to suggest that Cooley and O'Donnell knew each other, then Cooley was the likely bridge between Watkins and the ULA. That did not mean there was any evidence to suggest the link was real, but in several months they had discovered nothing else even close.

"Very well, David, what do you propose to do?"

"We'll plant microphones in his shop and his home, and tap all of his telephone calls, of course. When he travels, he'll have a companion.''

Owens nodded approval. That was more than he could do legally, but the Security Service didn't operate under the same rules as did the Metropolitan Police. "How about watching his shop?"

"Not easy, when you remember where it is. Still, we might try to get one of our people hired in one of the neighboring shops."

"The one opposite his is a jewelry establishment, isn't it?"

"Nicholas Reemer and Sons," Ashley nodded. "Owner and two employees."

Owens thought about that. "I could find an experienced burglary detective, someone knowledgeable in the field. . . ."

"Morning, Jack," Cantor said.

"Hi, Marty."

Ryan had given up on the satellite photographs weeks before. Now he was trying to find patterns within the terrorist network. Which group had connections with which other? Where did their arms come from? Where did they train? Who helped with the training? Who provided the money? Travel documents? What countries did they use for safe transits?

The problem with these questions was not a lack of information, but a glut of it. Literally thousands of CIA field officers and their agents, plus those of every other Western intelligence service, were scouring the world for such information. Many of the agents—foreign nationals recruited and paid by the Agency—would make reports on the most trivial encounter in the hope of delivering The One Piece of Information that would crack open Abu Nidal, or Islamic Jihad, or one of the other high-profile groups, for a substantial reward. The result was thousands of communiqués, most of them full of worthless garbage that was indistinguishable from the one or two nuggets of real information. Jack had not realized the magnitude of the problem. The people working on this were all talented, but they were being overwhelmed by a sea of raw intelligence data that had to be graded, collated, and cross-referenced before proper analysis could begin. The difficulty of finding any single organization was inversely proportional to its size, and some of these groups were composed of a mere handful of people—in extreme cases composed of family members only.

"Marty," Jack said, looking away from the papers on his desk, "this is the closest thing to impossible I've ever seen."

"Maybe, but I've come to deliver a well-done," Cantor replied.

"What?"

"Remember that satellite photo of the girl in the bikini? The French think they've ID'd her: Françoise Theroux. Long, dark hair, a striking figure, and she was thought to be out of the country when the photo was made. That confirms that the camp belongs to *Action-Directe*."

"So who's the girl?"

"An assassin," Marty replied. He handed Jack a photograph taken at closer range. "And a good one. Three suspected kills, two politicians and an industrialist, all with a pistol at close range. Imagine how it's done: you're a middle-aged man walking down the street; you see a pretty girl; she smiles at you, maybe asks for directions or something; you stop, and the next thing you know, there's a pistol in her hand. Goodbye, Charlie."

Jack looked at the photograph. She didn't look dangerous—she looked like every man's fantasy. "Like we used to say in college, not the sort of girl you'd kick out of bed. Jesus, what sort of world do we live in, Marty?"

"You know that better than I do. Anyway, we've been asked to keep an eye on the camp. If we spot her there again, the French want us to real-time the photo to them."

"They're going to go in after her?"

"They didn't say, but you might recall that the French have troops in Chad, maybe four hundred miles away. Airborne units, with helicopters."

Jack handed the picture back. "What a waste."

"Sure is." Cantor pocketed the photo and the issue. "How's it going with your data?"

"So far I have a whole lot of nothing. The people who do this full-time . . ."

"Yeah, for a while there they were working around the clock. We had to make them stop, they were burning out. Computerizing it was a little helpful. Once we had the head of one group turn up at six airports in one day, and we knew the data was for crap, but every so often we get a live one. We missed that guy by a half hour outside Beirut last March. Thirty goddamned minutes," Cantor said. "You get used to it."

Thirty minutes, Jack thought. *If I'd left my office thirty minutes earlier, I'd be dead. How am I supposed to get used to that?*

"What would you have done to him?"

"We wouldn't have read him his constitutional rights," Cantor replied. "So, any connections that you've been able to find?"

Ryan shook his head. "This ULA outfit is so goddamned small. I have sixteen suspected contacts between the IRA and other groups. Some of them could be our boys, but how can you tell? The reports don't have pictures, the written descriptions could be anybody. Even when we have a reported IRA contact with a bunch they're not supposed be talking to—one that might actually be the ULA—then, A, our underlying information could easily be wrong, and B, it could be the first time they talked with the IRA! Marty, how in the hell is somebody supposed to make any sense out of this garbage?"

"Well, the next time you hear somebody ask what the CIA is doing about terrorism—you won't be able to tell him." Cantor actually smiled at that. "These people we're looking for aren't dumb. They know what'll happen if they get caught. Even if we don't do it ourselves—which we might not want to do—we can always tip the Israelis. Terrorists are tough, nasty bastards, but they can't stand up to real troops and they know it.

"That's the frustrating part. My brother-in-law's an Army major, part of the Delta Force down at Fort Bragg. I've seen them operate. They could take out this camp you looked at in under two minutes, kill everybody there, and be gone before the echo fades. They're deadly and efficient, but without the right information, they don't know *where* to be deadly and efficient *at.* Same with police work. Do you think the Mafia could survive if the cops knew exactly where and when they did their thing? How many bank robberies would be successful if the SWAT team was waiting inside the doors? But you gotta know where the crooks are. It's all about intelligence, and intelligence comes down to a bunch of faceless bureaucrats sifting through all this crap. The people who gather the intel give it to us, and we process it and give it to the operations teams. The battle is fought here, too, Jack. Right here in this building, by a bunch of GS-9s and -10s who go home to their families every night."

But the battle is being lost, Jack told himself. *It sure as hell isn't being won.*

"How's the FBI doing?" he asked.

"Nothing new. The black guy—well, he might as well not exist so far as anyone can tell. They have a crummy picture that's several years old, an alias with no real name or prints to check, and about ten lines of description that mainly says he's smart enough to keep his mouth shut. The Bureau's checking through people who used to be in the radical groups—funny how they have mostly settled down—without any success so far."

"How about the bunch who flew over there two years back?" Not so long ago members of several radical American groups had flown to Libya to meet with "progressive elements" of the third-world community. The echoes of that event still reverberated through the antiterrorism community.

"You've noticed that we don't have any pictures from Bengazi, right? Our agent got picked up—one of those horrible accidents. It cost us the photos and it cost him his neck. Fortunately they never found out he was working for us. We know some of the names of the people who were there, but not all."

"Passport records?"

Cantor leaned against the doorframe. "Let's say Mr. X flew to Europe, an American on vacation—we're talking tens of thousands of people per month. He makes contact with someone on the other side, and they get him the rest of the way without going through the usual immigration-control procedures. It's easy—hell, the Agency does it all the time. If we had a name we could see if he was out of the country at the right time. That would be a start—but we don't have a name to check."

"We don't have anything!" Ryan snapped.

"Sure we do. We have all that"—he waved at the documents on Ryan's desk—"and lots more where that came from. Somewhere in there is the answer."

"You really believe that?"

"Every time we crack one of these things, we find that all the information was under our nose for months. The oversight committees in Congress always hammer us on that. Sitting in that pile right now, Jack, is a crucial lead. That's almost a statistical certainty. But you probably have two or three hundred such reports sitting there, and only one matters."

"I didn't expect miracles, but I did expect to make some progress," Jack said quietly, the magnitude of the problem finally sinking in.

"You did. You saw something that no one else did. You may have found Françoise Theroux. And now if a French agent sees something that might be useful to us, maybe they'll pass it along. You didn't know this, but the intel business is like the old barter economy. We give them, and then they give us, or we'll never give to them again. If this pans out, they'll owe us big-time. They really want that gal. She popped a close friend of their President, and he took it personally.

"Anyway, you get a well-done from the Admiral and the DGSE. The boss says you should take it a little easier, by the way."

"I'll take it easy when I find the bastards," Ryan replied.

"Sometimes you have to back off. You look like hell. You're tired. Fatigue makes for errors. We don't like errors. No more late hours, Jack, that comes from Greer, too. You're out of here by six." Cantor left, denying Jack a chance to object.

Ryan turned back toward his desk, but stared at the wall for several minutes. Cantor was right. He was working so late that half the time he couldn't drive up to Baltimore to see how his daughter was doing. Jack rationalized that his wife was with her every day, frequently spending the night at Hopkins to be close to their daughter. *Cathy has her job and I have mine.*

So, he told the wall, *at least I managed to get something right.* He remembered that it had been an accident, that Marty had made the real connection; but it was also true that he'd done what an analyst was supposed to do, find something odd and bring it to someone's attention. He could feel good about that. He'd found a terrorist maybe, but certainly not the right one.

It's a start. His conscience wondered what the French would do if they found that pretty girl, and how he'd feel about it if he found out. It would be better, he decided, if terrorists were ugly, but pretty or not, their victims were just as dead. He promised himself that he wouldn't go out of his way to find out if anyone got her. Jack went back into the pile, looking for that one piece of hard information. The people he was looking for were somewhere in the pile. He had to find them.

"Hello, Alex," Miller said as he entered the car.

"How was the trip?" He still had his beard, Dobbens saw. Well, nobody had gotten much of a look at him. This time he'd flown to Mexico, driven across the border, then taken a domestic flight into D.C., where Alex had met him.

"Your border security over here's a bloody joke."

"Would it make you happy if they changed it?" Alex inquired. "Let's talk business." The abruptness of his tone surprised Miller.

Aren't you a proud one, with one whole operation under your belt, Miller thought. "We have another job for you."

"You haven't paid me for the last one yet, boy."

Miller handed over a passbook. "Numbered account, Bahamian bank. I believe you'll find the amount correct."

Alex pocketed the book. "That's more like it. Okay, we have another job. I hope you don't expect to go with it as fast as before."

"We have several months to plan it," Miller replied.

"I'm listening." Alex sat through ten minutes of information.

"Are you out of your fucking mind?" Dobbens asked when he was finished.

"How hard would it be to gather the information we need?"

"That's not the problem, Sean. The problem is getting your people in and out. No way I could handle that."

"That is my concern."

"Bullshit! If my people are involved, it's my concern, too. If that Clark turkey broke to the cops, it would have burned a safehouse—and me!"

"But he didn't break, did he? That's why we chose him."

"Look, what you do with your people, I don't give a rat's ass. What happens to my people, I do. That last little game we played for you was bush league, Sean."

Miller figured out what "bush league" meant from context. "The operation was politically sound, and you know it. Perhaps you've forgotten that the objective is always political. Politically, the operation was a complete success."

"I don't need you to tell me that!" Alex snapped back in his best intimidating tone. Miller was a proud little twerp, but Alex figured he could pinch his head off with one good squeeze. "You lost a troop because you were playing this personal, not professional—and I know what you're thinking. It was our first big play, right? Well, son, I think we proved that we got our shit together, didn't we? And I warned you up front that your man was too exposed. If you'd listened to me, you wouldn't have a man on the inside. I know your background is pretty impressive, but this is my turf, and I know it."

Miller knew that he had to accept that. He kept his face impassive.

"Alex, if we were in any way displeased, we would not have come back to you. Yes, you do have your shit together," *you bloody nigger, he didn't say.* "Now, can you get us the information we need?"

"Sure, for the right price. You want us in the op?"

"We don't know yet," Miller replied honestly. *Of course the only issue here is money. Bloody Americans.*

"If you want us in, I'm part of the planning. Number one, I want to know how you get in and out. I might have to go with you. If you shitcan my advice this time, I walk and I take my people with me."

"It's a little early to be certain, but what we hope to arrange is really quite simple. . . ."

"You think you can set that up?" For the first time since he'd arrived, Sean had Alex nodding approval. "Slick. I'll give you that. It's slick. Now let's talk price."

Sean wrote a figure on a piece of paper and handed it to Alex. "Fair enough?" People interested in money were easy to impress.

"I sure would like an account at *your* bank, brother."

"If this operation comes off, you will."

"You mean that?"

Miller nodded emphatically. "Direct access. Training facilities, help with travel documents, the lot. Your skill in helping us last time attracted attention. Our friends like the idea of an active revolutionary cell in America." *If they really want to do business with you, it's their problem.* "Now, how quickly can you get the information?"

"End of the week good enough?"

"Can you do it that fast without attracting attention?"

"Let me worry about that," Alex replied with a smile.

"Anything new on your end?" Owens asked.

"Not much," Murray admitted. "We have plenty of forensic evidence, but only one witness who got a clear look at one face, and she can't give us a real ID."

"The local help?"

"That's who we almost ID'd. Nothing yet. Maybe they've learned from the ULA. No manifesto, no announcement claiming credit for the job. The people we have inside some other radical groups—that is, those that still exist—have drawn a big blank. We're still working on it, and we have a lot of money out on the street, but so far we haven't got anything to show for it." Murray paused. "That'll change. Bill

Shaw is a genius, one of the real brains we have in the Bureau. They switched him over from counterintelligence to terrorism a few years back, and he's done really impressive work. What's new on your end?''

"I can't go into specifics yet," Owens said. "But we might have a small break. We're trying to decide now if it's real or not. That's the good news. The bad is that His Royal Highness is traveling to America this coming summer. A number of people were informed of his itinerary, including six on our list of possible suspects."

"How the hell did you let that happen, Jimmy?"

"No one asked me, Dan," Owens replied sourly. "In several cases, if the people hadn't been informed it would have told them that something odd was happening—you can't simply stop trusting people, can you? For the rest, it was just another balls-up. Some secretary put out the plans on the normal list without consulting the security officers." This wasn't a new story for either man. There was always someone who didn't get the word.

"Super. So call it off. Let him get the flu or something when the time comes," Murray suggested.

"His Highness won't do that. He's become quite adamant on the subject. He won't allow a terrorist threat to affect his life in any way."

Murray grunted. "You gotta admire the kid's guts, but—"

"Quite so," Owens agreed. He didn't really care for having his next king referred to as "the kid", but he'd long since gotten used to the American way of expressing things. "It doesn't make our job any easier."

"How firm are the travel plans?" Murray asked, getting back to business.

"Several items on the itinerary are tentative, of course, but most are set in stone. Our security people will be meeting with yours in Washington. They're flying over next week."

"Well, you know that you'll get all the cooperation you want, Secret Service, the Bureau, local police, everything. We'll take good care of him for you," Murray assured him. "He and his wife are pretty popular back home. Will they be taking the baby with them?"

"No. We were able to prevail on him about that."

"Okay. I'll call Washington tomorrow and get things rolling. What's happening with our friend Ned Clark?"

"Nothing as yet. His colleagues are evidently giving him rather a bad time, but he's too bloody stupid to break."

Murray nodded. He knew the type.

Well, they wanted me to take off early, Ryan thought. He decided to accept an invitation to a lecture at Georgetown University. Unfortunately, it was something of a disappointment. Professor David Hunter was Columbia's *enfant terrible,* America's ranking authority on political affairs in Eastern Europe. His book of the previous year, *Revolution Postponed,* had been a penetrating study of the political and economic problems of the Soviet's unsteady empire, and Ryan, like others, had been eager to hear his new information on the subject. The speech had turned out to be little more than a rehash of the book, with the rather startling suggestion at the end that the NATO countries should be more aggressive in trying to separate the Soviet Union from her captives. Ryan considered that to be lunacy, even if it did guarantee lively discussions at the reception.

At the end of the talk, Ryan moved quickly to the reception. He'd skipped dinner to make it here on time. There was a wide table of hors d'oeuvres, and Jack filled his plate as patiently as he could before drifting off to a sedate corner by the elevators. He let others form knots of conversation around Professor Hunter. On the whole, it was nice to be back at Georgetown, if only for a few hours. The "Galleria" in the Intercultural Center was quite a contrast to the CIA institutional drab. The four-story atrium of the language building was lined with the glass windows of offices, and a pair of potted trees reached toward the glass roof. The plaza outside was paved with bricks, and known to the students as Red Square. To the west was the old quadrangle, and the cemetery where rested the priests who had taught here for nearly two hundred years. It was a thoroughly civilized setting, except for the discordant shriek of jets coming out of National Airport, a few miles downriver. Someone jostled Ryan just as he was finishing his snacks.

"Excuse me, Doctor." Ryan turned to see a man shorter than himself. He had a florid complexion and was dressed in a cheap-looking suit. His blue eyes seemed to sparkle with amusement. His voice had a pronounced accent. "Did you enjoy the lecture?"

"It was interesting," Ryan said diffidently.

"So. I see that capitalists can lie as well as we poor socialists." The man had a jolly, overpowering laugh, but Jack decided that his eyes were sparkling with something other than amusement. They were measuring eyes, playing yet another variation of the game he'd been part of in England. Already Ryan disliked him.

"Have we met?"

"Sergey Platonov." They shook hands after Ryan set his plate on a table. "I am Third Secretary of the Soviet Embassy. Perhaps my photograph at Langley does not do me justice."

A Russian—Ryan tried not to look too surprised—*who knows I've been working at CIA.* Third Secretary could easily mean that he was KGB, perhaps a diplomatic intelligence specialist, or maybe a member of the CPSU's Foreign Department—as though it made a difference. A "legal" intelligence officer with a diplomatic cover. *What do I do now?* For one thing, he knew that he'd have to write up a contact report for CIA tomorrow, explaining how they'd met and what they'd talked about, perhaps an hour's work. It took an effort to remain polite.

"You must have the wrong guy, Mr. Platonov. I'm a history teacher. I work at the Naval Academy in Annapolis. I was invited to this because I got my degree here."

"No, no." The Russian shook his head. "I recognize you from the photograph on your book jacket. You see, I purchased ten copies of it last summer."

"Indeed." Jack was surprised again and unable to conceal it. "My publisher and I thank you, sir."

"Our Naval Attaché was much taken by it, Doctor Ryan. He felt that it should be brought to the attention of the Frunze Academy, and, I think, the Grechko Naval Academy in Leningrad." Platonov applied his considerable charm. Ryan knew it for what it was, but . . . "To be honest, I merely skimmed the book myself. It seemed quite well organized, and the Attaché said that your analysis of the way decisions are made in the heat of battle was highly accurate."

"Well." Jack tried not to be overly flattered, but it was hard. Frunze was *the* Soviet staff academy, the finishing school for young field-grade officers who were tagged for stardom. The Grechko Academy was only slightly less prestigious.

"Sergey Nikolay'ch," boomed a familiar voice, "it is not *kulturny* to prey upon the vanity of helpless young authors." Father Timothy Riley joined them. A short, plump Jesuit priest, Riley had headed the history department at Georgetown while Ryan had gotten his doctorate. He was a brilliant intellect with a series of books to his credit, including two penetrating works on the history of Marxism—neither of which, Ryan was certain, had found their way into the library at Frunze. "How's the family, Jack?"

"Cathy's back to work, Father. They moved Sally over to Hopkins. With luck we'll have her home early next week."

"She will recover fully, your little daughter?" Platonov asked. "I read about the attack on your family in the newspaper."

"We think so. Except for losing her spleen, there seems to be no permanent damage. The docs say she's recovering nicely, and with her at Hopkins, Cathy's able to see her every day," Ryan said more positively than he felt. Sally was a different child. Her legs weren't fully healed yet, but worst of all, his bouncing little girl was a sad thing now. She'd learned a lesson that Ryan had hoped to hold off for at least ten more years—that the world is a dangerous place even when you have a mother and a father to take care of you. A hard lesson for a child, it was harder still for a parent. *But she's alive,* Jack told himself, unaware of the expression on his face. *With time and love, you can recover from anything, except death.* The doctors and nurses at Hopkins were taking care of her like one of their own. That was a tangible advantage of having a doctor in the family.

"A terrible thing." Platonov shook his head in what seemed to be genuine disgust. "A terrible thing to attack innocent people for no reason."

"Indeed, Sergey," Riley said in the astringent voice that Ryan had known so well. When he wanted, "Father Tim" had a tongue that could saw through wood. "I seem to recall that V. I. Lenin said the purpose of terrorism is to terrorize, and that sympathy in a revolutionary is as reprehensible as cowardice on the field of battle."

"Those were hard times, good Father," Platonov said smoothly. "My country has no business with those IRA madmen. They are not revolutionaries, however much they pretend to be. They have no revolutionary ethic. It is madness, what they do. The working classes should be allies, contesting together against the common enemy that exploits them both, instead of killing one another. Both sides of the conflict are victimized by bosses who play them off against each other, but instead of recognizing this they kill one another like mad dogs, and with as little point. They are bandits, not revolutionaries," he concluded with a distinction lost on the other two.

"Maybe so, but if I ever get my hands on them, I'll give them a lesson in revolutionary justice." It was good to let his hatred out in the open for once.

"You have no sympathy for them, either of you?" Platonov baited them. "After all, you are both related to the victims of British imperialism. Did not both your families flee to America to escape it?"

Ryan was caught very short by that remark. It seemed an incredible thing to say until he saw that the Russian was watching for his reaction.

"Or perhaps the direct victim of Soviet imperialism," Jack responded with his own look. "Those two guys in London had Kalashnikov rifles. So did the ones who attacked my wife," he lied. "You don't buy one of those at the local hardware store. Whether you choose to admit it or not, most of the terrorists over there profess to be Marxists. That makes them your allies, not mine, and it makes it appear more than a coincidence that they use Soviet arms."

"Do you know how many countries manufacture weapons of Soviet design? It is sadly inevitable that some will fall into the wrong hands."

"In any case, my sympathy for their aim is, shall we say, limited by their choice of technique. You can't build a civilized country on a foundation of murder," Ryan concluded. "Much as some people have tried."

"It would be well if the world worked in more peaceful ways." Platonov ignored the implicit comment on the Soviet Union. "But it is an historical fact that nations are born in blood, even yours. As countries grow, they mature beyond such conduct. It is not easy, but I think we can all see the value of peaceful coexistence. For myself, Doctor Ryan, I can sympathize with your feelings. I have two fine sons. We once had a daughter also, Nadia. She died long ago, at age seven, from leukemia. I know it is a hard thing to see your child in pain, but you are more fortunate than I. Your daughter will live." He allowed his voice to soften. "We disagree on many things, but no man can fail to love his children.

"So." Platonov changed gears smoothly. "What did you really think of Professor Hunter's little speech? Should America seek to foment counterrevolution in the socialist states of Europe?"

"Why don't you ask the State Department? That's not my part of the world, remember? I teach naval history. But if you want a personal opinion, I don't see how we can encourage people to rebel if we have no prospect of helping them directly when your country reacts."

"Ah, good. You understand that we must act to protect our fraternal socialist brothers from aggression."

The man was good, Ryan saw, but he'd had a lot of practice at this. "I wouldn't call the encouragement of people to seek their own freedom a form of aggression, Mr. Platonov. I was a stockbroker before I got my history degree, and that doesn't make me much of a candidate for sympathizing with your political outlook. What I am saying is that your country used military force to crush democratic feelings in Czechoslovakia and Hungary. To encourage people toward their own suicide is both immoral and counterproductive."

"Ah, but what does your government think?" the Russian asked with another jolly laugh.

"I'm a historian, not a soothsayer. In this town they all work for the *Post*. Ask them."

"In any case," the Russian went on, "our Naval Attaché is most interested to meet you and discuss your book. We are having a reception at the embassy on the twelfth of next month. The good Father is coming, he can watch over your soul. Might you and your wife attend?"

"For the next few weeks I plan to be at home with my family. My girl needs me there for a while."

The diplomat was not to be put off. "Yes, I can understand that. Some other time, perhaps?"

"Sure, give me a call sometime this summer." *Are you kidding?*

"Excellent. Now if you will excuse me, I wish to speak to Professor Hunter." The diplomat shook hands again and walked off to the knot of historians who were hanging on Hunter's every word.

Ryan turned to Father Riley, who'd watched the exchange in silence while sipping at his champagne.

"Interesting guy, Sergey," Riley said. "He loves to hit people for reactions. I wonder if he really believes in his system or if he's just playing the game for points . . . ?

Ryan had a more immediate question. "Father, what in the hell was that all about?"

Riley chuckled. "You're being checked out, Jack."

"Why?"

"You don't need me to answer that. You're working at CIA. If I guess right, Admiral Greer wants you on his personal staff. Marty Cantor is taking a job at the University of Texas next year, and you're one of the candidates for his job. I don't know if Sergey's aware of that, but you probably looked like the best target of opportunity in the room, and he wanted to get a feel for you. Happens all the time."

"Cantor's job? But—nobody told me that!"

"The world's full of surprises. They probably haven't finished the full background check on you yet, and they won't pop the offer until they do. I presume the information you're looking at is still pretty limited?"

"I can't discuss that, Father."

The priest smiled. "Thought so. The work you've done over there has impressed the right people. If I have things right, they're going to bring you along like a good welterweight prospect." Riley got another glass of champagne. "If I know James Greer, he'll just sort of ease you into it. What did it, you see, was that Canary Trap thing. It really impressed some folks."

"How do you know all this?" Ryan asked, shocked at what he'd just heard.

"Jack, how do you think you got over there in the first place? Who do you think got you that Center for Strategic and International Studies fellowship? The people there liked your work, too. Between what I said and what they said, Marty thought you were worth a look last summer, and you worked out better than anyone expected. There are some people around town who respect my opinion."

"Oh." Ryan had to smile. He'd allowed himself to forget the first thing about the Society of Jesus: they know everyone, from whom they can learn nearly everything. The President of the university belonged to both the Cosmos and University clubs, with which came access to the most important ears and mouths in Washington. That's how it would start. Occasionally a man would need advice on something, and being unable to consult the people he worked with, he might try to discuss it with a clergyman. No one was better qualified for this than a Jesuit, meticulously educated, well versed in the ways of the world, but not spoiled by it—most of the time. Like any clergyman, each was a good listener. So effective was the Society at gathering information that the State Department's code-breakers had once been tasked to break the Jesuits' own cipher systems; the assignment had started a small revolt in the "Black Chamber" . . . until they'd realized what sort of information was finding its way to them.

When Saint Ignatius Loyola had founded the order, the ex-soldier set it on a path to do only two things: to send out missionaries and to build schools. Both had been done extraordinarily well. The influence passed on by the schooling would never be lost on the men who'd graduated. It wasn't Machiavellian, not really. The colleges and universities plied its students with philosophy and ethics and theology— all required courses—to mute their baser tendencies and sharpen their wits. For centuries the Jesuits had built "men for others," and wielded a kind of invisible temporal power, mainly for the good. Father Riley's intellectual credentials were widely known, and his opinions would be sought, just as from any distinguished academic, added to which was his moral authority as a graduate theologian.

"We're good security risks, Jack," Riley said benignly. "Can you imagine one of us being a Communist agent? So, are you interested in the job?"

"I don't know." Ryan looked at his reflection in a window. "It would mean more time away from the family. We're expecting another one this summer, you know."

"Congratulations, that's good news. I know you're a family man, Jack. The job would mean some sacrifices, but you're a good man for it."

"Think so?" *I haven't exactly set the world on fire yet.*

"I'd rather see people like you over there than some others I know. Jack, you're plenty smart enough. You know how to make decisions, but more importantly, you're a pretty good fellow. I know you're ambitious, but you've got ethics, values. I'm one of those people who thinks that still matters for something in the world, regardless of how nasty things get."

"They get pretty nasty, Father," Ryan said after a moment.

"How close are you to finding them?"

"Not very close at—" Jack stopped himself too late. "You did that one pretty well."

"I didn't mean it that way," Father Tim said very sincerely. "It would be a better world if they were off the street. There must be something wrong with the way they think. It's hard to understand how anyone could deliberately hurt a child."

"Father, you really don't have to understand them. You just have to know where to find them."

"That's work for the police, and the courts, and a jury. That's why we have laws, Jack," Riley said gently.

Ryan turned to the window again. He examined his own image and wondered what it was that he saw. "Father, you're a good man, but you've never had kids of your own. I can forgive somebody who comes after me, maybe, but not anyone who tries to hurt my little girl. If I find him—hell, I won't. But I sure would like to," Jack told the image of himself. *Yes,* it agreed.

"It's not a good thing, hate. It might do things to you that you'll regret, things that can change you from the person you are."

Ryan turned back, thinking about the person he'd just looked at. "Maybe it already has."

20

Data

It was a singularly boring tape. Owens was used to reading police reports, transcripts of interrogations, and, worst of all, intelligence documents, but the tape was even more boring than that. The microphone which the Security Service had hidden in Cooley's shop was sound-activated and sensitive enough to pick up any noise. The fact that Cooley hummed a lot made Owens regret this feature. The detective whose job it was to listen to the unedited tape had included several minutes of the awful, atonal noise to let his commander know what he had to suffer through. The bell finally rang.

Owens heard the clatter, made metallic by the recording system, of the door opening and closing, then the sound of Cooley's swivel chair scraping across the floor. It must have had a bad wheel, Owens noted.

"Good morning, sir!" It was Cooley's voice.

"And to you," said the second. "Well, have you finished the Milton?"

"Yes, I have."

"So what's the price?"

Cooley didn't say it aloud, but Ashley had told Owens that the shop owner never spoke a price. He handed it to his customers on a file card. That, Owens thought, was one way to keep from haggling.

"That is quite steep, you know," Watkins' voice observed.

"I could get more, but you are one of our better clients," Cooley replied.

The sigh was audible on the tape. "Very well, it is worth it."

The transaction was made at once. They could hear the rasping sound of new banknotes being counted.

"I may soon have something new from a collection in Kerry," Cooley said next.

"Oh?" There was interest in the reply.

"Yes, a signed first edition of *Great Expectations*. I saw it on my last trip over. Might you be interested in that?"

"Signed, eh?"

"Yes, sir, 'Boz' himself. I realize that the Victorian period is rather more recent than most of your acquisitions, but the author's signature . . ."

"Indeed. I would like to see it, of course."

"That can be arranged."

"At this point," Owens told Ashley, "Watkins leaned over, and our man in the jewelry shop lost sight of him."

"So he could have passed a message."

"Possibly." Owens switched off the tape machine. The rest of the conversation had no significance.

"The last time he was in Ireland, Cooley didn't go to County Kerry. He was in Cork the whole time. He visited three dealers in rare books, spent the night in a hotel, and had a few pints at a local pub," Ashley reported.

"A pub?"

"Yes, he drinks in Ireland, but not in London."

"Did he meet anyone there?"

"Impossible to tell. Our man wasn't close enough. His orders were to be discreet, and he did well not to be spotted." Ashley was quiet for a moment as he tried to pin down something on the tape. "It sounded to me as though he paid cash for the book."

"He did, and it is out of pattern. Like most of us he uses checks and credit cards for the majority of his transactions, but not for this. His bank records show no checks to this shop, though he does occasionally make large cash withdrawals. They may or may not match with his purchases there.''

"How very odd," Ashley thought aloud. "Everyone—well, someone must know that he goes there.''

"Checks have dates on them," Owens suggested.

"Perhaps." Ashley wasn't convinced, but he'd done enough investigations of this kind to know that you never got all the answers. Some details were always left hanging. "I took another look at Geoff's service record last night. Do you know that when he was in Ireland, he had four men killed in his platoon?''

"What? That makes him a fine candidate for our investigation!" Owens didn't think this was good news.

"That's what I thought," Ashley agreed. "I had one of our chaps in Germany—his former regiment's assigned to the BAOR at the moment—interview one of Watkins's mates. Had a platoon in the same company, the chap's a half-colonel now. He said that Geoff took it quite hard, that he was quite vociferous on the point that they were in the wrong place, doing the wrong thing, and losing people in the process. Rather puts a different spin on things, doesn't it?''

"Another lieutenant with the solution to the problem." Owens snorted.

"Yes—we leave and let the bloody Irish sort things out. That's not exactly a rare sentiment in the Army, you know.''

It wasn't exactly a rare sentiment throughout England, Commander Owens knew. "Even so, it's not much of a basis for motive, is it?''

"Better than nothing at all.''

The cop grunted agreement. "What else did the Colonel tell your chap?''

"Obviously Geoff had a rather busy tour of duty in the Belfast area. He and his men saw a lot. They were there when the Army was welcomed in by the Catholics, and they were there when the situation reversed. It was a bad time for everyone," Ashley added unnecessarily.

"It's still not very much. We have a former subaltern, now in the striped-pants brigade, who didn't like being in Northern Ireland; he happens to buy rare books from a chap who grew up there and now runs a completely legitimate business in central London. You know what any solicitor would say: pure coincidence. We don't have one single thing that can remotely be called evidence. The background of each man is pure enough to qualify him for sainthood.''

"These are the people we've been looking for," Ashley insisted.

"I know that." Owens almost surprised himself when he said it for the first time. His professionalism told him that this was a mistake, but his instincts told him otherwise. It wasn't a new feeling for the Commander of C-13, but one that always made him uneasy. If his instincts were wrong, he was looking in the wrong place, at the wrong people. But his instincts were almost never wrong. "You know the rules of the game, and by those rules, I don't even have enough to go to the Commissioner. He'd boot me out of the office, and be right to do so. We have nothing but unsupported suspicions." The two men stared at each other for several seconds.

"I never wanted to be a policeman." Ashley smiled and shook his head.

"I didn't get my wish, either. I wanted to be an engine driver when I was six, but my father said there were enough railway people in the family. So I became a copper." Both men laughed. There wasn't anything else to do.

"I'll increase the surveillance on Cooley's trips abroad. I don't think there's much more to be done on your side," Ashley said finally.

"We have to wait for them to make a mistake. Sooner or later they all do, you know."

"But soon enough?" That was the question.

"Here we are," Alex said.

"How did you get these?" Miller asked in amazement.

"Routine, man. Power companies shoot aerial photographs of their territory all the time. They help us plan the surveys we have to do. And here"— he reached into his briefcase —"is a topographic map. There's your target, boy." Alex handed him a magnifying glass borrowed from his company. It was a color shot, taken on a bright sunny day. You could tell the makes of the cars. It must have been done the previous summer—the grass had just been cut. . . .

"How tall is the cliff?"

"Enough that you don't want to fall off it. Tricky, too. I forget what it's made of, sandstone or something crumbly, but you want to be careful with it. See that fence here? The man knows to keep away from the edge. We have the same problem at our reactor plant at Calvert

Cliff. It's the same geological structure, and a lot of work went into giving the plant a solid foundation.''

"Only one road in," Miller noted.

"Dead end, too. That *is* a problem. We have these gullies here and here. Notice that the power line comes in cross country, from this road over here. It looks like there was an old farm road that connected with this one, but they let it go to seed. That's going to be helpful.''

"How? No one can use it.''

"I'll tell you later. Friday, you and me are going fishing.''

"What?" Miller looked up in surprise.

"You want to eyeball the cliff, right? Besides, the blues are running. I love bluefish.''

Breckenridge had silhouette targets up, finally. Jack's trips to the range were less frequent now, mainly in the mornings before class. If nothing else, the incident outside the gate had told the Marine and civilian guards that their jobs were valuable. Two Marines and one of the civilians were also firing their service pieces. They didn't just shoot to qualify now. They were all shooting for scores. Jack hit the button to reel his target in. His rounds were all clustered in the center of the target.

"Pretty good, Doc.'' The Sergeant Major was standing behind him. "If you want, we can run a competition string. I figure you'll qualify for a medal now.''

Ryan shook his head. He still had to shower after his morning jog. "I'm not doing this for score, Gunny.''

"When does the little girl come home?''

"Next Wednesday, I hope.''

"That's good, sir. Who's going to look after her?''

"Cathy's taking a few weeks off.''

"My wife asked if y'all might need any help,'' Breckenridge said.

Jack turned in surprise. "Sissy—Commander Jackson's wife—will be over most of the time. Please thank your wife for us, Gunny, that's damned nice of her.''

"No big deal. Any luck finding the bastards?'' Ryan's day-hops to CIA were not much of a secret.

"Not yet.''

*　　*　　*

"Good morning, Alex," the field superintendent said. "You're staying in a little late. What can I do for you?" Bert Griffin was always in early, but he rarely saw Dobbens before he went home at seven every morning.

"I've been looking over the specifications on that new Westinghouse transformer."

"Getting dull working nights?" Griffin asked with a smile. This was a fairly easy time of year for the utility company. In the summer, with all the air conditioners up and running, things would be different, of course. Spring was the time of year for new ideas.

"I think we're ready to give it a try."

"Have they ironed the bugs out?"

"Pretty much, enough for a field test, I think."

"Okay." Griffin sat back in his chair. "Tell me about it."

"Mainly, sir, I'm worried about the old ones. The problem's only going to get worse as we start retiring the old units. We had that chemical spill last month—"

"Oh, yeah." Griffin rolled his eyes. Most of the units in use contained PBBs, polybrominated biphenyls, as a cooling element within the power transformer. These were dangerous to the linemen, who were supposed to wear protective clothing when working on them, but, despite company rules, often didn't bother. PBBs were a serious health hazard to the men. Even worse, the company had to dispose of the toxic liquid periodically. It was expensive and ran the risk of spills, the paperwork for which was rapidly becoming as time-consuming as that associated with the company's nuclear reactor plant. Westinghouse was experimenting with a transformer that used a completely inert chemical in place of the PBBs. Though expensive, it held great promise for long-term economies—and would help get the environmentalists off their backs, which was even more attractive than the monetary savings. "Alex, if you can get those babies up and working, I will personally get you a new company car!"

"Well, I want to try one out. Westinghouse will lend us one for free."

"This is really starting to sound good," Griffin noted. "But have they really ironed the bugs out yet?"

"They say so, except for some occasional voltage fluctuations.

They're not sure what causes that, and they want to do some field tests.''

''How bad are the fluctuations?''

''Marginal.'' Alex pulled out a pad and read off the numbers. ''It seems to be an environmental problem. Looks like it only happens when the ambient air temperature changes rapidly. If that's the real cause, it shouldn't be too hard to beat.''

Griffin considered that for a few seconds. ''Okay, where do you want to set it up?''

''I have a spot picked out down in Anne Arundel County, south of Annapolis.''

''That's a long ways away. Why there?''

''It's a dead-end line. If the transformer goes bad, it won't hurt many houses. The other thing is, one of my crews is only twenty miles away, and I've been training them on the new unit. We'll set up the test instrumentation, and I can have them check it every day for the first few months. If it works out, we can make our purchase order in the fall and start setting them up next spring.''

''Okay. Where exactly is this?''

Dobbens unfolded his map on Griffin's table. ''Right here.''

''Expensive neighborhood,'' the field superintendent said dubiously.

''Aw, come on, boss!'' Alex snorted. ''How would it look in the papers if we did all our experiments on poor folk? Besides''—he smiled —''all those environmental freaks are rich, aren't they?''

Dobbens had chosen his remark with care. One of Griffin's personal hobbyhorses was the ''Park Avenue Environmentalist.'' The field superintendent owned a small farm, and didn't like having some condo-owning dilettante tell him about nature.

''Okay, you can run with it. How soon can you set it up?''

''Westinghouse can have the unit to us the end of next week. I can have it up and running three days after that. I want my crew to check the lines—in fact, I'll be going down myself to set it up if you don't mind.''

Griffin nodded approval. ''You're my kind of engineer, son. Most of the schoolboys we get now are afraid to get their hands dirty. You'll keep me posted?''

''Yes, sir.''

"Keep up the good work, Alex. I've been telling management about you."

"I appreciate that, Mr. Griffin."

Dobbens left the building and drove home in his two-year-old company Plymouth. Most of the rush-hour traffic was heading in while he headed out. He was home in under an hour. Sean Miller was just waking up, drinking tea and watching television. Alex wondered how anyone could start the day with tea. He made some instant coffee for himself.

"Well?" Miller asked.

"No problem." Alex smiled, then stopped. It occurred to him that he'd miss his job. After all the talk in college about bringing Power to the People, he'd realized with surprise after starting with BG&E that a utility company engineer did exactly that. In a funny sort of way, he was now serving the ordinary people, though not in a manner that carried much significance. Dobbens decided that it was good training for his future ambitions. He'd remember that even those who served humbly still served. An important lesson for the future. "Come on, we'll talk about it in the boat."

Wednesday was a special day. Jack was away from both his jobs, carrying the bear while Cathy wheeled their daughter out. The bear was a gift from the midshipmen of his history classes, an enormous monster that weighed sixty pounds and was nearly five feet tall, topped off with a Smokey Bear hat—actually that of a Marine drill instructor courtesy of Breckenridge and the guard detail. A police officer opened the door for the procession. It was a windy March day, but the family wagon was parked just outside. Jack scooped up his daughter in both arms while Cathy thanked the nurses. He made sure she was in her safety seat and buckled the belt himself. The bear had to go in the back.

"Ready to go home, Sally?"

"Yes." Her voice was listless. The nurses reported that she still cried out in her sleep. Her legs were fully healed, finally. She could walk again, badly and awkwardly, but she could walk. Except for the loss of her spleen, she was whole again. Her hair was trimmed short to compensate for what had been shaved, but that would grow out soon enough. Even the scars, the surgeons said, would fade, and the pediatricians assured him that in a few months the nightmares would end.

Jack turned to run his hand along the little face, and got a smile for his efforts. It wasn't the smile he was accustomed to getting. Behind his own smile, Ryan's mind boiled with rage yet again, but he told himself that this wasn't the time. Sally needed a father now, not an avenger.

"We have a surprise waiting for you," he said.

"What?" Sally asked.

"If I told you, it wouldn't be a surprise," her father pointed out.

"Daddy!" For a moment his little girl was back.

"Wait and see."

"What's that?" Cathy asked on getting in the car.

"The surprise."

"What surprise?"

"See," Jack told his daughter. "Mommy doesn't know either."

"Jack, what's going on?"

"Doctor Schenk and I had a little talk last week," was all Ryan would say. He released the parking brake and headed off onto Broadway.

"I want my bear," Sally said.

"He's too big to sit there, honey," Cathy responded.

"But you can wear his Smokey hat. He said it was okay." Jack handed it back. The wide-brimmed campaign hat dropped over her head.

"Did you thank the people for the bear?" Cathy asked.

"You bet." Ryan smiled for a moment. "Nobody flunks this term. But don't tell anybody that." Jack had a reputation as a tough marker. That might not survive this semester. *Principles be damned,* he told himself. The mids in his classes had sent Sally a steady stream of flowers, toys, puzzles, and cards that had entertained his little girl, then circulated around the pediatric floor and brightened the days of fifty more sick kids. Smokey Bear was the crowning achievement. The nurses had told Cathy that it had made a difference. The monster toy had often sat at the top of Sally's bed, with the little girl clinging to it. It would be a tough act to follow, but Jack had that one figured out. Skip Tyler was making the final arrangements now.

Jack took his time, driving as though he were carrying a cargo of cracked eggs. His recent habits at CIA made him yearn for a cigarette, but he knew that he'd have to stop that now, with Cathy home all the time. He was careful to avoid the route Cathy had taken the day that— His hands tightened on the wheel as they had for weeks now. He knew he had to stop thinking about it so much. It had become an obsession, and that wasn't going to help anything.

The scenery had changed since the . . . accident. What had been bare trees now had the green edges of buds and leaves with the beginning of spring. Horses and cows were out on the farms. Some calves and colts were visible, and Sally's nose pressed against the car window as she looked at them. As it did every year, life was renewing itself, Ryan told himself. His family was whole again, and he'd keep it that way. The last turn onto Falcon's Nest Road finally came. Jack noted that the utility trucks were still around, and he wondered briefly what they had been up to as he turned left into his driveway.

"Skip's here?" Cathy asked.

"Looks like it," Jack replied with a suppressed grin.

"They're home," Alex said.

"Yeah," Louis noted. Both men were perched at the top of the utility pole, ostensibly stringing new power lines to accommodate the experimental transformer. "You know, the day after the job," the lineman said, "there was a picture of the lady in the papers. Some kid went through a window and got his face all cut up. It was a little brother, Alex. The lady saved his eyes, man."

"I remember, Louis." Alex raised his camera and snapped off a string of shots.

"An' I don't like fucking with kids, man," Louis said. "A cop's a different thing," he added defensively. He didn't have to say that so was the kid's father. That was business. Like Alex, he had a few remaining scruples, and hurting children was not something he could do without some internal turmoil.

"Maybe we were all lucky." Alex knew objectively that this was a stupid way for a revolutionary to think. Sentimentality had no place in his mission; it got in the way of what he had to do, prolonging the task and causing more deaths in the process. He also knew that the taboos against injuring children were part of the genetic programming of any human being. Mankind had progressed in its knowledge since Marx and Lenin. So whenever possible he'd avoid injuring kids. He rationalized that this would enhance his sympathy in the community he was seeking to liberate.

"Yeah."

"So what have you seen?"

"They got a maid—black o'course. Fine-lookin' woman, drives a Chevy. There's somebody else in there now. He's a white dude, big guy, an' he walks funny."

"Right." Alex made note of the former and dismissed the latter. The man was probably a family friend.

"The cops—state cops—are back here every two hours minimum. One of them asked me what we were doing yesterday afternoon. They're keeping an eye on this place. There's an extra phone line into the house—gotta be for an alarm company. So they got a house alarm and the cops are always close."

"Okay. Keep your eyes open but don't be too obvious."

"You got it."

"Home," Ryan breathed. He stopped the car and got out, walking around to Sally's door. He saw that the little girl wasn't playing with the seat-belt buckle. He took care of it himself, then lifted his daughter out of the car. She wrapped her arms around his neck, and for a moment life was perfect again. He carried Sally to the front door, both arms clasping her to his chest.

"Welcome back." Skip had the door open already.

"Where's my surprise?" Sally demanded.

"Surprise?" Tyler was taken aback. "I don't know about any surprise."

"Daddy!" Her father got an accusing look.

"Come on in," Tyler said.

Mrs. Hackett was there, too. She'd gotten lunch ready for everyone. A single mother of two sons, she worked hard to support them. Ryan set his girl down, and she walked to the kitchen. Skip Tyler and her father watched her stiff legs negotiate the distance.

"God, it's amazing how kids heal," Tyler observed.

"What?" Jack was surprised.

"I broke a leg playing ball once—damned if I bounced back that fast. Come on," Tyler beckoned Jack out the door. First he checked out the stuffed animal in the car. "I heard it was some kind of bear. That one must have played in Chicago!"

Then they went into the trees north of Ryan's house. Here they found the surprise, tied to a tree. Jack loosed the chain and picked him up.

"Thanks for bringing him over."

"Hey, no big deal. It's good to see her home, pal."

The two men walked back into the house. Jack peeked around the corner and saw that Sally was already demolishing a peanut-butter sandwich.

"Sally . . ." he said. His wife was already looking at him with an open mouth. His daughter's head came around just as Jack set the puppy on the floor.

It was a black Labrador, just old enough to be separated from his mother. The puppy needed a single look to know to whom he belonged. He scampered across the floor, mostly sideways, with his tail gyrating wildly. Sally was on the floor, and grabbed him. A moment later, the dog was cleaning her face.

"She's too little for a puppy," Cathy said.

"Okay, you can take him back this afternoon," Jack replied quietly. The remark got him an angry look. His daughter squealed when the dog started chewing on the heel of one shoe. "She's not big enough for a pony yet, but I think this is just the right thing."

"You train it!"

"That'll be easy. He comes from good stock. Champion Chesapeake's Victor Hugo Black for a father, would you believe? The Lab's got a soft mouth, and they like kids," Jack went on. "I've already scheduled him for classes."

"Classes in what?" Cathy was really befuddled now.

"The breed is called the Labrador *Retriever*," Jack noted.

"How big does it get?"

"Oh, maybe seventy pounds."

"That's bigger than she is!"

"Yeah, they love to swim, too. He can look after her in the pool."

"We don't have a pool."

"They start in three weeks." Jack smiled again. "Doctor Schenk also said that swimming is good therapy for this kind of injury."

"You've been busy," his wife observed. She was smiling now.

"I was going to get a Newfoundland, but they're just too big—one-fifty." Jack didn't say that his first wish had been to get a dog big and tough enough to tear the head off anyone who came close to his daughter, but that his common sense had prevented it.

"Well, there's your first job," Cathy pointed. Jack got a paper towel to clean up the puddle on the tile. Before he could do it, his daughter nearly strangled him with a ferocious hug. It was all he could do to control himself, but he had to. Sally would not have understood why her daddy was crying. The world was back in its proper shape. *Now if we can just keep it that way.*

"I'll have the pictures tomorrow. I wanted to get them done before the trees fill in. When they do, you won't be able to see the house from the road very well." Alex summarized the results of his reconnaissance.

"What about the alarm?"

Alex read off the data from his notes.

"How the bloody hell did you get that?"

Dobbens chuckled as he popped open the beer. "It's easy. If you want the data for any kind of burglar alarm, you call the company that did it and say you work for an insurance company. You give them a policy number—you make that up, of course—and they give you all the information you want. Ryan has a perimeter system, and a backup intruder system 'with keys,' which means that the alarm company has keys to the house. Somewhere on the property they have infrared beams. Probably on the driveway in the trees. This guy isn't dumb, Sean."

"It doesn't matter."

"Okay, I'm just telling you. One more thing."

"Yes?"

"The kid doesn't get hurt this time, not the wife either if we can help it."

"That is not part of the plan," Miller assured him. *You bloody wimp.* Sean had learned a new word in America. *What sort of revolutionary do you think you are?* he didn't say.

"That's from my people," Alex continued, telling only part of the truth. "You gotta understand, Sean, child abuse looks bad over here. It's not the kind of image we want to have, you dig?"

"And you want to come out with us?"

Dobbens nodded. "It might be necessary."

"I think we can avoid that. It just means eliminating all the people who see your faces."

You're a cold little cocksucker, Dobbens thought, though his words made perfect sense. Dead men told no tales.

"Very well. All we have to do now is find a way to make the

security people relax a bit,'' the Irishman said. "I'd prefer to avoid brute force.''

"I've been thinking about that." Alex took a moment before going on. "How do armies succeed?''

"What do you mean?" Miller asked.

"I mean, the great plans, the ones that really work. They all work because you show the other guy something he expects to see, right? You make him go for the fake, but it's gotta be a really good fake. We have to make them look for the wrong thing in the wrong place, and they have to put the word out.''

"And how do we do that?" After two minutes: "Ah.''

Alex retired to his bedroom a few minutes later, leaving Miller in front of the television to go over his material. On the whole, it had been a very useful trip. The plan was already beginning to take shape. It would require a lot of people, but that came as no surprise.

Curiously, his respect for Alex was now diminished. The man was competent, certainly, even brilliant in his plan for a diversion—but that absurd sentimentality! It was not that Miller reveled in the idea of hurting children, but if that was what the revolution took, then it was a necessary price to pay. Besides, it got people's attention. It told them that he and his organization were serious. Until Alex got over that, he'd never be successful. But that wasn't Miller's problem. Part One of the operation was now outlined in his mind. Part Two was already drawn up, already had been aborted once. *But not this time,* Miller promised himself.

By noon the following day, Alex had handed him the photos and driven him to an outlying station of the D.C. Metro. Miller took the subway train to National Airport to catch the first of four flights that would take him home.

Jack walked into Sally's bedroom just before eleven. The dog—his daughter had named him Ernie—was an invisible shape in the corner. This was one of the smartest things he had ever done. Sally was too much in love with Ernie to dwell on her injuries, and she chased after him as fast as her weakened legs would allow. That was enough to make her father overlook the chewed shoes and occasional mistakes with which the dog was littering the house. In a few weeks she'd be back to normal. Jack adjusted the covers slightly before leaving. Cathy was already in bed when he got there.

"Is she okay?"

"Sleeping like an angel," Jack replied as he slid in beside her.

"And Ernie?"

"He's in there somewhere. I could hear his tail hitting the wall." He wrapped his arms around her. It was hard getting close to her now. He ran one hand down to her abdomen, feeling the shape of his unborn child. "How's the next one?"

"Quiet, finally. God, he's an active one. Don't wake him up."

It struck Jack as an absurd idea that babies were awake before they were born, but you couldn't argue with a doctor. "He?"

"That's what Madge says."

"What's she say about you?" He felt her ribs next. They were too prominent. His wife had always been slender, but this was too much.

"I'm gaining the weight back," Cathy answered. "You don't have to worry. Everything's fine."

"Good." He kissed her.

"Is that all I get?" he heard from the darkness.

"You think you can handle more?"

"Jack, I don't have to go to work tomorrow," she pointed out.

"But some of us do," he protested, but soon found that his heart wasn't in it.

21

Plans

"He is thorough," O'Donnell observed. Miller had returned with the aerial photographs that Dobbens had copied, topographic maps, and photos of Ryan's home from the land and water sides. Added to these were typed notes of the observations made by his people and other data thought to be of interest.

"Unfortunately he allows his personal feelings to interfere with his activities," Miller observed coolly.

"And you don't, Sean?" O'Donnell chided gently.

"It won't happen again," his operations officer promised.

"That's good. The important thing about mistakes is that we learn from them. So let's go over your proposed operation."

Sean took out two other maps and spent twenty minutes running through his ideas. He concluded with Dobbens' suggestion for a diversion.

"I like it." He turned to his intelligence chief. "Joseph?"

"The opposition will be formidable, of course, but the plan allows for that. The only thing that worries me is that it will take nearly all of our people to do it."

"Nothing else looks feasible," Miller replied. "It's not so much a question of getting close enough, but of leaving the area after the mission is accomplished. Timing is crucial—"

"And when timing is crucial, simplicity is a must." O'Donnell nodded. "Is there anything else that the opposition might try?"

"I think not," McKenney said. "This is the worst-case expectation."

"Helicopters," Miller said. "They nearly did for us the last time. No real problem if we're prepared for it, but we must be prepared."

"Very well," O'Donnell said. "And the second part of the operation?"

"Obviously we need to know where all the targets will be," McKenney said. "When do you want me to activate our people?" On orders, the intelligence chief's penetration agents had been quiescent for some weeks.

"Not just yet," the Commander replied thoughtfully. "Again a question of timing. Sean?"

"I think we should wait until the mission is fully accomplished before moving."

"Yes, it proved to be a good idea the last time," the Commander agreed. "How many people are needed for your operation?"

"No less than fifteen. I think we can depend on Alex for three trained men, himself included. More than that—no, we should limit his participation as much as possible."

"Agreed," McKenney said.

"And training?" O'Donnell asked.

"The most we've ever done."

"To start when?"

"A month beforehand," Miller answered. "Any more time would be a waste of resources. For the moment I have quite a lot of work to do."

"So here are the plans," Murray said. "You can either let them stay at your embassy or we'll put them in Blair House, right across the street from the President."

"With all due respect to your Secret Service chaps—" The head of the Diplomatic Protection Group didn't have to go on. Their safety was his responsibility and he wouldn't trust it to foreigners any more than he had to.

"Yeah, I understand. They'll get a full security detail from the Secret Service plus a couple of FBI liaison people and the usual assistance from the local police. Finally we'll have two HRT groups on alert the whole time they're over, one in D.C., and a backup team at Quantico."

"How many people know?" Ashley asked.

"The Secret Service and Bureau people are already fully briefed. When your advance men go over, they ought to have most of the events scouted for you already. The local cops will not be notified until they have to know."

"You said most of the locations have been scouted, but not all?" Owens asked.

"Do you want us to check out the unannounced points this early, too?"

"No." The man from DPG shook his head. "It's bad enough that the public functions have to be exposed this early. It's still not official that they're going, you know. The element of surprise is our best defense."

Owens looked at his colleague, but didn't react. The head of the DPG was on his suspects list, and his orders were not to allow anyone to know the details of his investigation. Owens thought him to be in the clear, but his detectives had discovered a few irregularities in the man's personal life that had somehow gotten past all the previous security screenings. Until it was certain that he was not a possible blackmail risk, he would not be allowed to know that some possible suspects had already seen the itinerary. The Commander of C-13 gave Murray an ironic look.

"I think you're overdoing this, gentlemen, but that's your business," the FBI man said as he stood. "Your people are flying over tomorrow?"

"That's right."

"Okay, Chuck Avery of the Secret Service will meet your people at Dulles. Tell them not to be bashful about asking for things. You will have our total cooperation." He watched them leave. Five minutes later Owens was back.

"What gives, Jimmy?" Murray wasn't surprised.

"What further progress have you made on the chaps who attacked Ryan?"

"Not a thing for the past two weeks," Murray admitted. "You?"

"We have a possible link—let me be precise, we suspect that there might be a possible link."

The FBI man grinned. "Yeah, I know what that's like. Who is it?"

"Geoffrey Watkins." That got a reaction.

"The foreign-service guy? Damn! Anybody else on the list that I know?"

"The chap you were just talking to. Ashley's people discovered that he's not entirely faithful to his wife."

"Boys or girls?" Murray took a cue from the way Owens had said that. "You mean that he doesn't know, Jimmy?"

"He doesn't know that the itinerary has been leaked, possibly to the wrong people. Watkins is among them, but so is our DPG friend."

"Oh, that's real good! The plans may be leaked, and you can't tell the head of the security detail because he may be the one—"

"It's most unlikely, but we must allow for the possibility."

"Call the trip off, Jimmy. If you have to break his leg, call it the hell off."

"We can't. He won't. I spoke with His Highness day before yesterday and told him the problem. He refuses to allow his life to be managed that way."

"Why are you telling me this?" Murray rolled his eyes.

"I must tell someone, Dan. If I can't tell my chaps, then . . ." Owens waved his hands.

"You want us to call the trip off for you, is that it?" Murray demanded. He knew that Owens couldn't answer that one. "Let's spell this one out nice and clear. You want our people to be alert to the chance that an attack is a serious possibility, and that one of the good guys might be a bad guy."

"Correct."

"This isn't going to make our folks real happy."

"I'm not terribly keen on it myself, Dan," Owens replied.

"Well, it gives Bill Shaw something else to think about." Another thought struck him. "Jimmy, that's one expensive piece of live bait you have dangling on the hook."

"He knows that. It's our job to keep the sharks away, isn't it?"

Murray shook his head. The ideal solution would be to find a way to cancel the trip, thereby handing the problem back to Owens and Ashley. That meant involving the State Department. The boys at Foggy Bottom would spike that idea, Murray knew. You couldn't un-invite a future chief of state because the FBI and Secret Service didn't think they could guarantee his safety—the reputation of American law-enforcement would be laid open to ridicule, they'd say, knowing that his protection wasn't the responsibility of the people at State.

"What do you have on Watkins?" he asked after a moment. Owens outlined his "evidence."

"That's all?"

"We're still digging, but so far there is nothing more substantive. It could all be coincidence, of course . . ."

"No, it sounds to me like you're right." Murray didn't believe in coincidences either. "But there's nothing that I could take to a grand jury at home. Have you thought about flushing the game?"

"You mean running through a change in the schedule? Yes, we have. But then what? We could do that, see if Watkins goes to the shop, and arrest both men there—if we can confirm that what is happening is what we think it to be. Unfortunately, that means throwing away the only link we've ever had with the ULA, Dan. At the moment, we're watching Cooley as closely as we dare. He is still traveling. If we can find out whom he is contacting, then perhaps we can wrap up the entire operation. What you suggest is an option, but not the best one. We do have time, you know. We have several months before we need to do something so drastic as that."

Murray nodded, not so much in agreement as in understanding. The possibility of finding and destroying O'Donnell's bunch had to be tantalizing to Scotland Yard. Bagging Cooley now would quash that. It wasn't something that they'd simply toss off. He knew that the Bureau would think much the same way.

"Jack, I want you to come along with me," Marty Cantor said. "No questions."

"What?" Ryan asked, and got an accusing look. "All right, all right." He took the files he was working on and locked them in his file cabinet, then grabbed his jacket. Cantor led him around the corner to the elevator. After arriving on the first floor, he walked rapidly west into the annex behind the headquarters building. Once in the new structure, they passed through five security checkpoints. This was an all-time record for Ryan, and he wondered if Cantor had had to re-program the pass-control computer to get him into this building. After ten minutes he was on the fourth floor in a room identified only by its number.

"Jack, this is Jean-Claude. He's one of our French colleagues."

Ryan shook hands with a man twenty years older than himself, whose face was the embodiment of civilized irony. "What gives, Marty?"

"Professor Ryan," Jean-Claude said. "I am informed that you are the man we must thank."

"What for—" Ryan stopped. *Uh-oh.* The Frenchman led him to a TV monitor.

"Jack, you never saw this," Cantor said as a picture formed on the screen. It had to be satellite photography. Ryan knew it at once from the viewing angle, which changed very slowly.

"When?" he asked.

"Last night, our time, about three A.M. local."

"Correct." Jean-Claude nodded, his eyes locked on the screen.

It was Camp -20, Ryan thought. The one that belonged to *Action-Directe.* The spacing of the huts was familiar. The infrared picture showed that three of the huts had their heaters on. The brightness of the heat signals told him that ground temperature must have been about freezing. South of the camp, behind a dune, two vehicles were parked. Jack couldn't tell if they were jeeps or small trucks. On closer inspec-tion, faint figures were moving on the cold background: men. From the way they moved: soldiers. He counted eight of them split into two equal groups. Near one of the huts was a brighter light. There appeared to be a man standing there. *Three in the morning, when one's body functions are at the lowest ebb.* One of the camp guards was smoking on duty, doubtlessly trying to stay awake. That was a mistake, Ryan knew. The flare of the match would have destroyed his night vision. *Oh, well. . . .*

"Now," Jean-Claude said.

There was a brief flash from one of the eight intruders; it was strange to see but not hear it. Ryan couldn't tell if the guard moved as a result, but his cigarette did, flying perhaps two yards, after which both images remained stationary. *That's a kill,* he told himself. *Dear God, what am I watching?* The eight pale shapes closed on the camp. First they entered the guard hut—it was always the same one. A moment later they were back outside. Next, they redeployed into the two groups of four, each group heading toward one of the "lighted" huts.

"Who are the troops?" Jack asked.

"Paras," Jean-Claude answered simply.

Some of the men reappeared thirty seconds later. After another minute, the rest emerged—more than had gone in, Ryan saw. Two seemed to be carrying something. Then something else entered the picture. It was a bright glow that washed out other parts of the picture, but the new addition was a helicopter, its engines blazing in the infrared picture. The picture quality deteriorated and the camera zoomed back. Two more helicopters were in the area. One landed near the vehicles, and the jeeps were driven into it. After that helicopter lifted off, the other skimmed the ground, following the vehicle tracks for several miles and erasing them with its downdraft. By the time the satellite lost visual lock with the scene, everyone was gone. The entire exercise had taken less than ten minutes.

"Quick and clean," Marty breathed.

"You got her?" Jack had to ask.

"Yes," Jean-Claude replied. "And five others, four of them alive. We removed all of them, and the camp guards who, I regret to say, did not survive the evening." The Frenchman's regrets were tossed in for good manners only. His face showed what he really felt.

"Any of your people hurt?" Cantor asked.

An amused shake of his head: "No. They were all asleep, you see. One slept with a pistol next to his cot, and made the mistake of reaching for it."

"You pulled everybody out, even the camp guards?"

"Of course. All are now in Chad. The living are being questioned."

"How did you arrange the satellite coverage?" Jack asked.

This answer came with a Gallic shrug. "A fortunate coincidence."

Right, Jack thought. *Some coincidence. I just watched the instant-replay of the death of three or four people. Terrorists,* he corrected himself. *Except for the camp guards, who only helped terrorists. The timing could not have been an accident. The French wanted us to know that they were in counterterrorist operations for-real.*

"Why am I here?"

"But you made this possible," Jean-Claude said. "It is my pleasure to give you the thanks of my country."

"What's going to happen to the people you captured?" Jack wanted to know.

"Do you know how many people they have assassinated? For those crimes they will answer. Justice, that will happen to them."

"You wanted to see a success, Jack," Cantor said. "You just did."

Ryan thought that one over. Removing the bodies of the camp guards told him how the operation would end. No one was supposed to know what had happened. Sure, some bullet holes were left behind, and a couple of bloodstains, but no bodies. The raiders had quite literally covered their tracks. The whole operation was "deniable." There was nothing left behind that would point to the French. In that sense it had been a perfect covert operation. And if that much effort had gone into making it so, then there was little reason to suspect that the *Action-Directe* people would ever face a jury. *You wouldn't go to that much trouble and then go through the publicity of a trial*, Ryan told himself. *Goodbye, Françoise Theroux. . . .*

I condemned these people to death, he realized finally. Just the one of them was enough to trouble his conscience. He remembered the police-style photograph he'd seen of her face and the fuzzy satellite image of a girl in a bikini.

"She's murdered at least three people," Cantor said, reading Jack's face.

"Professor Ryan, she has no heart, that one. No feelings. You must not be misled by her face," Jean-Claude advised. "They cannot all look like Hitler."

But that was only part of it, Ryan knew. Her looks merely brought into focus that hers was a human life whose term was now unnaturally limited. *As she has limited those of others*, Jack told himself. He admitted to himself that he would have no qualms at all if her name had been Sean Miller.

"Forgive me," he said. "It must be my romantic nature."

"But of course," the Frenchman said generously. "It is something to be regretted, but those people made their choice, Professor, not you. You have helped to avenge the lives of many innocent people, and you have saved those of people you will never know. There will be a formal note of thanks—a secret one, of course—for your assistance."

"Glad to help, Colonel," Cantor said. Hands were shaken all around, and Marty led Jack back to the headquarters building.

"I don't know that I want to see anything like that again," Ryan said in the corridor. "I mean, I don't want to know their faces. I mean—hell, I don't know what I mean. Maybe—it's just . . . different when you're detached from it, you know? It was too much like watching a ball game on TV, but it wasn't a ball game. Who was that guy, anyway?"

"Jean-Claude's the head of the DGSE's Washington Station, and he was the liaison man. We got the first new picture of her a day and a half ago. They had the operation all ready to roll, and he got things going inside of six hours. Impressive performance."

"I imagine they wanted us to be impressed. They're not bringing 'em in, are they?"

"No. I seriously doubt those people are going back to France to stand trial. Remember the problem they had the last time they tried a public trial of *Action-Directe* members? The jurors started getting midnight phone calls, and the case got blown away. Maybe they don't want to put up with the hassle again." Cantor frowned. "Well, it's not our call to make. Their system isn't the same as ours. All we did was forward information to an ally."

"An American court could call that accessory to murder."

"Possibly," Cantor admitted. "Personally, I prefer what Jean-Claude called it."

"Then why are you leaving in August?" Ryan asked.

Cantor delivered his answer without facing him. "Maybe you'll find out someday, Jack."

Back alone in his office, Ryan couldn't get his mind off what he'd seen. Five thousand miles away, agents of the DGSE's "action" directorate were now questioning that girl. If this had been a movie, their techniques would be brutal. What they used in real life, Ryan didn't want to know. He told himself that the members of *Action-Directe* had brought it on themselves. First, they had made a conscious choice to be what they were. Second, in subverting the French legal system the previous year, they'd given their enemies an excuse to bypass whatever constitutional guarantees . . . but was that truly an excuse?

"What would Dad think?" he murmured to himself. Then the next question hit him. Ryan lifted his phone and punched in the right number.

"Cantor."

"Why, Marty?"

"Why what, Jack?"

"Why did you let me see that?"

"Jean-Claude wanted to meet you, and he also wanted you to see what your data accomplished."

"That's bull, Marty! You let me into a real-time satellite display—okay, taped, but essentially the same thing. There can't be many people cleared for that. I don't need-to-know how good the real-time capability is. You could have told him I wasn't cleared for it and that would have been that."

"Okay, you've had some time to think it over. Tell me what you think."

"I don't like it."

"Why?" Cantor asked.

"It broke the law."

"Not ours. Like I told you twenty minutes ago, all we did was provide intelligence information to a friendly foreign nation."

"But they used it to kill people."

"What do you think intel is *for,* Jack? What should they have done? No, answer this first: what if they were foreign nationals who had murdered French nationals in—in Liechtenstein, say, and then boogied back to their base?"

"That's not the same thing. That's more . . . more like an act of war—like doing the guards at the camp. The people they *were* after were their own citizens who committed crimes in their own country, and—and are subject to French law."

"And what if it had been a different camp? What if those paratroopers had done a job for us, or the Brits, and taken out your ULA friends?"

"That's different!" Ryan snapped back. *But why?* he asked himself a moment later. "It's personal. You can't expect me to feel the same way about that."

"Can't I?" Cantor hung up the phone.

Ryan stared at the telephone receiver for several seconds before replacing it in the cradle. What was Marty trying to tell him? Jack reviewed the events in his own mind, trying to come to a conclusion that made sense.

Did any of it make sense? Did it make sense for political dissidents to express themselves with bombs and machine guns? Did it make sense for small nations to use terrorism as a short-of-war weapon to change the policies of larger ones? Ryan grunted. That depended on which side of the issue you were on—or at least there were people who thought that way. Was this something completely new?

It was, and it wasn't. State-sponsored terrorism, in the form of the Barbary pirates, had been America's first test as a nation. The enemy objective then had been simple greed. The Barbary states demanded tribute before they would give right of passage to American-flag trading ships, but it had finally been decided that enough was enough. Preble took the infant U.S. Navy to the Mediterranean Sea to put an end to it—no, to put an end to America's victimization by it, Jack corrected himself.

God, it was even the same place, Ryan thought. "To the shores of Tripoli," the Marine Hymn said, where First Lieutenant Presley O'Bannon, USMC, had attacked the fort at Derna. Jack wondered if the place still existed. Certainly the problem did.

The violence hadn't changed. What had changed were the rules under which the large nations acted, and the objectives of their enemies. Two hundred years earlier, when a small nation offended a larger one, ships and troops would settle matters. No longer was this simple wog-bashing, though. The smaller countries now had arsenals of modern weapons that could make such punitive expeditions too expensive for societies that had learned to husband the lives of their young men. A regiment of troops could no longer settle matters, and moving a whole army was no longer such a simple thing. Knowing this, the small country could inflict wounds itself, or even more safely, sponsor others to do so—"deniably"—in order to move its larger opponent in the desired direction. There wasn't even much of a hurry. Such low-level conflict could last years, so small were the expenditures of resources and so different the perceived value of the human lives taken and lost.

What was new, then, was not the violence, but the safety of the nation that either performed or sponsored it. Until that changed, the killing would never stop.

So, on the international level, terrorism was a form of war that didn't even have to interrupt normal diplomatic relations. America itself had embassies in some of the nations, even today. Nearer to home, however, it was being treated as a crime. He'd faced Miller in the Old Bailey, Ryan remembered, not a military court-martial. *They can even use that against us.* It was a surprising realization. *They can fight their kind of war, but we can't recognize it as such without giving up something our society needs. If we treat terrorists as politically motivated activists, we give them an honor they don't deserve. If we treat them as soldiers, and kill them as such, we both give them legitimacy and violate our own laws.* By a small stretch of the imagination, organized crime could be thought of as a form of terrorism, Ryan knew. The terrorists' only weakness was their negativity. They were a political movement with nothing to offer other than their conviction that their parent society was unjust. So long as the people in that society felt otherwise, it was the terrorists who were alienated from it, not the population as a whole. The democratic processes that benefited the terrorists were also their worst political enemy. Their prime objective, then, had to be the elimination of the democratic process, converting justice to injustice in order to arouse members of the society to sympathy with the terrorists.

The pure elegance of the concept was stunning. Terrorists could fight a war and be protected by the democratic processes of their enemy. If those processes were obviated, the terrorists would win additional political support, but so long as those processes were not obviated, it was extremely difficult for them to lose. They could hold a society hostage against itself and its most important precepts, daring it to change. They could move around at will, taking advantage of the freedom that defined a democratic state, and get all the support they needed from a nation-state with which their parent society was unwilling or unable to deal effectively.

The only solution was international cooperation. The terrorists had to be cut off from support. Left to their own resources, terrorists would become little more than an organized-crime network. . . . But the democracies found it easier to deal with their domestic problems singly than to band together and strike a decisive blow at those who fomented them, despite all the rhetoric to the contrary. Had that just changed? The CIA had given data on terrorists to someone else, and action had been taken as a result. What he had seen earlier, therefore, was a step in the right direction, even if it wasn't necessarily the right kind of step. Ryan told himself that he'd just witnessed one of the world's many imperfections, but at least one aimed in the proper direction. That it had disturbed him was a consequence of his civilization. That he was now rationalizing it was a result of . . . what?

Cantor walked into Admiral Greer's office.

"Well?" the DDI asked.

"We'll give him a high B, maybe an A-minus. It depends on what he learns from it."

"Conscience attack?" the DDI asked.

"Yeah."

"It's about time he found out what the game's really like. Everybody has to learn that. He'll stay," Greer said.

"Probably."

The pickup truck tried to pull into the driveway that passed under the Hoover building, but a guard waved him off. The driver hesitated, partly in frustration, partly in rage while he tried to figure something else out. The heavy traffic didn't help. Finally he started circling the block until he was able to find a way into a public parking garage. The attendant held up his nose at the plebeian vehicle—he was more accustomed to Buicks and Cadillacs—and burned rubber on the way up the ramp to show his feelings. The driver and his son didn't care. They walked downhill and across the street, going by foot on the path denied their truck. Finally they got to the door and walked in.

The agent who had desk duty noted the entrance of two people somewhat disreputably dressed, the elder of whom had something wrapped in his leather jacket and tucked under his arm. This got the agent's immediate and full attention. He waved the visitors over with his left hand. His right was somewhere else.

"Can I help you, sir?"

"Hi," the man said. "I got something for you." The man raised the jacket and pulled out a submachine gun. He quickly learned that this wasn't the way to get on the FBI's good side.

The desk agent snatched the weapon and yanked it off the desk, standing and reaching for his service revolver. The panic button under the desk was already pushed, and two more agents in the room converged on the scene. The man behind the desk immediately saw that the gun's bolt was closed—the gun was safe, and there wasn't a magazine in the pistol grip.

"I found it!" the kid announced proudly.

"What?" one of the arriving agents said.

"And I figured I'd bring it here," the lad's father said.

"What the hell?" the desk agent observed.

"Let's see it." A supervisory agent arrived next. He came from a surveillance room whose TV cameras monitored the entrance. The man behind the desk rechecked to make sure the weapon was safe, then handed it across.

It was an Uzi, the 9mm Israeli submachine gun used all over the world because of its quality, balance, and accuracy. The cheap-looking (the Uzi is anything but cheap, though it does look that way) metal stampings were covered with red-brown rust, and water dripped from the receiver. The agent pulled open the bolt and stared down the barrel. The gun had been fired and not cleaned since. It was impossible to tell how long ago that had been, but there weren't all that many FBI cases pending in which a weapon of this type had been used.

"Where did you find this, sir?"

"In a quarry, about thirty miles from here," the man said.

"*I* found it!" the kid pointed out.

"That's right, he found it," his father conceded. "I figured this was the place to bring it."

"You thought right, sir. Will both of you come with me, please?"

The agent on the desk gave both of them "visitor" passes. He and the other two agents on entrance-guard duty went back to work, wondering what the hell that had been all about.

On the building's top floor, those few people in the corridor were surprised to see a man walking around with a machine gun, but it would not have been in keeping with Bureau chic to pay too much attention—the man with the gun did have an FBI pass, and he was carrying it properly. When he walked into an office, however, it did get a reaction from the first secretary he saw.

"Is Bill in?" the agent asked.

"Yes, I'll—" Her eyes didn't leave the gun.

The man waved her off, motioned for the visitors to follow him, and walked toward Shaw's office. The door was open. Shaw was talking with one of his people. Special Agent Richard Alden went straight to Shaw's desk and set the gun on the blotter.

"Christ, Richie!" Shaw looked up at the agent, then back down at the gun. "What's this?"

"Bill, these two folks just walked in the door downstairs and gave it to us. I thought it might be interesting."

Shaw looked at the two people with visitor passes and invited them to sit on the couch against the wall. He called for two more agents to join them, plus someone from the ballistics laboratory. While things were being organized, his secretary got a cup of coffee for the father and a Dr Pepper for the son.

"Could I have your names, please?"

"I'm Robert Newton and this here's my son Leon." He gave his address and phone number without being asked.

"And where did you find the gun?" Shaw asked while his subordinates were taking notes.

"It's called Jones Quarry. I can show you on a map."

"What were you doing there?"

"I was fishing. I found it," Leon reminded them.

"I was getting in some firewood," his father said.

"This time of year?"

"Beats doing it during the summer, when it's hot, man," Mr. Newton pointed out reasonably. "Also lets the wood season some. I'm a construction worker. I walk iron, and it's a little slow right now, so I went out for some wood. The boy's off from school today, so I brought him along. While I cut the wood, Leon likes to fish. There's some big ones in the quarry," he added with a wink.

"Oh, okay." Shaw grinned. "Leon, you ever catch one?"

"No, but I got close last time," the youngster responded.

"Then what?"

Mr. Newton nodded for his son.

"My hook got caught on sumthin' heavy, you know, an' I pulled and pulled and pulled. It come loose, and I tried real hard, but I couldn't reel it up. So I called my daddy."

"I reeled it in," Mr. Newton explained. "When I saw it was a gun, I almost crapped my drawers. The hook was snagged on the trigger guard. What kinda gun is that, anyway?"

"Uzi. It's made in Israel, mostly," the ballistics expert said, looking up from the weapon. "It's been in the water at least a month."

Shaw and another agent shared a look at that bit of news.

"I'm afraid I handled it a lot," Newton said. "Hope I didn't mess up any fingerprints."

"Not after being in the water, Mr. Newton," Shaw replied. "And you brought it right here?"

"Yeah, we only got it, oh"—he checked his watch—"an hour and a half ago. Aside from handling it, we didn't do anything. It didn't have no magazine in it."

"You know guns?" the ballistics man asked.

"I spent a year in Nam. I was a grunt with the 173rd Airborne. I know M-16s pretty good." Newton smiled. "And I used to do a little hunting, mostly birds and rabbits."

"Tell us about the quarry," Shaw said.

"It's off the main road, back maybe three-quarters of a mile, I guess. Lots of trees back there. That's where I get my firewood. I don't really know who owns it. Lots of cars go back there. You know, it's a parking spot for kids on Saturday nights, that sorta place."

"Have you ever heard shooting there?"

"No, except during hunting season. There's squirrels in there, lotsa squirrels. So what's with the gun? Does it mean anything to ya?"

"It might. It's the kind of gun used in the murder of a police officer, and—"

"Oh, yeah! That lady and her kid over Annapolis, right?" He paused for a moment. "Damn."

Shaw looked at the boy. He was about nine, the agent thought, and the kid had smart eyes, scanning the items Shaw had on his walls, the memorabilia from his many cases and posts. "Mr. Newton, you have done us a very big favor."

"Oh, yeah?" Leon responded. "What you gonna do with the gun?"

The ballistics expert answered. "First we'll clean it and make sure it's safe. Then we'll fire it." He looked at Shaw. "You can forget any other forensic stuff. The water in the quarry must be chemically active. This corrosion is pretty fierce." He looked at Leon. "If you catch any fish there, son, you be sure you don't eat them unless your dad says it's all right."

"Okay," the boy assured him.

"Fibers," Shaw said.

"Yeah, maybe that. Don't worry. If they're there, we'll find 'em. What about the barrel?"

"Maybe," the man replied. "By the way, this gun comes from Singapore. That makes it fairly new. The Israelis just licensed them to make the piece eighteen months ago. It's the same outfit that makes the M-16 under license from Colt's." He read off the number. It would be telexed to the FBI's Legal Attaché in Singapore in a matter of minutes. "I want to get to work on this right now."

"Can I watch?" Leon asked. "I'll keep out of the way."

"Tell you what," Shaw said. "I want to talk to your dad a little longer. How about I have one of our agents take you through our museum. You can see how we caught all the old-time bad guys. If you wait outside, somebody will come and take you around."

"Okay!"

"We can't talk about this, right?" Mr. Newton asked after his son had left.

"That's correct, sir." Shaw paused. "That's important for two reasons. First, we don't want the perpetrators to know that we've had a break in the case—and this could be a major break, Mr. Newton; you've done something very important. The other reason is to protect you and your family. The people involved in this are very dangerous. Put it this way: you know that they tried to kill a pregnant woman and a four-year-old girl."

That got the man's attention. Robert Newton, who had five children, three of them girls, didn't like hearing that.

"Now, have you ever seen people around the quarry?" Shaw asked.

"What do you mean?"

"Anybody."

"There's maybe two or three other folks who cut wood back there. I know the names—I mean their first names, y'know? And like I said, kids like to go parking back there." He laughed. "Once I had to help one out. I mean, the road's not all that great, and this one kid was stuck in the mud, and . . ." Newton's voice trailed off. His face changed. "Once, it was a Tuesday . . . I couldn't work that day 'cause the crane was broke, and I didn't much feel like sitting around the house, y'know? So I went out to chop some wood. There was this van coming outa the road. He was having real trouble in the mud. I had to wait like ten minutes 'cause he blocked the whole road, slippin' and slidin', like."

"What kind of van?"

"Dark, mostly. The kind with the sliding door—musta been customized some, it had that dark stuff on the windows, y'know?"

Bingo! Shaw told himself. "Did you see the driver or anybody inside?"

Newton thought for a moment. "Yeah . . . it was a black dude. He was—yeah, I remember, he was yellin', like. I guess he was pissed at getting stuck like that. I mean, I couldn't hear him, but you could tell he was yelling, y'know? He had a beard, and a leather jacket like the one I wear to work."

"Anything else about the van?"

"I think it made noise, like it had a big V-8. Yeah, it must have been a custom van to have that."

Shaw looked at his men, too excited to smile as they scribbled their notes.

"The papers said all the crooks were white," Newton said.

"The papers don't always get things right," Shaw noted.

"You mean the bastard who killed that cop was black?" Newton didn't like that. So was he. "And he tried to do that family, too. . . . Shit!"

"Mr. Newton, that is secret. Do you understand me? You can't tell anybody about that, not even your son—was he there then?"

"Nah, he was in school."

"Okay, you can't tell anyone. That is to protect you and your family. We're talking about some very dangerous people here."

"Okay, man." Newton looked at the table for a moment. "You mean we got people running around with machine guns, killing people—here? Not in Lebanon and like that, but here?"

"That's about the size of it."

"Hey, man, I didn't spend a year in the Nam so we could have that shit where I live."

Several floors downstairs, two weapons experts had already detail-stripped the Uzi. A small vacuum cleaner was applied to every part in the hope there might be cloth fibers that matched those taken from the van. A final careful look was taken at the parts. The damage from water immersion had done no good to the stampings, made mostly of mild steel. The stronger, corrosion-resistant ballistic steel of the barrel and bolt were in somewhat better shape. The lab chief reassembled the gun himself, just to show his technicians that he still knew how. He took his time, oiling the pieces with care, finally working the action to make sure it functioned properly.

414 • TOM CLANCY

"Okay," he said to himself. He left the weapon on the table, its bolt closed on an empty chamber. Next he pulled an Uzi magazine from a cabinet and loaded twenty 9-millimeter rounds. This he stuck in his pocket.

It always struck visitors as somewhat incongruous. The technicians usually wore white laboratory coats, like doctors, when they fired the guns. The man donned his ear protectors, stuck the muzzle into the slot, and fired a single round to make certain that the gun really worked. It did. Then he held the trigger down, emptying the magazine in a brief span of seconds. He pulled out the magazine, checked that the weapon was safe, and handed it to his assistant.

"I'm going to wash my hands. Let's get those bullets checked out." The chief ballistics technician was a fastidious person.

By the time he was finished drying his hands, he had a collection of twenty spent bullets. The metal jacket on each showed the characteristic marks made by the rifling of the machine gun's barrel. The marks were roughly the same on each bullet, but slightly different, since the gun barrel expanded when it got hot.

He took a small box from the evidence case. This bullet had gone completely through the body of a police officer, he remembered. It seemed such a puny thing to have taken a life, he thought, not even an ounce of lead and steel, hardly deformed at all from its deadly passage. It was hard not to dwell on such thoughts. He placed it on one side of the comparison microscope and took another from the set he'd just fired. Then he removed his glasses and bent down to the eyepieces. The bullets were . . . close. They'd definitely been fired by the same kind of gun. . . . He switched samples. Closer. The third bullet was closer still. He carefully rotated the sample, comparing it with the round that was kept in the evidence case, and it . . .

"We got a match." He backed away from the 'scope and another technician bent down to check.

"Yeah, that's a match. One hundred percent," the man agreed. The boss ordered his men to check other rounds and walked to the phone.

"Shaw."

"It's the same gun. One-hundred-percent sure. I have a match on the round that killed the trooper. They're checking the ones from the Porsche now.''

"Good work, Paul!"

"You bet. I'll be back to you in a little while."

Shaw replaced the phone and looked at his people. "Gentlemen, we just had a break in the Ryan case.''

22
Procedures

Robert Newton took the agents to the quarry that night. By dawn the next day a full team of forensic experts was sifting through every speck of dirt at the site. A pair of divers went into the murky water, and ten agents were posted in the woods to watch for company. Another team located and interviewed Newton's fellow woodcutters. More spoke with the residents of the farms near the road leading back into the woods. Dirt samples were taken to be matched with those vacuumed from the van. The tracks were photographed for later analysis.

The ballistics people had already made further tests on the Uzi. The ejected cartridge cases were compared with those recovered from the van and the crime scene, and showed perfect matches in extractor marks and firing-pin penetrations. The match of the gun with the crime and the van was now better than one hundred percent. The serial number had been confirmed with the factory in Singapore, and records were being checked to determine where the gun had been shipped. The name of every arms dealer in the world was in the Bureau's computer.

The whole purpose of the FBI's institutional expertise was to take a single piece of information and develop it into a complete criminal case. What it could not entirely prevent was having someone see them. Alex Dobbens drove past the quarry road on his way to work every day. He saw a pair of vehicles pulling out onto the highway from the dirt and gravel path. Though both the car and van from the FBI laboratory were unmarked, they had federal license plates, and that was all he needed to see.

Dobbens was not an excitable man. His professional training permitted him to look at the world as a collection of small, discrete problems, each of which had a solution; and if you solved enough of the small ones, then the large ones would similarly be solved, one at a time. He was also a meticulous person. Everything he did was part of a larger plan, both part of, and isolated from, the next planned step. It was not something that his people had easily come to understand, but it was hard to argue with success, and everything Dobbens did was successful. This had earned him respect and obedience from people who had once been too passionate for what Alex deemed their mission in life.

It was unusual, Dobbens thought, for two cars at once to come out of that road. It was out of the ordinary realm of probability that both should have government license plates. Therefore he had to assume that somehow the feds had learned that he'd used the quarry for weapons training. How had it been blown? he wondered. A hunter, perhaps, one of the rustics who went in there after squirrels and birds? Or one of the people who chopped wood, maybe? Or some kid from a nearby farm? How big a problem was this?

He'd taken his people to shoot there only four times, the most recent being when the Irish had come over. *Hmm, what does that tell me?* he asked the road in front of his car. *That was weeks ago.* Each time, they'd done all the shooting during rush hour, mostly in the morning. Even this far from D.C., there were a lot of cars and trucks on the road in the morning and late afternoon, enough to add quite a bit of noise to the environment. It was therefore unlikely that anyone had heard them. *Okay.*

Every time they had shot there, Alex had been assiduous about picking up the brass, and he was certain that they'd left nothing behind, not even a cigarette butt, to prove that they'd been there. They could not avoid leaving tire marks, but one of the reasons he'd picked the place was that kids went back there to park on weekends—there were plenty of tire marks.

They had dumped the gun there, he remembered, but who could have discovered that? The water in the quarry was over eighty feet deep—he'd checked—and looked about as uninviting as a rice paddy, murky from dirt that washed in, and whatever kind of scum it was that formed on the surface. Not a place to go swimming. They had dumped only the gun that had been fired, but as unlikely as it seemed, he had to assume they'd found it. How that had happened didn't matter for the moment. *Well, we have to dispose of the others too, now,* Alex told himself. *You can always get new guns.*

What is the most the cops can learn? he asked himself. He was well versed on police procedures. It seemed only reasonable that he should know his enemy, and Alex owned a number of texts on investigative techniques, the books used to train cops in their various academies, like Snyder's *Homicide Investigation* and the *Law Enforcement Bible.* He and his people studied them as carefully as the would-be cops with their shiny young faces. . . .

There could be no fingerprints on the gun. After being in water, the skin oil that makes the marks would long since have been gone. Alex had handled and cleaned it, but he didn't need to worry about that.

The van was gone. It had been stolen to begin with, then customized by one of Alex's own people, and had used four different sets of tags. The tags were long gone, underneath a telephone/power pole in Anne Arundel County. If something had resulted from that, he'd have known it long before now, Alex thought. The van itself had been fully sanitized, everything had been wiped clean, the dirt from the quarry road . . . that was something to think about, but the van still led to a dead end. They'd left nothing in it to connect it with his group.

Had any of his people talked, perhaps a man with an aching conscience because of the kid who'd almost died? Again, had that happened, he would have awakened this afternoon to see a badge and gun in front of his face. So that was out. Probably. He'd talk to his people about that, remind them that they could never talk with anyone about what they did.

Might his face have been seen? Alex chided himself again for having waved at the helicopter. But he'd been wearing a hat, sunglasses, and a beard, all of which were now gone, along with the jacket, jeans, and boots that he'd worn. He still had the work gloves, but they were so common an item that you could buy them in any hardware store. *So dump 'em and buy another pair, asshole!* he said to himself. *Make sure they're the same color, and keep the sales receipt.*

His mind ran through the data again. He might even be overreacting, he thought. The feds could be investigating some totally unrelated thing, but it was stupid to take any unnecessary risks. Everything that they'd used at the quarry would be disposed of. He'd make a complete list of possible connections and eliminate every one of them. They'd never go back there again. Cops had their rules and procedures, and he'd unhesitatingly copied the principle to deny its advantage to his opponents. He had established the rules for himself after seeing what catastrophes resulted from having none. The radical groups he'd hovered around in his college days had died because of their arrogance and stupidity, their underestimation of the skill of their enemies. Fundamentally, they'd died because they were unworthy of success. *Victory comes only to those prepared to make it, and* take *it,* Alex thought. He was even able to keep from congratulating himself on spotting the feds. It was simple prudence, not genius. His route had been chosen with an eye to taking note of such things. He already had another promising site for weapons training.

"Erik Martens," Ryan breathed. "We meet again."

All of the FBI's data had been forwarded to the Central Intelligence Agency's working group within hours of its receipt. The Uzi that had been recovered—Ryan marveled at how that had happened!—had, he saw, been fabricated in Singapore, at a plant that also made a version of the M-16 rifle that he'd carried in the Corps, and a number of other military arms, both East and West, for sale to third-world countries . . . and other interested parties. From his work the previous summer, Ryan knew that there were quite a few such factories, and quite a few governments whose only measure for the legitimacy of an arms purchaser was his credit rating. Even those who paid lip-service to such niceties as "end-user certificates" often turned a blind eye to the reputation of a dealer who never quite proved to be on the wrong side of the shadowy line that was supposed to distinguish the honest from the others. Since it was the dealer's government that generally made this determination, yet another variable was added to an already inexact equation.

Such was the case with Mr. Martens. A very competent man in his business, a man with remarkable connections, Martens had once worked with the CIA-backed UNITA rebels in Angola until a more regular pipeline had been established. His principal asset, however, was his ability to obtain items for the South African government. His last major coup had been obtaining the manufacturing tools and dies for the Milan antitank missile, a weapon that could not be legally shipped to the Afrikaner government due to the Western embargo. After three months' creative effort on his part, the government's own armaments factories would be making it themselves. His fee for that had doubtless been noteworthy, Ryan knew, though the CIA had been unable to ascertain just how noteworthy. The man owned his own business jet, a Grumman G-3 with intercontinental range. To make sure that he could fly it anywhere he wished, Martens had obtained weapons for a number of black African nations, and even missiles for Argentina. He could go to any corner of the world and find a government that was in his debt. The man would have been a sensation on Wall Street or any other marketplace, Ryan smiled to himself. He could deal with anyone, could market weapons the way that people in Chicago traded wheat futures.

The Uzis from Singapore had come to him. Everyone loved the Uzi. Even the Czechs had tried to copy it, but without great commercial success. The Israelis sold them by the thousands to military and security forces, always—most of the time—following the rules that the United States insisted upon. Quite a few had found their way to South Africa, Ryan read, until the embargo had made it rather more difficult. *Is that the reason they finally let someone make the gun under license?* Jack wondered. *Let someone else broaden the market for you, and just keep the profits. . . .*

The shipment had been five thousand units . . . about two million dollars, wholesale. Not very much, really, enough to equip a city police force or a regiment of paratroopers, depending on the receiving government's orientation. Large enough to show a profit for Mr. Martens, small enough not to attract a great deal of attention. One truck-load, Ryan wondered, maybe two? The pallets of boxes would be tucked into a corner of his warehouse, technically supervised by his government, but more likely in fact to be Martens' private domain. . . .

That's what Sir Basil Charleston told me at the dinner, Ryan reminded himself. *You didn't pay enough attention to that South African chap.* . . . So the Brits think he deals to terrorists . . . directly? No, his government wouldn't tolerate that. *Probably wouldn't,* Ryan corrected himself. The guns might find their way to the African National Congress, which might not be very good news for the government they were pledged to destroy. So now Ryan had to find an intermediary. It took thirty minutes to get that file, involving a call to Marty Cantor.

The file was a disaster. Martens had eight known and fifteen suspected intermediary agents . . . one or two in every country he sold to—of course! Ryan punched Cantor's number again.

"I take it we've never talked to Martens?" Ryan asked.

"Not for a few years. He ran some guns into Angola for us, but we didn't like the way he handled things."

"How so?"

"The man's something of a crook," Cantor replied. "That's not terribly unusual in the arms business, but we try to avoid the type. We set up our own pipeline after the Congress took away the restriction on those operations."

"I got twenty-three names here," Ryan said.

"Yeah, I'm familiar with the file. We thought he was passing arms to an Iranian-sponsored group last November, but it turned out he wasn't. It took us a couple of months to clear him. It would have been a whole lot easier if we'd been able to talk to him."

"What about the Brits?" Jack asked.

"Stone wall," Marty said. "Every time they try to talk with him, some big ol' Afrikaner soldier says no. You can't blame them, really, if the West treats them like pariahs, they're sure as hell going to act like pariahs. The other thing to remember is, pariahs stick together."

"So we don't know what we need to know about this guy and we're not going to find out."

"I didn't say that exactly."

"Then we're sending people in to check a few things out?" Ryan asked hopefully.

"I didn't say that either."

"Dammit, Marty!"

"Jack, you are not cleared to know anything about field operations. In case you haven't noticed, not one of the files you've seen tells you how the information gets in here."

Ryan had noticed that. Informants weren't named, meeting places weren't specified, and the methods used to pass the information were nowhere to be found. "Okay, may I safely assume that we will, by some unknown means, get more data on this gentleman?"

"You may safely assume that the possibility is being considered."

"He may be the best lead we have," Jack pointed out.

"I know."

"This can be pretty frustrating stuff, Marty," Ryan said, getting that off his chest.

"Tell me about it," Cantor chuckled. "Wait till you get involved with something really important—sorry, but you know what I mean. Like what the Politburo people really think about something, or how powerful and accurate their missiles are, or whether they have somebody planted in this building."

"One problem at a time."

"Yeah, that must be nice, sport, just to have one problem at a time."

"When can I expect something on Martens?" Ryan asked.

"You'll know when it comes in," Cantor promised. "'Bye."

"Great." Jack spent the rest of the day and part of another looking through the list of people Martens had dealt with. It was a relief to have to go back to teaching class the next two days, but he did find one possible connection. The Mercury motors found on the Zodiac used by the ULA had probably—the bookkeeping had broken down in Europe—gone through a Maltese dealer with whom Martens had done a little business.

The good news of the spring was that Ernie was a quick study. The dog got the hang of relieving himself outside within the first two weeks, which relieved Jack of a message from his daughter, "Daaaaddy, there's a little proooblem . . ." invariably followed by a question from his wife: "Having fun, Jack?" In fact, even his wife admitted that the dog was working out nicely. Ernie could only be separated from their daughter with a hard tug on his leash. He now slept in her bed, except when he patrolled the house every few hours. It was somewhat unnerving at first to see the dog—rather, to see a black mass darker than the night a few inches from one's face—when Ernie seemed to be reporting that everything was clear before he headed back to Sally's room for two more hours of protective slumber. He was still a puppy, with impossibly long legs and massive webbed feet, and he still liked to chew things. When that had included the leg of one of

Sally's Barbie dolls, it resulted in a furious scolding from his owner that ended when he started licking Sally's face by way of contrition.

Sally was finally back to normal. As the doctors had promised her parents, her legs were fully healed, and she was running around now as she had before. This day would mark her return to Giant Steps. Her way of knocking glasses off tables as she ran past them was the announcement that things were right again, and her parents were too pleased by this to bring themselves to scold the girl for her unladylike behavior. For her part, Sally endured an abnormally large number of spontaneous hugs which she didn't really understand. She'd been sick and she was now better. She'd never really known that an attack had happened, Jack was slow to realize. The handful of times she referred to it, it had always been "the time the car broke." She still had to see the doctors every few weeks for tests. She both hated and dreaded these, but children adapt to a changing reality far more readily than their parents.

One of these changes was her mother. The baby was really growing now. Cathy's petite frame seemed poorly suited to such abuse. After every morning shower, she looked at herself, naked, in a full-length mirror that hung on the back of the closet door and came away with an expression that was both proud and mournful as her hands traced over the daily alterations.

"It's going to get worse," her husband told her as he emerged from the shower next.

"Thanks, Jack, I really need to hear that."

"Can you see your feet?" he asked with a grin.

"No, but I can feel them." They were swelling, too, along with her ankles.

"You look great to me, babe." Jack stood behind her, reaching his arms around to hold her bulging abdomen. He rested his cheek on the top of her head. "Love ya."

"That's easy for you to say!" She was still looking in the mirror. Jack saw her face in the glass, a tiny smile on her lips. An invitation? He moved his hands upward to find out. "Ouch! I'm sore."

"Sorry." He softened his grip to provide nothing more than support. "Hmph. Has something changed here?"

"It took you this long to notice?" The smile broadened a tad. "It's a shame that I have to go through this for that to happen."

"Have you ever heard me complain? Everything about you has

always been A-plus. I guess pregnancy drops you to a B-minus. But only in one subject,'' he added.

"You've been teaching too long, Professor.'' Her teeth were showing now. Cathy leaned back, rubbing her skin against her husband's hairy chest. For some reason she loved to do that.

"You're beautiful,'' he said. "You glow.''

"Well, I have to glow my way to work.'' Jack didn't move his hands. "I have to get dressed, Jack.''

"'How do I love thee, let me count the ways . . .'" he murmured into her damp hair. "One . . . two . . . three . . .''

"Not *now*, you lecher!''

"Why?'' His hands moved very gently.

"Because I have to operate in three hours, and you have to go to spook city.'' She didn't move, though. There weren't all that many moments that they could be alone.

"I'm not going there today. I got stuck with a seminar at the Academy. I'm afraid the department is a little miffed with me.'' He kept looking in the mirror. Her eyes were closed now. *Screw the department* . . . "God, I love you!''

"Tonight, Jack.''

"Promise?''

"You've sold me on the idea, okay? Now I—'' She reached up to grab his hands, pulled them downward, and pressed them against the taut skin of her belly.

He—the baby was definitely a he, insofar as that was what they called him—was wide awake, rolling and kicking, pushing at the dark envelope that defined his world.

"Wow,'' his father observed. Cathy's hands were over his moving them about every few seconds to follow the movements of the baby. "What does that feel like?''

Her head leaned back a fraction. "It feels good—except when I'm trying to sleep or when he kicks my bladder during a procedure.''

"Was Sally this—this strong?''

"I don't think so.'' She didn't say that it wasn't the sort of thing you remember in terms of strength. It was just the singular feeling that your baby is alive and healthy, something that no man would ever understand. Not even Jack. Cathy Ryan was a proud woman. She knew that she was one of the best eye surgeons around. She knew that she was attractive, and worked hard to keep herself that way; even now, misshapen by her pregnancy, she knew that she was carrying it well. She could tell that from her husband's biological reaction, in the small of her back. But more than that, she knew that she was a woman, doing something that Jack could neither duplicate nor fully comprehend. *Well,* she told herself, *Jack does things I don't much understand either.* "I have to get dressed."

"Okay." Jack kissed the base of her neck. He took his time. It would have to last until this evening. "I'm up to eleven," he said as he stepped back.

She turned. "Eleven what?"

"Counting the ways," Jack laughed.

"You turkey!" She swung her bra at him. "*Only* eleven?"

"It's early. My brain isn't fully functional yet."

"I can tell it doesn't have enough of a blood supply." The funny thing, she thought, was that Jack didn't think he was very good-looking. She liked the strong jaw, except when he forgot to shave it, and his kind, loving eyes. She looked at the scars on his shoulder, and remembered her horror as she'd watched her husband run into harm's way, then her pride in him for what he had accomplished. Cathy knew that Sally had almost died as a direct result, but there was no way Jack could have foreseen it. It was her fault, too, she knew, and Cathy promised herself that Sally would never play with her seat belt again. Each of them had paid a price for the turns their lives had taken. Sally was almost fully recovered from hers, as was she. Cathy knew it wasn't true of her husband, who'd been awake through it all while she slept.

When that *happened, at least I had the blessing of unconsciousness. Jack had to live through it. He's still paying that price for it,* she thought. *Working two jobs now, his face always locked into a frown of concentration, worrying over something he can't talk about.* She didn't know exactly what he was doing, but she was certain that it was not yet done.

The medical profession had unexpectedly given her a belief in fate. Some people simply had their time. If it was not yet that time, chance or a good surgeon would save the life in question, but if the time had come, all the skilled people in the world could not change it. Caroline Ryan, MD, knew that this was a strange way for a physician to think, and she balanced the belief with the professional certainty that she was the instrument which would thwart the force that ruled the world—but she had also chosen a field in which life-and-death was rarely the issue. Only she knew that. A close friend had gone into pediatric oncology, the treatment of children stricken with cancer. It was a field that cried out for the best people in medicine, and she'd been tempted, but she knew that the effect on her humanity would be intolerable. How could she carry a child within her while she watched other children die? How could she create life while she was unable to prevent its loss? Her belief in fate could never have made that leap of imagination, and the fear of what it might have done to her psyche had turned her to a field that was demanding in a different way. It was one thing to put your life on the line—quite another to wager your soul.

Jack, she knew, had the courage to face up to that. This, too, had its price. The anguish she occasionally saw in him could only be that kind of question. She was sure that his unspoken work at CIA was aimed at finding and killing the people who had attacked her. She felt it necessary, and she would shed no tears for those who had nearly killed her little girl, but it was a task which, as a physician, she could not herself contemplate. Clearly it wasn't easy for her man. Something had just happened a few days ago. He was struggling with whatever it was, unable to discuss it with anyone while he tried to retain the rest of his world in an undamaged state, trying to love his family while he labored . . . to bring others to their death? It could not have come easily to him. Her husband was a genuinely good man, in so many ways the ideal man—*at least for me,* she thought. He'd fallen in love with her at their first meeting, and she could recount every step of their courtship. She remembered his clumsy—in retrospect, hilarious—proposal of marriage, the terror in his eyes as she'd hesitated over the answer, as though he felt himself unworthy of her, the idiot. Most of all, she remembered the look on his face when Sally had been born. The man who had turned his back on the dog-eat-dog world of investments—the world that since the death of her mother had made her father into a driven, unhappy man—who had returned to teaching eager young minds, was now trapped in something he didn't like. But she knew that he was doing his best, and she knew just how good his best was. She'd just experienced that. Cathy wished that she could share it, as he occasionally had to share with her the depression following a failed procedure. As much as she had needed him a few painful weeks past, now he needed her. She couldn't do that—or could she?

"What's been bothering you? Can I help?"

"I can't really talk about it," Jack said as he knotted his tie. "It was the right thing, but not something you can feel very good about."

"The people who—"

"No, not them. If it was them . . ." He turned to face his wife. "If it was them, I'd be all smiles. There's been a break. The FBI—I shouldn't be telling you this, and it doesn't go any farther than this room—they found the gun. That might be important, but we don't know for sure yet. The other thing—well, I can't talk about that at all. Sorry. I wish I could."

"You haven't done anything wrong?" His face changed at that question.

"No. I've thought that one over the past few days. Remember the time you had to take that lady's eye out? It was necessary, but you still felt pretty bad about it. Same thing." He looked in the mirror. *Sort of the same thing.*

"Jack, I love you and I believe in you. I know that you'll do the right thing."

"I'm glad, babe, because sometimes I'm not so sure." He held out his arms and she came to him. At some French military base in Chad, another young woman was experiencing something other than a loving embrace, Ryan thought. *Whose fault is that? One thing for sure, she isn't the same as my wife. She's not like this girl of mine.*

He felt her against himself, felt the baby move again, and finally he was sure. As his wife had to be protected, so did all the other wives, and all the children, and all the living people who were judged as mere abstractions by the ones who trained in those camps. Because they weren't abstractions, they were real. It was the terrorists who had cast themselves out of the civilized community and had to be hunted down one way or another. *If we can do it by civilized rules, well and good— but if not, then we have to do the best we can, and rely on our consciences to keep us from going over the edge.* He thought that he could trust his conscience. He was holding it in his arms. Jack kissed his wife gently on the cheek.

"Thanks. That's twelve."

The seminar led to the final two weeks of classes which led in turn to final exams and Commissioning Week: yet another class of mid-shipmen graduated to join the fleet, and the Corps. The plebes were plebes no longer, and were finally able to smile in public once or twice

428 • TOM CLANCY

per day. The campus became quiet, or nearly so, as the underclassmen went home for brief vacations before taking cruises with the fleet, and preparing for Plebe Summer, the rough initiation for a new class of mids. Ryan was incongruously trapped in his real job for a week, finishing up a mountain of paperwork. Neither the Academy's history department nor the CIA was very happy with him now. His attempt to serve two masters had not been a total success. Both jobs, he realized, had suffered somewhat, and he knew that he'd have to choose between them. It was a decision that he consciously tried to avoid while the proof of its necessity piled up around him.

"Hey, Jack!" Robby came in wearing his undress whites.

"Grab a seat, Commander. How's the flying business?"

"No complaints. The kid is back in the saddle," Jackson said, sitting down. "You should have been up in the Tomcat with me last week. Oh, man, I'm finally back in the groove. I was hassling with a guy in an A-4 playing aggressor, and I ruined his day. It was so fine." He grinned like a lion surveying a herd of crippled antelope. "I'm ready!"

"When do you leave?"

"I report for duty 5 August. I guess I'll be heading out of here on the first."

"Not before we have you and Sissy over for dinner." Jack checked his calendar. "The thirtieth is a Friday. Seven o'clock. Okay?"

"Aye aye, sir."

"What's Sissy going to do down there?"

"Well, they have a little symphony in Norfolk. She's going to be their number-two piano soloist, plus doing her teachin' on the side."

"You know they have the in-vitro center down there. Maybe you guys can have a kid after all."

"Yeah, Cathy told her about that. We're thinking about it, but— well, Sissy's had a lot of disappointments, you know?"

"You want Cathy to talk to her about it some more?"

Robby thought about that. "Yeah, she knows how. How's she making out with this one?"

"She's bitching about her figure a lot," Jack chuckled. "Why is it that they never understand how pretty they look pregnant?"

"Yeah." Robby grinned his agreement, wondering if Sissy would ever look the same way to him. Jack felt guilty for touching a sensitive topic, and changed the subject.

"By the way, what's with all the boats? I saw a bunch of yardbirds parked on the waterfront this morning."

"That's 'moored,' you dumb jarhead," Robby corrected his friend. "They're replacing the pilings over at the naval station across the river. It's supposed to take two months. Something went wrong with the old ones—the preservative didn't work or some such bullcrap. Your basic government-contractor screwup. No big deal. The job's supposed to be finished in time for the next school year—not that I care one way or another, of course. By that time, boy, I'll be spending my mornings at twenty-five thousand feet, back where I belong. What are you going to be doing?"

"What do you mean?"

"Well, you're either gonna be here or at Langley, right?"

Ryan looked out the window. "Damned if I know. Rob, we got a baby on the way and a bunch of other things to think about."

"You haven't found 'em yet?"

Jack shook his head. "We thought we had a break, but it didn't work out. These guys are pros, Robby."

Jackson reacted with surprising passion. "Bull-shit, man! Professionals don't hurt kids. Hey, they want to take a shot at a soldier or a cop, okay, I can understand that—it ain't right, but I can understand it, okay?—soldiers and cops have guns to shoot back with, and they got training. So it's an even match, surprise on one side and procedure on the other, and that makes it a fair game. Going after noncombatants, they're just fucking street hoods, Jack. Maybe they're clever, but they sure as hell ain't professionals! Professionals got balls. Professionals put it on the line for-real."

Jack shook his head. Robby was wrong, but he knew of no way to persuade his friend otherwise. His code was that of the warrior, who had to live by civilized rules. Rule Number One was: You don't deliberately harm the helpless. It was bad enough when that happened by accident. To do so on purpose was cowardly, beneath contempt; those who did so merited only death. They were beyond the pale.

"They're playing a goddamned game, Jack," the pilot went on. "There's even a song about it. I heard it at Riordan's on St. Patrick's Day. 'I've learned all my heroes and wanted the same/To try out my hand at the patriot game.' Something like that." Jackson shook his head in disgust. "War isn't a game, it's a profession. They play their little *games,* and call themselves patriots, and go out and kill little kids. Bastards. Jack, out in the fleet, when I'm driving my Tomcat, we play *our* games with the Russians. Nobody gets killed, because both sides are professionals. I don't much like the Russians, but the boys that fly the Bears know their stuff. We know our stuff, and both sides respect the other. There's rules, and both sides play by 'em. That's the way it's supposed to be.''

"The world isn't that simple, Robby," Jack said quietly.

"Well, it damned well ought to be!" Jack was surprised at how worked up his friend was about this. "You tell those guys at CIA: find 'em for us, then get somebody to give the order, and I'll escort the strike in.''

"The last two times we did that we lost people," Ryan pointed out.

"We take our chances. That's what they pay us for, Jack.''

"Yeah, but before you toss the dice again, we want you over for dinner.''

Jackson grinned sheepishly. "I won't bring my soap box with me, I promise. Dressy?''

"Robby, am I ever dressy?''

"I told 'em it wasn't dressy," Jack said afterward.

"Good," his wife agreed.

"I thought you'd say that." He looked up at his wife, her skin illuminated by moonlight. "You really are pretty.''

"You keep saying that—"

"Don't move. Just stay where you are." He ran his hand across her flanks.

"Why?''

"You said this is the last time for a while. I don't want it to be over yet.''

"The next time you can be on top," she promised.

"It'll be worth waiting for, but you won't be as beautiful as you are now.''

"I don't feel beautiful at the moment.''

"Cathy, you are talking to an expert," her husband pronounced. "I am the one person in this house who can give out a dispassionate appraisal of the pulchritude of any female human being, living or dead, and *I* say that you are beautiful. End of discussion.''

Cathy Ryan took her own appraisal. Her belly was disfigured by gross-looking stretch marks, her breasts were bloated and sore, her feet and ankles swollen, and her legs were knotting up from her current position. "Jack, you are a dope."

"She never listens," he told the ceiling.

"It's just pheromones," she explained. "Pregnant women smell different and it must tickle your fancy somehow or other."

"Then how come you're beautiful when my nose is stuffy? Answer me that!"

She reached down to twist her fingers in the hair on his chest. Jack started squirming. It tickled. "Love is blind."

"When I kiss you, my eyes are always open."

"I didn't know that!"

"I know," Jack laughed quietly. "Your eyes are always closed. Maybe your love is blind, but mine isn't." He ran his fingertips over her abdomen. It was still slick from the baby oil she used to moisturize her skin. Jack found this a little kinky. His fingertips traced circles on the taut, smooth surface.

"You're a throwback. You're something out of a thirties movie." She started squirming now. "Stop that."

"Errol Flynn never did this in the movies," Jack noted, without stopping that.

"They had censors then."

"Spoilsports. Some people are just no fun." His hands expanded their horizons. The next target was the base of her neck. It was a long reach, but worth the effort. She was shivering now. "Now, I, on the other hand . . ."

"Mmmmm."

"I thought so."

"Uh-oh. He's awake again."

Jack felt him almost as soon as his wife. He—she, it—was rotating. Jack wondered how a baby could do that, without anything to latch on to, but the evidence was clear, his hands felt a lump shift position. The lump was his child's head, or the opposite end. Moving. Alive. Waiting to be born. He looked up to see his wife, smiling down at him and knowing what he felt.

"You're beautiful, and I love you very much. Whether you like it or not." He was surprised to find that there were tears in his eyes. He was even more surprised by what happened next.

"Love you, too, Jack—again?"

"Maybe that wasn't the last time for a while after all. . . ."

23

Movement

"We got these last night." Priorities had changed somewhat at CIA. Ryan could tell. The man going over the photos with him was going gray, wore rimless glasses and a bow tie. Garters on his sleeves would not have seemed out of place. Marty stood in the corner and kept his mouth shut. "We figure it's one of these three camps, right?"

"Yeah, the others are identified." Ryan nodded. This drew a snort.

"You say so, son."

"Okay, these two are active, this one as of last week, and this one two days ago."

"What about -20, the *Action-Directe* camp?" Cantor asked.

"Shut down ever since the Frenchies went in. I saw the tape of that." The man smiled in admiration. "Anyway, here."

It was one of the rare daylight photographs, even in color. The firing range adjacent to the camp had six men standing in line. The angle prevented them from seeing if the men held guns or not.

"Weapons training?" Ryan asked cautiously.

"Either that or they're taking a leak by the numbers." This was humor.

"Wait a minute, you said these came in last night."

"Look at the sun angle," the man said derisively.

"Oh. Early morning."

"Around midnight our time. Very good," the man observed. *Amateurs,* he thought. *Everybody thinks he can read a recon photo!* "You can't see any guns, but see these little points of light here? That might be sunlight reflecting off ejected cartridge brass. Okay, we have six people here. Probably Northern Europeans because they're so pale—see this one here with the sunburn, his arm looks a little pink? All appear to be male, from the short hair and style of dress. Okay, now the question is, who the hell are they?"

"They're not *Action-Directe,*" Marty said.

"How do you know that?" Ryan asked.

"The ones who got picked up are no longer with us. They were given trials by military tribunal and executed two weeks ago."

"Jesus!" Ryan turned away. "I didn't want to know that, Marty."

"Those who asked had clergy in attendance. I thought that was decent of our colleagues." He paused for a moment, then went on: "It turns out that French law allows for that sort of trial under very special circumstances. So despite what we both thought all the time, it was all done by the book. Feel better?"

"Some," Ryan admitted on reflection. It might not have made a great deal of difference to the terrorists, but at least the formality of law had been observed, and that was one of the things "civilization" meant.

"Good. A couple sang like canaries beforehand, too. DGSE was able to bag two more members outside of Paris"—this hasn't made the papers yet—"plus a barnful of guns and explosives. They may not be out of business, but they've been hurt."

"All right," the man in the bow tie acknowledged. "And this is the guy who tumbled to it?"

"All because he likes to see tits from three hundred miles away," Cantor replied.

"How come nobody else saw that first?" Ryan would have preferred that someone else had done all this.

"Because there aren't enough people in my section. I just got authority to hire ten new ones. I've already got them picked out. They're people who're leaving the Air Force. Pros."

"Okay, what about the other camp?"

"Here." A new photo came into view. "Pretty much the same thing. We have two people visible—"

"One's a girl," Ryan said at once.

"One appears to have shoulder-length hair," the photo expert agreed. He went on: "That doesn't necessarily mean it's a girl." Jack thought about that, looking at the figure's stance and posture.

"If we assume it's a girl, what does that tell us?" he asked Marty.

"You tell me."

"We have no indication that the ULA has female members, but we known that the PIRA does. This is the camp—remember that jeep that was driving from one to the other and was later seen parked at this camp?" Ryan paused before going on. *Oh, what the hell . . .* He grabbed the photo of the six people on the gun range. "This is the one."

"And what the hell are you basing that on?" the photo-intel man asked.

"Call it a strong hunch," Ryan replied.

"That's fine. The next time I go to the track I'll bring you along to pick my horses for me. Listen, the thing about these photos is, what you see is all you got. If you read too much into these photos, you end up making mistakes. Big ones. What you have here is six people lined up, *probably* firing guns. That's all."

"Anything else?" Cantor asked.

"We'll have a night pass at about 2200 local time—this afternoon our time. I'll have the shots to you right after they come in."

"Very good. Thanks," Cantor said. The man left the room to go back to his beloved photo equipment.

"I believe you call that sort of person an empiricist," Ryan observed after a moment.

Cantor chuckled. "Something like that. He's been in the business since we had U-2s flying over Russia. He's a real expert. The important thing about that is, he doesn't say he's sure about something until he's *really* sure. What he said's true, you can easily read too much into these things."

"Fine, but you agree with me."

"Yeah." Cantor sat on the desk next to Ryan and examined the photo through a magnifying glass.

The six men lined up on the firing line were not totally clear. The hot air rising off the desert even in early morning was disturbed enough to ruin the clarity of the image. It was like looking through the shimmering mirage on a flat highway. The satellite camera had a very high "shutter" speed—actually the photoreceptors were totally electronic—that cancelled most of the distortion, but all they really had was a poorly focused, high-angle image that showed man-shapes. You could tell what they were wearing—tan short-sleeved shirts and long pants—and the color of their hair with total certainty. A glimmer off one man's wrist seemed to indicate a watch or bracelet. The face of one man was darker than it should have been—his uncovered forearm was quite pale—and that probably indicated a short beard. . . . *Miller has a beard now,* Ryan reminded himself.

"Damn, if this was only a little better . . ."

"Yeah," Marty agreed. "But what you see here is the result of thirty years of work and God only knows how much money. In cold climates it comes out a little better, but you can't ever recognize a face."

"This is it, Marty. This is the one. We have to have something that confirms that, or at least confirms something."

"'Fraid not. Our French colleagues asked the people they captured. The answer they got was that the camps are totally isolated from one another. When the groups meet, it's almost always on neutral ground. They didn't even know for sure that there was a camp here."

"*That* tells us something!"

"The thing about the car? It could have been somebody from the Army, you know. The guy who oversees the guards, maybe. It didn't have to be one of the players who drove from this one to the Provisionals' camp. In fact, there is ample reason to believe that it wasn't. Compartmentalization is a logical security measure. It makes sense for the camps to be isolated from one another. These people know about the importance of security, and even if they didn't before, the French op was a gilt-edge reminder."

Ryan hadn't thought about that. The raid on the *Action-Directe* camp had to have an effect on the others, didn't it?

"You mean we shot ourselves in the foot?"

"No, we sent a message that was worth sending. So far as we can determine, nobody knows what actually happened there. We have reason to believe that the suspicion on the ground is that a rival outfit settled a score—not all of these groups like each other. So, if nothing else, we've fostered some suspicions among the groups themselves, and vis-à-vis their hosts. That sort of thing could break some information loose for us, but it'll take time to find out.''

"Anyway, now that we know that this camp is likely to be the one we want, what are we going to do about it?''

"We're working on that. I can't say any more.''

"Okay.'' Ryan gestured to his desk. "You want some coffee, Marty?''

Cantor's face took on a curious expression. "No, I'm off coffee for a while.''

What Cantor didn't say was that a major operation had been laid on. It was fairly typical in that very few of the participants actually knew what was going on. A Navy carrier battle group centered on USS *Saratoga* was due to sail west out of the Mediterranean Sea, and would pass north of the Gulf of Sidra in several days. As was routine, the formation was being trailed by a Soviet AGI—a fishing trawler that gathers electronic intelligence instead of mackerel—which would give information to the Libyans. When the carrier was directly north of Tripoli, in the middle of the night, a French-controlled agent would interrupt electrical power to some radar installations soon after the carrier started conducting nighttime flight operations. This was expected to get some people excited, although the carrier group Commander had no idea that he was doing anything other than routine flight ops. It was hoped that the same team of French commandos that had raided Camp -20 would also be able to slip into Camp -18. Marty couldn't tell Ryan any of this, but it was a measure of how well *Action-Directe* had been damaged that the French were willing to give the Americans such cooperation. While it hadn't exactly been the first example of international cooperation, it was one of three such operations that had actually been successful. The CIA had helped to avenge the murder of a friend of the French President. Whatever the differences between the two countries, debts of honor were still paid in full. It appealed to Cantor's sense of propriety, but was something known to only twenty people within the Agency. The op was scheduled to run in four days. A senior case officer from the Operations Directorate was even now working with the French paratroopers who, he reported, were eager to demonstrate their prowess yet again. With luck, the terrorist group that had had the temerity to commit murder within the United States and the United Kingdom would be hurt by the troops of yet another nation. If successful, the precedent would signal a new and valuable development in the struggle against terrorism.

Dennis Cooley was working on his ledger book. It was early. The shop wasn't open for business yet, and this was the time of day for him to set his accounts straight. It wasn't very hard. His shop didn't have all that many transactions. He hummed away to himself, not knowing what annoyance this habit caused for the man listening to the microphone planted behind one of his bookshelves. Abruptly his humming stopped and his head came up. What was wrong . . . ?

The little man nearly leaped from his chair when he smelled the acrid smoke. He scanned the room for several seconds before looking up. The smoke was coming from the ceiling light fixture. He darted to the wall switch and slapped his hand on it. A blue flash erupted from the wall, giving him a powerful electric shock that numbed his arm to the elbow. He stared at his arm in surprise, flexing his fingers and looking at the smoke that seemed to be trailing off. He didn't wait to see it stop. Cooley had a fire extinguisher in the back room. He got it and came back, pulled the safety pin, and aimed the device at the switch. No smoke there anymore. Next he stood on his chair to get close to the ceiling fixture, but already the smoke was nearly gone. The smell remained. Cooley stood on the chair for over a minute, his knees shaking as the chair moved slightly under him, holding the extinguisher and trying to decide what to do. Call the fire brigade? But there wasn't any fire—was there? All his valuable books. . . . He'd been trained in many things, but fighting fires was not one of them. He was breathing heavily now, nearly panicked until he finally decided that there wasn't anything to be panicked about. He turned to see three people staring at him through the glass with curious expressions.

He lowered the extinguisher with a shamefaced grin and gestured comically to the spectators. The light was off. The switch was off. The fire, if it had been a fire, was gone. He'd call the building's electrician. Cooley opened the door to explain what was wrong to his fellow shop owners. One remarked that the wiring in the arcade was horribly out of date. It was something Cooley hadn't ever thought about. Electricity was electricity. You flipped the switch and the light went on, and that was that. It annoyed him that something so reliable, wasn't. A minute later he called the building manager, who promised that an electrician would be there in half an hour.

The man arrived forty minutes later, apologizing for being held up in traffic. He stood for a moment, admiring the bookshelves.

"Smells like a wire burned out," he judged next. "You're lucky, sir. That frequently causes a fire."

"How difficult will it be to fix?"

"I expect that I'll have to replace the wiring. Ought to have been done years ago. This old place—well, the electric service is older than I am, and that's too old by half." He smiled.

Cooley showed him to the fuse box in the back room, and the man went to work. Dennis was unwilling to use his table lamp, and sat in the semidarkness while the tradesman went to work.

The electrician flipped off the outside master switch and examined the fuse box. It still had the original inspection tag, and when he rubbed off the dust, he read off the date: 1919. The man shook his head in amazement. Almost seventy bloody years! He had to remove some items to get at the wall, and was surprised to see that there was some recent plasterwork. It was as good a place to start as any. He didn't want to damage the wall any more than he had to. With hammer and chisel he broke into the new plaster, and there was the wire. . . .

But it wasn't the right one, he thought. It had plastic insulation, not the gutta-percha used in his grandfather's time. It wasn't in quite the right place, either. Strange, he thought. He pulled on the wire. It came out easily.

"Mr. Cooley, sir?" he called. The shop owner appeared a moment later. "Do you know what this is?"

"Bloody hell!" the detective said in the room upstairs. "Bloody fucking hell!" He turned to his companion, a look of utter shock on his face. "Call Commander Owens!"

"I've never seen anything like this." He cut off the end and handed it over. The electrician did not understand why Cooley was so pale.

Neither had Cooley, but he knew what it was. The end of the wire showed nothing, just a place where the polyvinyl insulation stopped, without the copper core that one expects to see in electrical circuitry.

Hidden in the end was a highly sensitive microphone. The shop owner composed himself after a moment, though his voice was somewhat raspy.

"I have no idea. Carry on."

"Yes, sir." The electrician resumed his search for the power line. Cooley had already lifted his telephone and dialed a number.

"Hello?"

"Beatrix?"

"Good morning, Mr. Dennis. How are you today?"

"Can you come into the shop this morning? I have a small emergency."

"Certainly." She lived only a block from the Holloway Road tube station. The Piccadilly Line ran almost directly to the shop. "I can be there in fifteen minutes."

"Thank you, Beatrix. You're a love," he added before he hung up. By this time Cooley's mind was racing at mach-1. There was nothing in the shop or his home that could incriminate him. He lifted the phone again and hesitated. His instructions under these circumstances were to call a number he had memorized—but if there were a microphone in his office, his phone . . . and his home phone . . . Cooley was sweating now despite the cool temperature. He commanded himself to relax. He'd never said anything compromising on either phone—had he? For all his expertise and discipline, Cooley had never faced danger, and he was beginning to panic. It took all of his concentration to focus on his operational procedures, the things he had learned and practiced for years. Cooley told himself that he had never deviated from them. Not once. He was sure of that. By the time he stopped shaking, the bell rang.

It was Beatrix, he saw. Cooley grabbed his coat.

"Will you be back later?"

"I'm not sure. I'll call you." He went right out the door, leaving his clerk with a very curious look.

It had taken ten minutes to locate James Owens, who was in his car south of London. The Commander gave immediate orders to shadow Cooley and to arrest him if it appeared that he was attempting to leave the country. Two men were already watching the man's car and were ready to trail him. Two more were sent to the arcade, but the detectives arrived just as he walked out, and were on the wrong side of the street. One hopped out of the car and followed, expecting him to turn onto Berkeley Street toward his travel agent. Instead, Cooley ducked into the tube station. The detective was caught off guard and raced down the entrance on his side of the street. The crowd of morning commuters made spotting his short target virtually impossible. In under a minute, the officer was sure that his quarry had caught a train that he had been unable to get close to. Cooley had escaped.

The detective ran back to the street and put out a radio call to alert the police at Heathrow airport, where this underground line ended— Cooley always flew, unless he drove his own car—and to get cars to all the underground stations on the Piccadilly Line. There simply wasn't enough time.

Cooley got off at the next station, as his training had taught him, and took a cab to Waterloo Station. There he made a telephone call.

"Five-five-two-nine," the voice answered.

"Oh, excuse me, I was trying to get six-six-three-zero. Sorry." There followed two seconds of hesitation on the other side of the connection.

"Oh . . . That's quite all right," the voice assured him in a tone that was anything but all right.

Cooley replaced the phone and walked to a train. It was everything he could do not to look over his shoulder.

"This is Geoffrey Watkins," he said as he lifted the phone.

"Oh, I beg your pardon," the voice said. "I was trying to get Mr. Titus. Is this six-two-nine-one?" *All contacts are broken until further notice,* the number told him. *Not known if you are in danger. Will advise if possible.*

"No, this is six-two-one-nine," he answered. *Understood.* Watkins hung the phone up and looked out his window. His stomach felt as though a ball of refrigerated lead had materialized there. He swallowed twice, then reached for his tea. For the rest of the morning, it was hard to concentrate on the Foreign Office white paper he was reading. He needed two stiff drinks with lunch to settle himself down.

By noon, Cooley was in Dover, aboard a cross-channel ferry. He was fully alert now, and sat in a corner seat on the upper deck, looking over the newspaper in his hands to see if anyone was watching him. He'd almost boarded the hovercraft to Calais, but decided against it at the last moment. He had enough cash for the Dover-Dunkerque ferry, but not the more expensive hovercraft, and he didn't want to leave a paper trail behind. It was only two and a quarter hours in any case. Once in France, he could catch a train to Paris, then start flying. He started to feel secure for the first time in hours, but was able to suppress it easily enough. Cooley had never known this sort of fear before, and it left a considerable aftertaste. The quiet hatred that had festered for years now ate at him like an acid. They had made him run. *They* had spied on *him!* Because of all his training, all the precautions that he'd followed assiduously, and all the professional skill that he'd employed, Cooley had never seriously considered the possibility that he would be turned. He had thought himself too skillful for that. That he was wrong enraged him, and for the first time in his life, he wanted to lash out himself. He'd lost his bookshop and with it all the books he loved, and this, too, had been taken from him by the bloody Brits! He folded the paper neatly and set it down in his lap while the ferry pulled into the English Channel, placid with the summer sun overhead. His bland face stared out at the water with a gaze as calm as a man in contemplation of his garden while he fantasized images of blood and death.

Owens was as furious as anyone had ever seen him. The surveillance of Cooley had been so easy, so routine—but that was no excuse, he told his men. That harmless-looking little poof, as Ashley had called him, had slipped away from his shadowers as adroitly as someone trained at Moscow Center itself. There were men at every international airport in Britain clutching pictures of Cooley, and if he used his credit card to purchase any kind of ticket, the computers would notify Scotland Yard at once, but Owens had a sickening feeling that the man was already out of the country. The Commander of C-13 dismissed his people.

Ashley was in the room, too, and his people had been caught equally off guard. He and Owens shared a look of anger mixed with despair.

A detective had left the tape of a phone call to Geoffrey Watkins made less than an hour after Cooley disappeared. Ashley played it. It lasted all of twenty seconds. And it wasn't Cooley's voice. If it had been, they would have arrested Watkins then and there. For all their effort, they still did not have a single usable piece of evidence on Geoffrey Watkins.

"There is a Mr. Titus in the building. The voice even gave the correct number. By all rights it could have been a simple wrong number."

"But it wasn't, of course."

"That is how it's done, you know. You have pre-set messages that are constructed to sound entirely harmless. Whoever trained these chaps knew what they were about. What about the shop?"

"The girl Beatrix knows absolutely nothing. We have people searching the shop at this moment, but so far they've found nothing but old bloody books. Same story at his flat." Owens stood and spoke in a voice full of perverse wonder. "An electrician. . . . Months of work, gone because he yanks the wrong wire."

"He'll turn up. He could not have had a great deal of cash. He must use his credit card."

"He's out of the country already. Don't say he isn't. If he's clever enough for what we know he's done—"

"Yes." Ashley nodded reluctant agreement. "One doesn't always win, James."

"It is so nice to hear that!" Owens snapped out his reply. "These bastards have outguessed us every step of the way. The Commissioner is going to ask me how it is that we couldn't get our thumbs out in time, and there is no answer to that question."

"So what's the next step, then?"

"At least we know what he looks like. We . . . we share what we know with the Americans, all of it. I have a meeting scheduled with Murray this evening. He's hinted that they have something operating that he's not able to talk about, doubtless some sort of CIA op."

"Agreed. Is it here or there?"

"There." Owens paused. "I am getting sick of this place."

"Commander, you should measure your successes against your failures," Ashley said. "You're the best man we've had in this office in some years."

Owens only grunted at that remark. He knew it was true. Under his leadership, C-13 had scored major coups against the Provisionals. But in this job, as in so many others, the question one's superiors always asked was, *What have you accomplished* today? Yesterday was ancient history.

"Watkins' suspected contact has flown," he announced three hours later.

"What happened?" Murray closed his eyes halfway through the explanation and shook his head sadly. "We had the same sort of thing happen to us," he said after Owens finished. "A renegade CIA officer. We were watching his place, and let things settle into a comfortable routine, and then—zip! He snookered the surveillance team. He turned up in Moscow a week later. It happens, Jimmy."

"Not to me," Owens almost snarled. "Not until now, that is."

"What's he look like?" Owens handed a collection of photographs across the desk. Murray flipped through them. "Mousy little bastard, isn't he? Almost bald." The FBI man considered this for a moment, then lifted his phone and punched in four numbers. "Fred? Dan. You want to come down to my office for a minute?"

The man arrived a minute later. Murray didn't identify him as a member of the CIA and Owens didn't ask. He didn't have to. He'd given over two copies of each photo.

Fred—one of the men from "down the hall"—took his photos and looked at them. "Who's he supposed to be?"

Owens explained briefly, ending, "He's probably out of the country by now."

"Well, if he turns up in any of our nets, we'll let you know," Fred promised, and left.

"Do you know what they're up to?" Owens asked Murray.

"No. I know something is happening. The Bureau and the Agency have a joint task force set up, but it's compartmented, and I don't need to know all of it yet."

"Did your chaps have a part in the raid on *Action-Directe*?"

"I don't know what you're talking about," Murray said piously. *How the hell did you hear about that, Jimmy?*

"I thought as much," Owens replied. *Bloody security!* "Dan, we are concerned here with the personal safety of—"

Murray held his hands up like a man at bay. "I know, I know. And you're right, too. We ought to cut your people in on this. I'll call the Director myself."

The phone rang. It was for Owens.

"Yes?" The Commander of C-13 listened for a minute before hanging up. "Thank you." A sigh. "Dan, he's definitely on the continent. He used a credit card to purchase a railway ticket. Dunkerque to Paris, three hours ago."

"Have the French pick him up?"

"Too late. The train arrived twenty minutes ago. He's completely gone now. Besides, we have nothing to arrest him for, do we?"

"And Watkins has been warned off."

"Unless that was a genuinely wrong number, which I rather doubt, but try to prove *that* in a court of law!"

"Yeah." Judges didn't understand any instinct but their own.

"And don't tell me that you can't win them all! That's what they pay me to do." Owens looked down at the rug, then back up. "Please excuse me for that."

"Aah!" Murray waved it off. "You've had bad days before. So have I. It's part of the business we're in. What we both need at a time like this is a beer. Come on downstairs, and I'll treat you to a burger."

"When will you call your Director?"

"It's lunchtime over there. He always has a meeting going over lunch. We'll let it wait a few hours."

Ryan had lunch with Cantor that day in the CIA cafeteria. It could have been the eating place in any other government building. The food was just as unexciting. Ryan decided to try the lasagna, but Marty stuck with fruit salad and cake. It seemed an odd diet until Jack watched him take a tablet before eating. He washed it down with milk.

"Ulcers, Marty?"

"What makes you say that?"

"I'm married to a doc, remember? You just took a Tagamet. That's for ulcers."

"This place gets to you after a while," Cantor explained. "My stomach started acting up last year and didn't get any better. Everyone in my family comes down with it sooner or later. Bad genes, I guess. The medication helps some, but the doctor says that I need a less stressful environment." A snort.

"You do work long hours," Ryan observed.

"Anyway, my wife got offered a teaching position at the University of Texas—she's a mathematician. And to sweeten the deal they offered me a place in the Political Science Department. The pay's better than it is here, too. I've been here twelve years," he said quietly. "Long time."

"So what do you feel bad about? Teaching's great. I love it, and you'll be good at it. You'll even have a good football team to watch."

"Yeah, well, she's already down there, and I leave in a few weeks. I'm going to miss this place."

"You'll get over it. Imagine being able to walk into a building without getting permission from a computer. Hey, I walked away from my first job."

"But this one's important." Cantor drank his milk and looked across the table. "What are you going to do?"

"Ask me after the baby is born." Ryan didn't want to dwell on this question.

"The Agency needs people like you, Jack. You've got a feel for things. You don't think and act like a bureaucrat. You say what you think. Not everyone in this building does that, and that's why the Admiral likes you."

"Hell, I haven't talked to him since—"

"He knows what you're doing." Cantor smiled.

"Oh." Ryan understood. "So that's it."

"That's right. The old man really wants you, Jack. You still don't know how important that photo you tripped over was, do you?"

"All I did was show it to you, Marty," Ryan protested. "You're the one who really made the connection."

"You did exactly the right thing, exactly what an analyst is supposed to do. There was more brains in that than you know. You have a gift for this sort of work. If you can't see it, I can." Cantor examined the lasagna and winced. How could anybody eat that greasy poison? "Two years from now you'll be ready for my job."

"One bridge at a time, Marty." They let it go at that.

An hour later Ryan was back in his office. Cantor came in.

"Another pep talk?" Jack smiled. *Full-court press time . . .*

"We have a picture of a suspected ULA member and it's only a week old. We got it in from London a couple of hours ago."

"Dennis Cooley." Ryan examined it and laughed. "He looks like a real wimp. What's the story?"

Cantor explained. "Bad luck for the Brits, but maybe good luck for us. Look at the picture again and tell me something important."

"You mean . . . he's lost most of his hair. Oh! We can ID the guy if he turns up at one of the camps. None of the other people are bald."

"You got it. And the boss just cleared you for something. There's an op laid on for Camp -18."

"What kind?"

"The kind you watched before. Is that still bothering you?"

"No, not really." *What bothers me is that it* doesn't *bother me,* Ryan thought. *Maybe it should. . . .* "Not with these guys, I don't. When?"

"I can't tell you, but soon."

"So why did you let me know—nice one, Marty. Not very subtle, though. Does the Admiral want me to stay that bad?"

"Draw your own conclusions."

An hour after that the photo expert was back. Another satellite had passed over the camp at 2208 local time. The infrared image showed eight people standing at line on the firing range. Bright tongues of flame marked two of the shapes. They were firing their weapons at night, and there were now at least eight of them there.

"What happened?" O'Donnell asked. He'd met Cooley at the airport. A cutout had gotten word out that Cooley was on the run, but the reason for it had had to wait until now.

"There was a bug in my shop."

"You're sure?" O'Donnell asked.

Cooley handed it over. The wire had been in his pocket for thirty hours. O'Donnell pulled the Toyota Land Cruiser over to examine it.

"Marconi make these for intelligence use. Quite sensitive. How long might it have been there?"

Cooley could not remember having anyone go into his back room unsupervised. "I've no idea."

O'Donnell put the vehicle back into gear, heading out into the desert. He pondered the question for over a mile. Something had gone wrong, but what . . . ?

"Did you ever think you were being followed?"

"Never."

"How closely did you check, Dennis?" Cooley hesitated, and

O'Donnell took this for an answer. "Dennis, did you ever break trade-craft—*ever?*"

"No, Kevin, of course not. It isn't possible that—for God's sake, Kevin, it's been weeks since I've been in contact with Watkins."

"Since your last trip to Cork." O'Donnell squinted in the bright sun.

"Yes, that's right. You had a security man watching me then—was there anyone following me?"

"If there were, he must have been a damnably clever one, and he could not have been too close. . . ." The other possibility that O'Donnell was considering, of course, was that Cooley had turned traitor. *But if he'd done that, he wouldn't have come here, would he?* the chief of the ULA thought. *He knows me, knows where I live, knows McKenney, knows Sean Miller, knows about the fishing fleet at Dundalk.* O'Donnell realized that Cooley knew quite a lot. No, if he'd gone tout, he wouldn't be here. Cooley was sweating despite the air conditioning in the car. Dennis didn't have the belly to risk his life that way. He could see that.

"So, Dennis, what are we to do with you?"

Cooley's heart was momentarily irregular, but he spoke with determination. "I want to be part of the next op."

"Excuse me?" O'Donnell's head came around in surprise.

"The fucking Brits—Kevin, they came after *me!*"

"That is something of an occupational hazard, you know."

"I'm quite serious," Cooley insisted.

It wouldn't hurt to have another man. . . . "Are you in shape for it?"

"I will be."

The chief made his decision. "Then you can start this afternoon."

"What is it, then?"

O'Donnell explained.

"It would seem that your hunch was correct, Doctor Ryan," the man with the rimless glasses said the next afternoon. "Maybe I will take you to the track."

He was standing outside one of the huts, a dumpy little man with a head that shone from the sunlight reflecting off his sweaty, hairless dome. Camp -18 was the one.

"Excellent," Cantor observed. "Our English friends have really scored on this one. Thanks," he said to the photo expert.

"When's the op?" Ryan asked after he left.

"Early morning, day after tomorrow. Our time . . . eight in the evening, I think."

"Can I watch in real time?"

"Maybe."

"This is a secret that's hard to keep," he said.

"Most of the good ones are," Cantor agreed. "But—"

"Yeah, I know." Jack put his coat on and locked up his files. "Tell the Admiral that I owe him one."

Driving home, Ryan thought about what might be happening. He realized that his anticipation was not very different from . . . Christmas? No, that was not the right way to think about this. He wondered how his father had felt right before a big arrest after a lengthy investigation. It was something he'd never asked. He did the next best thing. He forgot about it, as he was supposed to do with everything that he saw at Langley.

There was a strange car parked in front of the house when he got there, just beyond the nearly completed swimming pool. On inspection he saw that it had diplomatic tags. He went inside to find three men talking to his wife. He recognized one but couldn't put a name on him.

"Hello, Doctor Ryan, I'm Geoffrey Bennett from the British Embassy. We met before at—"

"Yeah, I remember now. What can we do for you?"

"Their Royal Highnesses will be visiting the States in a few weeks. I understand that you offered an invitation when you met, and they wish to see if it remains open."

"Are you kidding?"

"They're not kidding, Jack, and I already said yes," his wife informed him. Even Ernie was wagging his tail in anticipation.

"Of course. Please tell them that we'd be honored to have them down. Will they be staying the night?"

"Probably not. It was hoped that they could come in the evening."

"For dinner? Fine. What day?"

"Friday, 30th July."

"Done."

"Excellent. I hope you won't mind if our security people—plus your Secret Service chaps—conduct a security sweep in the coming week.''

"Do I have to be home for that?''

"I can do it, Jack. I'm off work now, remember?''

"Oh, of course,'' Bennett said. "When is the baby due?''

"First week of August—that might be a problem for this,'' Cathy realized belatedly.

"If something unexpected happens, you may be sure that Their Highnesses will understand. One more thing. This is a private matter, not one of the public events for the trip. We must ask that you keep this entirely confidential.''

"Sure, I understand,'' Ryan said.

"If they're going to be here for dinner, is there anything we shouldn't serve?'' Cathy asked.

"What do you mean?'' Bennett responded.

"Well, some people are allergic to fish, for example.''

"Oh, I see. No, I know of nothing along those lines.''

"Okay, the basic Ryan dinner,'' Jack said. "I—uh-oh.''

"What's the matter?'' Bennett asked.

"We're having company that night.''

"Oh,'' Cathy nodded. "Robby and Sissy.''

"Can't you cancel?''

"It's a going-away party. Robby—he's a Navy fighter pilot, we both teach at the Academy—is transferring back to the fleet. Would they mind?''

"Doctor Ryan, His Highness—''

"His Highness is a good guy. So's Robby. He was there that night we met. I can't cancel him out, Mr. Bennett. He's a friend. The good news is, His Highness will like him. He used to fly fighter planes, too, right?''

"Well, yes, but—''

"Do you remember the night we met? Without Robby I might not have gotten through it. Look, this guy's a lieutenant commander in the United States Navy who happens to fly a forty-million-dollar fighter airplane. He probably is not a security risk. His wife plays one hell of a piano.'' Ryan saw that he hadn't quite gotten through yet. "Mr. Bennett, check Rob out through your attaché and ask His Highness if it's all right.''

"And if he objects?"

"He won't. I've met him. Maybe he's a better guy than you give him credit for," Jack observed. *He won't object, you dummy. It's the security pukes who'll throw a fit.*

"Well." That remark took him somewhat aback. "I cannot fault your sense of loyalty, Doctor. I will pass this through His Highness's office. But I must insist that you do not tell Commander Jackson anything."

"You have my word." Jack nearly laughed. He couldn't wait to see the look on Robby's face. This would finally even the score for that kendo match.

"Contraction peaks," Jack said that night. They were practicing the breathing exercises in preparation for the delivery. His wife started panting. Jack knew that this was a serious business. It merely looked ridiculous. He checked the numbers on his digital watch. "Contraction ends. Deep, cleansing breath. I figure steaks on the grill, baked potatoes, and fresh corn on the cob, with a nice salad."

"It's too plain," Cathy protested.

"Everywhere they go over here, people will be hitting them with that fancy French crap. Somebody ought to give them a decent American meal. You know I do a mean steak on the grill, and your spinach salad is famous from here to across the road."

"Okay." Cathy started laughing. It was becoming uncomfortable for her to do so. "If I stand over a stove for more than a few minutes, I get nauseous anyway."

"It must be tough, being pregnant."

"You should try it," she suggested.

Her husband went on: "It's the *only* hard thing women have to do, of course."

"What!" Cathy's eyes nearly popped out.

"Look at history. Who has to go out and kill the buffalo? The man. Who has to carry the buffalo back? The man. Who has to drive off the bear? The man. We do all the hard stuff. I still have to take out the garbage every night! Do I ever complain about that?" He had her laughing again. He'd read her mood right. She didn't want sympathy. She was too proud of herself for that.

"I'd hit you on the head, but there's no sense in breaking a perfectly good club over something worthless."

"Besides, I was there the last time, and it didn't look all that hard."

"If I could move, Jack, I'd kill you for that one!"

He moved from opposite his wife to beside her. "Nah, I don't think so. I want you to form a picture in your mind."

"Of what?"

"Of the look on Robby's face when he gets here for dinner. I'm going to jiggle the time a little."

"I'll bet you that Sissy handles it better than he does."

"How much?"

"Twenty."

"Deal." He looked at his watch. "Contraction begins. Deep breath." A minute later, Jack was amazed to see that he was breathing the same way as his wife. That got them both laughing.

24

Connections Missed and Made

There were no new pictures of Camp -18 the day of the raid. A sandstorm had swept over the area at the time of the satellite pass, and the cameras couldn't penetrate it, but a geosynchronous weather satellite showed that the storm had left the site. Ryan was cued after lunch that day that the raid was on, and spent his afternoon in fidgety anticipation. Careful analysis of the existing photos showed that between twelve and eighteen people were at the camp, over and above the guard force. If the higher number were correct, and the official estimate of the ULA's size was also accurate, that represented more than half of its membership. Ryan worried a little about that. If the French were sending in only eight paratroopers . . . but then he remembered his own experiences in the Marine Corps. They'd be hitting the objective at three in the morning. Surprise would be going for them. The assault team would have its weapons loaded and locked—and aimed at people who were asleep. The element of surprise, in the hands of elite commandos, was the military equivalent of a Kansas tornado. Nothing could stand up to it.

They're in their choppers now, Ryan thought. He remembered his own experience in the fragile, ungainly aircraft. *There you are, all your equipment packed up, clean utilities, your weapons ready, and despite it all you're as vulnerable as a baby in the womb.* He wondered what sort of men they were, and realized that they wouldn't be too very different from the Marines he'd served with: all would be volunteers, doubly so since you also had to volunteer for parachute training. They'd opted a third time to be part of the antiterror teams. It would be partly for the extra pay they got and partly for the pride that always came with membership in a small, very special force—like the Marine Corps' Force Recon—but mostly they'd be there because they knew that this was a mission worth doing. To a man, professional soldiers despised terrorists, and each would dream about getting them in an even-up-battle—the idea of the Field of Honor had never died for the real professionals. It was the place where the ultimate decision was made on the basis of courage and skill, on the basis of manhood itself, and it was this concept that marked the professional soldier as a romantic, a person who truly believed in the rules.

They'd be nervous in their helicopter. Some would fidget and be ashamed of it. Others would make a great show of sharpening their knives. Some would joke quietly. Their officers and sergeants would sit quietly, setting an example and going over the plans. All would look about the helicopter and silently hate being trapped within it. For a moment Jack was there with them.

"Good luck, guys," he whispered to the wall. "*Bonne chance.*"

The hours crept by. It seemed to Ryan that the numbers on his digital watch were reluctant to change at all, and it was impossible for him to concentrate on his work. He was going over the photos of the camp again, counting the man-figures, examining the ground to predict for himself how the final approach would be made. He wondered if their orders were to take the terrorists alive. He couldn't decide on that question. From a legal perspective, he didn't think it really mattered. If terrorism were the modern manifestation of piracy—the analogy seemed apt enough—then the ULA was fair game for any nation's armed forces. On the other hand, taken alive, they could be put on trial and displayed. The psychological impact on other such groups might be real. If it didn't put the fear of God in them, it would at least get their attention. It would frighten them to know that they were not safe even in their most remote, most secure sanctuary. Some members might drift away, and maybe one or two of them would talk. It didn't take much intelligence information to hammer them. Ryan had seen that clearly enough. You needed to know where they were, that was all. With that knowledge you could bring all the forces of a modern nation to bear, and for all their arrogance and brutality, they couldn't hope to stand up to that.

Marty came into the office. "Ready to go over?"

"Hell, yes!"

"Did you have dinner?"

"No. Maybe later."

"Yeah." Together they walked to the annex. The corridors were nearly empty now. For the most part, CIA worked like any other place. At five the majority of the workers departed for home and dinner and evening television.

"Okay, Jack, this is real-time. Remember that you can't discuss any aspect of this." Cantor looked rather tired, Jack thought.

"Marty, if this op is successful, I will tell my wife that the ULA is out of business. She has a right to know that much."

"I can understand that. Just so she doesn't know how it happens."

"She wouldn't even be interested," Jack assured him as they entered the room with the TV monitor. Jean-Claude was there again.

"Good evening, Mr. Cantor, Professor Ryan," the DGSE officer greeted them both.

"How's the op going?"

"They are under radio silence," the Colonel replied.

"What I don't understand is how they can do it the same way twice," Ryan went on.

"There is a risk. A little disinformation has been used," Jean-Claude said cryptically. "In addition, your carrier now has their full attention."

"*Saratoga* has an alpha-strike up," Marty explained. "Two fighter squadrons and three attack ones, plus jamming and radar coverage. They're patrolling that 'Line of Death' right now. According to our electronics listening people, the Libyans are going slightly ape. Oh, well."

"The satellite comes over the horizon in twenty-four minutes," the senior technician reported. "Local weather looks good. We ought to get some clear shots."

Ryan wished he had a cigarette. They made the waiting easier, but every time Cathy smelled them on his breath, there was hell to pay. At this point the raiding force would be crawling across the last thousand yards. Ryan had done the drill himself. They'd come away with bloody hands and knees, sand rubbed into the wounds. It was an incredibly tiring thing to do, made more difficult still by the presence of armed soldiers at the objective. You had to time your moves for when they were looking the other way, and you had to be quiet. They'd be carrying the bare minimum of gear, their personal weapons, maybe some grenades, a few radios, slinking across the ground the way a tiger did, watching and listening.

Everyone was staring at the blank TV monitor now, each of them bewitched by his imagination's picture of what was happening.

"Okay," the technician said, "cameras coming on line, attitude and tracking controls in automatic, programming telemetry received. Target acquisition in ninety seconds."

The TV picture lit up. It showed a test pattern. Ryan hadn't seen one of those in years.

"Getting a signal."

Then the picture appeared. Disappointingly, it was in infrared again. Somehow Ryan had expected otherwise. The low angle showed very little of the camp. They could discern no movement at all. The technician frowned and increased the viewing field. Nothing more, not even the helicopters.

The viewing angle changed slowly, and it was hard to believe that the reconnaissance satellite was racing along at over eighteen thousand miles per hour. Finally they could see all of the huts. Ryan blinked. Only one was lit up on the infrared picture. *Uh-oh.* Only one hut—the guards' one—had had its heater on. What did that mean? *They're gone—nobody's home . . . and the assault force isn't there either.*

Ryan said what the others didn't want to say: "Something's gone wrong."

"When can they tell us what happened?" Cantor asked.

"They cannot break silence for several hours."

Two more hours followed. They were spent in Marty's office. Food was sent up. Jean-Claude didn't say anything, but he was clearly disappointed by it. Cantor didn't touch his at all. The phone rang. The Frenchman took the call, and spoke in his native tongue. The conversation lasted four or five minutes. Jean-Claude hung up and turned.

"The assault force came upon a regular army unit a hundred kilometers from the camp, apparently a mechanized unit on an exercise.

This was not expected. Coming in low, they encountered them quite suddenly. It opened fire on the helicopters. Surprise was lost, and they had to turn back." Jean-Claude didn't have to explain that, at best, operations like this were successful barely more than half the time.

"I was afraid of that." Jack stared at the floor. He didn't need to have anyone tell him that the mission could not be repeated. They had run a serious risk, trying a covert mission the same way twice. There would be no third attempt. "Are your people safe?"

"Yes, one helicopter was damaged, but managed to return to base. No casualties."

"Please thank your people for trying, Colonel." Cantor excused himself and walked to his private bathroom. Once in there, he threw up. His ulcers were bleeding again. Marty tried to stand, but found himself faint. He fell against the door with a hard rap on the head.

Jack heard the noise and went to see what it was. It was hard to open the door, but he finally saw Marty lying there. Ryan's first instinct was to tell Jean-Claude to call for a doctor, but Jack himself didn't know how to do that here. He helped Marty to his feet and led him back into his office, setting him in a chair.

"What's the matter?"

"He just tossed up blood—how do you call . . ." Ryan said the hell with it and dialed Admiral Greer's line.

"Marty's collapsed—we need a doctor here."

"I'll take care of it. Be there in two minutes," the Admiral answered.

Jack went into the bathroom and got a glass of water and some toilet paper. He used this to wipe Cantor's mouth, then held up the glass. "Wash your mouth out."

"I'm okay," the man protested.

"Bullshit," Ryan replied. "You jerk. You've been working too damned late, trying to finish up all your stuff before you leave, right?"

"Got—got to."

"What you got to do, Marty, is get the hell out of here before it eats you up."

Cantor gagged again.

You weren't kidding, Marty, Jack thought. *The war is being fought here, too, and you're one of the casualties. You wanted that mission to score as much as I did.*

"What the hell!" Greer entered the room. He even looked a little disheveled.

"His ulcers let go," Jack explained. "He's been puking blood."

"Aw, Jesus, Marty!" the Admiral said.

Ryan hadn't known that there was a medical dispensary at Langley. Someone identifying himself as a paramedic arrived next. He examined Cantor quickly, then he and a security guard loaded the man on a wheelchair. They took him out, and the three men left behind stared at each other.

"How hard is it to die from ulcers?" Ryan asked his wife just before midnight.

"How old is he?" she asked. Jack told her. Cathy thought about it for a moment. "It can happen, but it's fairly rare. Somebody at work?"

"My supervisor at Langley. He's been on Tagamet, but he vomited blood tonight."

"Maybe he tried going without it. That's one of the problems. You give people medications, and as soon as they start feeling better, they stop taking the meds. Even smart people," Cathy noted. "Is it *that* stressful over there?"

"I guess it was for him."

"Super." It was the kind of remark that should have been followed by a roll-over, but Cathy hadn't been able to do that for some time. "He'll probably be all right. You really have to work at it to be in serious trouble from ulcers nowadays. Are you sure you want to work there?"

"No. They want me, but I won't decide until you lose a little weight."

"You'd better not be that far away when I go into labor."

"I'll be there when you need me."

"Almost got 'em," Murray reported.

"The same mob who raided *Action-Directe*, eh? Yes, I've heard that was a nicely run mission. What happened?" Owens asked.

"The assault group was spotted seventy miles out and had to turn back. On reexamination of the photos, it may be that our friends were already gone anyway."

"Marvelous. I see our luck is holding. Where did they go, you reckon?"

Murray grunted. "I've got to make the same assumption you have, Jimmy."

"Quite." He looked out the window. The sun would be rising soon. "Well, we've cleared the DPG man and told him the story."

"How'd he take it?"

"He immediately offered his resignation, but the Commissioner and I prevailed upon him to withdraw it. We all have our little foibles," Owens said generously. "He's a very good chap at what he does. You'll be pleased to learn that his reaction was precisely the same as yours. He said we should arrange for His Highness to fall off one of his polo ponies and break his leg. Please don't quote either of us on that!"

"It's a hell of a lot easier to protect cowards, isn't it? It's the brave ones who complicate our lives. You know something? He's going to be a good king for you someday. If he lives long enough," Murray added. It was impossible not to like the kid, he thought. And his wife was dynamite. "Well, if it makes you feel any better, the security on 'em in the States will be *tight*. Just like what we give the President. Even some of the same people are involved."

That's supposed to make me feel happy? Owens asked himself silently, remembering how close several American Presidents had come to death at the hands of madmen, not to mention John F. Kennedy. It could be, of course, that the ULA was back wherever it lived, but all his instincts told him otherwise. Murray was a close friend, and he also knew and respected the Secret Service agents who'd formed the security detail. But the security of Their Highnesses was properly the responsibility of the Yard, and he didn't like the fact that it was now largely in others' hands. Owens had been professionally offended the last time the American President had been in the U.K., when the Secret Service had made a big show of shoving the locals as far aside as they dared. Now he understood them a little better.

"How much is the rent?" Dobbens asked.

"Four-fifty a month," the agent answered. "That's furnished."

"Uh-huh." The furnishings weren't exactly impressive, Alex saw. They didn't have to be.

"When can my cousin move in?"

"It's not for you?"

"No, it's my cousin. He's in the same business I am," Alex explained. "He's new to the area. I'll be responsible for the rent, of course. A three-month deposit, you said?"

"Okay." The agent had specified two months' rent up-front.

"Cash all right?" Dobbens asked.

"Sure. Let's go back to the office and get the paperwork done."

"I'm running a little late, I'm afraid. Don't you have the contract with you?"

The agent nodded. "Yeah, I can do it right here." He walked out to his car and came back with a clipboard and a boilerplate rental contract. He didn't know that he was condemning himself to death, that no one else from his office had seen this man's face.

"My mail goes to a box—I get it on the way into work." That took care of the address.

"What sort of work, did you say?"

"I work at the Applied Physics Laboratory, electrical engineer. I'm afraid I can't be more specific than that. We do a lot of government work, you understand." Alex felt vaguely sorry for the man. He was pleasant enough, and hadn't given him a runaround like many real estate people did. It was too bad. *That's life.*

"You always deal in cash?"

"That's one way to make sure you can afford it," Alex chuckled.

"Could you sign here, please?"

"Sure thing." Alex did so with his own pen, left-handed as he'd practiced. "And that's thirteen-fifty." He counted off the bills.

"That was easy," the agent said as he handed over the keys and a receipt.

"It sure was. Thank you, sir." Alex shook his hand. "He'll probably be moving in next week, certainly by the week after that."

The two men walked out to their cars. Alex wrote down the agent's tag number: he drove his own car, not one belonging to the brokerage. Alex noted his description anyway, just to be sure that his people didn't kill the wrong man. He was glad he hadn't drawn a woman agent. Alex knew that he'd have to overcome that prejudice sooner or later, but for the moment it was an issue he was just as happy to avoid. He followed the agent for a few blocks, then turned off and doubled back to the house.

It wasn't exactly perfect, but close enough. Three small bedrooms. The eat-in kitchen was all right, though, as was the living room. Most important, it had a garage, and sat on nearly an acre of ground. The lot was bordered by hedges, and sat in a semirural working-class neighborhood where the houses were separated by about fifty feet. It would do just fine as a safehouse.

Finished, he drove to Washington National Airport, where he caught a flight to Miami. There was a three-hour layover until he took another airplane to Mexico City. Miller was waiting for him in the proper hotel.

"Hello, Sean."

"Hello, Alex. Drink?"

"What do you have?"

"Well, I brought a bottle of decent whiskey, or you can have some of the local stuff. The beer isn't bad, but I personally stop short of drinking something with a worm in the bottle."

Alex selected a beer. He didn't bother with a glass.

"So?"

Dobbens drained the beer in one long pull. It was good to be able to relax—really relax. Play-acting all the time at home could be a strain. "I got the safehouse all set up. Did that this morning. It'll do fine for what we want. What about your people?"

"They're on the way. They'll arrive as planned."

Alex nodded approval as he got a second beer. "Okay, let's see how the operation's going to run."

"In a very real sense, Alex, you inspired this." Miller opened his briefcase and extracted the maps and charts. They went on the coffee table. Alex didn't smile. Miller was trying to stroke him, and Dobbens didn't like being stroked. He listened for twenty minutes.

"Not bad, that's pretty fair, but you're going to have to change a few things."

"What?" Miller asked. He was already angered by Dobbens' tone.

"Look, man, there's going to be at least fifteen security guys right here." Alex tapped the map. "And you're going to have to do them right quick, y'know? We're not talking street cops here. These guys are trained and well-armed. They're not exactly dumb, either. If you want this to work, man, you have to land the first punch harder. Your timing is off some, too. No, we have to tighten this up some, Sean."

"But they'll be in the wrong place!" Miller objected as dispassionately as he could manage.

"And you want them to be running around loose? No way, boy!

You'd better think about taking them out in the first ten seconds. Hey, think of them as soldiers. This ain't no snatch-and-run job. We're talking combat here.''

"But if the security is going to be as tight as you say—"

"I can handle that, man. Don't you pay attention to what I'm doing? I can put your shooters in exactly the right spot at exactly the right time.''

"And how the hell will you do that!" Miller was unable to calm himself anymore. There was just something about Alex that set him off.

"It's easy, man." Dobbens smiled. He enjoyed showing this hotshot how things were done. "All you gotta do . . .''

"And you really think you can get past them just like that!" Miller snapped after he finished.

"Easy. I can write my own work orders, remember?''

Miller struggled with himself again, and this time he won. He told himself to view Alex's idea dispassionately. He hated admitting to himself that the plan made sense. This amateur black was telling him how to run an op, and the fact that he was right just made it worse.

"Hey, man, it's not just better, it's easier to do." Alex backed off somewhat. Even arrogant whities needed their pride. This boy was used to having his own way. He was smart enough, Dobbens admitted to himself, but too inflexible. Once he got himself set on an idea, he didn't want to change a thing. He never would have made a good engineer, Alex knew. "Remember the last op we ran for you? Trust me, man. I was right then, wasn't I?''

For all his technical expertise, Alex did not have tremendous skills for handling people. This last remark almost set Miller off again, but the Irishman took a deep breath as he continued to stare at the map. *Now I know why the Yanks love their niggers so much.*

"Let me think about it.''

"Sure. Tell you what. I'm going to get some sleep. You can pray over the map all you want.''

"Who else besides the security and the targets?''

Alex stretched. "Maybe they're going to cater it. Hell—I don't know. I imagine they'll have their maid. I mean, you don't have that kind of company without one servant, right? She doesn't get hurt either, man. She's a sister, handsome woman. And remember what I said about the lady and the kid. If it's necessary, I can live with it, but if you pop 'em for fun, Sean, you'll answer to me. Let's try to keep this one professional. You have three legitimate political targets. That's enough. The rest are bargaining chips, we can use 'em to show good will. That might not be important to you, boy, but it's fucking well important to me. You dig?''

"Very well, Alex.'' Sean decided then and there that Alex would not see the end of this operation. It shouldn't be too hard to arrange. With his absurd sentimentality, he was unfit to be a revolutionary. *You'll die a brave death. At least we can make a martyr of you.*

Two hours later Miller admitted to himself that this was unfortunate. The man did have a flair for operations.

The security people were late enough that Ryan pulled into the driveway right behind them. There were three of them, led by Chuck Avery of the Secret Service.

"Sorry, we got held up,'' Avery said as he shook hands. "This is Bert Longley and Mike Keaton, two of our British colleagues.''

"Hello, Mr. Longley,'' Cathy called from the door.

His eyes went wide as he saw her condition. "My goodness, perhaps we should bring a physician in with us! I'd no idea you were so far along.''

"Well, this one will be part English.'' Jack explained. "Come on in.''

"Mr. Longley arranged our escort when you were in the hospital,'' Cathy told her husband. "Nice to see you again.''

"How are you feeling?'' Longley asked.

"A little tired, but okay,'' Cathy allowed.

"Have you cleared the problem about Robby?'' Jack asked.

"Yes, we have. Please excuse Mr. Bennett. I'm afraid he took his instructions a bit too literally. We have no problems with a naval officer. In fact, His Highness is looking forward to meeting him. So, may we look around?''

"If it's all right with you, I want to see that cliff of yours,'' Avery said.

"Follow me, gentlemen.'' Jack led the three through the sliding-glass doors onto the deck that faced Chesapeake Bay.

"Magnificent!'' Longley observed.

"The only thing we did wrong is that the living and dining room aren't separated, but that's how the design was drawn, and we couldn't figure a graceful way to change it. But all those windows do give us a nice view, don't they?''

"Indeed, also one that gives our chaps good visibility," Keaton observed, surveying the area.

Not to mention decent fields of fire, Ryan thought.

"How many people will you be bringing?" Jack asked.

"I'm afraid that's not something we can discuss," Longley replied.

"More than twenty?" Jack persisted. "I plan to have coffee and sandwiches for your troops. Don't worry, I haven't even told Robby."

"Enough for twenty will be more than ample," Avery said after a moment. "Just coffee will be fine." They'd be drinking a lot of coffee, the Secret Service man thought.

"Okay, let's see the cliff." Jack went down the steps from the deck to the grass. "You want to be very careful here, gentlemen."

"How unstable is it?" Avery asked.

"Sally has been past where the fence is twice. Both times she got smacked for it. The problem's erosion. The cliff's made out of something real soft—sandstone, I think. I've been trying to stabilize it. The state conservation people talked me into planting this damned kudzu, and—stop right there!"

Keaton had stepped over the low fence.

"Two years ago I watched a twenty-square-foot piece drop off. That's why I planted these vines. You don't think somebody's going to climb that, do you?"

"It's one possibility," Longley answered.

"You'd think different if you looked at it from a boat. The cliff won't take the weight. A squirrel can make it up, but that's all."

"How high is it?" Avery asked.

"Forty-three feet over there, almost fifty here. The kudzu vines just make it worse. The damned stuff's nearly impossible to kill, but if you try grabbing onto it, you're in for a big surprise. Like I said, if you want to check it, do it from a boat," Ryan said.

"We'll do that," Avery replied.

"Coming in, that driveway must be three hundred yards," Keaton said.

"Just over four hundred, counting the curves. It cost an arm and a leg to pave it."

"What about the swimming pool people?" It was Longley this time.

"The pool's supposed to be finished next Wednesday."

Avery and Keaton walked around the north side of the house. There were trees twenty yards from there, and a swarm of brambles that went on forever. Ryan had planted a long row of shrubs to mark the border. Sally didn't go in there either.

"This looks pretty secure," Avery said. "There's two hundred yards of open space between the road and the trees, then more open ground between the pool and the house."

"Right." Ryan chuckled. "You can set up your heavy machine guns in the treeline and put the mortars over by the pool."

"Doctor Ryan, we are quite serious about this," Longley pointed out.

"I'm sure. But it's an unannounced trip, right? They can't—" Jack stopped short. He didn't like the look on their faces.

Avery said, "We always assume that the other side knows what we're up to."

"Oh." *Is that all of it, or is there more?* He knew it wouldn't do any good to ask. "Well, speaking as a has-been Marine, I wouldn't want to hit this place cold. I know a little about how you guys are trained. I wouldn't want to mess with you."

"We try," Avery assured him, still looking around. The way the driveway came through the trees, he could use his communications van to block vehicles out entirely. He reminded himself that there would be ten people from his agency, six Brits, a liaison guy from the Bureau, and probably two or three State Police for traffic control on the road. Each of his men would have both a service revolver and a submachine gun. They practiced at least once a week.

Avery still was not happy, not with the possibility of an armed terrorist group running around loose. But all the airports were being watched, all the local police forces alerted. There was only one road in here. The surrounding terrain would be difficult even for a platoon of soldiers to penetrate without making all kinds of noise, and as nasty as terrorists were, they'd never fought a set-piece battle. This wasn't London, and the potential targets weren't driving blithely about with a single armed guard.

"Thank you, Doctor Ryan. We will check the cliff out from the water side. If you see a Coast Guard cutter, that'll be us."

"You know how to get to the station at Thomas Point? You take

Forest Drive east to Arundel-on-the-Bay and hang a right. You can't miss it."

"Thanks, we'll do that."

The real estate agent came out of the office just before ten. It was his turn to shut down. In his briefcase was an envelope for the bank's night depository and some contracts he'd go over the next morning before going into work. He set the case on the seat beside him and started the car. Two headlights pulled right in behind him.

"Can I talk to you?" a voice called in the darkness. The agent turned to see a shape coming toward him.

"I'm afraid we're closed. The office opens at—" He saw that he was looking at a gun.

"I want your money, man. Just be cool, and everything'll be okay," the gunman said. There was no sense terrifying the man. He might do something crazy, and he might get lucky.

"But I don't have any—"

"The briefcase and the wallet. Slow and easy and you'll be home in half an hour."

The man got his wallet first. It took three attempts to loose the button on his hip pocket, and his hands were quivering as he handed it over. The briefcase came next.

"It's just checks—no cash."

"That's what they all say. Lie down on the seat and count to one hundred. Don't stick your head up till you finish, and everything'll be just fine. Out loud, so's I can hear you." *Let's see, the heart's right about there. . . .* He reached his gun hand inside the open window. The man got to seven. When it went off, the sound of the silenced automatic was further muffled by being inside the car. The body jerked a few times, but not enough to require a second round. The gunman opened the door and wound up the window, then killed the engine and the lights before going back to his car. He pulled back onto the road and drove at the legal limit. Ten minutes later the empty briefcase and wallet were tossed into a shopping center dumpster. He got back onto the highway and drove in the opposite direction. It was dangerous to hold on to the gun, but that had to be disposed of more carefully. The gunman drove the car back to where it belonged—the family that owned it was on vacation—and walked two blocks to get his own.

Alex was right, as always, the gunman thought. *If you plan everything, think it all out, and most important, don't leave any evidence behind, you can kill all the people you want. Oh,* he remembered, *one more thing: you don't talk about it.*

"Hi, Ernie," Jack said quietly. The dog showed up as a dark spot on the light-colored carpet in the living room. It was four in the morning. Ernie had heard a noise and come out of Sally's room to see what it was. One thing about dogs, they never slept the way people did. Ernie looked at him for several minutes, his tail gyrating back and forth until he got a scratch between his ears, then he moved off, back to Sally's room. It was amazing, Jack thought. The dog had entirely supplanted AG Bear. He found it hard to believe that anything could do that.

They're coming back, aren't they? he asked the night. Jack rose off the leather couch and walked to the windows. It was a clear night. Out on the Chesapeake Bay, he could see the running lights of ships plying their way to or from the Port of Baltimore, and the more ornate displays of tug-barge combinations that plodded along more slowly.

He didn't know how he could have been so slow on the uptake. Perhaps because the activity at Camp -18 almost tracked with the pattern that he'd tried repeatedly to discern. It was about the right time for them to show up for refresher training. But it was equally likely that they were planning something big. *Like maybe right here. . . .*

"Jesus. You were too close to the problem, Jack," he whispered. It was public knowledge—had been for a couple of weeks—that they were coming over, and the ULA had already demonstrated its ability to operate in America, he remembered. *And we're bringing known targets into our home! Real smart, Jack.* In retrospect it was amazing enough. They'd accepted the backward invitation without the first thought . . . and even when the security people had been here the previous day, he'd made jokes. *You asshole!*

He thought over the security provisions, taking himself back again to his time in the Corps. As an abstract battle problem, his house was a tough objective. You couldn't do anything from the east—the cliff was a more dangerous obstacle than a minefield. North and south, the woods were so thick and tangled that even the most skilled commando types would be hard-pressed to come through without making a horrendous racket—and they sure as hell couldn't practice that kind of skill in a barren, treeless desert! So they had to come from the west. *How many people did Avery say—well, he didn't say, but I got the impression of about twenty.* Twenty security people, armed and trained. He remembered the days from the Basic Officer's Course at Quantico, and the nights. Twenty-two years old, invincible and immortal, drinking beer at local bars. There'd been one night at a place called the Command Post, the one with a picture of Patton on the wall, when he'd started talking to a couple of instructors from the FBI Academy, just south of the Marine base. They were every bit as proud as his brother Marines. *They never bothered to say "we are the best." They simply assumed that everyone knew it. Just like us.* The next day he'd accepted the invitation to shoot on their range and settle a gentlemanly wager. It had cost him ten dollars to learn that one of them was the chief firearms instructor. *God, I wonder if Breckenridge could beat him!* The Secret Service wouldn't be very different, given their mission. *Would you want to tangle with them? Hell, no!*

If I assume that the ULA is as smart as it seems to be . . . and it is an unannounced trip, a private sort of thing. . . . They won't know to come here, and even if they did, if they're too smart to take this one on . . . it should be safe, shouldn't it?

But that was a word whose meaning was forever changed. Safe. It was something no longer real.

Jack walked around the fireplace into the house's bedroom wing. Sally was sleeping, with Ernie curled up on the foot of the bed. His head came up when Jack entered the room, as if to say, "Yes?"

His little girl was lying there, at peace, dreaming a child's dreams while her father contemplated the nightmare that still hovered over his family, the one he'd allowed himself to forget for a few hours. He straightened the covers and patted the dog on the head before leaving the room.

Jack wondered how public figures did it. They lived with the nightmare all the time. He remembered congratulating the Prince for not letting such a threat dominate his life: *Well done, old boy, that'll show them! Be a fearless target!* It was a very different thing when you were yourself the target, Ryan admitted to the night, when your family was the target. You put on the brave face, and followed your instructions, and wondered if every car on the street could hold a man with a machine gun who was bent on making *your* death into a very special political statement. You could keep your mind off it during the day when you had work to do, but at night, when the mind wanders and dreams begin . . .

The dualism was incredible. You couldn't dwell on it, but neither could you allow yourself to forget it. You couldn't let your life be dominated by fear, but you couldn't ever lapse into a feeling of security. A sense of fatalism would have helped, but Ryan was a man who had always deemed himself the master of his fate. He would not admit that anything else could be true. He wanted to lash out, if not at *them,* then at destiny, but both were as far beyond his reach as the ships whose lights passed miles from his windows. The safety of his family had almost been assured—

We came so close! he cried silently to the night.

They'd almost done it. They'd almost won that one battle, and they had helped others win another. He *could* fight back, and he knew that he could do it best by working at that desk in Langley, by joining the team full-time. He would not be the master of his fate, but at least he could play a part. He had played a part. It had been important enough—if only an accident—to Françoise Theroux, that pretty, malignant thing now dead. And so the decision was made. The people with guns would play their part, and the man behind the desk would play his. Jack would miss the Academy, miss the eager young kids, but that was the price he'd have to pay for getting back into the game. Jack got a drink of water before going back to bed.

Plebe Summer started on schedule. Jack watched with impassive sympathy as the recently graduated high school seniors were introduced to the rigors of military life. The process was consciously aimed at weeding out the weak as early as possible, and so it was largely in the hands of upperclassmen who had only recently been through the same thing. The new youngsters were at the debatable mercy of the older ones, running around with their closely cropped hair to the double-time cadence of students only two years their senior.

"Morning, Jack!" Robby came over to watch with him from the parking lot.

"You know, Rob, Boston College was never like this."

"If you think this is a Plebe Summer," Jackson snorted, "you should have seen what it was like when I was here!"

"I bet they've been saying that for a hundred years," Jack suggested.

"Probably so." The white-clad plebes passed like a herd of buffalo, all gasping for air on the hot, humid morning. "We kept better formations, though."

"The first day?"

"The first few days were a blur," Jackson admitted.

"Packing up?"

Jackson nodded. "Most of the gear's already in boxes. I have to get my relief settled in."

"Me, too."

"You're leaving?" Robby was surprised.

"I told Admiral Greer that I wanted in."

"Admiral—oh, the guy at CIA. You're going to do it, eh? How did the department take it?"

"I think you can say that they managed to restrain their tears. The boss isn't real happy about all the time I missed this year. So it looks like we're both having a going-away dinner."

"Jeez, it's this Friday, isn't it?"

"Yeah. Can you show up about eight-fifteen?"

"You got it. You said not dressy, right?"

"That's right." Jack smiled. *Gotcha.*

The RAF VC-10 aircraft touched down at Andrews Air Force Base at eight in the evening and taxied to the same terminal used by Air Force One. The reporters noted that security was very tight, with what looked to be a full company of Air Police in view, plus the plainclothes Secret Service agents. They told themselves that security at this particular part of the base was always strict. The plane came to a halt at exactly the right place, and the stairs were rolled to the forward door, which opened after a moment.

At the foot of the stairs waited the Ambassador and officials from the State Department. Inside the aircraft, security men made a final check out the windows. Finally His Highness appeared in the doorway, joined by his young wife, waving to the distant spectators, and descending the stairs gingerly despite legs that were stiff from the flight. At the bottom a number of military officers from two nations saluted, and the State Department protocol officer curtsied. This would earn her a reprimand from the *Washington Post*'s arbiter of manners in the morning edition. The six-year-old granddaughter of the base commander presented Her Highness with a dozen yellow roses. Strobes flashed, and both royal personages smiled dutifully at the cameras while they took the time to say something pleasant to everyone in the receiving line. The Prince shared a joke with a naval officer who had once commanded him, and the Princess said something about the oppressive, muggy weather that had persisted into the evening. The Ambassador's wife pointed out that the climate here was such that Washington D.C. had once been considered a hazardous-duty station. The malarial mosquitoes were long gone, but the climate hadn't changed very much. Fortunately, everyone had air conditioning. Reporters noted the color, style, and cut of the Princess's outfit, especially her "daring" new hat. She stood with the poise of a professional model while her husband looked as casual as a Texas cowboy, as incongruous as that might have seemed, one hand in his pocket and a relaxed grin on his face. The Americans who'd never met the couple before found him wonderfully easygoing, and of course every man there had long since fallen in love with the Princess, along with most of the Western world.

The security people saw none of this. They all had their backs to the scene, their eyes scanning the crowd, their faces stamped into the same serious expression while each with various degrees of emphasis thought: *Please, God, not while I'm on duty.* Every one had a radio earpiece constantly providing information that their brains monitored while their eyes were otherwise occupied.

Finally they moved to the embassy's Rolls-Royce, and the motorcade formed up. Andrews had a number of gates, and the one they took had been decided upon only an hour before. The route into town was its own traffic jam of marked and unmarked cars. Two additional Rolls-Royce automobiles, of exactly the same model and color, were dispersed through the procession, each with a lead- and chase-car, and a helicopter was overhead. If anyone had taken the time to count the firearms present, the total would have been nearly a hundred. The arrival had been timed to allow swift passage through Washington, and twenty-five minutes later the motorcade got to the British Embassy. A few minutes after that, Their Highnesses were safely in the building, and for the moment the responsibility of someone else. Most of the local security people dispersed, heading back to their homes or stations, but ten men and women stayed around the building, most invisibly hidden in cars and vans, while a few extra uniformed police walked the perimeter.

* * *

"America," O'Donnell said. "The land of opportunity." The television news coverage came on at eleven, and had tape of the arrival.

"What do you suppose they're doing now?" Miller asked.

"Working on their jet lag, I imagine," his chief observed. "Getting a good night's sleep. So, all ready here?"

"Yes, the safehouse is all prepared for tomorrow. Alex and his people are ready, and I've gone over the changes in the plan."

"They're from Alex, too?"

"Yes, and if I hear one more bit of advice from that arrogant bastard—"

"He is one of our revolutionary brethren," O'Donnell noted with a smile. "But I know what you mean."

"Where's Joe?"

"Belfast. He'll run Phase Two."

"The timing is all set?"

"Yes. Both brigade commanders, and the whole Army Council. We should be able to get them all. . . ." O'Donnell finally revealed his plan in toto. McKenney's penetration agents either worked closely with all of the senior PIRA people or knew those who did. On command from O'Donnell, they would assassinate them all, completely removing the Provisionals' military leadership. There would be no one left to run the Organization . . . except one man whose masterstroke mission would catapult him back to respectability with rank-and-file Provos. With his hostages, he'd get the release of all the men "behind the wire" even if it meant mailing the Prince of Wales to Buckingham Palace one cubic centimeter at a time. O'Donnell was certain of this. For all the brave, pious talk in Whitehall, it was centuries since an English king had faced death, and the idea of martyrdom sat better with revolutionaries than with those in power. Public pressure would see to that. They would *have* to negotiate to save the life of the heir to the throne. The scope of this operation would enliven the Movement, and Kevin Joseph O'Donnell would lead a revolution reborn in boldness and blood. . . .

"Changing of the guard, Jack?" Marty observed. He, too, had packed up his things. A security officer would check the box before he left.

"How are you feeling?"

"Better, but you can get tired of watching daytime TV."

"Taking all your pills?" Ryan asked.

"I'll never forget again, Mom," was the answer.

"I see there's nothing new on our friends."

"Yeah. They dropped back into that black hole they live in. The FBI is worried that they're over here, of course, but there hasn't even been a hint of it. Of course, whenever anybody's felt secure dealing with these bastards, they've gotten bit on the ass. Still, about the only outfit that isn't on alert is the Delta Force. All kinds of assets are standing by. If they're over here and they show anybody a whisker, the whole world is going to come crashing in on them. 'Call in the whole world.' We used to say that in Vietnam." Cantor grunted. "I'll be in Monday and Tuesday. You don't have to say goodbye yet. Have a good weekend."

"You too." Ryan walked out, with a new security pass hanging around his neck and his jacket draped over his shoulder. It was hot outside, and his Rabbit didn't have air conditioning. The drive home along Route 50 was complicated by all the people heading to Ocean City for the weekend, anything to get away from the heat that had covered the area like an evil spell for two weeks. They were in for a surprise, Jack thought. A cold front was supposed to come through.

"Howard County Police," the Desk Sergeant said. "Can I help you?"

"This is 911, right?" It was a male voice.

"Yes, sir. What seems to be the problem?"

"Hey, uh, my wife said I shouldn't get involved, you know, but—"

"Can you give me your name and phone number, please?"

"No way—look, this house, uh, down the street. There's people there with guns, you know? Machine guns."

"Say that again." The Sergeant's eyes narrowed.

"Machine guns—no shit, I saw an M-60 machine gun, like in the Army—y'know, thirty caliber, feeds off a belt, heavy bitch to pack along, a real friggin' machine gun. I saw some other stuff, too."

"Where?"

The voice became rapid. "Eleven-sixteen Green Cottage Lane. There's maybe—I mean I saw four of 'em, one black and three white. They were unloading the guns from a van. It was three in the morning. I had to get up an' take a leak, and I looked out the bathroom window, y'know? The garage door was open, and the light was on, and when they passed the gun across, it was in the light, like, and I could tell it was a sixty. Hey, I used to carry one in the Army, y'know? Anyway, that's it, man, you wanna do something about it, that's your lookout.'' The line clicked off. The Sergeant called his captain at once.

"What is it?'' The Sergeant handed over his notes. "Machine gun? M-60?''

"He said it was—he said it was a thirty-caliber that feeds off a belt. That's the M-60. That alert we got from the FBI, Captain . . .''

"Yeah.'' The Station Commander had visions of promotion dangling before his eyes—but also visions of his men in a pitched battle where the perpetrators had better weapons. "Get a car out there. Tell them to keep out of sight and take no action. I'm going to request a SWAT callup and get hold of the feds.''

Less than a minute later a police car was heading to the area. The responding officer was a six-year veteran of the county police who very much wanted to be a seven-year veteran. It took him almost ten minutes to reach the scene. He parked his car a block away, behind a large shrub, and was able to watch the house without exposing himself as a police officer. The shotgun that usually hung under the dashboard was in his sweating hands now, with a double-ought buck round chambered. Another car was four minutes behind his, and two more officers joined him. Then the whole world really did seem to arrive. First a patrol sergeant, then a lieutenant, then two captains, and finally, two agents from the FBI's Baltimore office. The officer who had first responded was now one of the Indians in a tribe top-heavy with chiefs.

The FBI Special Agent in Charge for the Baltimore office set up a radio link with the Washington headquarters, but left the operation in the hands of the local police. The county police had its own SWAT team, like most local forces did, and they quickly went to work. The first order of business was to evacuate the people from the area's homes. To everyone's relief, they were able to do that from the rear in every case. The people removed from their homes were immediately interviewed. Yes, they had seen people in that house. Yes, they were mostly white, but there had been at least one black person. No, they hadn't seen any guns—in fact, they hardly saw the people at all. One lady thought they had a van, but if so, it was usually kept in the garage. The interviews went on while the SWAT team moved in. The neighborhood houses were all of the same style and design, and the men made a quick check through one to establish its layout. Another set up a scope-sighted rifle in the house directly across the street and used his sight to examine the target home's windows.

The SWAT team might have waited, but the longer they did that, the greater was the risk of alerting their quarry. They moved in slowly and carefully, skillfully using cover and concealment until they were within fifty feet of the target house. Anxious, sharp eyes scanned the windows for movement and saw none. *Could they all be asleep?* The team leader went in first, sprinting across the yard and stopping under a window. He held up a stick-on microphone and attached it to the corner of the window, listening to an earpiece for a sign of occupancy. The second-in-command watched the man's head cock almost comically to one side, then he spoke into a radio that all his team members could hear: "The TV's on. No conversation, I—something else, can't make it out." He motioned for his team to approach, one at a time, while he crouched under the window, gun at the ready. Three minutes later the team was ready.

"Team leader," the radio crackled. "This is Lieutenant Haber. We have a young man here who says a van went tearing out of that house about quarter to five—that's about the time the police radio call went out."

The team leader waved acknowledgment and treated the message as something that mattered not a bit. The team executed a forced entry maneuver. Two simultaneous shotgun blasts blew the hinges off the windowless side door and it hadn't even hit the floor before the team leader was through the opening, training his gun around the kitchen. Nothing. They proceeded through the house in movements that looked like a kind of evil ballet. The entire exercise was over in a minute. The radio message went out: "The building is secure."

The team leader emerged on the front porch, his shotgun pointed at the floor, and pulled off his black mask before he waved the others in. His hands moved back and forth across his chest in the universal wave-off signal. The Lieutenant and the senior FBI agent ran across the street as he wiped the sweat away from his eyes.

"Well?"

"You're gonna love it," the team leader said. "Come on."

The living room had a small-screen color TV on, sitting on a table. The floor was covered with wrappers from McDonald's, and the kitchen sink held what looked like fifty neatly stacked paper cups. The master bedroom—it was a few square feet larger than the other two—was the armory. Sure enough, there was an American M-60 machine gun, with two 250-round ammo boxes, along with a dozen AK-47 assault rifles, three of them stripped down for cleaning, and a bolt-action rifle with a telescopic sight. On the oaken dresser, however, was a scanner radio. Its indicator lights skipped on and off. One of them was on the frequency of the Howard County Police. Unlike the FBI, the local police did not use secure—that is, scrambled—radio circuits. The FBI agent walked out to his vehicle and got Bill Shaw on the radio.

"So they monitored the police call and split," Shaw said after a couple of minutes.

"Looks like it. The locals have a description of the van out. At least they bugged out so fast that they had to leave a bunch of weapons behind. Maybe they're spooked. Anything new coming in at your end?"

"Negative." Shaw was in the FBI's emergency command center, Room 5005 of the J. Edgar Hoover Building. He knew of the French attempt to hit their training camp. *Twice now they've escaped by sheer luck.* "Okay, I'll get talking to the State Police forces. The forensic people are on the way. Stay put and coordinate with the locals."

"Right. Out."

The security people were already setting up. Discreetly, he saw, their cars were by the pool, which had been filled up only a couple of days before, and there was a van which evidently contained special communications gear. Jack counted eight people in the open, two of them with Uzis. Avery was waiting for him when he pulled into the carport.

"Good news for a change—well, good and bad."

"How so?" Ryan asked.

"Somebody phoned the cops and said he saw some people with guns. They rolled on it real quick. The suspects split—they were monitoring the police radio—but we captured a bunch of guns. Looks like our friends had a safehouse set up. Unfortunately for them it didn't quite work out. We may have 'em on the run. We know what kind of car they're using, and the local cops have this area completely sealed off, and we're sweeping the whole state. The Governor has even authorized the use of helicopters from the National Guard to help with the search.''

"Where were they?''

"Howard County, a little community south of Columbia. We missed them by a whole five minutes, but we have them moving and out in the open. Just a matter of time.''

"I hope the cops are careful,'' Ryan said.

"Yes, sir.''

"Any problems here?''

"No, everything's going just fine. Your guests should be here about quarter to eight. What's for dinner?'' Avery asked.

"Well, I picked up some fresh white corn on the way home—you passed the place coming in. Steaks on the grill, baked potatoes, and Cathy's spinach salad. We'll give 'em some good, basic American food.'' Jack opened the hatch on the Rabbit and pulled out a bag of freshly picked corn.

Avery grinned. "You're making me hungry.''

"I got a caterer coming in at six-thirty. Cold cuts and rolls. I'm not going to let you guys work all that time without food, okay?'' Ryan insisted. "You can't stay alert if you're hungry.''

"We'll see. Thanks.''

"My dad was a cop.''

"By the way, I tried the lights around the pool, but they don't work.''

"I know, the electricity's been acting up the last couple of days. The power company says they have a new transformer up, and it needs work—something like that.'' Ryan shrugged. "Evidently it damaged the breaker on the pool line, but so far nothing's gone bad in the house. You weren't planning to go swimming, were you?''

"No. We wanted to use one of the plugs here, but it's out too.''

"Sorry. Well, I have some stuff to do.''

Avery watched him leave, and went over his own deployment plans one last time. A pair of State Police cars would be a few hundred yards down the road to stop and check anyone coming back here. The bulk of his men would be covering the road. Two would watch each side of the clearing—the woods looked too inhospitable to penetrate, but they'd watch them anyway. This was called Team One. The second team would consist of six men. There would be three people in the house.

Three more, one of them a communicator in the radio van, in the trees by the pool.

The speed trap was well known to the locals. Every weekend a car or two was set up on this stretch of Interstate 70. There had even been something about it in the local paper. But people from out of state didn't read that, of course. The trooper had his car just behind a small crest, which allowed cars heading up to Pennsylvania to fly by, right past his radar gun before they knew it. The pickings were so good that he never bothered chasing after anyone who did under sixty-five, and at least twice a night he nailed people for doing over eighty.

Be on the lookout for a black van, make and year unknown, the all-points call had said a few minutes before. The trooper estimated that there were at least five thousand such vans in the state of Maryland, and they'd all be on the road on a Friday night. Somebody else would have to worry about that. *Approach with extreme caution.*

His patrol car rocked like a boat crossing a wake as a vehicle zoomed past. The radar gun readout said 83. Business. The trooper dropped his car into gear and started moving after it before he saw that it was a black van. *Approach with extreme caution. . . . They didn't give a tag number. . . .*

"Hagerstown, this is Eleven. I am following a van, black in color, that I clocked at eighty-three. I am westbound on I-70, about three miles east of exit thirty-five."

"Eleven, get the tag number but do not—repeat *do not*—attempt to apprehend. Get the number, back off, and stay in visual contact. We'll get some backup for you."

"Roger. Moving in now." *Damn.*

He floored his accelerator and watched his speedometer go to ninety. The van had slowed a little, it seemed. He was now two hundred yards back. His eyes squinted. He could see the plate but not the number. He closed the distance more slowly now. At fifty yards he could make out the plate—it was a handicap one. The trooper lifted his radio microphone to call in the tag numbers when the rear doors flew open.

It all hit him in a moment: *This was how Larry Fontana got it!* He slammed on his brakes and tried to turn the wheel, but the microphone cable got caught on his arm. The police officer cringed and slid down behind the dashboard as the car slowed, and then he saw the flash, a sun-white tongue of flame that reached directly at him. As soon as he understood what that was, he heard the impacting rounds. One of his tires blew, and his radiator exploded, sending a shower of steam and water into the air. More rounds walked up the hood into the right side of the car, and the trooper dived under the steering wheel while the car bounced up and down on the flattened tire. Then the noise stopped. The State Police officer stuck his head up and saw the van was a hundred yards away, accelerating up the hill. He tried to make a call on the radio, but it didn't work. He discovered soon after that two bullets had blasted through the car's battery, now leaking acid on the pavement. He stood there for several minutes, wondering why he was alive, before another police car arrived.

The trooper was shaking badly enough that he had to hold the microphone in both hands. "Hagerstown, the bastard machine-gunned my car! It's a Ford van, looks like an eighty-four, handicap tag Nancy two-two-nine-one, last seen westbound on I-70 east of exit thirty—fi-five."

"Were you hit?"

"Negative, but the car's b-beat to shit. They used a goddamned machine gun on me!"

That really got things rolling. The FBI was again notified, and every available State Police helicopter converged on the Hagerstown area. For the first time, the choppers held men with automatic weapons. In Annapolis, the Governor wondered if he should use National Guard units. An infantry company was put on alert—it was already engaged in its weekend drill—but for the moment, he limited the Guard's active involvement to helicopter support of the State Police. The hunt was on in the central Maryland hill country. Warnings went out over commercial radio and TV stations for people to be on the alert. The President was spending the weekend in the country, and that was another major complication. Marines at nearby Camp David and a few other highly secret defense installations tucked away in the rolling hills hung up their usual dress blues and pistol belts. They substituted M-16 rifles and camouflage greens.

25

Rendezvous

They arrived exactly on time. A pair of State Police cars remained on the road, and three more loaded with security people accompanied the Rolls up the driveway to the Ryan house. The chauffeur, one of the security force, pulled right to the front and jumped out to open the passenger door. His Highness came out first, and helped his wife. The security people were already swarming all over the place. The leader of the British contingent conferred with Avery, and the detail dispersed to their predetermined stations. As Jack came down the steps to greet his guests, he had the feeling that his home had been subjected to an armed invasion.

"Welcome to Peregrine Cliff."

"Hello, Jack!" The Prince took his hand. "You're looking splendid."

"You, too, sir." He turned to the Princess, whom he'd never actually met. "Your Highness, this is a great pleasure."

"And for us, Doctor Ryan."

He led them into the house. "How's your trip been so far?"

"Awfully hot," the Prince answered. "Is it always like this in the summer?"

"We've had two pretty bad weeks," Jack answered. The temperature had hit ninety-five a few hours earlier. "They say that's going to change by tomorrow. It isn't supposed to go much past eighty for the next few days." This did not get an enthusiastic response.

Cathy was waiting inside with Sally. The weather was especially hard on her, this close to delivery. She shook hands, but Sally remembered how to curtsy from England, and performed a beautiful one, accompanied by a giggle.

"Are you quite all right?" Her Highness asked Cathy.

"Fine, except for the heat. Thank God for air conditioning!"

"Can we show you around?" Jack led the party into the living/dining room.

"The view is marvelous," the Prince observed.

"Okay, the first thing is, nobody wears a coat in my house," Ryan pronounced. "I think you call this 'Planter's Rig' over in England."

"Excellent idea," said the Prince. Jack took his jacket and hung it in the foyer closet next to his old Marine parka, then got rid of his own. By this time Cathy had everyone seated. Sally perched next to her mother, her feet high off the floor as she tried to keep her dress down on her knees. Cathy found it almost impossible to sit comfortably.

"How much longer?" the Princess asked.

"Eight days—of course with number two, that means any time."

"I shall find that out myself in seven more months."

"Really? Congratulations!" Both women beamed.

"Way to go, sir," Ryan observed.

"Thank you, Jack. How have you been?"

"I suppose you know the work I'm doing?"

"Yes, I heard last night from one of our security people. I've been told that you located and identified a terrorist camp that has since been . . . neutralized," the Prince said quietly.

Ryan nodded discreetly. "I'm afraid that I'm not able to discuss that."

"Understood. And how has your little girl done after . . ."

"Sally?" Jack turned. "How's my little girl?"

"I'm a *big* girl!" she replied forcefully.

"What do you think?"

"I think you've been damned lucky."

"I'd settle for a little bit more. I presume you've heard?"

"Yes." He paused. "I hope your chaps are careful."

Jack voiced agreement, then rose as he heard a car pull up. He opened the door to see Robby and Sissy Jackson getting out of the pilot's Corvette. The Secret Service's communications van moved to block the driveway behind them. Robby stormed up the steps.

"What gives? Who's here, the President?"

Cathy must have warned them, Jack saw. Sissy was dressed in a simple but very nice blue dress, and Robby had a tie on. Too bad.

"Come on in and join the party," Jack said with a nasty grin.

Robby looked at the two men by the pool, their jackets unbuttoned, and gave Jack a puzzled look, but followed. As they came around the brick fireplace, the pilot's eyes went wide.

"Commander Jackson, I presume." His Highness rose.

"Jack," Robby whispered. "I'm going to kill you!" Louder: "How do you do, sir. This is my wife, Cecilia." As usually happened, the people immediately split into male and female groups.

"I understand you're a naval aviator."

"Yes, sir. I'm going back to a fleet squadron now. I fly the F-14." Robby struggled to keep his voice under control. He was successful, mostly.

"Yes, the Tomcat. I've flown the Phantom. Have you?"

"I have a hundred twenty hours in them, sir. My squadron transitioned into fourteens a few months after I joined up. I was just getting the Phantom figured out when they took 'em away. I—uh—sir, aren't you a naval officer also?"

"Yes, Commander, I have the rank of captain," His Highness answered.

"Thank you. Now I know what to call you, Captain," Robby said with visible relief. "That's okay, isn't it?"

"Of course. You know, it does get rather tiresome when people act so awkwardly around one. This friend of yours here actually read me off some months ago."

Robby smiled finally. "You know Marines, sir. Long on mouth and short on brains."

Jack realized that it was going to be that kind of night. "Can I get anyone something to drink?"

"I gotta fly tomorrow, Jack," Robby answered. He checked his watch. "I'm under the twelve-hour rule."

"You really take that so seriously?" the Prince asked.

"You bet you do, Captain, when the bird costs thirty or forty mil. If you break one, booze better not be the reason. I've been through that once."

"Oh? What happened?"

"An engine blew when I put her in burner. I tried to get back but I lost hydraulic pressure five miles from the boat and had to punch out. That's twice I've ejected, and that's by-God enough."

"Oh?" This question got Robby started on how his test-pilot days at Pax River had ended. *There I was at ten thousand* . . . Jack went into the kitchen to get everyone some iced tea. He found two security types, an American and a Brit.

"Everything okay?" Ryan asked.

"Yeah. It looks like our friends got spotted near Hagerstown. They blasted a State Police car and split. The trooper's okay, they missed this one. Anyway, they were last seen heading west." The Secret Service agent seemed very pleased by that. Jack looked outside to see another one standing on the outside deck.

"You sure it's them?"

"It was a van, and it had handicap tags. They usually fall into patterns," the agent explained. "Sooner or later it catches up with them. The area's been sealed off. We'll get 'em."

"Good." Jack lifted a tray of glasses.

By the time he got back, Robby was discussing some aspect of flying with the Prince. He could tell since it involved elaborate hand movements.

"So if you fire the Phoenix inside that radius, he just can't evade it. The missile can pull more gees than any pilot can," Jackson concluded.

"Ah, yes, the same thing with the Sparrow, isn't it?"

"Right, Cap'n, but the radius is smaller." Robby's eyes really lit up. "Have you ever been up in a Tomcat?"

"No, I wish I could."

"For crying out loud, that's no big deal. Hell, we take *civilians* up all the time—I mean it has to be cleared and all that, but we've even had Hollywood actors up. Getting you a hop ought to be a snap. I mean, it's not like you're a security risk, is it?" Robby laughed and grabbed a glass of tea. "Thanks, Jack. Captain, if you've got the time, I've got the bird."

"I'd love to be there. We do have a little free time. . . ."

"Then let's do it," Jackson said.

"I see you two are getting along."

"Indeed," the Prince replied. "I've wanted to meet an F-14 pilot for years. Now, you say that telescopic camera arrangement is really effective?"

"Yes, sir! It's not that big a deal. It's a ten-power lens on a dinky little TV camera. You can identify your target fifty miles out, and it's Phoenix time. If you play it right, you can splash the guy before he knows you're in the same county, and that's the idea, isn't it?"

"So you try to avoid the dogfight?"

"ACM, you mean—air-combat maneuvering, Jack," Robby explained to the ignorant bystander. "That'll change when we get the new engines, Cap'n, but, yeah, the farther away you can take him, the better, right? Sometimes you have to get wrapped up in the fur-ball, but if you do that you're giving away your biggest advantage. Our mission is to engage the other guy as far from the boat as we can. That's why we call it the Outer Air Battle."

"It would have been rather useful at the Falklands," His Highness observed.

"That's right. If you engage the enemy over your own decks, he's already won the biggest part of the battle. We want to start scoring three hundred miles out, and hammer their butts all the way in. If your Navy'd had a full-size carrier, that useless little war never would have happened. Excuse me, sir. That wasn't your fault."

"Can I show you around the house?" Jack asked. It always seemed to happen. You worked to have one of your guests meet another, and all of a sudden you were cut out of the conversation.

"How old is it, Jack?"

"We moved in a few months before Sally was born."

"The woodwork is marvelous. Is that the library down there?"

"Yes, sir." The way the house was laid out, you could look down from the living room into the library. The master bedroom was perched over it. There had been a rectangular hole in the wall, which allowed someone in there to see into the living room, but Ryan had placed a print over it. The picture was mounted on a rail and could be slid aside, Jackson noticed. The purpose of that was clear enough. Jack led them to his library next. Everyone liked that the only window was over his desk and looked out over the bay.

"No servants, Jack?"

"No, sir. Cathy's talking about getting a nanny, but she hasn't sold me on that idea yet. Is everyone ready for dinner?"

The response was enthusiastic. The potatoes were already in the oven, and Cathy was ready to start the corn. Jack took the steaks from the refrigerator and led the menfolk outside.

"You'll like this, Cap'n. Jack does a mean steak."

"The secret's in the charcoal," Ryan explained. He had six gorgeous-looking sirloins, and a hamburger for Sally. "It helps to have good meat, too."

"I know it's too late to ask, Jack, but where do you get those?"

"One of my old stock clients has a restaurant-supply business. These are Kansas City strips." Jack transferred them to the grill with a long-handled fork. A gratifying sizzle rose to their ears. He brushed some sauce on the meat.

"The view is spectacular," His Highness observed.

"It's nice to be able to watch the boats go by," Jack agreed. "Looks a little thin now, though."

"They must be listening to the radio," Robby observed. "There's a severe-thunderstorm warning on for tonight."

"I didn't hear that."

"It's the leading edge of that cold front. They developed pretty fast over Pittsburgh. I'm going up tomorrow, like I said, and I called Pax Weather right before we left. They told me that the storms look pretty ferocious on radar. Heavy rain and gusts. Supposed to hit around ten or so."

"Do you get many of those here?" His Highness asked.

"Sure do, Captain. We don't get tornadoes like in the Midwest, but the thunder-boomers we get here'll curl your hair. I was bringing a bird back from Memphis last—no, two years ago, and it was like being on a pogo stick. You just don't have control of the airplane. Those suckers can be scary. Down at Pax, they're taking all the birds they can inside the hangars, and they'll be tying the rest down tight."

"It'll be worth it to cool things off," Jack said as he turned the steaks.

"Roger that. It's just your basic thunderstorm, Captain. We get the big ones three or four times a year. It'll knock down some trees, but as long as you're not in the air or out in a small boat, it's no big deal.

Down in Alabama with this kind of storm coming across, we'd be sweating tornadoes. Now that's scary!''

"You've seen one?''

"More 'n one, Cap'n. You get those mostly in the spring down home. When I was ten or so, I watched one come across the road, pick up a house like it was part of a Christmas garden, and drop it a quarter mile away. They're weird, though. It didn't even take the weathervane off my pappy's church. They're like that. It's something to see, all right—but you want to do it from a safe distance.''

"Turbulence is the main flying hazard, then?''

"Right. But the other thing is water. I know of cases where jets have ingested enough water through the intakes to snuff the engines right out." Robby snapped his fingers. "All of a sudden you're riding in a glider. Definitely not fun. So you keep away from them when you can.''

"And when you can't?''

"Once, Cap'n, I had to land on a carrier in one—at night. That's about as close as I've come to wetting my pants since I was two.'' He even threw in a shudder.

"Your Highness, I have to thank you for getting all of this out of Robby. I've known him for over a year and he's never admitted to being mildly nervous up there." Jack grinned.

"I didn't want to spoil the image," Jackson explained. "You have to put a gun to Jack's head to get him aboard a plane, and I didn't want to scare him any more than he already is." *Zing!* And Robby took the point.

It helped that the deck was now in the shade, and there was a slight northerly breeze. Jack manipulated the steaks over the coals. There were a few boats out on the bay, but most of them seemed to be heading back to harbor. Jack nearly jumped out of his skin when a jet fighter screamed past the cliff. He turned in time to see the white-painted aircraft heading south.

"Robby, what the hell is that all about? They've been doing that for two weeks.''

Jackson watched the plane's double tail vanish in the haze. "They're testing a new piece of gear on the F-18. What's the big deal?''

"The noise!" Ryan flipped the steaks over.

Robby laughed. "Aw, Jack, that's not noise. That's the sound of freedom."

"Not bad, Commander," His Highness judged.

"Well, how about the sound of dinner?" Ryan asked.

Robby grabbed the platter, and Jack piled the meat on it. The salads were already on the table. Cathy made a superb spinach salad, with homemade dressing. Jack noted that Sissy was bringing the corn and potatoes out, wearing an apron to protect her dress. He distributed the steaks and put Sally's hamburger on a roll. Next he got their daughter in a booster seat. The one awkward thing was that nobody was drinking. He'd gotten four bottles of a choice California red to go with the steaks, but it seemed that everyone was in a teetotaling mood.

"Jack, the electricity is acting up again," his wife reported. "For a while there I didn't think we'd get the corn finished."

The Secret Service agent stood in the middle of the road, forcing the van to stop.

"Yes, sir?" the driver said.

"What are you doing here?" The agent's coat was unbuttoned. No gun was visible, but the driver knew it was there somewhere. He counted six more men within ten yards of the van and another four readily visible.

"Hey, I just told the cop." The man gestured backward. The two State Police cars were only two hundred yards away.

"Could you tell me, please?"

"There's a problem with the transformer at the end of the road. I mean, you can see this is a BG and E truck, right?"

"Could you wait here, please?"

"Okay with me, man." The driver exchanged a look with the man in the right-front seat. The agent returned with another. This one held a radio.

"What seems to be the problem?"

The driver sighed. "Third time. There's a problem with the electrical transformer at the end of the road. Have the people here been complaining about the electricity?"

"Yeah," the second man, Avery, said. "I noticed, too. What gives?"

The man in the right seat answered. "I'm Alex Dobbens, field engineer. We have a new, experimental transformer on this line.

There's a test monitor on the box, and it's been sending out some weird signals, like the box is going to fail. We're here to check it out.''

"Could we see some ID, please?''

"Sure." Alex got out of the truck and walked around. He handed over his BG&E identification card. "What the hell's going on here?''

"Can't say." Avery examined the pass and handed it back. "You have a work order?''

Dobbens gave the man his clipboard. "Hey, if you want to check it out, you can call that number up top. That's the field-operations office at company headquarters in Baltimore. Ask for Mr. Griffin.''

Avery talked into his radio, ordering his men to do just that. "Do you mind if we look at the truck?''

"Be my guest," Dobbens replied. He led the two agents around. He noted also that four men were keeping a very close eye on things, and that they were widely separated, with their hands free. Others were scattered across the yard. He yanked open the sliding door and waved the two agents inside.

The agents saw a mass of tools and cables and test equipment. Avery let his subordinate do the searching. "Do you have to go back there now?''

"The transformer might go out, man. I could let it, but the folks in the neighborhood might be upset if the lights went off. People are like that, you know? Do you mind if I ask who you are?''

"Secret Service." Avery held up his ID. Dobbens was taken aback.

"Jeez! You mean the President's back there?''

"I can't say," Avery replied. "What's the problem with the trans-former—you said it was new?''

"Yeah, it's an experimental model. It uses an inert cooling agent instead of PBBs, and it has a built-in surge-suppressor. That's probably the problem. It looks like the unit's temperature-sensitive for some reason. We've adjusted it several times, but we can't seem to get it dialed in right. I've been on the project for a couple of months. Usually I let my people do it, but this time the boss wanted me to eyeball it myself." He shrugged. "It's my project.''

The other agent came out of the van and shook his head. Avery nodded. Next the chief agent called the radio van, whose occupants had called Baltimore Gas & Electric and confirmed what Alex had told them.

"You want to send a guy to watch us?'' Dobbens asked.

"No, that's okay. How long will it take?" Avery asked.

"Your guess is as good as mine, sir. It's probably something simple, but we haven't figured it out yet. The simple ones are the ones that kill you."

"There's a storm coming in. I wouldn't want to be up on a pole in one of those," the agent observed.

"Yeah, well, while we're sitting here, we're not getting much work done. Everything okay with you guys?"

"Yeah, go ahead."

"You really can't tell me who's in the neighborhood?"

Avery smiled. "Sorry."

"Well, I didn't vote for him anyway." Dobbens laughed.

"Hold it!" the second agent called.

"What's the matter?"

"That left-front tire." The man pointed.

"Goddammit, Louis!" Dobbens growled at the driver. The steel belt was showing on part of the tire.

"Hey, boss, it's not my fault. They were supposed to change it this morning. I wrote it up Wednesday," the driver protested. "I got the order slip right here."

"All right, just take it easy." Dobbens looked over to the agent. "Thanks, man."

"Can't you change it?"

"We don't have a jack. Somebody lifted it. That's a problem with company trucks. Something is always missing. It'll be all right. Well, we got a transformer to fix. See ya." Alex reboarded the truck and waved as the vehicle pulled off.

"Good one, Louis."

The driver smiled. "Yeah, I thought the tire was a nice touch. I counted fourteen."

"Right. Three in the trees. Figure four more in the house. They're not our problem." He paused, looking at the clouds that were building on the horizon. "I hope Ed and Willy made out all right."

"They did. All they had to do was hose down one pigmobile and switch cars. The pigs here were more relaxed than I expected," Louis observed.

"Why not? They think we're someplace else." Alex opened a toolbox and removed his transceiver. The agent had seen it and not questioned it. He couldn't tell that the frequency range had been altered.

There were no guns in the van, of course, but radios were far deadlier. He radioed what he'd learned and got an acknowledgment. Then he smiled. The agents hadn't even asked about the two extension ladders on the roof. He checked his watch. Rendezvous was scheduled in ninety minutes. . . .

"The problem is, there really isn't a civilized way to eat corn on the cob," Cathy said. "Not to mention buttering it."

"It was excellent, though," the Prince noted. "From a local farm, Jack?"

"Picked 'em off the stalk this afternoon," Ryan confirmed. "That's the best way to get it."

Sally'd become a slow eater of late. She was still laboring at her food, but nobody seemed anxious to leave the table.

"Jack, Cathy, that was a wonderful dinner," His Highness pronounced.

His wife agreed. "And no after-dinner speechmaking!"

"I guess all that formal stuff gets to be tiresome," Robby noted, trying to ask a question that he couldn't voice: *What's it like to be a prince?*

"It wouldn't be so bad if the speeches could be original, but I've been listening to the same one for years!" he said wryly. "Excuse me. I mustn't say such things, even around friends."

"It's not all that different at a History Department meeting," Jack said.

At Quantico, Virginia, the phone rang. The FBI's Hostage Rescue Team had its own private building, located at the end of the long line of firing ranges that served the Bureau's training center. An engineless DC-4 sat behind it, and was used to practice assault techniques on hijacked aircraft. Down the hill was the "Hostage House" and other facilities used every day for the team members to hone their skills. Special Agent Gus Werner picked up the phone.

"Hi, Gus," Bill Shaw said.

"Have they found 'em yet?" Werner asked. He was thirty-five, a short, wiry man with red hair and a brushy mustache that never would have been allowed under Hoover's directorship.

"No, but I want you to assemble an advance team and fly them up. If something breaks, we may have to move fast."

"Fair enough. Where are we going, exactly?"

"Hagerstown, the State Police barracks. S-A-C Baltimore will be waiting for you."

"Okay, I'll take six men. We can probably get moving in thirty or forty minutes, as soon as the chopper gets here. Buzz me if anything happens."

"Will do. See ya." Shaw hung up.

Werner switched buttons on the phone and alerted the helicopter crew. Next he walked across the building to the classroom on the far side. The five men of his ready-response group were lounging about, mostly reading. They'd been on alert status for several days. This had increased their training routines somewhat, but it was mainly to defend against boredom that came from waiting for something that probably wouldn't happen. Nighttimes were devoted to reading and television. The Red Sox were playing the Yankees on TV. These were not Brooks Brothers FBI agents. The men were in baggy jumpsuits lavishly equipped with pockets. In addition to being experienced field agents, nearly all were veterans of combat or peacetime military service, and each man was a match-quality marksman who fired several boxes of ammunition per week.

"Okay, listen up," Werner said. "They want an advance team in Hagerstown. The chopper'll be here in half an hour."

"There's a severe thunderstorm warning," one objected lightly.

"So take your airsick pills," Werner advised.

"They find 'em yet?" another asked.

"No, but people are getting a little nervous."

"Right." The questioner was a long-rifleman. His custom-made sniper rifle was already packed in a foam-lined case. The team's gear was in a dozen duffle bags. The men buttoned their shirts. Some headed off to the bathroom for a preflight pitstop. None were especially excited. Their job involved far more waiting than doing. The Hostage Rescue Team had been in existence for years, but it had yet to rescue a single hostage. Instead its members were mainly used as a special SWAT team, and they had earned a reputation as awesome as it was little known, except within the law-enforcement community.

"Wow," Robby said. "Here it comes. This one's going to be a beauty." In the space of ten minutes, the wind had changed from gentle breezes to gusts that made the high-ceilinged house resonate.

"It was a dark and stormy night," Jack chuckled. He went into the kitchen. Three agents were making sandwiches to take out to the men by the road. "I hope you guys have raincoats."

"We're used to it," one assured him.

"At least it will be a warm rain," his British colleague thought. "Thank you very much for the food and coffee." The first rumble of distant thunder rolled through the house.

"Don't stand under any trees," Jack suggested. "Lightning can ruin your whole day." He returned to the dining room. Conversation was still being made around the table. Robby was back to discussing flying. The current war-story was about catapults.

"You never get used to the thrill," he was saying. "In a couple of seconds you go from a standstill to a hundred fifty knots."

"And if something goes wrong?" the Princess asked.

"You go swimming," Robby answered.

"Mr. Avery," the hand-held radio squawked.

"Yeah," he answered.

"Washington's on the line."

"Okay, I'll be there in a minute." Avery walked down the driveway toward the communications van. Longley, the leader of the British contingent, tagged along. Both had left their raincoats there anyway, and they'd need them in a few minutes. They could see lightning flashes a few miles away, and the jagged strokes of light were approaching fast.

"So much for the weather," Longley said.

"I was hoping it would miss us." The wind lashed at them again, blowing dust from the plowed field on the other side of Falcon's Nest Road. They passed the two men carrying a covered plate of sandwiches. A black puppy trotted along behind in the hope that they'd drop one.

"This Ryan fellow's a decent chap, isn't he?"

"He's got a real nice kid. You can tell a lot about a man from his kids," Avery thought aloud. They got to the van just as the first sprinkles started. The Secret Service agent got on the radiophone.

"Avery here."

"Chuck, this is Bill Shaw at the Bureau. I just got a call from our forensics people at that house in Howard County."

"Okay."

At the other end of the connection, Shaw was looking at a map and frowning. "They can't find any prints, Chuck. They have guns, they have ammo, some of the guns were being cleaned, but no prints. Not even on the hamburger wrappers. Something feels bad."

"What about the car that got shot up in western Maryland?"

"Nothing, not a damned thing. Like the bad guys jumped in a hole and pulled it in behind them."

That was all Shaw had to say. Chuck Avery had been a Secret Service agent all of his adult life, and was normally on the Presidential detail. He thought exclusively in terms of threats. This was an inevitable consequence of his job. He guarded people whom other people wanted to kill. It had given him a limited and somewhat paranoid outlook on life. Avery's mind reviewed his threat briefing. *The enemy here is extremely clever. . . .*

"Thanks for the tip, Bill. We'll keep our eyes open." Avery got into his coat and picked up his radio. "Team One, this is Avery. Heads up. Assemble at the entrance. We have a possible new threat." *The full explanation will have to wait.*

"What's the matter?" Longley asked.

"There's no real evidence at the house, the lab people haven't found any prints."

"They couldn't have had time to wipe everything before they left." Longley didn't need much of a hint either. "It might all have been planned to—"

"Exactly. Let's get out and talk to the troops. First thing, I'm going to get the perimeter spread out some. Then I'll call for more police backup." The rain was pelting the van now. "I guess we're all going to get wet."

"I want two more people at the house," Longley said.

"Agreed, but let's brief the people first." He slid the door open and both men went back up the driveway.

The agents on perimeter duty came together where the driveway met the road. They were alert, but it was hard to see with the wind-driven rain in their faces and the stinging dust blowing from the field on the other side of the road. Several were trying to finish sandwiches. One agent did a head count and came up one short. He sent a fellow agent to fetch the man whose radio was evidently out. Ernie tagged along with him; this agent had given him half a sandwich.

*   *   *

"You want to retire to the living room?" Cathy waved at the seats a few feet away. "I'd like to clear these dishes away."

"I'll do it, Cath," Sissy Jackson said. "You go sit down." She went into the kitchen and got the apron. Ryan knew for certain that Cathy had warned the Jacksons—Sissy at least, since she was wearing what on further inspection seemed an expensive dress. Everyone stood, and Robby walked off to the bathroom for a head call.

"Here we go," Alex said. He was at the wheel now. "All ready?"

"Go!" O'Donnell said. Like Alex, he wanted to be out in front with his troops. "Thank God for the weather!"

"Right," Alex agreed. He flipped the van's headlights to high-beam. He saw two groups of agents, standing a few yards apart.

The security force saw the approaching lights, and, being trained men, they kept a close eye on it despite knowing who it was and what it had been doing. Thirty yards from them there was a flash and a bang. Some men reached instinctively for their guns, then stopped when they saw that the vehicle's left-front tire had blown and was fluttering on the road as the driver struggled to get the truck back under control. It stopped right in front of the driveway. No one had commented on the ladders before. No one noticed their absence now. The driver got out and looked at the wheel.

"Aw, shit!"

Two hundred yards away, Avery saw the truck sitting on the road, and his instincts set off an alarm. He started running.

The van's door slid back, revealing four men with automatic weapons.

The agents a few feet away reacted in a moment, but too late. Barely had the door moved when the first weapon fired. A cylindrical silencer hung on the muzzle, which muffled the noise, but not the tongue of white flame that hovered in the darkness, and five men were down in the first second. The other gunmen had already joined in, and the first group of agents was wiped out without having fired a single return shot. The terrorists leaped out of the side and back doors of the van and engaged the second group. One Secret Service agent got his Uzi up and fired a short burst that killed the first man out of the back of the van, but the man behind him killed the agent with his weapon. Two more of the guards were now dead, and the other four of the group dropped to the ground and tried to return fire.

"What the hell is that?" Ryan said. The sound was hard to distinguish through the noise of the rain and the recurring thunder. Heads throughout the room turned. There was a British security officer in the kitchen and two Secret Service agents on the deck outside the room. Their heads had already turned, and one man was reaching for his radio.

Avery's service revolver was out. As team leader he didn't bother carrying anything but his Smith & Wesson .357 Magnum. His other hand was in any case busy with his radio.

"Call Washington, we are under attack! We need backup right the hell now! Unknown gunmen on the west perimeter. Officers down, officers need help!"

Alex reached back into the truck and pulled out an RPG-7 rocket launcher. He could just make out the two State Police cars two hundred yards down the road. He couldn't see the cops, but they had to be there. He elevated the weapon to the proper mark on the steel sight and squeezed the trigger, adding yet another thundering noise to the flashing sky. The round fell a few feet short of the target, but its explosion lanced hot fragments through one gas tank. It exploded, bathing both cars in burning fuel.

"Hot damn!"

Behind him, the gunmen had spread out and flanked the Secret Service officers. Only one was still shooting back. Two more of the ULA shooters were down, Alex saw, but the rest closed in on the agent from behind and finished him with a barrage of fire.

"Oh, God!" Avery saw it, too. He and Longley looked at each other and each knew what the other thought. *They won't get them, not while I'm alive.*

"Shaw." The radio-telephone circuit crackled with static.

"We are under attack. We have officers down," the wall speaker said. "Unknown number of—it sounds like a fucking war out there! We need help and we need it now."

"Okay, stand by, we're working on it." Shaw gave quick orders and phone lines started lighting up. The first calls to go out went to the nearest state and county police stations. Next, the Hostage Rescue Team group on alert in Washington was ordered out. Their Chevy Suburban was sitting in the garage. He checked the wall clock and called Quantico on the direct line.

"The chopper's just landing now," Gus Werner answered.

"Do you know where the Ryan house is?" Shaw asked.

"Yeah, it's on the map. That's where our visitors are now, right?"

"It's under attack. How fast can you get there?"

"What's the situation?" Werner watched his men out the window, loading their gear into the helicopter.

"Unknown—we just rolled the team from here, but you may be the first ones in. The communications guy just called in, says they're under attack, officers down."

"If there's any additional information, get it to us. We'll be up in two minutes." Werner ran outside to his men. He had to shout at them to be heard under the turning rotor, then ran back to the building, where the watch officers were ordered to summon the rest of the team to the HRT headquarters. By the time he got back in the chopper, his men had their weapons out of their duffles. Then the helicopter lifted off into the approaching storm.

Ryan noted the flurry of activity outside as the British officer from the kitchen ran outside and conferred briefly with the Secret Service agents. He was just coming back inside when a series of lightning flashes illuminated the deck. One of the agents turned and brought his gun out—then fell backward. The glass behind him shattered. The other two men both dived for the deck. One rose up to fire and fell beside his comrade. The last came inside and shouted for everyone to lie flat. Jack had barely enough time to be horrified when another window shattered and the last security man was down. Four armed figures appeared where the broken glass was. They were all dressed in black, except for the mud on their boots and chests. One pulled off his mask. It was Sean Miller.

Avery and Longley were alone, lying in the middle of the yard. The Brit watched as a number of armed men checked the bodies of the

496 • TOM CLANCY

fallen agents. Then they formed into two groups and started moving toward the house.

"We're too bloody exposed here," Longley said. "If we're to do any good at all, we must be back in the trees."

"You go first." Avery held his revolver in both hands and sighted on a black-clad figure visible only when the lightning flashed. They were still over a hundred yards away, very long range for a handgun. The next flash gave him a target, and Avery fired, missing and drawing a storm of fire at himself. Those rounds missed, too, but the sound of thuds in the wet ground was far too close. The fire shifted. Perhaps they saw Longley running back to the trees. Avery fired another carefully aimed shot and saw a man go down with a leg wound. The return fire was more accurate this time. The Secret Service agent emptied his gun. He thought he might have hit another of them when everything stopped.

Longley made it to the trees and looked back. Avery's prone figure didn't move despite the gunmen fifty yards away. The British security officer shouted a curse and gathered the remaining people. The FBI liaison agent had only his revolver, the three British officers had automatic pistols, and the one Secret Service agent had an Uzi with two spare magazines. Even if there weren't people to protect, there wasn't anyplace to run.

"So we meet again," Miller said. He held an Uzi submachine gun and bent down to pick up another from one of the fallen guards. Five more men came in behind him. They spread out in a semicircle to cover Ryan and his guests. "Get up! Hands where we can see them."

Jack stood, with the Prince next to him. Cathy came up next, holding Sally in her arms, and finally Her Highness. Three men spun around when the kitchen door swung open. It was Sissy Jackson, trying to hold some plates while a gunman held on to her arm. Two plates fell to the floor and broke when he jerked her arm up.

They have a maid, Miller remembered, seeing the dark dress and the apron. *Black, handsome woman.* He was smiling now. The disgrace of his failed missions was far behind him. He had all his targets before him, and in his hands was the instrument to eliminate them.

"You get over here with the rest," he ordered.

"What the hell—"

"Move, nigger!" Another of the gunman, the shortest of the bunch, roughly propelled her toward the others. Jack's eyes fixed on him for a moment—where had he seen that face before. . . .

"You trash!" Sissy's eyes flared in outrage at that, her fear momentarily forgotten as she wheeled to snap back at the man.

"You should be more careful who you work for," Miller said. He gestured with his weapon. "Move."

"What are you going to do?" Ryan asked.

"Why spoil the surprise?"

Forty feet away, Robby was in the worst part of the house to hear anything. He'd been washing his hands, ignoring the thunder when the gunfire had erupted at the home's deck. Jackson slipped out of the bathroom and peered down the corridor to the living room, but saw nothing. What he heard was enough. He turned and went upstairs to the master bedroom. His first instinct was to call the police on the telephone, but the line was dead. His mind searched for something else to do. This wasn't like flying a fighter plane.

Jack has guns . . . but where the hell does he keep them . . . ? It was dark in the bedroom and he didn't dare to flip on a light.

Outside, the line of gunmen advanced toward the woods. Longley deployed his men to meet them. His military service was too far in the past, and his work as a security officer hadn't prepared him for this sort of thing, but he did his best. They had good cover in the trees, some of which were thick enough to stop a bullet. He ordered his only automatic weapon to the left.

"FBI, this is Patuxent River Approach. Squawk four-zero-one-niner, over."

Aboard the helicopter, the pilot turned the transponder wheels until the proper code number came up. Next he read off the map coordinates of his destination. He knew what it looked like from aerial photographs, but they'd been taken in daylight. Things could look very different at night, and there was also the problem of controlling the aircraft. He was flying with a forty-knot crosswind, and weather conditions deteriorated with every mile. In the back the HRT members were trying to get into their night-camouflage clothing.

"Four-zero-one-niner, come left to heading zero-two-four. Maintain current altitude. Warning, it looks like a pretty strong thunder cell is approaching your target," the controller said. "Recommend you do not exceed one thousand feet. I'll try to steer you around the worst of it."

"Roger." The pilot grimaced. It was plain that the weather ahead was even worse than he'd feared. He lowered his seat as far as it would go, pulled his belts tighter, and turned on his storm lights. The only other thing he could do was sweat, and that came automatically. "You guys in back, strap down tight!"

O'Donnell called for his men to stop. The treeline was a hundred yards ahead, and he knew that it held guns. One group moved left, the other right. They'd attack by echelons, with each group alternately advancing and providing fire support for the other. All his men wore black and carried submachine guns, except for one man who trailed a few yards behind the rest. He found himself wishing that they'd brought heavier weapons. There was still much to do, including removing the bodies of his fallen men. One was dead and two more wounded. But first—he lifted his radio to order one of his squads in.

On O'Donnell's right, the single remaining Secret Service agent tucked his left side against an oak tree and shouldered his Uzi. For him and his comrades in the trees, there was no retreat. The black metal sights were hard to use in the dark, and his targets were nearly invisible. Lightning again played a part, strobe-lighting the lawn for an instant that showed the green grass and black-clad men. He selected a target and fired a short burst, but missed. Both groups of attackers returned fire, and the agent cringed as he heard a dozen rounds hit the tree. The whole countryside seemed alive with the flashes of gunfire. The Secret Service agent came around again and fired. The group that had been approaching him directly was running to his left into the brambles. He was going to be flanked—but then they reappeared, firing their weapons into the bushes, and there were flashes firing *out*. Everyone was surprised by that, and suddenly no one had control of the situation.

O'Donnell had planned to advance his teams on either side of the clearing, but unexpectedly there was fire coming from the woodline to the south, and one of his squads was exposed and flanked from two directions. He evaluated the new tactical situation in an instant and started giving orders.

*   *   *

Ryan watched in mute rage. The gunmen knew exactly what they were doing, and that reduced his number of options to exactly zero. There were six guns on him and his guests, and not a chance that he could do anything about it. To his right, Cathy held on to their daughter, and even Sally kept quiet. Neither Miller nor his men made any unnecessary sound.

"Sean, this is Kevin," Miller's radio crackled with static. "We have opposition in the treeline. Do you have them?"

"Yes, Kevin, the situation is under control."

"I need help out here."

"We're coming." Miller pocketed his radio. He pointed to his comrades. "You three, get them ready. If they resist, kill them all. You two come with me." He led them out the broken glass doors and disappeared.

"Come on." The remaining three gunmen had their masks off now. Two were tall, about Ryan's height, one with blond hair, the other black. The other was short and going bald—*I know you, but from where?* He was the most frightening. His face was twisted with emotions that Jack didn't want to guess at. Blondie threw him a bundle of rope. An instant later it was plain that it was a collection of smaller pieces already cut and meant to tie them up.

Robby, where the hell are you? Jack looked over to Sissy, who was thinking the same thing. She nodded imperceptibly, and there was still hope in her eyes. The short one noticed.

"Don't worry," Shorty said. "You'll get paid." He set his weapon on the dinner table and moved forward while Blondie and Blackie backed off to cover them all. Dennis Cooley took the rope to the Prince first, yanking his hands down behind his back.

There! Robby looked up. Jack had set his shotgun on the top shelf of the walk-in closet, along with a box of shells. He had to reach to get them, and when he did so, a holstered pistol dropped to the floor. Jackson winced at the sound it made, but grabbed it from the holster and tucked it into his belt. Next he checked the shotgun, pulling back the bolt—there was a round in the chamber and the gun was on safe. *Okay.* He filled his pockets with additional rounds and went back into the bedroom.

Now what? This wasn't like flying his F-14, with radar to track targets a hundred miles away and a wingman to keep the bandits off his tail.

The picture . . . You had to kneel on the bed to see out of it— *Why the hell did Jack arrange his furniture like this!* the pilot raged. He set the shotgun down and used both hands to slide the picture aside. He moved it only a few inches, barely enough to see out. *How many . . . one, two . . . three. Are there any others . . . ? What if I leave one alive . . . ?*

As he watched, Jack was being tied up. The Prince—*the Captain,* Robby thought—already was tied, and was sitting with his back to the pilot. The short one finished Jack next and pushed him back onto the couch. Jackson next watched the man put hands on his wife.

"What are you going to do with us?" Sissy asked.

"Shut up, nigger!" Shorty replied.

Even Robby knew that this was a trivial thing to get angry about; the problem at hand was far worse than some white asshole's racist remark, but his blood turned to fire as he watched the woman he loved being handled by that . . . *little white shit!*

Use your head, boy, something in the back of his brain said. *Take your time. You have to get it right on the first try. Cool down.*

Longley was beginning to hope. There were friendlies in the trees to his left. Perhaps they'd come from the house, he thought. At least one of them had an automatic weapon, and he counted three of the terrorists dead, or at least not moving on the grass. He had fired five rounds and missed with every one—the range was just too great for a pistol in the dark—but they'd stopped the terrorists cold. And help was coming. It had to be. The radio van was empty, but the FBI agent to his right had been there. All they had to do was wait, hold on for a few more minutes. . . .

"I got flashes on the ground ahead," the pilot said. "I—"

Lightning revealed the house for a brief moment in time. They couldn't see people on the ground, but that was the right house, and there were flashes that had to be gunfire, half a mile off as the helicopter buffeted through the wind and rain. It was about all the pilot could see. His instrument lights were turned up full-white, and the lightning had decorated his vision with a stunning collection of blue and green spots.

"Jesus," Gus Werner said over the intercom. "What are we getting into?"

"In Vietnam," the pilot replied coolly, "we called it a hot LZ." *And I was scared then, too.*

"Get Washington." The copilot switched frequencies on the radio and waved to the agent in the back while both men orbited the helicopter. "This is Werner."

"Gus, this is Bill Shaw. Where are you?"

"We have the house in sight, and there's a goddamned battle going on down there. Do you have contact with our people?"

"Negative, they're off the air. The D.C. team is still thirty minutes away. The state and county people are close but not there yet. The storm's knocking trees down all over the place and traffic is tied up something fierce. You're the man on the scene, Gus, you'll have to call it."

The mission of the Hostage Rescue Team was to take charge of an existing situation, stabilize it, and rescue the hostages—peacefully if possible, by force if not. They were not assault troops; they were special agents of the FBI. But there were brother agents down there.

"We're going in now. Tell the police that federal officers are on the scene. We'll try to keep you informed."

"Right. Be careful, Gus."

"Take us in," Werner told the pilot.

"Okay. I'll skirt the house first, then come around in and land you to windward. I can't put you close to the house. The wind's too bad, I might lose it down there."

"Go." Werner turned. Somehow his men had all their gear on. Each carried an automatic pistol. Four had MP-5 machine guns, as did he. The long-rifleman and his spotter would be the first men out the door. "We're going in." One of the men gave a thumbs-up that looked a lot jauntier than anyone felt.

The helicopter lurched toward the ground when a sudden downdraft hammered at it. The pilot wrenched upward on his collective and bottomed the aircraft out a scant hundred feet from the trees. The house was only a few hundred yards away now. They skimmed over the southern edge of the clearing, allowing everyone a close look at the situation.

"Hey, the spot between the house and the cliff might be big enough after all," the pilot said. He increased power as the chopper swept to windward.

"Helicopter!" someone screamed to O'Donnell's right. The chief looked up, and there it was, a spectral shape and a fluttering sound. That was a hazard he'd prepared for.

Back near the road, one of his men pulled the cover off a Redeye missile launcher purchased along with the rest of their weapons.

"I have to use landing lights—my night vision is wasted," the pilot said over the intercom. He turned the aircraft half a mile west of the Ryan house. He planned to head straight past the house; then he'd drop and turn into the wind and slide up behind what he hoped was a wind shadow in its lee. *God,* he thought, *this* is *like Vietnam.* From the pattern of the flashes on the ground, it seemed that the house was in friendly hands. The pilot reached down and flipped on his landing lights. It was a risk, but one he had to accept.

Thank God I can see again, he told himself. The ground was visible through a shimmering curtain of rain. He realized that the storm was still worsening. He had to approach from windward. Flying into the rain would reduce his visibility to a few feet. At least this way he could see a couple of hundred or so—*what the hell!*

He saw a man standing all alone in the center of the field, aiming something. The pilot pushed down on the collective just as a streak of red light rocketed toward the helicopter, his eyes locked on what could only be a surface-to-air missile. The two seconds it took seemed to stretch into an hour as the missile passed through his rotor blades and disappeared overhead—he immediately pulled back on the control, but there was no time to recover from his evasion maneuver. The helicopter slammed into the middle of a plowed field, four hundred yards from the Ryan house. It wouldn't move again until a truck came to collect the wreckage.

Miraculously, only two men were hurt. Werner was one of them. It felt as though he'd been shot in the back. The rifleman pulled the door open and ran out with his spotter behind. The others went next, one of them helping Werner while another hobbled on a sprained ankle.

*   *   *

The Princess was next. She was taller than Cooley, and managed a look that contained more than mere contempt. The little man spun her around roughly to tie her hands.

"We have big plans for you," he promised when he finished.

"You little scum, I bet you don't even know how," Sissy said. It earned her a vicious slap. Robby watched, waiting for the blond-haired one to get in the clear. Finally he did, moving back toward the others. . . .

26

The Sound of
Freedom

Pellets fired from a shotgun disperse radially at a rate of one inch per yard of linear travel. A lightning flash blazed through the windows, and Ryan cringed on hearing the thunder immediately after—then realized it had followed too quickly to be thunder. The shot pattern had missed his head by three feet, and before he understood what had passed by him, Blondie's head snapped back, exploding into a cloud of red as his body fell backward to crash against a table leg. Blackie was looking out the window in the corner and turned to see his comrade go down without knowing how or why. His eyes searched frantically for a second, then a red circle the size of a 45-rpm record appeared in his chest and he was flung against the wall. Shorty was tying up Cathy's hands and concentrating a little too much. He hadn't recognized the first shot for what it was. He did with the second—too late.

The Prince sprang at him, knocking him down with a lowered shoulder before himself falling on the floor. Jack leaped over the coffee table and kicked wildly at Shorty's head. He connected, but lost his balance doing so and fell backward. Shorty was stunned for a moment, then shook it off and moved toward the dinner table, where his gun was. Ryan lurched to his feet too, and threw himself on the terrorist's legs. The Prince was back up now. Shorty threw a wild punch at him and tried to kick Ryan off his legs—then stopped when the warm muzzle of a shotgun pressed against his nose.

"You hold it right there, sucker, or I'll blow your head off."

Cathy already had the ropes shucked off her hands, and untied Jack first. He went over to Blondie. The body was still twitching. Blood was still pumping from the surreal nightmare that had been a human face thirty seconds before. Jack took the Uzi from his hands, and a spare magazine. The Prince did the same with Blackie, whose body was quite still.

"Robby," Jack said as he examined the safety-selector switch on the gun. "Let's get the hell away from here."

"Second the motion, Jack, but where to?" Jackson pushed Shorty's head against the floor. The terrorist's eyes crossed almost comically on the business end of the Remington shotgun. "I expect he might know something useful. How'd you plan to get away, boy?"

"No." It was all Cooley could muster at the moment. He realized that he was, after all, the wrong man for this kind of job.

"That the way it is?" Jackson asked, his voice a low, angry rasp. "You listen to me, boy. That lady over there, the one you called *niggah*—that's my wife, boy, that's my lady. I saw you hit her. So, I already got one good reason to kill you, y'dig?" Robby smiled wickedly, and let the shotgun trace a line down to Shorty's crotch. "But I ain't gonna kill ya. I'll do somethin' lots worse—

"I'll make a girl outa you, punk." Robby pushed the muzzle against the man's zipper. "Think fast, boy."

Jack listened to his friend in amazement. Robby never talked like this. But it was convincing. Jack believed that he'd do it.

So did Cooley: "Boats . . . boats at the base of the cliff."

"That's not even clever. Say goodbye to 'em, boy." The angle of the shotgun changed fractionally.

"*Boats! Two boats at the base of the cliff*. There are two ladders—"

"How many watching them?" Jack demanded.

"One, that's all."

Robby looked up. "Jack?"

"People, I suggest we go steal some boats. That firefight outside is getting closer.'' Jack ran to his closet and got coats for everyone. For Robby he picked up his old Marine field jacket that Cathy hated so much. ''Put this on, that white shirt is too damned visible.''

''Here.'' Robby handed over Jack's automatic. ''I got a box of rounds for the shotgun.'' He started transferring them from his pants to the jacket pockets and then hefted the last Uzi over his shoulder. ''We're leaving friendlies behind, Jack,'' he added quietly.

Ryan didn't like it either. ''I know, but if they get him, they win— and this ain't no place for women and kids, man.''

''Okay, you're the Marine.'' Robby nodded. That was that.

''Let's get outta here. I have the point. I'm going to take a quick look-see. Rob, you take Shorty for now. Prince, you take the women.'' Jack reached down and grabbed Dennis Cooley by the throat. ''You screw up, you're dead. No fartin' around with him, Robby, just waste him.''

''That's a roge.'' Jackson backed away from the terrorist. ''Up slow, punk.''

Jack led them through the shattered doors. The two dead agents lay crumpled on the wood deck, and he hated himself for not doing something about it, but Ryan was proceeding on some sort of automatic control that the Marine Corps had programmed into him ten years before. It was a combat situation, and all the lectures and field exercises were flooding back into his consciousness. In a moment he was drenched by the falling sheets of rain. He trotted down the stairs and looked around the house.

Longley and his men were too busy dealing with the threat to their front to notice what was approaching from behind. The British security officer fired four rounds at an advancing black figure and had the satisfaction of seeing him react from at least one hit when a hammering impact hurled him against a tree. He rebounded off the rough bark and half turned to see yet another black-clad shape holding a gun ten feet away. The gun flashed again. Within seconds the woodline was quiet.

''Dear God,'' the rifleman muttered. Running in a crouch, he passed the bodies of five agents, but there wasn't time for that. He and his spotter went down next to a bush. The rifleman activated his night scope and tracked on the woodline a few hundred yards ahead. The green picture he got on the imaging tube showed men dressed in dark clothes heading into the woodline.

"I count eleven," the spotter said.

"Yeah," the rifleman agreed. His bolt-action sniper rifle was loaded with .308 caliber match rounds. He could hit a moving three-inch target the first time, every time, at over two hundred yards, but his mission for the moment was reconnaissance, to gather information and forward it to the team leader. Before the team could act, they had to know what the hell was going on, and all they had now was chaos.

"Werner, this is Paulson. I count what looks like eleven bad guys moving into the trees between us and the house. They appear to be armed with light automatic weapons." He pivoted the rifle around. "Looks like six of them down in the yard. Lots of good guys down— Jesus, I hope there's ambulances on the way."

"Do you see any friendlies around?"

"Negative. Recommend that you move in from the other side. Can you give me a backup here?"

"Sending one now. When he gets there, move in carefully. Take your time, Paulson."

"Right."

To the south, Werner and two other men advanced along the tree-line. Their night-camouflage clothing was a hatchwork of light green, designed by computer, and even in the lightning they were nearly invisible.

Something had just happened. Jack saw a sudden flurry of fire, then nothing. Despite what he'd told Robby, he didn't like running away from the scene. But what else could he do? There was an unknown number of terrorists out there. He had only three armed men to protect three women and a child, with their backs to a cliff. Ryan swore and returned to the others.

"Okay, Shorty, show me the way down," Ryan said, pressing the muzzle of his Uzi against the man's chest.

"Right there." The man pointed, and Ryan swore again.

In all the time they'd lived here, Jack's only concern with the cliff was to keep away from it, lest it crumble under him or his daughter. The view from his house was magnificent enough, but the cliff's height meant that from the house there was an unseen dead zone a thousand yards wide which the terrorists had used to approach. And they'd used ladders to climb up—*of course, that's what ladders are for!* Their placements were marked the way it said in every field manual in the world, with wooden stakes wrapped with white gauze bandaging, to be seen easily in the dark.

"Okay, people," Ryan began, looking around. "Shorty and I go first. Your Highness, you come next with the women. Robby, stay ten yards back and cover the rear."

"I am adept with light weapons," the Prince said.

Jack shook his head emphatically. "No, if they get you, they win. If something goes wrong, I'm depending on you to take care of my wife and kid, sir. If something happens, go south. About half a mile down you'll find a gully. Take that inland and don't stop till you find a hard-surface road. It's real thick cover, you should be okay. Robby, if anything gets close, blast it."

"But what if—"

"But, hell! Anything that moves is the enemy." Jack looked around one last time. *Give me five trained men, maybe Breckenridge and four others, and I could set up one pisser of an ambush . . . and if pigs had wings . . .* "Okay, Shorty, you go down first. If you fuck us up, the first thing happens, I'll cut you in half. Do you believe me?"

"Yes."

"Then move."

Cooley moved to the ladder and proceeded down backward, with Ryan several feet above him. The aluminum rungs were slippery with the rain, but at least the wind was blocked by the body of the cliff. The extension ladder—*how the hell did they get that here?*—wobbled under him. Ryan tried to keep an eye on Shorty and slipped once halfway down. Above him, the second group was beginning its descent. The Princess had taken charge of Sally, and was coming down with Ryan's daughter between her body and the ladder to keep her from falling. He could hear his little girl whimpering anyway. Jack had to ignore it. There wasn't room in his consciousness for anger or pity now. He had to do this one right the first time. There would be no second. A flash of lightning revealed the two boats a hundred yards to the north. Ryan couldn't tell if anyone was there or not. Finally they reached the bottom. Cooley moved a few feet to the north and Ryan jumped down the next few feet, gun at the ready.

"Let's just stay put for a minute."

The Prince arrived next, then the women. Finally Robby started down, his Marine parka making him invisible against the black sky. He came down quickly, also jumping the last five feet.

"They got to the house just as I started down. Maybe this'll slow them some." He held the white-wrapped stakes. It might make the ladders harder to find.

"Good one, Rob." Jack turned. The boats were out there, invisible again in the rain and shadows. Shorty had said that only one man was guarding them. *What if he's lying?* Ryan asked himself. *Is this guy willing to die for his cause? Will he sacrifice himself to shout a warning and get us killed? Does it make a difference—do we have a choice? No!*

"Move out, Shorty." Ryan gestured with his gun. "Just remember who dies first."

It was high tide, and the water came to within a few feet of the base of the cliff. The sand was wet and hard under his feet as Ryan stayed three feet behind the terrorist. *How far were they—a hundred yards? How* far *can one hundred yards be?* Ryan asked himself. He was discovering that now. The people behind him kept close to the kudzu-covered cliff. That made them extremely hard to see, though if there was someone in the boat, he'd know that people were coming toward him.

Krak!

Everyone's heart stopped for a moment. A lightning stroke had shattered a tree on the cliff's edge not two hundred yards behind them. For a brief instant he saw the boats again—and there was a man in each.

"Just one, eh?" Jack muttered. Shorty hesitated, then proceeded, hands at his side. With the return of darkness, he again lost sight of the boats, and Jack reasoned that everyone's night vision was equally ruined by the lightning. His mind returned to the image he'd just seen. The man in the near boat was standing at the near side, amidships, and appeared to be holding a weapon—one that needed two hands. Ryan was enraged that Shorty had lied to him. It seemed absurd as he watched the emotion flare and fade in his consciousness.

"What's the password?"

"There isn't one," Dennis Cooley replied, his voice unsteady as he contemplated the situation from rather a different perspective. He was between the loaded guns of two sides, each of which was likely to shoot. Cooley's mind was racing, too, looking for something he could do to turn the tables.

Was he telling the truth now? Ryan wondered, but there wasn't time to puzzle that one out. "Keep moving."

The boat reappeared now. At first it was just something different from the darkness and the beach. In five more yards it was a shape. The rain was pouring down hard enough to distort everything he saw, but there was a white, almost rectangular shape ahead. Ryan guessed the range at fifty yards. He prayed for the lightning to hold off now. If they were lighted, the men in the boats might be able to recognize a face, and if they saw that Shorty was in front . . .

How do I do this . . . ?

You can be a policeman or a soldier, but not both. Joe Evans' words at the Tower came back, and told him what he had to do.

Forty yards to go. There were rocks on the beach, too, and Jack had to be careful not to trip over one. He reached forward with his left hand and unscrewed the bulky silencer. He stuck it in his belt. He didn't like what it did to the gun's balance.

Thirty yards. He searched for and found the stock release switch on the Uzi. Jack extended the stock, planting the metal buttplate in his armpit and snugging the weapon in tight. *Just a few more seconds . . .*

Twenty-five yards. He could see the boat clearly now, twenty feet or so, with a blunt bow, and another just like it perhaps twenty yards beyond. There was definitely a man in the near boat, standing amidships on its port side, looking straight at the people approaching him. Jack's right thumb pushed the Uzi's selector switch all the way forward, to full automatic fire, and he tightened his fist on the pistol grip. He hadn't fired an Uzi since a brief familiarization at Quantico. It was small but nicely balanced. The black metal sights were nearly useless in the dark, though, and what he had to do . . .

Twenty yards. *The first burst has to be right on, Jack, right the hell on . . .*

Ryan took half a step to his right and dropped to one knee. He brought the weapon up, placing the front sight low and left of his target before he held the trigger down for a four-round burst. The gun jerked up and to the right as the bullets left, tracing a diagonal line across the target's outline. The man dropped instantly from sight, and Ryan was again dazzled, this time by his own muzzle flashes. Shorty had dived to the ground at the sound.

"Come on!" Ryan yanked Cooley up and threw him forward, but Jack stumbled in the sand and recovered to see that the terrorist was indeed running for the boat—*where there was a gun to turn against them all!* He was yelling something Ryan couldn't understand.

Jack had nearly caught up when Shorty got there first—

And died. The man in the other boat fired a long, wild burst in their direction just as Cooley was leaping aboard. Ryan saw his head snap over and Shorty fell into the boat like a sack of groceries. Jack knelt at the gunnel and fired his own burst, and the other man went down. Hit or not, Ryan couldn't tell. It was just like the exercises at Quantico, he told himself, total chaos, and the side that makes the fewest mistakes wins.

"Get aboard!" He stayed up, holding his gun on the other boat. He didn't turn his head, but felt the others board. Lightning flashed, and Ryan saw the man he'd shot, three red spots on his chest, his eyes and mouth agape in surprise. Shorty was beside him, the side of his head horribly opened. Between the two it seemed a gallon of blood had been poured onto the fiberglass deck. Robby finally arrived and jumped aboard. A head appeared in the other boat, and Ryan fired again, then clambered aboard.

"Robby, get us the hell outa here!" Jack moved on hands and knees to the other side, making sure that everyone's head was down.

Jackson moved into the driver's seat and searched for the ignition. It was set up just like a car, and the keys were in. He turned them, and the engine coughed to life as yet another burst of fire came from the other boat. Ryan heard the sound of bullets hitting the fiberglass. Robby cringed but didn't move as his hand found the shift lever. Jack brought the gun up and fired again.

"Men on the cliff!" the Prince shouted.

O'Donnell gathered his men quickly and gave out new orders. All the security men were dead, he was sure, but that helicopter had probably landed to the west. He didn't think the missile had hit, though it was impossible to be sure.

"Thanks for the help, Sean, they were better than I expected. You have them in the house?"

"I left Dennis and two others. I think we should leave."

"You got that right!" Alex said. He pointed west. "I think we have some more company."

"Very well. Sean, you collect them and bring them to the cliff."

Miller got his two men and ran back to the house. Alex and his man tagged along. The front door was open, and all five raced inside, turned around the fireplace, and stopped cold.

Paulson, his spotter, and another agent were running too. He led them along the woodline to where the driveway turned, and dropped again, setting his rifle up on the bipod. There were sirens in the distance now, and he wondered what had taken so goddamned long as he tracked his night-sight in a search for targets. He caught a glimpse of men running around the northern side of the house.

"Something feels wrong about this," the sniper said.

"Yeah," his spotter agreed. "They sure as hell didn't plan to leave by the road—but what else is there?"

"Somebody better find out," Paulson thought aloud, and got on his radio.

Werner struggled forward on the south side of the yard, trying his best to ignore his throbbing back as he led his group forward. The radio squawked again, and he ordered his other team to advance with extreme caution.

"Well, where are they, man?" Alex asked.

Miller looked around in stunned amazement. Two of his men were dead on the floor, their guns were gone—and so were . . .

"Where the hell are they!" Alex repeated.

"Search the house!" Miller screamed. He and Alex stayed in the room. The black man looked at him with an unforgiving stare.

"Did I go through all this to watch you fuck up again?"

The three men returned a few seconds later and reported the house empty. Miller had already determined that his men's guns were gone. Something had gone wrong. He took his people outside.

Paulson had a new spot and finally could see his targets again. He counted twelve, then more joined from the house. They seemed to be confused as he watched the images on his night-sight gesture at one another. Some men were talking while others just milled around wait-

ing for orders. Several appeared to be hurt, but he couldn't tell for
sure.

"They're gone." Alex said it before Miller had a chance.

O'Donnell couldn't believe it. Sean explained in a rapid, halting
voice while Dobbens looked on.

"Your boy fucked up," Dobbens said.

It was just too much. Miller slipped his own Uzi behind his back and
retrieved the one he'd taken from the Secret Service agent. He brought
it up in one smooth motion and fired into Alex's chest from a distance
of three feet. Louis looked at his fallen boss for a second, then tried to
bring his pistol up, but Miller cut him down, too.

"What the hell!" the spotter said.

Paulson flipped the rifle's safety off and centered his sight on the
man who had just fired, killing two men—but whom had he killed? He
could shoot only to save the lives of friendlies, and the dead men had
almost certainly been bad guys. There weren't any hostages to be
saved, as far as he could tell. *Where the hell are they?* One of the men
near the cliff's edge appeared to shout something, and the others ran to
join him. The marksman had his choice of targets, but without positive
identification, he couldn't dare to fire a shot.

"Come on, baby," Jackson said to the engine. The motor was still
cold and ran unevenly as he shifted to reverse. The boat moved slowly
backward, away from the beach. Ryan had his Uzi trained on the other
boat. The man there appeared again, and Ryan fired three rounds
before the gun stopped. He cursed and switched magazines before
firing a number of short bursts again to keep his head down.

"Men on the cliff," the Prince repeated. He'd taken the shotgun and
had it aimed, but didn't fire. He didn't know who it was up there, and
the range was too great in any case. Then flashes appeared. Whoever it
was, they were firing at the boat. Ryan turned when he heard bullets
hitting the water, and two thudded into the boat itself. Sissy Jackson
screamed and grabbed at herself, while the Prince fired three rounds
back.

Robby had the boat thirty yards from the beach now, and savagely
brought the wheel around as he shifted the selector back into drive.

When he rammed the throttle forward, the engine coughed again for one long, terrible moment, but then it caught and the boat surged forward.

"All right!" the aviator hooted. "Jack—where to? How about Annapolis?"

"Do it!" Ryan agreed. He looked aft. There were men coming down the ladder. Some were still shooting at them but missing wildly. Next he saw that Sissy was holding her foot.

"Cathy, see if you can find a first-aid kit," His Highness said. He'd already inspected the wound, but was now in the stern, facing aft with the shotgun at the ready. Jack saw a white plastic box under the driver's seat and slid it toward his wife.

"Rob, Sissy took a round in the foot," Jack said.

"I'm okay, Rob," his wife said at once. She didn't sound okay.

"How is it, Sis?" Cathy asked, moving to take a look.

"It hurts, but it's no big deal," she said through her teeth, trying to smile.

"You sure you're okay, honey?" Robby asked.

"Just *go,* Robby!" she gasped. Jack moved aft and looked. The bullet had gone straight through the top of her foot, and her light-colored shoe was bathed in dark blood. He looked around to see if anyone else was hurt, but aside from the mere terror that each felt, everyone else seemed all right.

"Commander, do you want me to take the wheel for you?" the Prince asked.

"Okay, Cap'n, come on forward." Robby slid away from the controls as His Highness joined him. "Your course is zero-three-six magnetic. Watch it, it's going to get rough when we're out of the cliff's lee, and there's lots of merchant traffic out there." They could already see four feet of chop building a hundred yards ahead, driven by the gusting winds.

"Right. How do I know when we've arrived at Annapolis?" The Prince settled behind the wheel and started checking out the controls.

"When you see the lights on the Bay Bridges, call me. I know the harbor, I'll take her in."

The Prince nodded agreement. He throttled back to half power as they entered the heavy chop, and kept moving his eyes from the compass to the water. Jackson moved to check his wife.

Sissy waved him away. "You worry about *them!*"

In another moment they were roller-coastering over four- and five-foot waves. The boat was a nineteen-foot cathedral-hull lake boat of a type favored by local fishermen for her good calm-seas speed and shallow draft. Her blunt nose didn't handle the chop very well. They were taking water over the bow, but the forward snap-on cover was in place, and the windshield deflected most of the water over the side. That water which did get into the back emptied down a self-bailing hole next to the engine box. Ryan had never been in a boat like this, but knew what it was. Its hundred-fifty-horse engine drove an inboard-outdrive transmission whose movable propeller eliminated the need for a rudder. The bottom and sides of the boat were filled with foam for positive flotation. You could fill it with water and it wouldn't sink—but more to the point, the fiberglass and the foam would probably stop the bullets from a submachine gun. Jack checked his fellow passengers again. His wife was ministering to Sissy. The Princess held his daughter. Except for himself, Robby, and the Prince at the wheel, everyone's head was down. He started to relax slightly. They were away, and their fate was back in their own hands. Jack promised himself that this would never change again.

"They're coming after us," Robby said as he fed two rounds into the bottom of the shotgun. "'Bout three hundred yards back. I saw them in the lightning, but they'll lose us in this rain if we're lucky."

"What would you call the visibility?"

"Except for the lightning"—Robby shrugged—"maybe a hot hundred yards, tops. We're not leaving a wake for them to follow, and they don't know where we're going." He paused. "God, I wish we had a radio! We could get the Coast Guard in on this, or maybe somebody else, and set up a nice little trap for them."

Jack sat all the way down, facing aft on the opposite side of the engine box from his friend. He saw that his daughter was asleep in the arms of the Princess. *It must be nice to be a kid,* he reflected.

"Count your blessings, Commander."

"Bet your ass, boy! I guess I picked a good time to take a leak."

Ryan grunted agreement. "I didn't know you could handle a shotgun."

"Back when I was a kid, the Klan had this little hobby. They'd get boozed up every Tuesday night and burn down a nigger church—just to keep us in line, y'know? Well, one night, the sheetheads decided to burn my pappy's church. We got word—a liquor-store owner called; not all rednecks are assholes. Anyway, Pappy and me were waiting for them. Didn't kill any, but we must have scared them as white as their sheets. I blew the radiator right out of one car.'' Robby chuckled at the memory. ''They never did come back for it. The cops didn't arrest anybody, but that's the last time anybody tried to burn a church in our town, so I guess they learned their lesson.'' He paused again. When he went on, his voice was more sober. ''That's the first time I ever killed a man, Jack. Funny, it doesn't feel like anything, not anything at all.''

''It will tomorrow.''

Robby looked over at his friend. ''Yeah.''

Ryan looked aft, his hands tight on the Uzi. There was nothing to be seen. The sky and water merged into an amorphous gray mass, and the wind-driven rain stung at his face. The boat surged up and down on the breaking swells, and for a moment Jack wondered why he wasn't seasick. Lightning flashed again, and still he saw nothing, as though they were under a gray dome on a sparkling, uneven floor.

They were gone. After the sniper team reported that all the terrorists had disappeared over the cliff, Werner's men searched the house and found nothing but dead men. The second HRT group was now on the scene, plus over twenty police, and another crowd of firemen and paramedics. Three of the Secret Service agents were still alive, plus a terrorist who'd been left behind. All were being transported to hospitals. That made for seventeen security people dead, and a total of four terrorists, two of them apparently killed by their own side.

''They all crowded into the boat and took off that way,'' Paulson said. ''I could have taken a few out, but there just wasn't any way to figure who was who.'' He'd done the right thing. The sniper knew it, and so did Werner. You don't shoot without knowing what your target is.

''So now what the hell do we do?'' This question came from a captain of the State Police. It was a rhetorical question insofar as there was no immediate answer.

''Do you suppose the good guys got away?'' Paulson asked. ''I didn't see anything that looked like a friendly, and the way the bad guys were acting . . . something went wrong,'' he said. ''Something went wrong for everybody.''

Something went wrong, all right, Werner thought. *A goddamned battle was fought here. Twenty-some people dead and nobody in sight.*

"Let's assume that the friendlies escaped somehow—no, let's just assume that the bad guys got away in a boat. Okay. Where would they go?" Werner asked.

"Do you know how many boatyards there are around here?" the State Police Captain asked. "Jesus, how many houses with private slips? Hundreds—we can't check them all out!"

"Well, we have to do something!" Werner snapped back, his anger amplified by his sprained back. A black dog came up to them. He looked as confused as everyone else.

"I think they lost us."

"Could be," Jackson replied. The last lightning flash had revealed nothing. "The bay's right big, and visibility isn't worth a damn—but the way the rain's blowing, they can see better than we can. Twenty yards, maybe, just enough to matter."

"How about we go farther east?" Jack asked.

"Into the main ship channel? It's a Friday night. There'll be a bunch of ships coming out of Baltimore, knocking down ten-twelve knots, and as blind as we are." Robby shook his head. "Uh-uh, we didn't make it this far to get run down by some Greek rustbucket. This is hairy enough."

"Lights ahead," the Prince reported.

"We're home, Jack!" Robby went forward. The lights of the twin Chesapeake Bay Bridges winked at them unmistakably in the distance. Jackson took the wheel, and the Prince took up his spot in the stern. All were long since soaked through by the rain, and they shivered in the wind. Jackson brought the boat around to the west. The wind was on the bow now, coming straight down the Severn River valley, as it usually did here. The waves moderated somewhat as he steered past the Annapolis town harbor. The rain was still falling in sheets, and Robby navigated the boat mostly by memory.

The lights along the Naval Academy's Sims Drive were a muted, linear glow through the rain and Robby steered for them, barely missing a large can buoy as he fought the boat through the wind. In another minute they could see the line of gray YPs—Yard Patrol boats—still moored to the concrete seawall while their customary slips were being

518 · TOM CLANCY

renovated across the river. Robby stood to see better, and brought the boat in between a pair of the wood-hulled training craft. He actually wanted to enter the Academy yacht basin, but it was too full at the moment. Finally he nosed the boat to the seawall, holding her to the concrete with engine power.

"Y'all stop that!" A Marine came into view. His white cap had a plastic cover over it, and he wore a raincoat. "Y'all can't tie up here."

"This is Lieutenant Commander Jackson, son," Robby replied. "I work here. Stand by. Jack, you get the bowline."

Ryan ducked under the windshield and unsnapped the bow cover. A white nylon line was neatly coiled in the right place, and Ryan stood as Robby used engine power to bring the boat's port side fully against the seawall. Jack jumped up and tied the line off. The Prince did the same at the stern. Robby killed the engine and went up to face the Marine.

"You recognize me, son?"

The Marine saluted. "Beg pardon, Commander, but—" He flashed his light into the boat. "Holy Christ!"

About the only good thing that could be said about the boat was that the rain had washed most of the blood down the self-bailing hole. The Marine's mouth dropped open as he saw two bodies, three women, one of them apparently shot, and a sleeping child. Next he saw a machine gun draped around Ryan's neck. A dull, wet evening of walking guard came to a screeching end.

"You got a radio, Marine?" Robby asked. He held it up and Jackson snatched it away. It was a small Motorola CC unit like those used by police. "Guardroom, this is Commander Jackson."

"Commander? This is Sergeant Major Breckenridge. I didn't know you had the duty tonight, sir. What can I do for you?"

Jackson took a long breath. "I'm glad it's you, Gunny. Listen up: Alert the command duty officer. Next, I want some armed Marines on the seawall west of the yacht basin *immediately!* We got big trouble here, Gunny, so let's shag it!"

"Aye aye, sir!" The radio squawked. Orders had been given. Questions could wait.

"What's your name, son?" Robby asked the Marine next.

"Lance Corporal Green, sir!"

"Okay, Green, help me get the womenfolk out of the boat." Robby reached out his hand. "Let's go, ladies."

Green leaped down and helped Sissy out first, then Cathy, then the

Princess, who was still holding Sally. Robby got them all behind the wood hull of one of the YPs.

"What about them, sir?" Green gestured at the bodies.

"They'll keep. Get back up here, Corporal!"

Green gave the bodies a last look. "Reckon so," he muttered. He already had his raincoat open and the flap loose on his holster.

"What's going on here?" a woman's voice asked. "Oh, it's you, Commander."

"What are you doing here, Chief?" Robby asked her.

"I have the duty section out keeping an eye on the boats, sir. The wind could beat 'em to splinters on this seawall if we don't—" Chief Bosun's Mate Mary Znamirowski looked at everyone on the dock. "Sir, what the hell . . ."

"Chief, I suggest you get your people together and put them under cover. No time for explanations."

A pickup truck came next. It halted in the parking lot just behind them. The driver jumped out and sprinted toward them with three others trailing behind. It was Breckenridge. The Sergeant Major gave the women a quick look, then turned to Jackson and asked the night's favorite question—

"What the hell is going on, sir?"

Robby gestured to the boat. Breckenridge gave it a quick look that lingered into four or five questions. "Christ!"

"We were at Jack's place for dinner," Robby explained. "And some folks crashed the party. They were after him—" Jackson gestured to the Prince of Wales, who turned and smiled. Breckenridge's eyes went wide in recognition. His mouth flapped open for a moment, but he recovered and did what Marines always do when they don't know what else—he saluted, just as prescribed in the *Guide Book*. Robby went on: "They killed a bunch of security troops. We got lucky. They planned to escape by boat. We stole one and came here, but there's another boat out there, full of the bastards. They might have followed us."

"Armed with what?" the Sergeant Major asked.

"Like this, Gunny." Ryan held up his Uzi.

The Sergeant Major nodded and reached into his coat. His hand came out with a radio. "Guardroom, this is Breckenridge. We have a Class-One Alert: Wake up all the people. Call Captain Peters. I want a squad of riflemen on the seawall in five minutes. Move out!"

"Roger," the radio answered. "Class-One Alert."

"Let's get the women the hell outta here," Ryan urged.

"Not yet, sir," Breckenridge replied. He looked around, his professional eye making a quick evaluation. "I want some more security here first. Your friends might have landed upriver and be coming overland—that's how I'd do it. In ten minutes I'll have a platoon of riflemen sweepin' the grounds, maybe a full squad here in five. If my people ain't too drunked out," he concluded quietly, reminding Ryan that it was indeed a Friday night—Saturday morning—and Annapolis had many bars. "Cummings and Foster, look after the ladies. Mendoza, get on one of these boats and keep a lookout. Y'all heard the man, so stay awake!"

Breckenridge walked up and down the seawall for a minute, checking fields of view and fields of fire. The .45 Colt automatic looked small in his hands. They could see in his face that he didn't like the situation, and wouldn't until he had more people here and the civilians tucked safely away. Next he checked the women out.

"You ladies all right—oh, sorry, Mrs. Jackson. We'll get you to the sick bay real quick, ma'am."

"Any way to turn the lights off?" Ryan asked.

"Not that I know of—I don't like being under 'em either. Settle down, Lieutenant, we got all this open ground behind us, so nobody's going to sneak up this way. Soon as I get things organized, we'll get the ladies off to the dispensary and put a guard on 'em. You ain't as safe as I'd like, but we're gettin' there. How did you get away?"

"Like Robby said, we got lucky. He did two of them with the shotgun. I got one in the boat. The other one got popped by his own man." Ryan shivered, this time not from wind or rain. "It was kinda hairy there for a while."

"I believe it. These guys any good?"

"The terrorists? You tell me. They had surprise going for them before, and that counts for a lot."

"We'll see about that." Breckenridge nodded.

"There's a boat out there!" It was Mendoza, up on one of the YPs.

"Okay, boys," the Sergeant Major breathed, holding his .45 up alongside his head. "Just wait another couple of minutes, till we get some real weapons here."

"They're coming in slow," the Marine called.

Breckenridge's first look was to make sure the women were safely behind cover. Then he ordered everyone to spread out and pick an open spot between the moored boats. "And for Christ's sake keep your damned heads down!"

Ryan picked a spot for himself. The others did the same, at intervals of from ten to over a hundred feet apart. He felt the reinforced-concrete seawall with his hand. He was sure it would stop a bullet. The four sailors from the YP duty section stayed with the women, with a Marine on either side. Breckenridge was the only one moving, crouching behind the seawall, following the white shape of the moving boat. He got to Ryan.

"There, about eighty yards out, going left to right. They're trying to figure things out, too. *Just give me a couple more minutes, people,*" he whispered.

"Yeah." Ryan thumbed off the safety, one eye above the lip of the concrete. It was just a white outline, but he could hear the muted sputter of the engine. The boat turned in toward where Robby had tied up the one they'd stolen. It was their first real mistake, Jack thought.

"Great." The Sergeant Major leveled his automatic, shielded by the stern of a boat. "Okay, gentlemen. Come on if you're coming. . . ."

Another pickup truck approached on Sims Drive. It came up without lights and stopped right by the women. Eight men jumped off the back. Two Marines ran along the seawall, and were illuminated by a light between two of the moored YPs. Out on the water, the small boat lit up with muzzle flashes, and both Marines went down. Bullets started hitting the moored boats around them. Breckenridge turned and yelled.

"*Fire!*" The area exploded with noise. Ryan spotted on the flashes and depressed his trigger with care. The submachine gun fired four rounds before locking open on an empty magazine. He cursed and stared stupidly at the weapon before he realized that he had a loaded pistol in his belt. He got the Browning up and fired a single shot before he realized that the target wasn't there anymore. The noise from the boat's motor increased dramatically.

"Cease fire! Cease fire! They're buggin' out," Breckenridge called. "Anybody hit?"

"Over here!" someone called to the right, where the women were.

Ryan followed the Sergeant Major over. Two Marines were down, one with a flesh wound in the arm, but the other had taken a round right through the hip and was screaming like a banshee. Cathy was already looking at him.

"Mendoza, what's happening?" Breckenridge called.

"They're heading out—wait—yeah, they're moving east!"

"Move your hands, soldier," Cathy was saying. The Private First-Class had taken a painful hit just below the belt on his left side. "Okay, okay, you're going to be all right. It hurts, but we can fix it." Breckenridge reached down to take the man's rifle. He tossed it to Sergeant Cummings.

"Who's in command here?" demanded Captain Mike Peters.

"I guess I am," Robby said.

"Christ, Robby, what's going on?"

"What the hell does it look like!"

Another truck arrived, carrying another six Marines. They took one collective look at the wounded men and yanked at the charging handles on their rifles.

"Goddammit, Robby—sir!" Captain Peters yelled.

"Terrorists. They tried to get us at Jack's place. They were trying to get—well, look!"

"Good evening, Captain," the Prince said after checking his wife. "Did we get any? I didn't have a clear shot." His voice showed real disappointment at that.

"I don't know, sir," Breckenridge answered. "I saw some rounds go short, and pistol stuff won't penetrate a boat like that." Another series of lightning flashes illuminated the area.

"I see 'em, they're going out to the bay!" Mendoza called.

"Damn!" Breckenridge growled. "You four, get the ladies over to the dispensary." He bent down to help the Princess to her feet as Robby lifted his wife. "You want to give the little girl to the Private, ma'am? They're going to take you to the hospital and get you all dried off."

Ryan saw that his wife was still trying to help one of the wounded Marines, then looked at the patrol boat in front of him. "Robby?"

"Yeah, Jack?"

"Does this boat have radar?"

Chief Znamirowski answered. "They all do, sir."

A Marine lowered the tailgate on the one pickup and helped Jackson load his wife aboard. "What are you thinking, Jack?"

"How fast are they?"

"About thirteen—I don't think they're fast enough."

Chief Bosun's Mate Znamirowski looked over the seawall at the boat Robby had steered in. "In the seas we got now, you bet I can catch one of those little things! But I need someone to work the radar. I don't have an operator in my section right now."

"I can do that," the Prince offered. He was tired of being a target, and no one would keep him out of this. "It would be a pleasure in fact."

"Robby, you're senior here," Jack said.

"Is it legal?" Captain Peters asked, fingering his automatic.

"Look," Ryan said quickly, "we just had an armed attack by *foreign* nationals on a U.S. government reservation—that's an act of war and posse commitatus doesn't apply." *At least I don't think it does,* he thought. "Can you think of a good reason not to go after them?"

He couldn't. "Chief Z, you have a boat ready?" Jackson asked.

"Hell, yes, we can take the seventy-six boat."

"Crank her up! Captain Peters, we need some Marines."

"Sar-Major Breckenridge, secure the area, and bring along ten men."

The Sergeant Major had left the officers to their arguments while getting the civilians loaded onto the truck. He grabbed Cummings.

"Sergeant, take charge of the civilians, get 'em to sick bay, and put a guard on 'em. Beef up the guard force, but your primary mission is to take care of these people here. Their safety is your responsibility—and you ain't relieved till *I* relieve you! Got it?"

"Aye, Gunny."

Ryan helped his wife to the truck. "We're going after them."

"I know. Be careful, Jack. Please."

"I will, but we're going to get 'em this time, babe." He kissed his wife. There was a funny sort of look on her face, something more than concern. "Are you okay?"

"I'll be fine. You worry about you. Be careful!"

"Sure, babe. I'll be back." *But they won't!* Jack turned away to jump aboard the boat. He went inside the deckhouse and found the ladder to the bridge.

"I am Chief Znamirowski, and I have the conn," she announced. Mary Znamirowski didn't look like a chief bosun's mate, but the young seaman—was seawoman the proper term for her? Jack wondered—on the wheel jumped as though she were. "Starboard back two thirds, port back one third, left full rudder."

"Stern line is in," a seaman—this one was a man—reported.

"Very well," she acknowledged, and continued her terse commands to get the YP away from the dock. Within seconds they were clear of the seawall and the other boats.

"Right full rudder, all ahead full! Come to new course one-three-five." She turned. "How's the radar look?"

The Prince was looking over the controls on the unfamiliar set. He found the clutter-suppression switch and bent down to the viewing hood. "Ah! Target bearing one-one-eight, range thirteen hundred, target course northeasterly, speed . . . about eight knots."

"That's about right, it can get choppy by the point," Chief Z thought. "What's our mission, Commander?"

"Can we stay with them?"

"They shot up *my* boats! I'll ram the turkeys if you want, sir," the chief replied. "I can give you thirteen knots as long as you want. I doubt they can do more than ten in the seas we got."

"Okay. I want us to follow as close as we can without being spotted."

The chief opened one of the pilothouse doors and looked at the water. "We'll close to three hundred. Anything else?"

"Go ahead and close up. For the rest of it, I am open to ideas," Robby replied.

"How about we see where they're going?" Jack suggested. "Then we can call in the cavalry."

"That makes sense. If they try to run for shore . . . Christ, I'm a fighter pilot, not a cop." Robby lifted the radio microphone. The set showed the boat's call sign: NAEF. "Naval Station Annapolis, this is November Alfa Echo Foxtrot. Do you read, over." He had to repeat the call twice more before getting an acknowledgment.

"Annapolis, give me a phone patch to the Superintendent."

"He just called us, sir. Stand by." A few clicks followed, plus the usual static.

"This is Admiral Reynolds, who is this?"

"Lieutenant Commander Jackson, sir, aboard the seventy-six boat. We are one mile southeast of the Academy in pursuit of the boat that just shot up our waterfront."

"Is that what happened? All right, who do you have aboard?"

"Chief Znamirowski and the duty boat section, Captain Peters and some Marines, Doctor Ryan, and, uh, Captain Wales, sir, of the Royal Navy," Robby answered.

"Is *that* where he is? I have the FBI on the other phone—Christ, Robby! Okay, the civilians are under guard at the hospital, and the FBI and police are on the way here. Repeat your situation and then state your intentions."

"Sir, we are tracking the boat that attacked the dock. Our intentions are to close and track by radar to determine its destination, then call in the proper law-enforcement agencies, sir." Robby smiled into the mike at his choice of words. "My next call is to Coast Guard Baltimore, sir. Looks like they're heading in that direction at the moment."

"Roger that. Very well, you may continue the mission, but the safety of your guests is your responsibility. Do not, repeat do not take any unnecessary chances. Acknowledge."

"Yes, sir, we will not take any unnecessary chances."

"Use your head, Commander, and report as necessary. Out."

"Now there's a vote of confidence," Jackson thought aloud. "Carry on."

"Left fifteen degrees rudder," Chief Z ordered, rounding Greenbury Point. "Come to new course zero-two-zero."

"Target bearing zero-one-four, range fourteen hundred, speed still eight knots," His Highness told the quartermaster on the chart table. "They took a shorter route around this point."

"No problem," the chief noted, looking at the radar plot. "We have deep water all the way up from here."

"Chief Z, do we have any coffee aboard?"

"I got a pot in the galley, sir, but I don't have anybody to work it."

"I'll take care of that," Jack said. He went below, then to starboard and below again. The galley was a small one, but the coffee machine was predictably of the proper size. Ryan got it started and went back topside. Breckenridge was passing out life jackets to everyone aboard, which seemed a sensible enough precaution. The Marines were deployed on the bridgewalk outside the pilothouse.

"Coffee in ten minutes," he announced.

"Say again, Coast Guard," Robby said into the microphone.

"Navy Echo Foxtrot, this is Coast Guard Baltimore, do you read, over."

"That's better."

"Can you tell us what's going on?"

"We are tracking a small boat, about a twenty-footer—with ten or more armed terrorists aboard." He gave position, course, and speed. "Acknowledge that."

"Roger, you say a boat full of bad guys and machine guns. Is this for real? Over."

"That's affirmative, son. Now let's cut the crap and get down to it."

The response was slightly miffed. "Roger that, we have a forty-one boat about to leave the dock and a thirty-two-footer'll be about ten minutes behind it. These are small harbor-patrol boats. They are not equipped to fight a surface gun action, mister."

"We have ten Marines aboard," Jackson replied. "Do you request assistance?"

"Hell, yes—that's affirmative, Echo Foxtrot. I have the police and the FBI on the phone, and they are heading to this area."

"Okay, have your forty-one boat call us when they clear the dock. Let's have your boat track from in front and we'll track from behind. If we can figure where the target is heading, I want you to call in the cops."

"We can do that easy enough. Let me get some things rolling here, Navy. Stand by."

"A ship," the Prince said.

"It's gotta be," Ryan agreed. "The same way they did it when they rescued that Miller bastard. . . . Robby, can you get the Coast Guard to give us a list of the ships in the harbor?"

Werner and both Hostage Rescue groups were already moving. He wondered what had gone wrong—and right—tonight, but that would be determined later. For the moment he had agents and police heading toward the Naval Academy to protect the people he was supposed to have rescued, and his men were split between an FBI Chevy Suburban and two State Police cars, all heading north on Ritchie Highway toward Baltimore. If only they could use helicopters, he thought, but the weather was too bad, and everyone had had enough of that for one night. They were back to being a SWAT team, a purpose for which they were well suited. Despite everything that had gone wrong tonight, they now had a large group of terrorists flushed and in the open. . . .

*   *   *

"Here's the list of the ships in port," the Coast Guard Lieutenant said over the radio. "We had a lot of them leave Friday night, so the list isn't too long. I'll start off at the Dundalk Marine Terminal. *Nissan Courier,* Japanese registry, she's a car carrier out of Yokohama delivering a bunch of cars and trucks. *Wilhelm Schörner,* West German registry, a container boat out of Bremen with general cargo. *Costanza,* Cypriot registry, out of Valetta, Malta—"

"Bingo!" Ryan said.

"—scheduled to sail in about five hours, looks like. *George McReady,* American, arrived with a cargo of lumber from Portland, Oregon. That's the last one there."

"Tell me about the *Costanza,*" Robby said, looking at Jack.

"She arrived in ballast and loaded up a cargo mainly of farm equipment and some other stuff. Sails before dawn, supposed to be headed back for Valetta."

"That's probably our boy," Jack said quietly.

"Stand by, Coast Guard." Robby turned away from the radio. "How do you know, Jack?"

"I don't *know,* but it's a solid guess. When these bastards pulled that rescue on Christmas Day, they were probably picked up in the Channel by a Cypriot-registered ship. We think their weapons get to them through a Maltese dealer who works with a South African, and a lot of terrorists move back and forth through Malta—the local government's tight with a certain country due south of there. The Maltese don't get their own hands dirty, but they're real good at looking the other way if the money's right." Robby nodded and keyed his mike.

"Coast Guard, have you gotten things straightened out with the local cops?"

"That's a roge, Navy."

"Tell them that we believe the target's objective is the *Costanza.*"

"Roger that. We'll have our thirty-two boat stake her out and call in the cops."

"Don't let them see you, Coast Guard!"

"Understood, Navy. We can handle that part easy enough. Stand by. . . . Navy, be advised that our forty-one boat reports radar contact with you and the target, rounding Bodkin Point. Is this correct? Over."

"Yes!" called the Quartermaster at the chart table. He was making a precise record of the course tracks from the radar plot.

"That's affirm, Coast Guard. Tell your boat to take station five hundred yards forward of the target. Acknowledge."

"Roger, five-zero-zero yards. Okay, let's see if we can get the cops moving. Stand by."

"We got 'em," Ryan thought aloud.

"Uh, Lieutenant, keep your hands still, sir." It was Breckenridge. He reached into Ryan's belt and extracted the Browning automatic. Jack was surprised to see that he'd stuck it in there with the hammer back and safety off. Breckenridge lowered the hammer and put the pistol back where it was. "Let's try to think 'safe,' sir, okay? Otherwise you might lose something important."

Ryan nodded rather sheepishly. "Thanks, Gunny."

"Somebody has to protect the lieutenants." Breckenridge turned. "Okay, Marines—let's stay awake out there!"

"You got a man on the Prince?" Jack asked.

"Even before the Admiral said so." The Sergeant Major gestured to where a corporal was standing, rifle in hand, three feet from His Highness, with orders to stay between him and the gunfire.

Five minutes later a trio of State Police cars drove without lights to Berth Six of the Dundalk Marine Terminal. The cars were parked under one of the gantry cranes used for transferring cargo containers, and five officers walked quietly to the ship's accommodation ladder. A crewman stationed there stopped them—or tried to. A language barrier prevented proper communications. He found himself accompanying the troopers, with his hands cuffed behind his back. The senior police officer bounded up three more ladders and arrived at the bridge.

"What is this!"

"And who might you be?" the cop inquired from behind a shotgun.

"I am the master of this ship!" Captain Nikolai Frenza proclaimed.

"Well, Captain, I am Sergeant William Powers of the Maryland State Police, and I have some questions for you."

"You have no authority on my ship!" Frenza answered. His accent was a mixture of Greek and some other tongue. "I will talk to the Coast Guard and no one else."

"I want to make this real clear." Powers walked the fifteen feet to the Captain, his hands tight around the Ithaca 12-gauge shotgun. "That shore you're tied to is the State of Maryland, and this shotgun says I got all the authority I need. Now we have information that a boatload of terrorists is coming here, and the word is they've killed a bunch of people, including three state troopers.'' He planted the muzzle against Frenza's chest. ''Captain, if they do come here, or if you fuck with me any more tonight, *you are in a whole shitpot full of trouble—do you understand me!*''

The man wilted before his eyes, Powers saw. *So the information is correct. Good.*

''You would be well advised to cooperate, 'cause pretty soon we're going to have more cops here 'n you ever saw. You just might need some friends, mister. If you have something to tell me, I want to hear it right now.''

Frenza hesitated, his eyes shifting toward the bow and back. He was in deep trouble, more than his advance payment would ever cover. ''There are four of them aboard. They are forward, starboard side, near the bow. We didn't know—''

''Shut up.'' Powers nodded to a corporal, who got on his portable radio. ''What about your crew?''

''The crew is below, preparing to take the ship to sea.''

''Sarge, the Coast Guard says they're three miles off and heading in.''

''All right.'' Powers pulled a set of handcuffs from his belt. He and his men took the four men standing bridge watch and secured them to the ship's wheel and two other fittings. ''Captain, if you or your people make any noise at all, I'll come back here and splatter you all over this ship. I am not kidding.''

Powers took his men down to the main deck and forward on the port side. The *Costanza*'s superstructure was all aft. Forward of it, the deck was a mass of cargo containers, each the size of a truck-trailer, piled three- and four-high. Between each pile was an artificial alleyway, perhaps three feet wide, which allowed them to approach the bow unobserved. The Sergeant had no SWAT experience, but all of his men had shotguns and he did know something of infantry tactics.

It was like walking alongside a building, except that the street was made of rusty steel. The rain had abated, finally, but it still made noise, clattering on the metal container boxes. They passed the last of these to find that the ship's forward hold was open and a crane was hanging over the starboard side. Powers peeked around the corner and saw two men standing at the far side of the deck. They appeared to be looking southeast, toward the entrance to the harbor. There was no easy way to approach. He and his men crouched and went straight toward them. They'd gotten halfway when one turned.

"Who are you?"

"State Police!" Powers noted the accent and brought his gun up, but he tripped on a deck fitting and his first shot went into the air. The man on the starboard side came up with a pistol and fired, also missing, then ducked behind the container. The fourth state trooper went forward around the deck hatch and fired at the container edge, covering his comrades. Powers heard a flurry of conversation and the sound of running feet. He took a deep breath and ran to the starboard side.

No one was in sight. The men who'd run aft were nowhere to be seen. There was an accommodation ladder leading from an opening in the rail down to the water, and nothing else but a radio that someone had dropped.

"Oh, shit." The tactical situation was lousy. He had armed criminals close by but out of sight and a boatload of others on the way. He sent one of his men to the port side to watch that line of approach, and another to train his shotgun down the starboard side. Then he got on the radio and learned that plenty more help was on the way. Powers decided to sit tight and take his chances. He'd known Larry Fontana, helped carry his coffin out of the church, and he was damned if he'd pass up the chance to get the people who'd killed him.

A State Police car had taken the lead. The FBI was now on the Francis Scott Key Bridge, crossing over Baltimore Harbor. The next trick was to get from the expressway to the marine terminal. A trooper said he knew a shortcut, and he led the procession of three cars. A twenty-foot boat was going under the bridge at that very moment.

"Target coming right, appears to be heading towards a ship tied to the quay, bearing three-five-two," His Highness reported.

"That's it," Ryan said. "We got 'em."

"Chief, let's close up some," Jackson ordered.

"They might spot us, sir—the rain's slacking off. If they're heading to the north, I can close up on their port side. They're heading for that ship—you want us to hit them right when they get there?" Chief Znamirowski asked.

"That's right."

"Okay. I'll get somebody on the searchlight. Captain Peters, you'll want to get your Marines on the starboard side. Looks like surface action starboard," Chief Z noted. Navy regulations prohibited her from serving on a combatant ship, but she'd beaten the game after all!

"Right." Peters gave the order and Breckenridge got the Marines in place. Ryan left the pilothouse and went to the main deck aft. He had already come to his decision. Sean Miller was out there.

"I hear a boat," one of the troopers said quietly.

"Yeah." Powers fed a round into his shotgun. He looked aft. There were people there with guns. He heard footsteps behind him—more police!

"Who's in charge here?" a corporal asked.

"I am," Powers replied. "You stay here. You two, move aft. If you see a head come out from behind a container, blow it the hell off."

"I see it!" So did Powers. A white fiberglass boat appeared a hundred yards off, coming slowly up to the ship's ladder.

"Jesus." It seemed full of people, and every one, he'd been told, had an automatic weapon. Unconsciously he felt the steel plating on the ship's side. He wondered if it would stop a bullet. Most troopers now wore protective body armor, but Powers didn't. The Sergeant flipped off the safety on his shotgun. It was just about time.

The boat approached like a car edging into a parking space. The helmsman nosed the boat to the bottom of the accommodation ladder and someone in the bow tied it off. Two men got out onto the small lower platform. They helped someone off the boat, then started to carry him up the metal staircase. Powers let them get halfway.

"*Freeze!* State Police!" He and two others pointed shotguns straight down at the boat. "Move and you're dead," he added, and was sorry for it. It sounded too much like TV.

He saw heads turn upward, a few mouths open in surprise. A few hands moved, too, but before anything that looked like a weapon moved in his direction, a two-foot searchlight blazed down on the boat from seaward.

Powers was thankful for the light. He saw their heads snap around, then up at him. He could see their expressions now. They were trapped and knew it.

"Hi, there." A voice came across the water. It was a woman's voice on a loudspeaker. "If anybody moves, I have ten Marines to blow you to hell-and-gone. Make my day,'' the voice concluded. Sergeant Powers winced at that.

Then another light came on. ''This is the U.S. Coast Guard. You are all under arrest.''

''Like hell!'' Powers screamed. ''I got 'em!'' It took another minute to establish what was going on to everyone's satisfaction. The big, gray Navy patrol boat came right alongside the smaller boat, and Powers was relieved to see ten rifles pointed at his prisoners.

''Okay, let's put all the guns down, people, and come up one at a time.'' His head jerked around as a single pistol shot rang out, followed by a pair of shotgun blasts. The Sergeant winced, but ignored it as best he could and kept his gun zeroed on the boat.

''I seen one!'' a trooper said. ''About a hundred feet back of us!''

''Cover it,'' Powers ordered. ''Okay, you people get the hell up here and flat down on the deck.''

The first two arrived, carrying a third man who was wounded in the chest. Powers got them stretched out, facedown on the deck, forwards of the front rank of containers. The rest came up singly. By the time the last was up, he'd counted twelve, several more of them hurt. They'd left behind a bunch of guns and what looked like a body.

''Hey, Marines, we could use a hand here!''

It was all the encouragement he needed. Ryan was standing on the YP's afterdeck, and jumped down. He slipped and fell on the deck. Breckenridge arrived immediately behind him and looked at the body the terrorists had left behind. A half-inch hole had been drilled in the man's forehead.

''I thought I got off one good round. Lead on, Lieutenant.'' He gestured at the ladder. Ryan charged up the steps, pistol in hand. Behind him, Captain Peters was screaming something at him, but Jack simply didn't care.

''Careful, we have bad guys down that way in the container stacks,'' Powers warned.

Jack went around the front rank of metal boxes and saw the men facedown on the deck, hands behind their necks, with a pair of troopers standing over them. In a moment there were six Marines there, too.

Captain Peters came up and went to the police Sergeant, who seemed to be in command.

''We have at least two more, maybe four, hiding in the container rows,'' Powers said.

"Want some help flushing them out?"

"Yeah, let's go do it." Powers grinned in the darkness. He assembled all of his men, leaving Breckenridge and three Marines to guard the men on the deck. Ryan stayed there, too. He waited for the others to move aft.

Then he started looking at faces.

Miller was looking, too, still hoping to find a way out. He turned his head to the left and saw Ryan staring at him from twenty feet away. They recognized each other in an instant, and Miller saw something, a look that he had always reserved for his own use.

I am Death, Ryan's face told him.

I have come for you.

It seemed to Ryan that his body was made of ice. His fingers flexed once around the butt of his pistol as he walked slowly to port, his eyes locked on Miller's face. He still looked like an animal to Jack, but he was no longer a predator on the loose. Jack reached him and kicked Miller's leg. He gestured with the pistol for him to stand, but didn't say a word.

You don't talk to snakes. You kill snakes.

"Lieutenant . . ." Breckenridge was a little slow to catch on.

Jack pushed Miller back against the metal wall of a container, his forearm across the man's neck. He savored the feel of the man's throat on his wrist.

This is the little bastard who nearly killed my family. Though he didn't know it, his face showed no emotion at all.

Miller looked into his eyes and saw . . . nothing. For the first time in his life, Sean Miller knew fear. He saw his own death, and remembered the long-past lessons in Catholic school, remembered what the sisters had taught him, and his fear was that they might have been right. His face broke out in a sweat and his hands trembled as, despite all his contempt for religion, he feared the eternity in hell that surely awaited him.

Ryan saw the look in Miller's eyes, and knew it for what it was. *Goodbye, Sean. I hope you like it there. . . .*

"Lieutenant!"

Jack knew that he had little time. He brought up the pistol and forced it into Miller's mouth as his eyes bored in on Sean's. He tightened his finger on the trigger just as he'd been taught. A gentle squeeze, so you never know when the trigger will break. . . .

But nothing happened, and a massive hand came down on the gun.

"He ain't worth it, Lieutenant, he just ain't worth it." Breckenridge withdrew his hand, and Ryan saw that the gun's hammer was down. He'd have to cock it before the weapon could fire. "Think, son."

The spell was broken. Jack swallowed twice and took a breath. What he saw now was something less monstrous than before. Fear had given Miller the humanity that he'd lacked before. He was no longer an animal, after all. He was a human being, an evil example of what could happen when a man lost something that all men needed. Miller's breath was coming in gasps as Ryan pulled the gun out of his mouth. He gagged, but couldn't bend over with Jack's arm across his throat. Ryan backed away and the man fell to the deck. The Sergeant Major put his hand on Ryan's right arm, forcing the gun downward.

"I know what you're thinking, what he did to your little girl, but it isn't worth what you'd have to go through. I could tell the cops you shot him when he tried to run. My boys would back me up. You'd never go to trial, but it ain't worth what it would do to you, son. You're not cut out to be a murderer," Breckenridge said gently. "Besides, look what you did to him. I don't know what that is down there, but it's not a man, not anymore."

Jack nodded, as yet unable to speak. Miller was still on all fours, looking down at the deck, unable to meet Ryan's eyes. Jack could feel his body again; the blood coursing through his veins told him that he was alive and whole. *I've won,* he thought, as his mind regained control of his emotions. *I've won. I've defeated him and I haven't destroyed myself doing it.* His hands relaxed around the pistol grip.

"Thanks, Gunny. If you hadn't—"

"If you'd really wanted to kill him, you would have remembered to cock it. Lieutenant, I had you figured out a long time ago." Breckenridge nodded to reinforce his words. "Back on the deck, you," he told Miller, who slowly complied.

"Before any of you people think you're lucky, I got a hot flash for you," the Sergeant Major said next. "You have committed murder in a place that has a gas chamber. You can die by the numbers over here, people. Think about it."

*   *   *

The Hostage Rescue Team arrived next. They found the Marines and state troopers on the deck, working their way aft. It took a few minutes to determine that no one was in the container stacks. The remaining four ULA members had used an alleyway to head aft, and were probably in the superstructure. Werner took over. He had a solid perimeter. Nobody was going anywhere. Another group of FBI agents went forward to collect the terrorists.

Three TV news trucks arrived on the scene, adding their lights to the ones turning night into day on the dock. The police were keeping them back, but already live news broadcasts were being sent worldwide. A colonel of the State Police was giving out a press release at the moment. The situation, he told the cameras, was under control, thanks to a little luck and a lot of good police work.

By this time all the terrorists forward were handcuffed and had been searched. The agents read off their constitutional rights while three of their number went into the boat to collect their weapons and other evidence. The Prince finally came up the ladder, with a heavy guard. He came to where the terrorists were sitting, now. He looked at them for a minute or so but didn't say a word. He didn't have to.

"Okay, we have things contained aft. There seems to be four of them. That's what the crew says," one of the HRT people said. "They're below somewhere, and we'll have to talk them out. It shouldn't be too hard, and we have all the time in the world."

"How do we get these characters off?" Sergeant Powers asked.

"We haven't worked that out yet, but let's get the civilians off. We'd prefer you did it from here. It might be a little dangerous to use the aft ladder. That means the Marines, too. Thanks for the assist, Captain."

"I hope we didn't screw anything up, joining in, I mean."

The agent shook his head. "You didn't break any laws that I know of. We got all the evidence we need, too."

"Okay, then we head back to Annapolis."

"Fine. There'll be a team of agents waiting to interview you there. Please thank the boat crew for us."

"Sar-Major, let's get the people moving."

"Okay, Marines, saddle up," Breckenridge called. Two minutes later everyone was aboard the patrol boat, heading out of the harbor.

The rain had finally ended and the sky was clearing, the cooler Canadian air finally breaking the heat wave that had punished the area. The Marines took the opportunity to climb into the boat's bunks. Chief Znamirowski and her crew handled the driving. Ryan and the rest congregated in the galley and started drinking the coffee that no one had touched to this point.

"Long day," Jackson said. He checked his watch. "I'm supposed to fly in a few hours. Well, I was, anyway."

"Looks like we finally won a round," Captain Peters observed.

"It wasn't cheap." Ryan stared into his cup.

"It's never cheap, sir," Breckenridge said after a few seconds.

The boat rumbled with increased engine power. Jackson lifted a phone and asked why they were speeding up. He smiled at the answer, but said nothing.

Ryan shook his head to clear it and went topside. Along the way he found a crewman's pack of cigarettes on a table and stole one. He proceeded out onto the fantail. Baltimore Harbor was already low on the horizon, and the boat was turning south toward Annapolis, chugging along at thirteen knots—about fifteen miles per hour, but on a boat it seemed fast enough. The smoke he blew out made its own trail as he stared aft. *Was Breckenridge right?* he asked the sky. The answer came in a moment. *He got one part right. I'm not cut out to be a murderer. Maybe he was right on the other part, too. I sure hope so. . . .*

"Tired, Jack?" the Prince asked, standing beside him.

"I ought to be, but I guess I'm still too pumped up."

"Indeed," His Highness observed quietly. "I wanted to ask them why. When I went up to look at them, I wanted—"

"Yeah." Ryan took a last drag and flipped the butt over the side. "You could ask, but I doubt the answer would mean much of anything."

"Then how are we supposed to solve the problem?"

We did solve my *problem,* Jack thought. *They won't be coming after my family anymore. But that's not the answer you want, is it?* "I guess maybe it comes down to justice. If people believe in their society, they don't break its rules. The trick's making them believe. Hell, we can't always accomplish that." Jack turned. "But you try your best, and you don't quit. Every problem has a solution if you work at it long enough. You have a pretty good system over there. You just have to make it work for everybody, and do it well enough that they believe. It's not easy, but I think you can do it. Sooner or later, civilization always wins over barbarism." *I just proved that, I think. I hope.*

The Prince of Wales looked aft for a moment. "Jack, you're a good man."

"So are you, pal. That's why we'll win."

It was a grisly scene, but not one to arouse pity in any of the men who surveyed it. Geoffrey Watkins' body was quite warm, and his blood was still dripping from the ceiling. After the photographer finished up, a detective took the gun from his hands. The television remained on, and "Good Morning, Britain" continued to run its live report from America. All the terrorists were now in custody. *That's what must have done it,* Murray thought.

"Bloody fool," Owens said. "We didn't have a scrap of usable evidence."

"We do now." A detective held three sheets of paper in his hand. "This is quite a letter, Commander." He slid the sheets into a plastic envelope.

Sergeant Bob Highland was there, too. He was still learning to walk again, with a leg brace and a cane, and looked down at the body of the man whose information had almost made orphans of his children. Highland didn't say a word.

"Jimmy, you've closed the case," Murray observed.

"Not the way I would have liked," Owens replied. "But now I suppose Mr. Watkins is answering to a higher authority."

The boat arrived in Annapolis forty minutes later. Ryan was surprised when Chief Znamirowski passed the line of moored boats and proceeded straight to Hospital Point. She conned the boat expertly alongside the seawall, where a couple of Marines were waiting. Ryan and everyone but the boat's crew jumped off.

"All secure," Sergeant Cummings reported to Breckenridge. "We got a million cops and feds here, Gunny. Everybody's just fine."

"Very well, you're relieved."

"Doctor Ryan, will you come along with me? You want to hustle, sir," the young Sergeant said. He led off at a slow trot.

It was well that the pace was an easy one. Ryan's legs were rubbery with fatigue as the Sergeant led him up the hill and into the old Academy hospital.

"Hold it!" A federal agent took the pistol from Ryan's belt. "I'll keep this for you, if that's okay."

"Sorry," Jack said with embarrassment.

"It's all right. You can go in." There was no one in sight. Sergeant Cummings motioned for him to follow.

"Where is everybody?"

"Sir, your wife's in the delivery room at the moment." Cummings turned to grin at him.

"Nobody told me!" Ryan said in alarm.

"She said not to worry you, sir." They reached the proper floor. Cummings pointed. "Down there. Don't toss your cookies, Doc."

Jack ran down the corridor. A corpsman stopped him and waved Ryan into a dressing room, where Ryan tore off his clothes and got into surgical greens. It took a few minutes. Ryan was clumsy from fatigue. He walked to the waiting room and saw that all his friends were there. Then the corpsman walked him into the delivery room.

"I haven't done this in a long time," the doctor was saying.

"It's been a few years for me, too," Cathy reproached him. "You're supposed to inspire confidence in your patient." Then she started blowing again, fighting off the impulse to push. Jack grabbed her hand.

"Hi, babe."

"Your timing is pretty good," the doctor observed.

"Five minutes earlier would have been better. Are you all right?" she asked. As it had been the last time, her face was bathed in sweat, and very tired. And she looked beautiful.

"It's all over. *All* over," he repeated. "I'm fine, how about you?"

"Her water broke two hours ago, and she'd be in a hurry if we weren't all waiting for you to get back from your boat ride. Otherwise everything looks good," the doctor answered. He seemed far more nervous than the mother. "Are you ready to push?"

"Yes!"

Cathy squeezed his hand. Her eyes closed and she summoned her strength for the effort. Her breath came out slowly.

"There's the head. Everything's fine. One more push and we're home,'' the doctor said. His gloved hands were poised to make the catch.

Jack turned as the rest of the newborn appeared. His position allowed him to tell even before the doctor did. The infant had already started screaming, as a healthy baby should. *And that, too,* Jack thought, *is the sound of freedom.*

"Boy," John Patrick Ryan Sr. told his wife just before he kissed her, "I love you."

The nearest corpsman assisted the doctor as he clamped off the cord and swaddled the infant in a white blanket to take him away a few feet. The placenta came next with an easy push.

"A little tearing," the doctor reported. He reached for a painkiller before he started the stitching.

"I can tell," Cathy replied with a slight grimace. "Is he okay?"

"Looks okay to me," the corpsman said. "Eight pounds even, and all the pieces are in the right places. Airway's fine, and the kid's got a great little heart."

Jack picked up his son, a small, noisy package of red flesh with an absurd little button of a nose.

"Welcome to the world. I'm your father," he said quietly. *And your father isn't a murderer. That might not sound like much, but it's a lot more than most people think.* He cradled the newborn to his chest for a moment and reminded himself that there really was a God. After a moment he looked down at his wife. "Do you want to see your son?"

"I'm afraid he doesn't have much of a mother left."

"She looks pretty good to me." Jack placed his son in Cathy's arms. "Are you all right?"

"Except for Sally, I think I have everything here that I need, Jack."

"Finished," the doctor said. "I may not be much of an OB, but I do one hell of a good stitch." He looked up to see the usual aftermath of a birth, and he wondered why he'd decided against obstetrics. It had to be the happiest discipline of them all. But the hours were lousy, he reminded himself.

The corpsman reclaimed the infant, and took John Patrick Ryan Jr. to the nursery, where he'd be the only baby for a while. It would give the pediatric people something to do.

Jack watched his wife drift off to sleep after—he checked his

540 · TOM CLANCY

watch—a twenty-three-hour day. She needed it. So did he, but not quite yet. He kissed his wife one more time before another corpsman wheeled her away to the recovery room. There was one thing left for him to do.

Ryan walked out to the waiting room to announce the birth of his son, a handsome young man who would have two complete, but very different, sets of godparents.